TINFOIL SOMBREROS

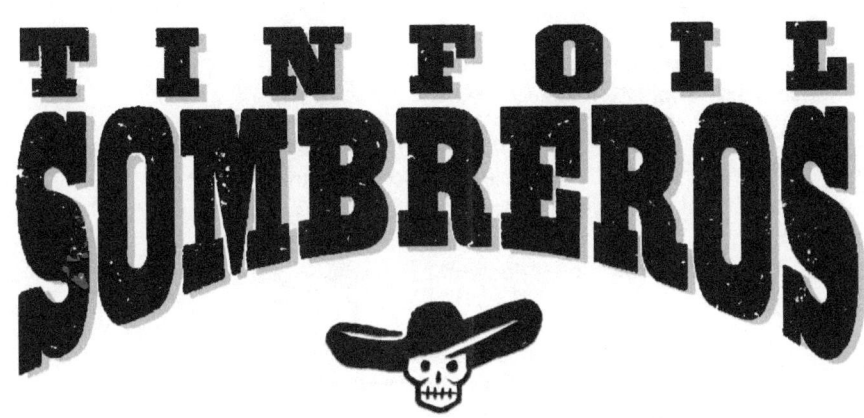

MARK TREMLETT

IRON HEAD BOOKS

PUBLISHER: Iron Head Books
EMAIL: mmrm9313@bigpond.net.au

EDITOR: Marcia Ruf
DESIGN/PRODUCTION: renodesign.com.au | R40001
DESIGNER: Graham Rendoth
ILLUSTRATIONS: Mark Tremlett
FONTS: Black Oak, Charter, Gotham

Images page 2: Modified Bronze Age Scandinavian
and Neolithic Celtic rock carvings

A catalogue record for this book is available
from the National Library of Australia
www.trove.nla.gov.au

ISBN 978-0-646-83809-0 (paperback)
ISBN 978-0-6451670-0-9 (ePUB)

A catalogue record for this
book is available from the
National Library of Australia

NATIONAL
LIBRARY
OF AUSTRALIA

For those that got off the bus.

Contents

The dice roll in the usual manner. Until that one unexpected time when they bounce from the table, flying off in different directions that you never imagined were possible.

WOLF

1

Broken

My name's Wolf. It's not my real name but kids at school started calling me that when I was about ten years old on account of a three-inch long mole in the shape of a wolf's head that grew on my lower-left arm. At first it looked pretty abstract, I guess. Nobody really paid it that much attention. But when it grew all hairy, except for a naked patch right where the teeth would have been, 'Wolfman' was born. I got ripped on for months, but they soon got tired of the teasing, and eventually everyone just knew me as Wolf.

Nowadays I'm tall and lanky and, according to some folks, kind of weird looking. A simple enough statement but you've only gotta take a look outside your front door to realize that's a pretty big order to live up to.

In the hair department, I sport a greying profusion of locks that stick up untidily from the top of my head. Most of the time I like to comb it up in that old fifties greaser style but now, down here in Sonora, the hot desert temperatures conspire to make that look almost impossible.

◆

I slowed the car to an imperceptible crawl and pressed the worn spring-loaded button on the cartridge player. The familiar *chi-chung* of ejecting plastic silenced the racketous music as quick as a thumb-dab on a candle flame.

The air-cushion tires pop-rocked the ground as I squeezed hard on the brake to completely shut down the slow forward movement. The '58 Fire Diamond hissed and spat like a dry thirsty beast. She was desperate for gas and water, so I let her sit for a few precious moments while I pondered our predicament. By *our*, I mean only the car and myself. There was nobody else onboard except for a giant black spider lurking in the back seat somewhere. I glanced across to the front passenger footwell where the old plastic cartridge tape had flipped itself out and onto the floor. An eight-track. A frick'n eight-track. Most people these days wouldn't have a clue what that was. But this old one was wired up sweet and could really pump out a sound. A good sound, granted, but the ancient system must be at least fifty years old now.

Six classic heavy-metal tapes were all I had to listen to. A trunk-sale flea-market bargain. That's the player, the speakers and the threadbare tapes all included. No, actually there were seven, my favorite one had taken the fly and disappeared somewhere under the front seat around the time when I crossed the border into Mexico.

The gear shift slid smoothly into first as I pressed on the gas pedal and pushed the growling '58 Fire Diamond Special on towards a little town that sat camouflaged in the fast-fading light about a mile straight ahead. I could feel the gnaw of hunger in my stomach. All I'd eaten in the last twenty-four hours was the little crispy bits in the corner of my eyes, but that did nothing to quell the pangs. As we picked up speed a plume of gritty black smoke trailed out behind, signaling to the town's folk that we were coming, like it or not.

Passing a handful of outrider dwellings something hit my windshield with a forceful *thud*, making me jump... like you do when you're attacked unexpectedly by a huge exploding sunflower. I flicked on the wipers and dragged two oily smears of petal mash across the glass blocking my vision almost completely.

My speed dropped off to a crawl, as we entered the canyon of two-story buildings. The few I could make out looked run-down and grizzly like a set from a gunslinger western. It was only the handful of cars parked along the street that marked this small desert town as being in the 21st century at all. Now and then I caught glimpses of people moving around outside in the darkness. One of them banged an impromptu *rap-a-tap-tap* on the trunk with a stick or something. I caught a fleeting glimpse in the rear-view mirror of a skinny-looking kid dissolving away into the blackness behind.

The Fire Diamond was parched. I could hear her expanding metals crying out for liquid. "There must be somewhere around here to fix you up, girl," I said. Like I believed it. With my night-eyes still on charge I jerked my head around desperate to see where I was in the dark.

Suddenly everything burst into light beneath a thousand electric globes that crisscrossed the street suspended beneath a gigantic spider's web of cables. Lamps lit up in windows and now I could clearly make out the jumble of huge paper mâché skulls and the multi-colored cut-out paper flags and stuff that hung haphazardly from wicker frames along the street. There were garlands of chrysanthemums and sunflowers dangling vibrant and beautiful amidst the sea of flickering lights and the voids of a hundred shadowy niches.

In all the unexpected visibility, it became obvious I could go no further. There were so many people roaming around I'd been lucky not to have run somebody down already.

On the brink of doing the car some damage, I flicked her out of gear and let her roll on to a stop. Right at that moment some asshole wearing a pull-on skull-head launched himself horizontally through my driver's side window showering me with a spray of razor-sharp glass fragments. It scared the frick'n daylights out of me. The ugly face twisted up towards me and like a creepy ventriloquist's dummy proceeded to mouth-off in Spanish. "Hola Señor, es el día de los muertos. *Yiiiihhhaaaaaaaa!*"

Then I remembered. It was the start of November, and down here in Mexico that could only mean one thing. It was Día de los Muertos – the Day of the Dead – and I'd driven myself smack bang right into the middle of it.

"*Ohhh* dear!"

The gasping Fire Diamond had reached its limit and burst into a cloud of hissing white steam. Skeleton-head had pulled himself out from the window and melted back into the reveling crowd but my entire body was now covered in tiny pieces of glass that had embedded themselves in my hair and were annoyingly working their way down inside my collar.

The interior of the car looked like it had been hit by a hailstorm. Glass was everywhere which was far more off-putting than anything else that was going on outside. I impulsively opened the door and jumped out shaking myself down like a crazy man covered in ants. Without thinking I leaned back inside and with a firm foolish swipe of my hand tried to brush the pieces from the front seat.

"You idiot," I mumbled scornfully as I became painfully aware of the skin-slicing lacerations that I had carelessly inflicted upon myself. My red blood-soaked hand rose ghoulishly back up to my face through the steamy vapors.

The festive crowd around me had swollen in numbers and was definitely becoming more boisterous. They were dancing and cavorting about wildly, even a gunshot or three went off in the excitement. It was only being so up close and personal that I realized these weren't ordinary face-painted town's folk, but skeletons. *Real frick'n skeletons!*

I freaked out and jumped back in the car, searching frantically for a handy gun or a club or something to protect myself from the walking dead, knowing full-well I had nothing.

By now everything outside had become a multi-colored swirl of fabric and freewheeling arm bones and tibias. Gaunt leering skull-heads would clunk unsettlingly up against the '58's windows, curious for a quick peek inside. My hand was still bleeding out, soaking through my clothes and staining the white seat upholstery. I'd grabbed the window rag for an emergency bandage, but it did little towards stopping the thin but constant red rivulets snaking their way down my fingers.

Out of the ruckus a fire-blackened skull with no teeth and putrid stinking breath lunged itself menacingly in through the shattered window, stopped short only by its broad bony shoulders and scorched sombrero.

I backed myself up along the glass covered seat and gave the big ugly bastard an almighty kick with the hard leather sole of my boot, right in its charred toothless face. To my horror it didn't budge an inch but hung there laughing and dribbling stuck tight inside the frame of the window.

"*Agggggghhh!*" I lost it completely and pummeled as hard as I could with a barrage of slams from the heels of my fast-moving Cubans. Finally, it gave way and fell like a limp sack of crap outside the door.

I could really feel the sharp bits of broken glass that were now pressing painfully into my back and the itchy warm blood tracks that kept running unabated.

This is ridiculous. Ten minutes ago, my biggest problem was a thirsty car and a hungry belly, now here I was rolling around on broken glass covered in blood beneath the tide of Día de los Muertos. I had no idea what to do next.

For a second the relentless swirling din of skeletal merriment parted as three lacy-fringed figures dressed in broad, sequined sombreros appeared along the front of the hood.

"Oh God no!" A mariachi band had materialized to serenade my moment of dejected misery. Yes, it was the three amigos resplendent in all their cliché glory: one guy feverishly sawing away on a fiddle, another strumming along on a steel guitar, and the third, a burly built hombre, belting away on one of those gigantic, wooden guitarróns. And to rub it in they were playing that *Manyana* song complete with all the actions. The skelly crowd was going nuts, all twirling around enthusiastically as they danced and sang right along with them. Then I noticed that the big burly guy wasn't a skeleton but a real living person. This brought me back to my senses. I moved across the seat to the broken window and poked my head out through the hole.

"Señor!" He didn't hear me above the racket. "Señor!" I tried again louder, gingerly waving my good arm about outside the window frame. The movement caught his eye and he looked straight at me and nodded as he kept on playing. I remembered the horn and gave it two sharp blasts. He must have heard it as he turned back towards me and smiled even more.

In exasperation I stuck my arm out again and waved him over. This time he nudged one of his amigos and never missing a beat they shuffled around the edge of the car to where I was sitting. As he bent down to say something, two inebriated skelly heads lunged up from the dirt below, between me and the underside of the big guitar, nearly deafening me in stereo with yet more almighty *Yiiihhhhaaaas!* The amigo pushed both of them roughly away and bent down a little lower towards me.

"Hola, señor, can I help you?"

He spoke English, I couldn't believe it. *"Yes,* yes please, I—"

"What seems to be the trouble, señor?" He interjected before I could get anything more out. He obviously saw nothing unusual about a lone blood-splattered gringo stranded in a vintage car amidst a sea of drunken, dancing skeletons.

He smiled like a loopy Cheshire cat and kept on playing on his big wooden guitar. His skeleton buddy with the furious fiddle leaned forward across the hood and shot me an extensive gold-toothed grin through the windshield all the time his stick arm going wild at ten to the dozen.

I looked at the big guy again and said, "Sir, I'm stuck here and need some gas and a bit of a—"

He interrupted me again, still smiling and joyfully playing his instrument.

"This is no problem; I will send for Luis Escoto. He will fix all of your problems, señor. You are a little lucky he is not so very far from here."

With that he straightened up, turned aside and before I could say anything else the whole trio had slipped away and merged seamlessly back into the crowd.

Great, my only chance of rescue and he just pisses off.

I had little faith in his half-hearted promise that this Luis – whoever – would really appear. I closed my eyes for a second, resigned to the fact that I was going to have to get out amongst this bunch of lunatics for better or for worse.

This is it, better to do it now. I leaned across to grab my stuff from the back seat when I noticed something slither from the roof and drop in through the window down onto the seat between my leg and the door. *BOOM! BOOM! BOOM! BOOM! KAPAT! KAPAT! KAPAT! KABOOM!*

"*Oh hell!*" A red millipede curl of high incendiary fireworks exploded like a long string of misery on the front seat beside me. Amidst an acrid pall of choking smoke, a fire storm of hot, burning sparks and ear-splitting noise blasted with force all around me. In an uncharacteristic display of agility, I lunged for the passenger-side door, pushed the handle down and roll-dived unceremoniously out and onto the ground. As I lay in the dirt, half in shock, a bony kick in the ribs from a passing reveler made me jerk my head up into the cloud of putrid smoke and pieces of scorched red paper that were drifting out from the car's interior. The smoke stung my eyes as I took a fleeting glance back at the damage. Exasperated, I climbed to my feet, leaned on the edge of the roof, and buried my face in my arms for a half-second respite against all of this Día de los Muertos mayhem.

My fragment of peace stopped abruptly when the Fire Diamond began rocking steadily from side to side. Lifting my head, I saw a young boy of about fourteen fanning the driver's side door determinedly as he extracted more of the remaining smoke. He ducked into the front and began adjusting the seat and fiddling with the column shift lever. I squatted down to confront him, but he just looked at me commandingly and made pointing motions towards the rear of the car yelling "Empujar. Empujar, señor. *Push! Push!*"

Without question I moved towards the trunk to do as he instructed. Hopefully, this was the Luis guy the big guitar playing amigo had promised, although it seemed more likely to be a brazen auto heist by some entrepreneurial local kid working surreptitiously amongst the carnival mayhem. Either way I was in no mind to debate the pros and cons of the situation and started pushing.

The boy released the handbrake and the old '58 began to slowly nudge her way forward. Distracted by everything that was going on, I was surprised to find someone else was pushing along right beside me.

Inclined at an angle almost parallel with the car, was a chubby shirtless fellow of about eighteen. He was wearing a purple flowerpot-like hat pulled down almost over his eyes and two brightly colored leis that half hid his man-boobs, giving him a somewhat disturbing appearance.

We both put our backs into it and in no time the Fire Diamond was getting up some speed and heading off down the street to a destination known only to my newly acquired driver and his accomplice. We pushed on for a few minutes, my vision limited to the dusty red duco of the Fire Diamond's trunk and the debris of the festival's discards strewn on the sandy road below.

I think my comrade in arms beside me was taking the bulk of the load. I tried to go easy on my wounded hand as occasional runs of blood still ran itchy down my arm. For no reason, the big fellow and I exchanged glances and he gave me a big cheesy grin, his eyes just squinting slits below the rim of his hat. Even in my horizontal position I was aware that the mayhem and incessant music were receding to our rear. I think we had passed through the eye of the storm and I began to feel a lot better. An unexpected left turn made me look up and I noticed we were heading to a place a yard or two back from the road. It wasn't the gleaming gas station that I was stupidly hoping for, but a nondescript wall, punctured by the gaping open hole of a double-sized roller door. We continued to push until my adolescent driver suddenly yanked on the handbrake and we came to a complete and definite stop right outside. The first thing I noticed was the two decrepit looking antique fuel pumps standing like double gatekeepers to the right-hand side of the hole. One was a cream color, and the other a dingy red, both irrevocably scarred by a patina of rust and the scrapes of long forgotten vehicles. My heart sank.

My grinning push-partner playfully slapped me on the back with his big chubby hand and steered me across to the side where my driver was already out and standing beside the open door. It was my first real good look at him, a small wiry kid, good looking with heavy dark eyebrows and amazingly white teeth.

"Hola, señor, this is my cousin, Bird." He gestured to my pushing buddy, who was already heading inside, but turned on hearing his name to wave.

"He is a little loco but very strong," he laughed affectionately and introduced himself. "I am Galo Escoto, I am the—"

His cell phone suddenly rang to the digitally bastardized tune of the 'William Tell Overture', so he cut dead his introduction, answered the call and walked off distracted by other business, either more important or immediate. Probably another salvage operation courtesy of the guy with the big guitarrón. I walked across to the light of the garage opening, which doubled as the epicenter of this little family run establishment.

Looking inside the garage I could see a couple of cars in various stages of repair parked down towards the back-end wall and an old pickup perched high on blocks. Its big headlight eyes and missing front paneling seemed to stare out fixedly in a forlorn, toothless gaze.

Everything else was the usual stuff you'd find in a mechanical workshop: a hoist, a couple of obviously new fifty-five-gallon drums (hopefully full of octane for the Fire Diamond), all kinds of tools, spare parts and tires, and one gigantic eight-foot piñata pig lying bright pink and prone on a blue canvas tarp.

Just inside the roller door tracks, next to a few plastic chairs, stood a glass fronted cola fridge. Only one of the shelves seemed allocated to the intended product, as apart from a marinating snake in a jar and an oily glass dish full of bolts, the others were all stacked with fruit.

Sitting on the chairs, and I swear they were not there earlier, were two people. One, a baby boy of about twelve months, goo-gahing away to himself, kicking and twisting around on his own axis like they do. And next to him on another, was a trim forty-odd-year-old man with a leathery complexion and a full black moustache, the ubiquitous look for many a middle-aged local. He was dressed in a crisp white shirt, a clean pair of oversized blue-jeans and sandals that showed off his ultra-white toenails. I figured this was most probably Luis Escoto.

As I made a forward gesture to shake his hand and say hello, he sprang quickly to his feet and came towards me. I was surprised when he didn't take my hand or engage in any conversation, but suddenly dropped down to a stoop and with notepad in hand began a slow examination along the length of the car.

Realizing that I was finally out of all of that mayhem, I turned my thoughts off for a moment, relieved that someone, anyone, was going to fix it all up so I could get the hell out of here.

Staring blankly, I followed Luis Escoto as he slowly in a chameleon like fashion, circumnavigated the entire perimeter of the Fire Diamond. The poor '58 was not looking good. She had a pulverized driver's door window, an interior that looked like it had been firebombed, a well-cooked radiator and God only knows what else.

Highlighted by an exploding rocket, the outlines of drunken skeletons cavorting around in the street snapped me back into a panic.

SKELETONS! What the? A hand placed on my upper arm immediately stopped me from going bananas. An attractive middle-aged woman stood beside me, smiling warm-heartedly.

"It is okay, señor, there is no problem."

With her other hand she offered me a burrito on a paper plate. Food! I grabbed it and shoved it greedily into my mouth. It barely touched the sides and was gone with two or three bites. I knew it was more of a courtesy thing, probably from the family's evening meal and I knew there would be no more.

"Thank you, señora. That was delicious."

Then a small girl of about four or five tugged impatiently at my jeans to get my attention. She handed me up a warm, moist hand towel then ran off immediately back into the adjoining living area. I wasn't sure if it was for me to wipe my face or not, but I thought my blood encrusted hand and forearm a better option and cleaned off most of the now congealed blood with a moment of vigorous rubbing. Only a couple of spots still persisted in bleeding, but nothing bad or deep enough to cause any worry.

"Su carro parece muy sucio," said the woman, then quickly realized I was just another dumbass, mono-lingual gringo.

"Your poor car looks very dirty and sad, señor. We will have it all fixed and cleaned very well for you tomorrow. Sorry, I do not speak inglés so well."

Luis Escoto had completed his circumnavigation of the car and scribbled more notes into his book. He spoke a few words in Spanish to the lady who was obviously his wife.

"It will be ready for you around mid-morning, señor," the woman reassured me.

"Do you possibly have any old leaded gas or octane? She definitely won't run on eth."

"Yes, of course señor, no problem. I suggest now that you go on a little down the way to The Pepper Coyote and get yourself a room for the night. They are good, clean rooms and you can relax a little and have some food and drink. Take it easy. Your automobile will be ready for you tomorrow."

Then as if to punctuate the moment, a spark-plumed rocket hurtled its way straight at us from the darkness outside. It flew like a thunderbolt over the roof of my car, before crashing hard into the far garage wall which cut dead its fiery momentum.

The Escotos seemed unphased and although the small boy fidgeting about on the plastic chair had been the cause for a moment's concern, luckily he was now sitting down on the floor, seemingly oblivious to the firework's last dying fizzes.

Bird stuck his head out through the fly screen door that adjoined the garage area and the family kitchen but pulled it back in again as nothing had exploded or noticeably burst into flame.

The Fire Diamond was ratshit. For a near concourse condition ride, there was a lot of fixing and cleaning needed just to make it look half decent. I was somewhat skeptical it would come up to much by mid-morning, even if they worked all through the night. It still had a busted window and there was no way on God's green earth that they were going to be able to fix that. I sighed in exasperation and leaned inside to get my stuff out from the back seat.

As I headed off to The Pepper Coyote, I saw an old man sitting with folded arms on one of the plastic chairs, who I swear was not there five seconds earlier. He just sat there grinning happily, with a smile identical to both Galo and Luis Escoto. The most impressive thing about him were the new and well-made cowboy boots he was so proudly wearing. They were a strange greenish-grey, tinged with a luminosity. He chuckled when he saw me looking at them.

"Chupacabra," he said.

I turned and set off.

2

The Pepper Coyote

I pushed my way in through the swinging doors like they do in the westerns. It was a big double-story space, with an old wooden verandah running precariously around the first-floor walls. I stood for a moment, fixated by the light cords that flowed like neon snakes around the handrails. At the far end stood the bar, it glowed with an eerie, electric blue color courtesy of the strip lights that edged all the shelves and the mirrors behind it.

The place was almost empty. Twenty or so tables were divided either side of the central walk that ran from the doors to the bar. On the left side, closest to the street end sat a couple of haggard looking skellies playing cards in slow motion. On the right side with his back to me, sat an old Mexican man having a heated conversation with someone sitting opposite who wasn't even there. His index finger wagging and punctuating the most important parts of his inaudible diatribe to his adversary.

Sitting at an adjacent table next to the man was another, much younger dude, half-lolling drunkenly across the back of his chair, his head bobbing approximately in rhythm to the irritating music that was coming from somewhere in the room.

Further towards the bar, I noticed two men half-hidden in the shadows beneath the left-hand side verandah. They were obviously gringos and definitely not from around here. I could feel their eyes following me as I walked on up to the bar.

As I stood there unattended, I glanced furtively along the counter at some mumbling drunk fixating on his likeness in the mirror.

"Yes señor, what can I get you?"

My head snapped back attentively when I heard the voice of an elderly woman on the other side of the counter. She was extremely short and at first, I inadvertently looked straight over the top of her.

"Um, give me a shot of Tequila, and a, *Oooh*—" Behind her was a fridge full of bottles. Even at that distance I could see what they were by the labels. Beers. European beers. "That one please, second shelf down, excellent!" I hadn't seen any of this particular beverage for eons, not even back in the States. I was amazed that they'd have it all the way down here in Sonora.

The familiar tap of an empty shot glass on the bar brought me back, but instead of the bartender there was now a taller, young Anglo girl standing there. Distracted by the beer hoard, I hadn't seen the change-over and found myself looking straight down her blouse. I adjusted my eyes upwards and grinned at her sheepishly in acknowledgement of my mistake.

She poured from an unlabeled bottle. I put the shot up to my lips and downed it in one, slamming the empty glass back on the bar with an unconvincing "*Aaagh!*", intentionally ignoring the saucer with the slice of lemon and the salt. Real guys don't jerk around with all that touristy, lick, sip, and suck crap. She took no notice anyway. I identified her immediately by her voice as American but couldn't quite place her accent.

"You want anything else with the beer mister, any food?"

"Yeah, whatever's going, some burritos, enchiladas, maybe some beans." My nonexistent knowledge of any other Mexican food was blatantly apparent.

"Sit yourself down somewhere and I'll bring something over to you."

She seemed a little distracted, even nervous. I caught the flick of her eyes as she dared a glance over towards the two men sitting in the shadows. As she turned to get my order, I followed her instruction and zeroed in on a spot three tables back behind the drunkard sitting at the bar.

Dropping my ass in the chair I could still feel the bead of the gringos burning a hole in my back, which I'd deliberately turned towards them, so I could check out the young American girl moving skittishly around behind the counter.

All of my energy seemed to drain from up top and pool in my lower legs and ankles.

"I'll be damned, didn't see this day coming," I thought to myself looking up at the surging wave of lights on the verandah rails above me.

"What *is* that frick'n awful racket?"

The all-pervasive music had become even more irritating now I was sitting down. I looked over my shoulder in the direction I thought it was coming from. Down in the far back corner, out of sight from the doors, was a tiny, makeshift stage, no bigger than a kitchen table, that stood about eight inches up off the floor. On it were two guys diligently plying their trade.

I turned my head a little more comfortably, as I felt compelled to get a better look at them. The tall one was playing a keyboard that sat on a thin, metal stand. To his left, just off the stage on the floor was his all-in-one amp and speaker combo. It was only the size of a small fruit box but was incredibly loud and turned all the way up to eleven.

He was wearing a saggy, threadbare hound-dog costume. Its minimal components included two droopy eye holes and a half-chewed piece of plastic that was supposed to be the nose. Although the mouth took the prize as the most artistic feature – a short, crooked gash drawn on with a felt tip pen – the most irritating thing though were the ears. Two sock-like shapes that swung limply in time to the music, as their owner's paws lunged maniacally along the length of the keyboard.

"What a dick!"

The other one was a skelly. Not a real one, but either a midget or a small fat kid dressed from head to toe in a cheap black ninja outfit. The green, fluorescent skeleton printed on it glowed menacingly by way of a strategically placed black-light bar down by his feet. He was armed with a crimson, twin-necked guitar and had absolutely no idea how to play it. He was totally crap and could barely manage a labored three-chord-riff. He wrestled with it constantly trying to keep it under control. This guy had no idea what he was doing.

Of course, the speaker units he had stacked up behind him were way too big and powerful for this pint-sized doof. The obligatory chrome script logo on the amp box had obviously given him some misplaced sense of talent and importance.

"What a dick!"

I turned back to the front in disgust, as the American girl arrived with my beer which she placed on the table in front of me. The top was already off, so I threw back my head and swigged down the chilled amber contents. It tasted like bliss and for a moment flushed all my worries away.

As I took another gulp the girl reappeared with a large plate of vittles. I wasn't quite sure what it was, but it was steaming and hot and there was a shitload of it. I concentrated on eating for a time without any other distractions, but the girl was still fluttering around the table trying to look busy but obviously trying to get my attention.

"Hey mister. Have you got a car? Can you give me a lift out of here?" She seemed both nervous and agitated, so I thought it best to answer rather than ignore her.

"Like where?"

"Anywhere. Just away from here."

"Yeah, I've got wheels, but they're screwed. No idea either how long it will take to get fixed," I lied to put her off. I wasn't really interested in getting any deeper into this discussion. As I hoed hungrily back into my food, I tracked her movements out of the corner of my eye for any signs of erratic behavior.

It was obvious she wasn't gonna take no for an answer. As she moved herself neatly around to my left, facing away from the two white guys back in the shadows. I remembered her furtive glance earlier and guessed she was in some kind of trouble.

"Please, can you get me out of here mister, I'd very much appreciate it ... really."

I figured she'd been hovering around me too long and so did the two men behind us. They suddenly stood up from their table and made their way over quite purposefully in our direction. As the girl took off, I kept on eating my food, mopping up the juice on the plate with the slightly stale corn tortillas. The gringos sauntered up next to me, their crotches hovering little more than a foot or so from my face. I tried to ignore them, but they weren't having any of that.

"Hey, how ya doin' buddy?" the shorter one closest to me said in a half disingenuous, half *Hi there! I'm your new best friend* kind of tone.

I put the last tortilla into my mouth and pushed the plate away. I looked up, exaggerating my chewing just to annoy him, and nodded.

He stepped back a little, spread his arms apart and placed his hands firmly down on the table. As he leaned forward his face was now only slightly higher than mine.

He was a smarmy looking character, fifty-something, with newly renovated, super-white teeth. He had an enormously big forehead, perfectly engraved with three symmetrical furrows that ran from one side of his big fat head to the other. I was enthralled with his unnatural looking hairstyle – smooth, black, and greasy with a slightly off centered mound on the top.

The other man had nudged himself around to the front of the table and stood looking down at me all-menacing, with both of his hands in his pockets. He was even uglier than his buddy. Mid-forties, a real frick'n pinhead, with thick horn-rimmed glasses and a droopy, ratty looking moustache, that acted as a counterbalance to the three shapeless, why-bother hair clumps that looked like they'd been stuck up on his head for a joke.

I glanced around the place surreptitiously for the girl, but she had vanished.

Unfortunately, the music hadn't. The irritating unrhythmic beat still pulsed on regardless and was really starting to settle perniciously behind my eyeballs.

Then the greasy-haired one spoke again. "So what brings you down here to these parts mister?"

"Who wants to know?"

That was his cue. "Martindale … *Special Agent* Martindale." He lovingly flipped his precious ID badge open like he had a thousand times before.

"And this is my partner, Special Agent Travers." His whiny voice was irksome.

I glanced momentarily at his ID. "Does that agency hold any sway here in Mexico?" I replied flippantly.

The chuckling bad cop face of his partner pulsed up and down in unison with the hands buried deep inside his trouser pockets.

"Oh yes it does mister. It has jurisdiction *everywhere* now, or haven't you heard? I'm sorry, now what was your name sir? I don't believe I heard it the first time."

His irritating grin had subsided, and his mood swung into the *You've had your fun, but now I'm getting annoyed and I'm going to get all nasty, unless you start to cooperate* mode.

His buddy leaned forward a touch, yanked his arms out from his pockets and folded them authoritatively in front of his chest.

"Wolf. My name's Wolf," I answered in a compliant but monotone voice.

Travers did a little wolf howl under his breath and sniggered his pin-sized head up and down again for a couple of seconds.

"Well Mr. Wolf, like I asked before, what brings a nice American boy like you all the way down here to Mexico?"

I was going to make some kind of smartass remark, but thought better of it, as it would only succeed in antagonizing this prick even further. I just wanted these two to go away as quickly as possible, so I could finish my beer and let my food go down in peace.

"I'm just travelling around, seeing the sights."

"Just travelling around, seeing the sights," grinned Martindale, bobbing his head up and down mockingly.

I was expecting some kind of grilling to get underway, when instead he reached into his jacket pocket and produced a five by four photo which he held up in front of my face.

"By any chance, do you happened to have seen this person any-where … while you were *just travelling around, seeing the sights*?"

The photo was of a girl about seventeen or eighteen years of age, attractive, beautiful actually, long fair hair, blue-grey eyes, broad smile, perfect teeth. It was obviously one of those fancy, upper class, high school photos: necktie, tailored blazer, antique bookcase in the background. A couple of areas had been digitally blurred out, obviously the school badge and some other tell-tale classified information objects, pertaining to either the girl or the school's identity.

"Nope, can't say I have. I'm sure I'd remember a pretty girl like that."

"This picture's a couple of years old now. Could you stretch your imagination to whether or not you might have seen someone with a slightly aged resemblance to this person?"

He never called her a girl, or a woman, just "this person". I could tell he didn't like this form of inquiry. He would probably rather have just pounded my head into the table until I confessed that I knew her name, age, shoe size and the coordinates of her immediate whereabouts.

"Sorry, I ain't seen anyone like that."

The American girl crossed my mind fleetingly, but apart from the closeness of age and hair color she bore no resemblance at all. Besides, these two had been eyeballing her since before I came into the place, so she was obviously not the one they were looking for.

"Well now, Mr. Wolf, if you do happen to—"

Right then a gun shot rang out loudly behind me, down near the swinging doors.

Instinctively I ducked and slid quickly off my chair to the floor.

The two special agents switched immediately into their action-man mode, all spread legged and crouching with handguns drawn ready to blast away at anything that moved. Acting all very "highly trained".

I glanced back through a forest of chair legs to where the shot had come from. An angry, heavy-set man, who I hadn't noticed the whole time I'd been there, (maybe he'd been taking a dump in the john or something) was now waving his smoking pistol menacingly above his head and swearing loudly in some swill-bucket version of Spanish.

In a flash Martindale and Travers had vaulted the length of the room down towards him. Even quicker had been the swan-diving Dog Man, who, judging by the smoldering hole in his terry toweling ear, had been the intended target of the well-placed gunshot and abuse. Swift retribution now fell upon Señor Shooter by way of an impromptu ashtray pounding. The weapon plucked handily from a nearby table.

The infuriating "music" had stopped, but the keyboard, pushed aside in the Dog Man's fervor had landed keys down on the floor and was now stuck hard on one shrill unending note.

Agent Travers held Señor Shooter's gun arm up vertically to stop him getting off any more rounds. Agent Martindale was wrestling unsuccessfully with both him and the Dog Man, who was going completely psycho yelling profanities in muffled English through a mouthful of terry toweling.

To make things worse, the half-drunk dude who had been sitting behind me bobbing away to the music when I first came in, had decided to join the fray and had launched himself, beer glass in hand, like an inebriated fighting missile right smack on top of the four already scuffling men. The now five combatants continued their fighting scrimmage down, and fortuitously out through the front entrance.

Thinking it a good time to get out of here and hit the hay, I picked up my stuff from under the table and snuck off crouching low towards the staircase over near the bar. I glanced back momentarily at the fracas, which had worked its way back inside the doorway. The swinging thumps of the spring-loaded doors added two more impartial combatants as they continued their oblivious fighting.

"Morons!"

I noticed the midget-man was calmly coiling up his leads. The double-necked guitar and his amp had already been zipped away safely in their protective vinyl covers.

Obviously, no bond of camaraderie between him and the Dog Man existed. He didn't even bother to move or pick up the fallen keyboard. Its piercing noise just kept screaming away, annoyingly loud, and relentless.

Breezing quickly past the drunken guy at the bar, I leapt athletically up the first few stairs determined to get away from all of this madness. The old wooden runs were worn out and springy and creaked ever louder the further up I went.

From out of nowhere, behind an old leather suitcase, appeared the

American girl coming down the stairs. She crashed herself hard against me like a sixty-pound sack of spuds. I could see in her eyes she was totally panic stricken and out of control. We jostled awkwardly for a moment as she pushed the suitcase into my face in her urgent need to get past me.

"They're looking for somebody else, it's not you, they—"

She flew on down to the bottom of the stairs and disappeared quickly out of sight somewhere behind the counter.

"Jeesh, what's her frick'n problem?"

I turned at the top of the stairs and followed the neon lights down the walkway in search of an empty room. Finding an open door with nobody inside I went straight in and threw my bag and jacket on the empty chair beside the bed.

The door had swung shut behind me, so I locked it and slid tight the bolt.

Luckily, there was a large wooden wardrobe standing right alongside, so in one last feeble act of exertion, I pushed it sideways in front of the door. One last barrier between myself and gun-totin' halfwits, drink-swilling skeletons, dog men, special agents, paranoid women, fireworks, blue-neon lights, and that god-awful, infernal music. I dropped down onto the bed like a long-hangin' side o' beef and fell instantly into a well-deserved, comatose sleep.

3

Flight

Five months earlier

No matter how many times she looked inside the bus's luggage compartment, the suitcase wasn't there. She knew it was pointless but hoped desperately that it would appear magically amongst all the other bags still in transit.

The initial sympathetic tone of the driver was now becoming terse. Although she understood little Spanish, she knew it was time to give up and concede that her suitcase was gone.

She glanced at the few remaining passengers staring blankly down at her from behind their windows, wishing her away and for the driver to get back onboard and continue at long last with their journey. He pushed her aside softly with his forearm, before locking the luggage compartment's door. Resuming his seat on the bus, the concertina door closed shut with a hydraulic hiss of finality as he engaged the drive, pressed the accelerator firmly and drove off into the invisibility of the hot dusty haze.

Containing her fury, she pivoted on her heels and moved across the dirt road to a low concrete wall that was part of the terminus building. She found a vacant spot amongst the jumble of people and their belongings, then flopped down defeated and let out a long-exasperated sigh. The acrid fumes belching from the idling bus exhausts had made her feel light-headed. She sniffed and wiped her eyes with a scrunched-up piece of tissue, extracted from up her sleeve, but there were no tears.

To reassure herself she looked down into the soft canvas shoulder bag that hung tightly against her side to see that everything in there was still safe. She pulled it back closed and zipped the top securely, wiped her nose and eyes again, then deep in thought, just sat there staring blankly out across the dusty street.

Finally, exhausted after days of constant travel, she had arrived at her destination but now without her bag. Acute tiredness had begun to take its toll, causing her head to nod up and down in a half sleep.

She knew it would be impossible to report the missing suitcase to the police or the bus company as it would only draw attention to her plight. Disheartened and weary she gazed out across the central square and recapped the timeline that had brought her to this point.

◆

It had been well over a week since she set out from Oslo. She remembered catching the last small ferry for the short journey across the harbor to the city from the leafy, exclusive peninsular where her father lived.

She remembered the peel of the bells from the city hall that started up as the boat neared the wharf, marking the hour. She remembered looking up at the Oslo Rådhus near the waterfront, where the Peace Prize laureates received their awards. She wondered when she would see its box-like facade again.

In no real hurry to disembark, she knew she would make it easily to the central bus station where the night bus would take her out of Norway and along the lower west coast of Sweden then across to Ystad on Sweden's Baltic coast.

Normally heads turned wherever she went, but she remembered how her good friend Gregers had walked straight past her on the Rådhusgata, deceived by her long golden hair now dyed a dull mousey brown and bundled up untidily beneath a large, knitted beanie. If this simple disguise atop an ill-fitting dress had fooled someone who knew her well, hopefully she'd blend into the building holiday crowds and leave unnoticed.

She had left on a Wednesday, the day before the annual Ascension Day holiday weekend. It had long been planned as the best time for her to slip away and get a good head start before anyone knew she was gone. Her departure was secret to all but three people, and she had no plans to return any time soon.

Her estranged father had shown little interest in her wellbeing and was only aware of her presence in his house by a phone call he'd made to the housekeeper. Informed that she had just dropped in for a few days, he never asked to speak to her, but learned she was heading to Drammen to spend the holiday with a friend and would then return to her job in the north.

Of course, this was not true, but it was her alibi to get away from

Norway unhindered. To add to her deception, she had charged up her phone and posted it by surface mail to a fictitious address. She hoped it would place her somewhere she wasn't for a few more days.

She remembered sitting quietly watching the sun come up at the ferry terminal at Ystad, then negotiating her way around the empty barriers that usually corralled the passengers onto the ferries. The one she had caught was quite small and fast, not one of the bigger liner-sized boats that crisscrossed the Baltic on the longer overnight routes.

The journey across to the fishing port of Allinge on the Danish island of Bornholm took only a couple of hours. She had been anticipating having a hearty breakfast when she got there, maybe some smoked herrings freshly prepared from the mornings catch, lots of cheese, toast, and coffee! Yes, three cups of hot, *real* coffee.

So far, she had managed to keep herself to herself. Nobody had paid her any unwelcome attention, apart from an over-friendly young Australian from Melbourne, who had gotten onto the bus at Gothenburg in Sweden. He had kept leaning annoyingly over towards her from his seat across the aisle in a futile attempt to try and chat her up, by enthusiastically extolling the virtues of "The Greatest Game on Earth", an obscure, antipodean football code that she'd never even heard of.

Nearing Allinge she thought happily of her best friend Elsbeth, who shared her twenty-four years of age to the day and knew she would be waiting for her, quietly watching her arrival somewhere off to the side, slightly back from the quay, which was her way.

It didn't matter if they hadn't seen each other for a month or even a year. So close was their friendship, they would simply take up and carry on their excited, animated discussion about some shared urgent news, personal melodrama, or the latest bit of earth-shattering gossip as if they had only been talking yesterday.

The visit to see Elsbeth had coincided well with her plans as it was en-route to her first destination. How glad she was to spot her friend in her long grey coat waiting patiently against the metal railing, motionless like a siren's statue.

She remembered her uncontainable excitement as she bounded up the last few concrete steps to meet her. The memory of those warm affectionate embraces and over excited laughter which came so easily from such a sincere and unconditional friendship on that dull and overcast morning would stay with her forever.

Elsbeth would surely be deeply missed.

The one day of fun and catching up with her friend had been planned as a considered luxury as well as a strategic imperative in her travelling schedule. Elsbeth did not live in Allinge, but further along the coast in Svaneke, a similar little fishing village that looked out directly east across the Baltic Sea to Russia, Lithuania, and Poland.

The trip across the island in Elsbeth's tiny old car had been blessed with the priceless gift of laughter, girlish fun, and pure enjoyment. They diverted south a little and drove as deep as they could into the heart of Almindingen, the remnants of the ancient forest that stands in defiance of the modern world right in the center of Bornholm.

As they walked silently along the little tracks beneath those beautiful green trees, she remembered how thoughtfully Elsbeth had dropped back a respectful distance and allowed her to wander ahead, alone for a while deep into the oldest and darkest corner of that most ancient and powerful Scandinavian place. To just sit and gather her thoughts and contemplate the ramifications of what she was planning and the uncertainty of the days and months that lay ahead.

She remembered the wonderful food Elsbeth had prepared and the expensive wine that she had so generously supplied until her mind's more critical faculties had been sloshed and distorted, subjecting her thoughts to the fluctuating emotions of uncontrollable happiness and laughter, nostalgia, sadness, panic and fear. And of course, the soppy and exaggerated tear-filled declarations of unequivocal love for her one true friend. She was a terrible drunk.

But before all that, before the wine had time to slowly soak its intoxicating spell upon her, they had discussed the seriousness of her flight and reiterated the most important details and pieces of information that had to be worked out and resolved. The things she knew she could only safely and secretly entrust to Elsbeth.

All of their correspondence for the past few months had been prudent and cautious. She knew they were not particularly good "spy types", but they did their best, keeping all communication as untraceable as possible against whoever was going to be looking for and coming after her in the not too distant future.

Urgent emails had only been exchanged from net-cafes, hot-spots or whatever other disassociated networks were available. All of their posts had been wiped and any phone calls were made only on land lines. When they'd tried making conversations in code, more often than not they deteriorated quickly into fits of hysterical laughter and confusion, as one, or both of them, would get the wrong end of the stick or otherwise just forget whatever it was they were supposed to have been talking about anyway.

They probably attracted more suspicion to anyone listening than if they'd simply come right out and said what they'd intended directly. But they'd tried.

Her most important ulterior motive for the short stopover had been delivered. A letter for her brother, which when the time was right, would tell him where he could find her. Secret and safe on Bornholm like the old, fabled Templar treasures hidden around the island's interior.

They had slept in the same bed that night, for no other reason than knowing they might not see each other again for months or even years.

The smoked herrings had not materialized on the day of her arrival, but on the morning of her departure she fondly remembered their early, slightly hungover stroll down the overcast beach, accompanied by a squawking flock of seagulls, to the herring smokers shack to buy some fish. Then, upon returning to eat, along with hot cups of coffee, the delicious Sunrise over Svaneke breakfast Elsbeth would prepare: a traditional local morning feast of smoked herrings, onions, chives, and radish slices, piled high up on rye bread and crowned on top with a raw, unbroken, golden egg yolk. Her last in her friend's company and the last before leaving the Nordic countries.

Parting was devastating and no matter how hard she had tried to put on a happy face she was overwhelmed by a feeling of sadness. Dear Elsbeth, how long would it be until she saw her again?

◆

The ferry from Bornholm to Kołobrzeg was her last trip by sea. It all seemed complicated and time consuming but getting to Poland without an ID trail was crucial to her plans. To board a flight from anywhere in Scandinavia or Europe was impossible now without submitting to the mandatory, full body holographic identification procedures. It was only due to a minor diplomatic rift between Poland and the rest of Western Europe, regarding some kind of ballistic missile deployment issue, that a technical loophole had left the door ajar for the moment, to still fly out to certain parts of the Americas without complying with the all-pervasive intrusion.

Upon disembarking at Kołobrzeg wharf beneath the watchful eye of the old city lighthouse, she had carried her small suitcase and shoulder bag the short distance to the railway station. Elsbeth had already booked a seat for her on the Ekspres Inter City in another name.

Collecting her ticket from the booking office, she boarded the already waiting train, found her seat, then settled herself comfortably by the window ready for the long eight-hour journey to Warszawa Centralna.

The trip was comfortable but emotionally troubling. For most of those eight hours she had gazed melancholic out beyond the train windows as the world flashed by. Unwittingly she could sense the ghostly presence of some of the innocent and unfortunate souls who had suffered and died so senselessly at the hands of others in this place at the crossroads of empires.

She knew she'd been charged way too much for the taxi ride to the airport, but she didn't care. Boats and buses and trains and taxis, she'd had enough, but unfortunately the journey was really only just beginning.

Although she did not have to go through the whole-body scanning process, she still had to use her Norwegian passport and a data trail of immigration and passenger list information would be unavoidable from here. She knew it might only delay her whereabouts for a time, but if she could get away quickly and quietly, she might have a good chance of reaching her eventual destination unnoticed.

Once she arrived at the airport, she knew she was going to have to wing it. Not having booked a seat she knew that getting a standby ticket would be purely a matter of luck. The airline office was virtually empty, so without delay she fronted up to the counter and in less than five minutes had purchased one economy class ticket, departure time: 2300 hours. Warsaw to Guatemala City via Casablanca. A mind numbing, thirty-five-hour endurance flight, but yes, luck was with her that day.

She found herself an out of the way corner on the floor of the airport until check-in time. After what seemed an eternity, she was finally in the air and able to kick off her boots, relax a little and even managed to nap for a while, before one of the flight attendants woke her with the obligatory barrage of questions, "The beef or the chicken? Tea, wine, or coffee? Would you like ice, milk or sugar?"

It was the announcement: "Ladies and Gentlemen, due to a small technical problem we will be making an unscheduled landing for as short a time as possible. We apologize for any inconvenience." That sat her bolt upright in panic. If the passengers were obliged to get off the plane somewhere in Europe, she would most certainly have to go through a holographic body-scanner to re-board, jeopardizing her whole covert plan.

Fortunately, it was only a minor alarm. The stopover was brief, and the passengers remained on the plane. She had never been so pleased to see an unwell person wheeled past her on a stretcher in all her life. She still felt pangs of guilt for allowing herself such a thought.

The rest of the flight to Casablanca and onto Guatemala City passed in a haze of half-sleep and boredom and the wish that it would finally come to an end. She watched the little screen on the back of the seat in front, mesmerized as she followed the little digital airplane on its journey across the pixel blue Atlantic Ocean, into the Caribbean and finally down into the 3D contours of Central America.

◆

She recalled how frenetic and energetic everything down on the ground was, compared to Europe or Scandinavia. The noise of the traffic; the heavy polluted feel of the air; the smells of the street; the color and the amount of people; it was just like it had been when she'd travelled to Southeast Asia.

Guatemala airport and city came and went. She remembered a cheap hotel room where everything was painted a purplish-blue color and all the fittings and bed linen were pretty much the same color too. But it was just a curio; she had slept like a baby that night after the seemingly endless flight across the broad Atlantic Ocean.

The old adage *It's not the destination, it's the journey* unfortunately didn't apply on this trip. Instead of just spending some leisure time to relax and checkout the city, she was back on a bus within hours for another grueling five-hour trip north west to Huehuetenago, better known as "Huehue", high up in clouds along the ridges of the Sierra de Los Cuchumatanes. A beautiful place, a coffee farming area still populated by the descendants of the Maya. But even more importantly a transit town for travelers heading on out towards the Mexican border.

Despite the tenacious travel schedule she had set herself, something magical about Huehue forced her this time to stop and unwind a little and allow herself the luxury of an impromptu visit to the Mayan ruins at Zaculeu just outside the city. She had always been curious about pre-Colombian cultures and was not going to let the opportunity go by.

Soon after her arrival she had been befriended by two local youths, who competed between themselves for her attention by taking her on motorbike rides around the mountainside places of Huehue. Eager to oblige, they had offered to take her on the two-hour journey further north to where they assured her they could drive her safely across the border into Mexico, without any police or authorities even knowing she was there. Which early the next morning they did.

◆

She sat patiently on the small concrete wall and began to drift into sleep with a precarious list off the vertical.

Her fragmented thoughts bobbed dreamily around her missing suitcase. Where was it that she last remembered seeing it in the bus luggage compartment? Who's faces could she recall on the bus and who had gotten off where? Her recollections were muddled with tiredness and made little or no sense at all.

With a jolt she looked up, suddenly aware of a cream and rust colored pickup truck that had appeared across the street from the bus depot. She shaded her eyes against the glare to get a better look. There it was, a piece of white ribbon tied unassumingly halfway up the radio antenna, just as she'd been expecting.

She stood up, brushed herself down halfheartedly with her hands and clutching her shoulder bag tightly against her side crossed over to where the pickup was parked.

Cautiously she walked to the open driver's window where a man in his late sixties wearing a tall, white cowboy hat sat quietly behind the steering wheel. As she reached the open window, he turned his gaze towards her, smiled kindly and spoke in a deep Texan accent.

"Well hello there, young lady, it's a pleasure to finally meet you!"

"Hello. Are you … The Mad Hatter?"

He didn't reply, but just raised his index finger up from below the window fame with a grin.

On the top of his finger sat a small, tinfoil sombrero modeled carefully from a discarded piece of chocolate bar wrapping.

She laughed with relief, then bounded sprightly around the front of the hood, where she opened the passenger door and climbed up into the seat right beside him.

4

Back to the Fire Diamond

I woke early. The one patch of sun coming in through the window was shining right on my face. I shifted away as disjointed recollections of the night before swirled through my head. With a roll I launched my legs over the side of the bed, the rest of me followed behind and came to rest in an unsteady upright position. Then came the morning's obligatory coughing and the sudden desperate need to go take a leak.

Standing with the agility of an eighty-year-old I zeroed my attention in on the wardrobe that I vaguely remembered pulling in front of the door. It stood there stoically like a heavy, wooden line-backer right between me and the can. Thankfully, it shifted back easily, so I tore down the stairs in search of the john.

All that aside, I walked back out into the saloon, which at this hour was quiet and totally still. The swirling light cables had been switched off, the chairs were all flipped up on the tables and not a skelly or drunk was around. I expected to see the short woman shuffling about behind the bar doing chores or something, but she was nowhere. The Pepper Coyote seemed deserted.

I scanned the room and flash-backed joyfully over last night's floor show. That Martindale guy and his God-ugly sidekick, the Dog Man and his ashtray pounding, the high-hip-gunslinger polka through the saloon doors and that neurotic, psycho bar chick. *Jesus, what a hole!*

Back in my room the bed had mysteriously been made, well maybe the top sheet tidied up a little, so I'd notice the piece of paper with a note on it. I picked it up and read: "Dear señor, please pay the balance of your hotel bill when you return to Luis Escoto's garage to pick up your car. Thank you."

The writing style was large and child-like. There was no name as to who it was from, so I folded it in two and slipped it into the pocket of my jeans.

It was the first time I'd really taken a look around the room. A bed, the line-backer wardrobe, wooden plank flooring with a threadbare mat and a big oblong shaped patch of light from the window that had shifted around from the bed and onto the wall. And apart from a chair and a little ol' water pitcher and bowl sitting on a dresser that was it.

Then I noticed something curious hanging off the picture rail at the end of the bed. It was a round wooden frame about the size of a dinner plate. Beneath the dusty glass was a time and sun-faded picture, like something from one of those old-fashioned children's books. The drawing itself was of two little kittens standing up on their back legs pulling a small toy wagon, in which sat a cute little wavy-haired girl. She was holding a posy of flowers in one hand and what looked like a snake in the other. It was pretty odd, but I gave it no more thought.

"Better get my sorry ass out of here." I took a quick look at myself in the dresser's mirror before I left. *"Holy Hell, what a sight".*

My face wore a three-day stubble and my hairstyle wasn't looking too good at all. The greying quiff had split in half and was pointing in two directions, one up, the other out semi-sideways. I made a half-baked attempt to rake it back into shape, "Looks like *The Quiff King Cowboy* will have to wait some," I said, self mockingly, and promptly plonked my old curl straw hat on my head.

Back on the street outside I realized it wasn't as early as I'd thought. The town was already going about its business. Above the sounds of the slow-moving traffic, even noisier kids were running amok through the street stalls like a whole bunch of high-octane loop fruits.

Other than a few overlooked decorations high up on light poles, it was as though the festivities of last night had never happened. And there was no sign of skeletons either.

"This place is all too frick'n weird for me!" I mumbled to myself and headed off in the completely opposite direction of Luis Escoto's garage.

Slinking down the street with some time to kill, I envisioned the fervid scene back at the garage. Whipping the poor old Fire Diamond back into some kind of shape would have been a big call considering the state I'd served it up in.

I realized then that Señor Escoto's mesmerizing appraisal of the car had somehow distracted me from the obvious. He hadn't even looked under the hood.

I thought for a second about a crack in the radiator or the possibility of a blown head gasket or even something worse. It was far too horrifying to think about, so I wiped it from my thoughts then and there.

Drawn on by the aroma of chargrilled chicken, I wasn't paying much attention to where I was going and with only a turn or two away from the main street, I'd walked myself into a part of the town where I knew I most definitely should not have.

The neglected walls of the surrounding laneways were covered heavily in posters and spray-painted slogans. Unwittingly, I'd turned into a small, confined plaza populated by stern-faced young men armed with an array of rifles and sidearms.

I wracked my brain in regard to cartels and street gangs, but that speedy cartoon mouse and "The King" in *Fun in Acapulco* was pretty much the extent of my knowledge of Mexico.

Gingerly I retraced what I thought were my footsteps, hoping that none of these guys had even seen me. Moving with stealth, I accidentally knocked one of the men's rifles with my bag as he stepped back unexpectedly. He spun his head around to look at me but being in the midst of a spirited dispute with his hombre, he turned instantly back to his wrangle. I knew from his demeanor that at any other time I would probably have been the recipient of some form of vehement redress.

The way out from here was near, but in my panic it all looked the same. All around I could feel the eyes and the curiosity of the men beginning to focus in on me. I heard a wash of angry Spanish that needed no translation. I dared not turn around but kept putting one foot in front of the other. Laughter broke out behind me. Whatever it was, their attention had thankfully been distracted and I was no more than two steps away from a corner around which I could make a bolt for freedom, when a hand slapped down heavily on my shoulder.

"So close," I thought. "So close. Now I've really had it." I turned to face my impending doom, only to be confronted by the grinning face of Bird.

I'd never been more relieved to see anyone.

"What you doin' down around here mister?" he asked me surprised. "You might get yourself in big trouble señor. Get on! We go back now to Luis Escoto's. Si?"

He had appeared so suddenly that I hadn't noticed he was perched up on the seat of an old stripped-down, step-through motorcycle, his substantial girth all but hid its fragile frame beneath him.

I jumped immediately on what was left of the back end of the seat. Even in my haste to escape I couldn't fail to notice the four inches of fleshy bum crack, smiling out at me over the top of his low riding, designer brand underpants.

Once we'd cleared the alleys, Bird pulled back the throttle and the whining motorcycle bolted us back in the direction of the garage.

The ride was most welcome, and Bird took up most of the seat; I hung on behind with my bag jammed down between us. My freehand held my hat on my head, while my legs dangled out at forty-five on either side. That poor old engine strained desperately beneath all the weight, but Bird just pushed it even harder.

Returning to *Casa de Escoto* took no time at all. It felt much less foreboding down this end of town, but I had no idea what marked the divide.

Bird hit the brakes with a vengeance, shifting his weight from the seat when it stopped. As a consequence, the rear of the bike sprang up a good ten inches and launched me right off the back. Due to some footwork that a Cossack would have been proud of, I kept my balance and was spared the humiliation of landing flat on my face. My undignified dismount had been the cause of impromptu laughter from Bird and some of the family who were hanging around out the front. I picked up my bag, stood straight and walked as unflustered as possible over toward the garage. I noticed Bird had taken off his flower-pot hat. It was the first time I'd seen his face properly and he really looked more Asian to me than Mexican.

"Thanks Bird. How'd you find me there?"

He giggled, "I saw you leave the Coyote bar and then go back the wrong way."

I knew what he meant. Bird's English wasn't perfect, but if I could speak Spanish even one tenth as good, I'd call myself bilingual, probably trilingual. I was already fluent in talking a whole load o' bull crap.

"Thanks Bird, I'm pretty sure you saved my bacon."

He grinned, looked at me kind of funny and wandered off inside, indifferent to my declaration of gratitude.

My early arrival didn't seem to bother the family, although when I looked inside the garage area, I couldn't see the Fire Diamond.

"Hello señor. How are you this morning?" Came the friendly greeting from young Galo. "I hope you had a good night's sleep at The Pepper Coyote."

"Yes, I did, thank you … wonderful place!"

He motioned with his hand towards the semi-circle of plastic chairs and invited me to sit. I nodded my head and plonked myself down on the one at the end beside the multipurpose cola fridge. Hearing the rusty squeak of the fly screen door opening I turned to see Mrs. Escoto.

"Hello Sir. I hope you had a pleasant stay at The Pepper Coyote?"

"Oh yes, very pleasant," I answered, lying through my teeth once again.

She asked me if I'd like a hot cup of coffee then turned and went back inside.

Looking down I saw the little baby boy from last night. With one hand he steadied himself on my chair leg, while with the other he was hitting the concrete with a small plastic discard he'd plucked from the floor of the shop.

Whack! whack! whack! he was a feisty little fellow, but when I bent lower towards him and said, "Well hello there, little guy, what's your name?" He looked up at me horrified and burst into tears as though I was the most terrifying creature ever spawned on the face of the earth.

The little bugger then started screaming so loudly that it seriously made my skull shake. His mother was soon on the scene. She handed me a mug of steaming, black coffee and bent down to pacify her traumatized child.

"I am sorry señor, he gets a little upset when he sees a strange face."

"No problem, yeah I certainly do have a strange one," I laughed, sipping timidly, and feeling like a three headed ogre. Meanwhile, post tantrum, the little guy had dropped the piece of plastic and waddled away happily into the care of his big sister.

"Well señor," smiled Mrs. Escoto. "Your car is all clean and shiny and the engine has been … serviced. And we had plenty of the right gasoline to put in the tank."

She gestured for me to come inside and take a look. I couldn't see it, but guessed it must have been the tarpaulin-covered car beside the goofy, grinning pickup.

We pulled the cover halfway back. The '58's chrome and bodywork was buffed to an immaculate sheen. Looking in through the sparkling windshield, I could see the white colored seats and interior looked almost brand new. I was impressed. I mean really impressed.

Galo re-appeared with Luis. They both seemed proud of all the work they'd done getting my car back in shape. Galo moved around to the driver-side door and released the hood catch. The massive piece of metal jolted upwards a few inches in readiness for his presentation.

But it was too late, the chill from an unexpected surprise surged right through me. The Fire Diamond's badge, the winged V decal that sat in the middle of the front of the hood wasn't there. It was beautiful; it was part of the car's whole identity and it was gone!

Luis and Galo seemed to move in slow motion, as they pointed and explained to me the finer points of the different mechanical services they had performed within the engine bay. I nodded my head. I smiled. I tried to look attentive and amazed at what they had done, but all I could think of was the badge. Where had it gone? I knew these guys wouldn't have misplaced it; they were far too thorough. I assumed it must have been pried off by one of the skellies when they swarmed around the hood last night at the festival.

I kept nodding and looking impressed at Galo and Luis's work, but the missing badge overrode everything. They pulled the tarpaulin back some more and continued their tour along the Fire Diamond's flanks, explained the temporary, polythene window they'd fixed into the hole and displayed with pride the now practically spotless interior which smelt citrusy and unnaturally clean.

But all I could think of was that damn, missing V badge.

"Umm, Galo, I noticed the Fire Diamond's decal wasn't there on the front when you lifted up the hood."

"Yes señor, we too had noticed that this was missing. We were unsure if it had fallen off at some time before?"

What could I say? I knew it wasn't their fault. I just thought of all those dancing frick'n skeletons and wondered which one of those assholes had pulled it off.

"Well a big thank you to everyone. You've done such a wonderful job, it's terrific. I'm *really* amazed, thank you all very much."

I laid on the gratitude and they seemed pretty pleased with my reaction. They deserved it. They'd obviously worked their rings off to fix up the wreck that I'd left them. It was a first-class effort, not some half-assed rush job. The Escotos were a good and genuinely nice family. I liked them all a lot. Stuffed if I'd work all night for twice the price.

That reminded me, what was the price? I hadn't even contemplated how much this was going to cost me, but I was sure it wouldn't be over the top.

I remembered the note in my pocket from The Pepper Coyote and handed it to Mrs. Escoto. She took it and began the inevitable process of tallying up my final bill.

"This letter is from my sister in law. She came here with your account earlier this morning while you were still sleeping so I could add it all up together."

She moved across to what looked like an upright piano that stood next to the family room door. Moving closer, I saw it was actually an old wooden writing desk with one of those flexible lids that slide up out of sight. Beneath its drab exterior the inside looked exactly like a high tech, city folk's workstation. A wide-screen computer, with a modem and printer, lit up here and there by blue electric dots.

I wouldn't have expected to see a set up like that out here in the Sonoran Desert. It was pretty self-evident that Mrs. Escoto was the managerial brain behind this little family business. She pulled up a stool, sat down and fired up the hardware.

As I stood watching a few paces behind, I noticed a little statue that stood on a small shelf up behind the screen. It looked at first like a Madonna figurine, but beneath the long white robes the head was not of a pious virgin, but a fleshless skull crowned with a radiating halo. In her hands she carried a scythe and an hourglass. It looked kind of creepy, but after some of the weirdo things I'd seen last night, I guess not.

I think Mrs. Escoto must have sensed me looking at it as she spoke to me without turning around. "She is Señora de las Sombras, the Lady of the Shadows. She grants favors of love, luck and protection in return for the faith of the believer."

I moved a step closer, curious to have a better look. Scattered around her feet on the little shelf, were a few modest offerings: two or three small flowers, a couple of filtered cigarettes, a tiny glass of alcohol, and some sugar-coated sweets.

This stuff was all kind of new and interesting, but I didn't have any frame of reference to go by, so I just made an amiable *Hmmm* noise.

I was sure she'd had the paperwork pretty much tallied up already. After a short burst on the keyboard she turned around and handed me the printed bill.

It was itemized in two different sections: one for the hotel stay, the other for all of the work on the car. I scanned through the list but was only really interested in the total amount. Bed, food, beer, car detailing, twenty gallons of fuel, etc., etc. Total: Four hundred and sixty-two dollars ... *holy Jesus.*

After the initial shock, I figured all in all it was a pretty reasonable deal. I pulled out my billfold expecting to settle up promptly. A sense of panic came over me as I realized I didn't have anywhere near enough.

She glanced down at the near empty cash compartment and threw up her arms in disbelief. Looking me straight in the eye, she let loose with an unexpected outburst.

"Why do you insult me? I treat you kindly, we have all worked hard to fix your broken car and then you try to cheat us and say you do not have enough money?"

She was really angry, but it wasn't her nature and she quickly reverted back to her usual pleasant and calm disposition. I could tell she had caught herself up and was feeling a little embarrassed.

I could feel the presence of the men of the family shifting around uneasily behind me, but I didn't look back. Reaching into my jeans front pocket I pulled out a couple of small notes that I remembered I still had, but their measly total only came to seven screwed up bucks. I'd spent most of my dollars filling up with gas back in Lukeville, just before I'd crossed over the Arizona border into Mexico.

Tapping my jacket all over and around the other pockets, I asked feebly if I could use their toilet. "I do have the money, *truly*. I just have to—"

Mrs. Escoto frowned with a look of revulsion. I think she must have thought that I had it stuffed down my crotch or shoved up my ass in a capsule. She gestured with her hand towards the small lavatory door in the workshop.

I felt their suspicious eyes following me as I opened it and went inside. Maybe they thought I was planning to escape out through the window or maybe a mouse hole. But that was impossible, the window was only a couple of narrow slits cut horizontally into the wall at head-height, looking out to the front of the shop. I assumed the position standing over the can, then undid my belt and carefully took it off. I turned and sat on the seat, straightening the belt out across my knees with my hands. Hidden along the underside, beneath a length of tape, I had my own little precious metals currency exchange. A dozen gold and silver coins of different sizes. It was my little secret and I was determined to keep it that way.

Apart from the Fire Diamond, this was all I had, not from any prudent acquisition or foresight on my part, but as an inheritance legacy from my dear old Dad. They were mostly an assortment of smaller value silver coins as well as three golden eagles and a one ounce Krugerrand that had come all the way up from South Africa.

I was frick'n loaded! (Well, relatively.)

Sitting there on the toilet, I tried to remember roughly what the coins were now worth and do some kind of conversions in my head. "Right, let's see, if I give her one of those coins, plus one of those? No hang on, I'll give her a—"

I felt like I'd been in there for an eternity, when I heard the sound of a car pulling up right outside.

Hearing two doors slam shut, I was reacquainted with that whiney unpleasant voice from last night. It was Martindale and his sidekick from The Pepper Coyote.

"Oh no, what the hell are they doing here?"

I plucked a couple of coins from the belt and pressed the black tape safely back into place. Fastening the belt quickly around my waist I stood up and took a peek back outside through the slits.

There they were all puffed up and strutting around for the benefit of the Escoto family, with Martindale going through his familiar spiel like a well-trained parakeet. The old interrogation and the inevitable color photo portrait quizzing: "Has anyone seen this person around here at all?" etc., etc., etc.

Indifferent to the unexpected questioning, the family members who were there just shook their heads upon being shown the photograph and soon drifted off back to their business.

I lifted myself quietly up onto the toilet so as to get a better look. There was no way I was going outside until they had gone. I'm fairly sure they weren't too impressed when the bar fight cut short their grilling and deprived them of pitching their hardballs.

"Now that looks like the sort of thing I could take a baseball bat to and cause some real fancy damage. What d' ya think Mr. Travers?" bleated Martindale.

"Oh yes sir, Mr. Martindale. You sure could make a fine mess out of that little beauty." They both laughed together in a weird and robotic fashion.

Like a half-sprung jack knife, I perched uncomfortably up on the seat looking through the slots as the bastard was pointing right at the Fire Diamond. Although from where I was, she was way out of eye shot.

"Damn you Martindale," I thought. He knows that I'm here and is trying to smoke me out. But then I thought about it a little more and realized he had no idea that the '58 Special was mine, or that I was anywhere near here at all.

Martindale spun around and walked self-assuredly towards the trunk of their browny-bronze Baybecker Prio. Returning immediately swinging a heavy wooden baseball bat in the air like a cheap Babe Ruth. "Don't you hit it," I mumbled to myself.

Then, surprisingly, without smashing or destroying anything, he simply stopped, handed over the bat to his partner and they got back into their car and drove off as quickly and unexpectedly as they'd arrived.

As I walked over to Galo and Mrs. Escoto inside the garage, I noticed that the Fire Diamond had been covered back over with the tarpaulin. Martindale must have been limbering up with his air swings to belt the crap out of the giant piñata pig that, unbeknown to me, had been plonked up on the '58's roof, but then thought better of it. I wondered for an instant if Señora de las Sombras had granted her favors and vibed off a positive outcome.

"How did *that* get there?" I said.

"Señor, we saw the gringo agents heading this way from further down the street. We thought your pretty red automobile would bring too many questions, so we put the large paper pig on the roof to hide it," explained Mrs. Escoto.

I was convinced... sort of. I hadn't been in the toilet for that long when they drove up, but Bird, aware of my conundrum, said simply, "Galo is a very fast man when he wants to be. He pigged on the roof of your car like an athlete."

Galo smiled and nodded his head in agreement. Then, without any preparation or run up, suddenly flipped himself head over heels in a full body somersault landing only a foot or so forward from where he started. I just stood dumbfounded, then applauded in genuine appreciation of such an unexpected show of fitness and agility.

Galo just grinned and took a bow.

"Now please, let me pay the money I owe you!" I raised the two gold coins in my fingers, relieved by the happy looks on their faces that this was definitely a much more acceptable form of currency in which to settle my account.

Back at the computer, Mrs. Escoto soon found the online exchange rate, but the value of the coins I had given her were still a little short of the total. I dived into my pocket for the screwed-up bucks to pay the difference, but she had other ideas.

"Señor. May I please make a suggestion? I am happy to forget the balance of your bill, if you would agree to give my nephew, Bird, a lift to another gas station further along the road where you will be travelling. I hope that as well as the badge they might also have the window glass to fit your beautiful car. You will have to stop there anyway to fill up with the old type gasoline that you need, which is not so easy to find further south."

Her English was still a little unsure and reserved, but she spoke beautifully.

"Sure. Sounds fine to me!"

I liked Bird, and we were both apparently going in the same direction and I'd be glad of the company. I did think for a second that he was a bit of a fat bastard and would make the car chew up too much juice, but I quickly dropped the nasty thought in the interests of good Karma and the long and open road up ahead.

Probably good to have someone riding shotgun this far south of the border, and someone who knew where the hell they were going. The discount on the final bill and the promise of a possible badge and window glass were the clincher.

Bird seemed to consider it a done deal, so with no hesitation moved across to the cola fridge and took out a package wrapped up in a plain green bin-liner.

Calmly he indicated for me to reach inside the car and pull on the latch of the trunk lid. Then he walked around to the back and placed his parcel carefully inside, while yelling commands out to Luis and Galo, to take down the piñata and pull off the tarp from the 'Special.

I looked at the gaping blank hole in the front of the hood and wondered if the promise of a decal from this alleged gas station was really just a ploy to get me to take him further down south.

I had another evil thought too. Maybe he was shifting ten or twenty kilos of coke or something in that package and I was the patsy mule with a whole lot o' trouble sitting right there in my trunk. He of course being only an innocent hitchhiker that I'd happened to pick up on the road.

"What's in the package Bird?"

"Only some skins señor. Do you want to see them? Do you think I am a big-time smuggler, heading off down to the south?"

The family laughed loud at that one.

Luis Escoto picked up my bag from under one of the chairs, where they had kindly nudged it out of sight during Martindale's visit and placed it squarely inside the trunk alongside Bird's mysterious package, and then closed the lid which resonated with a deluxe, old fashioned metal sound that you just don't get any more with the new plastic hybrids.

Bird was already up front in the seat searching around for the belt buckle. I had to say my round of goodbyes to the family, vigorously shaking hands and smiling out through the open door instead of the window because of the immovable polythene substitute.

I'd only known them for a few hours total, but I really had become quite fond of all of them. Closing the door, I fired up the ignition and the Fire Diamond roared with content, belching a plume of black fumes all the way back into the shop.

They all laughed at that too.

I tripped her into gear, nudged down on the accelerator and felt the first signs of movement as she rolled proudly forward and out through the door into the sunlight. With a glance in the rear-view mirror, I noticed the reflection of someone sitting small in the middle of the back seat. It was the old man wearing those memorable boots from last night. He caught my eye and smiled the family's pearly white grin. It was Luis Escoto senior.

Bird had seen him too and as we were heading to a stop, he opened the door, got out quickly and pulled his front seat forward and beckoned kindly to the old man in the back. Mrs. Escoto helped him out gently, his mischievous grin telling the whole story of how he *nearly* got away with it.

"We have to watch him, he's a real old trickster. Goodbye, señor."

With that Bird climbed back into the seat and resumed his search for the elusive seat belt. I looked out through the open passenger side window one last time at the old man waving goodbye. He pointed lovingly at his new ten-gallon cowboy hat, which I swear he hadn't had on ten seconds earlier and said that word again.

"Chupacabra." He chuckled for a second or two, then turned and shuffled off back inside.

5

Driving South

It was good to be back on the road. I sat behind the wheel feeling a lot more relaxed. Whatever they'd tweaked beneath the hood had given the old '58's engine that noticeable post-tune grunt. I guess that sounds like a simpleton's prognosis, but she was firing sweetly on all eight and that was good enough for me.

The transformation of the car's interior was incredible. The polythene window was a bit of a worry, I really didn't want it there, but hell, if a sandstorm blew in unexpectedly from the desert, I'll be the first one to thank the Escotos for fitting it.

Except for two tiny burn marks up above the busted window, everything else looked near enough perfect and the fragrance of the cleanser reminded me of the sweet-smelling fruit trees we had in the yard when I was a kid.

"Your folks sure did a good job fixing up my car," I said, looking at Bird. He sat staring straight ahead like a statue.

He seemed to ignore me, but then replied in a monotone voice. "Yeah señor, a good job, but that's what they do."

That was it. He seemed worried about something and looked like he wanted to be left with his thoughts. I said nothing else and just enjoyed the ride. I knew he would perk up when he was ready.

Apart from the odd person here and there, the landscape outside was flat and consisted of nothing more than an endless carpet of scrubby Chamisa bushes. The further we drove, all signs of people vanished completely, and it felt like we were the only ones out here.

After an hour or so, those typical long-armed cactus plants were starting to get more plentiful. This is how I'd imagined Mexico would look. I started singing a few bars of *South of the Border* for good measure.

I laughed at my own great wit and grinned blankly out towards the endless stretch of road up ahead. Stupid fool. Didn't have a frick'n clue.

Out of nowhere the unanswered question reared up again from my memory. *Skeletons?* I had important things to find out and now was the time to get answers.

"Hey Bird, what the hell was all that Day of the Dead stuff about yesterday? All those skeletons. Are they for real, or some kind o' trick? Do they just appear somehow magically on the night? They *definitely* weren't guys in costumes. Are they some kind of mass hallucination or what? I even had one of those ugly mother's heads stretched out across my lap, dribbling, and talking to me in Spanish. Scared the livin' you know what out of me."

He didn't answer.

"And what is the name of your little town back there anyway?"

Bird twisted in his seat and seemed to be preparing for a tell-all explanation, but it never came. "I do not know señor, Día de los Muertos, it's pretty strange stuff. All *very* Mexican."

"So, you don't know anything about the skeletons?" I persisted.

"No señor, they appear for the two nights of the festival and then we will not see them again until next year... usually."

If he did know anything, he wasn't in the mood to elaborate, so I shifted to something else that had intrigued me. "What's with that statue of Señora 'de Sombro' or whatever her name is?"

"Señora de las Sombras? She is another name for Santa Muerte, Saint Death. She is a most sacred figure with the Mexican people, she reminds them of their own mort...?" He was doing well, but the English tripped him up short.

"Mortality?"

"Yes, mortality. The cult was not...tolerated?...by the Catholic Church. But she is very accepted with many of the ordinary people. I hope your Santa Muerte will look out for you too, señor."

With a no effort flick of his hand he pointed up towards my rear-view mirror and a chill shot through my body. Hanging down on a thin leather strap was a small, three-inch, carved figurine of the Lady, swaying gently in unison with the rhythmic pitch of the car. Now I'd looked there a hundred times since I'd been driving, and I swear on my poor father's grave it most definitely wasn't up there before. There was no way I could have missed it and there was no way Bird could have leaned across and hung it up there without me noticing. That freaked me out. I shut up and tried to work out how the hell it had gotten there.

"Sometimes she will hold different things in her hands. They all have different meanings. Your Lady carries a lamp, which means smartness and spirit, a way through the darkness of ignorance and doubt. I know this, as mine holds a lamp too."

Eeesh! This was all very weird, but I figured it must have been put there by Mrs. Escoto sometime back at the garage and I'm sure with all good intent. How it had managed to remain invisible until the señora's name was mentioned was totally weird. I glanced up now and then if only to see if she really was there.

Changing tack completely I remembered my collection of eight-track cartridges that were down in the passenger side's footwell the last time I'd seen them.

"Hey Bird, what happened to the box of tapes that were down there last night?"

For the first time since we left, he actually turned his head to look at me, he was again wearing that stupid, purple flowerpot hat.

"They're here." He leaned awkwardly over the back and with one hand grabbed the box from behind my seat and placed it curiously on his lap. Bird's fingers flicked methodically through all the eight-tracks.

"This stuff is real olden days music, señor. I thought they were video cassettes."

"Eight-tracks. Yeah, well before your time Bird. All the petrol-heads back in the seventies had these things installed in their muscle-cars and big V8s. As far as I can remember they only ever seemed to play loud, heavy metal as well."

"What's this?" Bird turned one of the cartridges around curiously in his hand, as if it was a bygone relic unearthed from some technological graveyard.

"*Steppenwolf.* Yeah whack that one in."

Bird looked at me like I was a freak and pushed the cartridge into the slot.

"No, not like that, turn it around the other way."

He flipped the plastic and pushed it back in.

"Press that button right there with the arrow, move it on to track five, 'Born to Be Wild'."

The music blasted out loudly through the ancient, quadraphonic sound system.

"Yeah, I've heard that song before," commented Bird, nonplussed when it finished. Then he ejected the cartridge with that old familiar *chi-chung.*

"Have you got any twenty first century stuff? Any rap or hip-hop?"

I was mortified. Like a fool I almost believed I could transform him miraculously into an enlightened retro-rocker with one of the great, all time classics. No chance.

He caught me studying his face.

"*What!* Why are you looking at me like that?" he snapped defensively.

He seemed really pissed, but settled back down, not wanting to take it any further.

"Nothing, truly. I only looked at you."

He slotted the eight-track neatly back inside the box, placed it down on the floor near his feet and resumed his blank forward gaze ahead through the window.

"Yeah, I'm a big fat lard ass. *Ha, ha,* big-fat-Birdy!"

He was definitely on a slow burn and obviously self-conscious about his weight, so I thought I'd try and kill off any misunderstanding right then and there.

"I wasn't meaning to be rude Bird, but you don't seem to look as Mexican to me as the other Escotos, that's all. I wasn't even thinking about your weight. I'm sorry, really."

"That's because I'm *not* a Mexican," he barked out bluntly.

He paused for a few seconds, then in an unexpected motion ripped off his purple felt hat and lunged his face across the length of the bench seat towards me. He whispered a not too surprising revelation, "I'm *Japanese.*" Then he recoiled back perfectly into his previous position.

"I knew it! I was sure you weren't Mexican!"

"I'm *half* Mexican."

"'Wow, no kidding. How come? You're the first person I've ever met that's half Japanese and half Mexican."

He didn't seem to mind me asking, so I shut up and let him decide if he wanted to answer or not. He sat there looking glumly out ahead for a bit, then started talking again.

"It's a very sad story, señor…?"

Oh hell! After all this time I had been around Bird, I hadn't even bothered or had the good manners to tell the poor guy my name. "My name's Wolf. Of course it's not my real name but that's what they call me, just like they call you Bird I guess."

"Yes, Señor Wolf, as I have said, it is a sad story. My mother was an 'inmigrante ilegal'. She crossed into the United States to get work, but then got recruited into the army and was sent over to serve in Japan, where she met my father while stationed in Okinawa. He was a Japanese civilian. They were both killed in a car crash when I was just a small baby. None of my relatives in Japan were able to look after me, so I was sent back to my mother's sister, here in Mexico. I have lived with the Escoto family now for all of my life."

I was mortified when I heard Bird's tragic story. Man, how could you relay such a sad and horrendous event like that in a few matter of fact sentences? The poor guy, he'd probably told the story so many times before it had become an unemotional recap of the cold hard facts of his life. It was obvious his stoic expression concealed deeper emotions and a load of unanswered questions.

"Sorry Bird, that's a very unfortunate story to hear buddy. I'm truly sorry." He said nothing, so trying to lighten the mood a little I thought I'd try and change tack once again. "So how come they call you Bird?"

"It is my name, although it's not my real name." He said, ribbing me for what I had said to him earlier.

"So, what's your real name?"

"I don't know."

"You don't know your name?"

"Nope!"

He sat thinking, but I could tell that he was going to say more.

"All I was given from Japan was a small white envelope to keep. In it was a picture of my parents on their wedding day, my birth certificate, and a handwritten letter from those relatives. When I arrived here, I was too young to speak or read and nobody here in Sonora could understand Japanese, so they had no idea what it said or even what my name was. On the front of the envelope was a little drawing of a small bird, so everybody just called me Bird, or Pájaro in Spanish. I keep them all close and safe in an old metal cigarette case." He tapped the chest pocket of his denim jacket a couple of times with his fingers. "One day I will meet a Japanese person and I can find out what my real name is. And maybe something more about myself that might be written in the letter. How about you?"

"What?"

"Why do they call you Lobo?"

I knew lobo, it was Spanish for wolf. Just about the only word I did know. I lifted my left arm and showed him my hairy birthmark. He winced disapprovingly and pulled an unflattering face. "So where are you going with your car?"

"I'm heading on down further south to Puerto Cantaura near Guaymas to—"

"*Puerto Cantaura!*" He cut me short in an exaggerated exclamation of surprise. "That's about three hundred miles further down from here *Mr.* Lobo. You will definitely have to take me to The Alamo and buy lots and lots of gasoline!"

I immediately thought of the famous battle at The Alamo mission, but I was pretty sure that was further up north, somewhere over in Texas. He must have been reading my mind.

"Not *that* Alamo, Señor Lobo, but the gas station down past Santa Ana where you are so very kindly willing to take me." For some reason he burst into laughter.

"It's called The Alamo?" I asked, surprised.

"No, not really, but that's what some locals around there call it."

He said nothing else and resumed his stare straight ahead. Thankfully, the fast sinking sun had rolled all the way over to Bird's side. Sunsets really piss me off. They hurt my eyes big time whenever I'm driving.

◆

Apart from a truck up ahead that had turned off the road and disappeared into the desert and an old guy in a pair of white pajamas carrying a wooden rake, we saw nobody else at all for nearly two hours. The monotonous straight sections turned into broad sweeping curves and although the condition of the road was fair, the potholes increased the further we went south. We were travelling roughly parallel with what had been the old Highway 15, that ran fifty or sixty miles further off to the east. Highway 15 had been extensively upgraded as part of the North American Road and Highway network's Corridor One; a new superhighway that snaked from Whitehorse in Canada all the way down to Mexico City.

I had purposely avoided taking that route since setting out from Vegas. All vehicles travelling on the new corridor had a stack of different rules and regulations to follow and it was impossible for me to comply.

First, it was mandatory to have an electronic tagging device to debit your corridor usage fees from your personal account. Didn't have that.

Second, being a vintage car, the Fire Diamond required a special certificate of compliant roadworthiness.

And third, yet another damn certificate showing it had been converted to ACE. The stringent Authorized-Carbon-Emissions standard.

Nope, didn't have that either.

Finally, as if that wasn't enough, the whole system was surveilled by cameras which tracked all license plates 24-7. They knew everything about you and your vehicle – driving records, insurance status, make and model. All of it.

That's why I'd spent the last few days since crossing the border at Lukeville, driving around half lost on desert back roads. This was a one-way trip unfortunately, as there was no way I could keep the car back home in the States. The registration had almost run out, and when it did, I knew it would only be a matter of time before they'd catch up with me. I'd found myself an online buyer, supposedly somewhere down south in Puerto Cantaura, which was probably the only place I knew I'd be able to sell it.

We drove on for a while in silence, when Bird suddenly looked at me kind of inquisitively and asked if I wanted a smoke. I knew he wasn't talking filter-tipped, so I thought hard about it for at least two seconds.

"What is it?"

"It's just some home-grown," Bird replied nonchalantly.

Before I had a chance to answer he had a big fat pre-rolled doobie jigging up and down between his lips, while he waited patiently for the lighter to pop back out from the '58's chrome-plated dashboard.

Now I love the occasional puff, but I'd heard about this Mexican gear. I knew that Sinsemilla or that Mexican Haze stuff could blow your head right off and considering I was behind the wheel of a certified vintage automobile, I had to be responsible. There was no point getting completely off my tits and driving headlong into some giant roadside bolder.

Bird lit the joint, took a couple of long theatrical tokes and then handed it over to me. I glanced at it quickly and took a quick puff myself. It really stank, genuine Skunkweed. I just *knew* I was going to regret this. We passed it back and forth a couple of times then he unexpectedly tossed the blunt out through the window. No Bogarting down to a microscopic roach for this guy. That set me thinking, maybe that package in the trunk really was full of dope.

By now the car was full of smoke and needed a fresh gust of air. Bird's window was open but any intake on my side was stopped by the polythene stand-in. So, with a firm, impromptu elbow jab, I nudged it hard out into the desert.

"You sure that stuff's just home-grown?" I wasn't really expecting an answer.

As the smoke took effect, my body felt like a bag full of tiny glass marbles that ground up against each other when I moved. Luckily, all I had to do was steer and keep my foot on the accelerator, because I was pretty incapable now of doing much else. My brain felt like an oversized super ball bouncing around in my skull, pounding away at any coherent thought forms.

Then came the next phase – *The Fear!* That irrational smorgasbord of paranoia, anxiety and panic, that made me wish that I'd never puffed away on that god-awful thing in the first place. I was down there now in a deep pit of dread. Bird just sat there like a big girthy lump with a grin. It didn't seem to affect him at all.

"Hey Bird. How ya feelin' bro?"

"Good."

"I've gotta pull over and stretch my legs for a bit, I need to take a leak."

I really needed a moment to calm myself down a little. I didn't want him to think I was an absolute pussy who couldn't handle one little joint, which was the unequivocal, absolute truth.

A long stretch of open ground appeared by the roadside, so I steered the Fire Diamond over to a slow, easy stop. As I turned off the engine I was instantly hit by the silence. The only sound I could hear was the faintest hum from some midges. It was as eerie as the desert was awesome.

I walked over towards a few scattered bushes and went through the motions. Bird had the same idea and stood at a respectable distance away to my left. I was so frick'n stoned. The inside of my head felt like an all singing Bollywood roller-derby meets a whole drunken army of massed pipes and drums. Compared to that, coping with the all-imposing quietness of a broad Sonoran Desert landscape was nothing.

Bird and I walked back to the car now together.

"How is it?"

"Yeah, great Bird, thanks. I really need something to drink though; did you bring any water?"

He shook his head. "There's a small town not too far up ahead. We'll get something there."

I remembered the last time I pulled into a small town for water. "I think I'll probably keep on going, thirsty or not."

"You're really suffering from that little smoke aren't you señor," jibed Bird.

"Yeah a bit. That's pretty strong stuff *don Pájaro*."

He howled with laughter and got back into the car. I started up the engine and she tore off again without even missing a beat. The fuel tank was slightly over half and we still had some way to go until we reached The Alamo.

◆

We drove for a fair while longer when Bird said, "Hey Lobo, what's wrong with this car?"

I listened thinking there was some mechanical problem, then realized I was so ripped that I'd left it in second and forgotten to change up into third. Shit, what an idiot. I could have done some *real* damage or maybe even burnt the frick'n gearbox out if he hadn't noticed. I still had The Fear, so for the next quarter of an hour I listened very intently to see if I really *had* done just that. Luckily, it seemed okay, so I let it drop.

"I'm not smoking anymore weed," I said to myself, like I believed it.

Twilight had faded to darkness.

Bird's sudden outburst caught me off guard. "Did you hear that?" Judging by the way his head was bobbing around he was really distracted by something.

"What?" I couldn't hear anything; the massed pipes and drums were still playing rogue in my head.

"*Listen...*"

I slowed the car down and shifted my attention to the barely audible rumble that was building. I couldn't tell whether it was coming from somewhere really close by or from far away in the distance.

"What is it?" It was definitely getting louder and more intense.

"I do not like it don Lobo; it's coming towards us. It's coming from back down the road."

I got *really* worried. First thing I thought of was a gigantic alien mothership, cruising low above the road, sucking up everybody in its path for an ass-probe. Well, maybe not. It must have been the police or the military judging by the sound that just kept on building and building.

"Get off the road, NOW! Drive over there, down behind that. See it?"

Bird was pointing to a clump of cactus plants the size of a lounge room, sitting some thirty yards up ahead in a hollow. When we reached a place I could turn off, I cranked the steering wheel to the left and let the Fire Diamond roll down gently, feathering the brakes as I did so. Turning a little too sharp at the bottom I got a rear tire stuck in the sand, but with some urgent fender-rocking from Bird and a bit of hefty lead-footing on the gas pedal she soon came free and lunged herself forward well out of sight from the road.

Bird was away in a flash, hiding himself behind a small clump of rocks. I grabbed my hat and quickly followed. We crouched low and looked back towards the road from our hideout. It must be the Mexican army, a full armored division at least. But as it got closer it looked more like a monstrous glowing snake slithering purposefully along, its great length obscured here and there by the bends in the road and the voids of shadows cast behind roadside boulders.

"That's not the military," I said in a normal voice to Bird. There was no need to whisper, I could have yelled both my lungs out and nobody would have heard me above the noise. "They're motorcycles. I've never seen so many, ever."

A truly massive stream of bikers and their machines were cruising slowly past our hiding spot, in a loose three or four abreast formation down towards the south. There were literally thousands upon thousands of them. The whole colossus seemed to emanate with the energy of an overwhelmingly phantasmal presence, made all the more eerie by a million tiny pinpoints of light that twinkled and sparkled like a passing galaxy upon their dark sombreros and jackets.

Crouching low and keeping small between the rocks, I could feel my heart thumping hard in my chest. Bird was motionless in the shadows, only his eyeballs were moving watching the action up above. Suddenly, just as the great column seemed to be tapering off, a lone rider split away from the pack and in a zigzagging motion slid down the same sandy bank that I had rolled the Fire Diamond down earlier.

Bringing his heavy machine to a stop he dismounted and squatted down to make some adjustment to the still idling engine, all the while keeping a watchful eye on the passing stream of his brethren above.

Being only a few yards away it felt like he was right there upon us. Thankfully due to our rock-like stillness and the complete blackness of the shadows, the rider made no indication that he had seen us.

Apart from a pin line of reflected light along the brim of his pushed-back sombrero, he appeared as a total darkness. When he finally stood up again, a thin band of light shot down the entire length of his unfolding form, like fast-flowing mercury. He looked out over the bike and lowered his long heavy jaw in a crooked primal smile towards his companions. To my horror and surprise, it just hung there completely fleshless, obvious in its outline shape to be nothing more than bare teeth and bone. I was shocked at what I was seeing. He was a skeleton. They were *all* skeletons. Just bones.

He quickly jumped on his motorcycle and for one chilling instant turned his head directly towards us. Two pinpoints of pale-yellow light seemed to look knowingly right at us. Whether he knew we were there or not, I will never know, but he turned away, revved his bike triumphantly, engaged the gears and scrambled hastily back up to the road where he merged seamlessly back into formation with the tail-end riders.

We stayed there in silence as the full darkness settled back around us. Bird got to his feet but said nothing. Even though I couldn't see him properly, I sensed he was really unnerved and seemed in no hurry to get going. To be honest, neither was I.

The rumbling drone from the passing engines had now subsided and moved off into the distance. The empty silence of the desert chaparral had returned to fill the nighttime void.

"I've seen some frick'n weird stuff just lately, but that really takes the biscuit! *Who or what—*"

"Los Espectros Brillantes!" Bird interjected.

"Huh?"

"The Shining Specters, Mr. Lobo, they are called The Shining Specters. I have heard many stories of them, but I did not know if they were truly real."

"That was insane. I'm not even stoned anymore. Got another smoke Bird? I really think I need another joint now, just to calm me down." I was babbling.

He didn't reply but walked back towards the Fire Diamond.

"Tell me more about what just happened Bird, who the hell were they?"

"Come on, señor. We will be more comfortable sitting in your big red car than out here amongst the hard stones and *las plantas del cacto*."

I wanted five miles at least between us and them before we took off again. I was seriously thinking about heading back home, but then I remembered I didn't have one, so with a bit of self-persuasion I convinced myself to keep heading south ... but not for a while.

As we opened the doors and jumped into the car, the interior light brought us back into the real world, even if it was only 1958. Back in his seat, Bird promptly rolled himself forward, his head bending down as far between his knees as he could manage. I thought he was going to throw up, but he sprang back holding the Steppenwolf tape from the box.

"I will play that song again. It keeps on playing inside my head. I think I like it!"

"Yeah, good stuff Bird, crank it up *LOUD!*"

With an unexpected return of bravado, I fired up the engine and the Fire Diamond roared into life. The headlights cast long arching shadows, as I drove the car out from behind the cactus clump with a scything spray of loose sand and grit, but with the pedal to the metal and the quadra pumping we launched ourselves back up onto the road. We both laughed at the irony of the lyrics blasting from the speakers, but we soon settled back into silent running. The euphoria of hitting the road again was pretty short lived.

I pressed Bird a couple of times about what he knew about The Shining Specters, but he seemed to have clammed right up. We hadn't gone much further when he unexpectedly started talking again.

"They are the bone riders. Lost souls that have met with most violent deaths. Or so I've been told. They are united through their pain, their memories, and a shared collective suffering. Their alle …?"

"Allegiance?" I interjected.

"Their allegiance is unknown. I have been told they are very restless, waiting for the proper time to take revenge upon their enemies." His English was better than he thought.

"Yeah, what else?"

"I don't know."

"You said you'd heard lots of stories about them." He looked across at me with disdain and said no more.

The temperature had dropped quite a bit now and I was starting to regret my decision to elbow out the polythene window. I hadn't seen any sign of the riders, though I did glance more than a few times in the rear-view mirror expecting to see some tail-end stragglers sitting right on our tail. Thankfully, it never happened. All I saw was the total darkness outside and the reassuring figurine of Señora de las Sombras hanging down below the mirror listing gently to and fro at the end of her short leather chord.

We drove on quietly for about half an hour and fatigue was starting to set in. The terrain was all pretty much the same but now out in the desert we could see a scattering of low-lying light-colored lumps. It was only when we got up close that we realized exactly what they were. They were goats, or rather what was left of them.

Turning a rocky corner, we almost ran straight into a small truck lying on its side in the middle of the road. The vehicle must have lost control in some freak accident. Three occupants of a parked station wagon were already roaming the scene and shining their flashlights around in the darkness. An overweight man in a tracksuit approached Bird's window and the two of them spoke for a minute in Spanish. I hadn't a clue what they were saying but nodded along getting the gist solely from their gestures and solemn demeanor.

Unfortunately, the driver had been killed along with his truckload of goats. There was nothing we could do to help so we said adios and moved slowly on past the accident scene with Bird looking back until the lights had disappeared out of sight.

"What else did he say?" I asked with wincing curiosity.

"He said it was no *accidente*. The truck was attacked, and the goats were killed on purpose."

"Was it The Shining Specters?"

"No señor, this is not anything to do with them. It was chupacabra!"

Chupacabra. I'd heard that word somewhere only recently. I had to think hard where it was. That's what old man Escoto called his boots and also his cowboy hat.

"They are mysterious, dog-like diablo creatures that roam the darkness of the night and suck the blood from the still living livestock."

"Are you serious?"

"But this is very different, Mr. Lobo."

"Why's that?"

"Usually they roam the nighttime alone, looking for ... prey. But this looks like the work of a whole running pack, like lobos. Señor said they had found many, many tracks. This is exceptional."

By the look on Bird's face, I figured there was more to all this than he was letting on.

At first, I thought I was seeing things as the running form of a young woman appeared unexpectedly in the beam of the '58's headlights. She was about six feet up, stumbling along erratically, precariously close to the edge of the embankment that ran parallel down the left-hand side of the road. Caught in the lights she looked straight at us and ran off ahead, even faster.

In her right hand she was carrying an old-style suitcase. The lid was completely open and hung out at right angles. A few of the clothes and belongings that hadn't fallen out onto the ground were still lying on the inside of the lid, bouncing and sliding around as she ran. She was obviously pretty disturbed and in some kind of trouble.

"I recognize her!" I yelled to Bird. "That's the American girl from The Pepper Coyote. What the hell is she doing out here? She looks pretty messed-up."

Apart from the occasional panic-stricken glance back at us, she continued on unwavering in her single-minded effort to get away. As we kept pace with her, I leaned out through the missing window to try and coax her down. After a while, the bank petered out and she was back level with us on the side of the road.

"Hey, slow down, remember me? The guy in the bar last night, you served me a beer and some food."

I could see a couple of long, fresh blood streaks running down her arm and another one on the side of her head, half-hidden beneath her messed up hair. She took no notice, but struggled on, her suitcase flapping about awkwardly down beside her leg.

"Hey, slow down. Stop. You need some help. I can see you're bleeding. We'll take you somewhere and get you fixed up." It looked to me as though she had been attacked or maybe even involved in that accident.

"Come on miss, this is silly. Where are ya gonna go out here in the middle of the night?" I held my arm out towards her, encouraging her to stop and come on across to the car. Stumbling on for a few more paces, she stopped in her tracks, dropped to her knees, and then burst into tears. I got out and went over to help.

Lifting her back up onto her feet I steered her gingerly back towards the Fire Diamond. She was crying uncontrollably now and becoming more agitated and aggressive. Her arms were swinging around wildly and caught me hard in the face. Bird was not far behind. He'd picked up her suitcase and brought it back, lobbing it casually through the open door and onto the back seat. Desperately she kept fighting me as I pulled the front seat forward and tried to get her into the car.

"Let me go. Let me go. They'll come back again, they will. *They're here now! Can't you see them?*"

She was frick'n delirious. I could see raw panic in her darting eyes. I was pretty sure I knew what she was talking about but asked anyway. "What'll come back?"

"Those *things!* Those monster creatures, they're everywhere. They tried to kill me. They killed the driver. Yes, they did … yeah, ripped him to pieces." She wouldn't get into the back seat but kept hanging onto the door frame and getting even more fiery.

Bird shook his head despondently and clambered into the rear through the gap behind the seat.

"Please, get in. If they come back, it's safer in the car than out here."

This seemed to make some kind of sense to her back-to-front reasoning. She jumped straight in, grabbed the steering wheel and started looking for the ignition. I pushed her with both hands across to the other side and took the driver's seat. Hell, this sure was going to be some ride.

Her head was darting about like a maniac. "They're out there, mister, they're horrible. Close that window. Please. They'll get inside and get us. *Please close the window!*"

"Look, calm down. The window's broken, forget it. They won't get in here. Calm down, just relax."

My words had no effect. She really was in a state. Bird, who had been fumbling around in his denim jacket for a while, finally found what he had been looking for and handed it to her. Lying deep in a pocket was a long-forgotten wet wipe thing.

"Here miss, something to wipe—"

Ripping open the wrapper she twisted the rear-vision mirror around to inspect the wound on the side of her head. Señora de las Sombras swirled in response to her actions but her dance went unnoticed by the girl as she checked her face in the glass. It wasn't as bad as it first looked.

"How about your arm? I noticed you've got a bit of blood running down there."

"*Oh shit!*" I thought to myself, "not on the newly cleaned seats." I really am a selfish bastard sometimes. She wiped her arm with what moisture was still left on the wipe and surprisingly it seemed to mostly come off.

"It's not my blood," she said surprised. "It must have come from the driver of the truck. It was horrible… *those things!*" She started hyperventilating, her breathing was disturbed and uneven.

"Calm down, it's okay, calm down. Now tell us exactly what happened back there."

The fretting and crying kept up for a while but when Bird leaned forward and put his chin on the top of the front seat, as though to say *Well, we're waiting*. She settled down a little and started to tell us what had happened. I think she needed to get it off her chest and get the details straight in her own head too.

It seems she'd hid in a shed last night, out back of The Pepper Coyote. She'd thumbed herself a lift sometime today but had been dropped off at a desert crossroads. After a while she'd managed to pick up another ride but unluckily with the ill-fated goat truck. Everything had been quite normal until the goats started going nuts in the back as all of these creatures suddenly swarmed out of nowhere and massed in the road up ahead. In a panic the driver swerved hard to try and miss them, but fate flipped the truck over onto the passenger's side, so he fell on top of the girl where his body and the suitcase sandwiched between them had protected her from the attack. She told how the next few minutes were of absolute terror as the monsters tore up the goats and anything else with a pulse. She recalled how the unfortunate man's throat had been totally ripped out leaving his head hanging limply by some gristly sinews. Finally, after it had all gone quiet, she managed to get herself free by contorted wiggling from under the remains of his body and out through the smashed front windshield. The carnage had been too much to handle. She lost it completely, and just ran.

Wow! and I nearly crapped myself over a dribbling skeleton, no wonder the poor kid was in such a mess. "They're still out there, we'll never get away from them. *Please*, drive faster, will you? They're all over the place, can't you feel them?"

Bird put his hand on her shoulder in a gesture of condolence. He only meant it sympathetically, but for some reason that was the straw that broke the camel's back. She hit the roof and went totally ballistic. Her screams were so loud my ears rang.

"*Stop the car. Let me out. Let me out. LET ME FUCKING OUT!*"

I slammed on the brakes, not to let her out but only to try and shut her up. Big mistake! She pushed down hard on the handle, threw open the door and bolted out into the desert, completely hysterical.

Bird and I took off after her, calling out into the total darkness. Kind of pathetic really. "Miss, miss. Hey lady, where are you? Come back, it's okay, miss." We didn't even know what her name was.

After what seemed like an eternity of yelling ourselves hoarse, we knew it was pointless. She had completely vanished. All we could do was get back in the car and drive on in silence with her uncertain fate on our conscience.

I'd driven enough for one day and the old fuel gauge had dropped right down low and was sitting an ominous tad above empty.

"Hey Bird, how much further to go buddy? I'm gonna choke on my swollen tongue pretty soon if I don't get some water."

He didn't reply but just nudged his chin out at the road up ahead. I could see a tiny little pinpoint of light shining only a mile or so down the road.

"Is that it, don Pájaro?"

"That's it, Señor Lobo."

6

The Alamo

The light in the distance had become a line that pulsed on and off at one end. I couldn't work out what it was, but as we got closer, I could make out a neon-rocket-ship-thing that shot up in a glowing trajectory. Right at the top, below the high point was a single word – Joe's, spelled out in bright neon script.

The place was a round-cornered, old-time gas station with one of those slab awnings. The kind that thrust out over the driveway like a giant, gravity defying tongue. It even had an up-ramp to the roof, like the garage I had for my toy cars when I was little. Defining the outline of the building were long threads of retro electric light globes. The place looked great. It felt safe and welcoming and we hadn't even arrived there yet. We turned off the road and glided in the last few yards. Bird pointed to the space between the pumps, so I pulled up dead center, right in the middle of the driveway.

I fumbled around for a moment, so Bird would get out of the car first and lead the way over to the two guys who were sitting out front on a couch. I straggled along behind so as to let him get reacquainted with his buddies and say all of his happy hellos.

They both looked American; the older man seemed in pretty good shape for someone his age. He was wearing a brown army T-shirt, desert camo pants and a tall white cowboy hat. His face, what I could make out beneath the wide brim, appeared rugged and good looking. Even from that distance, I could see a genial smile grinning out towards us. I knew straight away he was ex-military. He just had that unmistakable presence of a Vet who'd been in the forces. An alertness those guys somehow always retain.

The other one was in his early twenties. He wore a tatty looking lumber jacket and a pair of faded yellow board-shorts that hung down past his knees. I couldn't see his face too clearly as he was bobbing in and out of the shadows where he was sitting.

Bird did the obligatory high-fives and a bit of the jostling-ritual stuff some guys like to go through when they meet up with their pals. The younger guy jumped to his feet, messing around, he laid a mock burst of punches right into Bird's stomach. Bird replied instantly with a feigned knee to the groin, then mashed his pals face for a second or two with his big spongy hand, pushing him away finally with a gesture of utter contempt.

"This is Wolf." He introduced me to the older guy who smiled sincerely and shook my hand with spirit.

"Heeeey, Saint Wolfgang, pleased to meet you." I didn't understand the reason for the name but felt comfortable with his friendly greeting. "I'm Joe. This is my place. Glad you two finally made it."

By now we'd all shifted back over to the car. I could see Joe had been enthralled with it from the moment we pulled in.

"Well, well, well. A 1958 Fire Diamond V8 Special. 366 cubic inch, 250 horsepower, and she's a manual transmission too. Wow! Everyone wanted automatics back then. I haven't seen one of these babies for years. She's a real beauty too. I love the red. Wow! My old man bought one of these brand new, when I was a knee-high, it seemed as big as a battleship back then. I ain't seen one in this good shape for decades. The way you've dropped the body down, looks *really sexy.* Did you do it all yourself?"

He was off and reminiscing in a yesteryear world of his own. He was crouching down enthusiastically examining all the chrome on the grill, looking in through the windows, carefully opening and closing the door, brushing his hand along the fenders, feeling all the contours. He even got down on the concrete and had a try at looking around underneath.

"*Beautiful!* What happened to the flying V from the hood?"

"Last night, back there in Birdtown, it got pinched by a dancing skeleton. I'm so pissed off."

"You're kiddin' me. Last night, after all this time? What a shame."

"How in the hell did they manage to pry it off anyway? It was all well-crafted back then, not like the plastic crap they make nowadays."

"I need a driver's side window too. One of those bastards smashed it to smithereens with its head."

"That'll be no problem but let me think about the badge. It rings a bell. I'm pretty sure there's one around here somewhere."

Like a fool, I'd imagined this place was going to have one of those display boards chock-full of retro Fire Diamond decals, sitting right up there on the counter.

I left Joe to himself as he wandered around to the other side and continued his meticulous inspection down towards the car's tail end.

"Señor Wolf, this is Vince," said Bird introducing me to the younger guy.

"Howdy Wolf, pleased to meet you man. That's a sick lookin' ride you've got there, bro'. What the hell are you doin' luggin' this fat-ass Japsican around in it?"

I looked at Bird, but he didn't seem to take any offence and instead just laughed.

Vince was obviously Joe's son. One of those guys you take a kind of curious liking to right from the start. He held a perpetual wicked grin on his lips and his eyes were kind of beady and intense. His facial expressions seemed to spring promptly back into a quizzical frown whenever he wasn't talking or fooling around. His straight brown hair was mid-length and completely unruly; it looked like it had never been combed since grade school. I had a feeling this guy was going to be a real frick'n handful.

Joe reappeared from behind us, clipping Vince playfully around the back of the head.

"Show some respect to your friend ya little turd. Come on, let's go get a beer."

Back over by the shop Vince lent deeply into a chest type cola fridge and started handing out the ice-cold bottles among the four of us.

"Get me one too little brother," spoke a voice from out of the dark. I turned my head as a taller man, about my age in his early thirties, sporting a wild four-inch beard came around the corner wiping his hands on a rag.

"Wolf, this is my eldest boy Charlie. Charlie, this is Wolf. He's brought Bird all the way down here to see us." Then he sniggered and took a swig on his beer.

"Wolf." Charlie nodded his head in recognition as he grabbed the bottle from Vince.

"Sounds like a frick'n menagerie: bird, wolf … aardvark." He mumbled away to himself and walked across the driveway to take a fleeting look at the Fire Diamond. "Nice."

Then he turned away, still drinking his beer and ambled across to the three adjoining motel rooms at the far end of the building.

"Don't take any notice of Charlie," said Joe. "He's okay, it's just—" he was going to say more but then changed the subject.

"Hey Bird, what did I hear you saying before to Vince about an accident and some chupacabras back there?"

Bird, happy to have Joe's undivided attention, urgently retold the whole dramatic story, but this time in more intense and gruesome detail. He told them about the girl from The Pepper Coyote and how we found her and lost her not long after the bloody accident with the goat truck and the chupacabras. Then when he'd finished, we both let rip with our recollections of our way more terrifying encounter with the phantom armada of Los Espectros Brillantes.

"Did you get to see any of them chooba-things?" Vince chimed in.

"No, but there must have been many, many of them."

"You guys really have had an interesting day." Joe squatted down on his haunches and stared pensively at the ground. I figured something we'd said must have struck a chord.

"Hmm, we'll see what we can find out in the morning." He stood back up and asked Bird about the bundle he was bringing down for him. Bird nodded and shuffled across to the Fire Diamond.

By now I seriously needed to go, so I asked Joe the way to the john. He pointed toward the far end of the building in the direction Charlie had headed. I crossed paths with Bird giving him a look that said, "If that is some kind of illicit booty you've made me haul all the way down here, *I'll, I'll—*"

◆

"Pull up a seat Wolf, and grab yourself another cold one," Joe said hospitably. I dragged the ubiquitous plastic garage chair around from beside the cola chest but declined another beer with a polite "No thank you."

"So, who was this crazy girl from The Coyote Bar then?" Joe asked, leaning towards me, his forearms resting across his wide splayed legs. "And why the hell did she run off into the desert in the middle of the night? Man, she must have been a frick'n mess, poor kid."

I told him about how she'd pestered me for a ride and how she'd made a runner from the special agents, mistakenly thinking they were out to get her. But I couldn't answer his question with any more detail than that.

"Yeah, while you were in the can, Bird told us about those agents turning up at Escoto's place too. This blonde girl in the photograph, did you ever see her…in real life I mean?" Joe asked.

"No, only on Martindale's picture, but even on a five by four, she still looked pretty hot."

They all burst out laughing together. I couldn't quite pick the thread of their in-joke, but I knew I was its unwitting butt.

"Only messin' with ya Wolf," said Joe. "Only messin' with ya."

"I hear she's a bit of a skank in real life!" laughed Vince, amused by his own nasty comment.

Looking around I noticed the package Bird fetched from the trunk had been left on the ground beside the cola chest. It hadn't been scurried away or treated with any kind of importance, so I thought it okay to ask what was in it.

"Nothing very exciting, just a bunch of skins," answered Joe flatly.

"I told him back at my aunt's place they were skins, but he thinks it's filled with *druuugs!*" jibed Bird.

"What sort of skins? Rabbit, coyote…chupacabra?" I said, sounding like I was well on top of things.

"*Oooh,* he's good," replied Joe fighting to hold down a grin, which was growing bigger by the second.

"Yeah, they're chupas, Mr. Clever-dick. We've got some folks here that, let's say, have more than a passing interest in them."

Another burst of laughter followed. I knew there was something else going on, but none the wiser, I sat there and grinned like a numbskull, prepared to bide my time.

"Yeah, they make real fancy looking cowboy hats to sell to all the loco gringos!" Bird was scoring off me big time and it was really startin' to annoy me. I decided right then and there, I wasn't going to help that asshole ever again with his English. No frick'n way!

"That reminds me Bird," said Joe in passing, "can you hand them on to Faye or MacElroy in the morning? They'll be pleased to get some fresh ones."

Then, seemingly out from nowhere, a little black cat jumped lightly up onto my lap.

"Hey she likes you," said Joe. "Never seen her do that to anyone before."

She sat there, bobbing her head around and just looking at me, sort of sniffing.

"What's it doing? I'm not big on cats."

"She's checkin' you out; you're lucky it's not the other one. The grey one would tear your fuckin' head clean off if it didn't approve," hollered Joe.

I noticed Joe's voice would build with contained excitement and then at the crucial moment ignite with an explosion of gut-busting laughter. I liked him a lot.

"Where's the other one? They're always lurking around together like a couple o' bad smells. Frick'n cats give me the jeebies," said Vince adamantly, pulling a stupid face and menacingly splaying his fingers open and closed like a pair of snapping talons. The cat took no notice whatsoever.

"Ah come on, they're good little guys. Faye would be really upset if she heard you talking about them like that," replied Joe protectively.

"Which one is this? I think it's Jenteka, the girl one," said Joe. "I can never remember which one's which. And what's the boy one called?"

"Gutteka. Say it like goo-te-ka," answered Bird, sounding studious.

"How the hell do you know that? Don't even know your own name, but you can remember the name of a stupid cat." I'm sure he understood what Vince had said, but Bird chose to ignore it. As much as I thought I liked Vince, he did seem to have a bit of a nasty streak.

"The other one's up there. It's been staring down at us for a long time." Bird pointed to the concrete roof above the driveway. We all looked up together. It sat motionless, slightly back from the edge. Something weird then took hold of me and I made up a few words in rhyme:

> *...Excluding reflections,*
> *from eyes full of light,*
> *it sat there unseen,*
> *in the darkness of night.*

"Oooh! seems we've got ourselves a regular Allen Ginsburg here boys," laughed Joe. "Come on Wolf, tell us another one."

"Oh, you're gonna just love their mommy," barked Vince.

Gutteka started to growl, sounding really pissed off about something. Vince flicked a bottle top up at it and it vanished like someone had turned off a switch. Jenteka, the one on my lap, jumped back into nowhere and was gone.

For a minute or two no one said anything, we just sat there listening to the night-time sounds of the chaparral out there in the darkness. My stomach broke the silence with a long, gurgling rumble complaining of its hunger.

"I'm with you there boy, I weren't being inhospitable or nothin'," explained Joe apologetically. "I asked one of the fellas back there to cook up something tasty, so we could have a bit of late supper to eat when you finally got here. Where the f—"

He was about to head off in pursuit of his missing vittles, when a middle-aged Mexican man scurried urgently around the corner, carrying a steaming hot, shallow pan. Both the handles were bundled up with a couple of dishcloths, even so, he was right at the end of his pain threshold, so reaching our position, he plonked the pan quickly and unceremoniously down on the concrete floor. He shook his hands in an exaggerated display of relief.

We leaned over towards the pan, curious to see what was down there beneath the plumes of fragrant steam. "Pollo mole. Chicken mole. Good call," enthused Joe. "Been hanging out for something to eat since before sundown."

"So sorry for the long delay, Señor Joe."

"Forget it Eduardo, looks great. Did you do any extra rice?"

"Sí señor, but I put it down back there. It was too hot to carry, *demasiado caliente*—" His words reverted to Spanish as he trotted off to retrieve the other part of the meal that had been left behind. He returned holding an enormous iron pot of rice, precisely as Bird came out of the shop carrying a handful of plates and a grab of forks and spoons.

Joe, me and the boys were all getting stuck in like we hadn't eaten for weeks.

"Es bueno, sí?" nodded Eduardo with a half-worried look on his face.

"Yeah, good," approved Joe without elaborating further.

Pleased with the approval, Eduardo looked on grinning as we gulped down the food like four greedy pigs at the trough. I loved the aroma from the cocoa and the chilies which really gave it some kick. The fresh chicken was cooked to the point where it fell apart when you put it in your mouth. Man, this was a tasty meal, easily the best thing I'd eaten in months. We even saved a helping for Charlie, but he never came back to eat it.

"Big thanks to Mrs. Eduardo too. Yeah gracias, Buenos Noches, see you tomorrow."

"He's a nice guy Eduardo," mused Joe. "Intense, but the absolute salt of the earth."

"Hey Wolf," Joe changed direction again, scraping the last bits of food from his plate. "Not being rude, but how come you're still wearing sunglasses in the middle of the night? Do you have some kind of problem with your eyes, or are you just being cool?"

Vince just laughed thinking it an obvious piss-take as Bird blurted out "Hey yes, Señor Lobo, that is right, I have never seen you without your shades, not even in the nighttime."

I ignored the other two but was intrigued by Joe's frankness and thought I should at least give him some kind of plausible answer.

"No, I'm not being cool. I do have a bit of an eye problem. But I don't really know what it is."

"Been to an eye doctor?"

"Nope, can't afford it."

"Gotta look after your eyes boy, ya gotta look after your eyes."

I was lying of course, bright lights did seem to faze me, but my eyes were really okay. Truth be known, my peepers looked like they belonged to some kind of insipid, little vole-rat creature so I guess I felt safe behind the shades. Probably just a symptom of a maladjusted psychosis I guess.

"Check out his hair though," blurted Vince. "He's some kind o' rocka-billy greaser. Of course he's trying to look cool. Take 'em off man, let's see if you've even got any eyes."

Without a second thought, I did just that.

"*Eeeesh!*" yelped Vince disdainfully. "Yeah, put 'em back on!" He was really starting to bust my balls.

It suddenly dawned on me that I never do take them off, not even in bed or the shower. I probably do need some kind of psychiatric counselling.

Vince left his plate on the arm of the couch, got up and announced he was going to bail and go play with his dickhead buddies out there in cyberspace.

"Come on Bird, I'll put you in your cage with some seed and help tuck you in!" Vince laughed at his own stupid joke, punched his old man in the arm as a good night gesture and sauntered off casually inside. Bird stacked the plates, then scurried away, leaving Joe and me and the near empty pan of chicken mole sitting alone out there beneath the stars.

"That means they're gonna be up all night, smoking dope," Joe said, disenchanted. "Thinks his old man's way too stupid to figure that one out."

"Sorry I can't offer you a decent shower tonight Wolf. The hot water isn't working, so unless you're tough enough to take a cold one, you'll have to wait until mid-morning. You can park the Fire Diamond around the corner and bunk down there if you like. The driveway 'll be closed, so the lights won't be on to keep you awake. Is that alright with you?"

I nodded in agreement, "Yeah fine, thanks."

He didn't seem to be in any hurry to head off himself just yet. In fact, he grabbed another beer out of the chest and sat back down on the couch to drink it.

Joe raised his bottle and asked me if I wanted another and once again, I declined.

I told him I had two questions that had been nagging at me and a third one that I wouldn't mind getting an answer to either. He looked straight at me and said "Sure kid, shoot. I'll answer them as best I can." He chuckled as though he knew what I was going to ask him and took another swig from his beer.

"So, why's this place called The Alamo when it says Joe's right up there?" I pointed to the sign atop the three-stage neon rockets.

He opened up his answer with a low rumble laugh: "Ah, we got called all kind o' names when we arrived here. The frick'n Alamo. Yeah, that's a good one. We tried to come up with a really good acronym for that but Americans-Living-A-Mexican-One was the best we could do."

"It wasn't very good, so we gave it away. One of the guys had a disgusting one about anuses and orifices, but I can't remember what it was. When I first came down here looking for somewhere to buy, I kid you not, this place was *already* called Joe's. So naturally I thought it was a good omen. Dunno what I'da thought if it had been called Funky Phil's or Twinkie-Dinkies or something. The *hijos de putas* was another one," he said with a shake of his head.

"I think it means sons of bitches, or worse. Fair call I suppose. All the locals suddenly get a deployment of ex-U.S. military types in their neighborhood gas station *Hi, how's it goin'?* Nowadays most folks just know it as Gringo Joe's. Yeah, Ted Johnston and Johnny Mason were with us back then. Both of 'em looked as if they'd just jumped straight out of a frick'n helicopter. Apart from T-shirts and sunscreen, none of us wore anything other than camo. Man, we brought a lot of hardware surplus down with us then too. A heck of a lot."

Joe grinned contentedly, reminiscing on fondly cherished memories. "Anyway," he slapped his thigh, punctuating a change of subject, "Your next question's about the chupacabras right?"

I nodded in agreement.

"I wish I could give you a serious answer to that Wolf, but to be honest I really can't. The media always makes out they're some kind of urban myth. But trust me they're not. Most folks come across a mangy, bloated carcass of a Xolo dog and think they've found a chupacabra. Have you seen them? Ugly hairless things. They're indigenous to Central America. The Aztecs and the Toltecs used them as hunting dogs, which they bred to eat back then as well. That reminds me..." continued Joe, his voice now starting to pressurize as it built up with one of his anecdotes. "Years ago, we all went over to this big feast thing, put on by some local families in a nearby village who we'd gotten pretty friendly with. They were being really hospitable serving up all these different types of traditional food and stuff. It was fantastic. I remember Johnny Mason, that guy could eat everybody else under the table. Anyway, he was filling his face with everything when they brought out this long spit pole with a well-roasted pig stretched out along it and started carving off strips right there at the table beside us. We were all stuffed-full by now and couldn't even manage a mouthful. But not Johnny, oh no. He piled it up on his plate and was eating away like there was no tomorrow. It turned out that it wasn't pork at all, but one of these frick'n barbecued Xolo dogs."

Joe exploded once again into laughter and took another gulp from his beer.

"Apparently, they're still regarded as a bit of a delicacy by some rural folks around here. Their meat is supposed to have some kind of strange medicinal qualities. When poor old Johnny finally figured out what it was that he'd been eating, he turned as white as a sheet and staggered away somewhere to throw his guts up. Man, he was pissed off. Sorry I went off on a bit of a tangent there, but which ever way you slice it that tasty little morsel was definitely not a chupacabra."

"So, what does a real chupacabra look like then?"

"Well let me just give you a little bit of background info." He leaned towards me for dramatic effect and then started to tell me what he thought I needed to know.

"These things first appeared back in the nineties, down in Puerto Rico where they started killing off sheep. Pretty soon reports started coming in from Columbia, El Salvador, Nicaragua, Mexico and everywhere else in Central and South America. As far as I can remember, the first ones started turning up in Texas back around 2004, but I think they were just pox-riddled coyotes or something. A bunch o' smart-ass scientists at some university conducted all these tests," Joe exclaimed derisively.

"They reckoned they were a freakish kind of coyote-canine-hybrid, but more and more of 'em kept on turning up. Some author called Radwood, Radrod, I forget, did this research project and came to the conclusion that people who thought they'd seen a chupacabra had all been watching too many sci-fi movies, and their delusions could be attributed solely to a log jam of computer-generated images clogging up their brains. When you consider the mindset of the general public, I reckon that's about 98.9% true." He chuckled away to himself at the apparent irony.

"But there are these *other* supposed chupacabra things out there, that are a completely different kettle of fish. They're a much more demonic looking creature that can stand upright and run around on their two hind-legs. They look kind of scaly and have this ridge of barbs running down the middle of their back. Some have tails, some don't, just depends. Either way, they're ugly-looking bastards, with razor-sharp teeth and a head that looks like a cross between a manic, rabid dog and a…a…" Joe pondered for a second but didn't come up with a likeness.

"How big are these things?"

"Varies, five to seven-foot tall on average, twice that if you add on the length of their tail."

"Holy moly!"

"Nah, I don't buy the attack you guys came across earlier had anything to do with the regular chupacabras. They don't hunt in packs. Sounds to me like it must have been the latter."

"Have *you* ever seen one?"

"Oh, shit yeah!" With one final gulp, he finished his beer and stared off into the distance.

"And what's your other question?"

"These goddamn skeletons. What the hell are they? I can't seem to get a decent explanation out of anybody. Bird reckons it's '*All very Mexican*'."

Joe laughed once again, and I continued. "I know it's got a lot to do with this Día de los Muertos festival and everything, but they are real, if that's the right word, aren't they? My half-trashed car and now this business with The Shining Specters. I just wanna know what it's all about. What's going on?"

Joe paused, searching for an answer. "I'll let you into a little secret Wolf. I've been living down here in Sonora for about eight years now and to be perfectly honest with you, I know as much about all that skeleton, Day of the Dead stuff as you do. Jack diddly squat. How about we continue our little discussion tomorrow, yeah? I'm going in ... still got a couple of hours of research to do."

"Sounds good."

He got up from the couch, feigning exaggerated feebleness and laid his hand firmly down on my shoulder. "Pull your car in over there across from the roller door and get yourself some sleep. You know where the john is, so I'll see you in the morning."

"Where're you from anyway, Wolf?" he asked as an extremely late afterthought.

"Las Vegas."

"The home of high kick'n Vicki, huh?" With that he went inside and pulled the screen door shut behind him.

7

Joker in the Back

I'd been having one of those anxious dreams, when I was woken by a finger tapping urgently on the top of my head. I opened my eyes to see the upside-down face of a very pretty blonde girl leaning over me through the open window, jabbering excitedly in a strange foreign language. The early morning sun shone gold through her hair and if it weren't for the constant poking and the verbal tirade, I could have sworn I must have died and gone up to heaven. She really did look like an angel.

Stretched out along the car's front seat with my head resting on my roadrunner pillow I tried to figure out what the hell she was getting so huffed-up about.

She reached determinedly over to the back seat. "Koffertten min, koffertten min. My suitcase, where did you find it?" She was buzzing like crazy with excitement.

She was after the suitcase the American girl had left behind when she did the bolt last night. I'd forgotten it was even there. I reached aimlessly across to get it, but she'd already grabbed it and was now hauling it out over my head.

She disappeared down beside the car, frantically opening the case right there on the concrete. I opened the door to get out, but the road-runner pillow beat me to it. Sitting on the edge of the seat I fumbled around trying to put on my socks and boots.

The girl was squatting down on her haunches, raking through the remaining items in the suitcase. She was wearing a tight-fitting pair of blue jeans and a mid-length vest that rode halfway up her lily-white back. Her unweaving braids were plainly the remnants of yesterday's perfect hairstyle.

It was certainly more appealing than yesterday morning's vision, perched behind Bird on his motorbike. Speaking of which, as if on cue, he appeared beneath the clatter of the ascending garage roller-door.

Dressed in a bright-yellow polyester tracksuit with that stupid purple hat pulled down tight on his head, he looked like one of those squeezy plastic lemon bottles you keep in the back of your fridge for emergencies. He really did look ridiculous.

He came over all flustered and straight away started explaining about the 'crazy woman' we'd come across by the side of the road. The more he babbled on it became clear that the case she'd left behind really did belong to the girl here beside me.

"Please don't worry Bird I have it now. Although there are only a couple of items here that are actually mine. You said there was lots of other things that had fallen out along the roadside?"

Bird went into more detail about the open lid and the stuff he'd picked up and put back into the case when the American girl finally stopped running and came over to us.

I watched as she cast aside a blouse and a couple of other bits and pieces that were obviously not hers. Then she closed the lid of the suitcase and examined the outside which had been damaged and darkened in places with the stains of splattered blood. Running her fingers lightly over the lid, she examined three tear marks that had been gouged out across its leather. She sprang to her feet and strode determinedly around the back of the car and into the mechanic shop, put the case safely beneath a workbench, twirled on her heels and returned at speed to the same spot she had left from only seconds earlier.

"Hello Mr. Wolf!" she said with a smile. "You found my case. Thank you so much, you don't know how much this means to me, but we must go back there at once."

With that proclamation she marched purposefully around the front of the Fire Diamond, opened the door and placed herself in the passenger's seat.

"There were some very important things in that case, which I thought had been lost forever. If there is the slightest chance that they are still lying back there on the roadside, it is imperative that we go there now so I can retrieve them. Come on Bird, get in, we have to go."

I'm still sitting there, sideways in the driver's seat, with one booted foot outside on the concrete and the other half-socked one still in my lap. "Hang on lady, I ain't even got both my boots on yet and the old Fire Diamond is sitting here on empty. EM-TEE."

"Well, back it up and fill it. We must get back there before all of my things disappear. *Please!*"

"So why can't you go there yourself in Joe's pickup?"

"It's not here, Charlie has taken it somewhere. Anyway it's too slow and your car will get there much faster." She stopped fretting for a couple of seconds and laughed. "Besides, I really love the look of your car and want to go for a ride in it."

I pulled on the boot and gave her a look to say "Well, with the price of gas at the moment I ain't got no interest in going on a twenty-mile joy-ride looking for lost pairs of frillies and fancy-pants-designer sunglasses, no matter how much you try to cajole me." Maybe that was a lot of information to try and get across with a single expression, but she must have gotten my drift as she said she'd pay for the gas when we got back. We had to get going immediately. Like *NOW!*

Reversing under orders to the pumps, I hadn't noticed Bird trying to squeeze inside through the gap behind my upright seat. I hit the brakes instinctively and he bowled straight on into the back.

"Hey Wolf, you imbécil! What are you doing? You could have crippled me. *Maldito idiota.*"

I took no notice and reversed the car back to the pump with the lead-based gasoline. I was surprised when I saw the pumps. I couldn't believe I hadn't noticed last night when we came in, they were the old Skull brand. As far as I knew, they'd gone out of business back in the seventies, but the pumps and their classic globe tops had been kept as a nice little touch by Joe. Skull...how ironic.

I only put in five gallons as quick as the old-style machine would pump it, hedging my bets, as I was sure I'd be left with the tab later on. I jumped back in the car, slipped her into first and the moment my foot hit the gas I had to slam down hard on the brakes.

"Holy je' Vince, *you idiot*, I nearly squashed you flat as a sandwich!" He had suddenly appeared out of nowhere, smack bang in front of the hood.

"What about me? (ridiculous puppy-dog pout) The three stooges going somewhere without their bestest, bestest buddy?"

The girl, who I'd guessed by now was Faye, stuck her head out of the window and screamed shrilly at Vince. "Get out of the way, will you please move out of the way."

"I wanna come, I wanna come." He was grinning and bouncing around annoyingly, countering any moves I made with the wheel so I couldn't steer around him. Naked to the waist, he was still wearing the same board shorts he had on last night. Vince had a pretty muscular build. That type of no-effort, well-proportioned body that chicks seem to dig. One of those guys who had no qualms about being picked for skins at high school sports, as opposed to the other 95% who looked like loaves of soggy white bread and would willingly sell their grandmother to play on the shirts side.

With an exasperated sigh, Faye relented just so we could get going. Vince pulled an exaggerated smile and moved around to the passenger side of the car in expectation that Faye would open her door and let him in.

"You're not sitting back behind me *boody boy!*" I think she was trying to say *Buddy Boy*, but I wasn't going to correct her, that accent was fantastic. I'd gotten the impression by now she was most probably Scandinavian. "You sit over behind Wolf; I'm not going anywhere with you carrying on like a fool right behind me. *You're so childish!*"

Vince dashed around my side and slid through the gap, spinning himself around in the seat next to Bird. "Howdy Birdy Boy. Where'd you all think you were going without old Vince?" He was extremely pleased with himself, like the Dalmatian who'd been allowed to sit up front in the firetruck, even if he was in the back.

Finally, we thundered off down to the roadside and we hadn't gone fifty yards when Faye yelled "Stop!" Jesus wept. We'd just spent the last ten minutes trying to get the most urgent mission known to man up and going, when suddenly we have to stop.

"Aaaah it's little Diego," bleated Faye. "He's going our way, let's give him a lift."

Shuffling along by the roadside was a boy of about ten wearing a ball cap and blue jeans and a Lupe Vélez sweatshirt. A new leather school satchel was slung casually over his shoulder.

"What the hell for, it's only a stupid kid," I yelled in an outburst of irritation. It takes me quite a while to get going in the mornings and today I'd been woken up from sleep by someone tapping me on the head like a woodpecker, fill her up with gas, go here, do it *NOW*, play driveway chicken with the grinning Adonis and now it's *let's stop for some local kid by the roadside.*

"Oooh Fenrir. Who's a little cranky this morning?"

To add insult to injury she was ragging on me for simply following orders. I pulled up alongside the boy who grinned at me with a dispro-portionately sized set of teeth. He opened the passenger side door and climbed in next to Faye.

"Hello foxy momma, you wanna..." Faye put her hand over his mouth to stop him from saying any more.

She turned around on the seat towards Vince and tried to belt him with her fist. Vince had already shrunk back deep into the upholstery in anticipation.

"What the hell have you been teaching him? He's supposed to be learning English you moron. My god I can't believe how incredibly stupid you are sometimes."

Vince's expression was one of bewildered innocence, he looked back at her indignantly as if to say, "*Me*. What have I done?" Bird just sat there; hat pulled down low over his eyes keeping silencio. Faye went through the motions of explaining to little Diego that what silly Señor Vince had told him to say was impolite, not good English, and not to repeat anything he tells you to anybody. Not ever.

"Stop here please," said Diego. "Thank you for the ride in your long, nice car." As he got out, he burst into another toothy grin, blew Faye an exaggerated kiss and said, "Adios foxy momma, *Te quiero a lo grande*." and slammed the door irritatingly behind him. Faye put her face down in her hands and let out a quiet scream of exasperation.

"Where's he going?" I asked somewhat mystified. "He was only in the car for thirty seconds and now he's heading off behind a pile of rocks."

"He's one of Joe's freelance spotters," said Bird, as if I knew what he was talking about.

"Spotters. What's he spotting behind a load of rocks and dirt. Bloody lizards? And what's he carrying in the fancy satchel then, a periscope?" I said trying to be funny.

"Diego's one of the best. He'll sit there for frick'n hours doing his shift. He watches the traffic and gives the old man the heads-up when someone that looks a bit sus' comes driving down the road. *There's a lot of cotton-pickin varmints passing through these here parts...yesireee!*" Vince perfectly imitated one of those old-timers from the black and white westerns, who always make those comical but highly prophetic statements.

"There's another stooge sitting a mile or two back in the other direction as well," he explained, all very matter of fact.

"So, what's inside the satchel?"

"One of Joe's antique laptops," answered Faye. "While they're on school holidays, Diego and his friend are supposed to be using them to help with their English lessons in exchange for their time on spotting duty," she said, directing a filthy look over towards Vince.

We drove on in silence for a while after that. I tried consciously to stop my gaze from drifting across to get an eyeful of Faye. It was hard, she was magnetic. I hadn't really clued-in to just how lovely she was until now. She really was something else. At least two or three leagues above any women I'd ever known. Two or three leagues above any women I think I'd even spoken to for that matter.

She was one of those girls that would make you suck your own gut in, under the self-delusion that the very act itself would somehow fool her into believing you were a trim and taut physical specimen, despite the indisputable proof to the contrary. I was sucking it in right then and there while I was driving … what an asshole.

"So, Faye," any excuse for another head turning look at her. "How did you know my name was Wolf?"

"No, not only Wolf, Fenrir. A fearsome wolf," she laughed playfully. The others both laughed along if only to score points. Vince naturally went one further and started howling like a four-footed leader of the pack.

I'd only been in Mexico a couple of days and I'd already gotten three new names. Señor Lobo. Saint Wolfgang. I seriously couldn't wrap my brain around that one, and now Fenrir?

"I'm sorry Wolf, Joe told me late last night that you had come down with Bird. Please don't be angry with me for being so bossy earlier on, but it is so important that I get there as quickly as possible to recover any of my missing things."

Everything looked completely different in the daylight and I could see now why Faye wanted Bird to come along. I was hoping he knew where we had picked up the American girl last night 'cos I didn't have a frick'n clue.

It was then I saw something quite curious. "Bird, look who it is." I pointed up ahead. Bird leaned forward across the seat and laughed. "It's the old señor we saw walking along with the rake yesterday, he must move very fast to have reached here already?" He leaned out the open window and gave him a wave as we passed, but the old man paid us no attention.

"How much further now?" asked Faye, I could see she was getting impatient.

"Pretty soon, about five more minutes I think," said Bird.

There was very little traffic at this time of the morning, so I hit the gas and picked up the speed to make Faye a little happier. She then discovered my box of eight-tracks on the floor. Picking them up, she gasped with surprise.

"You have Motörhead. *Ace of Spades*. Put it on. I LOVE THIS MUSIC." She wiggled the cartridge around in her hand exactly like Bird had done yesterday. A completely unknown relic from a bygone era.

I took it from her hand and flicked it into the player. The runner tape hummed through the car's four speakers, and as the guitar cut loose, Faye cranked up the volume to max. The heavy metal track came blasting in with an onslaught of deafening sound. It was heavy and hard and very, very fast.

Faye thrashed around in her seat like she'd shoved her fist in the mains. Her hair broke free from the failing braids as she scythed it around in time to the fast-playing metal. She was digging it.

The boys were getting off on it too. Probably more to do with watching Faye's little show, but they were both belting their brains around in their skulls like a couple of die-hard metal-heads. The effect that the unleashed guitar, bass and drums were having on my offside passenger was *perfectly disturbing*. Faye was going berserk. She stretched up over the seat towards Vince and Bird, her short armless vest left little to the imagination as she teased and taunted them. She had all the moves down pat and mimed along with the words perfectly, making all those sexy-pouty-type faces. Faye was winding us up, big time. Jesus H Christ she was hot.

Eventually, with two fast cord strikes on his axe, the guitarist signed-off and the track was suddenly over. Faye spun around forward, dropped back to her original position and pressed the eject button.

"Wow. That was fantastic! I really needed that," she said with a chuckle, regaining her former composure as if nothing at all had happened. "How much further?" Bird didn't reply.

"I thought you were supposed to be a doctor?" snapped Vince making a dig at Faye.

"You know I am, but that doesn't mean I always have to be little Miss Bookworm now does it?" she giggled and winked at me sideways. "What is it you say Vince? *'I'm up myself.'* You should have seen me back home when I was younger shaking my toosh in the speed-metal bars. No, I bet you only ever listened to that hop-hip'n type of music, didn't you, poor baby."

Vince pulled a face and said nothing. Of course, that only lasted about five seconds before they were at it again. Vince was always nig-gling, always trying to get something over on Faye, but she was always one step ahead and could play him like a five-dollar fiddle. I knew there was some kind of unresolved sexual tension between them, but definitely only on Vince's part. You could tell she had absolutely no interest in him whatsoever. I reckon Vince'd probably tried it on too fast when they'd first met and had been trying to compensate for the rejection ever since.

◆

We had only seen two other cars all morning, so when a third came towards us it caught my attention. It was boxy and brown, but still a little too far away to tell what it was. I watched, fixated, as it dipped low and out of sight in a trough in the road up ahead. I checked the rearview mirror and the eyes of Señora de las Sombras seemed to be glowing red, but I figured it was a trick of the light. Looking back to the road, the oncoming car was suddenly right on us and I recognized it immediately.

"Get down!" I yelled urgently, pulling Faye low across the seat. The side of her head landed roughly on my thigh amidst a tumbleweed of straw-like hair.

"*You da man Wolf. You da man!*" came the banal howling outburst from Vince.

"Sorry about that, it was Martindale and his pal in that Baybecker. I hope they didn't see you."

"Who's Martindale?" said Faye sitting herself upright.

"The two Feds who are sniffing around out there looking for you."

"*Me?*" she exclaimed with unconvincing surprise.

"Oh, come on. I'm not a complete frick'n tool. That is you in his photo, isn't it?"

With perfect timing Bird lunged forward and pointed to a spot beside the road. "*There* Señor Wolf, pull over there. That's where we picked up the girl."

I would never have recognized it even if my life had depended on it. It looked pretty much the same as everywhere else. I steered off the road and slammed on the brakes making sure of an impressive sliding stop. Faye took no notice and jumped immediately out of the car leaving her door wide-open but the seat still upright for the imbeciles in the back to negotiate for themselves.

◆

Faye by now was gone. She was up on the higher ground searching along the bank and diligently scanning the roadside below for her missing items. A couple of times I saw her bend down to pick something up and stash it in a white plastic shopping bag.

Vince and Bird had wandered only a short way ahead and were already taking their R&R, lolling around on a flat rock rolling up a doobie. As I passed, I scoffed in mock disapproval.

I walked on by myself for a while but felt a little uneasy as Faye had disappeared and the Fire Diamond was also out of sight. Something told me I ought to go back.

As I turned, I kicked a rock about the size of my fist. I was about to boot it on to oblivion, when I noticed it wasn't a rock at all, but a small, chunky statue. I knew it was bronze by its weight and the tell-tale sheen of metal that peeked out through its greenish-brown tarnish. The figure was some kind of ancient long-haired warrior-woman wearing a helmet and riding-high on a large charging boar.

This was *definitely* Faye's. I stuffed it in a pocket and headed back to the car.

I edged the Fire Diamond along the roadside at a crawl, with the passenger side door wide-open in case I came across any more of her stuff. When I drew up close to the stoners, they ambled over towards me. Vince raised his arms in the air, laughing and stretching the elastic of a skimpy pair of women's undies he'd just acquired.

"Hey Wolfie. Let me have a drive and I'll give you these," they both laughed hysterically, totally ripped off their tits. I ignored them.

Then, without the slightest consideration for the paintwork, the bastards both hauled their butts up onto the Fire Diamond's fender and looked in through the windshield expectantly, as if to say, *"Well we're ready now señor, drive on."*

Really pissed me off.

We crawled along for a couple of minutes; all eyes peeled for anything unusual. I took a look down at the little bronze figure on the seat beside me. It was intriguing, I liked it more every time I looked at it. Then right in front of me, Bird rolled over the side. I thought he was too stoned and had simply fallen off, but a couple of seconds later he reappeared holding a school exercise book and rejoined his pal on the hood.

There was still no sign of Faye, but I figured she was going to be around the next bend, standing there waiting for us to pick her up. As we turned the corner it was an altogether different picture. About a hundred yards up ahead the upturned truck was still on the road. We must have driven further than I thought. Whether the police had checked it out was impossible to tell, but I sure hoped those locals had taken care of the poor driver's body.

I saw Faye heading towards us from the accident site, retracing the American girl's steps. We drove on slowly, Bird leafing quizzically through the pages in the book, while Vince plotted his salacious underwear hand-over negotiations.

Then it happened.

As we got a little closer, the undulations of the road revealed a sight we were completely unprepared for. Down in a shallow, midway between the Fire Diamond and Faye appeared three ominous figures on motorcycles. I just knew they were Los Espectros Brillantes.

Vince and Bird saw them too and leapt off the hood and piled into the front seat beside me. The Fire Diamond was a pretty spacious ride, but this was a little too squeezy for my liking.

"What are we gonna do?" I said panicking.

"Oh relax!" said Vince, "Run right over the bastards if they try anything, this is a monster '58 Special ain't it?"

We crept along the dirt beside the road at a snail's pace getting steadily closer to Faye. She had stopped dead on the other side of the riders. They didn't seem to be moving or doing anything at all, so we crawled on a little further. The rider nearest to us jerked his motorcycle forward a little and just sat there, a sign for us to stop. That was good enough for me, I turned off the engine and wondered what in the hell to do next.

"Do you think they've got guns?" I asked naively.

"Of course they've got guns ya dipshit," exclaimed Vince condescendingly. "They're *Demon-Bikers-from-Hell* ain't they?" I had no answer to that.

"Just sit tight," said Bird. "Let's see what happens."

We sat gazing out through the windshield like three garden gnomes. The heat from the climbing sun distorted the ground into a shimmering mirage. Faye, still carrying the plastic bag, had moved to within a couple of feet of them. They seemed to be talking, but it was a little hard to tell. After a moment, the two riders close to her slowly dismounted from their motorcycles, but the one keeping an eye on us, stayed on his bike.

"They're gonna mess with her Wolf. We've gotta get over there and help," yelled Vince, showing the first real concern for anyone since I'd met him.

"No, wait, look at these guy's body language," said Bird. "They're not going to do anything to her, they're only standing there chatting."

In the daylight they appeared as darkish-grey, I couldn't put my finger on it, but they seemed to have the consistency of densely packed smoke. They really creeped me out. The other two riders now stood at arm's length on either side of Faye. She didn't look too fazed by them; in fact, she looked a little more relaxed. The one who I guessed was the leader was making some kind of speech. His movements as he spoke to her oddly took a turn for the theatrical, confirmed in one dramatic gesture as he unexpectedly moved back a pace, took off his black sombrero and bowed low and respectfully like some dude in a Shakespearean play.

"Far out!" Vince summed it up for all of us.

"What the hell was that all about?" I said relieved, feeling like I had to say something too.

"See, I told you. Just let it play out and see what happens. I knew it would be okay," piped in Bird.

"Piss off Bird, your professorship. You had no more idea of what was goin' down than me and the Wolfman," said Vince.

Pretty soon the two riders near Faye remounted their motorcycles and joined our guardian. Together the three rode north. Faye stood motionless as the dust settled slowly around her. She seemed to be in some kind of shock.

The boys and I got out and high-tailed it over to Faye who was now walking towards us. When we reached her she stopped and looked at us blankly. I couldn't tell if she was going to burst out laughing or burst into tears. It could have gone either way.

"I was so scared, I really thought I was in a lot of trouble when they first approached me, but they were not—" she didn't finish her sentence. "I think I just met Los Espectros Brillantes. They were all skjeletter. But then, you will never believe this, one of them spoke to me. He spoke to me in *Old Norse*." She was shocked and relieved all at the same time, I could see it in her face.

"What did it say?" asked Vince bluntly. "And what was all that bowing business about?"

She didn't reply but looked at us with an undefinable expression and changed the subject completely. "I found quite a few of my things, did any of you pick up anything?"

Bird flipped out the exercise book from a pocket deep within his baggy yellow tracksuit "Is this yours?"

"Yes. It's one of my notebooks, thank you Bird." She flicked through it quickly. "Fmoc and tBoc peptide synthesis, I'm so lucky I had most of my notes and data files on the flash drives in my shoulder bag, this is the only hard copy book that's left."

"Fmoc toc-boc what?" asked Bird, totally baffled, keeping her attention focused on him.

"It doesn't matter Bird, it's chemical formulas and stuff, all very boring." We had almost reached the car when Vince produced his trump card.

"What about *these*?" he twirled the flimsy underwear around on the end of his finger, obviously trying to provoke a reaction or cause her maximum embarrassment.

"You can keep those. Please be my guest." Vince was taken aback, that was definitely not the reaction he was expecting.

"They are not mine; they must belong to your little junkie friend," she said matter-of-factly.

Bird howled with laughter and pushed Vince sideways in ridicule making him half lose his balance. Vince dropped the item on the spot and wiped his fingers discreetly on the back of his board shorts. Bird nudged him once again, still laughing mockingly at his hapless friend. We all got back in the car as before, and I picked up the little bronze statue from the seat and handed it to her. "Is this yours?" I knew it was.

"Fenrir, I can't believe it!" she was suddenly ecstatic, bouncing up and down on her seat like an excited child. "It was one of the two things that I really, really HAD to find. Min bestemor, my grandmother gave it to me when I was a little girl. I thought I would never ever see it again, *takk*. Thank you. Thank you."

She leaned across and pecked me an excited kiss on the cheek. I really wasn't expecting that kind of reaction. I just thought it was some old piece of curio that she had been lugging around, but she was obviously very attached to it.

"So, what exactly was the other thing you just HAD to find?" enquired Vince snidely, trying to restore his damaged demeanor.

She was extremely happy now and gladly complied with answering his sarcastic question. Rummaging through the contents of the plastic bag she pulled out a pair of black, denim jeans. "Look what I found. My favorites. You wait till you see me in these Mr. Honky-doodle." She blew him a contemptuous kiss, giggled excitedly then resumed her search.

Man, I *loved* her accent.

"Here it is, finding this is so wonderful." Suddenly she pulled out a ragged, old hessian dolly. "This is Gersemi isn't she cute?" Faye held it up next to her smiling face, playfully nodding the doll's head quickly a couple of times with her finger as if to say 'Hello'. "I found her over there beside the overturned truck."

We all sat speechless, not even Vince could think of anything to say. We were completely dumbfounded.

"What? Why are you looking at me like that?" Faye seemed shocked by the bewildered expressions on our faces.

"A doll! The most important thing in the world and the whole reason for this morning's panic is a frick'n RAG DOLL?" I closed my eyes and banged my head on the steering wheel for effect.

"Oh, Fenrir, don't be so dramatic. It's not only Gersemi, although she is very cute, don't you think? It's what's *inside* her that's important as well."

"What? Nothing less than diamonds or, or—" I couldn't think of anything else quick enough.

Her face suddenly turned quite stern and upset, "Well it is."

"What the hell's inside it then?" barked Vince, trying to keep the ball rolling.

She looked at me, then over her shoulder towards the others, then back to me. "I can't tell you. I'll have to talk to Joe and MacElroy about it first." With that she turned, shoved the doll back in the plastic bag with the huff and sat looking straight ahead. My god she was gorgeous, even more so when she was annoyed.

We headed off back to The Alamo in silence, but it didn't last long. Vince was soon niggling away at Faye doing his utmost to provoke her, while Bird did his best to bring up all kinds of crazy left-field factoids in an attempt to keep the conversation rolling. I think if circumstances hadn't dumped him right in the middle of the Sonoran Desert that Bird would probably have been a pretty scholarly kind of guy.

I was curious about the connection between the American girl and Faye's lost suitcase. She explained how she had lost it on a bus trip many months earlier but seemed vague about the details. I told her all about what had happened at The Pepper Coyote, how the girl was terrified of the Feds and bolted, and how we'd picked her up after the accident and her midnight flight out into the desert.

Faye had nothing to add except that she'd found a syringe and some other bits of drug paraphernalia scattered out along the trail she'd so carefully retraced only a few minutes earlier.

"I think she was probably just an unfortunate junkie mixed up with the wrong people or some kind of deal that had gone bad. Who knows? What I can't understand is why she kept so many of my things for all this time. I cannot believe it; I am very lucky."

"Maybe she had jack to start with," I threw in flippantly.

"Who is Jack?"

"Doesn't matter, just an expression, it means *nothing*."

"I did find a few things of hers," said Faye "But not much, only a top and some bits of underwear. You can always go back later and get them if you want to Vince."

Bird roared with laughter and hit Vince with a pile-driver thump to the arm.

◆

The journey back to Joe's went incredibly quickly, like most return trips do. Apart from Vince's excitement at seeing a convertible crammed-full of big-breasted, hoochies hurtling off to God-knows-where, and "little Diego" who nearly sun-blinded us with a well-aimed piece of mirror from down behind his rock, nothing else happened at all.

I parked the Fire Diamond alongside the pumps, exactly where I'd first parked her last night. Joe had handed a stack of change to a customer and waved him off back to the road.

"How did you go darlin'?" he asked casually, turning to meet Faye as she was getting out of the car.

"I can't believe it. I am so happy. I found so many of my things, I even found Gersemi," she said completely thrilled.

"You found her. That's *fantastic!*" exclaimed Joe, equally enthused.

Vince looked at him as if he'd gone totally mad and walked off twirling his finger beside his head.

"Hey, don't go too far you, I want you to give me a hand with the hot plate. We're having barbecue today. Thought we'd grill up some lamb and have a TexMex BBQ. Tortillas, chilies, lots o' peppers and fresh vegetables … *beautiful*. Hope you guys are all hungry."

Vince was gone. Bird acknowledged approval with a clenched fist punch to the air and wandered off otherwise indifferent. I got the impression this was a fairly regular event.

"And Fenrir found *this!*" Faye excitedly held out the little figurine towards Joe.

"It belonged to min bestemor. I am just so happy."

Faye never mentioned her run-in with the three riders or anything about Martindale and Travers. I figured that might have been pretty important. Hey, I'd only known these people less than a day and I was already making assumptions about things I really knew nothing about myself. It wasn't any of my business anyway.

I could tell Faye wasn't intending to hang around and chat. Obviously, there were more important things on her mind.

"I must go," she said. "I still have a lot to do this morning, but I promise I'll be back by noon."

"Yeah 12.00 Faye. Tell MacElroy too," answered Joe flatly.

Then she picked up the plastic bag and took a step towards me. "Thank you Wolf, thank you for finding Gersemi and my little figurine and for taking me all the way back there in your beautiful car. Thank you for playing *Ace of Spades* for me too. I had so much fun going 'just a little crazy'. It was a very wonderful morning for me, *takk*. See you later."

I was speechless. With a disarming smile she picked up the plastic bag and disappeared out of sight somewhere beyond the rear of the building.

8

Home on the Range

Charlie had fixed the hot water system and I'd been given the honor to go test it out in the shower. So now, clean in my one change of clothes, I stood on the roof top and checked out the lay of the land. Joe suggested I park the Fire Diamond up here on the roof where it would be out of the way. She'd picked up a fine coat of grit this morning which now, thanks to Gutteka and Jenteka, had been embellished from hood to trunk with trails of little paw-prints.

The road out front ran parallel with the building some thirty yards beyond the driveway. Everything looked pretty much the same. Flat open desert covered in a patchwork of low-growing scrub. To the north, the only thing different were the boulders from where that Diego kid plied his trade.

At the rear of the building was the gas station's yard. Furthest out sat two or three neatly laid rows of cannibalized car bodies. The back row edging out into the scrubby undergrowth. In front of the wrecks, decades of hard work and traffic had pressed the ground solid and stained its surface a dark oily hue. The area now played host to an old fashion front-bucket tractor, building materials, two enormous spools of fencing wire and a neatly stacked pile of old tires. All kinds of crap like that. There was a half-crumbling adobe storage shed back there too. By the look of it, I figured it was probably the site's original building.

Back from the road to the south I could see an oasis of vegetation from which rose a bunch of tell-tale smoke plumes. I guessed it was some kind of a campsite.

I was snapped from my pondering by a handful of pronghorn antelopes, that had come bolting at speed from the scrub. Spooked by something. They ran momentarily into the yard area before quickly changing direction and heading off back into the desert. I was really starting to like being down here in Mexico.

◆

The barbecue was in full swing and Joe was having a ball. At ease behind one of those novelty plastic French maid aprons, he was the unchallenged master of the hot plate. I'm sure it was only a trick of the light, but his ten-gallon hat looked a whole lot bigger than it was, more like a fifteen. I laughed out loud as he happily flipped some oversized cuts on the grill. He grinned and looked at me kind of strangely.

We were standing around the barbecue that was nestled alongside a tall row of cactus plants. Arm's length from the grill stood an immovable rock and concrete picnic table, that could easily sit eight or nine people, and judging by its apparent industrial strength was probably built back in the fifties.

Faye was sitting at the head of the table. She had nothing on her plate but salad. Considering the copious amount of meat floating around, I presumed she must have been a vegetarian.

Vince had commandeered the inside seat as it offered the only worthwhile shade. He was busy hoeing into an enormous pile of lamb shanks and showed no interest in any other food on the table in front of him. Bird who was sitting between the two of them looked uneasy. Faye was nudging him with her elbow to shift around further, so she could move herself out of the sun. Poor Bird seemed worried about getting his chunkiness stuck between the immovable bench seat and the table and not being able to easily slide back out again.

Sitting adjacent on one of the latecomer chairs, eating his meal with a set of useless plastic cutlery was a man I hadn't seen before. He was a pudgy kind of guy in his mid to late forties, with one of those bullfrog-like throats that ran from the base of his chin to his collar. His receding hair was a light, ginger-brown, combed conservatively from left ear to right. His scruffy little moustache and seventies, oversized spectacles added credence to his unabashed nerdiness.

Mind you, not that I'd do any better, but the guy looked like he'd last about a day if he got lost out here in the desert. With my plate stacked high I sat next to him on the sun-drenched side of the table.

"Hello Wolf, nice to meet you, I'm MacElroy, Dr. Eugene MacElroy, and no I don't do ice-skating either. *Ha! ha!*" he laughed nervously.

I had no idea what the hell he was talking about. "Well hello there, Dr. MacElroy," I said raising a forkful of lamb. "It's nice to meet you too. Do you live down here, or are you just passing through?"

"Oh, I'll be staying down in Sonora for a while. You know, helping Joe and the boys out with things," he replied kind of skittishly.

"So how were those chupacabra skins me and Bird brought down for you?"

"Wha'?" he said kind of shocked as he swallowed a half-chewed mouthful. "What are you, um, talking about?" Eugene began fidgeting nervously, looked at Faye and wiped his forehead with his scrunched-up piece of napkin.

Vince started snickering. "Good one Wolf, you've freaked him out now."

Joe came striding over and swamped poor MacElroy with his shadow. *"You told him Eugene!"* Joe's voice climbed in pitch with excitement. *"You've gone and told him about the chupacabra skins."*

"I, I what, I didn't. What do you mean? He just came and sat down. I'd never—"

Joe couldn't pretend to be incensed any longer and burst into laughter.

"Oh, relax Eugene. I'm only pulling your leg. Wolf's a pretty clever guy, he knows what you're up to."

MacElroy babbled his innocence. I hadn't a clue what he was doing with the skins, but his reaction had really pricked my curiosity. He sure didn't look like the type of guy who'd be cutting and stitching them up into trashy, two-bit tourist wallets.

Faye, who had been holding back a grin, eventually came to his rescue. "Oh, leave poor Eugene alone. We all know he's right up to his tricky little eye holes in it." She then started laughing as well.

MacElroy sat there dejected, poking the remains of his lunch with his plastic fork.

◆

"Hey Wolf," Joe said casually as he finished cleaning up the hot plate. "Let's go for a walk. I've got something to show you."

Sticking the last charred piece of a lamb into my mouth, I got up and moved over towards him.

"We had a visit from your Fed buddies this morning while you were out," said Joe.

"Yeah! We saw them heading this way, I had to duck Faye out of sight so they wouldn't see her. All of that blonde hair and everything."

"So why do you think Martindale's looking for Faye?"

"Oh, come on Joe, I know it's none of my business, but she's obviously the girl in his precious little five by four. I'm not a complete simpleton.

All that carry on with their innuendoes last night, Vince and Bird are pretty hopeless at keeping anything secret."

Joe sniggered and nodded his head (and his hat) in agreement. "Yeah you're right Wolfman. They're a frick'n pair of twerps." I chuckled again at his hat, but he thought I was laughing along with him.

At first it seemed we were heading across towards the little camp site, but Joe turned right and guided me further away.

"That Martindale's a nasty little piece of work, hey? Comes driving in here with that gawky looking buddy of his, flashing ID and acting like some self-proclaimed king o' the boss hogs, asking all these bullshit questions. Charlie wanted to clock both of 'em on sight," Joe chuckled heartily at the thought. "It's gettin' harder keeping a lid on that boy I tell ya. Anyway, I'm sure we haven't seen the last of those two numbskulls."

"So I guess he made you look at Faye's photograph too."

"Oh yeah … frick'n creep. I just told him I'd never seen her."

Right at that moment we reached an area where the ground wasn't as pool table flat as everywhere else. "Here you go!" Joe said, happy to change the subject.

Like a scar the bumpy terrain ran parallel, between the edge of the campsite and the road.

"Someone in the past chucked heaps of old scrap iron and car bodies into this dried up water course. A lot of the surface fill had washed away when we got here, so we just plowed it back over and let it be. I'm sorry I can't pinpoint the spot exactly, but there's a Saratoga-J-Rider, a Belmoth Legeah and the front half of a '58 Fire Diamond with a V badge, buried more or less around here." Joe swept an arc with his hand.

"I don't know how much you want it, but if you're up for it you're more than welcome to dig it out." He shrugged his shoulders as if to say, "Sorry but that's really the best I can do." I started asking him a whole string of questions when suddenly a loud clanging alarm bell rang out from over at the garage.

"Damn!" barked Joe in annoyance.

"We've got a Code Yella. Hold that thought and we'll take it up later. I've gotta get back there." He turned and ran pretty quickly back the fifty odd yards in the direction of the building. I followed behind at a half-assed jog. I seriously couldn't keep up. Joe didn't turn around but told me to head for the garage and not to go anywhere near the driveway or the pumps.

The alarm bell stopped unexpectedly, as unfit and puffing I followed on a few ever-widening yards behind him. His 'size fifteen' blew off of his head straight towards me. I grabbed it and carried it back. It was the first time I'd seen him without it on since I'd arrived. Joe's hair was exactly as I'd thought it would be, a silver-grey, one hundred percent, military 'high and tight'.

I didn't go over to the garage like Joe told me, but skulked around out of sight behind the barbeque, curious to see what was happening. For a moment nothing seemed untoward until a black SUV of some humongous breed pulled up noisily on the further side of the pumps. This monster had tires the size of a tractor and a cabin that perched halfway up to the old driveway roof. Emblazoned across the black metal hood was the Jolly Roger, complete with obligatory crossed cutlasses. Yeah, the outside looked all very bad-boy. But I was far more intrigued as to what kind of life form lived within.

I noticed Vince dash quickly around to the rear of the vehicle carrying what at first looked like a 12-gauge shotgun. But seeing it had no stock I realized it was no more than a length of metal tubing.

At the same time Joe appeared and made a hurried movement towards the driver's side door. He had a firm grip on the end of a foot-long spanner, held tightly against the length of his inside forearm. He walked right up to the now opening door and forced his outstretched free hand into an emerging stomach of blubber that was about to pour itself down onto the tarmac. I could see Vince tapping his improvised weapon on the far side windows, menacingly holding the two rear passengers in check.

One of them then yelled shrilly from their seat, *"Hey Rastus, that scruffy-haired kid out there's got a shotty."* Despite Joe's efforts to prevent him, the oversized driver began to force his way out through the door.

"I'm sorry sir, please stay inside your vehicle and leave the premises immediately. There's nothing we can do for you here. You're obviously intoxicated and it's against Sonoran law for me to serve you."

As he said that, a near empty bourbon bottle tumbled down from the foot well and dropped with a thud on the concrete. *"Damn you boy!"* came the inebriated response from the driver. *"I want gas for my ride, and I wanna take a crap in your john. No, maybe I'll just take a crap on yaw head."* He laughed uncontrollably and looked back over to his buddies for a boost of bravado.

Even though Vince's bluff was holding up well, the two characters in the back were getting all fired up and would soon bust free from their seats. Right at that moment, a new player launched itself into the fray.

Coming in fast on a collision course with the rear of the SUV was the old tractor that I had seen from up on the roof. Its enormous dirt bucket thrust forward menacingly like some kind of medieval battering ram. It had no intention of stopping and appeared to be driven by an oversized, full giblet turkey. More likely I figured it was Charlie with one of those stupid, rubber party masks pulled over his head. But a two-meter gobbler did seem more exciting.

"Look!" yelled Joe. "The Spirit of Thanksgiving back there will push this hunk o' junk all the way down to Mexico City if he has to. You've got about five seconds before it opens up this wagon like a jumbo sized can o' spaghetti. So, get your fat ass behind that wheel, boy, and scram ... *NOW!*" Joe wasn't messing around.

When impact seemed imminent, Joe stepped back as the bad-boy driver somehow managed to jerk his vehicle forward, before revving its guts out and hurtling off at breakneck speed towards the road. Suddenly a loud flinching bang erupted as the fat man took a pot-shot through his SUV's window, zipping low over the top of Joe's head.

Joe made a downward swipe with the spanner as a gesture of a job well done. Vince wandered across towards him, casually resting his faux secret weapon on his shoulder. It was one of those flexible exercise bars without the black plastic hand grips.

"Did you see that guy?" asked Joe all pumped, "What a disgusting pile of crap. Man, he stank. I doubt if that bastard's taken a shower in months."

Joe lifted his hand to his nose. "*Phew-eee*, frick'n reeks! Bourbon and sweat. I need to go wash up. Good job boys, Vince, you did well. Charlie ... what's with the frick'n turkey head?" Joe shook his head and turned to go to the bathroom. "I'm gettin' too old for this kind o' crap!"

When he returned, I walked across to the driveway and handed him back his hat.

"Did you get a look at that guy? Holy Joseph, he must have weighed four hundred pounds at least, nearly broke my wrist trying to hold up all that blubber. Twenty bucks says we won't see those guys coming back this way again. They'll last two days if they're lucky down south. That was a no-brainer call by young Diego. He's got a knack for picking out the potential troublemakers. He hit the bell when those Feds came in earlier too."

Incident apparently over, Joe picked up and trashed the bourbon bottle, adjusted his hat, and completely changed the subject. "You told me last night that you're from Vegas. So, what the hell are you doing bringing that fancy little Fire Diamond all the way down here to Sonora?"

"I'm supposed to be down in Puerto Cantaura in a couple of days, I—"

"You're not going to that jumpin'-jalopy, low-rider, swap meet thing they put on every year down there, are you?" He interupted urgently.

"Well no, not exactly, I'm—"

"Don't go. *Forget it!* Those hombres down there will whisk that '58 out from under you before your boots touch the sidewalk. Yeah, they'll make you some really good offer to buy it, about a tenth of what it's really worth. But you'll be one lonely little gringo and you'll be in no position to bargain. Trust me, you'll be happy to get out of there with your head still facin' forward. A whole lot of villains flock to that little shindig."

"But I've got somebody I found online who is—"

"Yeah right," he interrupted me again. "*Online!* What the hell is that supposed to mean? Believe me, that little red Fire Diamond will be bouncing up and down like a frick'n jack-in-the-box full of bad boys, while you're still trying to fold your *Let's-Go-Mexico* map back up properly. Not my call Wolfman, but I reckon you'd be a whole lot better off staying right here and digging up your missing V badge. *Truly.*"

The assuredness of his warnings and the chicken shit realization that I really would be out of my depth if a situation like that eventuated, plus the fact I'd been having second thoughts about selling the Fire Diamond now anyway, didn't take much to persuade me. Besides, I really liked this place and the people here a lot and wouldn't mind hanging around for a little while longer. I was keen to know what that MacElroy guy was up too out here in the desert, and what Faye had to do with it too. I pretended to deliberate for about ten seconds but accepted his offer gracefully.

"How long do you think it would take me to dig that badge out? And where would I stay, I can't sleep in my car for too long?"

"We'll work something out," Joe said soberly. "What did you do back in Vegas?"

"I worked at Snake Eyed Jacks."

"No shit. You worked on the strip?" He started revving himself up for one of his big laughs. "What did you do there? Don't tell me you were one of the idiots that pranced around with those stupid hats on. Were ya?" Joe boomed loud with laughter.

Some of the floor staff at Snake Eyed Jacks had to wear fluorescent three-pointed jester hats, with round, shiny bells which they jigged and wiggled around like retards when somebody scored a big paying jackpot. They did look pretty lame, so Joe's ridicule was a fair call, I guess. "No, I worked there as a cleaner. Until I got laid-off."

Joe chuckled on for a few seconds more. "No that's great, we could do with a big-city, mop-jockey around here. A couple of hours work in the morning in exchange for your food and somewhere to stay. Not to mention a signed and certified Alamo digging permit." He squeezed out his last bit of laughter, then went back to being Mr. Sensible. "Let's go back over where we were and find you somewhere to live."

◆

We crossed the boundary path into the little camp site. Along the front, shaded by a random scatter of small Palo Verde trees were three vintage bullet style camper trailers. On the outside, two of them looked unkempt, their aluminum shells now a dull, weathered grey. But the highly polished surface of the third one gleamed brightly in the sunshine.

"That one there is McElroy's, and the shiny one is Faye's. The third one's empty but—" Joe paused mid-sentence, "But you're not important enough around here to take that." He chuckled jokingly, even though it was true.

As we passed behind the trailers, we walked through to what I'd guess was about a six-acre market garden area dotted here and there with little hut-like dwellings, most adorned in a hodgepodge of scrounged up bits and pieces or decorated enthusiastically with brightly colored house paint. There were even more modest lodgings made from old, gutted car bodies. Their only luxury being a simple cooking stove with a chimney sticking up from the now empty engine bays. From what I could see, most of these abodes had little more inside them than a few odds and sods, a mattress and a couple of blankets.

Considering the size of the settlement there seemed to be very few people around. I presumed they were out working on their plots or something, I really didn't know what to make of it.

"What exactly is this place Joe, and who are the folks that are living here?" I thought it an appropriate question considering he'd offered me the chance to move in.

"Vince calls it Beverly Hills. It's kind of like a retirement village, I guess. For all the poor unfortunate bastards that have got absolutely nowhere else to go. There are Mexicans who got shoved off their land and homes by the corporations. Some of our ex-army guys who've been cut adrift or screwed up badly in the wars. You know combat stress cases, nervous wrecks, even a couple of DU victims. Charlie's got that," mentioned Joe, his voice turning momentarily doleful. "Sucked in some of that shit when he was serving in Azmarakstan. Now he's ... We've even got some of the local Indians living down the back by the creek. They pretty much keep to themselves, but hey, it's their frick'n land. I'm the real trespasser."

"How many people live here then?"

"Ooh, thirty, thirty-five I guess ... no more than that. They're mostly self-sufficient. The only thing we get from them is a little bit of excess food stuffs, and some labor or expertise here and there. These dudes have got all kind-o' weird and wonderful skills. Such a frick'n waste of good folk really."

Unexpectedly Joe stopped walking. "What do you think of this then?"

We had arrived at an unoccupied 1970's camper van. Sky-blue and white in color, it had seen better days, but was by no means a rust-ridden wreck. Its shape reminded me of an oversized can o' dog food that had been left out to bloat in the sun. Even so, it sure looked a whole lot more inviting than the stripped out empty car body I'd been expecting. Joe fiddled around with the side door handle which was stuck, but it soon relented and slid back open. "It stinks a bit, but with a bit of a clean out she'll smell as sweet as a daisy in a day or two."

"Yeah, thanks Joe, she's a beauty. Fantastic." (I really meant it too.)

"I've gotta get back," Joe said out of the blue. "There's an amenity block over there, it's pretty basic but no worse than any family camping site back in the states. There's a big communal table just behind those trees, they bring out bread and rice and a couple of large pots of stew, or something tasty every evening around 1800. Everyone there will make you welcome, just dig in, you'll be fine. There're only five simple rules I expect everyone who stays here to abide by, okay?" Joe held up his hand and began ticking off the rules.

"ONE: Just do the chores or job you've agreed to do properly, and don't go skiving off.

TWO: No drunkenness ... well, unless you're back over there with all of us lot. That don't count.

THREE: No guns.

FOUR: You don't mess with anyone else or make too much noise. The biggest hassle we've had in the last three or four years was a half-assed bout of fisticuffs over a frick'n plastic bucket, so it's pretty cool; and

FIVE: No taking a dump or a leak anywhere except for where you're supposed to.

Apart from that, you can do pretty much what you like. I'll see you back over the shop at 0.700 to give you your cleaning stuff. And if you're lucky a shiny new mattock and spade. Come back over whenever you like and get your stuff. I'd rather you didn't bring the Fire Diamond here though. It's better to leave it where it is for the moment. Okay Wolf, I'm gone, check you later."

With that he turned and jogged briskly back over towards the building, his hat sitting tall on his head.

Climbing tentatively into the camper's interior I plonked myself down on the outstretched single bed. An aromatic cloud of dusty mildew wafted straight up into my nose, but considering the circumstances, it really wasn't all that bad.

Most of the little curtains were still there, although the wire runners had become unhooked and were hanging limp towards the floor. Down the back end beyond the sliding door was a skewed arrangement of wooden cupboards complete with a long dead, unopenable mini-bar fridge covered in those itsy-bitsy stickers that kids love to plaster over everything. The front seat section looked fine. A little dusty maybe, but nothing that a bit of elbow grease couldn't fix.

The promised evening meal came right at six sharp at one of the communal dining tables. I was served up a spicy bean soup and some bread by a couple of women who greeted me joyfully in Spanish. Nobody else paid me any undue attention and seemed to accept me as just a new face in their midst. I liked that a lot.

For the meantime anyway, this was it. I was home.

9

Dig!

I woke up early. Not out of any enthusiasm to go and get stuck into my unspecified chores, but on account of a moth the size of Wyatt Earp's moustache. The damn thing must have snuck in during the wee hours and had been fluttering about and dive bombing me ever since.

I left my boots off this morning and tried on a spanking new pair of those trainer things that I'd found abandoned beside the road in the middle of one those creepy UFO places back in Nevada. I figured their owner must have been abducted by aliens or something and it seemed like a waste to just leave them. Anyway, they fitted perfectly and seemed a far more sensible type of footwear to clean toilets in than a pair of Cuban heeled, stitched-leather cowboy boots.

I staggered across to The Alamo at around six-thirty. The strip lights that outlined the building had been left on all night. Their sharp white points looked pure and pretty against the orange-red glow of the still rising sun.

Walking across where the car bodies were buried, I realized the magnitude of the task I was in for. I hadn't so much as kicked a stone over yet and was already dreading the prospect of having to dig a hole the size of an Olympic swimming pool. Even then, there was no guarantee that I'd even find the frick'n Fire Diamond. Deep down I knew I wasn't up to it, but what the hell else was I gonna do?

About halfway over to the building I could see Joe sitting out the front on his couch reading and drinking a cup of coffee. We weren't the only ones up early either. I noticed someone walking almost parallel with me at some distance over to my right. It was Faye. She was wearing white track-pants and a tank top. Curiously, she was carrying a long wooden stick. I only saw her for a moment before she disappeared behind the car bodies at the rear of the building. I ambled up towards Joe who looked up from his book and gave me a good morning nod.

"That's what I like to see, keen and punctual," he smirked and offered me some coffee.

"No thanks, better get stuck into it."

"Nice pair o' shoes there, dude," he laughed sarcastically.

We wandered across to the diner, Joe pointing out what he wanted me to do as we went.

"Sweep and mop inside the dining room, give the chairs a quick wipe-down and do a bit of a tidy-up around this side of the service area." When we walked around to the public bathroom that I'd used yesterday, he unlocked it and gave me the key which was attached to a six-inch, flat metal rocket ship, a miniature version of the one on the sign out front.

"Just hang it up on the hook next to the cash register when you've finished. I know it's a hassle keeping tabs on it, but it sorta keeps us up to speed with who the hell is in here during the day. I won't go into the gruesome details, but the general public are absolute pigs… not all of 'em, but most of 'em!"

"Tell me about it, I worked down on the strip. Nothing I haven't seen before."

Joe unlocked another door with a key hidden out of sight on top of the light fitting.

"Here's the storeroom, got all of the latest hi-tech equipment in here for you Wolf." He chuckled and moved back out of the way. I flicked on the light. It was pretty much the same old stuff that I used back in Vegas, paper towels, half-empty bottles of chemicals, a broom and a crap looking mop and bucket.

"You'll only have to clean the motel rooms in the morning after someone leaves. We don't get folks staying here very often, but the rooms gotta be ready and clean just in case. Don't go near Charlie's room and if Vince tries to con you into doing his little pig-sty, tell him to naff off, lazy little so and so. I dunno, just do whatever you think needs doing. Mrs. Eduardo does the kitchen and the dining room tables herself. Oh! and take out the garbage on Thursdays." I think he was just being flippant.

"Hey, I saw Faye back there earlier, looking all sporty and carrying a long piece of stick."

"Yeah, she practices her martial arts most mornings," explained Joe soberly. "She trains with a bo staff. She's really getting good at it too, considering she's only been doing it for about six months."

"Who's she practicing with?"

"Sacramento from over at the little Indian settlement. He's a frick'n master at it, he's kind o' like Faye's sensei. He's a really funny guy, you'll have to meet him. I think he's the acting chief amongst his lot too."

"How come a Mexican Indian's a master of oriental martial arts, that's pretty weird isn't it?"

"I can answer that one, I asked him that exact same question a couple of years ago myself. I'm not sure which tribe he belongs to. Sometimes he says he's Yaqui, sometimes he says he's Mayo, or then he'll tell you he belongs to the Opata people. A few months back he told me straight-faced that he was *Onondaga* and those folks come from some-where up around the St Lawrence River, so I don't know. Anyway, he told me that at some time back in history his ancestors were supposedly visited by sea fairing Chinese who'd sailed across the Pacific to North America. Apparently some of the crew stayed behind, maybe they were shipwrecked or something, I forget. Sacramento said that they've passed down the story, Chinese genes, and the practice of using the martial arts bo staff ever since. Never know what to believe with that guy. C'mon, let's go up on the roof and check 'em out. We can see them practicing from up there."

I was puffing already as I scrambled up the concrete ramp a few paces behind Joe. He was twice my age and I was only half as fit.

"Jesus wept boy, you'll have to get yourself in some kind o' shape if you're gonna put in some hours with a shovel." He laughed again and pointed out back beyond the yard towards Faye and Sacramento. Although they weren't all that close, you could see them training to-gether quite clearly. The swoosh and clack of their bo staffs was distinct in the cool morning stillness.

I knew jack about martial arts, but I could tell by watching them that they were good, *really* good. Definitely not a couple of amateurish hacks. Even from this distance it was like watching one of those late-night kung fu movies but without the stupid sound effects and annoying sub-titles.

The more you watched, the more they seemed to morph into some kind of dualistic movement. Sacramento's skin was dark, and his black hair was pulled back into a ponytail like his opponent. His clothes were entirely black, in contrast to Faye who was pale and fair and dressed for the most part in white. It really did add something to their mystique and performance. We both stood there mesmerized. They were ... what's that old cliché? Poetry in motion.

"I took her on a couple o' times with my old army pugil stick," said Joe grinning. I looked at him blankly, I had no idea what he was talking about.

"You know, those things that look like giant cotton buds or a canoe paddle with a bag on each end. You always see grunts belting the crap out of each other in the boot camp films. Anyway, I couldn't get any-where near her. Never connected even once. She totally ran rings around me, and I could tell she was holding back too, taking pity on old gramps. When I asked her about it later, she said she didn't think we were fairly matched. Weapon wise that is. I was the platoon champ back in the day!" Joe shook his head and chuckled wryly to himself as he reminisced. "You won't hear Vince paying out or giving her any crap about doing this stuff. He knows too well she'd beat the livin' daylights out of him in three seconds flat."

Then, unexpectedly, Faye and Sacramento both stopped their dueling, faced each other some twenty feet apart and briskly bowed to one another. After a pause, they laid down their bo staffs, each picking up a different type of weapon and faced each other once again.

"Ah, they're using the naginatas. Now you'll really see something special."

"What's that?" I asked in ignorance.

"The naginata is a Japanese weapon. It's kind o' similar to the bo staff but completely different. Graceful, lots of sweeping movements. See the metal blade on the end, it's real and razor sharp. Most people practice using the wood or bamboo versions, but not these two, *they're frick'n crazy!*"

I was about to ask Joe more about the naginatas, but he seemed to read my thoughts.

"It was used to fight against mounted samurai in feudal Japan and is extremely lethal at close quarters, more than a match against a swords-man and popular with women fighters too apparently. Faye knows a lot of the history behind it. Sacramento admits himself he's a relative novice at using it. They reckon they're at about the same skill level, still just working it out together."

"What are they doing now then?"

"They're going through *Shikake-Oji*, a series of practice movements used to teach the basic techniques of the weapon. Lots of parries and stuff like that. There's a heck of a lot of discipline and etiquette involved in it too. All beyond my levels of attention I'm afraid."

We stood and watched them for a little while longer, but time was getting on, both of us had more mundane chores to attend to. I glanced over at the Fire Diamond, which was still where I'd parked it, although it's desert-dust coating had been trampled over even more with little paw prints by Gutteka and Jenteka.

As we turned away to leave, something dropped down from the sky directly above Faye and Sacramento. Due to its tremendous speed it appeared like a small, elongated teardrop, but it was obviously a wild bird of prey. From a distance Joe wasn't sure, but said it was either a hawk or a falcon. As it got closer it appeared to be aiming itself towards Faye, who was oblivious to its presence. Only a few feet above her, it suddenly pulled up gracefully from the dive, rolled elegantly into a sequence of spirals and then with a reverse, banking flip out, shot off like a bolt to the south.

Joe shook his head, bemused. "Come on Wolfman, show's over, let's get down and do some work. She's something else that kid, ain't she ... she's *really* something else."

◆

I'd made a concerted effort to look enthusiastic on my first day and finished my chores around noon. While I'd been cleaning the dining room, I met Mrs. Eduardo who was in the kitchen getting the breakfast menu ready. She was nice, even gave me a sly mug of coffee. "On the house for you Señor Lobo. *But don't tell Señor Joe.*"

When he came by, Joe seemed impressed. Reckoned he hadn't seen such a thorough job done for ages. With that endorsement he handed me a plate full of leftover mutton and a fresh bolillo roll. "You've earned your keep, now you can eat." He didn't actually say that, but that was the expression I read on his face. The food was appreciated, but I knew I couldn't forestall the inevitable. It was now time to dig.

◆

Standing there with a mattock and shovel I scanned the vast open area in front of me. Did I need a plan of action, or do I simply start digging and go hell for leather until I find something? Either way, it was going to be like looking for a needle in a haystack.

Thunk. Thunk. Thunk. Thunk. I'd swung the mattock four times now and was fed up already. What had I signed myself up for? I looked at the pathetic little pit I'd made so far and calculated it would take me about three hundred years to dig this lot up. More or less.

"Okay," I mumbled to myself as I stared at my Herculean task. "I'll mark out a grid with small holes and trenches. But I can't go too hard on the first day or my whole body will ache like buggery tomorrow. No, I think it's the day after when it goes all stiff. Everyone will come around and laugh at the imbecile lying incapacitated in the camper. Joe, Charlie, all the folks from Beverly Hills, oh god Vince! FAYE, she'll really think I'm pathetic... but I am."

I was really starting to panic. In spite of my catastrophizing heading right off the Richter scale, I did manage to work on for an hour, but my dig looked an absolute mess. Joe wandered over towards the end of my stint to see how I was going. He didn't say a word, just glanced between me and the ground a couple of times, shook his head poignantly and walked away in disgust. I felt like an absolute fool.

During day two, body-mind and spade came together, and I'd carved out a channel the length of three or four bathtubs. Nothing to start pulling crowds in, but at least I was making some headway. Seriously how hard can it be for a vertical standing male in his mid-thirties to dig a frick'n hole? By the end of day three I ached all over, my badly blistered hands had morphed into unfeeling lumps of flesh barely held together by a filthy, half sticking trail of plasters. Maybe that's an exaggeration but they were now getting pretty, bloody sore.

I hadn't seen much of Joe or the boys in the past three days, except when I'd been over doing my chores. Bird had returned to the Escotos, but said he'd be back before I'd even miss him. The only times I'd said a quick "Hi" to Faye was when she'd pass by with MacElroy doing whatever it was they were doing. With every turn of the shovel over the past few days, my mind jumped obsessively between the same three anomalies. Faye, Chupacabras and those damn walking skeletons. Strangely the long-buried V badge got barely any thought at all.

On the fourth day of digging I was starting to get jack of all this as I still hadn't found one solitary slither of metal, let alone a Fire Diamond. Feeling dejected I slumped down and rested my back against the side of my slowly expanding pit and chugged down some well needed water. The hole wasn't all that deep, but with my ass on the floor there was no way that anyone could see me. I could feel an end to this bullshit coming on soon. Yep, I'd had a gutful.

Plop!... plop!

Two little stones dropped one after the other onto my head. I looked up and once again saw the upside-down face of Faye peering down at me. Although this time her hair was not trailing freely on early morning sunbeams but was trundled up beneath a narrow-brimmed sombrero that billowed underneath with a bunched-up veil of mosquito netting. It was a practical piece of kit for someone of her complexion to wear out here in this desert, but as a fashion statement, most definitely not.

"Hello Fenrir," she laughed mischievously. "*It's me*, Faye."

Then another head popped over the edge to have a look at me sitting there. It was the impish smiling face of a young Indian girl of about eighteen who I'd seen Faye talking with earlier. Although, unlike her companion, protectively hidden behind the low-tech enviro-suit, she stood dressed in her normal everyday clothes, her long dark hair hung freely past her shoulders, down towards the gringo in the hole.

"Fenrir, this is my friend Oppuam, she lives here in the village."

The girl smiled her face into a ball of cheeriness and nodded briskly in recognition.

"We've been busy out there in the desert," explained Faye, "collecting a whole load of seeds and samples from the local vegetation. Oppuam found some medicinal power plants too. But phew! it's just so hot." Faye continued to gaze down at me somewhat perplexed.

"So, what exactly are you digging for Wolf?" She knew very well, but I answered anyway.

"I'm digging for my Fire Diamond badge that goes on the front of my car."

"Your Fire Diamond badge?"

"Yes."

"Why did you bury it there?" she grinned. "Are you just an old dog who likes to bury his bone?"

That was the best double entendre I could ever have dreamt of. The perfect retort came in a flash, and for one single moment I so, so wished I were Vince. But I just couldn't say it. Besides, it wouldn't have been very nice. She gave me a quizzical look that confirmed she hadn't the slightest notion of what she had said.

"No," I said, shifting gear. "I'm definitely not a dog! The badge is the same type that was on the front of the Fire Diamond, it got ripped off by the skeletons back at Birdtown."

"What does it look like Fenrir, I don't know that much about American cars, except that I really, really like them?"

I couldn't figure out if she was genuinely interested or reeling me in for some little joke she was concocting.

"It's the shape of a capital letter V, set between two outstretched wings."

"V?"

"Yes, V." I held up two fingers.

"Like V for Valkyrja?"

I didn't know what that was, but said yes anyway. "Yep, that's the one."

"Oh well, good luck Fenrir, happy hole digging. Woof, woof."

With that both of their heads pulled back from the edge and they disappeared into the glare of the afternoon sunshine.

As I took the last swig from my now empty water bottle, a curious sound caught my attention. It wasn't loud or disturbing, quite the opposite. A little rhythmic squeaking noise was building, and it sounded like it was only a yard or so to my left.

Hauling myself up for a look I was surprised to see Gutteka and Jenteka tethered lightly side-by-side, stoically pulling a small child's play wagon behind them. The sound I could hear came from one of the little metal wheels that squeaked distinctly every time it made a new rotation.

Gutteka was closest to me looking steely but determined with his lot, whereas Jenteka, who from my limited knowledge of cat expressions, seemed the happier of the two and had a playful skip to her stride. Piled high on the little shallow wagon were a heap of grasses and bits of vegetation that Faye and her helper Oppuam must have collected out in the chaparral. I wanted to laugh, but thought better of it, I didn't want to get on the wrong side of these two felines unnecessarily. Especially that Gutteka. I valued the duco on the Fire Diamond too much.

My thoughts went back to the room at The Pepper Coyote and that sun-faded picture hanging on the wall. I just knew deep down there was something more than sheer coincidence going on here.

10

Ground Swell

With literally my first shovel strike of the day I hit metal. But before I got the chance to see what it was, all hell broke loose.

The ground began pitching and rolling like the world's most terrifying carnival ride. I could see the earth splitting open, closing back up, then tearing itself apart again like a cake in the hands of a four-year-old sugar-junkie. For an eternity there seemed no up or down, no left or right, just the feeling of being trapped and hurtled around inside a humongous cocktail shaker. Not that I had any previous reference, but this quake felt like a 9.9. Nothing could be worse than this. Luckily, I'd lobbed myself out of the hole the second it started. Never moved that fast in my life, a primal instinct of self-preservation I suppose.

Foolishly, I tried to stand upright. It was impossible. My legs just buckled, and I dropped back down to the deck. The alarm bell over at The Alamo was ringing itself hoarse. It wasn't the same clanging sound for a code yellow, but not thinking rationally I presumed it was ringing for the imminent end of the world.

Finally, it all stopped. I found myself flat on my back, lying close to the trailers where Faye and MacElroy lived. *Holy mackerel!* the earthquake had pushed me fifty yards south. I staggered back onto my feet and tried to take stock of who or what was still there. Everything had turned dark and angry as plumes of churning sulfur billowed ominously from a long, jagged chasm that had opened up across the ground not ten feet away. Obscured by all of the muck and smoke in the air I couldn't see The Alamo at all, but I knew where it was thanks to that infernal alarm bell.

Having been rolled and pummeled along such a distance, I was surprised to find that my shovel had made the trip along with me. As for my hat and the mattock, I figured they'd probably succumbed to the bowels of the bottomless pit.

Picking up the shovel I turned and walked across to Faye's trailer to see if she'd been inside. "Faye. Are you in there, are you alright?" There was no answer. It was then that someone crawled out on their hands and knees from behind the tow-hitch. It was Oppuam.

"Hello Señor Wolf," she said politely, with her spring-loaded smiley face, although understandably in the present circumstances, a smidgen less enthusiastic than it might have been. "I am so happy to see you, I was so—"

Her pleasant expression turned to absolute horror as she pointed and screamed loudly "Look out, señor. *RUN!*"

Turning quickly, I was knocked flat on my back. Luckily, I had fallen, holding the shovel handle across my chest, it was all that stood between me and the face of some vile, demonic creature that now thrashed about in a manic rage up on top of me.

It was horrific, with beady-red eyes and a gnash of razor-sharp teeth that snapped frenziedly with the sole intention of ripping the face from my skull. Aided by a rush of freaked-out adrenaline I managed to somehow push upwards on the handle and force the disgusting thing off me. Next thing I know I'm standing back on my feet, I really don't know how I did it, caving the bastards head in with a downward blow from my shovel. It was only then that I saw the endless swarm of its buddies charging straight in towards me. Clueless to what I was doing fightin' wise, I just swung away for dear life and was surprised at how much contact I was actually making. No-way-Jose were any of these shitheads gonna take a chunk out of me with their choppers. I took a full roundhouse swing at one and lobbed its head off with the edge of the shovel and it shot off into the sky with a stupid expression on its face. The gunk spurting out of these creatures was a black kind of goo that looked like discarded engine oil.

For one fleeting moment I felt like Achilles, or some axe-wielding dwarf lord. Even so I was completely knackered and figured I had about ten seconds max before they overran me and slashed me to pieces.

It was then I heard the door of the trailer swing open and slam hard against the metal exterior. Looking back for an instant I saw Faye leap out through the open door and begin to carve a path with her bo staff through the onrushing creatures. Within seconds she was right there beside me wearing nothing more than an oversized t-shirt that hung like a flimsy mini dress. Her face and hair were streaked with blood which poured from a wound along her hair line and she was clearly limping, but right at this moment, she seemed nothing less than a heaven-sent angel of salvation.

Amidst all the fray I saw Gutteka and Jenteka launch themselves past me like two guided missiles. Whether I was tripping out on the acrid sulfur fumes or OD'ing on adrenaline, I wasn't sure. But with every leap forward the two little cats seemed to somehow double in size and after four or five strides had grown impossibly into a pair of fully-grown mountain lions. Each took a flank and threw themselves mercilessly at the oncoming creatures.

Faye stood her ground and fought hard in the center. Anything coming within an eight-foot radius of her was smashed hard or dispatched into the shredding talons of Gutteka and Jenteka. Rejuvenated by their presence, I stood beside Faye and hacked away at the still charging creatures, trying clumsily to keep clear of her bo staff's striking circle, which, although accounting for far more heads than my efforts, lacked that killer punch we needed to really help turn the tide. I could hear Faye's voice straining with exhaustion, there were just too many of them and I got the feeling things were starting to slip.

Suddenly from right out of nowhere this whoopin' ball of steel-edged humanity spins theatrically to the ground right beside us. *"How!* The redskins are here!" He winked in cheesy self-parody as he side-passed one of the two naginatas he was carrying to Faye. It was Sacramento.

Up until now Faye's stance had been stoic, although not all that deadly. But as soon as the two naginatas cut loose the scene changed to absolute bedlam. With no idea what was hitting them, the creatures were getting sliced up like spuds on a chopping board. There were heads and arms and chunks of flesh flying all over the place. More than once I felt an arcing spray of their oozy-black blood, and it stung like crazy. With the naginatas being so effective the attack soon petered out. Most of the horde retreated back into the dirt clouds, but some surged on relentlessly towards the camp site.

When it finally seemed safe, Faye dropped to the ground. She was a total mess, covered in her own blood as well as the oozie-black slime of the creatures.

Whether I'd imagined it or not, Gutteka and Jenteka had shrunk back to their normal size, although still highly agitated they continued to pace to and fro beside their mistress like a protective shield. From head to tail they were both drenched in the putrid black blood, which wisely neither had attempted to lick off.

Sacramento squatted down beside Faye to make sure she was okay, then took his leave and headed back at speed in pursuit of the still advancing attackers.

Oppuam appeared with a small bowl of water and squatted down beside Faye and began bathing the bleeding wound on her bedraggled friend's forehead. I just lay there on my back heaving with exhaustion, relieved this whole bizarre event was over. I looked around at the carnage of twitching body parts. A gruesome dismembered head lunged itself vengefully towards me like a demented Chuckie, still sparking on its last volts of spasmodic energy. With a well-aimed kick from my ooze-splattered trainer, I swiftly booted it all the way back to oblivion. "Eat polyurethane you bastard!"

Oppuam was still fussing over Faye who seemed a little delirious and wasn't really cooperating. I could hear her sort of sobbing and mumbling under her breath. Something like "I didn't want to kill them; I didn't want to kill them." But it wasn't all that clear.

Once the battle had ended, the reinforcements arrived. From out of the muck clouds came Vince on a low-rider motorcycle followed right behind by Joe and Charlie in the pickup.

Standing high on the foot pegs Vince rode nonchalantly through the mangle of body parts, over towards Faye and Oppuam. Wearing no more than a pair of multi-buckled motorcycle boots, a WW2 steel helmet, and a pair of nylon track shorts he balanced precariously for as long as he could right beside them. Either trying to show off his not so incredible motorcycle skills or more likely to make sure they both got an eye-full of his Kalvin-clad package that peeked out disturbingly through one of the wide-splaying leg-holes.

The pickup was right behind. Charlie was at the wheel while Joe, sporting the obligatory ten-gallon hat, stood leaning from his open door with a 12-gauge.

"Wow, looks like you folks copped a hammerin'." He jumped down from the vehicle and walked the few steps to where Faye was getting field-aid from Oppuam.

Gutteka and Jenteka let him come close to her side, but their low, uneasy growls made Joe aware of their vigilance.

"You okay darlin'? You sure look messed up," said Joe showing genuine concern. "What the hell just happened here? Did you fight off all these things on your own?"

"No, without Wolf and Sacramento's help I would have been totally overrun. I could never have kept on going."

Wow. I knew she was being generous, saying what she did, but I felt about twenty feet tall. Joe looked at me for a moment, but immediately turned his attention back over to Faye.

"Well you hold on there, sweetheart. We've gotta go check out the rest of the place and see what the hell's happening. You're in good hands with Wolf and Oppuam. We'll be right back ASAP, okay?"

With that he stood up and loped back towards the open door of the pickup. Right then, that infernal bell at The Alamo stopped ringing. It was amazing how quiet everything suddenly seemed.

"Thank God for that!" exclaimed Joe in his usual manner.

Vince seeing a good opportunity to score points with Faye, dismounted theatrically from his motorcycle and squatted down beside her, parroting his old man's good nature.

"Hey Pocahontas, what are you doin' this far off the reservation anyway?"

As one, the two girls looked at Vince in dismay. You could read him like a book. It was obvious he wanted Oppuam gone so he could try and hit on Faye by himself.

"Señor Vince, I am certain your remarks will not ingratiate yourself with Señorita Faye. As for myself, I am somewhat saddened at your complete lack of manners and respect. Your disparaging attempt to somehow belittle me by associating my name with probably the only Native American woman that you have ever heard of is truly abhorrent. No, Pocahontas for your information, was Matoaka, the daughter of Wahunsenacawh, the chief of a native Virginian tribe. She married an English settler named John Rolfe, which for most non-indigenous people became her enduring claim to notoriety. My name is Oppuam, which in the language of my people, the Yaqui, means tears. Tears I shed for you Señor Vince, and others like you, who just love to revel in their own self-ignorance."

Vince stood there dumbfounded. He thought he'd counter her by pulling a stupid face and wagging his hands in front of himself like a dog. That only made things worse. Oppuam was about to let rip with another serve, when the blast from a gun rang out in the distance.

"*Oh god!*" yelled Joe as the pickup passed alongside us. Then there was another shot, then another, followed soon after by three more. "I reckon I know what that is. Sounds like Oochie's got himself a handgun."

"Who's Oochie?" I said curious.

"Oochie-Cuchi. Old man Crawford, he's our resident Vietnam War tunnel-rat. We'd better go find him quick, he's a real frick'n worry when he's packin'."

A distant, blood curdling scream shrieked out from somewhere down the road to the south. Faye launched herself onto her feet.

"Give me the bike Vince!" Vince just stood gawking at her. "I need the motorcycle NOW!"

Faye picked up the naginata and leapt onto the still running bike.

"Do you think you can ride it?" His words fell flat as Faye tore off in a cloud of exhaust fumes and dirt.

"Get in you two," ordered Joe. "We'd better get after her."

Kaboom! Kaboom! Kaboom! I guess Oochie-Cuchi must have reloaded.

As Charlie hurtled off like a madman, Vince and I stood up in the truck bed, holding on to the roof of the cab. "Where'd you get that bike Vince?" I yelled loudly. "I've never seen you ride it before."

"Some old codger swapped it yesterday for sixty bucks worth of gas."

"*Sixty bucks!* must be a real piece-o'-shit."

"No way Wolfman, it's a—"

A massive lump of rubble kicked up our vehicle and slammed it back hard to the ground. Vince's helmet spun around on his head and then dropped to our feet with a thud. Despite the unexpected slam-dunk I continued my questioning.

"What kind o' bike is it?"

"A good old American softail. It's a bit of a rust bucket, granted, but it moves man, it moooves!" Vince changed the subject. "What the hell was Pocahontas crackin' a fat about? All the big words and the frick'n history lesson."

"Ah Vince, you're a classic, you learned nothing at all back there, did you?" I said somewhat judgmentally. He looked at me completely bewildered.

Sucking up the softail's exhaust, we pulled back onto the road some hundred yards behind Faye. "She sure can handle that bike, huh?" I said excitedly.

"Yeah, she's okay … for a chick."

"Jesus Vince, she's bloodied and wounded from the quake, just fought a massive battle with the horde from hell and she's wearing nothing more than a T-shirt!" He said nothing, but stooped to pick up his helmet, which he plonked back on top of his head.

As we rounded the next bend a horrific scene played out on the road up ahead. A small minibus had been flipped onto its roof in the earth-quake. Lying helpless like an upturned turtle, the bus was completely encircled by a surging mass of the same chupacabra things that had attacked us up at the trailers. It looked so unreal, like a scene from a video game.

Launching herself straight towards them, Faye dropped the motor-cycle in a scything curve that sent dozens of the creatures flying.

"Ah for fuck's sake!" screamed Vince in my ear. "The bitch just totaled my ride."

Now on her feet Faye unleashed the naginata like an unstoppable force of destruction. I looked on in awe from behind the cab's roof, mesmerized at the unbelievable speed she could wield it. In relatively no time at all Faye had cut down most of the immediate horde. She then let loose on the rest that were swarming towards her from around the far side of the bus. None got anywhere near her.

"Holy Saint frick'n Wolfgang!" yelled Joe as we pulled up behind the still squirming carcasses. "There must be a hundred of the ugly mothers and she's taken out every last one of 'em!"

Drenched in the filthy black slime, Faye had put aside the naginata and began pushing desperately at one of the mini-bus windows. "Come and help me, *quickly!* there are people still trapped inside here."

As we pulled the dead creatures away from the van, we discovered what was surely the source of the god-awful scream we'd heard before over at Faye's trailer. It was the body of a man, or what was left of one. He'd been dragged out through a smashed side window and torn up alive right there on the ground. As Charlie and I tried to move him, his intestines slipped sideways out onto the roadway. I almost puked, but it didn't seem to faze Joe or Charlie at all. Vince had selfishly run straight over to his precious bloody motorbike, which had skidded off away to the farthest side of the road. Joe was over at the van helping Faye. Through the blood smeared windows, they figured there were three more people inside, all hanging upside down in their safety belts, amidst a jumble of unsecured baggage.

Unexpectedly Joe came lurching back towards us, half supporting Faye with his arm.

"I've gotta get her back. The poor kid just passed out from exhaustion."

Joe reverted back into his military mode. "Vince, bring that bike over here *NOW!* I'm taking her to the Indian camp right away. You two get the survivors and their stuff out from the bus and move them across to the empty motel rooms. Cover up what's left of this poor bastard, and weigh it all down with rocks so it's coyote proof, okay? When I get Faye looked after I'll go and see how many 'Viet Cong' old Oochie's been blasting away at. God help us. I'll see you all back at The Alamo ASAP. Capiche? And don't forget to bring her naginata back either."

Charlie helped Faye onto the bike behind Joe and he roared off as soon as she clasped her ooze-blackened arms tight around him.

11

Mad Hatter's Council

I never did see Joe, back at The Alamo. I got a message from him via one of the little campsite kids that he'd called a meeting for 0.800 tomorrow morning, and I had to be there. But for the moment all I wanted to do was scrub this stinging black ooze off me so I could crash. Apart from my meagre belongings having been hurled all over the place, the camper was still in one piece and AOK for sleeping.

◆

I was in that lucid state where you're not quite sure if you're still asleep dreaming or really half-awake and aware of a constant *thump! thump! thump! thump! thump!* I lay there hypnotized by the beat and trying to figure out where it was coming from. Convinced it was almost outside I summoned up the strength to take a look out of the window at who the hell was banging away on a drum in the middle of the night.

Through the glass I could see a ribbon of flame torches that wound right along the edge of the earthquake crack down towards The Alamo. I couldn't make out any details in the dark, but the drumming was coming from somewhere amongst it.

Checking my watch, I saw it was just after five in the morning. Like a spoon to a magnet my bed drew me back. Resisting the urge, I threw my legs to the floor and got myself suited and booted. Cowboy booted. The sporty-dude trainers were now a thing of the past.

Outside, the air stank strongly of sulfur. *Thump! thump! thump!* I walked over to where the closest of the folks in the chanting torch-line were standing. I recognized some of them from over in the campsite.

"Hey, what's up, what's happening?" I asked smilingly at my immediate Beverly Hills buddy. He looked at me sternly and kept on incanting something under his breath, all the while precariously holding a two-foot high statuette of the Virgin Mary above his head. A little further along was an equally high-held assemblage of Señora de las Sombras figurines, with their bejeweled eyes glowing red and gold and green as they danced erratically amongst the torch lights. Making my way behind the line I reached the noise culprits, a small group of Indians banging away like mad on some drums. They paid me no attention, but as I watched them for a moment I realized that distracted in the dark by all of the flames and religious deities I hadn't noticed that down amongst the shadows at ground level there was a systematic operation underway to roll all the dead creature's bodies over the edge, back down to wherever they'd come from.

It was then that I saw Sacramento, completely absorbed in moving the carcasses up towards the abyss. He couldn't hear me over all the infernal drumming, so I waved both my arms to get his attention.

"Well hello there Mr. Wolf. It's nice of you to come along and help clean up some of your handiwork." He just laughed at his own joke, smiled high-spiritedly, and returned to what he was doing.

I asked if we could keep one at least, as Faye and Dr. MacElroy would need it for whatever it was they were doing. Sacramento looked kind of puzzled but gestured to me with his finger to come a few yards back to the rear.

"How about this one? He's a beauty, fry him up with some tabasco sauce, serve him up with some fresh guacamole and corn chips, *delicious*."

He went all wide-eyed and manic looking, licking his lips exaggeratedly, but he couldn't contain himself and soon burst out laughing.

"Be my guest. You can take this guy if you're really *that* hungry. But make it quick," he said all very seriously, "before someone else gets the same idea and beats you to it!" Once again he sniggered out loud and carried back on with his business.

I really didn't want to touch it with my bare hands, so I picked up a scrap of paper and used it to grip around the end of its tail. Unnoticed by the funeral crowd, I slipped away quietly dragging the dead weight of the wretched thing along behind me. I headed towards The Alamo, a little early for Joe's meeting perhaps, but at least I'd have something interesting when it came to show-and-tell.

The rows of electric lights that marked out the building were all out due to the quake, but I had a pretty good idea of the direction I was heading. A black silhouette against an even blacker background loomed up right in front of me, by the ubiquitous cowboy hat perched on its head, I guessed rightly that it was Joe.

"What's all that noise, who's banging those drums? Don't they know it's the middle of the night?" More startling than his unexpected appearance, was the fact that his gruff question had lacked the usual barrage of expletives.

"Jesus Christ can't a man get any sleep around here, I thought I'd let it go for a while but whoever these jokers are, they just don't know when to give it a rest!" He stood there in his ten-gallon hat, a dressing gown, and a pair of comfortable loafers. "And what's with—"

I cut him off mid-sentence. "It's the Mexicans and the Indians from the campsite, they're burying the Chupacabras. They're pushing them all back down the crack."

"*What?* They never said anything about this. MacElroy was expecting a whole pile of the bastards, he—"

I cut him off again and waggled the end of the creature's tail.

"It's alright, I've got one. Sacramento let me have it for my lunch."

Joe leaned forward and had a look at what I'd been dragging along behind me.

"Good man Wolf, this one looks pretty much intact. *And it's got a frick'n head!* We've never had one that's still attached. Eugene and Faye—" He stopped dead mid-sentence.

"It's okay Joe. I've figured out what's been going on. Faye and Eugene are making souvenir saddles for the tourist trade, right?"

"Yeah right, smart ass," he snorted defiantly. "Let's go back and get some coffee, it's freezin' out here."

We had a bit of a confab on the way and it seemed that apart from minor cuts and bruises just about everyone down at The Alamo was okay. Faye had been well looked after by Oppuam and the Indian women and was now safely back home in her trailer sleeping. It seemed she had smashed her head up inside the trailer's small bathroom during the earthquake. MacElroy apparently had been conked unconscious by a swinging cast iron lamp down in The Alamo's basement, hence completely oblivious to the whole frick'n shebang. Structurally, except for the old adobe storage shed which had all but collapsed, The Alamo was remarkably sound. Apparently, nobody down this end of the property had any idea of the Chupacabras at all. It seemed they had only come out of the ground pretty much where we had been attacked.

"You guys did a good job there yesterday Wolf, everyone's been talking about it."

I ignored the praise. I got the feeling that my klutzy participation in yesterday's battle had already been blown way out of proportion. Changing the subject, I enquired as to how the survivors from inside the minivan had fared. I knew already that apart from the poor guy that had been ripped to shreds, regrettably the driver had died from deep lacerations as well. The two women, an elderly Japanese lady and her younger travelling companion were pretty much okay and resting up at the motel. I thought of Bird and hoped he might get back to The Alamo in time to meet them.

As The Alamo loomed into view, I stopped dead and pointed up at the roof in disbelief.

"What?" barked Joe grumpily. "Oh yeah, you can thank Charlie for that."

During all of this upheaval the Fire Diamond had totally slipped my mind, but there, resplendent in a frozen air dive it balanced suspended halfway over the edge of the roof. Bounced about by the earthquake it had been lifted right up and plonked back down onto the low surrounding wall. The front half was hanging precariously out into space.

It had been Charlie who'd saved it from toppling over completely by propping it up makeshift with the extended bucket arm of the tractor.

"She's a bit rickety," said Joe. "But after we've finished this meeting, we'll haul her safely back down on all fours. What are the chances of it ending up there, hey? Charlie reckons it was rockin' and rollin' *right* on the edge. Hope there ain't no more aftershocks."

I acknowledged the deed with enthusiastic gratitude and asked him what we should do with my dead Chupacabra.

"Hmmm, better dump it here in the old drinks fridge, I guess. It'll scare the shit out of anyone diving in for a cola."

◆

Joe left me standing in his office while he went off to get properly dressed. I was really surprised. It wasn't what I'd expected. Not some pokey little backroom with a buckled, plywood desk and a couple of old sagging bookshelves. It was huge.

In the center was a large, wooden table covered with a scattering of unfolded maps and a couple of sheets of transparent film. Over against one of the walls facing outward was Joe's desk. It was ancient, it's time-worn leather top looked like it had been around The Alamo since the cowboy days. On the floor at either side teetered high stacks of books and a whole bunch of papers and files. The place looked more like some kind of scholastic workspace than your humble gas station backroom. Nothing seemed to be out of place, not even slightly askew, as if yesterday's tremor had never even happened.

A dozen chairs had been set out in three vaguely semi-circular rows facing the wooden table, which had been pulled back toward his desk to make space. On a side counter sat a pitcher of water, a portable coffeemaker and a stack of plastic cups. The whole set up convinced me he'd had these meetings before.

The thing that amazed me most about Joe's office, was the collection of pictures that crowded the walls. All types of framed photographs, paintings, and artworks as well as newspaper clippings, parts of old maps, all kinds of stuff that must have taken him years to assemble. I just stood there next to the table trying to take it all in. A ten by eight photo on one of the shelves caught my attention. It was a portrait photograph of a young U.S. soldier wearing a smart, class A uniform complete with a black beret embellished with the insignia patch of his regiment. At first, I thought it was Joe, but the print looked too sharp to be of his vintage, so I presumed it must have been Charlie.

"No, it's not Charlie," said Joe returning from somewhere behind me, like he'd read my mind. "It's Chester, my middle son, he was killed in Afghanistan fighting the Taliban."

"Oh, I'm really sorry Joe. I had no idea you even—" I felt really awkward and couldn't think what to say.

"Yep, killed by 'friendly fire' I was told. I tried for two years to find out more, but they wouldn't tell me anything. 'That information's classified.' Probably just as well, I would have jammed my fist down the bastard's throat and ripped his spine out through his face if I'd gotten hold of who did it." He stared at the photograph of Chester a little longer and then put it carefully back on the shelf. "Yeah … 'friendly fire'."

"This one here is me," he laughed, changing moods unexpectedly. He handed me one of those small standard-sized snaps you can tell were from the seventies by the way the color had been sucked out leaving that weird yellowy-brown glow creeping in from the edges. It was a dog-eared old photo of three young soldiers dressed in scruffy army fatigues posing casually in front of a nondescript background.

"That's me in the middle, handsome young grunt, weren't I?" he sniggered at his own observation. All three of them looked so young and skinny.

"When was this Joe?" I asked, genuinely interested. I could definitely see the likeness once he'd told me, but I don't think I would have recognized him otherwise. Although, apart from a bit more recession around the forehead and temples, he still had exactly the same haircut right now as in the frick'n picture.

"1971. Somewhere around Duc Pho. We were pretty much on the way out of Vietnam by then, but there was still a lot o' shit going down. I was so naive at the start, like a lot of us I went there with the best intentions, but when I got to see it all for myself—" Joe stopped mid-sentence, I could sense the anguish descending upon him.

"Who are the other guys?" I said trying to ease his solemnity.

"The one on the left, the black guy, that's Winston Warner, the nicest guy you'd ever wanna meet. Killed in an NVA ambush on a routine patrol about two weeks after that picture was taken. Poor bastard seriously wouldn't have hurt a fly. The other one, the guy wearing the boonie hat, that's Harry Pickles. He made it home, but the man's lost his mind now. Big time. His sister tracked me down a few years back and asked me if there was anything I could do. She was well into her eighties by then and way too poor to help him."

"What happened?"

"He's living in that hand painted camper van over in the campsite." Joe shrugged his shoulders and made a "What else could I do?" expression.

"His prize possession is one of those fake gold-plated skeet shootin' trophies that he'd picked up somewhere. He'll tell you straight up that it was presented to him by Gerry Ford for his heroic military service back in Nam. Yeah, he's got it sitting up there, wedged pride of place between the dashboard and the windshield, like it's the *Congressional Medal of Honor*. Work that one out. He's harmless enough, funny old guy, but you'd never, ever pick him, he looks about ninety years old now." Joe pulled an exaggerated grin of despair.

"They've finished. *About frick'n time*," barked Joe as the monotonous beat of the drums fell silent.

We both walked outside into the predawn light. The funeral detail had gone, but you could still pick out the tail-enders by their flickering torches. The gritty smoke had almost cleared and for the first time we could see clearly just what had happened.

A giant fissure had opened up and ran south towards the campsite along the line of the creek bed where I'd been digging. It looked like the little cracks you see in dry mud, only a million times bigger. We wandered across eager to get a better look.

"*Holy Smoke!*" exclaimed Joe in astonishment. "I knew it was pretty big, I could see it from the pick-up headin' over to the trailers. *But look how fuckin' wide it is!* And look, it must be a hundred yards long." His excited voice was rapidly heading up through the gears. "Man, that's amazing. Hey look. Look Wolf, over there!"

I didn't know what he was pointing at.

"No, there. Near the lumpy bit. Can you see it?" He was gesturing over to the far side of the crack. "Looks like old Mother Nature's done your digging for ya, you jammy bastard." He laughed so hard I thought he was going to have a seizure. Once I found the spot he was pointing at, I realized what he thought was so funny.

About a foot below ground level was a buried car. It's whole side-length ran parallel with the exposed dirt of the furthest wall of the fissure. But it wasn't the Fire Diamond. The Fire Diamond was pinned upside-down beneath it, the front end sticking out at ninety degrees over the abyss, with its hood hanging open like the tormented mouth of an underpinned wrestler. I saw my predicament immediately. I could hear Joe still laughing as he realized the same.

"You'll need a crash course in abseiling or tightrope walking, boy. Ain't no chance your gonna be able to just reach down and pluck it off like some free danglin' bunch o' bananas!"

He was right, I was hopeless at anything to do with climbing and screwing about with ropes. "*Hmmm*, I'll have to think about that one."

As I turned and headed back toward the building, I could still hear him chuckling as he followed a few steps behind me.

"Go and get yourself a snack or something, I'm gonna take Vince's bike and have a quick scoot around, judging by this, it could be a lot worse than I was expecting. See you back here in about twenty minutes."

◆

Joe came storming back in through the door and caught me by surprise as I was studying more of the pictures hanging around the walls.

"How's it looking?" I asked flatly.

"Not too bad, out here is the worst by a long shot. That whole area's just about useless now. I'll have to fence it off or something. Couldn't even see the frick'n bottom. There's a couple of smaller cracks over on the other side of the road and another one just beyond the Indian's camp, but they're nothing like this one."

"Is there much damage to anything else?"

"No, the rocket sign's listing a bit, but that's nothin'. The old shed out back has half-collapsed, but as far as I can tell, it's just all the crap and rubbish lying around that makes everything look a lot worse than it is. Anyway, I'm sure we'll get a lot more tales of woe when all the bods start rolling up."

Joe changed the subject and asked what I was looking at. "This picture here," I answered, "it's pretty freaky." He chuckled and asked why that one in particular. "Dunno, just creeps me out I guess," I responded.

I don't know anything about art, but it was obviously a reproduction of a painting from olden-days Europe. On the left-hand side, standing in front of some buildings was an important looking church guy, all dressed up in a long flowing robe with one of those tall, pointed hats on his head. On the other side of the picture was a horrible-looking devil-like creature, complete with bat-shaped wings, long-pointed horns, and beady little eyes. It also had two smaller eyes, one in the middle of each butt-cheek, but even stranger than that, it had a red-lipped, wide-gaping mouth for an asshole. It was holding open a giant-sized book showing something to the church dude, who was doing that dib-dob thing with his fingers.

"I mean, what the hell's that all about?" I blurted more forcibly than I'd intended.

"That's *Saint Wolfgang und der Teufel*," explained Joe, seemingly excited that I'd singled out this particular picture. "It was painted by Michael Pacher in Austria sometime in the late fourteen-hundreds."

I now understood the link with the curious name he'd called me that first night I'd arrived at The Alamo with Bird. And then I realized something else. "That ugly bastard looks like those things we got attacked by yesterday."

"You said it yourself Mr. Wolfgang. That handsome critter out there in the ice-box looks more like that thing than any bush-junk Sonoran hybrid."

I scanned around the room again and immediately more of the pictures in his seemingly random collection started to all pair up and make more sense. "What? You're not trying to tell me that thing out there is really from Hell, are you? Come on Joe, that's ridiculous."

"Where is Hell?" he asked me straight-faced.

"Down there, under the ground supposedly," I answered falling right into his little trap.

He shrugged his shoulders. "I ain't sayin' nothin'. You're making all the assumptions, but there sure weren't any frick'n cross-breed coyote-Xolo dogs running around in the woods of Europe in the middle ages."

"So, what's that devil showing the priest guy in the book that's so important?" I asked, sarcastically.

"Dunno, but I reckon I've come up with a pretty good theory."

"Like what?"

"Revelations. Chapter 12, verse 9: *And the great dragon was cast out, that old serpent, called the Devil, and Satan, which deceiveth the whole world: he was cast out into the earth, and his angels were cast out with him.*"

"You're serious aren't ya? I never took you for the religious type, Joe."

"I'm not religious. It's an analogy, an off-target metaphor that's been handed down for millennia. It chronicles something far more ancient and arcane."

"Such as?"

He was just about to explain his theory when there was a sharp, two-taps knock on the door. It opened quickly as someone, without waiting for a reply, let themselves in. It was MacElroy, his head was bandaged up like a hot cross bun, one long strip from ear to ear, another from front to back and a band around the perimeter holding it all together.

"Morning Eugene, how's your head?" Joe asked politely, but not sounding too concerned.

"Ah, I'll live. I copped a bit of a thump down in the basement yesterday," he said embarrassed, knowing we already knew all the details.

"Got a bit of a surprise for you later though, Eugene."

"What's that?"

"Out there in the ice-box, Wolf here's grabbed you a Chupa'. A nice juicy fresh one, although I don't think it's wha—"

"A whole one? Has it got a head?" he interrupted.

"Yep, got a head, guts and tail. It might even have a pair of luscious red lips for an asshole too, but we really didn't bother to look that closely."

"Can I see it?" Eugene was caught off guard by this unexpected revelation as his mind jumped two steps ahead of itself.

"Later Eugene, later," answered Joe, floating both of his hands up and down calmingly, surprised by MacElroy's enthusiasm.

"After the meeting's over, okay? It's not going anywhere. I want you to help me with these maps and charts before they all start turning up."

Poor MacElroy, he looked in vain towards the door like some excited kid who'd been told he's got a new pony out in the barn but had to eat up his greens before he was allowed out to see it. He reluctantly switched his attention back to Joe and whatever he was asking him to do.

While they were doing stuff up on the big table, I kept on looking at Joe's pictures. Another little painting, not much bigger than a bar coaster, looked to be from around the same time as Saint Wolfgang and the bible holding devil. This one was of Adam and Eve, standing beneath the apple tree *In-A-Gadda-Da-Vida*. I thought immediately of the namesake Iron Butterfly album outside in the Fire Diamond's cassette box. But instead of the usual old version of a serpent slowly winding its way down the tree trunk, Eve was talking to a much shorter creature who was female down to the waist but had scaly lizard-like legs and a matching tail that reached down to the ground at the back. I could see a recurring theme developing here.

"So, what's this one about Joe?"

He looked up distracted. *"What?"*

"Sorry. How come there's a half-woman, half-lizard creature instead of a snake?"

"How should I know, but ain't it interesting? Some say it's a depiction of Lilith, the demon of the night. Other scribe-types reckon it has something to do with Genesis 3:14."

"Pretty weird." My artistic assessment was basic at best. There was other stuff too, even more creepy. Bizarre little paintings of devils and demons hard at work torturing the naked flesh of their human captives. Either herding them into pits full of flame or throwing them into the wide-open mouths of monsters. I thought it best not to ask Joe any more questions but keep moving my way around the room in silence.

I'd found another black and white portrait photograph of a navy officer. This one was just a time blemished newspaper cutout in a thin metal frame.

"Who's this?" I barked out unthinking, immediately breaking my resolve to shut up and say nothing. Joe didn't even look up.

"Admiral Richard Evelyn Byrd," he replied emphatically. "Allegedly flew his plane in 1947 over the North Pole and down into the interior of the Earth through the North Polar Opening, where he found a lush, forested land and met the people who lived there, the Arianni. They escorted him to a crystal city where he met their master, who told of an impending dark age that would one day overtake all the surface people."

I was sorry I asked.

"When he got back to the states, less than a month later," Joe continued, "Byrd was summoned to attend a high-level meeting in DC where he was grilled by the brass and the spooks, and ordered to zip it and never mention it again. On behalf of all humanity. Some say it happened down at the South Pole during Operation Highjump, but I don't buy that."

The door opened once more, this time it was Charlie. Fronting up to the table, he unfolded a short, makeshift tripod made out of angle iron. "How's that?" he asked flatly.

"Perfect," responded Joe with only slightly more enthusiasm.

Within seconds the maps and their backing board had been put in place and not long after the other invitees started filing in on their own or in twos. There was a lot of good-natured banter and joking as they sorted themselves out and took seats in readiness for the meeting.

Apart from Joe, Eugene, Charlie, and me, I counted seven others that had arrived in the sudden turn up. I had no idea who was supposed to be there, but neither Vince nor Faye were amongst them.

"Where's Vince?" I asked Joe offhandedly, pretending not to notice Faye's absence.

"I only tell Vince stuff on a need to know basis. He's only interested in things that concern him directly. So—"

I took it that he wouldn't be coming. The others seemed to be a mixed group of folks from over in the camp site. Eduardo and his wife from the kitchen were there. They sat themselves down promptly on the front row of chairs. Sacramento had brought along another member from his tribe, a very serious looking man in his thirties, who, judging by the tense expression on his face, seemed a little anxious about being there. Sacramento introduced him with a straight face as Boof Head, but his real name was Takochai.

Oppuam had slipped in quietly on her own, seating herself on the end of the back row, almost unnoticed. The last ones to come in were an American guy called Wesley, who I'd said hello to a couple of times in passing. He looked kind of shell-shocked or something, as if in a permanent daze. But he hadn't lost it completely, I could see he still had that twinkle of wiseness, deep in the back of his eyes. But the guy that had brought him along was a classic. A chatty, feisty old guy who I guess would have been getting up there in his seventies. He stood about five foot nothing and was adorned right down his front with a straggly, grey beard and a thinning ponytail that hung down the middle of his back from beneath a shabby civil war cap.

This guy was a ripper. I really couldn't believe that I'd never seen him before. He was joking and carrying on, making more noise than everybody else in the room put together. He pushed his way through the chairs unperturbed, determined to get over by the wall to sit next to Sacramento. It had to be Oochie-Cuchi.

"Okay then, I think we're all just about here now," Joe said with authority as he picked up the minutes sheet and started the proceedings.

"Where's that pretty young blondie then Joe? She's the only frick'n reason I bothered to come along here," laughed Oochie.

"Hey, settle down Oochie, mind your language, there're ladies present. Now move yourself across and sit over there. I sound like some old grade-school teacher but I'm not having you and Sacramento sittin' together. You're as bad as each other. You're disrupting everybody else already and we ain't even started yet."

Joe's manner was friendly but firm. Oochie knew he meant it and made a real meal out of pushing his way back through the chairs. "Holy smoke Joe, me and the chief here weren't doin' nut'n."

"Oochie, the only reason I asked you here is to hand over that piece you've got hidden in that wooden leg of yours. Or have you already put your bong back there instead?"

Sacramento shuddered in silent laughter at that one. Oochie was unflustered.

"I'm serious, hand the gun over now, please. You know the rules and I'm not making any exceptions, even for you second-lieutenant Crawford."

"*Aaagh* but Joe, I bagged nine of those ugly bastards! Even got two with one shot."

"Hand it over and any more of your colorful language, you're *out*."

Oochie knew it was time to pull his head in, so finally seated, began fiddling around with the knee attachments of his prosthetic limb, through the hitched-up end of his long, baggy-short's leg.

"All right then folks, let's get started," said Joe. "Yesterday we all—" There was a light knock at the door. Everyone in the room turned to look as it opened and Faye poked her head timidly inside.

"*Hellooo,*" she said softly, stretching out the sound. "I'm very sorry I am late." Faye beamed a smile across the room and stepped softly down towards the central table. All eyes were still fondly on her, so she mimed a tap on the side of her hair with her knuckles as if to say, "It's made of wood."

Faye's lovely hair looked like a bundle of cut straw pulled back into a long, tapered mass. She had cleverly held it in place with a broad stretchy bandage that covered the wound on her hairline and doubled as a practical headband.

"It's all that gunky blood stuff, I can't seem to do a thing with it."

The whole room broke out in spontaneous applause. Her radiant expression changed to one of dismay and she looked a little uncomfortable. Word must have gotten around during the night about her valiant exploits and she was surprised by their most sincere exhibition of gratitude. Faye bowed her head beautifully in a gesture of humility, waving off the attention with a delicate little flutter of her hand as if to say: "Thank you, but *please* no more."

"Come on darlin', don't get embarrassed by this lot, come on in and sit yourself down right here," Joe said kindheartedly.

She happily took her place next to MacElroy, right in front of the central table. Being pretty close I overheard her delight as she fanned out three feathers in her hand.

"Look Eugene, they were right outside my front door, laid out deliberately on the ground in the shape of the old Nordic Fé rune."

"*Falco Peregrinus Anatum.* They're from a Peregrine Falcon," said MacElroy authoritatively, missing her bigger excitement regarding their arrangement. He turned his attention back to the front and whatever it was that Joe was about to say.

"Okay, thank you all for coming. I've just called this brief little gathering with all our representatives from over at the campsite. We're gonna have to come up with a proper name for it folks, sounds so, *hmmm*, … anyway. We'll talk about that some other time." There was no mention of Vince's Beverly Hills, I think the irony would probably have been lost on most of them.

"Firstly, and I'm glad to say right up front, that apart from one broken arm, a couple of nasty cuts and bruises and a star-seeing knockout, we all got off pretty lightly in yesterday's earthquake. However, when those devil things came pouring out of the ground and attacked, they killed two of the occupants of a passing minivan down on the road out front." He went on to mention how the police had already been notified and everyone agreed it would be best to leave it for the Sonoran authorities to handle.

Moving across to the tripod, Joe was keen to give his little presentation. Flipping a blank cover sheet back, he revealed a map of the North American continent beneath a piece of clear acetate.

"I'm not pretending to be a seismologist or an expert on tectonics, but I've been keeping an eye on all these earth changes and what could be happening."

"Okay, Professor Joe, let's have it. But keep it simple, so us ordinary lamebrains can follow," chuckled Oochie beneath his beard.

"Don't worry, there's only two people in this room with PhDs and I'm not one of them."

Joe's presentation was better than I had expected. First, he explained about the fault line cracks in the Earth's crust and how massive plates push up against each other causing earthquakes. I knew that, but he explained it really well for a layman. He drew big red rings on the acetate indicating the San Andreas fault line, where the North American plate pushed up against the Pacific plate all the way down the southern Californian coast. After that he started to lose me. He went on about Juan de something or other, and how the Cocos, the Caribbean and some other plate all linked up somewhere beneath more looping scribbles that ran all over the board. I'd never heard of any of 'em. He showed us some photographs of this giant crack that had appeared in the ground in Santa Maria Huejoculco back in 2011. It looked exactly like the big one that had opened up right outside. He talked for a while longer about tectonic plates and something called the Mid-Atlantic Ridge until the lecture moved somehow sideways to Chupacabras which then got *everybody* talking. The opinions and theories ranged from Indian legends, ridiculous urban myths to modern science and pure, unadulterated nonsense. Eventually the debate disintegrated into an inaudible rabble which ended abruptly with Joe's extremely loud, two fingered whistle.

"All right folks, settle down, settle down. As nobody can agree on what these goddamn things really are, let's just take a vote on what we're going to call them. Okay. I've made a short list of three names:

One – Chupacabras; which really is a bit of a mouthful and I for one ain't convinced that's what they are.

Two – Non-human life forms; NHLFs for short, thank you Eugene," Joe shook his head in despair.

"Or three – Diablos or devils; depending on your language of course."

The two dissenting voices were MacElroy making some nit-picky protest about "The flagrant disregard for scientific nomenclature" and Sacramento who was adamant we called them "The Spawn of Asencio." I think it was a relevant piece of local folklore, but due to his incessant laughing and tomfoolery, nobody would take him seriously. Anyway, the vote was taken, and 'devils' won out unanimously.

Joe had a few more points on the minute sheet, but now that the relatively short, but important part of the meeting had ended, everyone was getting fidgety and chatting amongst themselves willy-nilly. Dr. MacElroy was itching to get outside to collect his unseen prize from the icebox, but Joe had one more little surprise in store before we all disbanded.

"Okay everyone, thanks for coming, but before you go, I've got one more thing to show you all, thanks to our lovely Oppuam." Moving the tripod and maps from the table, he turned the computer screen on his desk around to face the audience. "Now don't blink folks or you'll miss it," he joked as he clicked the mouse. "It'll be over in seventeen seconds, so you won't be late for your breakfast."

I couldn't believe it. There I was on screen, paddling away like an imbecile against this oncoming wave of devils. Oppuam must have somehow shot it yesterday on her phone. The picture bobbed around erratically, and an enthusiastic cheer went up around me. I didn't know why but watching those few quick seconds made me feel more anxious than I had fighting against them for real.

What I saw next, totally blew me away. The screen then jumped to an angled shot of Faye and Sacramento in full combat mode with their naginatas. The two of them looked so synchronized and unconquerable. It was amazing.

More raucous cheering and eighteen seconds after Joe had clicked his mouse, the place jumped wild with excitement. Sacramento leapt up onto his chair and made three curt bows, while Faye bent forward, hiding her face in her hands, but within seconds she popped back up with a smile, bashfully accepting all of the sincere adulation.

"Play it again big fella, that was frick'n awesome." Everyone agreed with Oochie.

"Yeah Joe, play it again. Play it again!" Joe replayed it three more times before they had all seen enough and finally left.

12

·-Ih2

The last I saw of Faye was when she had ducked outside and disappeared around the back of The Alamo, twiddling the three falcon feathers in her fingers as she went. Although in passing she did unexpectedly invite me over to her trailer around four o'clock for afternoon tea and a chat. I think I'd only drunk the stuff once or twice in my life, but heck, that was one invitation I certainly wasn't going to pass up. Not for all the tea in China. *"Ha!"*

Eugene was frick'n around like a big girl trying to carefully lift the devil out of the ice box. Charlie, unable to watch his feeble efforts any longer, sauntered over to help. I hung around outside, as reluctantly Oochie handed over his firearm to Joe. It was a .44 Colby revolver with an eight-inch barrel. A beautiful, but deadly piece of artillery.

"How the hell did ya keep that inside that leg of yours? It weighs a ton. No wonder you're always listing over to the left," laughed Joe. Oochie grumbled and cursed and headed off back to the campsite.

"I bet something like that don't come cheap," I said, stating the bleeding obvious.

"No way Ooch would have paid anything like what it's worth though. Cunning old rascal probably wangled it out of someone for a song, don't you worry about that," smirked Joe. I could see he was way back there in reminiscence land.

"Were you in Vietnam with Oochie, Joe?"

"Nah, he was there way before my time. '66, '67? He was 1st Infantry, one of Westmoreland's boys. One of the Cu Chi tunnel rats, you know, down there just out of Saigon. That's where he got his nickname *and* lost his leg. Anyway," said Joe with resolve, "let's go and get that Fire Diamond of yours down from its perch, before it falls right off."

We headed back up the ramp to the roof, right as Charlie and

MacElroy were not so carefully dragging the devil's body into the garage workshop on a thick sheet of plastic. "Stretch that bastard out good and proper," ordered Joe. "I wanna' take a good look at that ugly bugger when we're through here."

◆

The Fire Diamond looked okay considering the force of yesterday's earthquake. I was worried it was going to be all dinged up, but there were only a few scrapes on the rocker panels below the doors where it must have slid along the top of the wall. I was amazed it wasn't a whole lot worse.

"Now, how the hell are we going to get it back down?" asked Joe.

It took a bit of planning and some delicate nudging of the tractor bucket by Charlie, but we managed to ease her clear from the wall and lower the rear end carefully down onto the roof. Joe used a couple of old tires to keep the Fire Diamond's long tail-end protected from scraping on the concrete. Eventually, after a lot of cussin' and man-handling the big red monster was safely back on four wheels.

"When you get a chance, go help Charlie with the tractor. It only goes forward; he's stripped the gearbox down twice and reckons reverse is completely shot. If Charlie can't fix it, nobody can. Just help him push it back a bit so he'll be able to drive it away. Anyway, come on over here, I've got something you might wanna see."

◆

The roof area of The Alamo was about the length of one of those interstate rigs and its trailer. Facing the road out front and hanging over the concrete awning was a semi-circular glass-windowed showroom, designed in its day to house two or three of the latest deluxe chrome-covered cars from Detroit. There was nothing on display up here anymore.

While Joe fumbled around with a bunch of keys, I sat on the wall and looked at the tall glass windows which had been whitewashed out years ago. The lower half of the closest pane had been scratched at artistically to display a crude but interesting gallery of daggers and skulls and stickmen with unnaturally large genitalia.

The roof side of the old show room was nothing more than a long row of glass concertina doors that looked like they hadn't been opened up fully for years. The old venetian blinds were all turned closed with some of the slats hanging bent or broken off completely. It gave away nothing of what was hidden behind their ranks of metal strips.

Finally, Joe unlocked the doors and pulled the first two open so that we could get inside. Expecting the showroom to be empty I was surprised to see a vehicle parked up against the far wall beneath a half-slipped cover sheet. The only other things in the room were a couple of old cardboard boxes and some rolled up banners or something that were now scattered across the checkered linoleum floor, but apart from that, nothing else.

"Holy, frick'n!" yelled Joe excitedly. *"That car was parked over here!"* his voice went amusingly high. "Lucky it didn't take some kind o' somersault leap right out through the window, I guess. Man, oh man." He walked determinedly across towards the car, grabbed hold of the thin nylon cover, and pulled it off onto the floor.

"What do ya think of *that* Mr. Wolf?"

"Wow! Is that yours?"

"Every last nut 'n bolt."

"Is it a real one?"

"Of course, it's a real one. Obviously, it's not an original, what do you think I am, a millionaire or something? But yeah, it's the 2006 model update, still cost me a pretty packet though."

What he was showing me was the Ouroboros, Twenty first century, V8 rebirth of the famous 1960's OB-359, an all-American super-duper classic. "That's one evil piece o' machinery there, Joe. Give me the specs, how fast does she go?"

"5.4-liter supercharged modular V8, six-speed manual transmission, 500 horsepower, puts out around 520-footpounds of torque. I've had her up to 200, but I reckon she could still go a *teensy-weensy* bit faster."

"Far out! I love how it's got the original color scheme too, white with the split GT racing stripe down the middle. That really looks something else."

"Yeah, it makes it go faster. Trouble is, the old girl's dead in the water. Stuffed. She's got a busted timing chain. It's a pain of a job, but Charlie'll fix it when he gets time."

I moved in close and through cupped hands peered into the driver's side window. "Looks like a jet fighter in there." It didn't, but it seemed like a good thing to say.

"Yeah, she's a real little beasty, shame she's not running. Anyway, I was thinking, you might want to back the Fire Diamond in here away from the elements and those frick'n cats." He laughed and pulled the cover back over the white, Ouroboros thoroughbred. "Come on, let's go back down. I need some food."

I chuckled to myself on the way out, as the crude little picture glyphs scratched onto the windows appeared more spectacular backlit in lines of glowing sunshine through the whitewashed glass.

◆

We'd barely sat ourselves down before Mrs. Eduardo was at our table with a steaming pot of hot coffee and mugs.

"Hola, Señor Joe, Señor Lobo, *mi valiente héroe!*"

She grabbed me on the cheek and gave it an affectionate squeeze. I wish she were just pulling my leg, but I could tell that she really did mean it. "And what would you like?"

"Same as usual please, Rosalina. He'll have the same as me," Joe answered hastily. Mrs. Eduardo made a little sigh of pure enjoyment, turned with a smile, and hurried off back to the kitchen.

"I suppose you wanna know what an old codger like me, is doing with a high-performance supercar down here in the middle of the frick'n desert, huh?"

"No, I think you're—"

"Well I'll tell ya anyway, it's got nothing to do with—" Joe made a wiggly movement with his pinky finger. "It's *much* worse than that. Pretty soon after Chester was killed my wife walked out and left me. Yeah, ran off with a full-bird colonel. Some starch-shirted, pencil-necked little prick that'd been gettin all goo-gah with her for years down at our local mega-market apparently. I always wondered why she loved going there so much. Anyway, after getting hammered with all that, I lost it big time. Went on the mother-of-all-fuckin'-benders, ended up in Vegas like you do and blew everything I had playing Blackjack. I was down to my last two hundred dollars, so I went for broke on one of those fancy one hundred bucks-a-shot, slot machines. Next stop was oblivion anyway, so I reckoned it didn't really matter. *I won three-hundred-thousand-dollars.* I couldn't believe it. That was the only time, the only time in my whole miserable damn life that I really believed there was a god. *Three-hundred-thousand-dollars.*" His voice went really high pitched as he reiterated the point.

"*Thank you, thank you, thank you!* God, I was an idiot back then. Anyway, that's what eventually led me all the way down here and this is where I stayed ... *for better or for worse.*" He said it in a sarcastic parody of the wedding vows. He clasped his hands together, as though in prayer, looked up at the ceiling and left me to figure out the rest.

I couldn't understand why, right out of the blue, Joe had suddenly decided to tell me all of this really personal stuff anyway. Then he changed tack.

"So now, Mr. frick'n Wolfgang, I think it's about time you spilled the beans and tell me what *really* brings you all the way down here. All the way down to the middle of nowhere." His questioning was direct, but still jovial and I could tell he would probably be okay with whatever I told him.

"All that Fire Diamond badge stuff is a good ploy mister, but I wanna know what you're *really* up to. I don't reckon it's got anything to do with a dame. Me thinks you're in some kind of trouble with the law. Am I right?"

I felt like I'd been put on the spot, so I had a long gulp on my coffee while I stalled for time.

"Come on Wolfie, you can tell Uncle Joe!" he said mockingly, in a tone of voice like you use when you try to sweet talk a confession out of a two-year-old.

"Well, yeah I am, but it's not what you think. Nothing major, I didn't kill anybody or rob a bank or anything."

Joe pushed his coffee mug to the side, folded his arms and lent forward towards me intrigued.

"Assault on a police officer," I blurted out beneath the pressure of his gaze. "But it's not what you think!"

"Go on."

"I was walking down Fremont Street one afternoon, just as you get to North Eastern, across from the market. I'm passing alongside of this parked black and white, when a police dog pokes its head out through the half open window and starts barking and carrying on like I'd just shoved a broom stick fair up its ass. Scared the living bejesus out of me. So, I start cussin right back with some four letter fruities. More out of shock than anything else. The next thing you know I'm spread-eagle across the hood of the cruiser, arms bent up behind my back with these two cops slappin' cuffs on me and charging me with *assault!* Assault on a Las Vegas police officer."

"You're shittin' me, for using harsh language on a K9?"

"Yep, I was supposed to front the judge a couple of weeks back now, but—"

"That's ridiculous. So you jumped into the old Fire Diamond and did a bolt all the way down south to Me-hi-co. Wow! Good one Mr. Wolf, good one."

"Yep, what an idiot. I really hadn't thought it through at all." Just then Mrs. Eduardo returned with a tray and unloaded two piled plates of fried eggs, bacon, and beans on the table in front of us. Joe happily picked up his fork and started hoeing in. He didn't speak for a bit as his mouth was continually full and he alternated his gaze up and down between me and his vittles.

"I've been meaning to ask, Joe," I said as I remembered something that had been drifting in and out of my memory. "How does this place get its electricity? There're no power lines coming in from anywhere and those two solar panels out back look pretty useless. One is hanging right off of its … thing." Sadly, I had as much grasp of electronics as someone from the dark ages.

Joe mumbled something indecipherable with a mouth full of food and waved his fork around, drawing some kind of invisible 3D diagram in the air out in front of him.

"Batteries. Sodium-sulfur batteries, they're about as big as this fried egg, look pretty much like one too, except they're all covered in silver foil and everything, they can store twenty or thirty kilowatts o' power each, for a day! And they don't even need any frick'n solar panels, grids or anything to keep 'em going. There's half a dozen of them downstairs in the basement going flat out. The only drawback is they're cook'n away at over six hundred degrees Fahrenheit, so you've got to keep the buggers somewhere cool and out of harm's way. When they start to go flat, all you've gotta do is lay 'em out flat in the hot midday sun to recharge them. They cost a shit-load when I bought them, but they keep this whole place and the campsite going 24/7.

"Anyway, glad you mentioned it, Wolf, I'd better go and check up on how they're going after that quake. Truth told, I forgot all about them," Joe laughed and shoved his fork back into his mouth. "You ain't got a clue what I've been talking about have you?"

"Nope."

Joe made a snort and kept on eating. We both sat there for a while happily munching, but there was something else still nagging me. "Yeah go on, ask away, what's on your mind?"

"Well, yesterday kinda freaked me out, you know."

"You got that right." Joe kept on eating.

"Those creatures, the *devils*. What are they *really*? I know they're not your 'Xolo-hyena chupacabra-whatevers'," I said doing that idiotic, inverted commas thing with my fingers, before thinking better of it. "They definitely looked more like the scaly, lizard-like ones you were telling me about earlier. And why are they coming up out of the ground? And all those old paintings in your office, what are they all about? Maybe they really are devil-devils. None of this makes any sense. Now I've seen 'em up close and had a bit of time to think about it, it's doing my head in. *I'm really starting to get the FEAR now, Joe!*"

He just looked up at me as he slipped a piece of bacon into his mouth. "Dunno."

"Don't know what?" I said peeved at his unhelpful answer.

"You asked me what they are, exactly, and I don't know. Once we've finished up here, we'll go down and see what Eugene's got to say. Did you see how excited he was when he realized he was gettin' one with a head?" he chuckled. "He's a clever old cookie Dr. MacElroy. Eugene knows everything about your regular critters, that's why he's so frick'n obsessed with your chupacabra stroke NHLFs stroke devils. He really wants to be the first mainstream scientist to get to the bottom of it all."

"How'd he end up here, anyway?"

Joe was busy mopping up the remnants on his plate.

"Long story, I used to be in an online forum group. It was centered around strange creatures and life forms basically. Yeah there were all kinds of folks on it. Scientists, amateur biologists, housewives, sasquatch-spotters, alien-spotters, all types. It was great. We'd all swap stories and sightings, upload pictures and stuff, some of the scientists were a bit of a pain in the ass, always trying to big note themselves with all these technical Latin names and confusing all of us simpletons. But mostly they were pretty good. I was Mad Hatter. Cut a long story short, MacElroy had almost gotten himself drummed out of his university so to speak, for going against the establishment and *'Virulently pursuing research not befitting someone of his academic position and standing.'* Some bullshit like that."

"He was looking into Chupacabras?"

"You got it in one. Anyway, I told him he was more than welcome to come down here to the desert and pursue his field research in whatever manner he deemed fit."

Joe's voice was starting to rise up in his usual excited manner.

"He was down here within a week and now I can't get rid of him even if I wanted to. No, he's a nice guy, Dr. MacElroy, a bit weird, but hey!" Joe pulled an expression as if to say "But who isn't down here."

"He's mellowed out a little now, but you should have seen him when he first got here." The voice was revving up nicely again for an imminent outburst of laughter.

"He was wearing one of those, what do you call them? Pith helmets? Long baggy shorts and socks and a pair of fuckin' tennis shoes." He roared with laughter. "I thought you've gotta be puttin me on. But no, he was the real frick'n deal. He wore that get up apparently all the way through the African Congo on the hunt for some long-lost horny frog or something. He's a gem, old Eugene. Oh yeah, and get this, he even carried around one of them giant magnifying glasses when he first got down here, but he got so much shit from Vince he keeps it well out of sight nowadays. Seriously he looked like a real-life cartoon character."

Joe was enjoying himself, and the way he told the story, albeit at poor old Eugene's expense, really was very funny. "I gave him about two weeks down here, but no, he stuck it out, he's like a pig in the poop when it comes to researching Chupacabras, frick'n loves 'em."

"What about Faye?"

Joe just smiled. "You mean Ice Maiden. That's another story, I'll let her tell you in her own good time."

"Anyway Joe, back to the devils."

"*Yeees?*"

"How did you get into all of this stuff in the first place?"

Joe leaned forward again as thought he was about to tell me the mother of all secrets. "It all started way down deep in the bottomless pit."

"What's that?" I said intrigued.

"Well, when I was a boy, we went on a family visit to stay with relatives up in Grayston County, Kentucky. Well a *must see* for out-o'-towners in Grayston County is Mastodon Cave National Park. It's the longest cave system in the world, not the deepest, that title goes to a cave somewhere near the Black Sea, but apparently Mastodon is the longest, with over six hundred miles of passageways. It's all limestone and sandstone. Tell ya when you're just a kid and the biggest hole you've been in up 'till then was an empty swimming pool, Mastodon Cave was exactly what they called it, the bottomless pit. I frick'n loved it, totally blew me away."

"What happened?"

"I'll tell ya," Joe said. "I was a little shit of a kid, I can still remember,

I got nagged the whole goddamn way from Texas to Kentucky by the old man for constantly putting my feet up on the upholstery."

"Was that in your dad's new Fire Diamond?"

"Sure was. By the time we got there the old coot was having conniptions, *'You're not coming on anymore holidays boy, you can't show any respect or do anything your eff'n well told, this is the last time, blah, blah, blah.'* You know the drill. He was adamant I wasn't going to be allowed to go the next day with everyone else to the caves, but luckily my mom and my little cousins were pretty persuasive and eventually talked the old man around to letting me come along. Anyway, I was on a short leash, as they say, and had to stay within arm's length so as not to fool around or get into any trouble *whatsoever*. But I tell ya, twenty minutes down into the caves and I'd already wandered off up a side turn on my own and the next thing you know I was lost. *Totally* lost. I could hear everyone shouting out my name, but I just couldn't figure out where they were, or how to get back. Everything all looked the same. I figured that if I were missing long enough, they'd be so relieved to find me that I wouldn't be in half as much trouble than if they found me straight away. So, I just went further and deeper down into the caves."

"Weren't you scared? I mean being only little."

"Ah shit no! I was off on an adventure; I had my trusty Space-Major flashlight. What could go wrong?" Joe paused to build the suspense.

"Well?"

"Well what?"

"What went wrong?"

Joe thought about it for a moment, I was expecting some really amazing answer. "Nothing went wrong, but something down there really scared the living daylights out of me."

I looked across the table at Joe with eager anticipation.

"After an hour or so the whole solo exploration thing didn't seem to be such a good idea. I was getting pretty hungry and the flashlight was starting to go. I never even thought of that when I decided to head off solo. Anyway, I found what I thought was the way back, totally wishful thinking on my part I'm sure, but I kept on that path until the flashlight was pretty much useless. Now I was gettin' worried."

Joe laughed once again, as he went back over his memories. "I was smart enough to know I couldn't just head off and stumble around blindly in the dark. I'd already seen some of the many bottomless drops in that place and I sure as hell didn't wanna go falling down one of those in a hurry. I sat down on the edge of the path in the darkness with my back against a rock and waited and waited and waited. Believe me it was *dark*, so frick'n black I couldn't see zip, not even my fingers in front of my face. By now I was really getting anxious, I started crying and having freaked out ideas about never being found at all. I can still remember just sitting there waiting and hoping for someone to find me. I was ready for the biggest whooping of my life, but I didn't care about that, just as long as they found me. After what seemed like an eternity my hearing had become so acute, I could hear everything, my heartbeat, even the blood swirling around in my head. *True!* There wasn't much to hear besides, so when I heard even the slightest sound it caught my attention immediately.

Somewhere off to my right I heard this ever so faint noise, I turned my head in that direction and instinctively flicked on my flashlight. It had about a millisecond's worth of light left in it, but that was enough, if I'd blinked I would have missed it, but about ten feet away from me I saw for an instant, this towering figure of something that *literally* made me shit my drawers. You're the first person I've ever admitted that to in sixty years Wolf, so if you *ever, ever* repeat that, you're gonna be a frick'n coyote's breakfast."

"What was it?"

"Dunno. Like I said, I only saw it for a millisecond, but I'll never forget it. Being just a kid and sittin' on my butt at the bottom of a cave, it looked about twenty feet tall. It had a huge scaly body and a head with evil yellow eyes. For years I just called it *the monster!* Pretty original huh."

"Did it attack you?"

"Nope, I went completely hysterical, I got up and ran like an idiot in the other direction. Next thing I know I'm surrounded by all these people. They were rangers from the national park being extremely attentive as they lifted me onto a stretcher. Man, I was never so pleased to see grown-ups in my life, ever. When the dust settled, I found out later that I'd run headlong into a rock wall and knocked myself out cold. Unbelievable. Still got a whooping from the old man, called me a reckless little idiot and banned me from doing *anything* for six months after." This time Joe didn't laugh, instead he looked thoughtful and said "So don't you go tellin' anybody about that. You hear?"

My next question was cut short as Vince came into the dining room shoveling breakfast cereal into his mouth from a bowl held high up under his chin. He was dressed in his yellow, low-rider, board shorts and an armless white T-shirt, but the kicker was on his head. Somewhere around the place he'd picked up Joe's prized ten-gallon hat and wore it into the dining room as nonchalantly as if it were his own. He made a nod of recognition towards us and munched his way over to the far side of the room.

"Where did you get my hat?" snapped Joe. "Give it here!" Completely defiant, Vince sat down at a table against the wall. "Useless idiot, I suppose you've just dragged your sorry ass out o' bed, have you?" Vince ignored him but looked up and smiled, dribbling a whole slosh of milk from his mouth. "Why you—"

Joe started up from his chair but froze when two dark haired women came in through the door. It was the Japanese ladies we'd pulled out of the upturned minibus yesterday evening.

Already half out of his seat Joe stood and turned to greet them. He motioned to me with his hand as if to say, "Get up, show some respect. *They're Japanese.*" The intention was good, but he was winging it with the etiquette.

The older lady who was somewhere in her sixties bowed respectfully once, but the other, a young girl of about eighteen seemed to bob up and down with me and Joe for as long as we were prepared to keep going. I think on her part more out of nervous politeness than anything else.

Vince took no notice and stayed put, slurping away on his cereal. I could see him smirking away at our folly.

The young girl was the only one who spoke. *"Ohayo gozaimasu"* she kept on saying, which I guessed must be Japanese for hello or good morning. Then she suddenly began speaking English.

"Hello sirs, how are you? *Arigato!* Thank you, kind sirs, for saving us from the evil demons arigato, arigato."

After her expressions of gratitude, she settled down a little and introduced herself and her older companion. She didn't speak perfect English, but like I always say, if I could speak Japanese even a tenth as good as that, I'd be calling myself trilingual.

"Please sirs, may I introduce my, *aaah?* ... Grand-o-mother, Hamada-san." The lady nodded her head slightly towards us. "I am Kudo Kiko." The girl bowed again.

"Hello, Miss Kudo, my name's Joe and this is Wolf. It's nice to finally make your acquaintance. I hope you slept well and are both feeling better?"

She quickly covered her mouth and did that embarrassed, giggling thing. "Please sirs, just call me Kiko. Japanese people say our names around the other way."

Hamada-san said something gruffly to her granddaughter in Japanese and they both sat down at a table half-way between Joe, me, and Vince, who sat over by the wall trying to remain unnoticed.

"Hamada-san and I would like to have something to eat right now, then maybe later on, we could have a pleasant … conversation?"

"Hai!" I sounded off loud and crisply like a Japanese speaker. Joe scoffed with a grunt at my idiocy. Just then Mrs. Eduardo arrived at their table with two steaming plates on a tray. We both sat quietly, craftily checking the visitors out from behind the rims of our mugs.

The girl was pretty cute, about five foot two, with long black hair and a fringe that hung right down into her eyes. She was wearing a white headband, a mid-brown tunic dress and those long, over-the-knee, white socks that younger Japanese women always seem to wear. Even out here in the Sonoran Desert. On the other hand, Hamada-san, the grandmother, was dressed in dark blue denim trousers and a green patterned blouse. Her demeanor was stern, almost grumpy.

Faye came rushing in from behind the counter. "Joe. Wolf. Quickly, come and take a look. Eugene has something *very* exciting he wants to show you. He's—" Her words were interrupted as a racket of scraping chair legs made her turn quickly and look towards the middle table. The appearance of Faye had been a complete surprise for young Kiko who had jumped to her feet in a panic-like state of excitement. She flew out from behind the table jabbering away at a million miles an hour in Japanese and bowing again with such zeal, it was hard to know if she was serious or was possibly having some kind of psychotic episode. I could see Vince across the room giggling hysterically to himself as he enjoyed this unexpected floor show. Kiko was nearly wetting herself with excitement.

Hamada-san berated her granddaughter angrily, obviously telling her to sit back down at the table immediately and behave herself. Faye looked totally surprised at what was happening, but she knew enough to be able to understand a few of the words that Kiko kept on repeating.

"Tomoe Gozen. Tomoe Gozen. Burondo no kami … Tomoe Gozen."

"I only know a tiny bit of Japanese," said Faye, "but she thinks that *I'm* Tomoe Gozen."

"Who?" Joe and I asked together.

"Tomoe Gozen. She was a legendary female samurai that lived in feudal Japan."

"What?" said Joe, taken aback.

"Burondo no kami. Blonde-haired Tomoe Gozen. I think?" elaborated Faye.

Kiko had calmed down a little now and was just sort of oscillating up and down on the spot, grinning so hard it looked like her face was about to explode. Suddenly it made sense, Kiko must have seen Faye fighting with the devils yesterday, while hanging trapped upside down in her seat in the overturned minivan.

Faye took a step toward her and held out her hand, Kiko bounced uncontrollably out to meet her, throwing her arms around her in an embrace. Faye looked back at us over the young girl's head and pulled an exaggerated face as if to say, "Oh dear, ... *help!*"

Hamada-san had given up on her irrational granddaughter and sat calmly at her table, her stern face unreadable as she fixed her gaze solely on the figure of Faye.

Kiko unlocked her grip and took a step backwards, she was about to start bowing again when Faye stopped her and kindly thanked her in English. Kiko's face balled up with emotion once again, and with that Faye took her leave and we both followed right on behind her.

◆

"Oooh! Tomoe Gozen, eh? You've got yourself a regular little one-woman fan club there," laughed Joe, as we went out through the back of the kitchen.

"I know, that was so strange, I didn't know what to do, poor little thing she was so sweet."

"She thinks you're a legendary superhero," I said attempting sarcasm.

"Oh, don't be so cruel Fenrir, she's probably still very shaken up. I feel so guilty now for just running away like that, but Eugene's down in his laboratory and has discovered something quite incredible about our cadaver."

We hurried out back to the workshop where Charlie was messing around with the tractor which he'd obviously moved on his own. Towards the far end of the garage were two, eight-foot stacks of brand-new truck tires sitting on a heavy wooden palette up against the wall. With the gentlest of flicks from Faye's hand, the whole thing rolled effortlessly sideways on some ingenious track system, revealing a narrow set of stairs that descended down into the basement.

Joe scurried down first, then Faye, and I followed along behind. The smell of those new rubber tires was heady and intoxicating.

I'd never been into the mysterious lab before, in fact I didn't even know where it was. Foolishly, I imagined it would have looked like those CSI ones you see on TV, chock-full of high-tech gadgetry. This wasn't like that at all. It was small and windowless with lumpy, whitewashed walls. From the gloom of the ceiling above hung six iron lamp shades complete with old-fashioned globes that bathed the room in a warm yellow light. I could hear an air conditioner sucking away up there in the darkness as well. Old wooden kitchen tables placed end to end hugged the walls and formed a continuous bench that held a selection of antiquated scientific equipment, racks of glass jars and beakers, ring-binder folders and random pads full of notes. There was one fairly modern-looking computer and a big old power-tower complete with a museum-piece, cream-colored monitor and a scattering of desk lamps that emitted a brighter, but unfriendly blue brilliance. Even though it looked pretty makeshift and smelt like a macrobiotic food shop, the place really had a serious feeling of work about it.

"Watch yourself," said Faye. "Be very careful. Eugene and I tried to sweep it all up but there are still little shards everywhere." At the bottom of the stairs was a broom and a dustpan full of broken glass. I had a sudden flash back to the Day of The Dead party when that big ugly skull busted in through the Fire Diamond's window.

On a table, in the middle of the room, lay a body-sized lump beneath a large sheet of pink colored bubble wrap. "Is that it?" I asked, eagerly.

"Yes, that's it. Come on across and have a look, but please put these on, you never know, what you might catch." Dr. MacElroy handed us each one of those paper facemasks.

We stood around the table while MacElroy carefully pulled back the plastic, making an over-exaggerated meal of it, as though he was unveiling the fragile remains of a million-year-old Chihuahua. Expecting to see its hideous face looking up at me, I was surprised that it was actually lying on its front. Faye maneuvered one of the cold blue lights into position so we could get a better look. Then MacElroy brought out his legendary giant magnifying glass, I sniggered unkindly, remembering how Joe had described him earlier.

"Now take a look at that!" Eugene pointed to the base of the neck with the tip of a sharpened pencil.

"What, I can't see nothin?" growled Joe. "What are ya showing me?"

"Look closely," insisted MacElroy, carefully moving the magnifying glass up and down into focus.

"Oh yeah I see it. *Holy smoke!* That's some kind of lettering," said Joe with renewed excitement, his voice already on the way up. "It looks to me like a tag or serial number." I'd noticed Joe was always careful not to swear too strongly around Faye. "Do you know what this means, do you know what this means? Someone or something has probably bred or made these things, that's—" He was so excited, he stood bolt upright and shook his head in dismay.

It was only then I put my face up close to its neck and I managed to take a look myself. The marks were really tiny, even with the aid of the powerful magnifier, I could only just make them out. "Those letters must only be about an eighth of an inch in size," I said amazed.

"Three millimeters to be precise," responded MacElroy.

"What does it say, are they numbers, letters?" Joe was flabbergasted and nudged me out of the way as he tried once again to scrutinize the markings.

"Well I've taken some hi-res photos with a 105mm macro lens and downloaded them to—"

Joe ignored the technicalities and made his way quickly across to the newer computer and waited for the rest of us to follow. Faye took control and brought up a beautifully sharp image of the highly enlarged inscription.

"Wow, that's great Eugene," complimented Joe. "What is it? It looks like ... *dot ... dash ... I ... h ... 2.*"

"Yeah that's exactly what I first read it as too."

"So, what does that mean?" I asked.

"Well," said MacElroy, "let's go through the symbols one by one. *Dot*, that could be anything, same with dash, although in Morse code, *dot* represents *E*, *dash* represents *T*, or together they make the letter *A*. But that's ridiculous, it's just conjecture. The *I* character, that's more interesting, obviously it could be interpreted as a capital I in the Latin script, or more interestingly it represents the character *Zai* in the ancient Phoenician letter forms that date back as far as around 1200 BC. It means weapon. The lower-case *h*, looks undoubtably like it belongs within the Latin scripts as well, but who knows? And lastly the number *2* as we have been calling it. But if you look closely, it isn't in fact a number 2 at all. The familiar ascending hook shape is there, but the horizontal foot or base bar is completely absent. This symbol is in fact also from ancient Phoenicia and it's called Pe or Peh … it means *mouth*."

"All I'm hearing is … *ET* … *weapon* … *mouth*, with 'h for horrible' thrown in for good measure! Good work Eugene, good work," said Joe impressed. By the expression on his face and the way he was scrutinizing the printout you could tell this was an important piece of the puzzle for him in his quest for answers to his ongoing questions.

13

Doin' the Do

Coming up from the lab I walked back through the garage and paused for a moment beneath the frame of the roller door. Outside the midday sun was getting hotter and brighter and painful to my eyes.

I heard a sound behind me. It was Charlie sitting on a fold-out chair, eating an orange. After swallowing a juicy mouthful, he looked up at me and said, "The time is nigh Mr. Wolf. Unless you've got any more little distractions, you'd better go rescue that little ol' V badge soon before it disappears down that bottomless pit forever. An aftershock could happen at any time you know."

He was right. Getting that badge off the hood wasn't going to be easy. Charlie had considered driving right up close to the edge and dangling me out on the tractor bucket but ruled it out categorically as the weight of the tractor would most probably collapse the unstable walls and send it and myself down the crack.

The new plan was to shove an aluminum ladder across the width of the void and jam it deep into the open window of the car directly on top of the upturned Fire Diamond, with the other end wedged firmly inside the bucket with the tractor parked as far back from the drop as possible.

◆

I was tied around the waist by some strong nylon rope. Charlie had anchored the other end securely around the hydraulic arm of the tractor. My instructions were to sit astride the ladder and edge myself slowly out across the chasm until I was above the Fire Diamond's upside-down engine bay and the half-opened hood.

Before I set out Charlie placed a thin, cord noose around my neck from which dangled three separate strings holding a pair of pliers, a screwdriver, and a small ballpein hammer. I was so impressed by his foresight. He was so frick'n organized.

The ladder felt pretty secure and after a couple of nervous ass-slides forward, I was ready. Charlie handed me a can of that wonder-spray, accompanied by a grumpy and prophetic warning. "I've got more of that stuff, but if you drop *any* of my tools, your gonna have to climb all the way down there and get 'em."

I nodded gingerly and wedged the can tightly into my shirt top pocket. Just past the half-way point I noticed my antics were drawing a bit of a crowd. Half a dozen dudes had wandered over from the camp curious to check out what the crazy gringo was up to.

"Right, that's far enough. Stop!" yelled Charlie authoritatively. "Now take out what I put in your other shirt pocket and don't drop it." I slipped my hand in and carefully pulled out what felt like a metal bath plug attached to a light length of chain. On seeing it I realized it wasn't a plug but a magnet. I didn't even know that he'd put it there."

"Okay. Now, lie yourself out along the length of the ladder and wrap some of the chain around your wrist. Carefully lower the magnet down as far forward as you can onto the inside of the Fire Diamond's hood. You'll probably only get one shot at this, so make sure you lock that magnet down as near to the front as you can. Cause once it's on it ain't comin' off in a hurry."

"Will-co!" The magnet twirled around like soap-on-a-rope for a while then with a mind of its own it found metal. "I've got it."

"Right, now *gently* wiggle the chain and see how much play you've got. Remember if you drop the chain it's game over Wolfman."

I followed his prompts and to my amazement the hood bobbed up with surprisingly little effort. "It's moving, it's moving really easily."

A clump of dirt exploded on the back of my head.

"Come on Wolf, ya big wuss. What the frick'n hell are ya doin' man, you should've had that dumb thing off at least ten minutes ago." It was Vince.

"Hey, cut it out you fool. Get back over here and leave him alone. Jesus! Sometimes boy, I really wonder where you get your mush-for-goddamn-brains from." It was Joe.

Apparently, my audience had grown to at least nine now, counting Charlie. But lying face down I couldn't see anyone. There could have been fifty. I was starting to get pretty edgy. Maybe Faye was up there too? Don't stuff this up, *be cool*. Don't stuff this up.

Surprisingly, the hood lifted easily, the old springs hadn't stiffened or rusted at all, so I went for broke and pulled hard till it almost closed. I looped and secured the rest of the chain around one of the ladder rungs to hold it tight.

And there it was at arm's length away, an exact match of the '58 badge that had caused all the fuss in the first place. "Charlie you're an absolute genius."

"You ain't got it off yet, sunshine. You're on your own now, *make me proud boy…make me proud!*" Charlie's sarcasm was eagerly appreciated by the others, as I could hear them laughing and joking behind me.

After "doing the do" with the tool kit, all the bashing and prying and twisting and whatever other desperate stuff I was trying, the V badge finally relented and just popped off the hood face. Aware of the sarcastic cheering, I got a little cocky and raised my trophy arm high, shifting my weight on the ladder.

And then it happened. Suddenly the entire thing dropped hard and quick to the left. It probably only shifted a few inches, but it felt like the world had just flipped upside down.

Like a complete idiot, yours-truly let go of the ladder and rolled like a turd off the side. It was only my foot and lower leg caught in the rungs that stopped me from falling off completely. I just hung there, dangling down into the pitch-black abyss with the nylon rope sawing itself back and forth through my crotch.

The good thing was I was still holding on tight to the V badge but only with the grip of terror. The bad thing was I screamed. Oh boy, did I scream. It wasn't your rugged *"AAAAAAAAAAGH!"* extended Wilhelm type scream you hear in the movies when the bad guy gets booted out of an airplane at thirty thousand feet. Nor like when a gun-totin' bandit plummets head-over-heels off a rooftop. It was a shrieking, high-pitched, little-girly-type scream. I just lost it completely.

Those few seconds hanging there upside down, scared the living daylights out of me like nothing before in my life. I felt like such an idiot. I felt so ashamed. But now it didn't matter either way, the damage was already done.

It was probably only a few seconds before the guys hauled me safely back topside. I thanked Charlie profusely as he disentangled me from the rope and all of his tools.

Vince thought the whole thing beyond hilarious, feigning genuine interest in replicating the *exact* pitch and tonal quality of my now infamous shriek. "I'm *just* not getting it right, how does it go again Wolf? *Aaaaaaaaaaaaaaaaaaaaaaaaagh!* Is that right?"

"Piss off!"

"No, no, you gotta get a much higher modulation," laughed Charlie.

I fiddled with the winged V badge in my pocket and wondered if it had really all been worth it.

"Hey Wolf!" cried Joe as an afterthought. "Now that you've got your Fire Diamond badge, I guess you'll be leaving. But if you want to stay on, you're relieved of all cleaning duties. From tomorrow you can help me get started fencing off this lot before some idiot falls over the edge."

Wait for it. One-two-three. *"Aaaaaaaaaaaaaaagh!"*

"Morons!" At least Faye wasn't there, I consoled myself. But I was sure she'd soon hear about my most disgraceful conduct.

14

Tea for Two

I'd spent at least half an hour combing and oiling up my hair into the quintessential, rockabilly quiff. I loved the way the strands turned a luscious, shiny black, even the grey ones if you roll them down inside the mix.

From my bag I pulled out my very best threads. A near new, black-denim, western shirt complete with red leather shoulder patches and lots of white embroidered stitching that swirled all the way down the front. Luckily it was folded flat and didn't need pressing. Just as well, as I didn't have anywhere to plug in a steam-iron, even if I had one. I gave the old cowboy boots a bit of a touch up too, with a luxurious lick o' deep red polish. I was lookin' pretty damn cool. Yeah, *cool-cat-cooool!*

Heading across to Faye's trailer I was trying to keep a low profile. I could see the shadow of my long pointy quiff bobbing about on the ground beside me like an excited mackerel surfing on the top of my head. I was dreading bumping into Vince or Charlie. I didn't care for any more of their nonsense at the moment, like the campsite hombres who'd just walked past me and let rip with a high-pitched scream. *"Aaaaaaaaaaaaaaagh!"* I was never, ever going to live this down.

Ah, didn't matter, I was suited n' booted and off for afternoon tea with the purdiest little filly in the whole damn county, yes siree! Stuff the lot of 'em.

Always one to be fashionably late I arrived at Faye's trailer at two minutes past four. The first thing I noticed was a spread of those falcon feathers she'd been showing to MacElroy, lying on the ground beside the bottom step. Being the quick-thinking smoothy that I am, I scooped them up and arranged them roughly into a wide sprouting bouquet of imitation flowers. I knocked on the metal door and backed myself down a step or two as footsteps came running along inside the trailer. The door opened outwards and all I could see were Faye's unclad legs.

"Hello Wolf, please come in."

As I vaulted back up the step, she gestured towards the little dining alcove directly across from the door.

"Please sit down, I won't be a minute, I'm running a little late. Thank you, put them down over there with all the others," she said seeing my posy of feathers. "There were more than a dozen lying outside when I came back earlier. I have *no idea* who keeps leaving them. Although I—" She was about to say something more but stopped short.

I sat on the right-hand seat at the table that looked along the entire length of the trailer. The other seat faced the rear-end window, a dead zone with nothing at all worth looking at. As she disappeared off down the other end, I noticed Faye was wearing the sweater she'd crammed into the plastic bag on the morning we'd retrieved her scattered possessions. I remembered its drab olive color.

While she was gone, I was happy to sit and take a bit of an eyeball around. She really had hit the jackpot scoring this little beauty. It was a twenty-five-foot late 1950's deluxe bullet trailer classic. Gorgeous. The whole interior must have had a total refit. All of the kitchenette cupboards and fittings were of fresh-hewn pine and the stove and sink gleamed bright with chrome. Everything inside looked neat and spotlessly clean.

Although still light outside, Faye had turned down all of the blinds. Only the defiant glow of afternoon sun still pushed its way in through the slats. Apart from a fitted wall lamp over the sink, the only other light came from three stocky candles. One sat high, flickering on a small quarter shelf beside the kitchen cupboards, another glowed somewhere further down the deep end and a third burned brightly on the window ledge beside me. They looked kind o' cool, I thought I'd steal the idea, it could only spruce up the mood inside my old van.

There was ambient music floating from somewhere. It was Brian Eno's *Music for Airports*. Brilliant. I recognized it from my youth back in Vegas, my roommate played it all the time. It was the complete opposite of Faye's head crackin' liking for metal.

She must have had a thing for skulls too, they were everywhere. Not real ones, these were the Día de los Muertos sugar type skulls. They were the size of golf balls with beady-black eyes, all lined up along the top of the cupboards and the windowsills gawking down at me. I managed to count around sixty or so before I got bored and looked away.

I knew those cats would be lurking around here somewhere too. I figured that if I took even one step down toward the other end, Gutteka would pounce out from some hidden place and rip my frick'n face off. The exact moment I thought it, Jenteka's little head popped up over the table from the opposite seat. She looked at me curiously for a moment, sniffed the air like she does, then bobbed back down and vanished. Still no sign of Gutteka, but I knew he was out there, I just knew he was out there.

On the windowsill beside me stood a short row of books with two sitting dolls as bookends. One was that raggedy old Gersemi, but the other one, apart from being the same size, had no common features at all. This one looked expensive. A fine porcelain face, locks of golden hair and embroidered clothes that were cut from velvet and lace. The two couldn't have been more different. I thought it curious, but I was much more interested in checking out her books.

There were five books in all. The first one was titled *Naginatajutsu*. That was the martial arts she practiced with Sacramento. *Skandinavisk Mytologi*. This was an incredibly old looking hardback volume. I figured it meant Scandinavian Mythology, I was clever enough to work that out by myself, but not quite enough to distinguish which Nordic language it was written in. *A Living History of South Western Tribes and Traditions*. She had obviously gotten right into all of the local native American stuff. *Ley lines, Standing Stones & Earth Energies*. Hmm, that sounded a bit cosmic. The last one closest to me was called *Chief Iron Eyes Little Eagle*. This one looked the most interesting. I could only see some of the cover poking out from behind the Hessian doll. I was just about to slip it out for a peek when Faye came back in a hurry. The long legs were gone, replaced by shapeless black track pants as she sat down opposite and smiled.

"So, Mr. Fenrir, it's very nice to see you, thank you for coming!" She leaned forward and made a playful little poke at the end of my quiff with her finger. *"I love it!"* she said, while she shrugged her head playfully into her shoulders and giggled. "You look like Juha Väinämöinen!"

"Who?"

She had that mysterious fragrance produced by the mixture of lotions and creams that all women dutifully apply to their skin. I breathed it all in. She wore no makeup at all. Her fine, strong features seemed as if carved from the finest alabaster.

Faye didn't have the customary heart-shaped face, the big round eyes and the cute little button-nose you usually associate with your typical good-looking blonde. She had a longer face that hung perfectly from well-defined cheekbones, her nose was distinguished and prominent, descending proudly from her brow at an angle that would best be described as classical. Her sumptuous lips could change in an instant from sensuous to stoic, then burst back into the radiance of an unexpected smile. But her eyes, those alluring blue eyes were the highlight feature of her exquisitely beautiful face, every glance, every look, every flutter and movement. Her whole persona was imbued with a dignity and an ethereal glow that women blessed with such natural beauty seem to possess in abundance. Her long hair, now clean of the disgusting slime, hung straight and loose behind her shoulders. When she pushed it back behind her ears, she really did look like an elf.

"Would you like to have some tea now?" Her words popped my mesmerization.

"*Yeah!* Sounds great."

"Would you like English tea or English tea? That's all I have," she laughed and jumped back out of her seat. I watched her as she turned to the kitchen bench, her hair swirled out in a trail of glowing yellow. Even from behind she was stunning.

"Guess what?" I said, playing my trump card early. "I got the Fire-Diamond's V badge." I pulled it from my shirt pocket and held it up under my chin. She leaned across the table appearing two feet away from my face.

"Fantastic, you are so clever." Her face ignited with a smile. After rolling it between her fingers for a moment, she handed it back to me and sprang back to the kitchen. (*Yep, seen that!*)

"I'm sure you'll hear all the gruesome details later on," I said prophetically. She took no notice. "Do you need a hand Faye? Is there anything you want me to do?"

"No Fenrir, I'm fine." She continued preparing the tea, darting back and forth happily between the kettle and a delicate array of unusual bone-china crockery.

"I didn't know the procedure would be so complicated."

"Oh, it's not Fenrir, it's so much fun and I really love tea."

"Is that what you folks drink up in Norway? I thought you mostly drank coffee." I had no idea at all. She didn't answer but soon sat down opposite, carrying a little wooden tray. I watched fascinated as she carefully laid it all out in front of me and methodically went through a whole set of pre-tea-drinking rituals.

"Aren't they cute?"

"What?"

"The little china cups, silly."

"Ugh, yeah, I guess." I never really thought of teacups as being cute. For me, the word only applied to small, fluffy gopher like critters, but whatever.

"Do you like chocolate biscuits? I have a whole unopened packet." She winked and wiggled her eyebrows.

"Oooh yeah, I love them."

The tea ceremony was a hoot. All that twisting of the pot and the pouring through a strainer, the delicate little sips, and the obligatory lifting of my pinkie. Not to mention the frick'n saucers. It was something else I tell ya. Once I'd found the optimum level of milk and dropped in these dice-like cubes of sugar the tea tasted pretty damn good.

"How's your leg?" I asked Faye, taking a sip.

"My knee?"

"Yeah, sorry I thought it was your leg."

"It's much better, thank you. I was really worried, I thought it was going to hurt for ages, but it was pretty much fine when I got up this morning. I was so glad."

"Oh Good. So now then Faye, what the hell are you doing out here in the Mexican desert with the feds on your tail?" I thought it might be a good time to cut to the chase.

"Who me?" She said in a good-humored pretense of denial. "It's a long story Wolf, but that's partly why you're here. I really have to tell someone."

"What about Joe, aren't you and him *Mad Hatter* and *The Ice Maiden*?"

Faye started laughing. "Who told you that?"

"I have my sources."

She rested her chin on the palm of her hand and strummed her teeth with her fingernails.

"You're funny, Juha Väinämöinen."

"That's the second time you've called me that. Who is it?"

"Oh Fenrir, he's brilliant, he's the lead guitarist in the Helsinki Quiff Lords. *You* should know that," she said poking at my drooping Atlantic mackerel again.

"More tea please Faye," I said, ready for a top-up. "So, how'd you manage to score this fab little trailer then Faye? Joe must think pretty damn highly of you. It's better than his place."

She flipped her hand dismissively towards me. "Joe has been wonderful to me Fenrir. He's such an old 'swear bear' but I love him to bits."

I laughed out loud, I'd never heard that expression before.

"*Fuck, fuck, fuck, fuck!* I love how he tries so hard to not use any profanities around me but always blows it, he's great!"

I decided to push my luck hard on the questions I still wanted answers to. "So, tell me about the connection between Ice Maiden and Agent Martindale, I'm still in the dark about that. And what's with all these feathers, the devil monsters and all that fuss about your suitcase? And this old sackcloth-dolly here?" I said jabbing it with my finger.

"Oh, leave Gersemi alone. You're such an old bully."

Faye put her elbows on the table, framing her face in her hands. After a long pause she asked, "Have you ever heard of Hvalrossøya?"

"Nope, can't say I have."

"Well it's an island roughly halfway between the most northerly part of the Norwegian mainland and the North Pole. There's an international seed repository located there; it's called IFD Hvalrossøya. It holds an extremely precious inventory of over two million agricultural seed samples from all across the world."

"What's it for?"

"It's been built as a kind of deep-freeze-ark, to act as a gene-bank to preserve the planet's biodiversity. In case of some calamitous man-made accident or natural disaster."

"What if a plane crashes into it or it catches fire?"

"Well it's been tunneled three hundred meters straight into the side of a mountain. All you can see on the surface is a gigantic metal door sticking out at the end. I think it's pretty safe."

"What about it?"

"It's where I used to work, well not there exactly, but it was the reason for my job on the mainland. I was a biochemist at the new laboratory in Tromsø. I worked within a team of scientists who processed and catalogued all of the deposits before they went off to IFD Hvalrossøya."

"So, you really are a doctor. Wow! I didn't think you were old enough."

"*Well shucks I ain't no dumb-ass, I'm a real clever girl Mr. Wolfmaaaaan!*" She said it in a perfect southern belle drawl. Faye scored a high-five with that one.

"So is Tromslow up in the northern part of Norway too?"

"Yes, it's on an island called Tromsøya, we're some three hundred and fifty kilometers inside the arctic circle."

I immediately thought dark choppy waters, icebergs and millions and millions of penguins. "What's that in miles?"

"*Oooh,* about two hundred and twenty I think, roughly."

"*God,* it must be *fu' freezing.* How many people live there?"

"Around seventy odd thousand I think.'

"*Geesh,* I thought you were gonna' say around a couple o' dozen."

"No, it's one of the larger cities in Norway."

"Isn't it dark up there all year round?"

"Only in mid-winter, but the good thing is, it never gets completely dark at all between April and mid-August. Tromsø is also a perfect placed to see the Northern Lights, they are just *so* beautiful."

"I should imagine that the Sonoran Desert makes a pretty big change from all the cold and darkness then ... *Ice Maiden*?" She took my question as rhetorical and didn't take the bait to answer. "So why did you leave and come all the way down here?"

"I had to run away."

"Run away. Why?"

Faye paused for a second, as if deciding whether or not to blab out the whole story, once and for all.

"I stole something."

"Go on." I was starting to enjoy this.

"Just some seeds."

I was expecting something more spectacular than seeds.

"Yes, I know it sounds boring, but there's a lot more to it than that."

"How so?"

"Well, for over two years I'd been involved with an online forum that covered a diverse range of subjects that I was interested in and a whole lot more. It was such an intelligent, well informed group and yes, during those long winter months their posts and online discussions kept me really enthralled."

"Mad Hatter being one, obviously."

"Yes, Mad Hatter, Menhir, Frau-Holle, Black-Bear, Eugenicus ... lots more."

"*Eugenicus!* that's gotta be Eugene."

"Yep," she giggled, pleased I'd guessed the connection.

"So, what the hell were you all into that made you wanna swipe seeds?" No answer.

"They were all so informative, there was so much incredible information being shared and discussed."

"Like what?"

"*Everything.* Ley lines, megalithic sites, Ásatrú and the runes, earth changes, mythology and ancient civilizations, archeoastronomy, astrotheology, extraterrestrials and UFOs, *all kinds* of esoteric subjects. It was great. I had found a really smart and diverse group of people who shared in all of my interests. I've always loved that kind of stuff, my knowledge and understanding of it all kept on growing day by day. It was just so liberating and enjoyable for me. Except for maybe one or two others, nobody I knew back in Norway had any interest in things like that. Most of my friends have handed themselves over willingly to the mindless, groupthink collective. They feel they've been victimized when they can't buy their favorite lip gloss anymore."

"I heard all you Scandinavians just stayed indoors during the long dark winters indulging in gratuitous free for all s—" She snapped those eyes towards me and glared with a powerful intensity. I just shut up dead.

"*No* Fenrir, you're such an idiot. We don't wear horned-plastic-helmets or skip around with baskets full of *Fjordie-Nordie* soap suds either. We don't all grin stupidly and say 'Yah!' every two seconds and although you'll probably find this very hard to believe, everyone from Scandinavia isn't called Helga, Björn or Anni-Frid either."

"I'm sorry Faye, I'm just a dumb-ass red-neck. You know, raised up on cheese-balls and burgers and American prime-time TV." I was capitulating shamelessly and sucking up *big time.*

"*Hmm.*" She squinted at me slightly pissed. But I knew I'd been forgiven. I thought I'd try and keep the ball rolling.

"So, did you take those seeds for one of your online friends then?"

"No not for any one person, but yes it was because of disturbing information I had found out from my contact with them."

"Please elaborate." I dunked a chocolate biscuit into my tea and took a tasty bite.

"Well even before I got involved with the online forum, I was naturally, because of my job, well aware of the detrimental effects that genetic mutations and hybrid crops were having on the entire biodiversity of the planet's ecosystems and its agricultural food production, especially the devastating toll it was taking on established traditional organic farming. Combine that with unseasonal weather anomalies—"

I was losing the thread, she could see my eyes glazing over, so she pulled up quickly.

"Am I talking too fast, I thought you were following me?"

"Oh yeah, I was, but you lost me a bit back there. What happened with the seeds then? What sort of seeds were they?" I thought a tactical change back to our original train of conversation would be a prudent move about now.

"Well in the chatroom, Mad Hatter had often brought up how many species of indigenous crops in rural Mexico were slowly disappearing and that in the last year or two some had died out completely. Especially some of the more exotic varieties of Zea Mays, which is a staple food crop and what people in this part of the world eat every day."

"What's *Zea Mays*?" I asked in all ignorance.

"Maize, corn, flour, bread … tortillas."

"Oh."

Faye went on, "I don't know whether it was pure coincidence or something much more synchronistic, but some of those exact same varieties of Zea Mays that we had been discussing online were amongst a consignment batch of maize kernels that had recently arrived at my laboratory in Tromsø. It was my responsibility to sort, test, prepare and make detailed inventories of all requisitioned seed strain batches that were heading off to the repository at Hvalrossøya. Unbelievably, the people I worked for in Tromsø knew nothing at all about the crop seed problems down here in Mexico. Nothing. Well, that was what they told me anyway. But I continued to question them about it and pursued my own enquiries for more peer review evidence that would convince them, but I got nowhere. They told me that I shouldn't believe all of this unsubstantiated garbage-science that I'd been reading on the internet. My god, I was their resident deputy biochemist after all, but they just treated me like I was totally crazy. By this time, I'd had enough, I'd been seriously thinking of leaving Tromsø anyway, even before all of this stuff started happening."

My head was nodding away in agreement, Faye was really on a roll.

"Talking to all these people on the forum had made me 'itchy feet', I really wanted to do some more travelling. To tell you the truth Wolf, I think I was bored to death with biochemistry, I had found other interests I wanted to pursue. I was still only twenty-four and I really don't think my heart was in it anymore."

"So, what happened then?"

"Well, for untrained amateurs Mad Hatter and Teosinte, another member of Joe's group down here, were just so well informed and between the two of them they sent me irrefutable photographic evidence of failed food crops, as well as leaked documents from the agricultural department. So much on-the-spot proof and convincing information. They even sent me a copy of a page from a school exercise book belonging to a little boy who had written that his parents had been forced to sell their farm because their maize crops had died out and never grew back at all the next season. He had little crayon drawings of himself and his little baby sisters too. It was so sad, it made me cry. Unfortunately, my so-called expert colleagues in Tromsø persisted with their denial that anything untoward was happening in Central America, they just rolled their eyes condescendingly whenever I mentioned the subject. I knew something definitely wasn't right and I became very suspicious and resentful. Eventually I was summoned, along with my boss, to the Facility Director's office and told bluntly that I should *'Desist with my unsubstantiated allegations'* or face immediate disciplinary action. I was so furious! After that I was determined to help out as best I could with the Zea Mays problem down here in Mexico despite the trouble I might get into."

"So that's when you took the maize seeds?"

"I made a conscious decision to never ever mention the subject again and to smuggle out a handful or two of the precious seeds every day. There were always more than what finally got sent off to IFD Hvalrossøya. It was a piece of cake to misappropriate the excess. Anything surplus to requirements were routinely destroyed anyway, so it wasn't stealing really. Within a week or two I had collected enough to send on down to Mexico. I called it *'Operation Yam-Kaax.'* After the corn god of the Maya."

"How did you get them out of there?"

"Never you mind."

"Well how did you get them down here to Sonora then?"

Faye glanced to her left for a microsecond as if to give me a clue.

"*No!*" I got it immediately. "You smuggled them here inside Gersemi?"

"Yes." She said flatly. I just loved her dry Nordic accent.

"Four different types of Zea Mays seed. Nine hundred and sixty grams in total."

"But we only found her a week or so ago, Gersemi I mean?"

"Yes Fenrir, that's why it was so urgent for me to get her back and get the seeds out quickly to Joe and Teosinte's farming contacts."

"So *that's* why you're down here and why Martindale's trying to find you!"

"Possibly…partly." She had finally admitted something on the subject, cryptic as it was. "There's *much* more to the story Fenrir but—" Faye pulled up mid-sentence again.

"Like what?"

She didn't reply for ages but stared at me deep in thought. "A man."

Oh of course, *a man!* A frickin, fuckin' man! It's always a man. I felt a rush of irritation and unjustified jealousy.

"Don't tell me, he's one of those guys, *whatever* he does, you just always—"

"No Wolf, it's nothing like you could ever *possibly* imagine."

I really had the shits now, I settled back, pretending uncomfortably to be mildly interested in the full unloading of Faye's entire boo-hoo, double-barreled sob story. Yeah, tell me everything woman. I'm just a big, stupid shoulder waiting like a giant-sized tool for you to do all your lovey-dovey crying onto.

"He is *evil* Fenrir; he is someone who has haunted me my entire life…even now."

Mildly promising, but brace yourself boy, for the whole *"But I just luv him!"* The old *"He's such a really misunderstood bad-boy"* spiel was about to commence. Dumb-ass Wolfman just sat looking across the table towards her, waiting all passive and accommodating for whatever chick-flick schmaltz was coming up next.

"I was *promised* to him Wolf. By my father." Her expression and mood changed to one of undeniable grief and foreboding.

"*What?* He can't do that, you come from Norway, that sort of thing only happens in those tribal, third-world places, you know, way out there in the sticks." I had no idea what I was even talking about.

"I know it's not what we'd normally call strictly legal or anything, but my father is involved in circles that you really don't want to know about. We all live our lives doing ordinary things. You know, going to work, cooking dinner, meeting up with friends and having fun. All of the everyday stuff people do. But then there's the sub-rosa world of shadowy fraternities that the vast majority of people don't even know exist. He's part of that world. They both are."

"Holy Jesus!" Once again, I realized my retort was woefully inadequate. "What's this guy's name and how come he thinks you should be *promised* to him?"

"His name is Mimas and he is much, *much* older than my father. He is multi-centennial. Although at the same time he takes on the appearance of a man in his mid-thirties, he always appears to be in his thirties ... he *never* ages."

I just stared at her gobsmacked. This wasn't following the script of the broken-hearted love saga that I'd been expecting at all. *"Far out!* So what is this guy, a frick'n demonic mage or something?"

With a tiny, fleeting glint of real self-pity, Faye looked intently up towards me. "I wish."

Somehow, I knew she wasn't reeling me in with a *"Ha-ha, tricked you"* joke. I could see, deep in her eyes that she believed one hundred percent in what she was telling me. I honestly didn't know what to make of it all.

"So why does this Mimas dude think he can make your old man promise you to him?"

"He out-ranks him, simple as that. He's further up the ladder or deeper down the hole of darkness, whichever way you want to look at it. Mimas is the one with the power to call all the shots. My father, despite his own delusions of grandeur and self-importance, is nothing but an expendable little minnow within their fraternity. A low-ranking gofer who was seduced by the riches and illusions of power to do the bidding of his masters. He's nothing more than a jumped-up servant for the harbingers of darkness ... *I hate him!"*

Man, this was gettin' pretty heavy. "So, what does your father *do* anyway?"

"He's a diplomatic attaché with an autonomous, international organization, whatever that means. He has never truthfully told me who he *really* works for. Never."

"Sounds like a government spook to me. Maybe he's involved with one of them secret societies. All those conspiracy theorists believe big time in how they're in league with those little grey saucer dudes."

Faye stared at me coldly with an expression of contempt. "Please don't make ridiculous comments like that Wolf, you have absolutely no idea about such things. It belittles you and makes you sound like a fool. You know Jack's shit about anything like that whatsoever."

"It's *jack* shit, not Jack's shit."

"What?"

"Nothing." I wasn't exactly sure what I'd said, but I could tell by her glare she was annoyed. "How often do you ever see this Mimas guy? Besides it's a bit of a limp-sounding name don't you think?"

"I've only ever seen him three times in my whole life."

"Three. Doesn't sound like he's that much of a nuisance then."

"I saw him first when I was only four, my parents, or should I say my father, often entertained guests late into the night at our house back in Oslo. One night they were making a lot of noise and it woke me up. I got out of bed and crept along the landing to the top of the stairs. I lay flat out on the carpet and looked down between the rails into the living room below. I thought no one could see me watching the pretty ladies in beautiful dresses and the old men in suits. I glanced at this younger man talking to an elderly woman when suddenly he jolted his head up and glared straight at me. I swear, I *swear* to this very day that for just a fraction of a second his eyes turned into those of a monster. I jumped up and ran terrified back to my bed."

"*A monster?* You were only little, don't forget."

"Oh, I didn't forget, the memory is as vivid now as when it happened."

"What sort of eyes?"

"Yellow and frightning like a crocodile. For years, I called him *the scary man.*"

Immediately I got another chill, as more pieces of the puzzle fell lopsidedly into place. Joe's twilight zone moment in the Mastodon caves, all that weird stuff up on his walls, earthquakes, unexplained battles with devil creatures and now this. My poor old normalcy meter was sittin' on empty.

"So, do you think it's this Mimas guy and not the whole Hvalrossøya thing that's got all the feds out there looking for you?"

"I'd be very surprised if he isn't involved in it somewhere, either way, Mimas will eventually track me down, when he feels the time is right. I'm only trying to make it as difficult as possible for him."

"So what happened the other times you saw him?"

"I saw him only briefly one afternoon, when I was walking home from the shops. He was sitting in the back of a limousine with the window wound down so he could see me. I remember how frightened I felt as his vehicle crawled slowly along the curb, right beside me. I can still feel those horrid, piercing eyes. He didn't say one single word, he just sat there in silence…*watching.*"

She didn't elaborate further, but I could see she was holding back and becoming more agitated and upset as she relived the event in her mind.

"The last time I saw him was when I was eighteen, *that* was the creepiest, it was only for a minute or so, he caught me completely un-awares as I cut through the sculpture gardens in Oslo. The park is very large and covers many acres. Inside the grounds there are many strange and unusual granite sculptures. Since I was a little girl, if ever I went there with school, or walked through the park with my mor, whenever I looked at them, they all seemed very scary, they *always* gave me the willies. He was waiting for me beneath the sculpture of a frightening creature embracing a seemingly reluctant young girl from behind. I disliked that one especially...but that's where he was, that's where he had planned to surprise me. I remember stopping dead in my tracks with fear, he had such a foreboding presence. I can still remember feeling chilled to my core."

"What did he say to you?"

She stared straight ahead at the empty seat beside me, she really looked petrified. "Not much. *'You are looking well my Freya. Remember, you will be mine and it will be time for us to depart, when next we meet.'* Something like that, I've tried so hard to block it from my memory."

I seriously didn't know what to say.

"Why *Freya*? Is that your real name?"

"Yes."

"Depart for where?"

"Mars."

I very nearly burst out laughing, but the expression on that lovely face of hers made me say nothing.

"Why did you not laugh then, Fenrir? I know you wanted to."

"Well I'm sure you wouldn't say something like that if you didn't have a very good reason." I lied pathetically.

"I'm glad, you've passed your first little test," she said, changing her mood a little and breaking out in a reserved half-smile. "Yes, I'm glad Mr. Wolf, thank you. I will tell you more someday soon, but for now maybe you should keep all of this little conversation to yourself...*please*. Is that okay?"

"Sure, no sweat." I shrugged my shoulders and pulled the face of compliance. "Well tell me more about the doll and how you managed to get it all the way here."

"Gersemi belonged to my grandmother, my great-grandmother made it for her from an old piece of potato sack during the second world war. That's the real reason why she is so precious to me, not the Zea Mays seeds, that was only the side event.

"My grandmother and her mor lived in a small village just outside of Steinau on the River Oder in Silesia, Eastern Germany. She was only six when the Russians finally came. She and my great-grandmother fled westward towards Berlin in early 1945, just a few days ahead of General Konev's 1st Ukrainian front. The little brown suitcase was hers too, that's why they both mean so much to me."

"So, your part German then?"

"Whatever gave you that idea Fenrir?" Another one of my more obvious "shootin' from the lip" ridiculous statements.

"So where was your grandfather, no sorry, your *great*-grandfather then?"

"He was missing, swallowed up by the Wehrmacht. The family had no word from him once he was sent off to Stalingrad in 1942. Nothing was ever heard of him again."

"I'm sorry Faye," I said as if it would make any difference. "What happened to your grandmas?"

"They both survived the battle for Berlin. When the war ended, my great-grandmother saw out the rest of 1945 and '46 as a trümmerfrau, a rubble woman, she was one of thousands of civilians ordered by the allies to work on the postwar cleanup of the ruined cities across Germany. After that she lived out her life in East Berlin in what became the DDR, the Deutsche Demokratische Republik. The same with my grandmother, although she was totally absorbed into the Young Pioneers and later the FDJ, the *Freie Deutsche Jugend*.

"When my own mother was born, she was indoctrinated into their brainwashing youth regimes as a child as well. But she went 'over the wall' when she was only seventeen, with Gersemi and the small brown suitcase. Well, actually she went through it. My father, the *diplomatic attaché*, saw her, pursued her, and stole her away to the West, for no other reason than her incredible beauty. He dwelt above all of that East versus West propaganda. My mor died in Oslo, of a broken heart, not long after the psychopathic bastard abandoned and discarded her for a younger, fresher model. She really *did* love him Wolf, although I have absolutely no idea why. He really is a swine." She just sat, deep in reflection, her thoughts at one with her dear departed mother.

"Anyway … would you care for a *real* drink Fenrir? Let's have a tequila!"

"What about Joe's rule number two?"

"Yes, I know, but he won't find out, will he? Anyway, he said no drunkenness, he didn't say anything about having one *iddy-biddy* little drink, now did he Mr. Wolfie?"

She giggled and jumped out from the table to go and fetch it.

"Only one, maybe two shots each Fenrir. We both have busy days tomorrow, so we can't risk getting blot-holed."

"Blottoed."

"What?"

"Nothing."

She returned with two little shot glasses and a local brand bottle of the good stuff.

"Where's the salt and lemon?" genuinely surprised she didn't have them on tap.

"Don't be silly, Fenrir." She quickly poured out two full shots.

"Skál!" Faye threw hers back, before I'd even had time to react.

"Skál!" I followed suit and did likewise.

"Aaaaaaaaaaaah! That was *good,"* Faye said excitedly, bursting back into life.

"So, now I know your little secret am I supposed to call you Faye or Freya?"

"No don't let on I told you that either please Wolf... not yet anyway."

"I promise I'll say nothing. But only if you tell me about your tattoo."

"Don't be silly Fenrir, I don't have a tattoo."

"Yes, you do ... the one down there on your lower back, just above your bum."

"I don't have a tattoo. Why do you say that?"

"You'd better go and have a look then. I saw it this morning at Joe's meeting when you lent forward. It's a circle, about the size of one of these saucers with a cross in the middle."

She sat looking at me, trying to figure out why I was so adamant about carrying on with an obviously pointless joke. Suddenly she burst out of her seat knocking one of the cute looking tea cups over in the process, turned back around to make sure it was undamaged, then tore off again like a wild one down towards her bathroom in search of a mirror.

A high-pitched scream radiated like a shockwave from the far end of the trailer. Faye came bounding back and stood dressed only in an armless top and a skimpy pair of black undies.

"It's a *tattoo* Fenrir, ... but I don't have a tattoo."

"Well you do now, maybe some sneaky little bastard snuck in during the night and drew it while you were asleep," I said trying to be funny.

She just stood there twisting and wriggling about, trying to get a proper look at the thing. Her near naked, bouncy little ass was almost right there in my face. Don't get me wrong, I wasn't complaining none, but *frick'n hell.*

"Do you know what this symbol is Fenrir?"

"Nope, I wouldn't have a—"

"It's a sun wheel. It's one of the most ancient symbols on Earth and goes all the way back to prehistoric times."

"*Obviously*, if it represents the Sun," I said, sounding incredibly scholarly.

"It's the sacred circle, the four equal lines point north, south, east and west to the ancient spirit world, they also represent the elements of earth, water, wind and fire."

"Where does it come from?"

"All over. It's found across Europe, the Nordic countries, the Mediterranean, it was even part of the native American medicine wheel rituals. It was used by pagan societies for transmitting the energies of the goddess and—" She stopped dead mid-sentence. *"Oh fuck!"*

I was shocked, apart from imitating Joe I'd never heard Faye use the F-word before. With that she dived across the table sending the tequila bottle flying. She grabbed the fancy doll and started pulling frantically at its clothing.

"What's that one's name?" I asked, but I was more curious to know why it needed such urgent attention.

"This is Hnoss."

"That's a dumb name for a doll," I said without thinking.

"Be quiet, Hnoss is just as important as Gersemi…they're sisters," said Faye removing the doll's blue, velvet coat and laying it out flat on the table. Hnoss sat by patiently watching.

The coat was lined in sky-blue silk with a hand-stitched seam down the middle. Faye soon unraveled the stitching and opened the silk lining to reveal fine embroidery worked meticulously onto the inside back of the coat. It was the sun wheel and some kind of Nordic writing. The symbol was exactly like Faye's tattoo.

"She was given to me by my other grandmother, on my father's side," said Faye "and I discovered this when I was a little girl and accidentally ripped the stitching open while I was playing. See these little pieces of amber?"

I leaned forward to take a closer look. Around the circle and along the arms of the cross were match-head-sized pieces of amber, all set carefully into tiny rings of burnished gold.

"I must have counted them a thousand times when I was a child, I couldn't read the runes until I was much older, but I could always remember how many little stones there were."

"How many?" I asked curiously. I kept losing count.

"Twenty-five. *Twenty-five!* Now I see it, now it's starting to make some kind of sense."

"What does? Twenty-five pieces of amber? What's that mean Faye?"

I leaned forward again to examine the delicately stitched silver characters that ran in a perfect circle around the sun wheel.

"I could read the runes when I was about twelve, but they didn't really mean anything to me back then."

"So, what the hell does it say then?"

Faye picked up the tequila, pulled out the cork and took a good hearty belt straight from the bottle.

"*Aaaaaaaaaaaaaaah!* That was even better."

She looked quickly once more at the runes and then cast her eyes straight at mine.

"*AT THE RISING OF THE HIDDEN SUN, BE READY FREYA, YOUR TIME HAS NOW COME.*"

"Far out ... what time?"

"Oh, Fenrir you can't be that stupid, the rising of the hidden sun, the tattoo, the twenty-five stones!"

"So, what does that mean?" I was failing badly at connecting all the dots. No pun intended.

"That's what they represent Wolf, years. I never knew what it all meant, 'til *your* time has *now* come', I'll be twenty-five in just a few weeks."

"Cool. But what time?"

"I don't know *exactly* Wolf, but I think I have a pretty good idea. I also have a horrible feeling that there's an even darker, hidden meaning in the message." With that she unexpectedly burst into tears and cried inconsolably.

Gutteka appeared out of nowhere to comfort his distressed mistress. I poured myself another shot and threw it down as discreetly as possible. The large grey cat rubbed up against Faye as he sat beside her, while still keeping a wary eye trained upon me. I could easily hear his low rumble growl, which in cat talk sounded pretty damn punchy.

While we were having our staring competition, the silky swathe of Jenteka's fur slithered between my boots beneath the table, before she popped up next to Faye and pummeled both her paws into the distraught girl's lap to show her affection.

I just sat there, unable to do or say anything.

"I'm sorry Wolf," said Faye finally, wiping her eyes. "I think I've known this was coming for most of my life. My Norwegian grandmother would say strange things to me when I was a little girl. I always thought she was a bit dotty. She would often call me names like The Great Dis. I had no idea what that meant. When I was about thirteen, I began to feel an imperceptible strangeness building up ever so gradually. Over the past few years, I've tried to ignore it and pretend it wasn't happening, but deep down I just knew it was really true. It was my calling, my destiny."

She could see I was totally confused.

"I'm being *channeled* Wolf. Possessed, taken over, whatever you want to call it. I am the predestined, physical vessel for the reincarnation of Freyja, Frøya, goddess of the Vanir, goddess of love, of beauty, war and death, the chief of the Valkyrjur, the ruler over the heavenly field of Folkvanger, where the ancient warriors slain in battle are received. The Great Dis. I'm not up to this Fenrir. I'm really, really not up to this ... I'm just *me*." With that she burst once again into tears, but this time worse than before.

This was all getting pretty frick'n weird to say the least. I thought maybe it was time to take my leave, so I stood up cautiously to avoid the wrath of the cats and made a half-assed attempt to say a thankful goodbye.

"I think I'd better get going now Faye, thank you for the tea and everything it was great." Faye's eruption of tears had now calmed.

"No Wolf, please don't go yet. I'm sorry, I'm a little overwhelmed by all of this. I know I'm behaving pretty silly, please forgive me. Let's have some more tea, I promise I won't cry anymore. Stay a little longer."

Well, what man could refuse a half-naked goddess pleading with him to stay.

I sat my sorry ass down and continued right on with the evening. The second round of tea was the same as the first, but for some reason it tasted a whole lot better. Faye was still a bit skittish after her "epiphany episode", so I made like nothing had happened in the strangeness department and carried on exactly where I'd left off.

"Have another belt o' the good stuff Faye. You look like you need it, one more's not gonna hurt you!"

"No Fenrir, I think I'll just stick with the tea."

"So why the hell are you being possessed by this goddess anyway?"

"I don't really know," sighed Faye. "Although I'm sure it is all for the good. When I was young, my grandmother would tell me all kinds of stories about Freya and the Vanir, but I thought they were only fanciful legends from the olden days. When she said my destiny was bound up with Freya as a war goddess, I tuned right out. I didn't want to believe those stories had anything at all to do with me. I was only a little girl and it was only the love and beauty side I wanted to hear about, especially the beauty.

"I was a haughty little brat, I really loved myself to death and thought I was totally shit-hot. I got everything she told me *completely*, how you say? Ass-about-face." She smiled in reminiscence.

"How's this? When I was about seven or eight, I was such a little bitch. I told all of the boys at school that I was *THE* Freya. There were two other Freyas in my year, but that didn't matter, and that I was so beautiful because Óðinn, the king of the gods had sent me down to the surface world to be their goddess and queen. And that they should all be ten-times nicer to me than any of the other girls … even Solveig. The amazing thing was they believed it. The boys made cardboard shields and helmets and followed me around the playground like my own private Viking bodyguard. They would form a semi-circle around me while I sat and ate my lunch. Amazing! It all came to a head one day when Håkon Drogsvold brought his father's replica battle axe into school. The teachers put an end to it, quick smart after that. The other girls totally hated me, it took ages to smooth things over and get things back to normal. I was dreadful."

I laughed long and loud. God, she was lovely. "So how did your grandmother know about all these things that were going to happen?"

"My bestemor was, is, a Seiðkonur, a shaman, a practitioner of the Seiðr, the old Norse Magick, so was her mor, and her mor before that. She told me that I was her one true progeny, her Neste i linjen. She would always tell me that. *'My Freya, you are the one true descendent of our line, your brother is good and true, but you are the one amongst us who is … special, my Neste i linjen'*. So, you can see why I was such a little cow. My brother Axel thought she was totally crazy but would always treat her very kindly."

"What about your dad?"

"She completely disowned him. My grandmother was horrified and distraught that his soul had chosen to cross over from the light and find kinship with the legions of darkness. I remember her saying that over and over again."

Pouring the last few drops of the tea into my cup, I'd forgotten to use the strainer, so I got nothing but a massive great dollop of tea leaves.

"I've only just realized Wolf; you've told me nothing about yourself. It's all been about *me! me! me!* I am sorry."

"Ah, forget it. I *hate* talking about me, besides there's Jack's shit worth knowing anyway, but there's just one more thing I want to ask you Faye—"

"What's that Fenrir?"

"Yesterday…that did really happen, didn't it? I mean the fight with the monsters and everything. If it did, I'm *absolutely* sure I saw those two cats on your lap turn into fully grown mountain lions, but that's impossible. Isn't it?"

"I was wondering if you'd seen that. Did you notice they didn't appear on Joe's screen at the meeting?"

"Yeah I did. I thought I was tripping out on the sulfur fumes or something and imagined the whole frick'n thing. I didn't bring it up, just in case."

"It's the Seiðkonur Fenrir, she's here and she's weaving her Magick."

"Wow!"

"Oh, that reminds me, I completely forgot," Faye said excitedly, "I have a little gift for you." Faye leaned across and grabbed something hidden on the shelf behind the candle. "Hold out your hand."

She gave me a quick kiss on the cheek and put something small, round and silver, smack in the middle of my palm. It was a quarter-sized dome of tinfoil.

"*Uh*…thanks."

I had the sudden notion it might have been a small block of hash or a wrap of marching powder, but my premature elation dropped off to zero when I realized it was neither, it was exactly what it looked like, a piece o' frick'n tinfoil.

"What the hell is that?"

"Well, after considering everything that you've put up with and gone through in the short time that you've been here. And taking into account all of the help that you have kindly given us, and not forgetting the fact that we think that you are a very nice guy as well, Joe and I have decided that you are now – providing that you're not about to leave tomorrow – a fully-fledged member of the infamous *Tinfoil Sombreros!*"

"Oh yeah, it is a sombrero. Thank you, Faye, that's really, *really* nice of you. Thank you." I didn't quite know what to say, I was never one for getting too excited or emotional, but believe me, her words of friendship sure meant a hell of a lot to me. And that little piece of shiny tinfoil suddenly grew in stature, trumping the Fire Diamond's V badge away into *"ah who cares"* oblivion. Getting it from Faye, I mean Freya, the goddess of love and beauty … well, I was stoked.

I soon took my leave, and with my tinfoil sombrero cupped carefully in my hand, floated back home to the camper.

15

Hildisvíni

As the dull red glow from the predawn sun turned to gold behind heavy winter clouds, I watched a little robin as it hopped around outside on the snow-covered window ledge, looking for scraps to eat.

I thought I sensed the presence of Brother Darius creeping silently up behind me and I quickly adjusted my gaze back to my work. Two gentle taps on the back of my head from a finger confirmed my suspicions.

"Pay more attention to your descenders Brother Wolfgang, keep them all even. That feeble scratching looks more like the work of the devil," scolded the old monk as he scrutinized my calligraphy. "You will never progress to falcon feathers if that's how you treat a poor old goose nib brother … *tut, tut, tut.*"

I had only become aware of the coldness in the priory kitchen since his arrival. The dying embers in the hearth had been left unattended during the long, dark hours of the night, as I toiled away, fixated in the effort to improve my clumsy, novice writing skills.

As Brother Darius turned away to leave, shaking his head in feigned displeasure. The loud, urgent toll from the bell in the rectory tower shattered the early morning stillness. It's untimely clanging could only mean one dreaded thing.

"Quickly Brother Wolfgang," barked Darius. "Pick up the books and hide them inside your tunic. We must leave now! Rovers are descending from the north, there is no time to dally, they will be here in only minutes."

We rushed outside to make our escape and were swept up amidst a gaggle of panic-stricken monks, carrying their last-minute-grabs of books and precious objects bundled hastily into sacks and wraps of old cloth. Tripping and stumbling, we ran westward, ungainly in the knee-high blanket of freshly fallen snow.

"Look! Up there," cried Brother Michael, lagging a dozen paces behind the rest of us. *"They are upon us!"* His free hand trembled wildly as he pointed up towards the sky. With a terrified shriek he was crushed deep into the icy ground by the most forward of the descending longboats. Behind it, three more of the massive, cloud-sailing vessels had dropped down upon us from the high-blue-yonder. Within moments the heavily armed Norsemen had piled out from their craft ready to unleash their pillage and terror on us poor, defenseless brothers.

Fueled with foreboding, I ran. And ran. And ran. I dared not stop until I was certain I was well out of danger. Slowing to take in some urgently needed breath, I was surprised to find that none of the others were with me. I looked back in horror to see them far off in the distance, bound together as captives of the marauding sky-lords. Thankfully, none had been maimed or brutalized. Instead they'd been stripped down to their undergarments and sent off into the snow in a full-stretch, high-kickin' conga line, much to the amusement of the hard-laughing Norsemen.

I paused for a moment longer and adjusted the downward slip of the books beneath my robe. Strangely everywhere in the direction I had been heading was now completely devoid of snow. In fact, the entire landscape had become a desert. Rock, dirt and sand, even the occasional cactus. This was good, now I could escape even faster. With my very first step, a heavy hand came down on my neck and stopped me dead in my tracks. A strong arm spun me around and brought me face to face with the band of fearsome Norsemen.

"Thought you could get away did you, *Saint* Wolfgang?" bellowed an angry, bug-eyed, colossus of a man. He held me in place with one hand around my throat, the other grasping the belly of a gigantic blood-axe.

"I should hack off your legs, gut you like a boar and feed your miserable entrails to the ravens!" he laughed loudly with his companions as they swiftly closed around me in a fast-forming circle of doom. How I selfishly envied the fate they had bestowed upon my brethren.

"What treasure does he hide there, concealed beneath his robe?" challenged an even angrier fellow as he lunged eagerly at what I was hiding.

"It's only a couple of books, nothing valuable. It isn't gold or anything." My voice quaked in fear.

A free-for-all grab ensued, but was interrupted when a screeching, unexpected metallic sound in the desert behind me got everyone's attention. I managed to turn my head and see what was happening. It was a car. All of its panels were covered in dust from a long-time stint in the desert, but it was unmistakably the bronzy, Baybecker Prio of agents Martindale and Travers, sitting there idling away like a rescue chariot, no more than four or five paces behind me.

The back door swung open.

"Quick, Mr. Wolf, run. Get in, get in!" motioned Martindale excitedly.

Seizing my chance, I broke free from the distracted Norseman's grip and vaulted the couple of steps to the Prio's wide open door. I jumped straight in. I was okay. The angered rovers lunged forward quickly to make their attack.

"I'm in, let's go!"

Mr. Travers, who was driving, hit the gas hard and the car hurtled off like a bullet. Only problem was, it was only the front-half of the car that was moving. The whole back seat section, the rear wheels and the trunk had snapped right off and just sat there going nowhere. I looked out ahead in surprise as the front half of the Baybecker Prio sped off amidst a plume of kicked up sand, offensive hand gestures and a spray of raucous laughter. This wasn't looking good. My seat belt had mysteriously buckled itself up and I sat there strapped fast and panicked. In unison the irate Norsemen thumped their drawn swords and axes upon their shields and moved the few remaining steps up towards me –*thunk!* –*thunk!* –*thunk!* –*thunk!*

I watched in terror as a man-mountain warrior stepped forward and slowly lifted his battle axe in what was obviously going to be my inevitable end. To my amazement as he raised it full-stretch up above his head the weapon somehow changed its shape. It had now become a massive iron hammer, square-shaped at the bottom and the size of a frick'n mini-bar fridge. It hung there in the air for what seemed an eternity. But right as the hammer began its death-dealing fall, out from behind the group of men stepped forward a more svelte figure enshrouded in a cape of white fur.

"STOP!" commanded the higher-pitched voice of a woman. "Let him be. Put down your weapon Håkon. He is not our enemy." It was Faye.

Moving quickly towards me she tossed the mantle of ermine back behind her shoulders, revealing a jerkin of shimmering samite beneath. Her arms and legs were swathed in fine, lustrous metal and upon her head sat a shining helmet of gold, adorned either side by wings of polished silver.

Thunk! –*thunk!* –*thunk!* The beating on shields continued unabated. Faye grabbed the book from my hand and turned to show it to her kin.

"You see, he's reading *Chief Iron Eyes Little Eagle* ... He's one of us!"

With that I woke up.

I lay there quietly and kept my eyes closed for a short while longer. It had been one of those rare dreams where you wake up and remember the details perfectly. Half a moment ago I was a hapless character starring in my own little freaked-out mini-drama set in some far-away land, half-full of snow and half-full of desert, about to get my head caved in by a four-hundred-pound sky-rover dude wielding a mini-bar fridge. I was kind o' glad I'd woken up when I did, it all seemed so real. The thumping of the raiders' shields turned out to be the repetitious chugging of an old water pump somewhere over on the edge of the campsite –*thunk!* –*thunk!* –*thunk!* –*thunk!*

Most of the dream had faded, except for that one unforgettable vision of Faye clad in dazzling armor that was now etched indelibly into my mind.

◆

I was up, dressed and halfway to the gas station before I'd realized how early it was. Didn't really matter, force of habit, I guess. As I got closer, I could see the silhouette of someone standing up on the garage roof, peering intently over to where Faye and Sacramento were already belting the daylights out of each other with their martial weapons. It was Hamada-san. She stood motionless, totally absorbed, following their every action.

Regular as clockwork, Joe was sitting right out front as usual, reading a book and drinking his morning brew. I could tell it was newly made, even at twenty yards, I could see the hot, steamy tendrils curling up from his favorite mug.

"*Hey,* Wolfman," Joe acknowledged my presence.

"Mornin' Joe," I replied with a nod.

"Grab yourself a cup, it's fresh. You ready to do some work today, my friend? I've locked the '58 away up top, so don't even think of doing a runner or anything stupid like that," he chuckled.

I'd noticed on the way over a pile of ten-foot star-poles and a massive coil of fencing wire, so it was obvious we had a real day's work ahead of us.

"No problem, boss. As long as I don't have to dangle over that pit again, I'll be okay."

"Good man, good man," said Joe. "*No fuckin' screaming either!*" He went apoplectic with an outburst of laughter. "I'm sorry Wolf, couldn't resist that one."

I feigned an inaudible scream and joined in too.

"Hey Wolf, we had a visit from the Sonoran Police last night, they came and retrieved the bodies of the two poor souls from the mini-bus. Took 'em back to Hermosillo in one of those new police ambulance things. It looked like a frick'n tank. They cleared the bus off the roadway too, lifted it straight up onto the back of a flat bed with an onboard crane. *Yeah.* The Mexican cops were amazing, I was dreading a whole lot of snooping around and an interrogation over the accident report, but these guys were really cool. They didn't even ask about cause of death. I picked up a few bits in Spanish between them and I figured this wasn't the only case of devil mayhem they had on their plate. I got the feeling these guys just wanted it all taken care of with as little red tape as possible, probably so they could get home and look after their own families. I do feel sorry for the two men that died. But now it's over it's one more thing off my mind anyway."

I felt terrible, to be honest. I'd hardly given it any thought at all.

◆

Joe's plan with the fence was pretty straight forward. Pacing out strides along the length of the crack, we laid out a long line of star poles positioned roughly eight feet back from the crumbling edge of the abyss. Nothing slap-dash or cowboy about it though, Joe scrutinized every last one's verticality and alignment to its immediate neighbor before giving it the final nod of approval.

We'd done pretty well. By noon, Joe and I had gone all the way along the near side and had come a few yards back towards the building on the other. Joe seemed pretty pleased and was confident that we'd have the whole thing pegged out by sunset.

"We'll get stuck into all that wiring tomorrow," Joe said optimistically.

We'd slapped ourselves down from dirt and sand and were heading back to the kitchen to get some lunch, when Charlie waved us over.

"Hey pops!" he yelled as we got close. "Come over here and take a look at this."

He'd been working out the back pulling down the remains of the old adobe shed that had copped a hammering during the earthquake. The shed was toast. Only half of the walls and the roof were still standing, but only just. The rest had collapsed completely. The heavy, central beam holding up the roof had fallen down at one end. It's only movement in over a century had blindsided an old, upright piano that had sat silent and unsuspecting beneath it. One end of the keyboard was pulverized into a mash of busted up walnut splinters and ivory. The rest of the shed was a fallen muddle of bricks and caved-in roof and whatever else Joe and the boys had been piling in there for near on a decade. Back in the real world it would have been called a hard-hat zone, but out here, that was all bullshit.

"Check this out." Charlie ducked his head under the fallen beam and moved across to the wall where two packing crates, both the size of a wardrobe had fallen over. The shaking had tumbled the furthest one onto its back and the near one lay across it at a precarious angle.

Right then, Vince lobbed himself in from the sunny outside.

"Hey, wha's up losers?"

"Well howdy there, little brother," said Charlie sarcastically. "How you doin'?"

I'd never heard Charlie talk like that before. He was winding something up.

Joe stood back quietly and checked the whole scene out, the fingers of his left hand tapping away enthusiastically to some rhythmic, inaudible tune. The ones on his right were busy squeezing a candy along its paper tunnel and all the way down to his mouth. It doesn't sound that funny, but I almost burst out laughing. I loved watching Joe, he cracked me right up. Some of the poses he could strike were absolute gems. For this one, he was the all-time Mr. Funky cowboy dude.

Joe knew his boys really well. I figured by the rascally little grin simmering away on his face, he knew something was about to go down.

"Do you remember when we found these crates and all that other stuff inside that hijacked trailer?" Charlie asked Vince.

"Yeah, they'd already grabbed all the good stuff. Greaser bandits. A crappy TV, half a box of stupid toy dogs and these two frick'n crates full of cans of pickled cow guts. *Whoopie!* I told you back then, sight unseen, it wasn't going to be worth the hassle of bringing 'em back here."

"You did check them though, didn't you?" quizzed Charlie.

"Yeah, I told you, just cans full of pickled entrails. I tried to flog 'em to the stooges over in Beverly Hills for a buck each, but *they* wouldn't even take 'em for free. *Assholes!* Maybe we should stack 'em up high and give one away for every ten bucks spent buying gas, or maybe we should just toss the whole frick'n lot down the pit as an offering to the creatures." Vince snorted self-congratulatory at his own brand of humor.

Charlie bent down and examined the hole Vince had carelessly ripped across the middle of the crate's outer plywood. The geometric pattern of the stacked metal cans highlighted the obvious few that were missing.

"So, did you even bother to have a look inside of this one?" he tapped his hand on the crate underneath.

"Nah, waste o' time," smirked Vince.

"*Hmm* ... well give me a hand moving this one out of the way and we'll have a bit of a look inside box number two, shall we?" responded Charlie unperturbed. It was patently obvious he'd found something in there and was reeling Vince in for some unexpected surprise.

Vince and Charlie heaved the first crate back upright, the momentum tipping a couple of cans onto the ground through the hole.

"*Eeeesh*, Italian offal," said Joe, picking one up. "Pickled entrails and organs. You should have taken it over to Oochie, he would have woofed half of this down by himself."

Back at crate two, Charlie bent down with his pinch bar and pretended to open up the corner. He'd obviously taken a sneak-peek inside already.

"Looks like you're right *again* little buddy, nothing in here but big old cans of pickled offal. No, hang on a minute, what's that? I think I can see something else wrapped in plastic underneath. Whatever it is, it's red."

Vince leaned across for a second to look as if he was interested as Charlie deliberately pulled out two or three more cans from the crate.

"Hey, it's got some writing on it. What's that say?" He was really trying to get Vince to nibble. "Uuum? ... 'elus? Hang on a second, let me pick some of this plastic away, 'ngelus, yeah there it is, *Angelus*. What's that then Vince?"

Vince was wising up. He didn't know exactly what was going on, but he knew he was being played.

"I dunno! Sounds like a—" I think the word rang a distant bell somewhere, but for the moment Vince drew a blank.

Charlie pulled out more of the cans tossing them theatrically back over his shoulder onto the floor of the shed.

"Look Vince, here's some more writing right alongside it, it says 'llare? Hang on, no it's *Marte-llare*. Wow! *Martellare*? I think I've found some carbon fiber side panels. Maybe there's even a whole goddamn motorcycle stashed away down here?"

Charlie plucked carefully at more of the protective plastic.

"*Phhhh*, big deal, a frick'n Euro-donkey, I'll take the gizzards thanks," answered Vince belligerently.

Pretending not to hear, Charlie picked out most of the still remaining cans and dropped them on the ground beside him.

"Look little brother, it says right here, it's a *Martellare Angelus MCLV*. Now I'm not sure, I could be totally wrong, but if my memory serves me correctly, this is a classic, Benevento-built, pedigree Italian superbike. But as I said, I could be totally wrong."

Charlie stood up and backed away from the crate. He gazed down admiringly at what he had just uncovered. Lying in its box, preserved in a swathe of thick protective packing was indeed the magnificent form of a brand new half-disassembled motorcycle. The front wheel, forks and carbon fiber nose fairing had all been taken off and placed around the outer edges of the crate for a more compact fit. Even wrapped tight in its plastic cocoon, it was a magnificent sight to behold.

"*Whoooh!*" whistled Joe, impressed. "You trying to tell me that little beauty's been laying out here in the shed for what? *Three frick'n years?*"

"Yes sir-ee!" replied Charlie grinning broadly and taking a well-orchestrated swipe at his younger brother. "Five hundred cans o' pickled offal and a *classic* Martellare superbike."

"Holy Joseph, you're an idiot, boy!" Joe bawled incredulously.

"How the hell would I know it was under there!" snapped Vince defensively, now fully aware he'd been stooged.

"But you said you'd checked it out … didn't you? Oh no that's right, it was a waste o' time."

"Piss off Charlie, you're such a know-it-all ain't ya. How come you didn't know it was stashed there then Mr. Clever-dick? And why's it got such a stupid name anyway? You can't even say it properly."

"*Marter-lah-ray An-jealous*," Charlie said in an exaggerated Italian accent. "What's so difficult about that?"

"Well what the fuck does that mean?"

"*Hammering* Angel."

"Yeah right, frick'n great name that one, why the hell would you call a motorbike *that*? Even a plastic 'I-tie' one."

"Well, the story I heard, was that when Celino Moretti fired up his prototype Martellare back in Benevento, Italy, in the thirties, it made such a hell of a racket it frightened his youngest daughter, who put her hands to her ears and said his new machine sounded like hammering. When her older sister saw the look on her father's face, she felt sorry for him and said, "No papa, it sounds like an angel." Signor Moretti laughed his head off and supposedly he joined both the words together and the Hammering Angel, The Martellare Angelus was born. Ain't that a good little story?"

"*Nuh!* Sounds like a bunch o' bullshit to me," scoffed Vince, being the total prick that he was.

Faye appeared unexpectedly amidst the uprights of the half-fallen door frames. Her tall silhouette cut a striking outline against the glaring, midday sun.

All jaws hit the ground, even Joe's, as she cautiously stepped her way over the rubble and mayhem. No exaggeration, Faye's legs looked like two shapely stove pipes in a pair of skintight, black denim jeans. She really looked amazing in her blue jeans, but these were in a frick'n league of their own. And I tell you straight up, if they were cut any lower, it would have been *truly* indecent.

"What are you all doing in here?"

Before anyone had time to answer, Faye's eyes fixed on the open crate and she gasped in surprise at seeing the motorcycle.

"*Hildisvíni!*" she yelled excitedly in what I presumed was Old Norse.

"What?" both Charlie and Joe said as one.

Faye picked her way urgently through the mess in the shed, bending gracefully like a willow as she ducked beneath the fallen beam that stood between her and the brand new Martellare Angelus. Awestruck she crouched down before it. The sun wheel tattoo on her lower back now visible for all to see.

Vince of course mumbled the obligatory, crude innuendos, whereas Charlie just looked away, put a hand across his brow and shook his head in subtle torment. Of course, Joe and I looked on with complete indifference.

Faye spread her arms out wide, slowly placing the palms of her hands down reverentially upon the Martellare's carbon fiber flanks.

"This is Hildisvíni. The war boar... Freya's battle swine!"

We all looked at each other bemused.

"What's she on about?" said Joe, cutting straight to the point.

I at least knew a *part* of the script, but remembering my promise back at the trailer, stayed mum and shrugged my shoulders just like all the rest of them.

"He's beautiful, can I have him Joe? *Please.*"

Joe stood there gawping. It was the first time I'd ever seen him speechless. Not so Vince. He just burst out laughing and went apoplectic.

"Oh yeah. *Sure*, right on, knock yourself out woman, what a frick'n hide. Can I have him Joe? *Pleeease*. Jeeesh. I've only laid eyes on it just this second but I *really, really want it!*"

"Shut up Vince," said Joe, sounding irritated. "You seriously do want it don't ya?"

"It is *Hildisvíni*," said Faye in a stolid monotone.

Joe could see the urgency in her face and that this meant something *much, much* more than some spoilt little girly whim. She wasn't like that, and the firmness of her request had really taken him aback.

"Okay darlin' it's yours."

"Thank you, Joe. Thank you!"

"*Aaah*, you've gotta' be kidding. *'Thank you Joe, thank you!'* Guess who's been stooged, big guy...*what the fuck!* What about me? What if I want the frick'n thing? I've got more right."

"Zip it, Vince, it's just a plastic donkey, you'd rather have all those cans of gizzards, remember?" Joe said defiantly.

Charlie howled with laughter. Vince just got more irate.

"Crap! That's just bullshit, and you know it. I've got ten times more claim to the thing than she has, I bet she couldn't even ride it properly anyway. Remember what she did to the softail, I'm not—"

"You bet your boots I can ride him; I could wipe the floors with you *boody-boy!*" replied Faye, getting somewhat annoyed at his petulance.

"No sweat, sister. We'll have a frick'n race to decide it then, winner takes all! Marta-fuckin'-Laree, cans o' fuckin' offal, whatever, I reckon it's..."

Vince just went *on* and *on* and was really starting to piss us off, when Charlie, who had returned to his chore of emptying out the last remaining cans, turned around to show us what else he had found buried deep down in the corner of the crate.

"Check these out." Charlie had uncovered a little stash of fancy Italian shirts, all boxed up and sporting trendy labels. "Wow, these are top drawer, designer names here boys," he said passing them back to the rest of us. "Shame none of you scumbags would appreciate them though."

There were four in total. Joe and Vince were arguing over which colors they liked the most and whether or not they would fit.

"Hoo-ee, *get some!*" blurted Charlie finding something else. He held up a grab of half-a-dozen packets of fancy-looking nylons.

"Some pervy bastard sure must have been upset; one undelivered Martellare Angelus, no trendy Italian shirts to wear to his gangster bash and his hoochi mamma's lingerie didn't get there either. *Man*, he must have been pissed." Unusual for Charlie, he started laughing again.

Faye leaned across Charlie to pick up something else from the crate. It looked from where I was standing like a bundle of belts, but when she shook it out and held it down the length of her body, it was clearly one of those sexy-looking body harness things, a crisscrossed bodice of black leather strapping all held together at the junctions by an array of little metal rings the size of silver dollars.

"I'll have this too," pronounced Faye.

"*Woo-hoo!* Someone's in for a hiding!" chuckled Joe.

Faye pulled a snarky face and turned her attention back to Hildisvíni.

"Will you put him back together for me please Charlie? I can help."

"No sweat. Be glad to. Only thing is, I promised the old man I'd get started on the—"

"Don't worry about that," interrupted Joe, anticipating what he was about to say. "The GT can wait, let's get this little red beast up and runnin' first, hey?"

"There you go. No hay problema." Charlie cracked a wry smile. He was trying to act kind o' cool, but I could tell he couldn't wait to get it out of the box and back over into the workshop. "I'm tellin' you now though, if those engine valves are out o' whack that really is a job for a Martellare specialist."

"I know that Charlie, but let's hope there's no problem and it will be okay." Faye smiled thankfully at Charlie and I could see him melt like a dropped ice cream.

"Isn't he beautiful?" Faye said excitedly. "And still lying asleep in his box. My brother had a Martellare Angelus 750. It was such a wonderful machine. This is the last incarnation of that particular model. I think it's his *grandson?*" she chuckled at her own analogy.

"Oh, it's not yours yet *doll-face!*" chimed in Vince only two clicks short of a tantrum. "16.00. Out front. *Winner takes all*, okay?"

"Okay," Faye replied, trying hard not to burst out laughing.

With that Vince stomped out of the shed like some dumb-ass, belligerent, grade-schooler.

16

It's On

Faye headed back with Joe and me to get something to eat, as Charlie had politely declined her offer to help unpack the bike. All the way over she'd been telling Joe who Hildisvíni was in Nordic mythology. How when Freya wasn't riding her chariot pulled by cats, she was gallivanting across the sky on the back of the golden bristled boar, who incidentally just happened to be made out of metal. Joe listened intently, but I think a little bemused as he couldn't see the connection between Faye, a mythological flying boar, and a red Italian Martellare Angelus MCLV superbike.

Faye still hadn't told Joe about her manifesting entwinement with the Vanir goddess Freya. I wondered whether he would really take her seriously, despite his fascination with all things esoteric. Changing the subject Joe quizzed Faye about the afternoon's scheduled race.

"You really don't have to go through with it, Faye. I told you the bike's yours."

"Oh, it's only a time trial," smiled Faye. "I've walked across the motorcycle track with Oppuam countless times. I've even run some of the way around it before training with Sacramento. It's a scaled-up version of the Indianapolis circuit but with two much-longer straights. It's really quite good, but obviously nowhere near as fast as the real one. Vince gets so worked up, he won't be able to settle and concentrate on his riding anyway. I'm sorry Joe, he's so unbelievably *childish!*"

"Concentrate!" laughed Joe. "That'd be a first."

Back in the kitchen we whipped up some cold cut sandwiches and gobbled them down in no time flat with a pitcher of lemon-flavored ice water. *Dee*-licious!

"Come on Wolfman we'd better get back to those frick'n star p—" Joe cut off mid-sentence as the dining-room door opened behind him. Once again in came Hamada-san and her granddaughter Kiko.

"Konnichiwa. Hello gentlemen, hello Miss Faye." Her cute little head was grinning profusely and bobbing up and down as she began to wind herself up again.

Joe and I nodded politely and scurried off around the corner, stuffing the last of our lunch into our faces. Faye, suddenly stranded on her own, grabbed a handy kitchen apron and tied it quickly around her waist, then walked out into the dining room, bowing politely to both of them. I guessed her thinking straight away. Such a low-cut pair of jeans might not be deemed appropriate for greeting an elderly Japanese lady.

Out of sight around the corner, Joe and I took a sly peek to see what was going on. Neither of us were in the mood for Kiko's high-octane effervescence.

"Hello Miss Faye." Kiko was shaking again with barely contained excitement. "My grandmother, Hamada-san would like to say something important to you and she would like me to aah? ... translate for her, as she does not speak any English."

Hamada-san had seated herself at a table and stared unflinchingly across the room towards Faye. "My grandmother says that she thanks you for your courageous efforts to save us from the demons, when we were both trapped inside of the minibus. She says that from her ... *perspective?* of being upper-side-down, she had a most unique view of your Zen Shin and fighting technique and your unusual abilities with the naginata." Kiko beamed a smile and nodded abruptly with self-satisfaction. Hamada-san interjected, saying something quickly to Kiko in Japanese.

"My apologies Miss Faye, my grandmother says that it is important for me to tell you that in Japan she holds the rank of *Hachidan*, the eighth level Dan in Naginatajutsu."

I heard a gasp of surprise from Faye. This was synchronicity on a double-dose of steroids. I remembered her telling me once that to get some instruction from a real life naginata sensei would be truly fantastic.

Kiko continued. "Hamada-san says that she finds you ... extremely—"

The girl turned back to her grandmother very distressed. I could hear by the tone of her voice that she was pleading with her not to have to relay to Faye what she'd been instructed to. Hamada-san barked back at the girl, slightly annoyed. I don't understand Japanese, but it was obvious what she had said. *"Don't be stupid girl, just tell her exactly what I have told you!"*

I couldn't help myself; I ducked my head back around the door to see what was going on.

"What's happening?" asked Joe.

"Faye's at the table with her back to me opposite Hamada-san, and Kiko's standing between them, bouncing around like she's got an electrode up her backside!"

"Uggh!" said Joe, satisfied with my description of the proceedings.

Kiko continued. "Hamada-san says that she finds you...extremely *unusual*...and..." The girl went through the whole protest thing again, but her objections were once more sternly rebuked by Hamada-san "...if you displayed such terrible, unorthodox techniques in one of her training sessions in Japan, she would...throw you out of her dojo!"

Kiko burst into tears and started apologizing again, carrying on like she'd just said the worst thing in all the history of mankind.

"God that kid's highly strung!" whispered Joe, up close to my ear.

Through her blubbering Kiko continued. "However...Hamada-san says that, despite your obvious lack of proper instruction and allowing for your complete, ummm, *strange* and unconventional style, she feels that you would be a match for *any* of her most accomplished students."

Kiko's face burst back into sunshine. "She says that she is completely...*baffled?*...and has never, in all of her years, seen anybody in her dojo fight anything like you. My grandmother says she is aware of your very capable abilities with the Chinese bo staff, that you have obviously studied and practiced for some time with your training partner. She is familiar with the weapon and sees that he is *very* well skilled and an obvious master of the discipline. Please Miss Faye, my grandmother would like you to explain where you, and ahhh...*him*, have learnt from such an unusual school of Naginatajutsu."

"We've been trying to teach ourselves the discipline...from a book."

Kiko translated Faye's words enthusiastically back to the sensei. Hamada-san roared with laughter. That and the sound of chair legs scraping on the wooden floor seemed reason for me to take another look. Hamada-san suddenly rose to her feet and moved towards Faye embracing her warmly in a somewhat reserved but genuine show of affection.

"She's giving Faye a *frick'n hug*," I relayed back to Joe. His eyes bulged in complete surprise.

"That kid sure is somethin' else Wolf. She *sure* is somethin' else."

Kiko was as happy as a pig in the proverbial now, her mood had changed completely.

"Hamada-san thinks that is very, very funny and...*commendable*. Now you have explained, Miss Faye, that your practice has come from a book, she can see a little more clearly how and why you have gone...I do not know the exact words in English. Is it … *completely off* the railway tracks?"

Faye laughed, the sensei laughed and Kiko went completely supernova. It seemed fairly obvious that Hamada-san was going to put Faye "back on the rails", so to speak. Joe and I had heard enough, so we slipped away unnoticed through the rear of the building and back outside to the fencing.

"Holy cow!" said Joe, completely bemused. "An eighth dan, sixty-plus, super-serious Japanese sensei. Faye the falcon and frick'n giggle-pot, clown trousers Sacramento, that's gonna be one hell of a goddamn early morning's entertainment. I just can't wait to see *that* going down. I give Sacramento about five minutes before Hamada-san boots him all the way back into Beverly for acting like he's OD-ing big time on nitrous frick'n oxide … just gotta see that!"

As we reached the back door, that infernal alarm bell started up again, but this time with a different ear-splitting ring.

"Ah hell. A Red Alert! That's all we frick'n need," blurted Joe, turning on his heels and rushing back through the kitchen to where the others were still hanging around, wondering what on earth was happening.

"Faye, take Hamada-san and Kiko down into the lab and keep them there. MacElroy too if he's there. Don't even think of leaving until I come and get you. Anyway, you know the other way out if things go pear-shaped, this one could get nasty kid. Be careful." With that he ran to the front and ushered in the guy who'd been working his shift on the driveway.

"Take young Castano here with you too. Settle down Kiko it's fine, it's fine. Go with Faye and just do as she says."

"Wolf, shut that goddamn bell off, will ya! It's the white switch next to the rocket key. Grab that too and give it to Charlie who'll be on his way in from outside. Do whatever he tells you and when you see Vince, tell him to get his ass over to the taps. Understood?"

"Roger!" I said trying to sound kind o' military.

Charlie was right where Joe said he'd be. I gave him the key and we headed off towards the motel toilets. I followed dutifully wondering what was going down and why the hell we needed the key to the frick'n bathroom.

"Come on Wolf, this one's gonna be fun."

Charlie grabbed the little key hidden above the light fitting and opened the door to the store's cupboard. He quickly pulled the cleaning trolley out of the way and swept aside a stack of toilet rolls to reveal a square metal drain in the floor. Lifting away the grill he pulled out what looked to me like a chainsaw case and a metal box, almost the size of a suitcase. He passed that one back to me and I immediately let it drop. It was incredibly heavy.

"Careful Wolfman, take it outside and wait by the door." Charlie was right behind, carrying his "chainsaw". He ran ahead and positioned himself at the far corner of the wall facing back towards the driveway. I stuck my head out for a look but felt a tug on my shirt as Charlie yanked me back out of eyeshot.

"Pull your head in fool," he said very quietly.

I felt like a fool. That short glance had shown me a lot. Eight or nine vehicles had descended on the driveway, some were at the pumps, others parked all around, wherever they wanted to. These hombres didn't look like anybody I'd seen before. They were obviously a gang or maybe something worse. From what I could hear, their accent was so unusual I wasn't even sure if they were speaking Spanish. Who are they Charlie?"

"God you're a dumbass Wolfman, they call themselves *Acciones más allá del mal*. Trust me, they come from somewhere way, way south of the Mexican border."

I was such a gringo novice when it came to the realities of living in Mexico.

"So, what are they doing up here?"

"How do I know, now shut up."

Charlie had unpacked his case and was expertly assembling the pieces stashed inside.

"What's *that* thing?" I said, forgetting again to speak in a whisper.

"It's a RODS-7d mini-gun, better known as 'The Gee-Gee'. Six rotating barrels that can pump out six thousand rounds per minute. It'll mash these groovers into a hot-spicy-purée if they take a crack at the old man. Now *please*, shut up and unclip that frick'n ammo case ... *quietly!*"

I followed Charlie's instructions and left him to do the tricky mechanical business and connect up the seemingly unending belt of ammunition that was coiled up carefully inside the metal box.

"Where did you get it?"

"Army surplus store, where else?"

"How's it work?"

"It's electric powered, but this one's hooked up to a filthy, heavy duty battery. *Anything else?*"

Charlie was flat on his stomach at forty-five degrees to the wall with the tip of his Gatling gun inching out around the corner, covering the driveway.

I was lying there flat out beside him ready to feed out the ammo belt and trying desperately to bury my head into the ground by way of my chin. I didn't know whether to feel foolishly exhilarated or just crap my pants. It could have gone either way.

"Are you really going to shoot them?"

"I'll give a short, sharp blast over their heads into the underside of the overhang first, a hundred rounds per second concrete shower ought to make 'em back off. If they wanna take it further, well we'll have to wait and see."

From where I was, and Charlie assured me we were definitely out of eyeball, I could see Joe mixing it bravely out on the driveway. I was amazed at how many of these guys dressed like good old American home boys, while some looked like skin heads and others had long, greasy hair and tattoos. They didn't seem to follow any particular pattern at all, except all were packing guns and strapped up heavily with ammunition belts across their chests and shoulders.

Joe was being courteous and in broken Spanish, asking what type of gas they wanted and how they intended to pay. The gang were moving around trying to give off an air of unpredictability and intimidation. Charlie and I lay there watching and waiting.

Unexpectedly something blocked out the sun from above us. It was Vince.

"Get down you idiot!" growled Charlie under his breath. "Hell, you're as stupid as this guy. Work your way back around behind the motel rooms and man the taps, you know what to do."

"No way, big guy. I wanna have a crack on the '7d. *Frick'n awesome!*" He stood there, frantically shaking and going all spaz, like some poor dude being riddled by a burst of machine-gun fire.

Charlie pulled rank. "Pull back Vince and get over there NOW!"

Vince was a belligerent little shit, but he knew better than to argue with Charlie at moments like this, he wasn't completely devoid of any sense of responsibility. He flipped us both the bird and disappeared off somewhere behind us.

Charlie shook his head, regained his concentration and wiggled himself further into the ground.

Voices were raising over at the pumps and from what I could see, the body language was becoming more aggressive. I could hear Joe yelling, "*¡Pare! ¡Pare!* Stop! Stop!" Things were getting ugly.

The ones filling their tanks kept yanking the nozzles in and out checking if the gas was actually pumping. Even from here, we could see the fuel spurting out intermittently. I had visions of Vince peering out from some evil genius control panel hidden somewhere out in the scrub, antagonizing the bad-boys with a tap-turns-off, tap-turns-on, tap-turns-off scenario. He was perfectly gifted to excel at that kind of irritation.

Sidearms started appearing and irate voices began sounding off in Spanish. Joe's voice raised in unison "You want free gas? *You want free gas?* I'll give you free gas!"

He pulled out the nozzle from the far-end pump and started spewing fuel all over the driveway and around the wheels of their vehicles. Then, completely unexpectedly, he raised it up over his head and doused himself down beneath a gush of raining fuel.

Charlie wiggled into position and started clicking switches in preparation for firing the mother of all machine guns. My heart was thumping at a million beats per second and the needle on my courage meter was dropping rapidly towards the yellow end of the spectrum. The whole thing seemed unstoppable and about to kick off into a shit-fight.

Charlie started choking and tried desperately to hold back an outbreak of uncontrollable coughing which undoubtedly would compromise our position. He pulled back around the corner and hacked out his tortured lungs into the sleeve of his jacket. Down at the pumps the gang were all switched on, guns drawn, itching to cut loose with a testosterone fueled re-enactment of the O.K. Corral.

Joe stood firm, brandishing the dowsing gasoline pump in one hand and an unflicked lighter in the other.

"Well what's it going to be boys? Piss off outta here now, or we'll *all* go up together?"

Charlie was in a really bad way. He was coughing up blood and crawling on all fours like a dog back along the edge of the wall. It wasn't merely a case of bronchitis; it was the depleted uranium eating away at his insides. I had no idea *what* to do, I was panicking severely.

"Take the gun. Cover the old man," Charlie choked thinly between bursts of raw, painful hacking. "If you have to, push the button on top of the hand grip."

I nodded and got behind the gun in readiness for an all-out assault. What should I do? Do I start shootin first or wait until they have a pop at Joe? I had no idea what I was supposed to do. I really wanted Vince to come back, grab the thing out of my hands and palm all responsibility off onto him. I even looked over my shoulder to check he wasn't already standing there.

I'd never even fired a gun before, well, nothing bigger than a .22 shooting soda cans off a farmyard fence, let alone this baby. One quick look and you knew it would, as they say on TV, "unleash hell!"

"I can't handle any of this. I'm not a goddamn grunt."

Then, completely against the run of play, I noticed a distraction amongst the gang members. Some seemed preoccupied, and one by one they turned their attention away from Joe to whatever was going on down by the roadside. A few stood high on their open-door frames uncertain about what they were looking at.

I couldn't see jack, so I edged up close to the wall and peered out towards the road. I saw what had caught their attention immediately. A yard or two from the edge, stood a solitary figure dressed in robes, that shimmered amidst the rising heat.

"Holy shit!" I crossed myself like a true non-believer and stared mesmerized at the specter that now stood silent and ghostly.

The figure carried the scythe, for the moment of death, and the globe for death's sweet dominion. It was the skinny one, the lone skeletal incarnation of Señora de las Sombras.

I could hear Charlie barking his lungs out behind me, I knew I should have done more to help him, but the mysterious image somehow held me captive.

The apparition started moving and drifted out across the roadway. The interlopers seemed completely unnerved by the señora's presence and I could tell that from either reverence, fear, or confusion they were getting edgy and ready to bolt.

As the Lady of The Shadows headed ever closer, the gang had seen enough. This was the clincher. Gesturing wildly to each other, they piled unceremoniously back into their vehicles, fired up the engines and turned out onto the road heading north towards the U.S. border.

I laid the gun down carefully and ran towards Joe. He was standing there motionless, soaked in fuel watching what I'd thought to be an apparition but, in reality, was an old Indian woman who I'd seen once or twice on the fringes of the camp site. What I thought was as a scythe and globe were nothing more than a thin crooked stick and a bulging bag full of cuttings. The old woman continued on behind the line of cactus plants at the back of the concrete table. She turned to look at us momentarily and chuckled knowingly to herself about something our "chatterbox" minds could not grasp.

"You okay?" I asked, reaching Joe. He didn't move but turned his eyes to acknowledge my presence. "I'm far too old and decrepit for this nonsense."

I smiled and tried hard to make light of all that had just happened. "You'd better get out of those clothes Joe before that gas burns half your skin off."

Joe pulled a wicked grin, wiped his face with his hand. "Thanks for your concern Mr. Wolf, but no immediate problem, it's only diesel. I told you it came from the end pump." He hadn't, but it didn't matter.

"You old bastard, so this whole thing was just a ruse?"

"Yeah, worked though didn't it?" sniggered Joe. "Those jokers saw only what they *think* they saw. They must have thought the poor old gal from the Indian camp was a frick'n witch or something."

"I thought that too. So I'm obviously as stupid as they are," I said self-mockingly.

"Anyway, do you *really* think I'm such a dick that I'd douse myself with gasoline?" He looked at me with an expression that made me laugh out loud for the absurdity of it.

Then I remembered, "Oh shit. *Charlie!* We'd better go help him. He had a serious coughing fit. I left him around the side of the building." Joe turned around and bolted immediately off to his aid.

We found him sitting on the back-step sipping gingerly on a tall glass of water. His voice was still a little raspy but almost back to normal. "So, you pulled the old human torch ploy then," said Charlie when he saw Joe drenched from head to toe. "Gets 'em every time!"

"You okay son? I think you need a bit of R&R behind the old oxygen mask boy."

"Yeah sure, I'm sorry I went AWOL pops. If I'd have spewed my lungs up anymore, I would have brought 'em down on top of us, especially if they'd seen me there with the RODS'."

Suddenly the penny dropped. "So you weren't manning the Gee-Gee during my little performance?"

"Nope. As far as I know it was in the capable hands of the Wolfman here, sorry boss, but what else could I do?"

"Yeah, no problem Joe, I was packin' that RODS-7d thing, I had your six! *Sorry*, no what is it? Your *four*?" I said, sounding pretty foolish.

Joe turned white, dropped his ass on the step and chugged the rest of Charlie's water. Next thing, Faye comes hurtling upstairs from the lab, jabbering away to all and nobody in Norwegian. She was livid.

"What was happening? Why did you leave us down there so long?" She looked Joe up and down, curious as to why he was completely soaked.

Joe explained it all to her, but seeing Charlie with his head between his knees, Faye immediately forgot her displeasure and knelt down to see what she could do to help him.

"He's okay darlin'. He's *okay*, really. He just had one of his awful coughing fits. We're taking him inside soon for a couple o' bangs on the bottle."

"Aaaagh, you bloody fools, poor Charlie is in a bad way here, he really needs medical attention. Not 'a couple o' bangs' on the oxygen … stupid men."

Faye berated me and Joe with a full-on serve in her mother-tongue and mollycoddled Charlie back inside. As they disappeared through the doorway, Charlie gave us a sly wink over the top of Faye's arm which she had placed caringly around his shoulder.

"Come on Wolf," said Joe in a pragmatic tone. "Let's go and pack that RODS-7d away before you-know-who gets his greasy little paws on it."

◆

Considering all that had happened, I was amazed how quickly the afternoon returned to normal. The Japanese ladies had disappeared back to their room, MacElroy had stayed down in his hole playing the mad scientist and Charlie, after some impromptu nursemaiding from Faye, had carried on in the workshop as usual.

Joe called off any more work on the fence until tomorrow and took on the role of martial for the impending time trial race across the road at Indianapolis.

With nothing else to do, I sat stretched out on one of the chairs inside the garage listening to Vince hassling Charlie to make a few minor adjustments to his bike.

"Hey Vince," called Joe, walking in from outside, "lend me your ride. I'll do a quick circuit and make sure there's nothing out there on the track."

Vince looked baffled.

"You know, potholes boulders dead sheep crashed satellites stuff like that."

"I checked it already, no problem. I'll be sweet."

"It's not you I'm particularly worried about, besides I wanna go check on young Diego and his buddy. He made a good call earlier. I'll give 'em the rest of the week off." With that Joe mounted the bike, fired her up and disappeared out of sight.

◆

It was close to four in the afternoon, when Faye, pulling on a pair of fingerless leather gloves, appeared outside the garage doors. She was wearing the tight black jeans, short heeled boots and a brown leather jacket that was so well-worn that the arms easily hitched up to the elbows. The lapels were invisible beneath her main of long blonde hair which hung loose and untethered. Beneath the jacket she wore nothing but a plain black bra, a couple of strings of beads and my frick'n hat on her head.

"Hey!" I said, walking out from the shade to greet her. "Where'd you find it?"

"What?" she said, acting all innocent pretending she didn't know what I was talking about.

"My curl straw hat."

"This one?" She went all wide eyed and tried to hold back an impish smile.

"Finders are keepers, Fenrir. I found it hiding underneath Eugene's trailer, I like it quite a lot."

"Anyway Faye, it's *finders* keepers."

"What?"

"Just finders keepers, not … oh doesn't matter, it's yours. It looks a whole lot better on you than it does on me by a long shot."

Faye took it off and giggled. "I was only joking Wolf, I'm glad I found it for you."

"No, it really suits you." What didn't. She'd look amazing wearing a feed sack. She slipped the hat back on her head, pulled the front down over her eyes and made a sassy little smile that would have buckled an eight-inch I-beam.

Then it arrived. Lord Vince pulled up amidst a pall of smoke and dust on his rusting machine. He was wearing a full set of racing leathers, buckled motorcycle boots and a full-face helmet. The *whole* kit and kaboodle. He even had on a pair of frick'n knee sliders. Joe and Charlie emerged from inside the garage at precisely the same moment.

"Oh God help us," said Joe. "Look, it's star-spangled Evel himself."

Charlie stood there, arms folded shaking his head and Joe, not one to miss a dig at his youngest, took a couple of half-hearted swipes at Vince's padding with his fists.

"You idiot. What are you? Scared of losing to a lil' ol' *girly*, are ya?" Needless to say Joe howled with laughter at his own observation.

Faye took a leggy couple of steps away from the action. I could see her trying hard to hold back her laughter.

Vince flipped up his visor. You could see he was deadly serious, waving his arms around and yelling something incoherent to the guys. I moved in closer.

"*Bullshit!* All's fair in love and war ain't it? I'm goin' for it! *I'm frick'n goin' for it!* You know that Euro-donkey belongs to me, you're rippin' me off big time. If frick'n Goldilocks over there thinks she can beat me, well she's—"

"Ah shut ya whining boy!" Joe slammed the visor back down and clipped him around the ear, well the helmet anyway. Despite the high waving arms, the rest of Vince's indignant tirade went unheard inside his muffled cocoon. Our bemusement only made him angrier.

"Okay, that's enough. Settle down, settle down," pronounced Joe authoritatively as he put his invisible race marshal's hat back on.

"I think it's only fair, Faye gets to do a trial lap first, since she's only done the bugger on the soles of her shoes. Then we'll flip a coin and see who goes first, okay?"

Vince threw his hand disrespectfully into the air, dismounted the still idling bike and marched himself across to a plastic chair inside the garage. Faye walked over and nestled her rear end onto the seat. She certainly looked more the part today than that afternoon when she rode off to fight the devil creatures wearing nothing more than an oversized T-shirt.

"Just do a quick lap darlin' and come back up here to the pumps. We'll do a Mason start, yeah?"

Joe both announced and asked the question together. Vince and Charlie nodded, and Faye sped off on her trial lap. My hat blew straight off her head. I think she forgot she was wearing it.

"What's a Mason start?" I asked walking over to pick it up.

"Johnny pegged out and graded the whole damn track not that long after we got here. He was a real motorhead, old Johnny Mason. He'd be out there beltin' around on those two old Jap bikes we had back then, remember that Charlie? God he was quick. Neither of us could ever catch him. Slammed into one of those stupid long horn sheep one time. *Smack!*" Joe punched his fist hard into his palm, "I was coming up behind him when he hit it. I thought there'd be nothing left but a mangled pile o' jelly gizzards with four frick'n hoofs. Three seconds later the dumb thing jumps up out of the dust and runs off like nothing had happened." Joe started his chuckle motor up, then shook his head at another one of his priceless memories.

"Oh yeah, a Mason start was from right there between the pumps. We'd head off down to the road, then straight across and into the first left hand turn on the track. There's a couple of rights and lefts, immediately after, over in that direction and then, see over there, the extended back straight that runs south parallel with the road. Look there's Faye now. Once she goes down there, you can see a glimpse through the chaparral as she'll take the turns all the way down to the end and then merges back onto the road for the final straight that runs right past the front of The Alamo. We've got sixteen turns, just like Indianapolis, but our two straights are twice as long. The main one down there on the road is a mile and a half."

I was totally confused ... left turn, ... right turn, ... but I could pick out Faye by her hair and the long trailing dust cloud that sprayed out from behind the motorcycle. Soon she returned and pulled up as though she'd just done a feisty little spin around the yard.

"Any problems?"

"Nei!"

I couldn't get over the way even a simple no, could sound so sexy in her Norwegian accent.

"Okay Charlie, get down ... Oh, he's onto it."

Charlie had walked off in the direction of the road, right in front of the building.

"We scratch a line across the dirt down there for the finish line ... it's a *tradition*."

Charlie held up his arm and waved a piece of cloth in the air.

"Son-of-a-gun's remembered to fetch the old Indi' checkered flag as well."

Joe was loving it.

"Vince, Faye, this is a one lap time trial. The one who pulls the fastest lap gets to keep the Martellare Angelus. Okay? Simple as that. Charlie and I will adjudicate, our word is *final*. No whingeing, whining or chuckin' a hissy will in any way influence our decision if things don't go your way. Okay?"

Faye and Vince both nodded in agreement.

"Wolf, lend me a coin please."

I dug deep in my pocket and handed Joe a quarter.

"Right Vince, you call, winner picks either first or last run."

Joe flicked the coin high in the air and trapped it on the back of his hand.

"Heads!" snapped Vince emphatically.

"Tails it is."

I was expecting a flurry of displeasure, but he said nothing.

"Faye, first or last?"

"I'll ride last."

"No problemo!" said Vince, sounding incredibly smug. "You're goin' down blondie, I've got it in one."

Faye stood unperturbed and watched as Vince clambered onto the seat of his old softail.

"Sure Vince, but when I win, I'll take those red multi-buckled boots you're wearing as well…yes?"

"Yeah, yeah, sure, whatever. But you're goin' *down!*"

"Right, bring her over here." Joe marshalled the bike and rider over to a line, mid-way between the pumps. Vince was revving the shit out of the bike, making lots of unnecessary smoke, basically to make it more unpleasant for the rest of us.

Joe pulled out a stopwatch from his shirt pocket. *"Ten seconds!"* He then moved forward to a starter's position slightly ahead of the pumps. *"Five seconds!"*

It was hardly worth saying it, the revving was deafening, and the exhaust fumes forced Faye and me to move away from the pumps completely. Joe chopped the remaining seconds with his arm. On *"GO!"* he thrust it out straight, clicked his thumb on the stopwatch, as Vince tore off making an overzealous wheel skid amidst a cloud of foul-smelling smoke.

We moved on down to where Charlie was, but kept our attention on Vince. There wasn't that much to see, but we could hear him. Oh yes, we could definitely hear him alright.

"He's overworking the engine, it's totally unnecessary," said Faye concerned.

"Idiot!" said Charlie, less sympathetic. "He's got no idea how to ride a bike."

Occasionally his dirt trail would pinpoint his position, but we lost him completely when he entered the turns down the southern end. Charlie pulled out a pair of mini binoculars from his army pants and got the bead on his progress.

"Here he comes, check out all that goddamn smoke, the rate he's going you won't get a chance to ride before he blows the frick'n thing up, jeeesh!"

Vince crossed the line at a good speed, but none of them seemed particularly impressed when they checked out his time. Vince got back to the pumps before we did. He was looking pretty pleased with himself; you could tell by his demeanor that he was sure he had it in the bag.

"What are you lookin' so smug about, that was some pretty piss poor riding dude," said Charlie.

Vince grabbed the watch from Joe's hand.

"Hmmm, not as fast as Johnny's record, granted, but he was riding a faster bike. Anyway, I'm sure it'll do the job."

Contemptuously he turned the wheel of the softail and pointed it in the direction of Faye who was standing off to the side.

"There you go toots … knock yourself out!"

I don't know if it was the words he used or the condescending manner in which they were spoken, but I could tell that she wasn't impressed. Faye snatched the handlebars, threw a denim-clad leg over the seat, and snuggled herself down in position.

"Okay Joe, whenever you are ready. I've *really* had enough of this guy's crapping."

◆

What can I say? There's no point in recapping every single detail. Faye took off cleanly and looked impressive in the glimpses we managed to catch of her out in the scrub. She didn't over tax the engine and her final bolt down the straight was low, tucked in tight and ridden with a minimum of fuss, like a pro. It was beautiful. Suffice to say, she completely hammered Vince with her run.

As Faye crossed the finish line, I was about halfway back towards the building. I figured what was about to go down and I was right. Vince went totally ballistic. I could see Joe and Charlie shaking their heads and showing him the stopwatch, reminding him about the rules of the race.

Vince wasn't having any of it. He was shouting and arcing back and forth between them, slamming his helmet into the ground and using language that even those two deemed way-out-west. I've seen people pissed before, but Vince had lifted the art to a whole new level.

But something else made his anger rage even more. Not only had Faye snatched the MCLV from his grasp, but once she had crossed the finish line, she took his own precious bike and thundered off towards the north showing no indication of coming back.

17

Entourage

The sun was sinking fast and Faye had not returned. Vince was nowhere to be found either. Joe thought he'd taken the pickup and shot off looking for his bike, but then remembered he'd lent it to Eduardo earlier to go fetch supplies for the kitchen.

Charlie and I had shifted the disassembled Martellare over from the shed to the garage on a pallet trolley. We'd laid a square of fresh green plastic out on the floor in readiness. He'd grabbed a blue piece at first, but I thought the green was more appropriate considering the motorcycle's prestigious pedigree and its country of origin. Joe was adamant I suffer from "suppressed artistic pedanticism." As we were lifting the bike's frame up and onto the wheel stand, MacElroy popped his head out through the not-so-secret stairwell and started babbling at a million miles an hour.

"Slow down Eugene, slow down. I can't understand a damn thing you're saying," interrupted Joe.

"You're not going to believe this but something completely tragic has happened. *Unbelievable*, I—"

"What's up Eugene? Don't tell me Frankenstein's monster is still beating you at checkers."

MacElroy was in no mood for jokes. *"It's gone!"*

"What's gone?"

"Dot-dash-I-h-2. The cadaver, the unidentified, biological specimen. I just opened up the freezer chest for the umpteenth time and now it's gone."

Joe walked over and squatted at the top of the stairs. I could sense his methodical logic, paddling across non-existent data like a duck.

"Hmmm. Okay. Either *one*: it's been taken; or *two*: it's come back to life, crawled out of the ice box and run off into the desert by itself; or *three*: it's vanished into thin air like a puff o' smoke! My money's on

Vince though. The crafty little shit. That's probably where he is right now, flogging its mangy carcass to a bunch o' free-range new-agers. Yeah, that's another thing he let slip during his hissy-fit. Did you hear him? Had no intention of riding the Martellare at all. Reckons Charlie, me and Faye had all conspired to rip him off the twenty-somethin'-grand he figured he was gonna pocket when he sold it," Joe shook his head in amazement. "Unbelievable. Damn fool's just like his mother."

"I really don't think it was Vince, Joe. As far as I'm aware he had no idea the cadaver even existed." MacElroy was no great fan of Vince at the best of times, being the hapless brunt of his infantile teasing, but in this case, he was quick to rule him out as the most likely suspect.

Joe thought for a moment. "Hmm, yeah, your probably right Eugene, I think his dumbass behavior of late may have somewhat clouded my judgement."

Suddenly we all jumped as the alarm bell started ringing and then stopped almost immediately. "What was that? Why'd it cut out?" asked Charlie puzzled.

"Could be a false alarm. I've got young Raul up at the northern end, he's not quite as clued in as Diego. I'd better go check it out."

With that Joe stood up, turned on his heels and jogged back through the building towards the driveway. Me and Charlie followed right behind. Eugene was in two minds, but quickly disappeared back down into his bunker. Somewhere in the short distance from the garage to the driveway, Joe managed to find his precious hat and stuck it high on his head. It always gave me a chuckle whenever I saw him wearing that thing.

The glare outside was unbelievable. It was that exact moment of a desert sunset when the intensity of the light, combined with the sun's low angle, would fry the living eyeballs of anyone stupid enough to look directly into it.

With three pairs of eyes adjusting to the brightness, we could barely make out a circling horde massing out front along the roadside. Obscured behind the dust filled glare, the dark fluttering shadows seemed like an enormous flock of descending vultures. It was impossible to see exactly what they were but the unmistakable shudder that thundered long and loud from their engines confirmed their true identity. These were no birds of prey…these folks were bikers.

Me, Mo and Larry stood there like statues, a couple of paces outside the shop.

"First time ever at ol' Joe's Gas 'n' Grill, someone's managed to get the jump on me. Completely my fault though," said Joe. "I put too much faith in the young muchachos and the electric bell warning system, I guess. No matter. What ya gonna do? Couldn't see this lot off, anyway. This isn't Rorke's Drift and I sure ain't Lieutenant John Chard neither."

I didn't get the obscure reference, but I'm sure he had some sort of appropriate picture hanging on the wall of his office.

"So, should I just leave the bathroom key where it is then?" said Charlie sarcastically.

"This one'll be on the house, boys. They can do whatever they frick'n well like!" Joe said, only half joking. By now, he had produced his serious, military version binoculars and was busy scanning the roadside and the perimeters.

"*Jesus*, these guys are one hell of a bunch o' freaky lookin' dudes, I'll give 'em that. But what are they up to? Why the hell are they here?"

"Maybe they've just pulled over to go pick those pretty desert marigolds," said Charlie, being cute.

"My ass! These guys really give me the creepin' willies. *Holy frick'n* ... check those two out, over there, down by the rocket."

"Yeah, the two furthest on the left." Charlie was driving the binoculars now. "They've got severed devil heads strung around their handlebars with sidearms shoved down their throats like a couple o' holsters."

Right then, a fast-moving group of about a dozen riders turned away from their buddies and headed at speed straight towards us. Emblazoned with the sun's searing rays behind them, their trailing dirt cloud kicked high into fire. They split into two lines of six, escorting one central rider. Either the emissarial party or the one-stop, head-hunter squad were about to pay us a visit. The thundering charge would be on us in a heartbeat.

"I really hope this won't get ugly," sighed Joe. "I think we should kind o' back ourselves up a little now fellas. Better safe than sorry!"

"No! Don't you see the signs? Stay put," I said, sounding pretty ridiculous.

"Signs. What signs?" said Joe. "Don't you go all hippy-trippy on me Mr. Wolfman."

"Over there, look. Sitting beside the pumps, it's Gutteka and Jenteka. They're all revved up about something, look at their tails going crazy."

The riders tacked slightly in their course. Then, amongst a sea of swirling shadows, as if a beacon had been ignited, the unmistakable mane of Faye's long golden hair, flew up high and bright into the sun making her presence known from within the ranks of her dark and mysterious entourage.

"*It's Faye!*" blurted Joe excitedly, stating the bleeding obvious. "How'd she get a ring-side seat with this ugly lookin' bunch o' goofers?"

All thirteen riders pulled up hard in a staggered, angled formation no more than a tall-man's length from the edge of the driveway. Faye was sitting up there on Vince's softail as cool as you like, smack bang in the middle. She had acquired a pair of wrap-around shades, that gave away nothing of the wearer's mood behind them. I'm telling you straight, she fitted in perfectly, she looked like a real bad ass mamasita.

The dirty dozen remained astride their massive, idling machines. They looked like the mutated love children of the horsemen of the apocalypse and the grittiest, meanest, late-night spaghetti western hombres. Faye cut the engine and stepped away from her bike. Immediately, the two adjacent riders dismounted their still running motorcycles and followed her up to the edge of the driveway, not as a captor's response but more as a gesture of high regard. The riders stopped shy of the pumps. Faye stayed with them, as if to make known the bond that had now been forged between them. She spoke calmly and introduced us to her companions.

"Joe, Wolf, Charlie, please meet my new friends. They insisted on escorting me safely back home. I think it was really very nice of them. These are the riders of Los Espectros Brillantes," Faye pronounced theatrically.

"*It's The Shining Specters,*" I whispered from the corner of my mouth to Joe.

"No shit!"

As we shuffled closer, you could tell by Faye's demeanor she was caught somewhere between exhilaration and a well-controlled bout of unease.

"This is Valasco, a captain within their ranks and this is Mercio, his sergeant at arms."

The captain tipped his fine, bejeweled sombrero courteously, but showed no expression on his smoke-like, skeletal face. He didn't appear hostile but emitted an unsettling sense of foreboding. I felt the same creepy feeling run through me as I did that night when Bird and I saw them heading en mass along the highway.

"Please see my friends. *Be aware!*" Faye stretched out her arm and gestured to the others to look in our direction. "I bid you watch out for them and see that no harm should befall them."

"She's got 'em hanging off her every word," Joe said in a whisper.

"Yeah, they sure seem kind of smitten with her alright," sniggered Charlie.

After a final exchange between Faye and Valasco, the riders took their leave, remounted their motorcycles and together with their squad thundered off into the last failing rays of the sunset.

Faye staggered forward out into the center of the drive, relieved it was over. She stood there staring blankly down the road after them, then bent forward to stroke her cats, who had both run out to greet her. She turned back towards us and spoke ever so softly.

"What do you think?" said Faye with a half-smile. "I've got myself an army. It sounds really silly I know, but they told me I've been sent here by higher forces. By the gods! That's what they said. It's predestined, and I have been chosen as their ... leader."

With that, Faye sunk to her knees and hung her head in confusion.

18

The Monster and the Beast

The evening of Faye's return was pretty full on. Faye handed Vince's bike over to Joe so he could pick up the boys from their roadside hides. When they got back, poor Raul was bawling his eyes out and apologizing for messing up his watch call. Joe soon calmed him down and reassured the youngster that he'd done okay. He explained how anyone could have gotten a bit muddled if they'd spotted Señorita Faye riding amongst such a massive group of bikers. Mrs. Eduardo had cooked them both a special supper and Joe, who should have known better, loaded them up with a couple of bottles of soda each before sending them off home reasonably happy. It was nice.

Thankfully, Faye had changed into her old blue-jeans. Too much visual exposure to the black ones really wasn't good for a poor boy's health. She was bouncing off the walls in the garage with excitement as she helped out Charlie with the Martellare's assembly. He'd reassured her a hundred times that he was fine, completely over his coughing fit and was feeling A.O.K. I could see by the glint in his eye he was having a great time as the center of attention. He was lovin' it.

Encircled by an assortment of unattached motorcycle pieces, the MCLV stood high and central on a sea of green plastic. Charlie and Faye moved methodically around it's chassis like a pair of spider technicians, weaving the machine together as they checked and inspected every last mechanical component, oblivious to me, Joe or any other distractions.

Joe cranked up the music from an old, greasy radio that sat mumbling away to itself on the bench top. Then he handed around cold beers between the four of us from a six pack that he seemed to pull out of nowhere. Finally, with nothing else left to do, Joe plonked his backside down onto a chair, made a weird kind of grunting exhalation and took a long swig from his beer. He took another gulp, wiped his mouth with the back of his hand and then started talking.

"You know Wolf, the more I think about what happened to Eugene's missing devil, the more I'm convinced it could only be *option three*."

"Why so?"

"Just a logical process of elimination really. It's pretty damn obvious nobody's taken it. Nobody even knew it existed besides us four and Eugene."

"What about Sacramento?"

"Yeah, he's not stupid, he knows something was going on down there, but he wouldn't want it."

"What about option two?"

"I can't see any indication of option two either. There's nothing to show it suddenly came back to life, busted out of the icebox, and high-tailed it back home to its buddies. I think the disappearing into a puff o' smoke option is the most logical. It's what their kind does. To put it simply, demons are nasty little motherfuckers that live deep below the ground with the sole intent of coming up to the surface one day to steal you out of your bed and haul your ass back down to Hell and everlasting damnation." Joe chuckled wryly at his almost fairy tale explanation.

"But I thought you didn't know what their kind was?"

"No, not their exact genus, but whatever, they're still frick'n demons." He turned his head away, stared across towards Charlie and Faye and appeared to sink deep into contemplation.

I still needed clarification. "Okay. So you say it disappeared into a puff of smoke, but what you really mean is that it dematerialized and transporter-beamed itself somehow back down below the ground to demon central. Yeah?"

"*Exactly!* And don't forget it had those tag marks, remember? Dot-dash-I-h-2. Someone or something probably wanted it back."

Joe was either joking, deadly serious or had gone completely insane. I wasn't blind to the fact that this whole conversation was making me sound just as crazy as him. I pulled an unconvincing face and turned my attention back to the action over at the bike.

Charlie and Faye had made heaps of progress. There was a lot of talk about the pros and cons and the differences between racing slicks and multifunctional tires, which I had worked out on my own, was what the Martellare Angelus was already fitted with. But as for the "Breath of the Angels" exhaust, the swing arm suspension system, and the M.A. treno valvole, all of that techno babble went completely over my head.

But anyway, within a couple of hours the bike looked almost complete.

Both the forks and the front wheel were attached, only the fairing, the cables and other little bits and pieces seemed all that was left to do. But to be honest I really had no idea. It still might take the rest of the night for all I knew.

As I sat there zoned out, watching Faye diligently adjust something or other with a baby-size spanner, a classic rock track came blasting loud through the radio.

From her squatting position beside the bike Faye leapt to her feet and had a bit of a dance. It lasted only a couple of seconds, but to watch that gorgeous creature dance, walk, move, smile or do anything was a priceless treat. One of mother nature's little gifts to be savored.

Faye crouched back down beside the Martellare and returned her attention to whatever it was she'd been doing.

"Just *luv* The Billy Man!" she said without even missing a beat. But pretty soon she bounced back up for a longer, wilder encore. God she was amazing, every single inch perfection. As I sat there distracted amidst my fantasies, Joe came back to life and started talking again.

"Anyway, whatever they are, there's something in the wind Mr. Wolfgang, something is *definitely* in the wind and I'm pretty damn sure by a Texas mile we haven't seen the last of those nasty little buggers."

He made another strange snorting sound with his nose, finished off his beer and hauled his well-built frame up from his seat.

"I'm off inside for a bit of R&R. That's readin' and research, not, ah doesn't matter, I'll leave you kids to it."

He started to head inside through the garage but turned abruptly and spoke to me in a loud whisper.

"Oh yeah, be early Wolf, Faye and Sacramento are having their first training session in the morning with sensei Hamada-san. Faye 'll be fine, but I reckon Sensei 'll haul Sacramento's ass right out of there when he starts carrying on like an idiot. It'll be fun to watch. I'll meet you over the back behind that old white transit, we'll get a close-up view from there and still be right out of sight."

Joe turned, said good night to the others and lobbed inside to his digs.

Once he'd gone, I leaned forward intent on rejoining the mechanical action happening out front on the green drop sheet. But as I did, even from halfway across the workshop, Charlie shot me that almost imperceptible, but completely unmistakable glance, that said, *"Hey Wolf, when are you gonna piss off too?"*

I felt like some three's-a-crowd-turkey perched up high on his chair with a beer. Rightly or wrongly I got a case of the guilts. Seriously, why wouldn't the guy want me out of his face. I'd had my tea and tequila moment and he deserved some time alone with Faye. After all he's the one doing her all the favors, I was just an unneeded sideline spectator.

Chugging my drink, I mumbled some hasty "I've-decided-to-leave-right-now" goodbyes and began my retreat back home. As I left, Faye looked up, smiled goodnight and got on with her work.

I was snookered by circumstance; this wasn't what was supposed to happen. I tried hard to act cool and convince myself that all was well, but I wasn't doing a good job of it. In truth I felt sick and kind o' foolish.

Halfway back to the camper I heard the first straining sounds of the Martellare's engine as they tried to kick it over and fire the machine into life. Then it stopped. A couple of seconds later it started up again, but to no avail. On the third attempt the beast did roar and for the first time Hildisvíni barked his mechanical lungs out for all the world to hear. Well anyone within a mile or so radius of The Alamo at least.

The sound was incredible. Charlie and Faye had raved on about the fabulous, unmistakable sound of a Martellare engine, but hearing it for yourself you could appreciate exactly what they'd been on about.

As they revved it high into full boar mayhem, it sounded like contained thunder being forced hard from the depths of its mechanical body. The idling growl, a low bass rumble ready to unleash its fury at a split second's notice. The stillness of the night now trembled beneath its awesome resonance.

Without even thinking, I turned one eighty degrees ready to head straight back over to share in their achievement but stopped dead when I heard the engine cut out and the garage door come crashing shut. I felt the green-eyed monster surge up through my body and settle in the vacuous gables of my heart. This was one of those "to the victor go the spoils" kind o' moments and there was jack diddly squat I could do about it.

I'd already been on the ass end of unrequited love a dozen times in my life, but it was apparent that my woes were now akin to the tally of a baker. The vassal incarnate for the goddess had taken root under my skin and was aching like frick'n crazy.

19

Peas in a Pod

First thing in the morning, Joe and I arrived at our spotter's hide almost together. It was perfect. We were only about twenty yards or so back from the little grassy patch where Faye and Sacramento always did their practice.

I was expecting our covert view of their training session to be from behind the transit van, with both our heads poking discreetly out from either side, but instead the van was facing forward and Joe had already opened up the passenger side door and gestured to me to slide on in quickly before they had a chance to notice us.

"Just keep quiet," said Joe below his breath. "They'll never know we're in here."

I was a little miffed that my side of the windshield had a stack more grime caked on it than Joe's, so I edged myself further across to his side. It reminded me of a couple o' lovelorn teenyboppers sitting up front and personal at a drive-in movie. Joe must have had the same idea as he piped up quickly.

"Now don't you start gettin' any of your wicked ideas there Wolfie baby. I *never* put out on a first date ever, so be nice and behave yourself."

I could see he wanted to burst out laughing, but knowing how loud he could be, settled for a face scrunching, low impact snigger instead.

Outside, a drift of distant clouds hung low in the eastern sky obscuring the morning sun from blinding our view of the impending proceedings. It seemed we'd taken our ring-side seats right on time. Faye and Sacramento stood side by side down one end of the grassy patch, while Hamada-san took up her position some ten yards directly opposite.

I was surprised Kiko wasn't out there somewhere, acting as interpreter, but then I figured martial arts were more about correct actions than a constant running stream of verbal commentary.

They began proceedings with a respectful bow towards an improvised, little wooden altar, a sign of respect to the spirits, which must have been important to Hamada-san's outdoor Sonoran dojo. Then they turned back and made an abrupt midsection bow towards each other and I noticed they never broke eye contact.

"That's in case of an unexpected attack," Joe filled me in authoritatively.

They started with a slow-paced set of warm up moves but curiously it wasn't with the naginatas, but the Chinese bo staffs that Hamada-san had chosen to work with first.

Joe reckoned this part of the process was called Saburi but in the next breath said they were now doing katas. I think he knew a fair bit about all of this martial arts stuff but would get a little mixed up with some of the names and what was what.

Hamada-san was well in control as she assessed them, diligently correcting their posture and movements. Faye and Sacramento were completely unaccustomed to formal procedure and I was sure she was cutting them slack. But don't get me wrong she was tough. *God* she was tough. You could see she'd done this a thousand times and knew precisely how to cajole her students to the limit of their abilities and beyond. When the action heated up Hamada-san showed no mercy to either of them. Very little honey, but a whole lot o' vinegar.

I was impressed by Hamada-san's skill with the bo staff, but when they eventually changed over to the naginatas, the intensity cranked up immediately. She may have looked like a sedate little Japanese grand-mother in her sixties, but Hamada-san was unquestionably a full-on, power-packed, fighting-machine.

We watched enthralled as she alternated between fending off the vigorous onslaughts of Faye and Sacramento and then standing aside to observe her two new students as they beat the living bejesus out of each other. Thankfully, their previous foolhardy practice of training with live, naked blades had been curtailed and their weapons were now sheathed with leather protectors.

"Man she's good," said Joe excitedly. "She's the perfect example of *Zen Shin*."

"What is that? You mentioned it before."

"Well it's focus. A state of awareness. Through Zen Shin you harness and use the vital energies of Chi to progress. You know, advancing forward step by step and gradually getting more proficient over time. The younger dudes are full of raw speed and energy but have relatively lesser skill and control. Obviously after a lifetime of practice, an older artist's agility starts to wane, but they develop the ability to compensate against a tide of unfocused, youthful exuberance by focusing and utilizing Zen Shin. It builds and gets exponentially more powerful the older and more proficient you become. It projects itself in the dojo like some kind of cosmic, almost impenetrable force field."

"You mean it's like what that little green dude with the pointy ears in those Star—"

"Where do you think they got that whole idea from in the first place Wolf? This is the *real* deal, right here in front of you."

I wasn't sure if what he told me was gospel, but it sounded pretty convincing.

Joe and I sat there engrossed as Hamada-san fought on tirelessly with Faye and Sacramento. After nearly two hours of full-on training, Faye was looking pretty ragged and her master-class partner-in-arms wasn't looking that much better. I think they'd both been pushed to their limits.

Suddenly Hamada-san stopped all proceedings and with an extended arm, forcefully pointed the tip of her naginata directly at where we were hiding. Whether she knew we'd been there all along was hard to tell, but either way she'd decided we'd seen quite enough and was inviting us to take our leave immediately.

Feeling like a couple of naughty schoolboys, Joe and I jumped out of the transit van and scurried away under the steely gaze of Hamada-san.

"That reminds me Wolf, lucky she gave us the flick, I promised young Kiko I'd print something out for her this morning on the computer and I *completely* forgot about it." Joe's mind had already moved on, or so I thought.

On one hand I was surprised at how quickly he bailed, but on the other hand I was conscious of Joe's steadfast respect for appropriate conduct. I'd half been expecting him to make light of the whole situation, but he made no disparaging comments at all.

"What's up?" I said, genuinely curious.

"*Aggh!* Nothing to do with Hamada-san. I was thinking about what I said last night about Sacramento, making him out to be a flipper and a bit of a buffoon. I'm the one who's the real dickhead, Wolf. I still keep taking the piss and making folks out to be idiots, even at my age."

"Well we all do that," I blabbed straight off the cuff.

"That's just it, but why? It's totally ridiculous, we behave like stupid little monkeys, always jumpin' on each other's heads for no good reason. Don't know about you, but I never, *ever* seem to learn."

I was surprised at Joe's unexpected candor.

"Did you see him out there earlier. No clowning around, no fear, no giant ego. *Look at me lady, I'm a frick'n bo staff master!* No sir. He was the essence of humility and fully in the moment. He was flawless. *A warrior.* And by that, I mean a *real* one, not some candy-ass wannabe with a shooter stuck down his Y-fronts. He told me once that he walks shoulder to shoulder with death. I mean he feels completely at ease with his own mortality. For Sacramento, every single day alive on this earth was gratefully accepted as a blessing and a sacred gift. There's a lot to learn from all the old Indian stuff Wolf, but we never bother to take the time to get into it. We never take the time."

We picked our way through the old car bodies and rounded the corner of the building nearest the garage. The roller door was still pulled shut. Jealous, illogical notions would have flooded my thoughts, but for the distraction of someone quietly sitting on the ground with his back propped up against the metal roller. He looked like he'd been out there all night.

It was Sacramento's buddy from over at the campsite. My mind went blank, trying to remember his name, but Joe saved the day.

"Well howdy there Takochai, what can I do for you?"

He jumped to his feet holding a large, plastic lunch container which he handed quickly over to Joe.

"Ooh, something tasty?" Joe said lightheartedly, trying to crack the iron-hard expression riveted onto the face of the serious young man.

It must have come from Sacramento, but due to his prior engagement with Faye and Hamada-san, had probably asked his friend to deliver it *"First thing in the morning"*, which Takochai had taken quite literally.

Joe's eyes lit up when he looked inside. It wasn't chocolate brownies, quite the contrary, its contents looked pretty damn disgusting. It was a claw from a devil with three inches of forearm still attached. The flesh at the stump end appeared partly dissolved by a powder leaking from a folded paper envelope inside the box.

"MacElroy's gonna go ape when he gets his mitts on this little beauty. I'll make sure he gets it as soon as he arrives," said Joe with a grin.

We both said our thanks to Tokochai and he bolted off back to the camp without saying a single word.

"Go see if Rosalina or Eduardo are ready to give you something to eat.

I'll come and join you as soon as I've run out a print for little Kiko, that's if I can remember where I've stashed my pack of the good A3 paper."

◆

Entering the dining room, I came face to face with dopey and dozy. Vince and Bird were over by the wall, one drinking a luminous green juice and the other hoeing enthusiastically into his usual gigantic bowl of cereal.

"Ayh! How's it hangin' dudes?" I thought it a befitting greeting for these two amigos.

Even from across the room I could tell they were both off their faces. Bird sat their grinning and theatrically raised the palm of his hand in a low exertion sign of recognition. Vince babbled something short and incoherent and returned to his milky trough.

I pulled out a chair and sat down at the table beside them. Neither seemed particularly capable or willing to start up any further conversation.

Bird was wearing that ridiculous lemon-yellow polyester tracksuit again, but instead of his flowerpot hat he now donned a kid-sized, fake-straw sombrero embellished with cotton stitching that spelled out FUN IN THE SUN. But if that didn't look stupid enough, he'd also managed to grow himself one of those Van Dyke moustaches, complete with that skinny little bit of hair that ran vertically from his bottom lip to the end of his chin. He looked like some kind of comic book villain. Vince on the other hand looked his usual untidy self, although curiously he did have on a brand-new shirt, one commandeered earlier from the packing crate booty in the shed.

It wasn't long before Rosalina arrived with some toast and a coffee. A welcome distraction from the stimulating banter going down with these two dropkicks.

Joe came bursting into the dining room.

"Oh for God's sake! What rock have you two crawled out from?"

I laughed at his bluntness. Bird clammed up and Vince just sat mute, sniggering.

"They're out of their melons as well." Joe shook his head in disgust. I could imagine steam hissing out through pressure valves in his ears.

"Tell me boy, you didn't take the slipper out on the road did ya?"

Vince grinned to the affirmative as he munched away happily on his breakfast.

I figured the slipper must have been the rusting remnant of an old

European car that sat hidden amongst the other wrecks around the back. I'd only noticed it because of the unusual, rounded body shape. It's roof and windshield supports had been chopped right off to the level of the doors and it did look exactly like an old man's carpet slipper on wheels.

"This might be the backwoods of Sonora, sunshine, but *holy Moses!* If any passing patrol car caught you driving that heap o' crap out there, they'd have thrown the goddamn book at you. Not to mention the fact that you're both completely off your stupid noggins. And this one here looks like an escapee from Good King Willie's Asylum Circus. You're complete imbeciles, the pair of ya."

After his tirade Joe poured himself a glass of juice and stormed back inside.

"So Bird, you must be champing at the bit about meeting Hamada-san and Kiko then?" I said, changing the subject and thinking it was the obvious reason he'd come back so soon. Bird looked at me puzzled. He had no idea what I was talking about.

"You didn't know they were here? … Obviously not."

Vince continued slurping away, looking up occasionally at the sound-less pictures flashing across the TV screen on the wall.

"Who are these, Kiko and … ?" asked Bird.

"The two Japanese ladies that have been staying here since the earthquake," I said, surprised that nobody, especially Vince had filled him in already. Bird didn't fall off his chair with enthusiasm or even ask any more questions. Then Vince finally spoke.

"I picked him up yesterday evening from that truck station up north. Couldn't go and fetch him on the softail 'cos *Goldilocks* pissed off with it, remember?"

"I got dropped off yesterday afternoon, but none of the truckers would take me any further," Bird said indignantly and then took a guzzle on his drink.

I wasn't that surprised. He did look pretty bizarre.

"Things are very bad back home. The little town of Tocoa near our place, it was attacked by Chupacabras. They came from inside the ground, there were people killed everywhere, twenty or more. The grietas, the cracks, had taken many people too."

Then Vince got excited. "Even saw this annihilated mash of a gas truck that had plowed full-on into a boulder. *Smack!* frick'n awesome." Bird copped a sudden thump to the upper arm as Vince reenacted the impact.

I turned my head as someone came in from the kitchen. Expecting it to be Joe, I was surprised to see it was Kiko. She seemed a little dis-orientated and startled by our presence. She oscillated in her tracks but then plucked up the courage and steamed on over. She wasn't holding any kind of printout, so I presumed Joe hadn't found any of the good A3.

I couldn't believe what she had on. Starting at the top, her hair was like usual, hanging down long, with a fringe that seemed to saw away irritatingly right at the level of her eyeballs. The T-shirt was one of those "Hi there, Catty" things, the giant cartoon head crossed out anarchically with a black, hand-painted X and the words I HATE scrawled across the top in English. The short, little skirt was made of lime green plastic, not completely see through, but not totally opaque either, it had a flecky kind of retro pattern all over and a shaggy, dancing fringe around the bottom like an off-cut from Grandma's good-room lampshade. But the legs took the cake. Imagine two, upturned, fur-covered wastepaper baskets with a row of Styrofoam cup-like claws spread out evenly around the fronts where the toes should be. Well that's what they looked like. I think they were supposed to be a pair of genuine, reproduction dinosaur feet. But they didn't look very convincing to me.

With a nervous smile Kiko made a couple of clipped-off little half-bows to me and Vince, but on coming face to face with Bird for the first time, she went all kind of, I dunno... weird. Mixing together a more erratic, urgent bowing with an indecipherable sort of gibberish that I could only presume was some kind of shorthand Japanese teen-slang.

Bird reciprocated immediately, jumping up from his chair and almost knocking over the table and everything on it in the process. He did a clumsy kind of first time, belly-crunch bow, but then gave up and held his arms out unusually wide on either side in a pose that suggested either "Come on down to Daddy" or that he was some kind of new age, born-again messiah. Vince almost choked trying to hold down his laughter.

Judging by their awkward and stranger than usual behavior and the ga-ga expressions plastered across both Bird and Kiko's faces, it was pretty obvious I'd just been witness to that rare but undeniable phenomena known as two-way love at first sight. It was all a bit too much for Kiko, she looked like she was about to pass out at any moment. With one last bow and an embarrassed smile hidden behind her hand, she turned and bolted for the door as quickly as her imitation dinosaur legs could carry her.

"*GO BIRD* ... She's hot for you, bro. Big time!" came the inevitable, insensitive, expert summation of the incident from the now empty mouth of Señor Vince. "She can tell you your name and yell it in Japanese while you're doin' the wild-thing!" He burst out laughing, pushed his bowl away and wandered off somewhere out towards the front of the building.

Poor Bird stood there stunned pondering the chirping tune of the cartoon love birds that swirled endless and imaginary above his head.

"I've gotta scoot and give some stuff to Joe," I lied. I didn't have the cool dude skills to encourage Bird and I felt a bit mean. "Okay. Check ya later then Bird. Whenever you're ready, big guy, I'll get Kiko to help you out with the stuff you need to know."

I headed out back through the kitchen and was pleasantly surprised when I saw Faye sitting quietly on the edge of the step. She looked up and gestured that I sit down beside her.

"Look Wolf, look what Kiko has done." I noticed a large piece of paper lying flat across the top of her legs.

"Isn't it fabulous? She only just gave it to me."

"*Yeah*, I know."

"You've seen it?"

"No, but can I have a look? *Wow!* Kiko did that?"

Drawn in manga style, Kiko had created an amazing piece of artwork. It was a sci-fi, action-figure depicting Faye as a blonde-haired Tomoe Gozen leaping out of the page towards you. I was impressed.

"Don't you love those big doe-eyes and all that long, wispy hair. *I love it, love it!*" The joyous expression of the real-life Faye was priceless. "Kiko drew it on her tablet." Beneath the flowing mane of long golden locks, Faye's pale blue T-shirt had been upgraded to a space-age, plastic minidress with a neckline that plunged low between two pert grapefruit-sized breasts. She was wearing a shiny pair of thigh-high boots with needle-point toes and heels. Faye pointed to them with a bit of a giggle.

"Could you imagine fighting the monsters wearing those little numbers? They look really great, but I don't think they'd be very practical." She moved her face closer to mine and whispered, "I'd wear them though, if I had a pair." But then her expression changed to concern. "I don't *really* look like that though, do I?"

I laughed out loud at the ludicrous question. Faye had hardly any boobs at all and as for hips, she didn't really have much in that department either. To be honest she looked more like a long, straight stick of tasty cheese. But apart from the dramatic, doe-eyed, leaping figure of Tomoe Gozen and three very manga-styled demons, the unifying link in the whole scene was the powerful scythe action of the heroine's long and sweeping naginata, which in Kiko's imagination had been beefed up very considerably with the addition of a—

Right then the fly screen door scraped open behind us. It was Vince. Nothing particularly exciting about that but dangling from his hand was the well-worn pair of motorcycle boots from yesterday's wager.

"Well *uuur*, howdy there, folks!" Vince said in that old-time prospector voice he does. "Seems *uuur*, Miss Faye, you won that little ol' motorcycle bet fair and square, so *um*, here's what I reckons that I owes ya."

Despite the silly voice and the reluctant, halfhearted show of contrition, Vince handed the pair of boots over to Faye, which she accepted gracefully but with a justifiable modicum of suspicion.

"There you go missy, a crappy pair o' boots to go with an even crappier bike."

Poor old Vince couldn't resist one final dig, then he dropped the voice and said, "What was that picture you were looking at before?"

"*Nothing*, just a page from a magazine," Faye said as she slipped it quickly out of sight. Vince was completely uninterested anyway and turned to go back inside.

"I'm gonna go get the Bird Man and drag his sorry ass over to see that Japanese chick again." He chuckled at his impending intentions.

"*Bird is here?*" Faye sparked up, totally surprised.

"Oh yeah, he's here alright," I answered somewhat sardonically "and you wouldn't believe it, him and that Kiko are made for each other. They're like two frick'n peas in a pod. *Ha!*"

20

Metamorphose

We were only ten minutes back into the fence building when Hildisvíni awoke from his night-time slumber. Released from the stand he now stood free outside the garage supported firmly between the slender long legs of his mistress.

The bestial roar of the engine turned the heads of everyone towards the arrowhead shaped headlamps that shone menacing like a pair of untamed eyes.

Charlie was right there too, gesturing instructions above the Martellare Angelus engine like a pit crew boss to his rider. Faye sat impatient, champing at the bit, then took off like a bat out o' Hades.

"*Hooo-weee!* You see that? Kid's a frick'n lunatic," Joe yelled excited.

We could hear the gorgeous whine of the Hammering Angel as Faye shot away south and out of sight.

"Couldn't see her putt-putting around on one of those little two-stroke moped things now could ya?" smirked Joe. "Come on Wolf, let's get stuck into this dumbass job or we'll *never* get it finished."

Faye's initial foray was short, as we soon heard the sound of the MCLV returning. She was probably about where the minibus had over-turned when the ground around us started shaking. The rumble was lower this time but still the dreadful unmistakable din of an earthquake. Joe let the coil of fencing wire drop and signaled to me to move away from the crack. The previous quake was still fresh in my mind and I felt the gut-wrenching fear of having to go through another. Then as quickly as it started it stopped.

Joe moved further over towards the building. "Over here Wolf, it's probably run its course, but—"

We both squatted low to the ground. I could feel my heart beating like crazy and I started to fixate on the crack expecting another on-slaught from the devils. But nothing.

"What ya gonna do? Where can you run from an earthquake?" I didn't reply. After a few long minutes my heartbeat had returned almost back to normal.

"Aftershock," stated Joe confidently. "I was wondering when it would happen."

"Do you think there'll be any more?"

He didn't answer but shrugged his shoulders and pulled his wide-eyed face of uncertainty. The returning sound of Hildisvíni snatched our attention as Faye veered off the road and hurtled back towards us. Slowing to a crawl, she glided up close and shut down the engine completely.

"Wow! That was more of a ride than I was expecting. Are you both okeydokey?"

"Oh yes. *Shaken*, not bacon," answered Joe comically in his best Scottish brogue.

Charlie emerged from inside the garage and wandered somewhat disheveled towards us. He was soaked from beard to midriff with oil.

"Dumbass bowl o' multi-grade took a dive right off the shelf on top of me."

"Aaah, poor Big Dain," said Faye in a sexy lighthearted voice.

BIG-DAIN! What the hell does that mean? I've never heard Faye call him *that* before. It was definitely the big that really got my attention. The green-eyed monster stirred again, in the pathetic little recess of my brain space.

"I think we got off lightly that time folks," Joe said, checking out his hat for any sign of damage. "But I'd better go inside and check if they're all *okeydokey!*"

Faye poked her tongue out; she knew he was pulling her leg.

Joe had started off towards the building when Dr. MacElroy came out holding his head. Faye kicked down the stand on the bike and jumped off to go and help him.

"Eugene! Take your hand away, let me see your head. What happened?" she fussed.

"I'm okay, I'm okay…*I guess?* I took another belt on the head from that swingin' lamp shade."

Seeing it wasn't serious, Faye planted a kiss on his forehead.

"You'll live. It's only a bit of a scratch."

"Thank you, Faye," interjected MacElroy, his thoughts distracted elsewhere. "I'm fine, really, but I've got something important to tell you."

Joe's ears pricked up. Eugene sounded excited.

"I think the powder sample we received this morning has provided us with a possible and I do stress *possible*, bio-agent. All my preliminary tests so far indicate an extraordinary propensity for effective repellency towards the NHLFs."

"What the hell is he on about?" snapped Charlie mouthing his question to Joe.

"He's finally found a bug spray for the devils."

"Guys a frick'n tool, pops."

"That's amazing Dr. Egghead you've figured it out already. You're pretty damn good. I only gave it to you an hour ago. So, tell us what the hell is it then?"

"Well, not really. It wasn't all that hard to figure out," said MacElroy staving off any undue credit. "It was printed on the wrapper inside the envelope. It's powdered sodium fluoride."

"So what can you bake out o' that?" I said trying to sound like a wit, but quickly wished I hadn't.

"It's the stuff they put in the water," piped up Joe. "You'll never have to worry about your teeth going rotten. A frick'n industrial waste product. It's poison, messes up the brain, dumbs people down, causes all kinds o' mental and physical problems. They used it in the camps and the gulags to keep all the inmates docile. Besides, any pest exterminator will tell you it's the best thing to use as rat poison," Joe said matter-of-factly.

"Bullshit!"

"All true. Go check it out for yourself if you don't believe me."

"But they wouldn't be allowed to do that nowadays, ... would they?"

"Oh of course not Wolf, I'm just pulling your leg, as if they'd ever do that."

Joe, Faye and MacElroy started grinning and I got the feeling I was somehow an integral part of the joke.

Immediately the two PhDs locked horns, hotly contesting the wisdom of using such an insidious chemical. Dr. MacElroy seemed completely in favor of using the sodium fluoride, counting up on his fingers a whole list of other stuff they'd tested, that had failed to come up trumps. Faye on the other hand was dead against it and argued to keep on searching for something more natural and less toxic in its makeup. She was convinced that the answer would come from pursuing her collaboration with the local Indians and their knowledge of indigenous plants and medicines. Most of their boffin-banter went straight over our tiny laymen brains and we soon got bored and wandered off.

It wasn't until later in the afternoon when I met up with Joe that he asked me to take the pickup down to Hermosillo in the morning. Apparently, the decision had been made to collect a couple of sacks of sodium fluoride from a man called Señor Chachi. I couldn't shake the image of him looking exactly like that kid on that old TV comedy, except with a big black Mexican moustache.

Anyway, the fly in the ointment was that Vince, against Joe's better judgement, had been seconded into coming along, as he, for reasons unknown, was the only one who knew exactly where this Señor Chachi's storage yard was located amongst a maze of indistinguishable back streets.

◆

I sat behind the wheel of the pickup ready and waiting to leave. His lordship still hadn't appeared, so I passed the time ripping out hairs from the inside of my nose. Suddenly the passenger door opened. I turned, expecting it to be Vince, but with two fingers jammed halfway up a nostril, I cringed with embarrassment when I saw it was Faye.

"It's a guy thing," I said trying hard to sound kind o' jocular as she pulled an aversive face.

I presumed she was returning from her morning training and was surprised when she climbed up onto the bench seat beside me. She was wearing trainers, a drab pair of garage coveralls and an ill-fitting beanie with her hair tucked up beneath it. Even when she tried to look plain and dowdy, she still looked hotter than an Indiana blast furnace.

"Are you ready? Let's go then ... or do you still have more nose hairs to pluck out?"

She smiled, but then apologized playfully for being so mean.

"Well um, uh, I'm waiting for Vince. I had no idea you were coming too, Faye."

"Vince!" she said surprised, then sighed with exaggerated woe. "I thought it was you and me driving to Hermosillo."

"No, Joe told me that he had to come, as Vince is the only one who knows the place where we—"

"... have to pick up the sodium fluoride," said Faye, finishing off my sentence.

"So why are you coming? I thought you were dead against it."

"I am, but I'm on a shopping mission of my own."

"*Yeah*, what's that?"

"Nothing you'd be interested in. Women's business."

"Oh." I said no more.

With his usual impeccable timing, Señor Vince's head lunged right in through Faye's open window.

"Well howdy there, partners."

He caught her off guard and she nearly jumped out of her skin.

"*Shift on over there blondie, y'all gonna let me in or not?*"

He was back doing that stupid, old-timer, prospector voice again. I was in two minds as to whether it was some kind of retro-linguistic anomaly from smoking too much dope or more likely just a conscious effort to be bloody annoying.

Faye opened the door and jumped down out of the cab.

"Well I'm not going if I have to sit next to boody-boy here for a hundred bloody kilometers. I'm *seriously* not in the mood for his adolescent nonsense."

Oh yes, it was *on*. They were instantly back to their perpetual bickering. This time about who was supposed to be going, who should be doing the driving and who should, would or wouldn't be sitting next to who. I couldn't believe it. I thought I'd resolve the quarrel by starting up the motor and making like I was heading off solo. BIG MISTAKE.

Now Joe's pick-up sounded pretty damn noisy at the best of times and with Vince babbling on in old-timer talk, the running engine made it even harder to make out exactly what the hell he was crapping on about. So, when Vince suddenly pipes up with.

"*Well ur, missy, you can always climb up on back and park your taut little fanny on thur bed.*"

Faye hit the roof. She could speak better English than any of us, but this time our good old American vernacular got *completely* lost in translation.

Faye went bananas, shrieking at Vince in Norwegian. I had no idea what she was saying, but I was damn sure it would have made a frigate-full of one-eyed sailors blush, and then some. *Man*, she was pissed.

It wasn't until Joe, hearing all the ruckus, came hurrying out from inside and explained to Faye exactly what Vince had said regarding the colloquial name for the rear-end of a pickup truck and more importantly the slang term for the human posterior that she eventually calmed down and climbed stoically back up into the cabin. Finally, after fifteen minutes of ridiculous delay, we were off.

Thankfully, from then on, things weren't quite as frosty between them as I'd been expecting. I think Faye seemed a teeny bit embarrassed about her fiery, overreaction, but hey, if Vince has anything to do with anything, you can be certain it would be pretty much warranted. Although stranger things have happened, bizarrely, by the time we were a dozen or so miles north of Hermosillo, they were both chatting away quite happily. Probably the most civil I'd seen them towards each other since I'd met them.

◆

We drove down along the Solidaridad, a long major road which entered into the outskirts of Hermosillo from the north. This was the first large sized city I'd visited since coming to Mexico and I was a little unsure about what to expect. We were looking for a particular turn off, supposedly located close to where we were already, so we had no need to venture further south, down into the city's main center.

Vince was useless. Like an idiot I was expecting concise, *"Turn left, turn right, proceed half a mile forward, left again, bingo! Señor Chachi's place,"* type of directions. He hadn't a clue.

The one thing I will concede though is that to the unfamiliar eye, everything really did look pretty much the same. The surrounding streets were a warren of barbed wire topped brick and concrete walls, iron gates and grill work, the occasional tree and a confusing array of poles and overhead wires. But Vince's claim of knowing where this elusive place was, really didn't hold much sway.

After what seemed an eternity of going back and forward, up and down the Solidaridad, Vince *finally* recognized an old, lime-washed building with a crooked blue water tank on the roof. This was the landmark he'd been looking for.

Now with a reference point, it still didn't get any easier. It was *"Turn left, keep going, keep going, no go back, keep going, left again, no right, no left."* You get the picture. Then finally – I'm one hundred percent sure it was a fluke – we pulled up tetchy and irritable right out the front of Señor Chachi's, sheet-iron, lock up gates. Before we even got out, I could hear the loud, incessant barking of a guard dog.

Great! Ever since I was a kid, I had this love-hate relationship with the wretched things. *All dogs*, not just the guards. They *loved* me, as something to bark at, growl at, wipe their dirty mitts on, sniff, slobber over, or if they can get away with it, rip a tasty little chunk out of me with their nasty mashing teeth. Needless to say, I frick'n *hated* them.

As Vince climbed out of the pickup, a face appeared at one of those little peep-hole doors that sat flush in the center of one of Señor Chachi's gates.

It wasn't a man, but that of a young señorita. Seeing Vince she smiled enthusiastically, shut the little peephole and began to open the left-side gate from inside. She only had it open six inches when the snarly, barking business-end of the guard dog shoved its fang-filled face as far out into the street as the slightly opened gate would allow.

"Fuck that!" I said emphatically. "There's no way on earth I'm going *anywhere* near that thing."

"Me neither," Faye said thankfully in a show of support.

The girl, seeing our unease, yanked the dog back inside, while giving it the old stock, standard lecture to *"Shoosh, behave, keep quiet,"* that sounds exactly the same whether it's in Spanish, English or whatever. If the girl came back with the dog owner's credo of *"It's alright, he won't hurt you,"* I was going to simply start up the truck and head straight on back to The Alamo.

The dog, now under control, still barked and barked as if it somehow knew it would choke itself to death if its relentless yelping should stop, even for one iota.

"Come on you two," signaled Vince as he casually slipped his arm around the girl's waist, who had squeezed out through the gate and now stood on the street beside him.

"Diablo's cool. *He won't hurt you.*"

"Uuugh, dogs."

Faye, having decided it was now safe to get out, slid herself over towards the door. "Come on Fenrir, I'm sure she's put it back somewhere safe and out of reach."

Out of sight, but definitely not out of ear shot.

"Do I really have to? I just – don't – like – dogs. I can cope with the little fluffy ones, *sometimes,* but these big, smelly, agro bastards really give me the creeps. The last time I had a run in with a frick'n dog, I ended up getting arrested."

"What?" said Faye.

"Long story, I'll tell you about it later."

"Oh come on Wolf, this is silly, I'll protect you," Faye said half-teasing.

Feeling pretty stupid, I finally opened the door. By now Vince's tongue was halfway down the young señorita's throat while still keeping a vigilant eye out for Señor Chachi, who I figured was most probably her father.

"Hey Dudes, this is my *lovely* chica hermosa, Marlina."

The girl, a year or two younger than Vince, was tall and shapely with wavy chestnut hair. She was exactly the type of sexy señorita that I'd imagined Vince would go for.

"Marlina, this is Wolf and the lady over there wearing the attractive coveralls is Faye."

"¡Hola! Encantado de conocerle, ¿Cómo estás?" said Marlina happily with an air of brazen confidence.

I knew her words meant pretty much, "Hello, how are you, pleased to meet you." But all I could say in reply was "Buenos días." I was so pathetic. Of course Faye answered Marlina's next words fluently with "Lo siento, no hablo Español."

I didn't know what she said, but it sounded really cool. Meanwhile, by the not so subtle way Vince and his señorita were pawing at each other, it was obvious that they communicated in a different language entirely. But that was by the by.

Interpreting and obviously speaking in tongues, Vince explained that Señor Chachi wasn't quite back *yet*, from being somewhere else. But he would probably be back very soon.

Vince reached into his pocket and peeled off some cash, then handed Marlina a note written in Spanish by Joe. She read it quickly and dragged Vince excitedly by the arm into the yard. Faye followed next and I tagged uncomfortably along at the rear. And all the time, that goddamn dog, wherever it was, barked and barked and barked and barked. It was really doing my head in.

You wouldn't believe all the gear that was stacked in this Señor Chachi's yard. It spanned everything from building and farming equipment to bald-headed mannequins and a whole squad of concrete pelicans. Truly, I'm sure whatever you could think of, it was stashed in here somewhere. Señor Chachi had the lot. Sitting on a palette, thankfully close to the gate was a stack of hundred-pound bags of sodium fluoride ready and waiting to go. Me and Vince went totally macho and heavy-hauled three of those mothers up and onto the truck bed in less than a Mexican minute, leaving the girls to stand and admire our taught, ripped guns in the process. Well, Vince's anyway.

I thought it was all a done deal and we were about to leave when Marlina informed us, using Vince as a questionable translator, that there was a Saturday market only a few blocks away and wondered if maybe we might want to go.

Faye was all for it. We had nothing else scheduled, so hey, why not? Besides, it wasn't hard to spot a thinly veiled plot to ditch me and Faye for an hour, so Vince could disappear somewhere else for a more private chat with Marlina.

◆

The marketplace was nothing like I'd been expecting. We'd entered through one of the service alleys, which, like gaps in a smile, broke up a continuous L-shaped row of shops that formed one side of the square. The whole place had a kind of upbeat, festive feel about it. There was such an unexpected energy with music and people milling around beneath a warm and sunny sky. It was great.

We couldn't have been there more than a minute when Vince tapped me on the shoulder and said, "If we get separated, we'll meet under the tree over by the food stalls. Yeah?"

"Yeah right."

As I'd predicted, the next time I turned around Vince and Marlina were gone. To be honest, the old adage two's company, four's a crowd really did apply in this case.

Faye and I gave the market a bit of a once-over. There was all the predictable stuff, fruit and vegetables, your standard homewares, linen, plastic bowls, plastic chairs and of course every conceivable piece of cheap electrical crap you could imagine.

Most of the stalls didn't really grab us, although we did seem to share a liking for weird stuff and anything that stood out as genuine-imitation-wild-west. I even saw a fashionable selection of hand-stitched chupacabra billfolds.

We soon gravitated over to where two lines of cars were parked for a tailgate sale. There was some great stuff to rake through. The trash and treasure cast offs from a hundred different lives and for a hundred different reasons. It was all there.

I found one guy selling off his entire vinyl collection who also had a bunch of old eight-track cassettes in a box, not that dissimilar to mine. I had a flick through, but found nothing that squared with my particular tastes. Faye had zeroed in on a chock-full rack of clothing that even to my eye didn't look half bad. I could see by the way she was rifling through them that she'd stumbled on one of those unexpected gold mines you always hope one day you'll find. The vendors of these good-looking clothes were a middle-aged couple who'd set up their stall right out back of their humongous-sized camper van, which stuck out like dog's balls amongst all of the other vehicles along the line. The lady who was doing all the selling was a tall, rakish woman with white cropped hair, who I guessed was in the twilight of her forties. Sadly though, her over-cooked roast-like skin, obviously from an idle life of sun-drenched pleasure, made her look almost as old as her husband. He was about sixty and looked for all the world like some grey-haired, shipping tycoon relaxing on the back of a yacht with a brandy. You could tell by his demeanor that he *really* didn't want to be there at all. This was all far too common and beneath him. I couldn't help wondering what roll of the dice had cast this seemingly well-to-do couple in such an obvious, fish out of water predicament.

In any event, the woman was cheerful and very friendly. She joked and chatted freely with Faye and seemed genuinely keen to offer her advice and opinions. It was obvious we were going to be hanging around here for ages, so I resigned myself to make like I was the enthusiastic boyfriend doting on my super-hot girlfriend's impeccable fashion choices. Yeah pathetic I know, but what can ya do?

Faye grabbed a long, black coat off the rack. The line of brass buttons that ran from the neck to the naval gave it an obvious military look. Very last century. But when she slipped it on, even over those ungainly coveralls, you could see its well-cut tapered waist made it a garment of obvious quality.

I watched fascinated as she experimented with the collar and lapels flipping and turning them into different looks and styles. Once the coat was acquired, Faye unexpectedly changed her approach and no-nonsense-like plucked out a few more keen-eyed selections from the rack.

"I'll also have *this, this, this* and *this,* and ... hmmm ... yes, I'd better take *that!*"

All the while the woman was complimenting her wholeheartedly and speaking in what I'm certain was Italian. "Bello, bello, favoloso, magnifico!"

Even her husband was in on the act. I could see him over on his fold out chair nodding enthusiastically, all the while gobbling Faye up with his piggy-pervy eyes. I could read him like a book. "*Delizioso!* What is such a magnificent young beauty like her doing with *him*, and why that ridiculous hat and those unsightly looking coveralls?"

Once the lady was paid and the not so fashionable bin-liner full of clothes handed over, Faye did that strange European air-kiss-thing and said her goodbyes in Italian.

"She was nice," Faye said chirpily. "I can't believe it Wolf, I just bought some really lovely stuff."

"Yeah, I liked the coat."

"I know, I couldn't believe it, it's *haute couture*."

"What's that, Italian?"

"No that's French … but yes the coat is Italian."

I was lost.

"What's the big deal with you and all things *Italian*?"

"Belleza, qualità e sofisticazione!"

"Just as a matter of interest Faye, how many languages *do* you speak?"

She sucked her bottom lip, went all girly and gazed up cutely towards the sky. *"Umm?"* She started counting on her one free hand, but soon ran out of fingers. "Six … and two others, but only just a little."

"So what are they, all these different languages?"

"Well, Norwegian obviously. Danish, Swedish, Deutch, English and *Old Norse*. I still have trouble with Icelandic for some reason, even though it is much more similar in form to Old Norse than the rest."

"What are the other two then? The only just 'a littles'?"

"Like I said, basic Icelandic and a teeny-weeny bit of Italian."

"Spanish?"

"Nope, hardly anything more than hello, goodbye, and how are you?"

"Well, I have no problems at all with either Spanish or Icelandic, I'm beginning to think Miss Faye that you're not really as smart as I thought you were." She jabbed me playfully in the ribs and laughed out loud at my nonsense.

Our drifting around had brought us back to the shop buildings where we had first come in. Knowing pretty much where we were, I stopped to check out a table stall of Día de los Muertos figurines and skulls. Some were exactly like the little painted ones Faye had lined up along the shelves in her trailer.

Thinking she was right beside me I turned to point one out but noticed she wasn't there. Presuming she'd moved on ahead to look at something else I didn't take much notice. All the little skeleton señors and señoritas were mesmerizing and they'd bewitched me for longer than I'd thought. It was only when I felt an electric jolt from the fire-bright eyes of the Lady of the Shadows that I snapped back to reality and urgently began looking around for Faye.

Then I spotted her through a momentary gap in the crowd. My heart started pounding with shock and fear and confusion. Faye had been grabbed by two human gorillas who were forcibly dragging her towards the open doors of a van parked down one of the alleyways.

With his gnarly right hand clamped over Faye's mouth and his left hand crudely under her crotch, one of the men bounced her hurriedly sideways in the direction of their vehicle, while his no-nonsense buddy used his massive girth like a muscle-bound bulldozer shoving and wrangling them all together as one big mass. I could see Faye desperately trying to resist but against the combined size and strength of these two men it was impossible.

With my legs feeling like two useless jellies I ran suicidally towards her. I would be there in seconds. I had no idea what I would do when I got there and was sure they would probably shoot me or at best leave me a bloodied and broken wreck. All I wanted right now was for something or someone to magically appear and save Faye from danger and make this unreal nightmare go away.

The thug holding Faye unexpectedly yelled in pain and pulled his hand away from her mouth. She must have got a bite on his fingers. That move was crucial. Instantly she sprung her head forward and smashed it forcefully back into his face. The violence of her action caught him completely off guard, hammering his big ugly head hard into the bricks of the alleyway behind him. It knocked him out cold and he slid down the wall to the deck. With an angry vicious pile-drive his buddy punched Faye hard in the stomach and she began to arch over winded. I desperately threw myself at him, but he simply thrust out an elbow which knocked me sprawling backwards. Distracted, he grabbed at the top of Faye's head, ready to smash her hard in the face with his fist, but was surprised to find the only thing he held was her beanie.

Poor Faye had buckled and rolled off to one side. I thought she was finished, but I gasped in disbelief when, in one fluid movement she continued her roll, grabbed an empty iron crate from the ground and slammed it up hard and ferociously into his face sending her jumbo-sized assailant on a back-flip down to the concrete.

Like a resurrected phoenix beneath a swathe of golden hair, Faye jumped back to her feet, once again strong and fully attentive, but now on the attack. She offered neither mercy nor quarter and slammed the iron crate down viciously onto the stunned unfortunate's head.

SLAM! SLAM! SLAM!

Then her gaze fell on an irrelevancy, right there in the way. *Me.* For one timeless second, she locked her cold piercing eyes onto mine. The look was wild, distant, and *very, very* threatening. This wasn't Faye. This was *Freya*, the goddess of war, now incarnate.

She raised the crate high above her head in readiness for a fourth strike and an undoubted kill. Foolhardily I lunged myself forward between her and her prey and yelled *"NO FAYE, STOP! Stop! Enough ... enough!"*

Then as if someone had flicked off a switch, I saw her revert back to her normal self. Looking confused and disorientated Faye promptly dropped the iron crate on the ground when she saw the bloodied body beneath her. The guy looked fucked. I don't think he was dead, but he certainly wouldn't be winning any more beauty prizes.

"Come on Faye, let's get out of here."

Faye was babbling and going all wide-eyed and spooky from the shock.

"HE's here Wolf, *HE's here* ... I can feel his presence ... HE's here! *SHE's* here too! She did this ... yes *Freya* did this. Oh dear, dear Óðinn, what has she done?'

As curious onlookers were beginning to show a bit of an interest, a chubby, middle-aged Mexican man with greying unkempt hair stepped out from behind a box-laden trolley that he had parked strategically to hide us from further prying eyes.

The expression on his face flashed disconcertingly back and forth, between one of geniality and one of concern. Now he's happy, now he's worried, now he's happy, now he's worried. But strangely, a quick rotating movement that he made with his index finger seemed to somehow calm Faye down considerably. The devilishly handsome face of his iconic namesake printed right across his T-shirt told me *exactly* who he was, and I submitted us both unquestioningly into his charge.

He promptly indicated in one of the "now he's happy!" phases it was definitely time to go.

"Rápidamente! rápidamente!"

I picked up Faye's bag and hat from the ground as he ushered us over into the shadows and quickly away from the scene.

After running down a bunch of alleyways and side lanes we burst back out into the street only thirty yards up from Señor Chachi's. I could see Vince acting the dude, he was lolling back across the hood of the pickup tapping away on Marlina's neck and shoulders with his fingers as though she was some kind of drum kit.

Two other girls were also there, the four of them all flirting and laughing and carrying on so much that none of them heard nor saw us coming.

Señor Chachi clipped Vince contemptuously on the back of the head and berated the three girls gruffly in Spanish. One of them took off quickly, while Marlina and the other who I presumed was her sister were told sternly to get back inside and pull the metal gates shut behind them.

"Hey, how's it goin' Señor Chachi, what's happ—"

Vince's shameless *"Well hi there!"* ruse came quickly to naught. Except for another, even harder, whack on the back of his head Señor Chachi ignored him completely.

The three of us were bundled quickly back into the pickup and sent hurriedly on our way. All the time, Señor Chachi's expression switching back and forth between one of serious concern and one of unabashed excitement as he did so.

Oh yeah, the whole time all this was happening, that infernal Diablo just kept on barking and barking and barking and barking.

◆

It wasn't until we were twenty minutes out of Dodge and totally convinced that no one was behind us, that we stopped. I pulled over at a section of road where we could see anyone coming for miles in either direction.

Faye was going nuts. Her blurred memories of what had happened at the marketplace were quickly sharpening up. She insisted on asking me all these dumbass questions and saying things like, "I killed them, didn't I? We have to turn around *immediately* so I can hand myself in."

She was working herself into a state and started hyperventilating. It all came to a head when suddenly she opened the door, bailed from the cab, and threw her guts up.

"What's wrong with her?" I was amazed at Vince's uncharacteristic restraint. He'd sat there looking totally bemused saying nothing at all since we'd left.

"We had a bit of an *incident,* back there at the market."

"No!" Vince said sarcastically.

I thought it best to tell him quickly what had happened before Faye got back in the truck.

"She beat the living daylights out of a couple o' bad boys who tried to drag her off into a van."

"Seriously?"

"Yeah! You should have seen these two monsters, I kid you not, they were the size of Sherman tanks. They picked on the wrong one there."

"Far out, I figured something *large* had happened. She was frick'n losing it back there!" sniggered Vince.

"And yeah, who's this Freya chick she was crapping on about? *'Freya she sees all, through my eyes!'* Hooley frick'n Dooley, she's gone nuts."

Vince, finding it all very amusing reclined back on the seat and chuckled his scruffy-looking head off.

"And yeah, this Mee-merz dude. *Wow,* she don't seem too fussed about catching up with him any time soon."

"It's Mimas, Me-mus. Please don't mention either of them, especially him. They're as best as I can figure, a friend and a foe. I dunno? *From some other space and time.*"

Vince rolled his eyes with contempt, exactly like I'd expected him to.

21

Hnefatafl

I'd been expecting our return to The Alamo to be met with a modicum of interest, but three bags of sodium fluoride were obviously nothing to get worked up about. The reception committee of two hoity cats with a single-minded interest in greeting their *mommy* wasn't quite what I'd imagined.

Vince had vanished, and Faye had slipped groggily back to her trailer with Gutteka and Jenteka. I hung around for a while but apart from a guy called Tisac who was manning the pumps, there was no one else to be found. He didn't speak any English and formed his words slowly, as if that would somehow transcend any language barrier. Didn't work on me though, I couldn't understand one single word he said.

It was only when I got back to the camper van that I heard some laughter and a little music drifting over from the campsite. I figured that it was probably where they all were, but I really couldn't care less. The van door slid open easily and I crashed out for a well-earned siesta on my skinny single bed.

I lay there thinking about how frail Faye had looked when she climbed back up into the cab. I remembered how she pulled the black coat from the bag, wrapped it around herself and stared silently out of the side window for the rest of the trip home.

It was obvious that the first incarnation of Freya had been *way* too intense. The whole thing couldn't have lasted more than ten seconds total, but it had completely shaken her up.

◆

The devils were pounding hard on the walls and trying to get in. No matter how hard I tried, it was impossible to completely pull the sliding door shut. To my horror one of them managed to jam its arm through the gap and was poking me hard with its claw. That woke me up immediately, but instead of devils I was confronted by my arch nemesis, the giant flying moustache-moth hurtling around fitfully on the roadrunner pillow just an inch or two from my face.

"Hello Mr. Wolf."

The unexpected voice made me sit up immediately. It was Faye.

"Holy Joseph! You scared the you-know-what out of me."

"I'm sorry Fenrir, I thought you were only resting. I didn't know you were asleep."

"Nor did I, I must have dozed off."

Judging by the gloomy darkness inside the van and the failing light outside I figured I must have been out like a light for a couple of hours at least. Faye was holding a dinner plate covered with a clean and neatly folded dish cloth.

"What's that?"

"It's a couple of slices of barbecued meat..."

She hesitated for a second and thought carefully about the end of her sentence.

"It's Asian influenced. I knew you would like some so I brought a couple of pieces over for you. It is very tasty."

"Well thank you Faye," I was touched. "Where did you get it?"

I initially thought that Hamada-san or Kiko had cooked up something exotic while we'd been down in Hermosillo. Faye giggled as a preempt to answering.

"Oh, I brought it across from the campsite, they were having a little commemorative lunch party."

"Hmm, I thought I heard a bit of frivolous *yeeha-ing!* coming from over that way."

"I was fast asleep earlier too, but Joe came by and insisted that I had been *'most cordially invited by the host'* to come along to his little get together."

"So what was it for?" I said as I shoved a chunky slice into my mouth. "Wow, that is delicious, what sort of meat is it?"

"Oochicoochi's leg!" Faye burst out laughing.

"What?" My mouth dropped open mid-chew.

"No, not his *real* leg silly, well in a way it was, but only... *symbolsk?* Symbolically."

It was great to see the old Faye was definitely back amongst us. She couldn't stop laughing. "Well, apparently, Oochie, Lieutenant Crawford has this little anniversary celebration every year on the day that he lost his leg in the Vietnam war," Faye was in hysterics. "I'm sorry Wolf I'm not laughing at him or that the poor man lost his leg but the whole thing was just *so* funny. It seems so *morbid* really but Oochicoochi thought it was *GREAT.*"

I loved her accent and her laugh was completely contagious.

"You should have seen it when they brought the barbecued pig leg out to the table. It was standing upright on a platter with a life-size army boot made from the crispy, over-cooked crackling at the bottom and a single sparkler stuck ceremoniously on the top." Faye was inconsolable with laughter. I ate another slice of the meat and chuckled along with her.

"Seriously Wolf, he was just so, so funny. He was having a wonderful time, cracking jokes, being obnoxious, telling old stories, offering everyone, *'Hey Goldilocks, don't be shy, please, just help yourself. Have another piece of my tasty ol' leg!'*"

I smiled, impressed with her perceptive and excellent mimicry.

"He looked like, what is that saying? The pussy cat who got all of the cream."

I was going to correct her but, hey.

"Anyway, I'm heading back home now," Faye announced. "What are you doing later?" The question took me by surprise.

"*Uuur*, well, nothing really."

"Well how would you like to play a game?"

What do you frick'n think? My imagination shot up like that sideshow attraction where you hit the giant hammer and try to make the bell ring, but an overwhelming sense of reality hurled it back down to earth just as quickly.

"Sure, what do you have in mind?" I thought that sounded pretty cool, with a non-committal air of indifference.

"Hnefatafl."

I suddenly had an overwhelming urge to wield the giant hammer again.

"Nefa— what?"

She took no notice but turned to walk away.

"I'll come back in an hour or so, okay?"

"Yeah … sure."

◆

She'll be back in an hour, maybe two. *Hmmm.*

I ran the palm of my hand, flat-iron style across the grubby cover of the camper's tortured mattress as if it might somehow miraculously turn into a crisp-sheeted bed from a five-star hotel.

Oh, give it a rest tiger. I squashed my ridiculous train of thought immediately. You're so far out of her league, you couldn't even score a cheap seat, high up in the bleachers. I've never really been a glass half-full kind o' guy, although a rogue vein of self-delusion has always run contradictory to the hard facts of reality.

Didn't matter. I grabbed my soap and towel and a spare pair of boxers and hightailed it over to the campsite showers, all the way across evaluating the likelihood of a logjam of soaped-up jolly hombres luxuriating in the novelty of the recent abundance of hot water, courtesy of Joe's new sodium-sulfur powered boiler. I figured even in a worst-case scenario I'd at least have time to send a steaming hot face cloth on a joyride up between my ass cheeks once or twice.

I couldn't believe it, except for some poor soul scowling at himself in the mirror, the shower block was completely empty. Less than ten minutes later, I was back at the ranch, oiling up the quiff and looking as cool as the proverbial cucumber. It was five forty-five, the place looked like shit and darkness had almost settled. And what the hell is Nefenatafal, anyway?

◆

"Hello Fenrir, I'm back."

"Howdy Faye, you look a *treat*." I suppose that sounded pretty corny, but I wasn't that much of a silver-tongued charmer.

Faye was wearing her olive-green sweater and her regular blue jeans and trainers, but her hair was different. It was all piled up on top of her head in a messy looking bundle and held in place by one of those spring-loaded comb things. She even wore a tiny pair of earrings that looked like two sparkling apple seeds.

"No Mr. Wolf they're not real." She'd noticed me checking them out. "They're only zircons, but they *are* very shiny."

Under one arm Faye was carrying three cardboard egg cartons, and in her hands she had a plastic shopping bag and a long roll of cow-hide leather.

"This looks nice," Faye said, almost sincerely.

I'd used my "suppressed artistic pedanticism" skills to ring the immediate area around the door of the camper with a whole bunch of stubby little candles. She sat down with all of her bits and pieces on the out-stretched blanket that I'd laid out earlier.

"So. Are you ready to play Hnefatafl?"

By now, all my most ludicrous delusions of anything touchy feely happening had crumbled into microscopic dust.

"You bet." Although I hadn't the faintest idea what it was.

Faye unrolled the piece of leather and laid it out flat in front of her. It had those irregular edges you get on a rough-cut hide, obviously local and definitely not Norwegian. Right in the middle was a carefully hand-drawn grid of about twelve squares by twelve squares along each side. A few of the outer squares were tooled in some kind of swirling design and another bunch of squares made up a diamond shape in the middle. It was a board game!

"So what do you use for the playing pieces Faye, counters? Are there any dice?"

"Hold the horses Fenrir, let's have a hit or two of the good stuff first, yeah?"

With that she pulled out a tequila bottle and a couple of glasses from the plastic bag and poured two shots.

"Skál!"

I was impressed. She had already poured herself another while I was still raising the first one up to my lips.

"Come on Wolf, you big girly…" Faye mocked cheekily. "Let's see a bit of that old Viking spirit. *"Skál"* She slammed down the second and then sat frozen for a moment as if she'd been magically turned into stone.

I stole those precious seconds to feast my eyes on her loveliness. The light from the candle flames twinkled in the apple seed earrings and danced amongst the random slithers of hair that had freed themselves from the comb and hung wispily down around her ears. Man she was gorgeous.

"Buuuurp! Okay Wolf, you light the fire, while I set the pieces up on the board."

"Sure," I said casually. I'd lit my fire a couple of times since I'd been here, but success was mostly hit and miss. My cub scout skills were on par with a first week rookie. Thankfully, this time the flame took straight away.

"Greetings golden haired goddess, warm thyself beside the roaring hearth of my hallowed halls," was the kind of greeting that should have cascaded from my lips, so I was annoyed with myself for sprouting the

bleeding obvious. "Fire's going," I said, as if it's doing was as easy as turning on the TV.

"Come on Wolf, let's have another shot."

For a millisecond, the rogue vein of self-delusion resurfaced assessing the odds of an inebriated goddess incarnate throwing herself wantonly upon yours truly, but my lecherous thought vanished with a speedy, self-delivered boot up the backside. Metaphorically speaking of course.

"Do you think that's wise to have a third one? I mean quite so soon."

"*Umm*, maybe not, you're probably right. I do have to train in the morning, but I'll have another as soon I thrash you at Hnefatafl."

"Sounds good."

Faye was unsettled and I figured this whole board game thing was only a ruse, a distraction from the incident at the market. It didn't take a genius to see that it was a way to keep some company and her mind on something else. Not that I'm complaining, but I figured it best if she worked through it in her own way and time.

"Wow, that's awesome!" I gasped. The set-up board looked truly amazing. Twenty-four red skulls were now positioned on the swirly squares around the outer edge. White skulls sat on the diamond formation in the middle with a larger, apple-sized skull sitting smack in the center. The flickering firelight shimmered brilliantly on the thousands of tiny inlaid shards of mirror that covered all of the pieces. The effect was hypnotic. I would never have guessed that the little skulls from inside Faye's trailer were the players. It was obvious now what had been stored in the egg cartons. Faye motioned for me to sit down at the opposite end of the board.

"Okay, so what are the rules then? How do you play?"

"*Right*. Hnefatafl is a Viking board game from the Dark Ages that—"

"How come the red side's got twice as many pieces and who's the big dude in the middle of all the white ones?"

Faye looked up at me annoyed.

"Have you finished? I was about to explain all that before you so rudely interrupted."

"Sorry. Go ahead...*please*."

"Unlike chess or checkers, the size of the opposing armies in Hnefatafl are unequal. The red side are the attackers, their four flanking positions around the edge of the board represent ships and they are out to capture the king, that's the *big dude* sitting in the middle. The white side's objective is to escort the king to safety as he makes his escape from the board by reaching any one of the corners."

"Why is the king's side white?"

"It doesn't matter, the colors can change, even the board size can change, they're just variations. Don't confuse yourself with any of that right now."

Faye told me how all the pieces could move and be captured and although on face value it seemed fairly simple to play, the beauty of the game lay in the tactics and strategy.

"Who goes first?"

"The attackers. I'll play them, and you can take the king's side."

"But that's unfair, isn't it? You've got twice as many men as me."

"No Wolf, this isn't sjakk, I mean chess. It might surprise you, but the king's side nearly always wins in tafl, that's why it's courteous to take it in turns to play each side alternately."

"What's tafl?"

"*Uugh*. Tafl just means table and Hnefa refers to the king piece. Hnefa-tafl."

"So the king's side can still win, being outnumbered two to one?"

"I just told you they could, it wouldn't be much of a game if they couldn't now, would it? Although personally, I hardly ever get beaten playing attack."

"So you're pretty good then?"

"I'm more than pretty good Mr. Wolf, I'm *fantastic*."

"Yeah?"

"If I may tune my own bugle, I was all fylker, sorry, *counties*, high school champion of Norway."

"Are you serious? That's frick'n amazing. And it's not tune your own bugle, it's ... ah, doesn't matter."

"I didn't have much of a choice, I played so much I couldn't help but always win."

"What do you mean?"

"My bestemor, the Seiðkonur would always make me play tafl with her whenever she came over or we went to visit. Not only one quick game, but game after game after game. Axel thought it was hilarious. He would always fetch the box and set up the board in readiness, just to annoy me. I would sometimes burst into tears or try to run and hide. I can still hear her now: *'Hello dear Freya, let's have a quick game of tafl.'* ... or ten!"

"I bet she was an ex-champ and wanted you to be like her?"

"No, she would say, *'Learn the subtleties of tafl my Freya, pursue it as a virtue. Someday it will serve you well.'* I didn't mind it at first, then I absolutely *hated* it, but then as I got a little older, I began to understand and really like it."

"Was all the constant practice, practice, practice that made you a winner?"

"*Hmm*, yes and no. The Seiðkonur would always keep encouraging me to *'Use the Triskele Freya. Use the Triskele.'* I hadn't a clue what she was on about until I was nine or ten. But when I did figure out what she meant, I realized that I'd been doing that all along anyway. Axel used to make me laugh, he would stand behind her and pull faces like a wild berserker. She caught him once and told him that she would turn him into a toad."

"*So—*"

"What's the Triskele? It's an ancient symbol found across western Europe. Its origins are lost to millennia, *'Far, far, back in time before the Neolithic,'* as my bestemor would always tell me. Although its original meaning is unknown, its symbology is very profound and steeped in spiritual significance. The particular aspect of it that I was concerned with, was the triple unfolding spirals and the transference of their mathematical patterns into the movement strategies of Hnefatafl."

"*Wow!* What does this Tris' thingy symbol look like?"

She tried unconvincingly to make the shape with her fingers, while explaining that it was, "Three spirals that all seem to join up and form a triangle."

I could see she was getting sick of all the questions.

"And what has all that got to do with tafl?"

"It's a kind of… *sequence* if you like, I can *SEE* the mathematics, I can SEE the unfolding patterns. Don't ask me how I do it, I really don't know that myself, but I've usually got most of my games won right from the onset. Basically I divide my forces into three and play a rotating spiral tactic, not unlike the Triskele. It *completely* bewilders opponents who just charge out willy-nilly with a more standard, four-sided frontal attack."

I hadn't the foggiest idea what she was on about.

"Well then, knock yourself out *Ice Maiden*, let's play Hnefa-*frick'n*-tafl."

"No more questions?"

"Nope."

"Okay. Attacker moves first. I'll help you out Wolf, as we go along."

Game One lasted about a minute, I got slaughtered. Faye apologized profusely and admitted that her embarrassing, unsociable flaw was that she just couldn't *EVER* consider going easy on an opponent playing tafl, even a first-time beginner.

I feigned indignity, demanded a shot of tequila, and set up my next round of attackers. To be honest, I couldn't give a rat's ass about losing, sitting there throwing down tequilas with the gorgeous Faye was more than I could cope with anyway.

"How old is this game?"

"I told you, it dates back to the Dark Ages, somewhere around the 8th century in Scandinavia. But the Seiðkonur adamantly disagrees with that, of course. She says it is 'much, much older.' But she *would* say that. She says that about everything."

For the next game we switched sides as was the custom.

"Okay, my red guys are all in their ships, so why's your king not in his castle?"

At the moment I said it, Faye pulled something wrapped in newspaper, out from her shopping bag.

"What's that?" I said curiously.

"I never play the king. I always play *Freya.*"

It was the little metal figurine of the woman riding the boar that I'd picked up from the side of the road that first morning I arrived here.

"*Far out!* Is that allowed in the rules?"

She looked at me as if I were joking. Faye placed the statue down carefully on the center square amidst her guard of the smaller-sized skulls and smiled.

It hit me like a hammer, Thor's frick'n hammer.

"*That figure is you!* That's *YOU* riding Hildisvíni."

"Your perception is keen, my dear little minion. *Now,* let the *real* games begin."

Stunned, my mouth fell totally open.

"What?" said Faye.

"I think your buddy Freya just spooky-spoke to me."

"Oh don't be ridiculous, you're only making that up."

But the expression on my face said I wasn't. "So what did she say?"

I relayed the sentence and Faye's mood turned quickly sullen. Then unexpectedly she jumped to her feet and began pacing around in what I can only describe as a panic. It was obvious she'd been brooding over what had happened down in Hermosillo, but I wasn't expecting any mention of Freya to spark a reaction like this. Luckily, it was nowhere near as intense as before and within a minute she had calmed herself down. More or less.

Faye sat herself beside the fire and gazed forlornly into the flames. I thought she was about to burst into tears, but she simply sat there.

"I'm frightened Fenrir … *please* forgive me."

"Uum, yeah, no problemo."

"Now she's arrived. I can feel her warlike aggression running cold and rampant through my veins. It grows stronger and more lethal as the hours pass now, but at the same time I'm being overwhelmed as her *incredible* goodness and love surges around inside my psyche like, I can't describe it, it's frightening and incredibly exhilarating at the same time, she's just so, so powerful. I feel like I'm one of those lava lamp things, with her swirling around deep inside of me. But what truly scares me the most, isn't Freya, … it's HIM, he terrifies me. He knows near enough where I am now. It will only be a matter of time before he finds me."

I was hopeless. I had no idea what I should say. "Did you see him Faye? Back there at the market?"

"No, but he was there, he was there. Those two kidnappers were merely hired goons, but his *spirit* was there. I could feel his malevolent powers engulfing me."

"Sooo … is it you or is it Freya, that he's after?"

Faye just stared deeply into the fire. "He wants to subdue and overcome her, to capture and control the divine female energy for his own means, but to do that he needs *my* physicality. To him we are both goddess and mortal, divine and terrestrial, both one and the same."

"Does he still want to take you to …?"

"Mars," said Faye.

"Is it only demonic beings that live there?"

"Of course not. There are many different races and life forms that inhabit the fourth planet."

"Does that include humans?"

"Hominins have been there for eons."

"Are they from Earth?"

"Some are, some aren't."

"How'd they get past the Van Allen Belts, then?" I'd catch her up on this one.

Faye shook her head with disdain and said nothing.

"What about the Moon?"

"What about it?"

"Are there bases and people living on the Moon as well?"

"Oh yes!" she said flippantly. "It's teeming with all kinds of people. On the dark side, the front side and deep beneath the surface structure. People from Earth have been up there since the fifties. It's very interesting where the Moon came from, how it got there, and what its true purpose is."

"Hmmm, it's probably made of frick'n cheese as well," I said bitchily under my breath. "Have you ever been there?" I took a sixty-forty punt on what she would answer.

"No, not me, but Axel has."

I was convinced all this Freya possession business was sending Faye completely loopy.

It was bizarre how completely nonplussed she seemed about all of these wacko, ridiculous things she was saying. Faye suddenly broke out with a smile. I was glad to see she was fine. Well, mostly anyway.

"Come on Wolf, we've still got Hnefatafl games to play." She moved away from the fire and we took our previous positions in readiness.

"Faye, I've got one more question."

"What's that?"

"Who exactly is this Mimas guy then, and who or what is the power behind him?"

She didn't answer straight away, but I could tell that just hearing his name made her feel very uneasy.

"You really wouldn't understand Wolf. Besides, you don't believe anything that I tell you anyway, *Mr. 'made-of-cheese'."* Faye looked hard and probing across the tafl towards me. She was about to say something but stopped and I could tell by her face, there was no way on earth she would speak of it.

"Let's just say … the terrible, terrible, darkness."

◆

We played two more games of Hnefatafl. I lost them both. It took longer to reset the pieces than the time we'd spent actually playing.

"Okay, that's it, you're going down Faye, this time you're going *down*."

I had made my first move when a swirling, black dot appeared out of nowhere right above the Hnefatafl board. Leaning forward I swiped the air with my arm to make it go somewhere else.

"NO, don't do that!" Faye urgently scolded my action. "It's a bee!"

"I'm only trying to make it piss off."

"Fenrir, you should never ever swipe like that at a bee."

It circled around for a few seconds longer then landed right on top of the Freya statue.

"*Huuuugh!*" Faye gasped long and excited. "I think he's come here to see *me.*"

"What?"

Faye sat with a grin from ear to ear, memorized as it wiggled around and marched all over the little figurine's head.

"Neith might have sent him from Sais. But this little fellow's *definitely* got that unmistakable Minoan shimmy when he dances. Don't you think?"

"Oh *definitely,*" I said snidely. "It's just a bee Faye, not Mr. Bojangles." Once again, she ignored me.

"Yep, I'm pretty sure he's one of Rhea's. She would have asked him nicely to come and see me," Faye beamed excitedly.

"I wonder if she still gets mistaken for Cybele, that used to drive her crazy. When I was a little girl, she would sometimes turn my tears into little golden bees that buzzed and tickled as they rolled down my cheeks. It used to make me laugh and I would always stop crying."

"I thought Minoans lived thousands of years ago."

"Oh Wolf, you really don't get it do you? This little bee was sent here through Seiðr."

She sat there transfixed and smiling as it shimmied and did its little dance.

"I like bee's, they're busy, they do things. I like ants too; they cart stuff away."

For an instant I was witness to the beautiful loving side of Freya. I saw in Faye an innocent child, lost in wonder in a sun-filled meadow amidst tall, swaying flowers in a world both now, but also somewhere distant, a *long, long* time ago.

Then Faye went bonkers. Apparently their "little chat" had taken an unexpected twist.

"Oh wow! wow! *Of course, of course, of course!* How on earth could I have forgotten? *Oh yippee! Yippee-doodle!*"

"What?"

"They're coming Wolf. They'll be here TOMORROW."

"Who?"

"The Tire Boys!"

With that little excited revelation she jumped to her feet and did a little jig.

"*Tire boys*, tire boys, *tire boys*, tire boys. You'll LOVE it Fenrir! Can you get the time off to come along and watch?"

"*Uuur*, yeah, I guess so. Joe's pretty slack when it comes to—"

Faye stopped her jig and started packing up the little skulls and putting them into the empty egg cartons.

"Suppose we can finish the tafl some other time then … maybe?" I said, baffled.

Things were going pretty well until Mr. frick'n Buzz-boy blew in and stuffed up proceedings with his important "yippee-doodle" revelation. Irrespective, I suppose I should have felt somehow grateful at being invited along to whatever it was. All I could think of was an all-boy, tire-changing Indy 500 pit crew, but that made no sense. I couldn't see any through line between bees, boys, and tires.

"So, just exactly who—"

"Who are the tire boys? You'll see tomorrow. They're *truly, truly* amazing."

I was still none the wiser.

"I'm sorry Wolf, I know this seems rude, but it is getting late and I *do* have to train in the morning with Hamada-san, so I'd better be going."

"No problem," I said feeling a little bit miffed. Obviously, the dubious shimmy-shake announcement by a bee, regarding the impending arrival of tire boys trumped a pleasant evening playing Hnefatafl with boring yours truly.

"Oh yes," she said, remembering something at the bottom of her plastic bag. "Here's the book you wanted to read. It belongs to Sacramento, but he said you were welcome to borrow it."

Faye handed me the copy of *Chief Iron Eyes Little Eagle*, one of the books I'd noticed on her kitchenette table.

"I'm sure you will like it." She kissed me on the forehead and scurried off with her things. "See you around noon!" Faye yelled back as an afterthought.

I sighed with resignation and looked despondently at the cover. The subtitle read: *An illustrated retrospective of Native American peoples portrayed through popular culture.*

Once I started flicking through the pages I was hooked. This was obviously where Sacramento had been scoring heaps of his wise-cracking material. Then amongst other things I found the pertinent chapter on

Chief Iron Eyes Little Eagle. The guy was a legend. He'd been in frick'n countless TV westerns and films that I'd watched as a kid. I never knew that his fame had allowed him to work as a tireless fundraiser for a whole bunch of Native American charities or that he taught "Indian" culture on reservations and helped to rid them of the scourge of the white man's fire water. My belated opinion of him had gone up tenfold. The book was amazing, I didn't put it down 'till well after midnight.

22

The Tire Boys

I was glad to have spent a couple of hours working on the fence with Joe, so I didn't feel too guilty about dropping tools and heading off to wherever with Faye. Besides, we'd more or less run out all the wiring and were only tying off loose ends and straightening up a couple of poles that still looked a tad lopsided.

We had wandered down the south end of the now completely fenced off crevice, to take a better look at the trinkets that the locals had started to hang off the wires. Garlands of plaited straw, brightly colored string, sunflowers and marigolds, all kinds of stuff like that. Joe quite liked a small child's drawing of himself holding hands with the Lady of the Shadows. He was in two minds as to what it really meant, but he still thought it was great, especially the fifty-gallon cowboy hat sitting monumentally on top of his head with energetic, crayon speed lines radiating off it. He told me straight up it was already earmarked for a prime spot on the wall in his office.

I grabbed my jacket and was heading back over to the garage when Vince came chugging past on his rusty old classic.

"Wanna ride dude?"

"Sure, thanks," I gladly accepted, if only to break the routine. I was climbing back off not twenty seconds later, when Vince cocked his head up and grinned.

"Hey Wolfman, check out 'John and Kiko'."

Vince laughed in his usual lukewarm manner as Bird and Kiko walked arm in arm towards us. I hadn't seen either of them since their meeting in the dining room. Obviously, things had moved on in leaps and bounds between the two of them. They stopped, bowed, and together bade us good morning in Japanese, like a long-time, old-married couple.

Vince was grinning. You could see he was waiting for any chink in their bi-fold armor to pounce.

"Hey Birdman, Kiko. How's it going?"

They stood grafted as one at the hip and they both looked as happy and content as you could ever wish on anybody.

"Please Señor Wolf, I am pleased to tell you ... I now know my *real* name." Bird grinned in self-satisfaction and Kiko's face screwed right up into a cheery smile-ball.

"Wow, nice one. About frick'n time!" Vince said, sounding surprised. "What is it?"

Bird stood tall and puffed out his chest. *"Shintarō.* That is my name!"

"Bullshit!" yelled Vince.

"Wow! Shintarō the mist," I said trying to help push up the big fellow's gusto.

"No-no-no-no-no!" chimed in Kiko. *"Tombei* the mist, he was an Iga Ninja. *Akikusa* Shintarō was the name of the samurai on Japanese TV."

I think Kiko was pleased and amused that we could actually connect the obscure 1960's pop culture icon with Bird's real name.

"Shin-bloody-tarō. You cruiser," said Vince, now sounding excited.

Making that *Ah, before I forget,* expression, Shintarō dipped his hand deep into his pants pocket for something.

"I found this in the road close to Luis Escoto's, do you want it?"

I couldn't believe it, he casually handed me the '58 Special's missing V-badge as though it was nothing more valued than a dropped plastic comb. Everything from that horrible night trapped inside the Fire Diamond at the skelly-fest up until now flashed through my head.

"Yeah thanks," I said somewhat blasé. I slipped the badge into my jacket's chest pocket and did up the button. I thought it pretty ironic that I now had two of the damn things.

The sound of Faye's voice snapped me back as she appeared right beside us and gave Kiko and Bird a big hug. Kiko was shaking like a leaf again. Man, she was so frick'n awestruck every time she saw Faye, it was scary. As usual there was a lot of bowing, buckets of smiles and the excited words spoken quickly in Japanese all peppered with the familiar *Tomoe Gozen! Tomoe Gozen!* I always got a kick out of being around Kiko, she was great.

Faye looked frosty. I don't use words like that often. She wasn't just cool; she was Ice Maiden cool. She wore a rainbow-unicorn T-shirt beneath her brown-leather jacket, those wicked black jeans and her newly acquired motorcycle boots. Her hair hung loose, and she was wearing *my* hat.

"You like that hat of mine, don't ya?" I asked. Not that I minded, I said she *should* wear it, it looked ten-times better on her than it ever did on me. I knew for a fact that I'd flung it down the back of the camper yesterday afternoon and I distinctly remember it spinning on the bench above the bar fridge when it landed.

"You said I could wear it," Faye said flatly.

"That's fine, no problem, I'm glad. I just wondered how you got it?"

"Gutteka sort of fetched it home with him last night I suppose ... sorry."

"Gutteka and Jenteka weren't there! Were they?"

"Oh yes they were, just out of sight in the shadows. You can be sure about that."

"Oh I believe you. I believe you."

Shintarō then handed Faye a folded piece of paper. "Who drew that?" said Faye.

Kiko couldn't catch her breath quick enough to affirm that it was drawn by her new beau. "Shintarō is a *very, very* good ... artist."

"That's great Bird," I yelled genuinely impressed. It was outstanding, a stylized picture of a falcon in full flight.

"Yeah, the big guy's a living legend back home when it comes to Day of the Dead Week," blurted Vince, almost but not quite complimentary.

"Why's that?"

"All those paper skeletons and skull faces they hang everywhere. Old blubber-guts here draws most of that." He was now giving praise, as only Vince could.

"Shintarō this is beautiful, thank you very much," Faye said sincerely. "Why did you not ever show me your artwork before? I had no idea."

He shrugged his shoulders and went all kind o' shy and embarrassed. Faye refolded the paper and slipped it gently into her jacket's inner pocket.

"You are a dark horse. I'd really like to see some more. Thank you," she said. "Are you ready Wolf?" she asked me in monotone.

"Yeah, but I've still gotta go find Joe and get the keys to the truck."

"I thought I'd take you for a ride on Hildisvíni. Is that alright?"

"Uh?" I was completely surprised. "But your bike's only got that one seat and—"

Faye interjected, "Well it *should* be okay to pillion, I know it doesn't have any rear foot pegs, but keep your daddy-long-legs out of the way and I'm sure it will be fine. Come on."

She turned and walked towards the open garage door. The gleaming

Martellare Angelus stood ready on its wheel stand inside. Faye called out a casual word of thanks to Charlie who'd obviously done a bit of mechanical prep on the bike beforehand but being preoccupied somewhere down the deep-end acknowledged her words with a half-hearted raise of his hand and a distant *"No problem"*.

Gutteka and Jenteka caught our attention. They were both standing up on their hind legs like a couple of prairie dogs doing that snarly, ears back boxing thing cats do. It was all very playful, *whack! boof! whack!* until Jenteka caught Mr. G off-guard with a crafty left hook. Then it was on. I'd never seen anything like it. I swear to God the two of them turned instantly into a swirling, basketball-sized fur-blur of fighting cat.

"Jentekatt, Guttekatt, nok nå." Faye knelt down and spoke gently as both cats immediately stopped their scrapping and made up quickly with a lot of nuzzling and preening stuff.

"They are restless Fenrir. They sense things are changing and are readying themselves now for battle." She was talking about two cats, but the mood of her remark was unsettling. Faye picked up a small backpack and told me to put it on.

"What's that?" I said stupidly.

"Stuff for the trip, what do you think?"

"So what about me then Faye? I'll need protection out there in that midday heat, I don't want to get sunstroke you know … not having a hat of my own to wear or anything."

She took the bait and stormed over to some metal shelves stuffed with junk and pulled out this revolting floppy brimmed hat.

"What the hell is *that*?"

"Oh be quiet, it's not the fanciest hat in Mexico but it will keep the sunstroke away from your milky white skin." Touché.

One side was bent up at a peculiar angle, which to my eyes didn't look very fetching at all. Faye noticed me subtly fiddling with it, trying to make it somehow go straight.

"Fenrir, it's got one of those pull cords to keep it attached to your head, trust me that's all you will need. When we're on the road the wind will bend it into much more contorted shapes than that! Now, stop your complaining or I'll go by myself."

I never said a word. So, it was crappy hat on, with cord string up.

Faye threw her leg over the bike and expertly rolled it forward off the rear wheel stand. Then she fired up the engine, revving the throttle quite excitedly. The sound was magnificent.

"Okay?"

"Yep!"

"Well, get on the bike then!"

I lifted my leg awkwardly over the top of the cowling behind Faye's seat and plonked my ass down right behind her. One glance down at that gorgeous, lower back and her taught denim butt made me wanna cry.

FRICKING HELL!

Faye took off like an unleashed typhoon. *"STOP! STOP! STOP!"* She slammed on the brakes. I skidded right down the shiny polished seat cowl, my forward momentum stopping only when my junk slammed smack into Faye's tattoo.

"What the hell are you doing?" Faye turned her head, looking at me baffled.

"I nearly went flying off the back."

Okay. As wussy as it sounds, including Vince's dink about five minutes ago, this was only the third time in my entire life that I'd actually ever been on a motorcycle. The first time, not that long ago either, was when I caught that ride with Bird back to Luis Escoto's place. If plonked behind the big fella felt like serving as an auxiliary anchor on the back of a slow-moving putt-putt, *this* ride was akin to being strapped to a hell-fire missile. Without the straps. Man, when Faye took off, I nearly had a frick'n heart attack.

"Well hold on properly then, dum-dum."

"Where?"

"Grip your fingers into those two slots below your thighs, but don't go too low or you'll burn your skin off on the exhausts."

Stuff that. I nudged myself forward to the back of her seat and curled both my arms right around her. She never said a word, just clicked the bike in gear, let out the clutch and we both thundered off into oblivion.

◆

We headed north for a while and, feeling more relaxed, I'd long since let go of Faye's waist and now clung casually onto the seat cowl like she'd told me to. My lanky legs settled into an awkward wishbone position and stuck out ungainly on either side. Faye said I could easily get a job as a high-wire freak act.

Apart from an old Belworth Smokey-Joe creeping south and a hapless farmer doing a twenty-point turn in the middle of the road for no apparent reason, there was nothing else moving. The only thing of interest we'd passed was the burnt-out remains of the gas tanker, who's demise had been re-created so accurately by Vince's punch on Bird's fleshy arm.

But now we sat stopped and silent about a half mile from the truck-checking station ahead. There was a wash of flashing red and blue lights. Policia. I presumed they were Mexican, but with this many units, the chance of some of them having come south from over the U.S. border seemed highly likely. Something big was up and there was no way we were going one single tire roll closer.

"What's that's all about?" I said.

"I don't know, but I think it's time we left the road. There was a track heading off about a kilometer back, I think that will take us roughly where we want to go. Anyway, how is your hat holding up?" Faye jibed me sarcastically.

"S'allright!" I said like that cartoon donkey.

♦

This was pretty much the first time I'd ventured any real distance away from a road. The slow speed felt like some leisurely, nature-channel trip through the desert, the only thing missing was a narrator and the soundtrack.

At first the ground was more or less scrubby, but it soon gave way to a compacted sandy terrain. The long-armed Saguaros cactus plants were everywhere, and their size was impressive. This was excellent. Lost in a Mexican desert with an Ice Maiden goddess from Norway. The heat, the solitude, the deafening silence. We cruised on just sucking in the views, when Faye slowed the bike to an unexpected stop.

"What is it?"

She ignored me but held her gaze to the north.

"Faye."

Purposefully she cut the engine, pushed down the foot stand and dismounted. She walked over to what looked like the edge of a gentle ridge off to our right.

Feeling like a pickle on a cupcake, I clambered down off the bike and followed on behind. Other than a wide-open vista of sand and rocks, there didn't seem much out there. But after a while, it didn't seem unreasonable to figure that we were standing on the weather-worn lip of a very shallow, mile-wide depression. I'm no geologist, but if you slotted in a couple of the missing sections from around the edge, you could almost convince yourself that this was once the rim of some ancient, long-extinct volcano that had eons since returned itself to the desert.

Faye was scouring the ground along the edge of the rim and ventured further down onto the shallow drift of the side slope. She seemed pretty intent. I hadn't a clue what she was looking for. At one point she moved to a large, flat bolder which stuck out beyond the lip. Then, finding nothing, she headed to another similar boulder, which sloped down at a much steeper angle. She ducked out of sight but quickly reappeared and signaled excitedly for me to come on over.

"I think I've found some old rock carvings. If I'm right, they're extremely ancient, but it's almost impossible to see them in this bright desert sun."

I was one step ahead. I took off the backpack and dived inside for the water bottle.

"Here, splash some of this over it. That's what they do in all those archaeology documentaries."

"We're in the *desert* Fenrir. Only a fool would do such an idiotic thing." She then changed her mind and said, "Oh go ahead then, but only a sip … or maybe a mouthful."

The wet scratchy lines looked only slightly more visible than before.

"I knew it!" Faye beamed excitedly. "This place is *old* Wolf. Not only the geology, the human connection here is prehistoric. Those rock markings look Clovis to me."

"What's Clovis?"

"The Clovis people were big-game hunters of the late Pleistocene."

"The what?"

"The end of the last ice age, when the great ice sheets began to recede."

"Far out! So were these the dudes who killed off the mammoths?"

"Well, Clovis people had bifacially flaked projectile points on their weapons, a super technological advancement back in the Stone Age. So yes, they do think it was possible. Although it would be ironic if such a mass extinction could have been caused by something so simple as a chipped piece of stone don't you think? Either that, or the mammoths and the other megafauna died out through catastrophic changes in the ecosystem during what they call the Late Quaternary extinction event." Faye was preoccupied and stared straight past me. "I tend to favour J Harlen Bretz's glacial-meltwater-floods theory myself," Faye commented, reengaging.

"Were these Clovis the first Americans?"

"No, there were people here many thousands of years before them.

There is still a lot of speculation regarding their origins. Many archae-
ologists now propose they *may* have been the people of the Solutrean
culture, who migrated from Europe at least 17,000 years ago by following the edge of the Laurentide ice sheet in tiny skin-covered boats. It's
all quite interesting … well I think it is anyway."

I wandered back over to take another look at the marks that Faye
said were Clovis, I couldn't see anything. They looked more like the
scratches left by some idiot going nuts in an all-wheel-drive to me.

"What was it that made you stop here exactly?"

"I don't know. I somehow felt it. Something irresistible drew me
here." Faye looked me straight in the eye. "*This* will be the place Wolf …
I know it!"

The tone of her words sent a shiver right through me.

◆

I was getting a bit bored with riding pillion until a desert mesa loomed
out of the shimmering heat up ahead. I'd never been this close to one
before, in fact I'd only ever seen them further off in the distance. This
thing was massive.

"*Man, oh man.* That looks amazing."

Faye pointed some thirty yards up ahead to where the ground unexpectedly fell away into a canyon that stretched between us and the mesa.

"This is close enough, we'll stop here," she said.

We walked close to the edge and had a look down. I'd been expecting a drop into Hell, but surprisingly the bottom seemed no more than
a hundred feet. The broad canyon snaked its way in a gigantic lazy S
between where we stood and the towering mesa opposite. It looked like
the course of an old dried-up river.

Faye took off her jacket, laid it leather side down and then sat her
butt on the silk-padded lining. With a change of heart she slid back a
yard further away from the edge. I just plonked my ass down on the
dirt. After a quick glance over her shoulder at Hildisvíni, Faye adjusted
her hat and sunglasses and settled herself for the show.

"This will be great Fenrir. We can see the whole canyon perfectly."

I was keen alright, but I still had no idea what was going on.

"Hand me the backpack please Wolf. I *really* need a drink."

"Yeah what other stuff have you got in here, for its size it's as heavy
as all f—"

I cut my profanity dead. She noticed, but that was it.

"There's a couple of liters of water, not much, but that's all there is. Two pairs of binoculars, I dib Joe's, but the other pair are good too."

"What else?" I'd suddenly gotten pretty hungry.

"I suppose you mean food. It's okay Wolfie, I've packed a healthy salad bolillo roll and an apple."

"That all?"

"Yes but there's one of each, … one each?" Faye started giggling. "Uh! I get tangled up sometimes with the English grammar."

"What else?"

"What else what?" Faye laughed again, "You see! *Sprøtt språk*, crazy language. Oh, only a mini-sized first-aid kit and Joe's old dinosaur cell phone."

"Why did he give you that?"

"*Maybe* just in case we break down or even get lost in the desert," the look on her face said it all. "My god Wolf, can you really be that dumb?"

"No, I thought a funky kind o' babe like you would be packing her own little wafer-thin smartphone."

"The last one I owned, I posted off before I left for Mexico, as a decoy. I don't care, I really don't want one anymore."

This was bizarre. I'd never-ever heard such heretical nonsense.

"Oh of course they have their practical uses Fenrir, I'm not disputing that, but to align yourself so willingly with a 24/7 tracking and monitoring device is a little naïve, don't you think? People of my generation have never known a life any different. You've seen them – two thirds of the population can't even bear to let them out of their sight. They wander around with one clutched so lovingly in their hands, it's become the absolute hub of their existence. But don't ever question or criticize it, they'll defend it tooth and nail. 'You *have* to have one, everybody else has got one. How could you *possibly* survive?'" Faye pulled a mocking expression as her thumb bounced aimlessly around on an imaginary smart-screen.

"But it's technological progress, you sound like a bit of a Luddite, Faye."

"Oh progress, *phhh!* First they were holdable, then they were wearable, now they're implantable. All gradual steps in turning everyone into compliant cyborgs if you ask me. I mentioned in conversation once to a friend of mine in Berlin, who I thought was reasonably intelligent, how the Stasi would have done anything to have such a device at their disposal. She just looked at me. She hadn't a clue who the Stasi were or what I was talking about. A complete ignorance of history. It will always come back and bite you if you choose to stay so willfully uninformed." Faye went all sullen and stared out across the canyon towards the mesa.

"But do you know what really made me never, ever want to have another phone again? I was waiting for the start of a cultural parade back home earlier this year, when a sweet little toddler of about one or two waddled a few steps forward from her mother's care, excited to show off her first bunad. That's a traditional Norwegian costume, that she had been so cutely dressed in. She was the epitome of life and joy and innocence. She looked up, smiled gorgeously, and waved her little flag at a young man passing by. *'Look at me sir, don't I look pretty?'* she seemed to say. She was so very excited and happy. The young man walked straight by and completely ignored her. The poor little girl looked so sad and confused. No, the young man didn't even see her. He was far too preoccupied with his electronic 'death-score' as he played on his little plastic phone. I felt really sorry for him. I'd decided right then and there, these things weren't for me. Anyway, enough of my deluded preaching. What about you?"

"What? Oh *my* phone. I don't have one either. Although not by choice. One of my halfwit friends shoved mine, halfway up where the sun don't shine in a drunken dare to see if it would still ring."

Faye laughed. "Did it?"

"You'll never know Faye, my lips are forever sealed … even so, for some reason I never really felt like using it again after that."

"You're an idiot Wolf. Just eat your roll."

We ate the food and drank a little water. The sun had started to sink in front of us. I figured we must have been facing south-west.

"How long now Faye? When does whatever-it-is happen?"

"Soon. You'll certainly hear it coming."

I stared out across the canyon towards the mesa and watched the shadows lengthen and the color of the rocks turn a vivid orange. I became aware of a distant rumble which grew louder and louder and louder. It was obvious that whatever it was would be coming into view within seconds, down below in the canyon. I reckoned I'd figured it in one. This was going to be a pre-scheduled controlled release of water from some dam or catchment basin further up north. It was the tire part that threw me. Any minute now, some crazy bunch of assclowns would come hurtling around the S-bend of the canyon riding a fast-flowing wave on lashed-up inner-tube rafts.

How wrong was I.

There was no gushing torrent of water. This massive, rumbling, dust-shrouded torrent bursting headlong into the canyon below, really was … tires.

I couldn't believe it.

Faye stood up excitedly, punched the sky with her fist and screeched out a cheer.

"Woo-hoo! Go you frick'n Tire Boys!"

It was only after my initial surprise that I started to work out what was going on.

Down amidst all the noise and the kicked-up dust from this stampeding armada of tires, you could make out the fleeting shapes of people down in the canyon moving right along with them. Not safely off to the sides, but ducking and weaving, right in amongst it, keeping them all on track and somehow constantly moving.

Now don't get me wrong, this wasn't some minor, stick and hoop, roll down the hill type job. This bull run of old cast-off rubber was really shifting. If any of these guys had tripped or fallen, I reckon the sheer pace and size of this fast running horde would have squashed them as flat as a tortilla. The rolling rubber was all grouped together into manageable pods numbering maybe fifteen to twenty tires in width. They were all kept in line by long steel chains that ran through the center holes and held relatively taut by a round metal plate at each end. In turn, each and every pod was connected in ranks and rows to each other by even more chains which kept this whole massive juggernaut together … more or less. It was an ingenious engineering feat on its own, let alone the expertise needed by the guys down there to maneuver and somehow keep the entire behemoth under control. It was incredible.

"Use the binoculars Wolf, you can see much more that way."

Faye was right, it felt like you were right down there with them. They were moving on what looked like giant two-wheeled roller-blades, one on each foot, a bit like those old pump-up scooters the kids used to ride back in the sixties, only longer with a lot more flex and bounce in the foot plate. They skated effortlessly and kept up with the thundering pace. These guys were insane.

They picked up speed on the straight coming towards us and it was only as they came out of the shadows that I became aware of their unusual clothing. I could see about twenty of them all dressed in leather tunics with short, dark gloves and bindings strapped all the way along their arms and legs. On their feet they wore close-fitting shin-high boots that looked perfect for the job. Their hair, for the most part, was piled up high in a kind of oiled-up ponytail which tumbled down behind them from the top of their heads. These dudes looked like some wheel-footed legion of ancient Greeks. They looked great.

"What's going on Faye? Fill me in on the specs."

Faye didn't hear me; she was too busy jumping up and down excitedly cheering them on.

"Aren't they fabulous Fenrir, *look, look!*"

Faye pointed to the midst of the action where half a dozen Tire Boys had all leapt as one, like a human wall, to push down a substantial renegade section of tires that under its own momentum had kicked off on a rhythmic, ten-foot bounce into mayhem. They looked just like a troupe of acrobats or a line of ancient mariners lunging up over the yardarm together to secure down a storm lashed topsail.

Faye was really digging this. I yelled at her above all the noise.

"I don't understand why these guys are risking their necks for a bunch of worn out old tires?"

"There's more to it Wolf. Tire Boys is only their slang name, their street name. I suppose it's a silly tradition, but now that you've seen them in the flesh, I can tell you their real name. These are *The Honey Rollers!*" Faye announced excitedly. "Although Honey Rollers still isn't their *real* real name. This is the second of their biannual runs, it's a tradition that goes back centuries. They pack the honey and lash it carefully inside old tires and roll it for a couple of hundred kilometers from the hives up in the mountains to a village down on the coast."

"They didn't have tires—" Faye cut me dead.

"Back in the old days they made the wheels from woven grass and hardened sections of cactus skin. This is the modern adaptation. Even the honey is packed in old plastic milk cartons now, they waste *nothing.*"

"What about the—"

"The tires? That's the funniest part. They sell them off to an online cult invented by some zillionaire social-media mogul. They're building a kind of adobe tire-stacked pyramid as a monument to his self-aggrandising contribution to 21st century society. I've heard, when it's finished, it'll be even larger than The Pyramid of The Sun at Teotihuacán."

"So how much honey?"

"Each tire holds eight to ten liters, along with all the packing of course. God knows how much they are rolling all together."

"Do you have to be an Indian?"

"No, there's Hispanics, white guys, Native Americans. It's not about race to be a Honey Roller you just need to have a particular kind of *pizzazz* and a bonkers devil-may-care attitude."

"How do you know all this stuff Faye?"

"Sacramento told me, he used to roll with them, but quite a few years ago now." She giggled about something but didn't take her eyes from the action down below.

"Aaaagh! did you see that? That poor guy nearly got flattened."

"How come Sacramento used to—"

"He's so funny, whenever I ask him about it, he holds his back comically, bends over forward and says 'Ooh, it's only for the younger men.' And that he's *'Far too old now, to roll'.*"

"Wow!"

Faye got excited again. *"Look, look, look, look, look!"*

"Holly-Hell!" I kid you not, some guy had just pulled off a high-wheeling back-flip right in the nick of time and somehow managed to get clear only a second before a high-bouncing bunch of tires pummeled him flat into the mesa wall.

"That was Prins Eugen," Faye said, sounding like she must have known him personally.

"Wasn't that a German battleship?"

"No, heavy cruiser."

"I only call him that because of the horizontal stripy thing that he wears across his chest. It reminds me of a tunic the Swedish prince was wearing in a photo in one of my school textbooks."

I was about to ask Faye what the small shields they carried on their backs were for. They looked like a cross between a catcher's mitt and a regular trash can lid, but then a bouncing pod of tires suddenly broke loose. A couple of the Honey Rollers reached around, drew down their shields and I watched enthralled as they physically pummeled the unruly section back down to earth and under control. Then without a second thought they let their shields go and like magic they retracted to their original position on their backs connected by what looked like a spring-loaded cable.

"So why are half of the guys in brown and the others in black?" The Rollers seemed to fall into two definite camps.

"The ones wearing the sandy brown leathers are DOAX, while the—"

"What? I missed that." The noise was horrendous.

"*Doe-Axe*, the brownish colored ones are the DOAX."

"And?"

"The ones wearing black are the HEXO."

"What does that mean?"

"The DOAX derive their name from the ancient Minoan double axe. It is a stylized symbol believed to represent bees."

"What about HEXO?"

"Their name comes from the hexagon combs made by the bees in their hive."

"So what's the difference?"

"DOAX are the show-offs, they're a little crazier and daring. Their role is to respond instantly to sudden breakouts and unexpected calamities. DOAX take the most heart stopping risks. HEXO are a little more prudent, more ordered, and careful. They keep a watchful eye on the pack and try to avert anything from getting too far out of control in the first place, but they all work together as a cohesive unit and complement each other perfectly. Something like the strikers and defenders on a football team. I've adopted these rollers as my very own little *Azzurri*," Faye giggled, but once again I had no idea what she meant, but judging by the way she pronounced it, I presumed it was obviously something fancy, classy, and *most definitely Italian.*

"Ay, ay, ay, *hubba bubba!* Look over there, Wolf. It's Commodore Jack!"

I spun my binoculars over to where she was looking. This dude was HEXO and he looked to me like he was trapped with his back hard up against the rock wall. He was Caucasian, looked about nineteen or twenty and had shortish black hair with one of those long, wispy fringes, the kind of hair that *always*, even when it was messy, looked kind of *au naturel* and kick-ass perfect. Around his throat he wore a thin white neckerchief that gave him an old-time navy, midshipman look. To top all that, his eyes were baby-blue, and he had that high cheekboned face and white gleaming teeth. His slim muscular torso fitted perfectly into his black leather tunic. This guy was so unbelievably good looking it couldn't *possibly* be true. *Hmmm*, frick'n eye candy, toy boy. I hated him already.

"*Cradle snatcher!*" I called out to Faye, but I guess she didn't hear me.

The action was heating up down below. I saw two guys come sliding in low on their haunches, like surfers on boards. I think they were HEXO, but with so much dust in the air it was pretty hard to tell. A massive, breaking wave of rubber tires was about to flip over on itself, when they both grabbed the running-chain that ran along the length of the outer-edge tire plates, and with a whole lot of wrenching managed to somehow steer it straight and roll it all back into line again. These guys were fearless, they had frick'n guts alright.

"Hey Faye, I bet Sacramento was DOAX?"

"No, HEXO."

"Wow!"

"Who are those three guys over there with the quiver-like backpacks?"

"They're the mechanics, it's their job to do all the running repairs. They carry giant bolt cutters, spare chains and U-bolts, stuff like that. They have to be so quick witted and careful. I think they have the scariest and most dangerous job of them all."

"Are they DOAX?"

"No, HEXO."

"Can a woman be a Honey Roller?"

"Oh yes, but only one. She's the Melissae, she acts as a kind of queen bee. I saw her over there only a moment or two ago—"

"*HOLEY frick'n MOLEY!*" I cried out. Two rollers had just collided in a bone jarring accident. One of them was Commodore Jack. He'd taken a chance with a break in the traffic to swoop down from the wall and leap over a pod to get into a different part of the pack, meanwhile a DOAX doing something crazy, didn't see him coming and *SMASH!* a wicked full-blown, mid-air collision.

They both stood up, a yard or two apart and made that animated, palms-up expression of surprise to each other with their hands. I could clearly see through the binoculars, the post-collision expression on their faces and their indignant mouthing-off. With no harm done, I couldn't help but laugh and imagine their dialog. *What? I didn't see you bro. What the hell were you doing?* "You're a worry dude, watch where you're frick'n going man, reckless DOAX!" Five seconds later they were off again. It was all incredibly entertaining.

"Oh, a collision between *two* of my favorites," fluttered Faye as she pressed her hands together angelically, like she was praying.

"Who was the other guy then?"

"Y-B-D!"

"Who's he when he's at home?"

"*Young Brad with Dreads.*" The green-eyed monster knew exactly what she meant. Enough said.

"Look, there she is Fenrir! Over there, up on that small ridge. There's the Melissae."

"Wow!" I wasn't expecting her to look like that! She was the most intimidating of them all.

The Melissae was a very tall, imposing black woman. She reminded me of that singer-actress lady from the 1980s, especially with the flat top hair and her long, shapely legs. I wished I could think of her name.

The Melissae stood high up on a sand ridge scanning her minions with a pensive all-seeing stare. It was hard to tell, but she seemed to be sending out instructions by way of extended arm gestures aided only by a pair of short golden batons. I was enthralled by the look of her dress. Well it wasn't really a dress, more like alternating hoops of black and brown leather that formed her impressive tunic. Even from here, she looked strangely reminiscent of an abstract, regal bee.

"What exactly does she do Faye?"

"She's the boss. She's neither DOAX or HEXO, but she calls the shots and controls every aspect of the run. She keeps a watchful eye on the handful of redcaps, they're the young guys trying out. If they measure up, she, and only she decides if they will be permitted in the future to roll. If so, she decides what clan they will be initiated into as well. The Melissae's word is final."

Faye was preoccupied, as though looking out expectantly for something or someone. Then, a few seconds later... "*LOOK* Fenrir, see that man over there, I call him *Tauro-kathapsia* or Tauro for short. The first time I saw him he somersaulted three hundred and sixty degrees, way up into the air, to safety over an out of control stampede. It was *unbelievable,* he virtually flew. He is fantastic, the most daring, *the bull leaper!* The most fearless DOAX of all!"

Move over Commodore Jack and BP-with D or whatever his name was, this guy was *really* getting two thumbs up reaction from Faye. I now *hated* him most of all.

Seriously, this guy *did* stand out. I think he was Mayan or Aztec or something like that, he looked like a combination of all those colorful men on the temple walls. Not only the Mezzo-American ones, he really did remind me of those bull leaping guys from the old Minoan frescoes. I'd seen them a million times on my old cookie tin back home in Vegas.

This guy, Tauro, had the supremo hairdo as well. It was black as pitch and oiled up high in an ancient looking ponytail style like you wouldn't believe.

"Isn't he *fabulous* Wolf. Just watch the magnificent way that he moves."

Why do women always say things like that to guys? Do they really think they'll get an honest answer? Seriously, Faye was going ga-ga. And yes, exactly right on cue, frick'n Lord-God-Tauro pulled another incredible dare-devil feat from his legendary box of tricks and rescued an inexperienced redcap from an imminent and untimely death. All, of course, right under the watchful eye of the Melissae.

I wasn't in the mood.

"Yeah, he's great, Faye."

I think the bulk of the pack had passed us now, only the tail-enders were still coming through.

Faye took a swig from the water bottle, but her eyes were still glued on The Honey Rollers. "That was so great. What did you think, Fenrir?"

"Those guys are amazing, thanks for bringing me … I think I'll have that apple now."

As the rumble of The Rollers tapered off a silence crept back across the desert. I stared at the shadows on the high mesa walls that stretched ever longer as the sun dropped low in the west.

Suddenly, a whiney, nasal voice destroyed the moment.

"*Well, well, well.* Look-ee here Mr. Travers, if it isn't little Miss Goldilocks and our old friend the big, bad Wolf!"

It was Martindale and Travers. In all of the commotion they had somehow snuck up behind us and now stood with their guns pointed right at our heads.

"Look Mr. Travers, he's even wearing one of grandma's old bonnets. I think Wolfie here must have dropped in on granny on his way over here and gobbled her up whole."

Martindale was getting off on all of this double meaning bullshit and he wasn't even any good at it. I couldn't believe how much this tool loved the sound of his own whiney voice. When I'd met him before I thought he was pretty creepy, but this time he seemed ten times worse. He'd adopted this weird, bouncy stance and kept thrusting his gun about excitedly looking for any excuse to blast off some rounds. This guy was mental and capable of anything.

Travers was doing that weird thing where his whole body jiggles up and down in a silent snigger. He was revving up and down now like he'd been privy to the world's funniest joke.

Eeesh. What a couple of fruitcakes.

"Mr. Wolf must be a *real* nasty piece o' work, don't you think Mr. Travers? How's about we keep young Goldilocks here for ourselves and you can have the honor of throwing this useless jerk off the cliff." Travers jiggled once again in agreement.

A charge of terror surged through me as I knew this clown really meant it. In panic, I glanced at Faye for help, but she stood braced and still as a statue with Martindale's gun pointing straight at her head.

Travers took a step towards me and I was sure that he was going to do it, but right at that moment something slammed hard into his face. He started shrieking his head off and flapping around like a big crybaby. A *Falco Peregrinus* had swooped out of the sky like a silent thunderbolt and began ripping into Travers with eight razor-talons and a sharp-hooked beak. His face, or what was left of it, now looked like a bloodied dollop of uncooked mince and his demeanor completely destroyed for such a wannabe, big-time bad guy.

Obviously, the bird had been keeping a watchful eye on Faye from high above and struck on impulse when it saw she was in danger.

Martindale started shooting up into the air, more or less aiming at the falcon. With one shot he nearly blew Travers head off. Then he fired off another couple of shots that went absolutely nowhere. This guy wasn't even thinking. Faye and I would be lucky if we both didn't end up dead. Bobbing about looking for a better angle, one of Martindale's boots planted itself down firmly onto the upturned lining of Faye's leather jacket, then for an instant he placed his other boot right alongside it.

Faye had been watching. She lunged forward, grabbed the bottom end of her jacket and with one god-almighty heave pulled it hard along the ground towards her. Martindale's size fourteen clods got caught up in the shoulder curl and the force of Faye's action flipped the imbecile over and crashed him down hard onto the deck.

But Faye hadn't finished. As he lay there writhing around in the dirt trying to figure which way was up, in one feisty movement Faye struck out mercilessly and kicked the vicious bastard as hard as she could in the balls.

"And that was for Wolfie, you evil, fucking prick!"

I swear to God, for one split second that dude's ghoulies popped out where his eyes used to be. I was honored with Faye's dedication, but I *never* expected such colorful language.

Travers lay there screaming and wriggling like an oversized maggot. Peregrinus had long since flown off but he still hadn't noticed. Martindale's face had turned a deep purple-red and he was choking and grunting like a twice-hammered pig. I'm not a vindictive person ordinarily, but under the circumstances seeing those two bastards squirming around in pain was excellent.

"*Quickly Wolf!*" said Faye as she stooped down to pick up her jacket. "Pick up the pack and the binoculars. We're out of here. *Let's go, let's go, let's go!*"

I did as she said and ran fast towards the Martellare Angelus.

"*Give me the bag!*" Faye reached in, grabbed a bottle of water and the first-aid kit and skidded them along the ground towards the agents.

"It won't help much … but *hey!*"

She sounded just like yours truly. Even Faye was scoring off me now.

For a moment I felt the rising heat of a panic attack. Maybe those two had been cute enough to have taken the Martellare's key. When Faye pulled it out of her pocket, I was so relieved. She wasn't so stupid as to leave it in the ignition for all eyes to see. Feeling safe now, I started babbling to Faye.

"How was that falcon of yours, huh? Far out! Do you think it was sent down by Freya?"

"Possibly, but I think min bestemor more likely had a hand in it. Either way it was definitely guided by Seiðr."

Hildisvíni roared loud into life and we hightailed it out of there so fast I nearly spun a-over-t. A hundred yards away we found Martindale's car parked sneakily in a shallow depression. Faye pulled up beside it, reached in through the open window and pulled out the keys.

"Please let me have 'em," I begged. "I wanna chuck 'em somewhere where they'll *never-ever* find them."

Faye ignored me and tossed them under the car, cranked up the revs and sped off. It was only when we got back in sight of the road that she stopped.

"Pass me the water please Wolf, I'm really in need of a drink."

"Man, *that* was somethin' else. Do you *always* intend to beat the shit out of someone, whenever we go out on a date?"

Faye laughed, but her mood had become serious.

"How could I have been so stupid," she murmured berating herself. "How could I have been so *stupid!* Never again, never, *ever* again."

"What?"

"This might sound like some kind of excuse, but in a way I'm glad all of that just happened. How could I have allowed myself to have been caught so *completely* off guard. I could have gotten you killed. I'm so sorry Wolf, forgive me."

"Hey Faye, I'm a big boy, not your problem."

"Oh yes, it is, that was totally unacceptable. That's twice now. I have to accept the magnitude of this. This whole frick'n saga! I've got to get my act together. Oh, and another thing—"

"Yes?"

"Please tell me whenever I say frick'n. It's getting to be a habit and I'm starting to say it as much as you lot do."

◆

Now she'd read herself the riot act Faye seemed much calmer. I noticed it in the more relaxed way she rode home. It was only when we reached spittin' distance from The Alamo that things took an unexpected turn.

Three riders from the ranks of Los Espectros Brillantes were waiting down by the road on their motorcycles. I got the feeling right then, that things would soon start to change and probably not for the better.

Faye slowed to a crawl, then fifty yards short, she stopped and asked me politely to get off so she could ride up and meet them alone. That suited me fine. I slid off the side of the seat cowl and cut my way across towards the pumps on foot. I recognized Mercio, Captain Valasco's sergeant at arms, but I didn't know the others. Even from here they gave me the willies.

Halfway back to the building I noticed Joe and Charlie up on the rooftop scrutinizing the riders. Looking back I saw Faye sitting poised and attentive locked in conversation with the shadow-veiled sergeant at arms. I'd reached the edge of the driveway when I heard the Martellare engine reignite. I spun on my heels to watch her head off but unexpectedly she rode over and drew up beside me. Faye didn't say a word, just handed me my curl straw hat and powered on up into the garage. A moment or two later she came hurtling back out, but this time armed with her deadly eight-foot-long naginata.

23

Dixie Belle

The first thing Joe asked me when I got to the roof was "Where was she going?" I had no answer as it was the same question I was about to ask him. From the conversation that followed, it seemed that all kinds of mayhem had broken out while me and Faye had been gallivanting about in the desert.

Apparently, another big earthquake had happened around some place near Sieta Cerros. Joe told me how four cars, jam-packed full of terrified locals all fleeing north, had pulled in for gas. They told stories of massive swarms of diablos rising from the depths, attacking and devouring anyone or anything unable to flee.

"The poor bastards were petrified," chimed in Charlie. "One of them pulled out his wallet to hand me some money but he was shaking so much he fluffed the few paltry pesos he had everywhere. We gassed 'em up for free and gave 'em some food for the kids." Charlie never showed much emotion but the expression on his face said a lot.

"Tell him what happened with the green Montargo," said Joe.

Charlie kept up his narrative. "I was halfway through filling up the tank when the trunk lid pops open and out rolls a blood-soaked old grandma."

"Was she dead?" I asked, riveted.

"I think so, 'cos half a second later, out flops her head onto the ground."

Joe slapped Charlie hard but sympathetically on the shoulder. "Yeah, it was the first time I've ever seen old Chucky boy here turn forty shades of green."

They both laughed kind o' nervously. But I knew they weren't being callous.

Joe picked up the threads of their recap. "We put the OUT OF GAS sign up, soon after because the next few cars that pulled in had already heard we were giving out free fuel. *As if!* One smarmy dude got really shitty and in near perfect English called us 'Imperial misogynist bastards.'

Work that one out," Joe shook his head indignantly. "We're not a frick'n benevolent society you know." I felt sorry for Joe. As gruff as he made himself out to be, he was really just a big softy.

"How were the roller boys?" Joe said changing the subject. "Did they put on a show?"

I answered to the affirmative but was more keen to go into the details of what had happened with Martindale and Travers. Both Charlie and Joe roared with laughter when I told them how Faye booted the special agent so mercilessly in the nuts.

"He was a clown that guy. Man, I would have loved to have seen that." Joe's internal chuckle motor had revved up again just thinking about it. But beyond all that, they seemed concerned and were already quietly ascertaining what further fallout could possibly come from it.

"How long had Mercio and the other riders been sitting out there?" I said steering the conversation back towards Faye.

"Couple of hours," answered Charlie. "They never came right up here though. I think they somehow knew she wasn't around and sat there waiting patiently by the road. Well, I'm getting back to work. Tell me if MacElroy comes up from his little hole will you, I dug out that old backpack spray gun rig for him. See you at dinner." Charlie turned away and headed off back down the ramp.

Joe and I stood there for a little longer looking silently out across the road towards the last red glow on the horizon.

"How's she coping?" Joe said, sounding concerned.

"She's alright. I think she's more terrified about all this Freya and the Seiðr business than anything to do with The Shining Specters."

Joe looked at me kind o' puzzled, then I remembered Faye hadn't filled him in on the more esoteric aspects of her being down here in Sonora. He didn't press me on what it was I was talking about, so I didn't elaborate and let the topic slip.

"Come on let's go down. Charlie's found something for you too."

"Yeah, what's that?"

"Driver's side-window glass. It's not from a Fire Diamond, but I'm pretty sure it'll fit."

◆

I was in that half-sleep state around four in the morning when I became aware of soft, drifting music. The lovely melody seemed to float away but would always return like a circle. The sound was so pure it wasn't coming from a radio, this was the twinkling of piano keys. But that made no sense. The only piano I knew was over behind the garage inside the half-collapsed shed and this music was coming from somewhere not that far away. Eventually curiosity got the better of me and like a spellbound sleepwalker I slithered out of bed and followed the melodic sound back to its source.

I was amazed to find its player was Faye. At some time, probably while we'd been out in the desert, the damaged piano had been saved from its allotted trashing and had been brought over and left outside the unoccupied trailer next to Faye's. I walked quietly to where she sat completely engrossed in her playing.

"Hello Wolf," Faye whispered gently without turning around.

"Howdy ... I didn't know you played the piano. It sounds lovely."

"Not really. I can only remember the first few minutes properly."

"What is it?" I said with my usual ignorance.

"Sonata al Chiaro di Luna."

"It's nice, I'm sure I've heard it somewhere before ... is it Italian?"

"No ... it's not Italian, it's Beethoven. The Moonlight Sonata, first movement. My mother taught me how to play it."

I moved the last steps closer and stood beside her. Something was wrong, I could hear it in the tone of her voice. Faye turned her head towards me and made a forced smile. Tears were streaming down her face and mixing with the telltale spatters of oily-black devil's blood. I'd never seen her look so forlorn.

"I miss her Wolf. I miss my mother so much." Her voice quivered fitfully as she spoke those despairing words. I just stood there dumbstruck listening as she played that magnificent tune.

"She taught me how to play. I would sit beside her on the piano stool as she patiently showed me the keys. My mother was so loving, so kind, but I just didn't have her musical gift. That's why I can only play the first two minutes over and over."

Faye wiped her face with her hand. The tears and blood merged into an ugly grey smear, but she kept on playing and the melody circled around and around.

"It was terrible, Wolf. Last night I saw shocking things. *Horrific* things. Things I wasn't prepared for. Those monsters, there were *thousands and thousands* of them. They came up from inside the ground and slaughtered everything that lived or breathed. Adults, children, livestock, even the plants. *Everything.*"

"Tell me what happened … if you like. If it helps. If it makes it any easier." She responded despite my clumsy overture.

"When I left yesterday evening with Mercio and the other two escorts, we snaked our way down towards the south-west. We eventually rode into the midst of a brigade of mounted Los Espectros Brillantes. As one, they all turned towards me, raised their machete weapons and hailed me with an overwhelmingly ardent salute. Oh Fenrir, it was so surreal, so unexpected. At one point I came this close to losing my nerve and bottling out completely. Why me? *Why me?* I said over and over to myself. Then SHE took over. *My god!* I felt this indescribable rush of power suddenly surge right through me. It was so intense that all I could do was just hang on tight and go along for the ride. And it's like the Specters *knew* she was there. They fell into chapter and rank behind me and we rode headlong into a vicious, nighttime engagement with those creatures. I rode at the head of captains. Upon Hildisvíni I led the charge of Los Espectros Brillantes. Without hesitation their leaders and a two thousand plus force of skeleton riders followed. I led them Wolf … *me!* We showed the horde no mercy. This army in battle is ruthless and brave and a most deadly host. They regard me as their rightful queen. They said they've been waiting many lifetimes. Waiting for now. Waiting for *me!*"

Faye's anguished mood swung between confusion and panic.

"Freya made *ALL* of this happen. She is so powerful, so immense. It was terrifying but exhilarating … Exhilarating like you wouldn't believe!"

For one miniscule moment, I noticed a rise in her voice that despite all of her protestations, hinted that maybe she might have actually enjoyed it. Suddenly Faye stopped playing the piano, turned her bedraggled face completely around towards me and burst once again into tears.

◆

"Oh no, Joe's gonna kill me."

I'd slept in and was over an hour and a half late. As I staggered over still fiddling around with the buttons on my shirt, I was surprised to see a hive of activity out the front of the garage.

"Good afternoon Wolfman, nice of you to join us," Charlie said wryly as he swerved up beside me on the tractor hauling a trailer-load of rubble.

Vince pulled an infantile face at me from inside the garage where he was mucking around with his softail.

Over by the row of old car bodies, MacElroy was getting ready to test out his newly acquired spray gun on a freshly skinned devil hide. He was wearing a perished rubber biohazard suit which was unfortunately devoid of its essential face mask and hood. To compensate, he'd pulled a tight-fitting plastic bag completely over his head with gouged out eye holes to allow better visibility through an oblong pair of swimming goggles. Completing the ensemble, he had on a pair of pink rubber kitchen gloves and concrete-splattered galoshes. Being generous, he looked like some madcap professor from a low-budget, sci-fi movie. Being brutally honest he looked like a complete frick'n idiot.

Shintarō was pacing up and down beside the ice box like he was about to become a father, or that the world was going to end. Either way, if he'd had a pack of those rapid-smoke cartoon cigarettes jiggling around in his mouth they wouldn't have looked out of place. But whatever it was that was worrying him was going down at the concrete table.

Sitting around on the back bench, where they couldn't get out, were Hamada-san and Kiko. Joe was on the near-edge seat with his back towards me and opposite him down the far end was Faye.

Kiko was distraught, I mean really, *really* distraught. The poor girl had obviously been crying and howling so much that all the accompanying sound effects had ceased, leaving only a crimson pulsating face. She looked like a soft-boiled frog. Unexpectedly she slammed her forehead twice and extremely hard into the mosaic top of the table, but even so, only a tear-choked gurgling sound whimpered out of her mouth. Angrily, Hamada-san pulled Kiko back upright and berated her sternly in Japanese.

I glanced over at Faye, I guessed she hadn't slept at all last night, she sat there looking exhausted. Joe got up from the table and headed over towards me.

"*Phew-eee!* Is that kid highly strung or what? Oh, by the way Wolf, I've got a small favor to ask you. Would you mind going back to your old cleaning job? Only for today though. The place isn't looking too bad, but it just needs that … professional touch." I knew he'd passed the job on to that Tisac guy but I think Joe was having second thoughts. He might be okay at pumping gas but as for cleaning, Tisac sucked.

"Sure, no sweat. What's up with—"

"Agh, Hamada-san has just told me she needs to make arrangements to leave the day after tomorrow and head on up to Puerto Penasco to catch their flight back to Tokyo. You know Hamada-san sacrificed a couple o' weeks relaxing up there on the beach, so she could pass on all of that naginata instruction to Faye and Sacramento. She might seem a bit of a cold fish, but she really does think a lot of our girl."

"Would I be right in thinking that Kiko doesn't wanna go?"

"Yeah, her and young Romeo over there look like they're about to try something stupid if they—"

"Do you think they'd stay on longer if they could? Is it only a matter of tickets and money, or do they really have to go?"

"Kiko reckons she was gonna run off and hide out in the desert somewhere if her grandmother forces her to leave. She is eighteen, but I know nothing about Japanese laws, so I really can't tell you. As for Hamada-san, she's pretty hard to get any clear information out of anyway. Her interpreter is, well, take a frick'n look for yourself."

Suddenly I had an idea. "Excuse me Joe, I've *really* gotta do something," I said making tracks to the bathroom.

"Yeah, no problem Wolfman, but don't forget the rocket key."

Two minutes later I'm sitting down beside Faye. I don't know what came over me, but for once in my life I thought I had the means to really help someone. I slipped her a couple of my coins.

"*Please*, don't argue. Make sure they stay put until those two lovebirds work something out and your naginata training is through. I got up quickly and left before she had time to say no. Shintarō had been watching us like a hawk and tried desperately to quiz me as to what was going on. I played dumb and headed back to the cleaner's storeroom.

◆

My work was finished around one, so I cleaned myself up and wandered over to the couch where Joe was sitting reading one of his books.

"Hey Wolf, good job man, thanks."

I appreciated that. He wasn't the type to run around and check, he knew I wasn't a shirker and trusted that I'd done a proper job.

"Go on in and grab yourself something to eat and come back out and join me. Help yourself … whatever you want."

I wrapped some cold cuts in a tortilla and grabbed the last can of cola that was lurking down the back of the fridge. By the time I got back outside to eat my lunch with Joe, I was surprised to find that Faye was there too.

"Thank you Wolf, thank you so much," said Faye overjoyed. "Your super-kind generosity was very appreciated. Although it did take a lot of persuading to get Hamada-san to finally accept. I think she had a bit of an issue about it being some kind of charity."

Despite the fact that Faye looked ragged with tiredness, she was absolutely beaming.

"So what happened?" I said curious as I sat on the arm of the couch.

"She's agreed to stay," Faye jigged up and down on the spot and clapped her hands together cutely. "Well, for two more weeks anyway."

"*Excellent*. How 'bout Kiko?"

"Hmm, she can stay on, if..." Faye looked all big-eyed and pleading at Joe.

"Fine by me."

Faye got excited and started all that girly type clapping again. Man, she was so frick'n gorgeous. I couldn't take my eyes off her.

"Kiko's going to defer her art college course. Do you call it her freshman year? And she is going to help Bird, sorry, I mean Shintarō get his passport, so he can travel over to Japan with her."

"That'll be an eye opener for the dude," said Joe with a chuckle. Faye was absolutely thrilled and bounced around with excitement.

"*Right*. Now listen here missy," Joe feigned a stern commanding tone. "Head off back to your trailer, take a nice hot shower and get yourself a few hours shut-eye... that's an order private."

Faye acquiesced, tugged the brim of Joe's hat playfully and as quick as a wisp disappeared.

"*Wow*, she's a darlin'." Joe shook his head paternally, and promptly reopened his book.

"What are ya reading?"

"*Ha!* Me and young Faye had a little bit of a chinwag soon after the concrete table summit. She apologized to me for holding back earlier but then she confided everything and spilled *ALL* o' the beans."

"She's told you about Freya?"

"Yep." Joe held up the book's cover and looked at me resignedly. *The Compendium of Scandinavian Mythology*.

"Excellent. Where did you get that?"

"Had it for ages. It was stashed down deep in one of my book piles. I thought I'd better do some boning up on who's who and what's what, up there in the nine Norse worlds. If our girl had told me all that stuff about herself and Freya, or should I pronounce it *Freyja*, *Frøya*, or *Frøjya*, even two years ago, I would have laughed my ten-gallon hat off and told her she'd gone totally, bat-shit crazy. But *now*, aaagh!" He shrugged his shoulders and made his wide-eyed expression.

A sneaky bit of cunning flashed into my mind.

"What does it say about Big Dain?"

"Big Dain? Big Dain?" Joe mumbled to himself as he thumbed through the index at the back.

"No Big Dain, but there is just Dain."

"What's it say?"

Joe adjusted his glasses and turned to the page.

"Dain. *'One of the dwarves from the poetic Eddas...'*, blah, blah, blah, *'... who with his brother Nabbi created Hildisvíni, Freya's gold-bristled boar'*. Why for?" Joe asked curiously.

"Oh nothing. I've heard the name somewhere before, that's all." *The dwarf who built Hildisvíni*. I felt really pathetic and ashamed.

"Yeah, it's pretty interesting stuff all this Germano-Scandinavian mythology," Joe said as he casually flicked his way through the pages.

I'd finished off my tortilla when the shape of someone else unexpectedly appeared right beside us.

"Look out, here's trouble," Joe said with a friendly quake in his voice as he looked over the top of his specs and saw that it was Sacramento.

"Well howdy pilgrims!" he greeted us theatrically in his John Wayne style.

"Hey thanks for lending me your book," I jumped in quickly. "I loved it. I'll give it back to Faye when I've finished off the last couple of pages."

"Well make sure ya do!" Sacramento persisted with his imitation of the Duke. *"Us Injuns take scalps now if your book's over-dooh!"*

Joe liked that one and laughed. "So what can I do for you Sacramento?" he asked, tucking his book down the side of the couch.

"Well I've come to... Sensei and Super-chick have conspired against poor, poor Sacramento and I've been ordered to hand over my pointy-stick... *sniff, sniff.*" Horsing around he milked it for all it was worth. He screwed his knuckle into the corner of his eye in a comical act of crying.

Apparently, Hamada-san had told Faye and I quote *"That her unorthodox amalgam of bo staff and naginata fighting techniques made a case for the forging of a single weapon that would combine and maximize her proficiency with both weapon styles simultaneously."* Basically, a naginata with a blade at each end. The exact same weapon Kiko had already drawn in the artwork she had made for Faye.

Sacramento finally stopped his mucking around and pulled the naginata literally out of thin air and handed it over to Joe.

It seemed Big Dain had been requested to forge the new twin-bladed ultra-weapon, ASAP. I had a vision of Charlie wearing a floppy gnome's hat hammering away at an anvil amidst a flurry of fire-sparks and smoke.

"Thanks Sacramento, I'll get this to Charlie right away," Joe said responsibly. "*Oh yeah!* If you're not busy tomorrow afternoon, come on over. It's Vince's birthday and a few of his buddies are coming around for a couple o' beers. And tell Takochai and Oochie to drag their sorry asses over here too."

Sacramento nodded, pretended to be excited, and vanished around the side of the building.

"That goes for you too Wolf, but don't bother gettin' all hair-styled up. The bunch of hombres Vince's picked up around here ain't nothing like the yuppie-scum types you're used to hobnobbing around with back in Vegas."

I laughed out loud at that one. "Any of your friends coming?"

Joe's expression turned suddenly pensive. "I don't have any friends."

"Cut it out, I bet a great guy like you has buddies from here all the way up to Saskatchewan."

Joe sniggered and cast his attention onto the slow-curving razor-sharp blade of the naginata.

"No, not me. I was given the elbow years ago, like the proverbial turd in the punch bowl."

I loved the eloquent way Joe used the metaphor. "How come?"

"Well, if for some reason or other you begin to wonder what's *really* going on, and start looking into things for yourself, don't go telling anyone else because they're not interested. Don't even try to have a conversation that's not one hundred percent authorized, certified and straight through the Overton Window. You know, sold to you by some smarmy lookin' dude that *'Brings it to you first'* and *'Tells it like it is'*… 'Sport next!'" added Joe sarcastically. "Hell, most people couldn't care less about the truth. 'I surrender my intellectual sovereignty to him. Yes HIM, to do *all* my thinking for me. I ain't got the time and quite frankly, I really couldn't give a shit anyway. It's a great big scary world out there and I don't want to know about it. If it ain't on TV it just isn't true. End of story'."

"So, who are you talking about Joe?"

"Ah, most of the normies in general, really. They know *everything*, can't tell 'em nothin'. Especially the Mr. Smarty-pants ones with all their degrees and diplomas. They're always first with the rolling eyeballs and their pre-programmed little catch cry. *'Conspiracy theory! Conspiracy theory! … Where's ya tinfoil hat buddy?'*" Joe said in a childlike whine. "If you ask them to elaborate, they'll usually just waffle on with no idea what they're talking about but insist that their own favourite legacy media propoganda stories are all one hundred percent indisputable facts."

Joe hadn't finished yet. "They'll cut you off dead quick, if something you try to talk about contradicts or challenges them. 'Don't confuse me with your drivel, I've already made up my mind. Go peddle your snake oil somewhere else. I'm kickin' back, watchin' the game and drinking my aspartame soda with my five hundred best buds on the phone right here beside me!' Don't get me started Wolf. Just *don't* get me started … pain in the ass the lot of 'em."

Frick'n hell! I only asked him if any of his friends were coming.

"Come on Wolf, I'll take the pointy stick over to Charlie, then we can have a crack at fitting that window glass into the Fire Diamond."

◆

Joe said something out of the box always seemed to happen on Vince's birthday. The forecast on the radio said today would be hot, a real stinker. Considering it felt like noon when the sun had been up for less than an hour, I guess things were going to plan.

I loved the early mornings outside the garage, you could never predict what things would be like. Some days it seemed like everyone had moved out during the night. The roller door would still be down and not a creature would stir until ten. Other mornings it was like a regular carnie town. Yesterday was like that. The jury was still out on today.

Faye came striding towards me as if she had walked right out of the morning sun. I thought she had a jacket flung over her shoulder but as she got closer, I could see it was actually a half-filled hessian sack. My unspoken question was answered with a roll of her eyes and two words.

"Falcon feathers. This lot must be the mother lode. I'm certain I know why they keep turning up now too," she said resignedly as she hurried off towards her trailer to stash this load of feathers with all of the others.

"Hey Faye!" I yelled before she'd gotten out of earshot. "Are you coming over for a drink at Vince's birthday bash?"

"Maybe later. I'll be out for most of the day with Oppuam. We're heading back into the desert to try and find the elusive power plants that the wise woman said she had seen on her wanderings."

I don't know for sure, but I strongly suspected that this might be her last-ditch attempt to discover a more natural alternative to MacElroy's recent chemical warfare. I think Faye had very little interest in Eugene's preoccupation with the sodium fluoride experiments. It was obvious it made her feel uncomfortable.

"Okay, Faye, be careful out there. Don't forget your hat, ... and take lots of water." She ignored me and kept walking.

"Oh put your little peepers back in their sockets boy," Joe said catching me checking out Faye's exit for a moment too long.

"Come on Mr. Wolf-whistle, I think we'll do a bit of tidying up around here—" He stopped mid spiel. "Well bejesus! Take a look at that?" Joe pushed the rim of his hat back like an old-time cowboy. He was looking at MacElroy who was back out on the testing range bright and early.

"What's that he's using?" quizzed Joe.

Eugene overheard him as he wasn't too far away.

"I did a bit of tinkering with the spray gun last night and I think I've come up with a more efficient design."

Tinkering! He'd completely revamped it. He'd enlarged the tank and beefed-up the motor which now hummed like an unstable reactor. The thing looked not unlike a WW2 era flamethrower.

"Give it a burst Eugene," Joe cheered him on enthusiastically.

MacElroy pulled the trigger and the unexpected kickback blew him completely ass over tit.

Joe shook his head despondently. "The guy's a frick'n doofus."

◆

We were about fifteen minutes into our clean up when a shirtless Vince came staggering out of the garage, yawning his head off.

"Well if it isn't the birthday-boy himself," berated Joe. "If you're too goddamn idle to get out o' bed and pull your finger out, I'm not wasting my time or the Wolfman's here trying to help you out." With that he threw down the broom he was using and headed off towards the kitchen. Vince just stood there looking nonplussed.

Joe soon returned with a coffee. "You watch, he's gonna want the keys to the truck next so he can go and pick up his precious kegs."

"Will you give 'em to him?"

"Yeah, of course. Only frick'n way I can get rid of him."

True to his word, Joe gave Vince the truck but refused to do any more fixing.

"Besides none of his so-called buddies would even notice the damn difference anyway."

The heat was looking to blow the top out of the thermometer. Joe said I should sit it out on the couch in the shade and finish reading my book, with the one proviso that if any customers pulled in, I'd pump the gas. Sounded fine to me, if only to keep up with that Tisac guy.

◆

Around eleven-thirty, an orange work van turned off the road and hurtled up towards the driveway. It didn't stop for gas but gave a familiar beep on the horn and sped past towards the garage.

"Who's that?" I asked.

"The Four Señors," Joe snorted unexcited. "Although there'll probably only be one or two of them inside. A couple of them are Vince's ... well, let's just say acquaintances."

"They're a bit early, aren't they?"

"Nah, they're setting up the music or something. It's too frick'n hot and I'm really not in the mood for all of that howdy-doody bullshit at the moment. I think I'll go over and pay my respects to Hamada-san and warn her about some of the insalubrious types she might run into if she wanders too far over this way. Wanna come?"

After spending much longer than we'd intended visiting the Japanese ladies, we were saying our goodbyes when Vince came charging back in the truck.

"Come on Wolf, no peace for the wicked. We'd better get around there and see what those turkeys are up to."

Vince was already out of the cab and in the back unloading his newly acquired kegs of beer. He seemed quite determined to get his precious cargo off and out of the sun as soon as possible.

"Only time that boy moves is if he's got a vested interest in something," Joe mumbled under his breath.

The Four Señors were in the garage talking to Charlie, we could hear a bunch of laughter and the usual howdy-ho catch up banter coming from inside. They soon came out still joking and carrying on and made a B-line towards Vince. From all of the rowdiness I was amazed to see that there was, as Joe had predicted, only two of them. Going by the name I was expecting to see a couple of young Mexican guys. But one of them was a tall, athletic Afro-American and the other one was a dwarf.

"*B-a-n-k-s-i-e-!*" Vince growled best-mate-style over the side of the truck to the black guy. They did all the obligatory fist bumping stuff plus a bit of robust back slapping for good measure. They were clearly pretty tight and glad to see one another.

"Señor Cheerful," Vince said more reservedly as he acknowledged the dwarf, who responded with a peculiar grin and a slow rhythmic nod of his head. I got the impression that these two weren't *quite* as chummy as Vince and Banksie, but they both seemed okay with their stilted greeting and left it at that.

"How's it goin' n-word?" Vince jibed affectionately to Banksie who by now was helping to carry a keg over into the shade.

"Hey, careful there boy, you're only two vowels and three consonants away from walking the line in the big house if you continue with all that racist banter." Banksie's retort was completely lost on Vince. Joe shook his head and motioned me over to have a closer look at the visitor's vehicle.

The Four Señors' van was a two-ton double-cab with a flatbed section in the rear. Its most impressive feature was a steel-mesh, runway-like, roof-rack that ran the entire length of the vehicle. There was only a ladder and a few coils of electrical cable up there at the moment, but you could easily stash an entire full stage sound system up top if needed.

"So, where's the other two?" I questioned Joe.

"The other three. Banksie's not one of them, he's just a ring-in. The Four Señors are a frick'n stingy bunch o' bastards who don't put themselves out for nobody unless there's mucho dinero involved. I don't have anything to do with 'em. They've always got some kind o' weird shit going on. Search me how Banksie's got himself involved. He's a really nice guy. As best as I can make out, he couldn't stand living up there in Portland anymore and headed as far down south as he could."

◆

Banksie was great. Very intelligent, and along with his funky tongue-in-cheek quips he had that disarming charm that made you feel pretty special. I warmed to him immediately. As for Señor Cheerful, he'd obviously been given the name as a joke. I've never encountered a more churlish person before in my life. I was pretty certain there was a lot more to the story behind his unfortunate manner. Even so, I said very little to the man and avoided him as much as possible.

It was only when Banksie started sliding a small subwoofer off the flatbed of the van that it struck me. I suddenly realized exactly who these two guys were. How could I *not* have seen it before? It was The

Dog Man and the fluro-skelly with the double-necked guitar from my night at The Pepper Coyote. Far out! So why the full body disguises? A truckload o' reasons flashed through my brain. I gave up and asked Joe if he had any insights.

"Dunno? … Maybe they just like dressing up."

We'd left Vince and the others to their own devices as Joe had decided we should get to work fixing one of the water pumps that serviced the irrigation ditch running along the edge of the campsite. It was beneath a small spread of trees in the shade and had a conveniently clear view of everything that was going on over at the garage. I figured we were only here so Joe could keep a watchful eye on Vince and whatever the others were getting up to.

"Ignore those frick'n clowns and pay attention to what you're supposed to be doing," Joe said after he caught me gawking over one time too many.

Judging by the ear-splitting feedback and the obligatory *Test-one-two* of a sound check, I'd been expecting Dog Man and Señor Cheerful to play more of their excruciating free-form racket that I'd experienced. But instead it seemed that Banksie had slipped on his DJ hat and that good old vinyl on the turntable would be the means to pulse up the party.

It was around half past two when Vince's guests began to arrive. The first was an SUV full of rowdy young chicas and one poor guy who looked like he'd been conscripted as the designated driver. Another car arrived soon after but this time the noise factor had tripled.

"Ah, *Saint Sebastian*, I'd forgotten all about those mamas," said Joe despondently. "It looks like Vince has invited the 'adrenalin sisters' and their boyfriends over from Pesqueira. One of 'em's called Esmeralda. She's got the highest-pitched wail of a voice you could possibly imagine." Joe stood up straight and looked back over towards the new arrivals. "Yeah that's her. See the one with the big hair and the flowery dress? Wait 'til she gets a few tequila mojitos inside of her. I bet you ten bucks she'll try and mesmerize you blind with her twin double-D thrusters."

He was just about to say something else when a stretch Red-Hawk Emporia convertible pulled up and a skeletal looking gringo and his girlfriend got out.

"Ah great, it's Johnny frick'n Hollywood and his little sweetkins. Man, watch out for that prick. He'll be watching and waiting for any opportunity to pull some kind o' scam on you."

"Why's that?"

"Because he can."

"What about the girl?"

"Oh Nevette, don't worry about her. She'll probably try to entice you with her scrawny little carcass and stooge you up for something. She even tried it on with me once for some reason. Well at least I *think* she did. Now I could be wrong, but either way, I'm old enough to be her frick'n father. No hang on make that her *grandfather!* Uugh."

"She sounds delightful. I'll keep that in mind."

"Hey, here's someone that's a really nice guy," Joe chuckled enthusiastically as a heavy-set Mexican man in his thirties alighted from his car. "That's Enrique, he's about the only one of Vince's friends, not counting Banksie or the Birdman that I actually like. Smart guy. Travelled all the way down to Quito in Ecuador and didn't get kidnapped or killed."

"So, what's so unusual about that?"

"He set off south from Santa Ana when he was only seven years old with his four-year-old sister and twenty American dollars in his pocket, after gangsters murdered his parents. I'd like to see Vince try that. He'd need a top-o-the-line air-conditioned camper, at least twenty grand and a multilingual all-girl road-crew." He roared with laughter at that one, and before he'd even stopped to draw breath, unexpectedly said, "That'll do for today, I'm parched. Let's go get ourselves a nice cold beer and see who else he's dragged in over there."

◆

Approaching the action, I noticed that the Four Señors' van was now parked around the back and had a shade cloth stretched from its roof-rack over to the rear of the building. It gave perfect protection from the sun's scalding rays and all of Vince's party crew had congregated beneath it. By now they were all boozing and bouncing away happily in front of Banksie's turntable platform.

I was amazed. There must have been thirty or forty people there by now. Joe couldn't figure out where they had all come from. Banksie's music was kicking off too. So far it was sounding pretty good, not exactly to my retrospect tastes but it was definitely pumping, and the guests seemed to be getting off and having a pretty good time, to say the least.

On our way over to get ourselves a beer we walked straight into Johnny Hollywood and his girlfriend. He was a bit of a dude. He looked seriously emaciated clad in a matching black T-shirt and jeans and a pair of white English brogues. Beside the heavy-framed glasses, his most noticeable feature was the washed-out tabby-cat hairstyle, all combed forward and making his head look like it had been spat out backwards by a gigantic carnivorous flower.

I got a disingenuous nod of recognition when Joe introduced me, but that was deemed sufficient and all I was entitled to. He quickly turned on a dime and moved on to somewhere more worthwhile. Nevette had those quick darting eyes that never once stopped moving. I definitely got the feeling I was surreptitiously being scanned from top to toe and assessed as to whether or not I had the makings of an unsuspecting mark.

She looked like a collage of C-grade celebrities arranged ad hoc into one single person. Her hair was the color of peroxide-snow and it looked just like a crisply ironed pillowcase draped symmetrically over the top of her head. Her skin, discounting the rose-pink lips of her fully ripened trout-pout, glowed unnaturally orange and clung like re-used shrink-wrap against her boney carcass. In one hand she was holding a bottle of some brightly colored alcopop. The other clung for dear life onto a cell phone which she habitually and irritatingly looked at every ten seconds, as though she was expecting someone extremely important, or more likely someone equally as fatuous as herself, to call at any moment. I just wanted to wrench the thing out of her grasp and hurl it as far into the desert as possible. Having said that, she wasn't all bad. At least she said more than half a dozen words to me. I think they were "Hello Wolf, very nice to meet you."

Joe had bolted seconds earlier and was steaming his way over to the booze table to confiscate a beer that Vince was gladly pouring for young Diego into a gigantic stein glass that even a seasoned Bavarian bierkeller patron would have had trouble managing. When he returned a couple of minutes later with two enticing cold ales he was fuming.

"Jesus wept! That boy ain't got the faintest notion of *any* common sense. If young Diego got wasted drinking beer *I'd* be the one in the shit with his mother." Handing me my beer Joe changed the subject. "Dunno about you, but I'm sittin' over there on those chairs under that umbrella."

◆

Sitting beneath the umbrella was great, you could sit back in the shade and soak up all of the action.

"How'd you go with Nevette?" Joe asked me with a grin as he took a few long gulps from his beer.

"Great. Had a riveting conversation."

With his glass Joe pointed towards another couple that were heading on in to the party. "Hey Wolf, check out those funky chickens!"

Kiko looked great. She had bundled her hair up into two black spheres on the top of her head. Her fringe hung low as usual and down into her eyes, the combined effect gave her the look of some kind of anime character. The bin-liner micro-mini dress was fantastic. It was set off nicely by a six-inch wide patent belt and knee-high white socks that shot straight up like beanstalks out of fat-soled school girly shoes.

Shintarō had definitely dressed down. He was wearing that stupid yellow polyester track suit with bare feet and for some reason known only to himself had artistically twirled up the ends of his moustache. Within minutes they were chatting away happily and mixing in like seasoned party veterans.

Charlie slipped over to join us where he could sit and drink his double bourbon in peace.

"Frick'n Banksie's working the room alright. He's already got a couple o' floozies over there goin' gaga and miming all these lurid suggestions at him."

Joe said something that I missed but I dare say it wasn't worth repeating.

"And *man*, that Señor Cheerful's a miserable son of a bitch ain't he?" said Charlie, astonished. "Not two minutes ago I told him what a great job he'd done engineering the music and how good it all sounded. He just frick'n dissed me and waddled off smirking like his shit don't stink. God he's a little prick." Charlie shook his head bewildered and then turned his attention back to his drink.

Apart from the surprise inclusion of a DJ, the party was pretty much like I'd expected; stinking hot and pretty rowdy. If you took away the dust it was almost like what I was used to back home. Not that I really ever went to many parties though. I even found myself tapping along with all the doof, doof stuff. It was like an acquired infusion into my time-capsule 1970's and eighties taste I suppose.

As the sun started sinking westward everything took on a golden glow. The beer flowed freely and was going down fine. The laughter was getting louder. Everyone was talkin' turkey and I was amazed at how much fun I was having. Even Gutteka and Jenteka were keeping an eye on proceedings. I could see their little heads poking out over the edge of the sunshade watching it all from above.

Charlie was the first to notice. He pointed to the rising dirt plumes that trailed behind three motorcycles heading in towards the party from the road. At first, I thought they were a squad of Los Espectros Brillantes coming to find Faye, but the bikes sounded entirely different to anything that I'd ever seen the skellies ride. These men were on two-wheeled high-performance thoroughbreds built for the open road. They didn't come charging right up like I'd expected but steered over to the left of the driveway for an impromptu display of high-spirited burnouts and donuts. It was all in good fun, like some shit kicked-up announcement of their most venerated arrival.

"Who are *these* guys?" I asked like you do.

"Oh, I wouldn't bother getting too excited," said Charlie contemptuously. "The chunky little guy with the bandana, that's La Bamba. That Jap bike he's riding there could kick the ass of anything on two wheels from here down to Mexico City. But look at it. *Seriously*. It's a no-class ride. Just a crafty porked-up rip-off of the latest Martellares. It doesn't look *nowhere* near as mean as Faye's MCLV."

"That's for sure." Joe raised his drink and took a long gulping swig in agreement.

"The one with the mohawk riding that other rice rocket. That's Lil' Pepe."

Charlie was about to point out who the third rider was when a whole bunch of partygoers all whooping and hollering came rushing over ready to watch the spur-of-the-moment high-octane dirt show.

I was surprised at how single-minded their enthusiasm was. I figured these three must have been some kind of local celebrities, either that or the sun and all the booze had driven the whole frick'n lot of them stark raving mad. For the moment Los Trios had drawn the crowd away from Banksie. He knew they'd be back, but for the time being he'd brought down the tempo, held onto the beat and just kept it all cool.

Charlie, Joe, and I eventually succumbed to our curiosity and wandered up for a bit of a look. Unfortunately, about five seconds after we got there the guys decided that their little shit-storm had now been concluded. So, amidst a raucous barrage of whistling and cheering, they shut down their engines, got off of their bikes and with drinks thrust appreciatively into their hands held court around their most impressive machines.

Without any warning I was deafened by an ear-splitting howl as a screaming mouth lunged past my face. Looking down, I was privy to the big-haired Esmeralda's quivering rack sliding beneath my eyes as she pushed herself urgently into the throng desperate to make her way to the front of the crowd.

"*Aghh, Le quiero! Le quiero, él es maravilloso!*"

"What's she saying?"

"She's *in LOVE!*" Charlie said mockingly, "She literally worships the ground the frick'n dude walks on. He's her hero, her numero uno, her *chico maravillo!*"

It was the *third* rider, the obvious leader, who Esmeralda was completely besotted with. His features were strikingly handsome in that strong Mesoamerican way. High-sculpted cheekbones, a proud prominent nose and black piercing eyes that seemed to mesmerize and hold the gaze of everyone he spoke to. The man was in his late twenties and stood nearly seven feet tall. His broad upper torso tapered sharply to a very thin waist which was emphasized by the dark-green motorcycle leathers which gave his body an almost insect like appearance.

From all of the sycophantic chit-chat going on around him, I'd overheard that his *real* name was Lucien. But the green-eyed monster had already recognized him as Taurokathapsia or that frick'n-bull-leaper-DOAX-guy for short.

◆

It was only after we'd reclaimed our chairs that we noticed Faye and Oppuam heading back in from the desert. Crossing the road, they came as far as the rocket sign but then changed direction and slipped out of sight behind the high row of cactus plants.

I plotted their position in my head, waiting to see if they'd reemerge at the point where the track headed off towards the campsite. My timing was perfect but so was Oochie-Cuchi's. By pure chance he'd been hobbling over to the party from the opposite direction and had unexpectedly walked right into them.

Oochie was adamant that they should both come along too. Poor Faye was trying so hard to be polite but you could tell all she really wanted to do was just get away. Oochie wouldn't take no for an answer, especially as he'd made the effort to comb out his beard. It looked impressive, exactly like a skateboard hanging from the end of his chin.

Eventually Faye relented and the three of them came over to where we were sitting. Like true gentlemen, Charlie and Joe offered their seats but Faye shook her head and declined, saying that she had no intention of staying.

It was pretty obvious by the way she managed to keep her back turned to Lucien that Faye wasn't at all comfortable standing so close to him. I guessed it was what she was wearing.

Faye didn't usually fuss too much about how she looked but today's improvised sun protection outfit really wasn't all that flattering. She had on a baggy camo' jacket that completely shielded the sun's searing rays from her fair skin. Add to that knee-length peasant pajama pants with pulled-up green socks, dusty white trainers and her hair tucked up into a boonie hat perched above oversized sunglasses and iridescent sunscreen and you begin to get the picture.

Right out of nowhere the prodigal son appeared to say his hellos to his old man. One hand was draped around the waist of a pretty girl and the other was grasping the stein Joe had taken away from young Diego.

"Waaazzz-upp!" yelled Vince, enthusiastically raising his drink above his head and spilling half in the process. He was getting pretty drunk by now and had a grin on his face like a retard.

Joe shook his head in despair and gave him a patter on the ribs as he wished him a happy birthday. Rising to the occasion Vince thought it only fitting to introduce everyone there to everybody else. I knew that if he'd been sober, he really wouldn't have given a shit. He caught sight of Lucien holding court behind him and dragged him over to meet us. I got the feeling Lucien was glad of any momentary distraction, if only to get away from the fawning attentions of the big sized everything Esmeralda.

"Lucien, this is my old man Joe."

"Hey, how's it going Lucien, long time no see?"

"Hola cómo estás?" Lucien smiled and nodded his head respectfully.

"I'm sure you remember my big ugly brother Charlie."

"Hola lo recuerdo Charlie."

Charlie just said "Howdy!" in English.

"This is the lovely chica Suzelly from Carbo."

"Hola mi lindo joven durazno," I don't know what he said but the girl blushed, and her eyes went all kind o' glazey.

"This old rascal here is second lieutenant Crawford. He might only have one leg but he's still a bit of a fox when it comes to the ladies." All the guys laughed at that one, especially Oochie.

"This here is Poca' ... *Oppuam.*"

"Hola," mouthed Lucien, now bored and uninterested.

"And last but not least, this is Faye."

I saw her wince, embarrassed, but she smiled undaunted and thrust her hand out happily to shake Lucien's.

"Hello Lucien, it really is a pleasure to meet you!"

But by now Lucien had had enough. Lured by the beckoning calls from his flunkies he glanced indifferently at Faye then turned and walked off somewhere else. Faye stood there open mouthed with her hand still extended out front. Oh god, did she look pissed.

"Well! The *arrogance* of that man!" She spun on her heels and stormed off back to her trailer.

◆

It was about half an hour later and I'd just got another round of drinks in for me and Charlie. Banksie had long since lured his audience back to the fold and now only Los Tres Jinetes and a few of their hard-core groupies were still mooching around out front. From the corner of my eye, I caught a glimpse of a long-legged blonde chick cutting around behind our chairs and making a B-line over to the drinks table, on her way relieving a hapless Johnny Hollywood of a bottle of fluorescent-pink alcopop that was obviously destined for the awaiting hand of Nevette. I almost choked on my beer when the blonde turned around and I saw it was Faye.

Her outfit was skimpy and trashy and way, way south of her pay grade. The turquoise ruffled skirt was short, to say the least, and sat so far down her naked belly that it had nowhere still half-descent left to go. Her cropped white T-shirt had an emblem or something on the front that I couldn't make out from where I was standing. At the ends of her long, bare legs a pair of low-heeled slip-on sandals adorned her feet, their tacky flower embellishments matched perfectly with the hair ties holding her two extra-long pigtails in place. To top it off she'd scribbled on a whole lot of trashy eyeliner and painted her lips bright red. *Man she looked good!*

I noticed Nevette thrust forth the poisoned apple, so to speak, the moment she cast her quick darting eyes upon Faye and the hijacked drink. The self-deluded fantasy as fairest in the land had crashed hard, like broken mirror shards around her feet.

I nudged Joe for an urgent heads-up as he still hadn't noticed. His mouth dropped open and his eyes nearly popped from his head. I cracked up laughing at his gawk under that crazy-looking cowboy hat and the funny way his ass poked out when he slid up to the edge of his chair. He shot me a sideways look completely baffled as to what I was laughing at. Oochie had now seen Faye too and let out that old stock standard wolf-whistle.

"Look at that pretty little filly will ya. Now if I was twenty years younger, I'd—"

"Give it a rest Ooch, more like *fifty*, you old perv." Charlie shut him up quickly before he started getting all graphic.

Faye steamed straight up to Lucien and for some unknown reason started talking to him in a southern-belle accent. Pretty convincingly too. "Well howdy there Mr. Lucien. *Oh lawdy, lawdy*, I've just been *dyin'* to meet you!"

Joe's jaw dropped even further and the look on his face was priceless.

"I heard the king of the donuts was comin' to this li'l ol' party an' when I seen y'all doin' that twirly-whirly stuff over yonder in the dirt patch, *I just knew* it had to be *YOU!*" she said, tapping him playfully on the chest with her finger.

Faye was doing great. She had all the girly moves down pat from the see-sawing sexy little hip-pivots to the stupid looking grin plastered right across her face. Lucien just stood there speechless, totally perplexed by this six-foot-tall blonde gringo-bimbo.

"Oh, I'm sorry Mr. Lucien, I'm just so excited I plumb forgot to properly introduce myself. My name's Tammy-Faye Jackson and I'm from South Carolina 'n Dixie! *Two-time winner, one-time runner-up, Miss Cotton Queen, Madison County!*" Faye whispered quickly behind her hand as it was obviously an important side issue.

"So what's with blondie and all that southern talk Joe?" asked Oochie looking totally baffled.

"Dunno. But keep your voice down, don't let's blow her little game."

Esmeralda was definitely not impressed and with an accompanying tirade in Spanish, she squeezed herself into the gap right between Lucien and Faye. It was only the raise of his god-like hand that stopped the enraged Esmeralda from grabbing Tammy-Faye and dragging her away like a fully triggered door-bitch.

"*Woo-ee!* that sure is an impressive lil' ol' motorcycle y'all got there Mr. Lucien. I bet y'all move like shit off a shovel 'specially when y'all wearin' that fancy lil' ol' spidey-man outfit there. I knows a thing or two 'bout motorcycles but I ain't never seen one like *that!*" Faye said to Lucien, now all fired up and *really* pushing her luck with this southern belle thing. For a second there I thought she was going to blow it and burst out laughing.

"It's a Donau. A Tri-Spiker-Eleven-fifty," said Lucien warily. I couldn't place his accent, but he did speak pretty good English.

"What's a Donau?" I whispered to Charlie in total ignorance.

"They're from Austria. Damn good bikes too, don't you worry about that."

Lucien just stood there staring down at Faye's chest.

"What is this?" he asked curiously running his finger across her T-shirt, "I know Martellare of course, but what are these words here?"

I'd never seen Faye wear the shirt before and guessed it must have come from the Italian lady's market stall in Hermosillo. It was a vintage version of the Martellare Angelus logo. But Lucien was underlining the words underneath.

Faye looked blankly at Lucien. She yanked the shirt up theatrically and took a better look at it herself.

"*Moretti treno valvole*? Well I'm not rightly sure Mr. Lucien. I think it's got sup'm to do with them lil' ol' valve thingies swishin' around in them there Martellare enj'ns."

"She knows *exactly* what it means," whispered Charlie choking down a smile.

Lucien nodded slowly. His attention now focused completely on Faye.

"Y'all like what you see Mr. Lucien?" She beamed a big cheesy smile and swirled enticingly from side to side. It was *then* that Faye made her move.

"Ya know, Mr. Lucien, I reckon this might sound kind o' stupid, y'all bein' famous an everythin' and me bein' just a gal. But I got me a motorcycle over yonder. How 'bout I go fetch him and maybe we could have ourselves a lil' ol' race?"

Lucien's mob howled with laughter at that one. Charlie informed me hurriedly before the heckles died down that Lucien was widely acclaimed as the Lord-God-Living-Legend of the racing bike fraternity around Sonora and except for La Bamba with his two hundred miles-an-hour-plus-road-missile, ol' spidey-rider here would leave all challengers who fancied their chances sucking up the Tri-spiker's wake.

Lucien stood there smirking, wallowing in his own self-assuredness and the absurdity of such a suggestion. Tammy-Faye's offer was deemed nothing more than an attention seeking joke.

"Well how-bout you then, Mr. Mohawk?" Faye cunningly switched her attention over to Lil' Pepe. "If Mr. Lucien here is *scared* of lil' ol' me, maybe we could head over yonder and race it out for a lap or two?"

That was completely unexpected. The eye of attention had swung away from Lucien but being the big-cheese-El-Tauro, he closed down Lil' Pepe, re-engaged himself back into the spectacle and then fell straight into Faye's little ploy.

"Okay, miss. Let's pretend for a minute that we do race," his entourage laughed again predictably. "What kind of a wager do you think would maybe make it a little more interesting?"

"*Woo-ee!* If that ain't slicker than snot. I ain't one to beat around the bush none, Mr. Lucien. I reckons if I win y'all have to strip yourself out o' that lil' ol' spidey-man outfit, all the way down to ya shorts. I'd sure as hell 'd like to see *that!*" Faye announced boldly, trying her hardest to act dumb and in character.

With a contemptuous expression on his face Lucien sounded his inevitable reply. "And, if *I* win?"

Tammy-Faye said nothing but in a 'blink and you missed it' moment, she flicked the hem of her short skirt skywards and did the exact same thing with her eyes. Some of the quicker ones caught it, Lucien most certainly did.

> *... And so the falcon lured the spider*
> *who mistook her for a fly.*

The rider feigned total inexperience as the red Martellare Angelus chugged drunkenly out of the garage. Tammy-Faye gripped tightly onto the handlebars, her legs standing straight on the foot pegs with her butt sticking high in the air. The Lucienites all jeered and laughed but played along with this ridiculous farce. With a final unsteady wiggle, the motorcycle crawled to a halt. Tammy-Faye dropped clumsily back down into the saddle only stopping the bike from falling over completely with some deft and lucky footwork.

"Oops, nearly lost it there didn't I, Mr. Lucien?"

I chuckled at that stupid looking grin she'd managed to keep on her face throughout this whole charade as I knew the intelligence of the brain behind it. Faye had completely hoodwinked them all. Joe, Charlie and Oochie were enjoying all of this immensely.

"Are y'all ready Mr. Lucien?"

To his credit Lucien must have taken pity, and concernedly enquired if she had any other more appropriate clothing to wear. Tammy-Faye admitted that all this excitement had made her go "a little bit dipsy" and that she'd be "back for some racin'" in the "shake of a puppy dog's tail." With that, Faye puttered away to the garage where her gear was assumedly waiting for her.

◆

When Faye returned a few minutes later, she was no longer playing games. With a foreboding roar from Hildisvíni's engine she forcefully pounced her motorcycle out of the garage and slammed on the brakes only inches from Lucien's feet. The full compression of the front wheel shocks momentarily pushing the nose of the bike as far down the forks as it would go. Lucien didn't flinch. That move was no accident. He knew he'd been punked.

Faye had kept the Martellare T-shirt but had exchanged the sandals for her dark-red motorcycle boots. Instead of the skimpy dress she now sat astride her machine clad in a pair of creamy-white racing leathers embellished with an elongated arrowhead that ran down the side of each leg.

"Where'd she get them snazzy lookin' britches?" Joe asked excitedly.

"They were either Johnny's or Ted's. I really can't remember," answered Charlie.

"Probably Johnny Mason's," chuckled Joe. "Before he put on thirty pounds eatin' all those frick'n Xolo dogs. Charlie, you'd better go get the flag and head on down to the line. This whole thing's about to kick off and it'll all be over in five minutes." Joe jumped up from his chair and dubbed himself supreme-boss marshal of all proceedings.

By now, word had spread, and a second wave of onlookers had shifted over from the drinks and music side of the party excited by the promise of an imminent motorcycle race. With sheer exuberance, Vince fell right into the core of the revelers. It was hard to say who he'd be putting his money on. Being the little shit that he was, my guess was he'd probably be rooting for Lucien. But you never can tell with Vince.

"So who's got the best bike then?" I said naïvely to Charlie.

"*Hmm?* Well they're both around the same vintage. On paper the Martellare's got a little more speed and engine capacity but Lucien's been tweaking and tuning that Tri-Spiker to within an inch of its life for near on half a decade now. I dunno? I'd say they're pretty much even. It all comes down to the riders now," Charlie said emphatically.

"*Okay.*" Joe was in his element. "La Bamba, you go do a fast reckon and make sure there's no rocks or dead stuff lying across the track. Yeah?" Joe quickly answered La Bamba's reply. "Don't worry about it.

How the hell could we start if you're still out there riding around?"

Charlie came back holding the checkered flag and cadged a lift down to the road with La Bamba where he proceeded to scratch out the finish line with the heel of his boot.

"Right, you both know the track. This'll be a two-lap race. We'll go with a Mason start. For all you clowns that don't know, that's from right up here on the driveway and straight out between the gas pumps. No kickin' or gouging (Joe threw that in for a joke) and no whining or crying foul if either of you falls off, runs out o' gas or misses a turn on the track. Yeah?"

Both heads nodded in agreement.

Lucien had long since mounted and started up his machine. I hadn't taken that much notice of it before, but in my layman's opinion the Tri-Spiker was sharp and angular, kind of space-age-looking, even insectoid, completely different to the rounded muscular lines of Faye's Martellare.

Excited by the loud rumbling of engines, the crowd surged forward towards the driveway where the two riders maneuvered their machines up into position on the starting grid.

Being such a short ass, and one of the only four or five people in the crowd that was barracking for Faye, I helped Oochie climb up onto the back of Joe's couch so he could at least see the bikes get away.

The noise beneath the concrete roof was horrendous but amongst all of the commotion and racket I saw Faye suddenly turn her head towards Lucien and say something like "Let's see how good you really are then DOAX." And then she just took off. A spontaneous cheer went up from the crowd.

"What the...?" Joe gasped surprised, his head twisting every which way with his hand still raised high ready to drop for the start. Faye shot out towards the road like an unleashed banshee, but Lucien had not been caught napping and clung perilously close to her tail.

The two racers shot across the road at a ridiculous speed and launched themselves straight into the first gradual turn of the track. Faye was still in front, with Lucien less than a bike-length behind her. They thundered on for two-hundred yards before taking a right-hand turn that led into a tight hairpin bend.

Man, this was amazing! The agile way they threw their body weight from one side of the bike to the other looked almost choreographed and the angles they managed to lay their machines down going into the turns seemed impossible. Just an inch or two lower and the whole frick'n bike would surely have slid completely out from under or plowed itself deep in the dirt. These two really meant business. As they came out of the hairpin, they were obscured by a cocktail of dirt and red setting sun, but in seconds they swept back into view and out into the desert on the long-arcing curve of the turn.

I heard Vince yelling *"Up on the roof! Up on the roof!"* A horde of about twenty people, Joe and me included, charged up the Alamo's ramp intent on getting a better view of the action. I felt a bit guilty leaving Oochie down below, but he didn't seem to care. He was far too busy chatting up a couple of young babes who'd jumped up on the couch right beside him.

By the time we'd reached the roof, Faye and Lucien were back in sight and leaning their machines low through turn six, a steep left-hand curve that momentarily brought them heading straight back in towards us. The noise from their straining engines was still pretty loud even at that distance. I reckoned they were about three hundred yards away. Through the haze you could pick out the blurry red shape of Faye and the smudgy black one that was Lucien.

They twisted and dueled their way through turns seven and eight still heading more or less in our direction. A manic cheer went up from the Lucienites when they saw for the first time that their hero had taken his rightful position and was now in the lead.

The bikes dropped down low into the tight right-hand corner of turn nine and then launched themselves noisily off at full-throttle into the near mile-long back-straight that ran dead parallel with the road going south.

Disgruntled voices around me seemed upset that the race had inconsiderately headed off out of sight and they'd been deprived of any more action. I heard Johnny Hollywood whining that he felt "ripped off".

I'm sure that when Mason was plotting out this desert-bash racetrack all those years ago, he must have somehow overlooked the fact that a day like today might arise and he would be beating himself up that he hadn't considered the spectator satisfaction of the likes of Johnny Hollywood and his blow ins.

Hindered by the fast setting sun, all eyes were squinting for the imminent return of the racers who, after negotiating the far-end series of turns, would soon come hurtling back towards us along the mile-long straight that doubled as a public roadway. Then they would peel off back into the desert for the second and final deciding lap.

Joe tapped me on the shoulder and pointed down towards Charlie.

"Look, it's La Bamba, he's going ballistic. He's pissed we didn't wait for him to get back before the race started," Joe roared with laughter. "The guy loves all that respect bullshit. He'd do frick'n *anything* to be worshipped like Lucien... never could understand why people have that kind o' mind-set."

"Here we go!" Joe said blankly as the rising sound of the engines signaled their return.

"*Ooh-ee* listen to that *sweet,* sweet music," came an unfamiliar voice from behind us. It was Banksie. "The bikes I mean, not that old-school psycho-trance bullshit Señor Cheerful's playing around the back."

He'd answered my question without me even asking.

"I didn't know you liked motorcycles Banksie," Joe said straining to catch the first sight of the riders.

"I don't, but all these jive-ass-mothers dissed me and came charging up here, so I thought I'd better come and see what all the damn fuss was about."

Joe grunted, uninterested as the Martellare and the Donau hurtled back into view. Lucien was about four or five lengths ahead of Faye now and looked determined to hang on tight to his lead.

"*Holy shit,* they're coming in fast. If they don't ease off soon, they're gonna zoom right past and overshoot the turn completely."

Joe's worries were unfounded as both riders dropped skillfully back down through the gears and took the left-hand turn in their stride. Considering the speed these two were moving Lucien's line of entry had drifted wider than it should have, allowing Faye to close the gap between them. She sat right on his ass through turns two and three. Then, with both bikes decelerating into the tight hairpin bend, Faye took her chance and gracefully guided the Martellare right in between Lucien and the inside curve of the track, emerging out onto the sweeping turn back in front.

"*Oh lordy, lordy me, did you see that?*" exclaimed Joe in awe. "*Gorgeous!* Even a pro would've been proud of a maneuver like that. Absolute cream-cake perfection."

Even the staunchest Lucien fans (except Esmeralda), applauded and nodded their heads in approval at such a stunning piece of bravado. "Wow that bimbo chick can ride okay, as well as being a hot lookin' piece o' pu—"

"Hold that thought right there Hollywood," Joe interjected immediately.

"Say one more syllable and I'll throw you right off this roof."

Johnny laughed it off, but he couldn't keep his mouth shut for long. "Ah this is all bullshit dude, half a minute's action then all you get is a cloud of dirt and a bunch o' far away motorbike noises."

I couldn't believe it, next thing you know he'd be asking for his money back.

"Fifty bucks says Lucien's already got this thing won anyway."

Joe responded quickly "I'll take that bet. You *obviously* don't know my girl."

They did that spit and the high five thing and then ignored each other completely.

By now the sun was fast sinking low and the duel through the back turns was almost impossible to make out. The one thing I did notice as they came around nine and headed off south was that Lucien was back in the lead. His upper body strength and years of constant familiarity with his Donau motorcycle were now definitely starting to tell. We could still hear their engines okay, but until they tore along that final mile to the finish, all we could do now was wait.

"*Aquí vienen!* Here they come!" yelled the youngsters with the keenest eyes. The engines were screaming and although the distant motorcycles grew larger with every second it was still pretty hard to make them out. They looked like two noisy squiggles bouncing up and down in the near extinct light.

This would all be over in a matter of seconds. As the shapes became more solid another roar of excitement exploded from inside the gallery as it was clear that Lucien was right out in front. The noise was incredible as the two high-performance engines whined at their upper-most limits. They were now *eight – seven – six* hundred yards out and Lucien was a good four Tri-Spiker lengths in the lead.

"*Lucien! Lucien! Bravo Lucien!*" His fan club were now jumping up and down on the show-room roof and leaning right out from the wall like an overzealous mob at a soccer game, ecstatically cheering on their hero to his inevitable victory. The Martellare and the Tri-Spiker were flat-chat now and just three-hundred yards from the line.

"*COME ON DARLIN'! COME ON DARLIN'! you can do it; you can take him!*" Joe yelled his wholehearted encouragement.

With only two hundred yards left to go Faye crouched even lower calling on all last reserves from the MCLV's bursting engine and then charged right up level with Lucien's Tri-Spiker. It was only then Faye dropped the hammer *completely* and red lined the screaming Hildisvíni right past Lucien to win by a half-second gap on the line.

At the exact moment they both crossed an all-horns-blasting road-train heading in the opposite direction roared right between them sending the riders out wide to either side of the road. They must have seen the thing plowing headlong straight towards them while they were still racing. What a couple o' maniacs.

"YEAH! fuckin' YEAH!" Joe threw his precious hat in the air and was bouncing around punctuating his victory dance with his trademark upper-cut air-swings. *"Man, that kid's somethin' else, ain't she?"*

Apart from me, Joe, Kiko and Bird, sorry Shintarō, the rest of the crowd just stood mumbling in a state of stunned disbelief. As they all started heading back down in disappointment, I noticed a solemn Hamada-san standing half-way up the ramp gazing serenely down towards the roadway. She turned and caught my eye before she descended. I was kind o' glad she'd been there to witness the blond-haired Tomoe Gozen's victory and a completely different side of her pupil's many attributes.

By the time we'd left the roof, the riders had still not returned. Joe reckoned the speed Faye was doing when she crossed the line would have been well over two-hundred miles per hour. Charlie said that was all bull as the top speed possible for a factory Martellare was one-ninety-five at best. So I don't know exactly, somewhere around that number, but I tell you straight, it was ridiculously fast. She was *flying*.

◆

Faye returned from the road and pulled up short of the driveway. She shut down the engine and with arms fully locked on the handlebars and her legs grounded securely on either side of her champion Hildisvíni, she just sat there still and silent. Everyone felt a little intimidated and thought it best to leave her alone.

When he got back, Lucien rode up confidently and stopped not too far from Faye. I could only guess at his torment, the king defeated by a *girl*. The crowd had quickly gathered into a semicircle around the two protagonists, intrigued to see what would happen next. Poor Esmeralda, whose world had all but crumbled before her, now feigned unconscious-ness as she listed uncomfortably across a pink plastic chair.

They all started clapping and chanting something in Spanish. Lucien, now off his bike, walked up to within a few yards of Faye, who still sat there unstirring.

"What are they saying?" I asked Joe, being a devout monolingual.

"Agh. *Get 'em off, get 'em down,* something like that. This lot are a bunch of flip-flopping turncoats. They're all wanting to see Lucien pay up and strip on down to his undies."

The look on Lucien's face was of someone who'd been nudged a few rungs down the ladder of his own pier's prestige. I figured he felt damned if he didn't, but he'd probably have more chance of coming up trumps if he did. The very second he laid his hand on the zipper of his spidey-like leathers, Faye kicked down the foot stand, dismounted her motorcycle and bade him to stop.

"I don't want to see you in your shorts Lucien. I've made a mountain out of a molehill with this whole thing anyway. I'm sorry. I suppose *technically*, I threw the race by jumping the start, but I know you're too much of a gentleman to insist—"

She cut her sentence short, and then continued on a different track. "All you had to do was shake my hand and say hello. Was that really too much to ask?" With that Faye raised her head and walked quietly off to her trailer.

24

Joy Ride

Joe said it was pointless skulking around looking for a sneaky hidey-hole to watch Faye and the others train from, as Hamada-san would undoubtedly spot us, and it might really get her miffed. But even from our old vantage point up here on the roof, we still had a pretty good view of proceedings. Charlie was with us this morning, keen to see how his crafting of the new double-ended naginata would perform on its debut outing. Apparently, it had even been given a name, not the jokey, unflattering, pointy-stick that Sacramento had called it, but something old and Nordic. Charlie couldn't for the life of him remember what it was, but he seemed pleased with his handy work and impressed with what he was seeing.

Already Faye had taken to this deadly new weapon like she'd been wielding it all her life. But now, once the kata sequence of naginata attack and defense movements had been completed, Faye moved out into a central position between Sacramento and Hamada-san for what was going to be a two against one, freestyle bout between herself and both of her sensei. It was a test of sorts to let them see exactly what she was capable of. Having nothing comparable to counter with, Hamada-san and Sacramento had armed themselves with stout wooden staffs easily as thick as your wrist.

When given the command, Faye unleashed the double bladed naginata into a whirlwind of movement and power with a most deadly grace. We'd been expecting something impressive, but this was unbelievable. The speed was truly staggering. In a matter of seconds Faye had sliced both sensei's staffs into a scatter of kindling before finishing her attack sequence abruptly with a most theatrical pose that screamed, all skill, all class, and most of all don't even *think* about messing with ME.

"Holy frick'n Moly!" laughed Joe impressed, in a voice that spoke for all of us.

"*Geirahöð!* That's it," blurted Charlie, excitedly remembering the weapon's name. "The geirahöð. The battle spear."

"Technically it's not *really* a spear," Joe said, completely missing the moment.

Whether it was sheer coincidence or a sign from the spirits there was no way of knowing. But right at the moment Faye bowed with respect to her mentors, the ground started rumbling and shaking.

Once more I felt the gut-wrenching uncertainty of how long the tremor would last and how strong it was going to be. Standing up on the roof was a particularly uncomfortable feeling. It wasn't hard to imagine that at any second the concrete underfoot could split wide open, swallow you whole and then come crashing down on top of your head for good measure. Instinctively we turned and headed back down the ramp. Charlie lost his balance and bounced all the way down on his butt. The tremor shook hard, but thankfully didn't have the same intensity to start hurling stuff around like the first one did. By the time we'd reached the bottom the shaking had stopped, completely, as if nothing had happened at all.

"You okay, Charlie?" Joe asked, concerned for his eldest.

"Yeah. Grazed half the skin off of my hand, but I reckon I'll probably live."

"How 'bout you Wolfman?" Joe asked me in turn.

"I'm fine although I—"

He wasn't really interested as his attention had already moved elsewhere. "*Hmm,* I don't think the epicenter was anywhere near here. I've got a hunch it was over in that direction, south-west and more towards the ocean."

His assumption seemed correct, as he pointed excitedly in the direction of the Pacific. "Look at that will you. The horizon's on fire." Well it wasn't exactly on fire, but a fifty-mile stretch of smoky-black plumes had shot high up into the sky, making a hell of a mess as they did so.

"Right, let's get things organized around here. Charlie, go check inside the building and get whoever's still in there outside. Once you've done that, better get the old Gatling gun out too. You never know, some of those devil bastards might feel like coming back up for a rematch," Joe whispered cautiously under his breath. "I'd rather have it up here nice 'n handy than hidden beneath a whole pile o' bog rolls."

"Onto it pops," said Charlie.

Then unexpectedly, Faye appeared with the geirahöð in her hand.

"I was just getting to you darlin'," Joe said, caught off guard but glad to see she was okay. "Where's Sacramento?"

"He went back to the campsite."

"Good, he's the best one to sort out what's going on over there. Wolf, I'd like you to go and find Hamada-san and Kiko and check that they're both safe and well."

Faye grabbed my arm.

"Before you go, would you please hold onto this for me Wolf. I shan't be a moment," Faye said, casually handing me the geirahöð as if it held no more importance than an old mop handle. The very sight of that thing filled me with dread, let alone having it thrust into my hand. I ran my eye along the gentle curves of the naginata's eighteen-inch blades. The weapon was extremely forboding.

I glanced at Faye as she ducked low beneath the partially open roller-door and disappeared out of sight.

A woman screamed, as suddenly the fly-screen door burst open and a near naked man came charging out wearing only a pair of cruddy looking briefs, an untied pair of combat boots and one of those floppy winter hats on his head. He stumbled blindly out to where we were standing, tripped on the laces and landed face first in the dirt. The scary part was the 12-gauge shotgun he was carrying, but scarier than that it was Vince.

Poking her head out through the door right behind him was a shocked Mrs. Eduardo. She clasped her hands to her mouth with concern but retreated back inside on seeing that Joe was already there to meet him.

With a jolt, Vince lurched his head up drunkenly and slurred *"Where are they? Where'z those monster things? … jus' le' me at 'em!"*

Joe automatically put his boot down hard on the barrel of the shotty before the idiot managed to get a blast off. *"Holy mother of God, what the HELL are you doing boy?"* Joe was fuming. He bent down and relieved Vince of the weapon.

"How in tarnation did you get this out of my gun case ya clown?" Vince just grinned pathetically and tried unsuccessfully to sit up straight. It was only then that we realized how inebriated he actually was.

"How old are you, boy?" Vince didn't answer – he was incapable of constructing a coherent sentence.

Joe was about to let rip when, for a second time, the fly screen flung open and a young woman hastily swaddled in a gathered-up bed sheet came trotting out. She was just as drunk as Vince and surprised to find a reception committee unexpectedly standing around her alcohol-sodden true-love's body.

"Oh for God's sake! Anyone else you've got back there Vincent? Nevette in there too, is she? Johnny, *'You owe me fifty bucks'* Hollywood maybe?" Joe growled sarcastically.

The girl staggered around for a moment with an expressionless look, leaned down and delicately placed the palm of her hand upon Vince's head, then calm as you like, without saying a word, turned and sauntered her way back inside.

Joe stood there seething like he was about to explode. But rather than lose it completely, he abruptly stormed off around the ramp to the driveway.

"OH, FOR F—" We heard the cry from out the front. Joe came racing back towards us, now twice as angry.

"The dining room door and shop window have been pulverized. Smashed to frick'n smithereens … *Uuuuuuuuuugh!*"

Vince raised an arm in a pathetic attempt to try and console his old man.

"Shut up you idiot. Get your sorry ass back inside, clean yourself up and by the time I get back I want this whole damn place lookin' spotless. And if there's any more of your so-called friends still in there they'd better make themselves pretty damn scarce. Understood?"

The sound of clattering metal turned our heads as the half-opened roller-door began to slide up. I expected to see Faye, but instead it was Charlie walking out a disorientated looking Shintarō from somewhere inside. Wearing nothing more than a long pair of boxers and a cone shaped towel around his head, I figured the poor guy must have been getting dressed after his shower when the tremor started.

Shintarō and Charlie were half-way towards us when Kiko unexpectedly came running around the corner draped in a flimsy silk kimono and those oversized dinosaur clods on her feet, with her hair trailing long out behind her. She was reciting impassioned words in Japanese to her newly found sweetheart like odes from a love-torn-saga. Upon seeing Kiko, Shintarō broke free from Charlie's grasp and ran towards her with equal emotion.

The resulting conclusion as they came together was truly breathtaking. As if to savor each other's vision they stopped a few feet apart for an instant, before meshing as one in an embrace that would have put any daytime soapy actor and actress to shame.

It was touching. To tell you the truth I was just jealous. Joe looked at me with an expression that summed up his opposite opinion.

Once again the beast did roar as the sound of the Martellare reverberated loudly inside the garage. Faye steered the growling motorcycle right up beside us. She had changed into the black jeans and motorcycle boots but still wore the T-shirt she had on during training. Gone was the Tammy-Faye look of yesterday, replaced by a speedy, hand-painted, slash of black across both eyes, that looked crude but very intimidating.

"You've got another tattoo," I said, not knowing for certain if she was aware of it.

"Oh no, I've got *two* new ones. I noticed them this morning."

Faye pulled up her short sleeve that was partialy hiding it from view. At the top of her left arm, on the round of her shoulder was an intricate tattoo the size of your hand.

"Wow, it's the ancient Triskele," I said, impressed.

"Very good Fenrir, you remembered its name."

"What about this one?" quizzed Faye, exposing a counter-balancing disc on her right arm.

"The Ying and The Yang. No! The *Yin* and The Yang. The symbol for the eternal duality of everything."

"Very good Wolf, now return the geirahöð back to me please."

I was startled, I had completely forgotten I was still holding it.

Faye had a quick word to Joe and then on to Charlie. Something complementary about the excellent craftsmanship he'd performed on her new weapon, although I couldn't hear exactly what she was saying over the noise of the Martellare's throbbing engine.

"Goodbye for now. I have been called and must urgently attend."

Faye anticipated our next remark and raised her head momentarily to the sky. Far above, like a patient escort circled *Falco Peregrinus*, eager to guide her charge to wherever it was she was needed. Right at the second before she took off, she called out commandingly, *"Jentekatt, Guttekatt, komme!"* The two felines appeared out of nowhere and leapt up obediently onto the motorcycle's seat cowl behind their mistress.

Before leaving she glanced down at Vince who was still lolling about like a waste of space in the dirt. It only lasted a moment but the look on her face as she sat there proudly upon Hildisvíni firmly holding the impressive geirahöð was one of utter contempt. The flash of self-realization that shot across Vince's face as his drunken eyes looked up to meet hers was definitely something more haunting.

◆

After an uncertain moment Shintarō roughly lifted Vince back up onto his feet and hauled him away with Kiko fluttering around behind them like an anxious Kabuki dancer.

Joe came rushing back outside after locking the shotgun away and grabbing his precious cowboy hat.

"Don't get me wrong. I'm not defending the idiot but turns out it was *my* fault Vince got his mitts on the shotty. I'd left the frick'n key in the cabinet door, stupid old fool."

One thing I liked about Joe was that he would always admit his own mistakes. "Where is he anyway?"

"Shintarō and Kiko have dragged him around the back for a good hosing down," Charlie joked spitefully.

"*Shintarō*. I still can't get used to that name," Joe chuckled wryly as he fiddled with the dimples in his hat. "Try and stay outside as much as possible. Just in case. And Charlie, make sure little brother pulls his finger out and cleans up that glass and any other stuff that still needs doing. Me and Wolf are taking the kegs back and having a bit of a recon."

As Joe headed off to go and get the truck, I had a brainwave.

"Hey Joe, do you wanna take the Fire Diamond out for a spin? She needs a bit of a run and there's bucket loads of room in the trunk."

Joe turned on his heels. *"You can do the driving,"* I said in a tempting, syrupy voice.

"Good call Wolfman," Joe said excitedly. He threw me his key bunch and told me to go fetch her out of the showroom.

"Don't leave the key sittin' in the door lock now will ya," he said self-mockingly as he disappeared around the back to get the kegs.

◆

The three of us headed south. That was Joe, me and the ten-gallon hat that I'd buckled up pride of place in the middle of the bench seat between us. He wasn't amused.

Joe was having a ball at the wheel. He'd wound the new window down fully so he could stretch his elbow right out and do that funky-dude-tapping-thing that he does with his hand on the ledge. Even when I looked the other way, I could still hear the rhythmic patter and found it hard not to burst out laughing.

"So where exactly are we going?" I asked.

"Agh, just some old roadside beer-barn not far from here. One of the bar staff hires out kegs on the sly but you get charged a frick'n king's ransom if you don't fetch 'em back right on time though. You're forced to pay *la pena por la falta de respeto*."

"What's that?"

"The penalty for disrespect!"

"Sounds like a real piece o' work."

"Nah, Prisciliana's a little darlin'. She's really got her head screwed on right for a twelve-year-old. She wasn't there yesterday when Vince picked up the kegs. Pity really, they would've gotten on like a house on fire."

"This ol' Fire Diamond purrs along like a kitten, Wolf. Sure leaves that old bucket of bolts I chug around in for dead. Thanks a bunch for letting me drive her. Anyway, I'm sure the old carbies could do with a bit of a blowout. Yeah, she's okay."

"Speaking of blow outs, what happened to Banksie last night? I never thought he would have been the type to just split and run."

"Ah, Banksie would still be out there playing his frick'n records now if you let him. It would have been Cheerful that decided to leave. He probably had to go to some other job this morning with his three amigos. Banksie acts like a big shot pretending he's the boss and everything but he really only works for them," said Joe. "Yeah, they're an industrious little gang o' dudes I will give 'em that."

"Did you know it's Faye's birthday in a couple of weeks, Joe?"

"Seriously? It's the first I've heard of it." He sounded genuinely surprised.

"That means she's a Sagittarius like Vince, doesn't it?"

"Well no, actually. Faye reckons her star sign is Ophi… Ophur… somethin' or other? Ophiuchus! that's it."

"Crap! There's no such sign," Joe snapped assertively.

"Well that's what I said, but she insisted there is. Although she didn't seem all that interested or bothered about it either way."

"What's its symbol?"

"Well it's a capital U with a wiggly line running right across it."

"No! What's it a depiction of dumbass. A pig with a violin, a two-headed monkey?"

"Oh, it's a man in a loincloth wrestling with a gigantic snake. The Snake Handler."

"Well, come on Wolf, what else did she say? Faye wouldn't make stuff like that up," Joe insisted, curious and impatient.

"I can't remember much. She said there used to be thirteen zodiac signs a couple of thousand years ago but for some reason or other they decided to give one the flick."

"And that would be Ophiuchus, right?"

"Yep!"

"So who gave it the flick?"

"Dunno, a bunch o' beards, I guess. But apparently it's been shoe-horned back in now between Sagittarius and…what's the one that comes before it?"

"Scorpio?"

"Yeah, but it's reinstatement has thrown all the other signs right out of whack. Most folks have no idea that their zodiac sign is something completely different now."

"Yeah, well thank you for that erudite elucidation of all things astrological, Professor Wolfgang. It's obvious you're a veritable fountain of knowledge on the subject."

◆

We drove on in silence, keeping an occasional eye on the horizon and the ominous plumes of dark smoke that bellowed thick into the sky.

"Looks like Kuwait in '91 when they set the oil fields alight," Joe mentioned authoritatively, crouching down to see how they were fairing higher up above the roof line.

"Were you there then? The Gulf I mean."

"Nah, I was well out of it. I was back home by then playing daddy-cakes with my two little boys."

I didn't want to risk opening up any old wounds, so I quickly shifted the subject.

"What do you think about all this *Freya, goddess of the Vanir* business, Faye's got herself tangled up in?"

"To be honest Wolf, at first I thought she was messin' with me. It all sounded so farfetched but *look at her*. Listen to her. Everything about her screams that it's gotta be true. Like I said before, I'm just your average meat and two veg kind of guy and all this cosmic other-worldly stuff don't sit right with my reasoning. The thing that *really* bugs me about it all, and I can't make any sense of, is why here?"

"How do you mean?"

"Well, what the hell is the reincarnate vassal of a mythological Nordic goddess doing charging around with a phantom bunch of bonehead motorcycle riders down here in the middle of the Sonoran Desert? Shouldn't she be up there somewhere near the North Pole flying around with Eric Bloodaxe and an equally disagreeable looking bunch of Viking berserkers or something? It just don't add up."

Bingo! Joe had hit the nail on the head.

"You know, that's *exactly* what's been bugging me too. Still, I'm sure she'd tell us why, if we asked her."

"*Oooh* ... I've had a flashback or one of those déjà vu thingies," Joe zinged excitedly, coming right out of left field. "Did you see the way our little goddess slipped right inside Lucien and took him on that hairpin turn yesterday? *Man that was excellent.*" Joe shook his head and grinned, savoring the memory and filing it away carefully under *Recently Acquired Favorites.* "She sure can ride, that kid. She sure as hell can ride." Joe soon dropped back into silence except for that incessant tap, tap tapping of his hand on the window frame.

Throwing one back outta left field myself, I asked Joe if there was anything else that he knew or had forgotten to tell me about the devils.

"Well I told you, they're just a bunch of assholes. No seriously, I'm no expert, although I really wish I was. I try and piece together all the bits and pieces of information that I hear and discover about them. There's always been stories about devils and other nasty critters living under the ground. Although to be fair, not *all* of them are considered completely malevolent either. Take the peoples of the south western desert for example. Most of them will tell you that their ancestors came up out of the ground to live on the surface at some point. A whole lot of them went back down too, deep into the bowels of the earth to live with a mysterious race of friendly snake people, so they could escape a barrage of falling stars or meteorites or something."

"*Truly?*"

"Oh yeah, there are hundreds of stories and legends about Native Americans having encounters with subterranean races. I've heard there are ant people, mantis people and supposedly even a race of incredibly wise giants living down there as well. They come up now and then for a visit and teach all kinds of amazing knowledge and stuff to the Indians."

"Are the ant and the mantis people evil?"

"*How the hell would I know?*"

"Do you think any of them might have once been extra-terrestrials?"

"Possibly. You should hear some of the stories an old Apache and his son I know up in New Mexico have to say about all that kind o' stuff. That'll *really* make the hairs on your neck stand up."

I probed him immediately, but he quickly changed tack. "Have you ever heard of Xibalba?"

"Nope. What's that?"

"Part of the Mayan underworld. Xibalba means *'the place of fear'*. It's a massive system of subterranean caves somewhere down in the Yucatan peninsula. The Popol Vuh, the creation texts of the Maya, say it's the domain of fierce and terrifying overlords who rule a race of creatures that worship only death and ritually practice all kinds of gruesome human torture and sacrifice."

"Bullshit!"

"Well, that's exactly how it went when my ex-wife got a job there!" chuckled Joe.

I'd noticed he was checking the rearview mirror more than usual. "What is it?" I said turning around to see if there was anyone behind us.

"I think we've got company." There were a few lazy bends in the road so whenever I looked back, whoever it was lagged behind just out of view.

"Check out Señora de las Sombras." I glanced up at the little figurine and felt a sudden jolt of disquiet when I saw those beady red eyes glowing menacingly back down at me.

"Oh, Santa Muerte, what's it gonna be this time?"

When the road straightened out, Joe gestured with his eyebrows up towards the mirror. Through the rear window I could now see a peppering of little black dots a mile or two back behind us.

"Is it The Shining Specters?" I said, certain I already knew the answer.

"Reckon so," Joe grinned.

"What should we do?"

"Relax Wolf. I don't think they're gonna chop our heads off or anything if that's what you're worried about. I've got a feeling they probably know we're pretty tight with super-chick and they'll just carry on their merry way straight past us."

"But what if it isn't Valasco's men and these dudes don't know who we are?"

"Well then they'll scoop out your brain and use your lily-white skull for an ashtray." Joe roared with laughter at that one. It didn't take long before the point riders were sitting right up on our tail.

"Oh for God's sake quit turning around will ya. You might start pissin' 'em off big-time and then they *will* have reason to go at you."

At best, I was convinced Los Espectros Brillantes regarded our relationship with Faye as being merely tenuous. As the Fire Diamond became steadily engulfed by the closely packed contingent of skjeletter, an all-pervasive feeling of unease descended throughout the car. Even Joe said he could sense it. This was the closest yet that I'd been to a rider. I felt more than a little apprehensive when I realized that the only thing preventing one of them from busting in and murdering me was a single pane of glass.

When I dared to peek, I could clearly make out the details of their dark leather clothing and wide-brimmed sombreros embellished with swirling brocade and tiny gems that glinted in the sunlight. I even caught the occasional glimpse of their smokey-grey skulls peering out from their shadowy masses. It seemed safe to assume that they had no intention of harming us, although I must admit, the fear surged high when one of them unexpectedly thrust his head, well his skull, right up against my window for a look-see. I didn't know whether to wave or smile or what. I figured the most prudent option was to stay calm, look straight ahead and do absolutely nothing. I'm telling ya straight, having one of those dudes inches from your face felt really frick'n creepy and reminded me a little too much of that wretched first night I'd spent in Mexico with a babbling, bad-breathed skeleton sprawled out across my lap. I was even more horrified when I looked across at Joe and caught him pulling dumbass faces and giving the thumbs up sign to the ones alongside him. He reckoned they had bigger fish to fry than us and besides there were far too many of them to be concerned with a couple of gringos out for a mid-morning joyride. Eventually the entire squadron had overtaken completely, leaving us chugging along behind in their wake.

"I told you we'd be sweet," Joe said annoyingly, just to rub it in.

"Yeah, easy to say that in hindsight. Did you get a look at all that artillery they had tucked away inside their belts? Not to mention those frick'n machetes. *Eesh!*"

◆

We'd only gone about a mile or two further when Joe, straining his eyes over the top of the dashboard, pointed straight ahead. "Hey Wolf, what in the wild-west is *THAT*?"

"Looks like a wall," I said hastily without taking much notice.

Joe downshifted into second and edged the Fire Diamond closer to whatever it was stretched long and black across the roadway.

"*Whoa!* It's another earthquake crack," I yelled over-excitedly. As we inched the car closer, the wide, dark crevasse became clearer.

"That's twelve feet wide at least! Do you want me to back up some and go for a flying leap?" Joe sounded serious, but I'm sure was only joking.

"Uuur, no thank you," I said looking about to see if we could drive off-road somewhere and take a short, little detour around it.

To the left, on the driver's side, the crack jagged its way steadily uphill. It was far too scrubby and rocky for the Fire Diamond to make it more than a couple of feet away from the roadside.

"I know it's still pretty early, but I can't believe there's nobody here yet, no cops, no cars, no nothing," Joe said surprised. "What about down there?" he asked pointing to a hazy spot maybe two hundred yards away to our right where the crack seemed to have run its course.

"*Hmm?* Looks okay I guess but it might be the lay of the land. For all we know the thing might run all the way down to the ocean," I answered sounding somewhat negative.

Joe made movements to get out of the car and wander down for a look.

"Oh don't worry," I said, trying to make amends. "The ground looks *fairly* clear, let's just take it easy."

Joe nudged the gas pedal and steered the car off into the desert maintaining a healthy thirty-foot gap between us and the edge of the zig-zagging crack. I was impressed how any rocks or shrubs larger than the head of a cabbage were piloted around accordingly.

"That's definitely the end of the fissure there, boy. *All the way to the ocean*," mocked Joe.

I felt a lot better knowing we'd soon be over on the other side and Joe would be spared the wrath of this Señorita Prisciliana. I had a construct in my head of a pint-sized tyrant with an eye-patch puffin' away on a half-smoked Cuban cigar.

"What was that?" Joe scowled looking concerned.

Straight away I noticed the murmur of another tremor. The shaking grew rapidly louder and I was certain the crack was about to widen and swallow us whole, but it was worse than that. Something solid slammed hard into Joe's door. I jerked my head around to see what it was.

Spewed up by the tremor, an enormous tsunami of pissed-off devils was attacking en masse along the driver's-side length of the car. I watched dumbstruck as their hideous teeth-filled faces and talons hammered furiously against the window glass. "They're swarming around the back now Joe! They're climbing up on the trunk. *Aaaagh!*"

Thankfully, Joe wasn't a panic-merchant and didn't go straight into a hissy like yours truly. Instead he rammed the Fire Diamond determinedly into reverse, turned the wheel to full-lock and accelerated back through the horde as fast as the gearbox could manage.

"What are ya doing?" I shrieked hysterically.

"Gettin' as close to the edge as possible so the bastards don't swamp us! Now get over in the back and pull the middle of the rear seat down so you can reach into the trunk," Joe commanded, bobbing his head around urgently trying to see where he was steering.

"DO IT! DO IT!" I was over the front bench and had yanked the back-seat thing down before I'd even realized it.

"Pull in those two carry bags on top of that shit between the kegs."

"Got 'em!" I said, trying to regain a modicum of composure.

"Open the grey one and take out the lil' G-G."

I did as he said. The lil' G-G was a long cylindrical metal apparatus the size of someone's fist and forearm. It didn't take long to figure it was the junior-sized version of Charlie's full-scale cleaner's cupboard Gatling gun.

"Now unzip the other bag and grab the stripy yellow and black feeder end of the ammo belt."

"Got it!"

"Now pull back the yellow slider on the side of the G-G and stick the belt end straight in. Flick the green power switch to ON and then do the same with the one on the outside of the ammo case. *QUICKLY!*"

Considering the erratic manner that Joe was fishtailing the car plus the unnerving racket from the onslaught outside, I was amazed that I'd managed to do exactly what he'd asked of me without stuffing it up. "Okay. It's on. It's humming."

"On the count of two, I'm gonna pop the trunk. So keep your finger on the trigger and just keep on shootin'. You've got ten seconds of ammo, max!"

"Roger!"

The moment the lid sprung open the sheer force from the oncoming devils was way more intense than I'd expected. My heart was beating like gangbusters as I wielded the noisy lil' G-G back and forth for what seemed like a frick'n eternity. The devastating effect of six extremely fast-firing machine gun barrels against a tightly entangled wall of organic matter was not a pretty sight, let me tell you. It was something like shoving your face into the top of a gigantic food processor for a peepshow and witnessing what was literally a swirling mass of exploding devil parts and gizzards garnished liberally with an endless slurry of high-velocity splattering blood-oil. Mix that with Joe's evasive driving skills and thousands of red-hot free-flying ammo cartridges bouncing and ricocheting all around the trunk and the kegs, this was unquestionably the *worst* little side-show ride that I'd ever been on.

Suddenly one of the demon spawn lunged straight at me through the open gap in the seat. The G-G was aimed point blank at the snarling asshole's head and I squeezed one last time on the trigger. I'll spare you the gruesome details but just envision an acrid-smelling light grey mist. That final half-second burst had completely used up all of the bullets. Luckily, our hasty retreat had taken us back behind the oncoming demons. Even so, Joe kept the car fishtailing in reverse plowing over innocent rocks and boulders that he might have inadvertently missed on the way down. With only a glancing look out across toward the crack I was amazed at how many bodies were banked up like a swathe of dark-grey snow along the edge of our escape route. Joe's reasoning to mow a path back through the onslaught now seemed the most logical action to take, if he hadn't, the sheer number of devils would have quickly swamped us dead in our tracks. He only slowed down and stopped when we were safely back on the road.

"Well that was different," said Joe. "Let's do it again, huh?"

I laughed at realizing we *had* escaped without being eaten alive but my concerns about the state of the Fire Diamond now began to filter in. What I could see through the gap into the trunk was bad enough, I dreaded to think what she looked like on the outside.

"You did well, Wolf," Joe said nodding and holding up his hat to inspect it for any signs of damage. "I'm glad I brought the lil' G-G along, just in case. Sorry about the state of your car though." Through the windshield we could see the charging swarm as it relentlessly headed west, straight out into the desert as if on a predetermined program.

"What are the chances, hey?" I said, feeling a little cockier. "That we drive smack-bang right into the middle of where these mongrels decide to stream back up to the surface."

Joe agreed, but his mood changed noticeably as he became preoccupied with something off in the distance. *"Oh no, no, no!"* he muttered urgently under his breath. Without any warning he pressed the pedal to the metal and we hurtled off back down the road at speed.

"What is it?" I said watching him scour the side of the road for a place to get an unobstructed view.

Joe slammed on the brakes and brought the car to a gravel-sliding stop and immediately got out and walked over to the edge of a ridge. I climbed out from the back seat and followed him.

"See those plumes of smoke over there? That's Casa de Huérfa. It's a tiny hamlet that don't even rate itself a dot on the map. It's where the orphanage is. The folks there take care of all the kids who've lost their parents to the drug wars and all that bullshit. Those bastard devils can smell their young blood and are making a B-line straight towards 'em."

I felt totally sick. I didn't know what to say. We stood there useless staring forlornly as the long-trailing dust cloud of doom headed rapidly westward and out toward the innocent.

"That's what they do," he despaired. "There's no conscience, no feeling … it's just what they do."

Then something else caught Joe's eye out on the chaparral. He began bobbing his head around, desperately trying to somehow conjure himself up a better look. "I wish I had my field glasses so I could see what the f—"

"I've got some. They're in the glove compartment, they're not as good as the—"

"Well go get 'em then, quickly!"

Joe held my crappy little binoculars up to his eyes and focused them smartly on whatever it was he'd spotted. "Oh lordy, lordy, lordy, *I don't believe it!"*

"What?" He ignored me and kept on looking. "What is it, what's going on, Joe?" His new excitement had cranked up my curiosity.

"THE CAVALRY'S ARRIVED!" Joe slammed home the point with one of his exuberant air-swing punches and handed me back the binoculars. "Look down there! No, over *there* ya doofus. See that long grey line? Over there towards the right! The one with all the dirt and shit streaming out behind it."

"It's—"

"Yeah, it's The Shining Specters. Those bad boys are gonna kick those frick'n slimy bastards' asses! *GO YOU BONEHEADS! … YEAH! … FUCK'N YEAH!"*

Once he'd *more* than enthusiastically pointed it out, it all became clear. Two straight lines each of about fifty motorcycle riders were moving at speed in a tight formation straight toward the horde of on-coming creatures.

"Oh *please* gimme the binoculars back Wolf, I gotta see this."

I handed them back to him gladly. I couldn't help smiling. Joe had braced himself wide-legged and was pivoting from side to side in eager anticipation of the imminent engagement.

"Man, this is like the frick'n Charge of the Light Brigade," Joe yelled excitedly.

"There doesn't seem that many of 'em though. The riders I mean, compared to—" I commented needlessly.

Joe wasn't hearing my armchair quarter-back opinions anyway, he was right down there on the field with the riders. The two opposing forces were only moments away from impact. Even without the use of the glasses I noticed a momentary ripple run along the ranks of the oncoming riders and when the front lines were no more than fifteen or twenty yards apart, a massive explosion from their pistols blasted devas-tatingly deep into their onrushing enemy. From up here they looked like the ranks of a pistol cavalry regiment from some bygone era.

The impact of the gun blasts thumped a noticeable gap in the forward ranks of the devils but seemingly not enough to faze them. Within seconds the mounted skeletons plowed headlong into the seeth-ing swarm, their quickly drawn machetes flashed brightly in the sunlight turning the fight into one of cold hard steel against a huge, frenzied force of razor-sharp teeth and talons.

The mêlée was full on and vicious. The Shining Specters, although strong and powerful on their motorcycles, were vastly outnumbered and quickly became engulfed. Up until now Joe had seemed impressed with their resilience but I was surprised when he agreed with my comment and said, "There just ain't enough of 'em to whip their asses proper."

Then, as if the gods had thrown in an unforeseen wild card, a tumultuous rumble began shaking the very ground we stood on.

"Oh not again." I rubbed my face with my hand expecting the worst.

Positioned where we were along the edge of that small ridge, I expected at any moment to be either bounced right over the edge or swallowed up whole by a fissure. A feeling of relief and surprise wiped the slate when it wasn't a tremor at all, but unbeknown to us from right beneath where we stood, a second wave of riders materialized seemingly out of nowhere and thundered off like an unleashed torrent down the slope to reinforce their kin in the battle.

"*Over there, look.* Over on the far side," pointed Joe enthusiastically. There was another wave, but this one came storming straight towards us from half a mile away, over on the western side.

"Alright, *two-sided flank attack!* Classic cavalry maneuver, been used since—" Joe's mouth dropped open mid-spiel and he hastily pulled the binoculars back up to his eyes.

"Holy frick'n smoke, *it's our girl. It's our girl!*" I snatched the glasses back and brought them up, focused exactly where I was supposed to.

My knees almost buckled when I saw that it really was Faye leading the oncoming force of The Specters. Front and center amidst the outstretched ranks of the machete wielding riders, she stood out like a glorious jewel. Her long sun-kissed hair flowed wild and shone magnificently in the fresh morning wind. The occasional flash from the geirahöð's swirling blades dazzled, as one-handed, she whirled the deadly weapon fast and proficient high above her head. She was the embodiment of Freya, the Great Dis.

"Wow! Did you see *that?*" exclaimed Joe, getting more and more excited. "Looked like two bouncing bombs or something rolling along on either side of her."

I wasn't sure if Faye had filled Joe in *completely* when they had their little chat, but I knew exactly what it was. "It's Seiðr Joe … that was Gutteka and Jenteka."

He looked across at me blankly, so I explained as best as I could.

"Unbelievable," he answered in a tone of soft amazement.

We stood and watched as the opposing flanks of mounted motorcycles smashed like two razor sharp walls of destruction into that wretched horde of devils. I think Joe and I shared a moment of deep trepidation seeing our dear friend seemingly vanish headlong into that scene of deadly mayhem, obscured behind high swirling sand and black smoke.

"Come on Wolfman, I've seen enough. Nothing we can do from here … she'll be okay. It's been a *long* morning and I need a drink. Oh shit, that reminds me, what about Prisciliana's kegs? She's gonna frick'n … well, you know."

25

Show and Tell

Our arrival back at The Alamo was nothing out of the ordinary apart from the five-foot square, 1960's advertising billboard that now stood in for the shop front's shattered glass window. It seemed like a perfect fit. The rest of the area looked spotless. Vince really had pulled his finger out and Joe seemed reservedly impressed, but knew his youngest better than anyone.

"*Hmm*, I doubt if the little prick did it out of any feeling of remorse, probably got that little squeeze of his to do it for him while he sat back eating his cereal."

We were about to do a Luis Escoto, three-sixty-degree damage type inspection around the Fire-Diamond when a brand new, whale-sized mobile home turned off from the road and pulled tightly into the driveway.

"Jupiters," Joe said soberly.

The occupants were the embodiment of the near extinct American family unit. Mum, dad and two twin boys of about ten or eleven who sat buckled up, side by side in the back seat of the cab compartment with their identical ball-capped and headphoned craniums bowed low, engrossed in some inane game on their identical laptop tablets. They never took a peek out the window or even looked up from their screens.

"How ya doing? What can I get you?" Joe asked courteously when the man alighted from the huge white contraption.

"Fill her up and clean the windshield," commanded Daddy Jupiter handing the appropriate key over to Joe.

Joe just looked at him. "Uh, how do you intend to pay? ... *sir.*"

"What do you mean, how do I intend to pay? ... *Pinky-Pay* of course," he said, doing the obligatory cutesy little curl-swirl thing with his hand, exactly like the grinning idiots hyping up this "new way to pay" on his ninety-inch TV had trained him to do. *"Forget about cash, forget about cards, carry your wealth in your palm or your pinkies. ... Oh yeah!"*

A microelectronic nanochip implanted into the soft fleshy spot between the ring and little fingers. I'd seen those commercials a frick'n trillion times. Ad nauseam. *'Carry your wealth in your pinkies!'* ... yeah, right. People back home were climbing all over each other to get one.

"I'm sorry sir," Joe replied eloquently, "we're not geared up for that type of service out here."

"Phhh!" Daddy Jupiter made a breathy, disparaging comment with his lips.

"Cash only," Joe said trying hard to suppress a wicked, rising smile.

"Oh how quaint, how so last century." Mr. J walked back around to Mrs. J's side of the big-white-whale and proceeded to rummage through the glove compartment like he'd been asked to pay with gold doubloons or pieces of eight or something.

He was wearing a pair of those silly-daddy cargo pants that stopped about six inches below the knee, highlighting the hairless milky-white calves that protruded tantalizingly out from his shin-high cotton socks and the brand new four-hundred-dollar trainers below. The T-shirt and matching ball cap had some trendy, corporate slogan emblazoned across the front engendering a feeling of smug self-importance to those in the know and warning everybody else that you're an absolute dipshit. It was the regulation look for those IT desk jockeys let loose on Saturday mornings wandering the cavernous isles of hardware stores on their ill-advised hunt for power tools, destined to slice off at least half of their keyboard-tapping digits come Sunday.

Jupiter emerged victorious and flashed a bill or two of some hard-excavated cash. Only then did Joe engage the gas pump nozzle and start filling up the tank.

"Where you heading?" Joe asked, trying to make small talk.

"We're going to the pyramid. The boy's keep naggin' me to take 'em down to see it."

"The Pyramid of the Sun ... at Teotihuacán? You won't get down there this way unfortunately. There was an earthquake earlier this morning and it's chopped a great, wide canyon right across the roadway."

"No, *not there*, we're going to the new great adobe pyramid at Recados Tontos."

"I knew it!" whispered Joe under his breath. "He's one of those social media zealots."

"You won't get to Recados Tontos this way either. You'll need to head back north to Cabaña Roja, turn right there and follow the road due east until you pick up Highway 15 and then, when you get down to Hermosillo swing back south-west again on Highway 26 where you—"

"Well, thank you for your advice," interrupted Daddy Jupiter, "but I'm sure we'll be fine."

The snide contemptuous smirk on his face was one I'd seen a million times before working back at Snake-Eyed Jacks. This dude was exactly the self-opinionated know-all Joe had been talking about that time he spat the dummy about having no friends.

I watched this guy pull his cell phone slyly out of his pants pocket and do that sneaky little dance of delight with his thumb across the screen. Obviously, there was no such mention of any road closure on the most trustworthy oracle, so Joe's first-hand advice was regarded as nothing more than local-yocal, hillbilly-hoo-ha.

By now, Mrs. Jupiter was out of the cab compartment and demanding the key to the bathroom. She was obviously a one-time trophy wife, long since fallen from the glitzy shelf, who now suffered on, down amongst the empty drink bottles at the back of the bar. Her upper half was busty and purposefully ambiguous beneath a loose-fitting floral blouse. The bottom half was encased in some stretchy white slacks that the TV ads promised *one hundred and ten percent* to compress and eradicate *all* tell-tale signs of a paunchy stomach or a rapidly south-shifting buttock. A feat which modern elastic technologies were obviously still incapable of doing. At ground level, its dainty little trotters were encased in snow-white ballet pumps, the perfect choice of footwear for a whale ride down through the harsh and rocky Mexican desert. Mrs. Jupiter sauntered off towards the bathroom with the rocket key in one hand and her jewel encrusted cell phone in the other.

> *...And the faux diamonds*
> *sparkled as she did so.*

Mr. Jupiter was handing over the money to Joe as if the very concept of cash was irrevocably linked to the bubonic plague or something equally as nasty.

Not long after, Mrs. Jupiter returned, her demeanor held precariously in place by a fragrant interlocking shroud of aerosol sprays and gels.

"Your toilets are filthy and disgusting," she proclaimed contemptuously flipping the rocket key back at Joe while *never* letting her eyeballs stray from her all-important phone. "I intend to report this hideous little, *uugh!* gas station to the authorities."

The accusation really ticked me off because I knew for a fact that unless someone had just ducked in and punched one out, that her sanctimonious comment was total nonsense. On the other hand, maybe that was how she got her jollies. Go take a dump, don't pull the chain, and then straight-faced blame it on somebody else. I'd seen that one a thousand times, cleaning the loos at The Jacks. Otherwise why would she be bothered using the ones in a hideous little, *uugh!* gas station? I'm sure she had her own gold-plated bathroom suite hidden somewhere deep inside the whale.

Mr. and Mrs. Jupiter got back into the driver's cab and without a by your leave started up the engine and hauled the big white wagon back toward the road. They turned defiantly towards the south exactly in the direction where Joe had politely advised them not to.

We both stood speechless, deep in thought as they disappeared out of view.

"What a prick!" said Joe with impeccable timing.

"You got that right, but they'll be back when they come face to face with the Crack of Doom."

"No way! Not *THAT* guy. He'll cut out into the desert and go overland rather than eat crow and have to admit he was wrong. Probably kill himself and his whole frick'n family while he's at it."

"Anyway Joe … why Jupiters?"

"Agh, it's a name I give to that particular hybrid-species of off-the-peg, mainstream, middle class know-it-alls … completely lost in space! Anyway, where is everybody? Where's Vince and Charlie?"

Surprisingly, it was Dr. MacElroy who turned up first, stepping urgently back outside through the glassless dining room door. He was carrying a large, steaming saucepan of water in one hand and a bunch of folded up towels in the other.

"Joe, Wolf, you're back," gasped Eugene, sounding relieved to see us.

"What's up, someone having a baby?"

"No, it's Charlie, he's had another turn about an hour ago. One of his coughing fits, and he's vomited up a fair bit o' blood as well. I helped him over to his room and laid him out on the bed. I'm no MD but I thought it better to wait a little longer to see how he fared. Do you think I should have called a doctor?"

"Thanks Eugene, you're doing fine. I'll come over with you now." Joe patted the concerned man affectionately on the back as they went off together to see Charlie.

There was no point in me heading over as well so I stayed where I was and tried to work up the courage to check out the state of the car and take an unwelcome look inside the trunk. The old steel panels, as best as I could tell, hadn't sustained too many dints, probably due to the way they built these babies back in the fifties. The same, sadly, could not be said for the duco. The sides and tail-end were so scratched up you could see all the way down to bare metal. The still attached pieces of devil came in two different varieties, the stubborn fleshy bits wedged in tight amongst the chrome work or smears of mucus like slime splattered disgustingly along the side and rear-end of the Fire Diamond. It reminded me of rotten cabbage leaves gone off in the sun.

As I poked at it gingerly with a small piece of stick, I heard a mournful groan wafting out from inside the dining room. It was Vince lolling in a chair with his arms sprawled out across a long rectangular box on the table in front of him. Both his eyes were shut tight, but he was obviously awake.

"Howdy Vince! Got a bit of a hangover there, bro'," I yelled at double volume just to rub it in.

"Piss off."

"What's in the box?"

"Wha'?"

"The box your leaning on."

"I dunno … flowers."

"Who are they for?"

"Ugh … never heard of her?"

I looked at the little card tucked discreetly into the ribbon. It said Tammy-Faye Jackson and I immediately started wondering who had sent them, obviously someone at the party and I reckoned I had a pretty good idea who.

"Looks like you've done a handy job tidying up out there Vince, did you do it all by yourself?" He flipped me the bird, so obviously he hadn't.

Back out front I noticed Tisac's hat sitting on top of his neatly folded jacket down behind the couch. So, knowing Vince and judging by the condition he was in, I guessed it must have been poor old Tisac who he'd conned into doing most if not all of the work.

"Get your good for nothing ass out here boy!" Joe bellowed, poking his head into the dining room after looking in on Charlie. "I know you got Tisac to do it, but I'm more annoyed with myself that I *actually* *believed* you might have done something that I asked you to do yourself."

Vince never appeared. He'd already slipped unnoticed out through the back.

"How's Charlie?" I asked Joe.

"He's okay. Well he's not really, but that awful coughing has stopped, thank God, he'll be out and about soon. I'm just hoping for now, he can get an hour or two of some shuteye."

"The poor ol' car looks like crap," Joe said concerned. "It's mostly superficial, nothing a brand-new paint job couldn't take care of though. Young Galo Escoto's a bit of a legend with a spray gun, he'd have her back, ship-shape in no time." Joe then paused for a moment, rubbing his chin in contemplation. "Tell you what, I can't afford to buy this old jalopy with cash, but I've got a little quarter-acre piece of land on the beach just north west of Guaymas. It's pretty remote but it's got an old shack on it and I doubt if I'll be going down there again in a hurry, so, maybe we could do an outright swap. Anyway, just an idea, have a bit of a think about it Wolf."

Well that one came right out of nowhere. I immediately envisioned tall swirling palm trees and raunchy bikini babes doing the hula-hula down in the shallows. I soon conceded that the odds of it being even remotely like that were probably zero to none.

"Hello Joe, hello Wolf," came the pleasant tones of a young female voice from behind us. It was Oppuam.

"*Hey*, how you doin' sweetheart?" came an always sincere greeting from Joe.

"I am well, thank you."

"Everything okay, with you and your folks after that earthquake?"

"Yes, we are fine, it caused no problems at all." Oppuam's diction and pronunciation were always perfect.

"Please Joe, I was wondering if you knew where Miss Faye is right now as I cannot seem to find her anywhere. I have a most important message from the old, wise woman to relay to her as soon as possible."

"Well, no Oppuam, right at this moment I don't. Wolf and I saw her earlier today, she was leading a force of Los Espectros Brillantes into a battle with a marauding army of devils."

Oppuam didn't bat an eyelid. Joe's statement seemed as normal as mentioning he'd just seen her head off down to the corner store to buy a loaf of bread and a carton of milk. "Hmm. Well do you mind if I wait here for her please, it's vital I speak to her the moment she returns."

"Of course you can darlin', no problem. Why don't you sit yourself down over on the concrete table and I'll go fetch you a nice cold drink and something to eat."

"If you don't mind Señor Joe, Sacramento told me that you have a hardcover book pertaining to the Nordic pantheon and all of the associated myths and legends. Would it be okay if I sat and read some of it while I waited?"

"Sure can. I'll go get it and fix you up a nice glass of juice to sip on as well."

◆

In the course of the afternoon, me, Joe and a near-useless Vince got stuck into boarding up the broken window and door with some sheets of half-inch plywood we'd found around the back. The old, advertising billboard fell out the minute we touched it. We didn't blame Tisac, he'd been stooged into doing it anyway. But even so, to expect that a five-foot square of half-inch ply would stay held in place by a couple of three-quarter-inch nails was optimistic at best. Even Eugene pitched in to lend a hand but when Joe and I told him about everything that had happened earlier, he soon became distracted. He drifted across towards the Fire Diamond where, like a kid in a candy store, he helped himself to a smorgasbord spread of mangled-up bits of devil. Each to his own I suppose.

It was way past five-thirty in the evening when the tranquility of a desert sunset gave way to darkness, and the thunderous ever-growing sound of approaching motorcycles. Upon arrival, the escort turned in from the road and delivered their well-guarded general safely back to her home and friends.

It reminded me of my old neighborhood and how the in-vogue girl-next-door would be dropped off home at any godforsaken hour by a whole pack of rap-happy muscle-car wannabes. I knew this whole setup wasn't going to last, a nagging voice inside me said that sooner or later Faye would move out to be with her riders and possibly never return.

I didn't recognize any of this particular contingent, neither Captain Valasco nor his sergeant at arms were amongst the dozen or so riders who had escorted Faye home. As before, they came no closer than just beyond the pumps. There they sat parked, engines idling in their usual staggered line, facing towards us on either side of their leader.

Faye spoke confidently to the rider beside her on her left, who, judging by his manner and the finery of his clothing, was a commander of undoubtedly equal, or maybe even higher rank than Captain Valasco. She bade him and the others farewell and, as quickly as they had arrived, they turned away on their machines and departed noisily back into the darkness.

"She's got them dudes under control," grinned Joe.

The goddess lunged the Martellare Angelus forward and brought it to a dead stop right in front of the three of us. Gutteka and Jenteka jumped off, one on either side and vanished in the blink of an eye.

Faye looked totally haggard. But considering she'd just come straight from one almighty battle, and God knows wherever else since the last time we'd seen her, I was amazed she didn't look a whole lot worse. Her hair looked like it had when she'd done her little Mötorhead dance routine, that morning in the Fire Diamond. She was covered in a powder fine coating of dust. Even so, she looked great, reminding me big time of some wasteland warrior babe you see in those fast action sci-fi flicks.

Faye handed the geirahöð over to Vince to look after. "Did you? Did you really?" Vince seemed more than impressed but couldn't string the mule train of appropriate words together to say so. He stood there in awe, studying the weapon carefully from one end down to the other.

"Here you go Faye." Joe handed her a tall glass of water that he'd hurriedly ducked back into the kitchen to fetch. Faye gulped it down and let out a sigh of satisfaction when she'd finished. *"Aaagh … thank you, my mouth was so dry."*

"We saw you this morning, out there on the plain. That was *awesome!"* I said, wishing instantly that I could have pressed *text-edit* and not sounded so banal.

"You saw us, you saw the battle?" Faye responded, sounding surprised.

"Oh yeah! It was outstanding, a two-sided flank attack," bounced back Joe. "Me and the Wolfman here even backed ourselves up into a bit of a skirmish with those ugly looking critters ourselves."

Faye became quickly concerned. "Are you okay? Were either of you injured? … and by the way, where is Big Dain, is he okay?" she said, urgently looking around for Charlie and starting to get anxious.

"He's fine, he's fine. Relax. He just had another one of his bad turns, but he's having a bit of a sleep now … he'll be alright."

"Hello, Miss Faye." In all the excitement we'd forgotten about poor Oppuam who we'd left by herself, sitting over at the concrete table.

"Hello gorgeous," Faye said sincerely, clasping her battle-weary arms, lightly but affectionately around the neck of her small young friend.

"It's very important Miss Faye, I must speak to you *immediately."* Faye and Oppuam moved a few paces away from our prying ears, so the young girl could relay her message in private.

"I must go now," Faye said, returning very quickly. She took the geirahöð back from a reluctant Vince who'd been messing about trying to make it twirl, more cheerleader style than in a manner befitting a lethal weapon of war.

"Don't forget your flowers, Faye," I yelled out, as the two girls quickly left. She came storming back and looked at me strangely as if to say, "Well why didn't you just go inside and get them for me."

Glares aside, there was no way on this earth, I could hand a woman another man's bunch of flowers. It just isn't done. "Don't worry, they're from Lucien." Faye smiled teasingly as she turned and disappeared back around the corner of the building.

"Don't worry!" What the hell does that mean? "You know I could never have eyes for Lucien. You know you're the only man for me Wolf." or "Don't worry, it's really got 'Jack's shit' to do with *you anyway*." The possibility of any other interpretation didn't exist.

◆

I was heading back to the van after a well-earned, scorching-hot shower. The day had been stressful and all I wanted was for every last trace of splash back from those creatures completely washed from my body. Twenty yards shy of Faye's trailer, I heard her metal door slam shut. Within a second or two, her lean shape appeared from around the far side and came heading towards me on the path.

The strings of little electric lights that outlined the edges of The Alamo had been left on again this evening. The effect was amazing. Faye's moving silhouette appeared perfectly over the top of them as she moved, giving the appearance that she was walking through a sky of twinkling stars. When she saw me coming towards her, she playfully tipped her head from side to side as if to say, "I've got my hands full."

In one hand she was carrying her grandmother's precious suitcase, in the other, the hessian sack that contained the countless dozens of accumulated falcon feathers. The practical function of the shapeless item seemed somehow demeaning to the magnificence and individual finery of the beautiful, precious feathers they held unseen within its confines.

"Hello Faye," I said enthusiastically as we came up together. "I thought you'd already gone."

"Well I'm *finally* on my way over there now, you know what they say, a woman's work is never done."

She looked kind of strange but, as always, enchanting. Her hair had been woven in two long braids that hung all the way down to her waist. She was wearing a plain cotton dress that stopped in its formless descent somewhere past her knees and a pair of well-worn flat-soled gardening boots on her feet. The overall effect was an intriguing combination of Southern country farm girl meets Nordic goddess.

"What's with the luggage?"

"I was asked to bring them along … and a couple of other things too."

"Such as?"

"Never you mind, you ask far too many questions Fenrir."

"Sorry … so what is it you're going over there for?"

"There you go again. Let's just say it's *women's business*."

Faye giggled and rubbed me lightly on the shoulder. "Bye Wolf. I'll drop by first thing in the morning after training and we'll have a nice cup of coffee."

"I'd like that. Sounds great." (*Like it*, I'd crawl over red-hot coals for it.)

Faye really looked exhausted. I hoped she wasn't in for too late a night. I stood and watched her leave and for one, strange, out of time moment, I saw Faye, her mother, her grandmother and her great grandmother, all as one, carrying that ordinary little suitcase along with every first-hand memory of hardship, misery and the precious, precious love its very existence contained.

◆

The morning seemed chillier than usual. Probably because I was up early trying to kid myself that I was one of those pre-dawn outdoor type dudes who'd already skinned a buck, wrestled with a grizzly and paddled upstream backwards through the rapids and still had time for bacon and beans before the sun had rolled its big fat ass out of bed. In reality I was bent over on my knees shaking the shit out of a disposable lighter trying like mad to get the damn thing to work so I could get a cozy looking fire started, just in case Faye actually did turn up like she said she would. (A willing accomplice to my own naive sense of optimism.)

I was huffing and puffing like a big bad wolf on a single glowing twig that so far was as close as I'd come to starting a fire. Suddenly, out of the corner of my eye I noticed Faye waving her arms around, running towards me extremely excited.

"*Wolfie! Hi, hi, hi!*" she said in that gorgeous Norwegian accent as she happily hurled herself right up against me.

What's this all about? I thought, presuming she must have been drunk, but naively hoping deep down, that the worm had finally turned.

"I missed you so much Fenrir."

(What?)

"I have so much to tell you, but what's been happening here?"

"You mean *here*, right in front of the van?"

"No silly, back at the ranch. How is everyone? How's Joe? How's Charlie? How's Eugene? Oh, it seems like ages."

"Are you serious, it's been, what, twelve, fourteen hours max?"

"Since what?"

"Since I last saw you, walking over towards the camp site yesterday evening with your case and the sack full of feathers."

"Last night? *Nei det er umulig.* No that's impossible, I've been gone for three whole weeks?"

"What's up Faye? Did you have some kind of weird dream last night or something?"

Faye, bobbing around all excited, suddenly turned as still as a stone. I figured she was having some insightful moment of realization. "Oh *dritt* ... it must have been the suppe. The foul tasting suppe!"

"You keep slipping in tongue to Norwegian, woman."

"Do I?" she said surprised, comically bugging out her eyes as she did so. "It was that horrid soup ... you're right. You do know the old woman is a shaman, a Seiðkonur just like the bestemor? That soup must have had some type of a magic potion mixed in with it ... *Ooooh, magisk drikk!*"

(Magic potion! Huh! This gal's got a PhD in biochemistry.)

"Oppuam told me many times that the old woman has an extensive knowledge of the psychoactive properties of all the local power plants. No wonder I can't make down from day, and up from night. *You're right.*"

"There you go again. I never said anything. What the hell *have* you been doing over there Faye?"

"Drinking suppe," she answered crisp and matter of factly.

I had no idea what it was, but she was definitely coming down on a soft, spiral landing from something. Some of these new wide-eyed facial expressions Faye was pulling were somehow both gorgeous and frick'n hysterical.

"What are you smiling at Fenrir?"

"You."

"*Why?* Do you think I'm gal?"

"What's that?"

"Umm ... *crazy!*"

"Definitely." She punched me playfully on the arm.

"So come on, for your own benefit, retrace exactly what you did over at the Indian camp?"

"When?" She said it as innocent as a forgetful child.

"Well, last night in *this* dimension, or three weeks ago, in the *post-soup* other."

"I can't tell you."

"And why not?"

"It was a secret. Secret women's business. Yes, hemmelige kvinners virksomhet."

"Alright, so where have you been for the last three weeks then?"

"Oh! Maybe *that's* why Lucien's roses were all still fresh and alive this morning."

"What?"

"Because I never went anywhere." Faye seemed more confused about it all than I was.

"Okay. Supposing you had been somewhere, where do you think it might have been?"

"You'll never believe me!"

"Try me."

"I WAS IN THE NEOLITHIC. I lived for three weeks by the sea in a tribal village, way, way back in the astrological age of *Taurus.*" Faye was firing on all cylinders now. I felt like a bit of a dick, but I still had to ask.

"You know I'm a bit of a boof-head, woman. Refresh me on what and when was the Neolithic?"

"The time of the late Stone Age. In Scandinavia ... *oooh* four, five, maybe seven thousand years ago. Before that was the Mesolithic period."

I was getting confused. "Okay, so there was a Mesolithic and a Neolithic. So what the hell was the other one, the *Megalithic*?"

"The later period of the Neolithic. The time when the ancient stand-ing stones and circles were erected by the tribes of Western Europe and Scandinavia."

I remembered one of Faye's books back at her trailer was all about that kind of stuff. "And you were just there?"

"Ja!"

"So what language did you speak?"

"I don't know exactly Wolf, that's a very good question. It was a kind of mixture of all the languages that I could already speak and some that

I'd never ever heard before at all."

"But you all got on okay?"

Faye scowled and looked at me fiercely. "You don't believe me. *You're making fun of me.*"

I was, but I was also a pathetic groveler and turncoat. "*No, no.* Just curious to know whether you had any adverse communication problems or not… while you were there."

"It was fine," Faye answered tepid and toneless.

"So where was this village? Was it in Norway?"

"I don't know. It might have been, but everything looked so completely different back then. I know it was on the sea and facing due south. If it was in Norway, it could have been either Vestfold, Telemark, or Vest Agder. Maybe it was Lolland in Denmark? But I had an inkling it was most likely on the southern coast of Scania in Sweden. That's where the ley line current is very prominent and powerful. But if it was, I'm certain it was still way back in time before Ales Stenar, the megalithic stone ship at Kåseberga was erected. Everything was so *quiet* then Wolf. If you listened very carefully you could hear a humming sound coming from the stones that stood along the ley lines. It was—"

"*Whoa, whoa!* Back up a little. That's twice you've mentioned it now, what the hell are ley lines?"

"Oh, they are a system of geo-magnetic energy paths that encircle the planet. Power currents if you like. The Chinese called them Dragon lines. You'll only laugh and mock me when I say this, but the Earth is *anything but* a ball of inanimate rock just out there circling the sun. She is a living, sentient being like you and me. As well as all the ley lines, she has important chakra points around the planet too, nodes where intersecting—"

I could tell where all this hippy hocus-pocus stuff was heading so I rudely butted in and hijacked her train of thought completely. "So I guess you must really like all of these standing stones and circles, especially if you've got a book about them?"

"Like them. *I LOVE THEM!* I remember when I was very little, the first thing I did when my bestemor took me to a stående stein was to totter straight over and hug it."

"Sounds like a Nordic version of your good old American tree hugging hippy to me Faye."

"You really are an absolute twerp sometimes Fenrir." (Point duly taken.)

"Axel, myself and a few others would often take the bikes for a run down the E-18 from Oslo to Vestfold. It was only a couple of hours ride but sometimes we'd stay the weekend at Elsbeth's brother's house in Tjølling. We'd always try and set off early in the morning so we could see as many of the sites as possible. Isterhågen was always my favorite. There were so many other places too. Grøtte standing stone, The Nybo standing stone, The Stoplesteinan circle, *I LOVE that!* There's one stone … although I can't remember its name? It looks like a gigantic spear point sticking up out of the ground only a meter or so back from the side of the road. I took a fabulous picture of Axel sitting up alongside it on his 750-Martellare. I'm really into all the prehistoric sites; dolmans, barrows, henges, cairns, anything from the Stone or Bronze Ages, and of course, not forgetting the Iron Age Viking places too. I really am a full-on hard-core Víkingr girl, you know Fenrir," laughed Faye impishly.

"Are there still many of these stones and things up in Scandinavia?"

"Fenrir, there are hundreds, *thousands* especially when you include the British Isles. On longer trips we would ride up through the mountains, across to Bergen and take the ferry across to the Orkneys where we'd visit Skara Brae, the stone rings of Stenness and Brogdar and the site of the Neolithic temple complex down on the Ness. We've been up to the Shetlands, across to the Isle of Lewis in the Outer Hebrides to see the stones of Callanish. We've been to Ireland, England everywhere. *I LOVE IT!* It's a *far* more exhilarating way to spend your time than sitting around in a cafe somewhere, acting all cool and staring at a stupid smartphone."

Her little up-tempo admonishment at the end made me laugh out loud. (Sorry, *LOL.*) "I've never done either, but I think I'd probably concur," I said in a plummy British accent, for no reason.

"You're crazy Wolf. Would you like to come back to my trailer? I have something *very* exciting to show you."

"Sounds good, let's go." I almost used that tired old gag about having to rearrange my sock drawer but thought better of it.

◆

"Would I be correct in saying, that last night's 'secret women's business' was an all gal, soup-sipping soirée where those who drank the old woman's brew scored a full packaged holiday back to the Stone Age?"

"How dare you!" Faye reproached me sternly. My joke was a total launch-pad miss-fire. Faye turned on her seat and sprang up towards the little kitchenette. I dredged up every last ounce of self-rebuking drivel

that I could think of, but it was totally unnecessary as thirty seconds later she'd forgotten all about it and returned to the table carrying two chunky mugs and a pot of steaming hot coffee.

"You still haven't told me much about what happened after you went over to the camp."

"I told you, it was women's business." She soon relented as I knew she was dying to tell me.

"Oppuam was there, she was translating back and forth between myself and a couple of Native American women who I'd never met or seen before. One of whom was very, *very* old. The others all held her in high esteem and doted on her continuously. She had such a presence. I knew undoubtedly that she would be the guiding force of whatever it was that was going to happen. She was so small and frail. The deep wrinkled lines of her time weathered face gushed with kindness and affection whenever she smiled. And her eyes, oh those eyes, so old, so probing and so full of infinite wisdom. They truly seemed to shine from within. I couldn't break away from her gaze, it was so hypnotic and mesmerizing. It warmed me right to my core. At one point—"

"Was this before or *after* the soup?"

Faye ignored my interruption. "…she beckoned me to sit down beside her. She gently held both my hands between her arthritic fingers which sadly were little more than withered twists of skin and bone, but the power, wow! I felt such an overwhelming surge of love and the presence of the Great Spirit that it just blew me away. Do you know what she said to me then? You'll never believe me."

I figured the question rhetorical, so I didn't even bother to answer.

"She smiled and then spoke frailly in her own language. Oppuam relayed her words to me in English as she said it. *'At the rising of the hidden sun, be ready Freya, your time has now come'.*"

"Seriously!"

"I got gåsehud from tip to toe."

"Gasehud?"

"Umm … Goose lumps."

"Goosebumps."

"What?"

"Doesn't matter. What happened then?"

"I don't know exactly. The next thing I remember I was sitting cross-legged on soft green grass in the presence of a circular council of *truly* magnificent women."

"Were they Indians?"

"They were *goddesses!*"

"Pte Ska Win was there, the White Buffalo Calf Woman. The mother of life, the spirit woman who brought the seven sacred rituals to the Lakota people of the great American plains. She looked radiant. Rhea and Neith were there too, so were Qamaits, Mari, Zonget, Jörð, the mother of Thor, Nane, Arduinna, and many, others."

"Were there any male god's there?"

"Fenrir, don't you ever listen, this was an 'all gal, goddess *soirée*' as you so ineloquently put it. Although a rowdy contingent of the girls was there, and they're not strictly goddesses. That was at least until Herja and Ölrún started playing up big time and Brynhildr sent every last one of them back home to Valhöll in disgrace."

"Who are the girls?"

"The Valkyrjur dumbo, the Shield Maidens, the Choosers of the Slain."

"Oh!"

"And *SHE* was there too."

"Who?"

"The Celt! ... *The Morrígan*. Even Freya is cautious and decidedly wary of Her."

"Why?"

"Like many in attendance at the council, she is a fearsome goddess of war, a frightening and formidable adversary. Even though they are 'friends', the two of them have got history. *Oh boy*, have they got history. They've been banging heads together for a *long, long, long* time, believe me. Thankfully, for the moment anyway, she is still on our side."

"Where was this council?"

"Back in the Neolithic of course. We sat amidst a breathtaking circle of soft glowing stones."

"Why were they glowing?"

"Back then, stående steiner looked completely different to the way we see them now. The stones were all highly polished and glimmered radiantly beneath a massive and most luminescent full moon. It was *wonderful* Fenrir. You could hear the hum and crackle as the earth currents surged up through them and activated the towering columns of quartz."

"It must have been a high-powered meeting ... no pun intended."

"Oh it was, trust me."

I waited.

"Well, are you going to tell me what it was about?"

Faye gave me that long pensive look she does when she just can't decide. "Considering that you're not particularly interested in anything that I tell you anyway, and when I do, you either rudely interrupt me or dismiss it as either hippie-dribble or with some other ignorant derogatory comment, why on earth would I bother?"

She had me dead to rights on that one.

"Let's just say, for the last five thousand years, more or less, we've been living in the cosmological dark age of the demon. The age of the Kali Yuga. The last of four yuga stages where the sequence of human decline has very nearly stripped virtue and goodness from the face of Mother Earth. The true spiritual path of her people has all but acquiesced to the inimical powers of a most malevolent fraternity. Well this age is ending."

Unexpectedly Faye's voice changed back into that of a southern belle. *"So like you Yankie boys always say. The lil' ol' Mother Goddess and her kin are gonna have to step right on in and kick some serious butt, before these self-serving overlords will let HER back in to redress the balance ... comprende?"*

Frick'n hell! Faye had gone bonkers. Whatever it was she just said went completely over my head. "What is it with you and southerners, don't you like them or something?"

Faye just laughed, not at my pathetic remark but at my obviously transparent avoidance and inability to comment on *anything* vaguely deep and meaningful. She knew my question was merely deflective, but she indulged me with an answer anyway.

"It's the only English-speaking accent that I can do. We had an exchange student from South Carolina who came into our year for a term when I was still in secondary skole back in Norway. We'd all been expecting an Elly-May or a Becky-Sue or a girl with some other exciting southern belle name like that. Can you imagine the disappointment when her name just turned out to be *Debbie*? Didn't matter though. She was a real sweetheart and within a week *all* of the girls were trying to copy her accent and change our looks to how we thought southern girls would probably dress. Debbie said we were way off-track and had all been watching too many of those Beverley Hillbilly reruns. None of us took any notice. Can you imagine Fenrir? A dozen, fifteen-year-old Norwegian girls with adopted TV names like Pammie-Lee or Patsy-Jane or Tammy-Faye, *that was me of course*, Bobbie-Jean, Bobbie-Jo, Kitty-Lou, Bessie-Jo and a few others. All struttin' around like little hussies with teased up hairstyles, high knotted shirts and rope-tied jeans. All blowing bubble gum and twirling it out with our fingers. The boys thought it was *hilarious*. Luckily, so did Debbie. But just like my Viking entourage from primary school, the teachers put an end to it sooner than later, as they were at their wit's end from not understanding a word we were saying. It was all very funny. So to cut my long-winded answer short, yes I do like people from the southern states Fenrir... *especially Debbie*."

"What is it you wanted to show me... Tammy Faye?"

"Come over here and set yourself down on the comfy."

"Can I bring my coffee?"

"Yes." There was that monotone accent again, I frick'n dug it.

Sitting on "the comfy", I took a gulp from my still hot drink while Faye got down almost flat on the floor so she could reach and pull something out from beneath a row of shelves. She made me promise, "hope to die", that I wouldn't tell anyone about it.

"Oh of course, I *promise*."

I was a little disappointed to see it was nothing other than the old brown suitcase. It didn't take two brain cells to figure out though that there must have been something far more exciting inside. Faye placed it on the little coffee table right in front of me.

"Look Wolf," she said running her fingers softly over the lid on the place where the claw slashes were.

"Wow," I said, feigning mock enthusiasm.

"Isn't it amazing? One of the old woman's friends who was there last night repaired the damage with this beautiful tiny, tiny stitch work." Faye was beaming.

"Where are all the falcon feathers then?"

I was about to say something stupid about Indian head-dresses and the Rio Mardi Gras but luckily, she put a finger up to my mouth and stopped me. "They are in good hands, I can assure you."

"Women's business?"

"Yes. Secret women's business."

"Okay, ... *Wa'z in the case, wa'z in the case?*"

The moment Faye opened the lid, the only thing inside was a bundled-up piece of cloth. It was old and obviously Native American. When she unraveled it, I wasn't all that fussed with what was inside that either.

"What is it?"

"What does it look like?"

"A box." Faye took no notice and set it down beside the case on the table. "Is it a musical box?"

"Ten points Fenrir. Go to the top of the class."

I couldn't believe it. I really didn't know what to expect... *but a musical box?*

"This looks like it's from Europe or Scandinavia to me, am I right?"

"It's Norwegian. It's decorated in the Rogaland folk art style. I think probably it must have originally been brought out to the Americas by the Sloopers, sometime around the mid-eighteen hundreds."

"What's a Slooper, Faye?"

"Norwegian settlers. At first, they settled in the north-east area of the United States of America but eventually, over the decades, they pointed their wagons to the south and the west and ventured out all over the country."

"Close your eyes for a second Wolf, it's old, I have to set it up." I did as requested. "Okay, you can look now. Tell me if you recognize anything? *Isn't it wonderful?*"

I studied it carefully. The box was old, black, and wooden and beautifully decorated with carefully hand-painted flowers that had dulled and been worn away in places by over a century and a half of handling. The inside was lined with blue velvet padding. A circular mirror sat prominently in the center of the recessed lid. But the most enthralling feature by far was the little figurine that turned slowly around in front of it to the tune of her own accompanying music. She was beautiful. The more I watched her the more she drew me in, and I couldn't take my eyes away. Undoubtedly fashioned long ago by her creator as a labor of love, her hair was carved long and flowing and fair. It somehow seemed to merge as she moved with her lithe and willowy arms, one raised high above her head, the other trailing low and harmoniously down by her waist. The effect when she danced was hypnotic. Enchanting. Maybe even magical.

And then suddenly I got it. It all became clear. The haunting, mechanical melody drifting out from the box was the same tune I'd heard that early morning when I'd found Faye sitting alone playing the piano. It was the *Sonata al Chiaro di Luna.*

"That's Beethoven's 'Moonlight Sonata'!... But how? I mean, *that's* pretty freaky."

Faye went big-eyed and stared right into my face. "*Synchronicity Juha Väinämöinen.* Pure, unadulterated synchronicity."

"Hmm." What could I say?

"I *do* like the little dancer though … she kinda reminds me of you."

Faye pretended to be disappointed and pulled a sulky but cute face.

"Your obviously far too *cool* for musical boxes," she said sarcastically. "But I still have one thing left to impress you."

With that she took a shiny, silk handkerchief with something wrapped inside, out from the recess in front of the little dancer. At first, as the silk unfolded I thought she was just holding a handful of rocks but as she laid them out carefully in a semi-circle on the table, it was obvious they were all joined together and part of a most stunning necklace.

"EXCELLENT! I *really* like that."

Heading inward from each end, the necklace was made up of two very different types of polished stones set out in an alternating pattern that increased in size from that of a pea to one very impressive almond shaped stone at the center. One type of stone was a deep blue-black in color and speckled with tiny white dots which gave each piece the appearance of a star-filled sky. It was weird. They all seemed to sparkle and shine like individual little galaxies.

"The blue stones come from only one special place in the world," Faye said, seeing that I was showing at least some kind of interest.

"Where's that?"

"The Preseli Mountains in Cymru, or as you'd call it, Wales. It's a particular type of dolerite that is charged with unusual magnetic properties. These intense deep blue stones come from an ancient long-mined-out vein. Preseli stones nowadays are more or less grey. Believe me, they possess some very special energies and powers that influence the chakras and have healing effects on the body. When some people come into the presence of the blue stones, they sense a strange intuitive connection within themselves to the remote primordial past … I know I do."

I couldn't feel jack.

"I bet you didn't know that the original outer ring at Stonehenge was built with Preseli Bluestone centuries before the trilithon circles were raised into place."

"No I can't say I did."

"Why do the stones glimmer like that Faye?"

"Flecks of pyrite, or is it augite? I'm not very good at petrology."

"These other stones, the golden-yellow ones, they're amber right?"

"Very good, but not just any old amber, this is Succinite, Baltic amber. Elektron, as it was known to the ancient Greeks. Ultra-hard fossilized resin, tens of millions of years old that came from the ancient forests. Amber plays a role in magick where the elements of light and fire contained within are released as a guide in the Astral darkness. Like the blue stones, it also possesses properties that affect the chakras and the body in mysterious ways."

I could hear her babbling on beside me but the thing that had grabbed my attention was the central stone in the necklace. Although it was the largest and obviously the most impressive, not only for its size and its amazing translucent quality, but for what was frozen deep inside it. Laid out, smack in the center as if it had been placed there by a skilled human hand, was the perfect shape of a honeybee.

"Isn't he magnificent?" Faye asked excitedly, noting that her in-depth explanation of the various histories and therapeutic properties of rocks was completely lost on me.

"Yeah, I like him, he's *really* good." A pattern soon formed in my mind. "That night when we played Hnefatafl, there was the bee. Then there were the Honey Rollers and now this little guy here turns up. Is that synchronicity ... or what?"

"*Synchronicity.* Oh yes, all the connections are there in spades, but you still don't quite get it, do you?"

"Get what?"

"The Eddas tell of a necklace of gold that was forged by Dwarves. Obviously, this is not it. This is its *far more ancient* predecessor, made even before the Neolithic by nomadic hunters of the frozen north. It seems, according to the Indian women, to have come to the Americas during the time when the ice sheets were still receding. As the old woman handed it to me last night she said softly. 'It has taken countless summers and crossed many different paths on its long, long journey but this ring of power stones has slowly made its way safely down here to us for safekeeping. Take it my child, it is rightfully yours. It is well known that it was first brought over to this land by your kin, the ones our own ancient ancestors called, the sky-eyed people.'"

"So why did *you* get it? ... I'm sure other Nordic types have been around these parts too. What about the Slopers?"

"*Sloopers.*" Faye shook her head and just looked at me with an expression of complete and utter bewilderment. "This is Freya's necklace ... *this is The Brísingamen.* This is all part of the unfolding. I'm here, the necklace is here and if I may say so, you do still seem *completely* unaware that this whole Freya saga will very soon come to an unstoppable end."

I looked down at the table at the necklace and tried to think of something relevant to say. "Why don't you put it on, so I can see how it looks."

"*I can't.* Well at least not yet. Anyway, look at the time, half the morning's gone already. I'd better get going." Faye suddenly re-wrapped the necklace, tucked it snuggly into the music box and then bundled the whole lot back into the case. "Would you mind putting it back under there where I got it from please, while I quickly go and get changed."

It was only then that I noticed she was still in the same get-up that I'd seen her wearing last night. I did as she asked, and then picked up the coffee mugs to go and rinse them out in the sink. In doing so, my sudden unexpected burst of movement had set off the low rumble growl from one of Faye's pet lions who, judging by the direction of the sound, was positioned right above me somewhere up on top of the kitchenette cupboards. I stood there frozen, fearful that any untoward movement would condemn the top of my head to share the unwelcomely fate of a soft-boiled egg.

"*Gutteka,* shoosh!" Luckily, Faye came back out of the bedroom wearing her blue jeans and a bra, lining up the neck of a sweatshirt before carefully pulling it over her head in the way that only women do.

"Excellent. You kept them a secret. Look at all those tattoos!"

"Aren't they wonderful? *I got ink,* back in the Neolithic," Faye giggled warmly. "If I said they've 'grown on me', then that's probably more to the truth."

Both Faye's arms were now completely covered with an assemblage of greenish blue bands, that flowed boldly along and around her limbs in a complex interwoven system of spirals, curves, and standalone marks. They were undoubtedly talismans of power from a more ancient time under Taurus.

Faye pulled her sweater on quickly. "Sorry, I'm supposed to try and keep them covered up ... well for now anyway."

"Good idea, those babies would definitely attract some attention. There's a lot of folk around here who might get the wrong idea completely if they suddenly see you looking like *that.*"

"Exactly! Come on Wolf, I can't wait to catch up with the others."

26

Freya's Ride

"What else did you and all those goddesses get up to in the Neolithic Faye?" I asked, as she pulled the trailer door shut behind her and locked it.

"Well, immediately after the night of the council, they all shot through and left me there on my own."

I was surprised, not at her answer but at the matter of fact way she'd said it. "Why did—"

She already knew my next question. "Because that was the place where I was..." Faye paused, searching for the appropriate word. "I don't know, pre-ordained if you like, to remain behind in the village by myself."

"And the reason being?"

"To summon the powers of the Triskeli."

"How'd you do that?"

"Up on a small hilltop overlooking the village, three conjoined giant spirals, each thirty meters wide had been carved into the earth and marked out boldly in white with finely crushed seashells and bones. The site was regarded as highly sacred to the villagers and they would never walk upon it, only their livestock graze there. Right in the center where the three spirals meet is where I was encouraged to... well, train."

"With a spear?"

"I wish. The staff they gave me to use up there was almost as long and nearly the weight of a frick'n flagpole."

I laughed out loud at the unexpected outburst and the expression on her face. "Are you serious?"

"*Ohhh* yes, I did this for two hours at sunrise and for two more hours at sunset. Every single day I was there... except one."

"Which one was that?"

"The first one after the council. It was an orientation day of sorts."

"So how did you train and what was it all about?"

"I'm sorry, I don't fully understand the why myself yet and I don't think Freya does either, but the how … *uugh!* I was encouraged to hold the long wooden staff up above my head and rotate it around and around in a swirling circular motion for as long as I could manage."

Faye took a deep breath and considered her next words. "It was always when I was right at the point of collapse with its weight that the staff seemed to take pity on me." Faye paused again, not quite certain of how to describe it.

"In some mysterious way its bulky shape somehow morphed into a much lighter and streamlined device that would enable me to spin it much faster and execute that endless rotating motion more easily. It became the geirahöð and there is *nothing* I know of that is more perfectly designed for such a task. It's so obvious to me now why I was attracted to the bo staff and then drawn towards the naginata and finally to the ultimate symmetry and balance of the hybrid double blade. Obviously, the presence of Sacramento and Hamada-san is no coincidence and I'm blessed that they have both been here to help me."

I gaped at her blankly. Whenever she started talking like this, I never knew what I was supposed to say. It always seemed a bit too new-agey and out there for me. "Were there other things going on in the Stone Age beside your training?"

Judging by the contemptuous look on her face I knew I'd been seen as a fool. "I bet when you say Stone Age you imagine brutish unkempt cavemen skulking about in long shaggy mammoth furs, right?"

"Indubitably."

"That's so wrong. You couldn't be any further from the truth if you tried. The people who I lived with showed a genuine sense of respect and concern for each other that reminded me so much of the traditional Native Americans. They would carry themselves with poise and a humble dignity and, believe it or not, they really had an amazing sense of style back then too. Skins, wood, rock, bone, feathers, and shells, that's all they had. It was all so much more natural and … earthy. If I didn't have to leave my eyelash curler and the fondue set behind, I'd go back there in a heartbeat. It was definitely no paradise living so close to the elements. Conditions were very, very hard. I only saw a handful of people who were older than forty the whole time I was there. Have a guess what their clan totem was?"

I could tell by her excited expression what the answer was already but just to be annoying I said, "I dunno, some type of arctic moose?"

"No stupid, it was a peregrine falcon." Faye then explained that there was a glaringly obvious etymological through line (whatever that meant) from their word fali-*kah* to fálki which means falcon in old Norse. Faye kept yappin' away excitedly about all things Neolithic and it was only the unusual scene going on right outside the garage that made her finally shut up.

Vince was swinging the bo staff wildly above his head in what was an obviously futile attempt to get a hit in on Hamad-san who, for some unknown reason, was indulging him in an impromptu sparring session. Although he was the same hight as Faye, Vince seemed to completely tower over Hamada-san due to his gangly all-over-the-place ineptness.

The miss-match was comical enough without Sacramento's participation as an additional wildcard, which had turned the whole thing into a theatre of the absurd. Foregoing the role of an all attentive sensei keeping a close and watchful eye on proceedings, he had opted instead to play the part of an over excited chimpanzee.

Sacramento was a master mimic. He lurched from side to side and bounced up and down with such an ease you'd swear he had some kind of springs attached to his feet. He had that animated slapping himself on top of the head thing down pat and his outstretched lunging arm-pokes to the back of Vince's legs were more monkey-like than human.

Vince was hopeless. He was completely flustered by Sacramento bobbing around his ankles and couldn't keep any focus at all. For her part, a stone-faced Hamada-san looked completely unfazed as she effortlessly blocked Vince's erratic parries and snuck in the occasional little jab here and there for good measure. But it was only when Sacramento started screeching loudly and making all kinds of outlandish primate noises that Vince completely got the shits and lost it. In frustration he lashed out with the bo staff and took a wild air-swing at his chimpanzee tormentor. Sacramento was far too quick. From a bouncing squat position he launched himself clear with an unbelievably acrobatic backflip. Vince hurled the bo staff angrily away, made a token head jerk bow of recognition to Hamada-san and stormed off around to the pumps with a still in monkey-mode Sacramento bobbing up and down right behind him.

Joe, who'd been sitting quietly watching proceedings from the concrete table, shook his head in bewilderment as he stood up and came across to where Faye and I now stood with Hamada-san.

Faye seemed over excited to see them both as though she really had been gone for weeks. The three of them seemed indifferent as to whether I was there or not so when they all toddled off together to see Charlie, who was in the garage working on Faye's Martellare, I took my leave and wandered out front to see what was happening with Vince and the monkey man.

Sacramento was gone but Vince was sitting on the ground out in front of the pumps smoking a cigarette and flicking stones at a renegade chicken from the campsite that was pushing its free-range roaming liberties somewhat past the extreme.

"How's it going?" I said sounding all chummy as I came up on Vince unexpectedly. He looked up at me suspiciously.

"I thought it was dick-wad again."

I grimaced and waited to see if he was in any kind of civil mood to talk.

"What was all that bullshit about? The guy's a frick'n tool. All I wanted was a quick kind of intro lesson with the Jap' lady when he comes sticking his nose in like big-chief-circus-monkey."

"Well, I don't think he meant any harm by what he was doing Vince. To me it seemed to be some kind of abstract part of the lesson."

"What?" Vince barked irritably without even thinking.

I couldn't believe he had missed the whole point of what Sacramento was up to. "I can't say for sure, but what I think he was trying to get across with all of that distraction was the first lesson."

Vince just looked at me blankly. "What d' ya mean?"

"Don't worry about what I'm doing. Concentrate on what you're doing." As much as I liked Vince, he really was annoyingly thick sometimes.

"Ahh, he's still a frick'n dipshit." With that he got up, hurled his remaining handful of stones at the chicken and stormed off somewhere around the far side of the building.

◆

Sitting down in the sunshine was nice, so I stayed a while longer and soaked up some rays. I had fallen under the mesmerizing spell of "el chicken". I knew it was more cunning than dumb, as it always stayed just out of range of a stone's throw.

The squeal of worn brakes caught my attention as a distant car pulled up hard and let someone out. As it drove off, I saw a man standing alone down by the roadside.

I watched him like a hawk as he walked determinedly straight towards me. He had nothing with him other than the dark blue pants, the plain white T-shirt, and the shiny black shoes he was standing in. As he came closer, I could see he was a tall Caucasian in his mid to late twenties with a short-cropped head of light sandy hair. He looked like a god. When he came within a few close paces he stopped and stood there calmly smiling at me. I knew who he was immediately.

"You're Axel, aren't you?"

"Yes … I've come to find Freya." That flat Nordic accent and the tiny piece of sombrero shaped tinfoil he was wheeling around between his fingers was proof enough for me. I jumped to my feet and shook his hand with pleasure.

"My name's Wolf … although that sister of yours calls me Fenrir. Please come with me, I know one little Viking goddess who'll be very, very happy to see you."

We had almost reached the garage door when Faye came bounding out holding a bag full of trash. At first, she did a double-take then gasped in disbelief, dropped the bag and immediately ran towards him screaming loudly and almost knocked the poor guy over as she leapt on him with excitement. The others came out to see what all the commotion was about and within half a minute the assembled throng had grown to six.

Faye was over the moon. She was jumping up and down and hugging and kissing Axel with an unabashed delight while at the same time trying to introduce him to everyone present.

"What are you doing here? How did you find me?" Faye was totally ecstatic.

"I had to come and see my little søster, *not* because I like you so much," Axel said teasingly. "But to warn you that Mimas is zeroing in on where you are and—"

"Oh, I know he's close alright, he's really close. I've already had two very scary run-ins with a couple of his hired goons and these totally mental case Feds," Faye cut in excitedly.

"Yes but there's *more*, something much—"

Axel cut his sentence short and made an almost imperceptible sideways glance at Hamada-san before looking straight back to Faye where he asked her a very short lightning-fast question in Norwegian so as not to appear rude to the rest of us.

Nei, nei, were the first and only words I could decipher of Faye's equally rapid answer. But judging by the way she vehemently rebuffed his question my intuition told me it had something to do with her sensei.

"Do you have any access to the internet? I'm sorry to bring this up, before I've even had time to meet everyone properly, but there's something I must show you straight away," Axel said very seriously.

"We sure as hell do. Got all them trendy gizmos down here at The Alamo," Joe said comically as he generously offered up his desktop computer for Axel to use.

"Do you want *all* of us, or just ...?" Joe left the question open.

"No please, everybody. I think you'd all better come and take a look." Intrigued, we made our way over to Joe's office. Faye was quizzing Axel as to how he got here and more intriguing than that, how in all of Mexico he knew exactly where she was. She badgered him before he finally relented.

Axel looked at his wristwatch and told us straight-faced that exactly two hours and twenty-five minutes earlier he'd still been in Norway. The only reason he'd gotten here so fast was that he'd stowed away on one of the classified, underground, maglev trains. Apparently, he'd spent the last forty-five minutes trying to hitch a ride from where he'd gotten off, some ten or fifteen miles north of that truck station further up the road.

"I knew it," Joe whispered quietly to me as we were going in through the door. "Did ya notice the little outline tattoo of a rabbit jumping through a circle on Axel's arm?"

"No."

"Well he's got one."

"What is it?"

"He's Svarte Kaniner."

"Which is?"

"A *Black Rabbit*," Joe answered, sounding puzzled as if I was a complete simpleton for not knowing exactly what he was talking about.

"They're an amalgam of loosely related groups that share a common interest in the underground tunnels of Europe. You know, historians, archeologists, cave explorers, folks like that. And *of course* the military. Apparently, there's two or three completely independent networks down there that stretch from Scandinavia all the way over to Turkey. Some of the tunnels date back as far as thirteen or fourteen *thousand* years. Can you believe that? There are some that were dug out in the medieval ages which they think were escape routes from all the religious persecutions of the time. And then there's the new high-tech modern ones like Axel was alluding to that are spread out all over the globe."

"Really?" He was ready to keep on talking but with the others gathering curiously around his desk, Joe put his tongue on pause and shifted his attention to the computer. Once it was up and running, Axel took over and in no time brought up whatever it was that he seemed so anxious for us all to see.

The site was a blog and most of the text was written in Japanese except for the fluorescent pink English subtitle bar which read "My Friend Faye. The Viking Blonde Haired Tomoe Gozen".

Faye lent across the desk and stuck her face up close to the screen. "Kiko, what have you done? She must have been running this blog from her tablet since she's been here." She explained to Axel quickly who Kiko was and that Hamada-san standing beside him was indeed her grandmother.

"They'll know *exactly* where I am when they see this. I can't believe they haven't come and grabbed me already." Faye turned white and was looking quietly panicked.

Joe could see she was getting herself all worked up, so he gently put his arm around her shoulders and with a few kind words calmed her down.

"Now settle petal. As far as I can figure, *they, he,* whoever it is, knows you're down in Sonora *somewhere* ... but that's about it. If they knew where you were exactly, they'd be down here goin' ape shit *on all of us*. Now that ain't happened, has it? *Has it?*"

"Nei." Answered Faye cutely.

"And as for those other two dipshits out there. Swaning up and down the highway, dishing out aggro like it's going out o' fashion. They've already been down here snooping around and found nothing. If you ask me, neither one of them have got enough brain cells floatin' around in their melons to know their ass from their elbow. So, don't go worrying your pretty little head over those two dodos."

Even though she had no understanding of English, Hamada-san had read what was on the screen and more or less got the gist of what had happened. She said something softly in her native tongue, the tone of her voice sounded concerned and very apologetic. Axel answered her calmly and reassuringly in fluent Japanese. Even Faye seemed impressed.

Axel scrolled down and found a post of particular interest. "This was the first thing I saw when I was shown this last week. Please little søster, what exactly *have* you been doing down here for the last six months?" Axel enlarged the image to full screen.

"*Look, look, look!*" cried Faye with an instant rush of excitement. "This was when the first earthquake happened, and I fought with the monsters over at the minibus. Kiko must have shot this video when she was still trapped inside hanging upside down in her seat."

On the screen we could see that Kiko had flipped the image the right way up showing a static image of dangling seat belt straps and fallen travel bags, while behind it an overexposed image of Faye was locked in fast-action combat with a truly disturbing and seemingly overwhelming onslaught of devils. The picture was not all that clear and jumped and jarred up and down. All anyone would have had to do was freeze frame the image and they'd know it was Faye in an instant.

"I think all this hot, desert sun has sent you a little crazy Frey'. Demons, Naginatajutsu, what else don't I know?"

"You don't know the half of it," laughed Charlie. "Tell him about your skeleton army."

Axel looked back at Charlie who was standing behind him and rolled his eyes comically with an expression of sheer disbelief. "It's true!"

"Look Wolf, there's the anime artwork that Kiko gave me."

Poor Faye looked completely frazzled. Scrolling on further, Axel found a couple more posts and translated them back into English. *'I now live in Mexico with my dear friend Faye who is the most beautiful looking girl in the whole wide world.'* Axel grinned and winked at his sister teasingly. Faye just sighed and put her face in her hands.

"Here's one. 'Blah, blah, blah … *Faye told me yesterday that Norway was far too cold … blah, blah, blah … and so now, after a lengthy talk she has taken my advice and decided that Mexico is really the best place to stay.'* etc., etc."

"I never said that. The poor kid's making stuff up."

"Here's a good one," said Axel. "This is one of her blogger friends replies. *'Dear Kiko, I love to follow all of your wonderful stories and adventures with Faye Tomoe Gozen. I love her too. I would like to someday come to visit and stay with you both in Mexico. Could you please post a couple of photos of her training with her naginata or riding on her red, Martellare Angelus?'* What the hell does that mean?" Axel looked completely enthralled.

"Do you really have a Martellare? I would have come down here ages ago if I'd known you had one of those." Faye answered back quickly in Norwegian and judging by the way Axel's face lit up, he was obviously impressed.

Charlie had seen enough and excused himself, saying he'd better get back to work. Hamada-san did likewise. With a brisk and straight-faced goodbye, she bowed collectively and took a step towards the door. Faye looked worried, she moved with her trying hard to impress on Hamada-san that she really wasn't *angry* and despite how it seemed, there was no reason for Kiko to get in any kind of trouble.

Suddenly Joe's phone started ringing. He picked it up quickly and I could tell by the wincing expression on his face that whoever it was had really made him wish he hadn't.

Axel closed down the computer and then curiously lifted the underside of the mouse up close to his face. "This thing has still got a ball?" His expression was one of amazement, energized with a handsome smile of good humor.

Joe grimaced as he put the phone down. "Oooh, that was Prisciliana. She's frick'n ropeable. She wants those two kegs back *TODAY!* Before her boss gets back from Guaymas. Apparently, a temporary bridge has been set up over the crack and the road down her way is back open. I'll send Vince, he can deal with Prisciliana, after all, the beer was for his little shindig." Joe then changed tack, "Tell you what Faye. Why don't you take Axel into the garage and introduce him properly to Charlie and let him have a good look at that little ol' motorcycle you've got sittin' out there as well."

"Yes," said Axel excitedly. "Let's go. You've *really* got a Martellare?"

"Wolf, you come with me," ordered Joe. "We'll brew up a fresh pot and steal a few of Rosalina's hotcakes. We'll see you two back out there in five."

Crashing about in the kitchen Joe gave me a point by point summation of what he thought about Kiko and the whole internet thing and whether or not there could still be any possible blow back. He didn't seem too concerned, but his overriding comment boiled down to a simple. "Kids, they're *all* frick'n self-obsessed." Granted, it was a bit of an overgeneralization, but he did have a point.

Joe stepped into the garage carrying a tray stacked high with all the coffee stuff as Faye, Axel and Charlie were all doting over the Martellare Angelus in the way that only true motorcycle aficionados do. I was surprised to see Dr. MacElroy had emerged from his bunker and standing alone down the back, staring curiously at Joe's white OB-359 Ouroboros.

"Hey Eugene," Joe yelled gruffly. "Come on over here and meet Faye's brother Axel."

Dr. MacElroy couldn't believe it and came bounding over like a shot. "Well hello Axel, this really is a surprise. It's so nice to meet you. Your sister has told me so much about you. My name's MacElroy and before you ask—"

"*NO!* Not that stupid gag about ice-skating Eugene, it's wearing a little thin," Joe growled cutting him off quickly. Eugene just stood there grinning and staring up at Axel like he frick'n well loved him. "Wow, you sure are the male equivalent of your good-looking sister, aren't you? I'm sure your intelligence would be the equal of Faye's also."

"*No!*" said Axel feigning indignity. "I'm *much* more intelligent, and ten times better looking." Faye kicked Axel playfully in the shin, but Eugene burst out laughing and pushed the whole thing completely overboard.

"Give it a rest," scowled Joe. "You sound like a frick'n wuss." But Eugene wasn't finished. He pointed casually back to Joe's car.

"Do you see the intrinsic irony of a GT Ouroboros motorcar with a broken timing chain Axel? The eternal re-creating cycle of Jörmungandr has inexplicably come to an end."

"*He* was one of Loki and Angrboða's three monster kids," Joe mentioned matter of factly as he filled up the mugs. MacElroy's blatant attempt at sounding like a well-rounded smart-ass had fallen flat as no one had bothered to tell him that the Ouroboros had since been repaired and was now in full working order.

With her arms spread-eagle and a piece of cake in her mouth, Faye was riding the Martellare in and out of the garage, trying the new cruise control gizmo that Charlie had adapted to the throttle. Faye thought it was brilliant and said that most of the Los Espectros Brillantes riders had their motorcycles modified this way already so both hands could be kept totally free for fighting.

Cutting the motorcycle's engine Faye kicked down the foot-stand and flicked a long denim leg back across the seat. In no time the conversation became a warts and all recap of some of the bizarre exploits that had happened to her since she'd been in Mexico. None of which surprised Axel. In fact, knowing full-well his little sister's pedigree, he just took it all in his stride.

One of the things that puzzled him, along with the rest of us, was why Freya had decided to run with a band of undead skjeletter motorcycle riders all the way down here in the middle of the Sonoran Desert.

"This particular spot was designated to her by the Elders of the High Council, it's as simple as that," said Faye. "Los Espectros Brillantes had been assembled here too. Although many, many years previous. They are the anguished souls of innocent peasants tortured and murdered by the cruelty of dark and merciless despots. They say they will not pass over until they have reaped their long-sought revenge."

"Yeah but why a *Nordic* goddess Faye, and not some local indigenous deity?" quizzed Joe, still none the wiser.

"When you cross over, you *actually* see it; you do. Your ethnicity and geographic location is completely irrelevant. All that matters at a point in time like this, is the collective protection of the Earth's sacred hoops and the vehement suppression of this global demonic onslaught. Evil is still an integral part of the great duality. Freya's task, along with the many others present on the High Goddess Council, is to maintain the balance and to ruthlessly help keep it in check." Somehow, I actually understood what Faye had just said.

"And what about *THE DEVILS*?" Joe said, stealing the very next words from my mouth. "What in tarnation are they?"

"Manifest clusters of unadulterated evil," came Faye's unequivocal answer as she took another nibble on her fruit cake.

"They've been down there for eons you know, lying dormant in a state of deep hibernation. Completely forgotten, *except* by the Dark Lords who are now manipulating the planet's current geomagnetic anomalies to draw them up to the surface as a pestilent shock-trooper army for evil. The reason they appear as devils is because *that* is the predominant archetype the collective psyche still associates with any kind of demonic entity that rises up out of the ground. Although having said that, if you go further north, relentless, mass entertainment brainwashing has repro-grammed younger members of the public to now more readily identify with these god-awful creatures as *zombies*."

"That makes sense," I said in agreement. Faye said no more and took a long hearty gulp from her coffee.

"*The Dark Lords?*" whispered Joe, frowning and still somewhat skeptical.

"Oh yeah, Mimas is one of them, big time," I blabbed back without even thinking.

"Axel, that rabbit tattoo on your arm, that's Svarte Kaniner," Joe said, changing the subject and keen to have a talkfest with Faye's brother.

"You know about Svarte Kaniner?"

"Oh sure, but not as much as I'd like to," he said with a probing grin on his face.

"Black ears mean you're military, right?" While we were back in the kitchen, Joe had told me that he'd heard how different parts of the outlined rabbit tattoos would be filled in solid to identify one particular group of Svarte Kaniner from another. Some had colored ears, others tails, front legs, back legs or whatever. He had no idea which was which, but Joe was adamant Axel was in some way involved with the military.

"Yes, did Freya tell you?" said Axel.

"Nope, worked it all out on my lonesome. A guy like you has special forces written all over him."

"No, well yes, *in a way*... I'm ex-Jegerkompaniet, Arctic Rangers. They're pretty special."

Joe laughed accordingly. "So what are you doing now then Axel?"

"I'm still a ranger, but now I'm with national parks. That's why my rabbit tattoo also has little black feet."

For some reason Joe thought that was hilarious and slapped him on the back with a warm seal of approval.

"You came down here in the tubes?"

"Yes."

"Where'd you leave from Axel?"

He seemed surprised at Joe's candidness. "Somewhere far up north."

"Oh come on son, you can do better than that," Joe smiled questioningly, expecting a full debriefing.

"It's okay Axel, there's *nothing* you can't tell Joe... *he's* The Mad Hatter," Faye said affectionately. Axel's face lit up with another handsome smile as he replied, "AC-68-L."

Joe thought about it for a second or two. "Maybe I'm wrong but the alphanumeric of that cryptic coordinate sounds like it was somewhere right up close to the circle."

"Your right, I left from the underground submarine base in the Lofoten."

"Wow! It really is there. I knew it was all bull when they said it didn't exist. I wondered why you were half-dressed up like a sailor."

"I buried the shirt and hat in the sand as soon as I got off."

"So how'd you get clearance to catch a ride on the shuttle?"

"Svarte Kaniner. We've got all kinds of connections and ways of doing things."

"Fantastic." Joe was completely engaged. All this stuff was right up his alley.

Faye didn't seem all that interested and made moves to persuade Dr. MacElroy to go down with her into the lab. "Nice to meet you Axel," said Eugene. "I'm sure we can catch up and have a bit of a chinwag later."

"Okay, that sounds good," Axel replied in a reassuring tone.

"You were saying how Svarte Kaniner got you onto the shuttle." Joe was determined to not drop this thread.

"There was this one particular navy guy we had contact with who wanted to go AWOL. In fact he was aware that he was being set up as a patsy for something or other and wanted to disappear completely. He and I looked fairly similar, so it wasn't all that hard to switch places physically."

"Surely catchin' a shuttle from inside a base like that means passing through some kind of hi-tech biometric security system."

"Only on the ultra-classified routes, surprisingly. The standard maglev system is pretty old technology now. Fortunately, the sailor's level two clearance swipe-card was all I needed. It was getting myself down to the tube bays undetected that was the hard bit."

"Yeah, how'd you get yourself inside a secret submarine base anyway?"

"Decades ago, when the facility was still only a plan on the drawing board, Svarte Kaniner made sure they had their own people working inside every department from engineering all the way through to construction and fit outs. Intuitively they worried that foreign elements hostile to our national security might at some time in the future infiltrate or succeed in taking over down there. So right from the start they took the precautionary measures of building a covert network of secret tunnels and entrances to get themselves in and out of the base in times of need. The Svarte Kaniner are great patriots you know."

"What happened to the navy guy then?"

"The sailor who I did the swap with, lived in readiness to go at a moment's notice. The Kaniner got me in through the same tunnel hatch that they used to get him out. We only crossed paths for a second when he handed me his swipe card before I hitched myself a ride down here on the shuttle."

"How long did it take you … to get to Sonora I mean?"

"Less than two hours."

"Man, that's incredible. Those things must really frick'n shift. Did you run into any kind o' trouble?"

"No thank God, but at one point the shuttle pulled up beside a platform somewhere and just sat unmoving for the longest three minutes of my life. I was sure I'd been detected."

"Where was that?"

"All I know is the air smelt incredibly foul and the whole place *really* gave me the creeps."

"Incredible! You've sure got some guts there boy. Was there anyone else on the shuttle?"

"There could have been, but all I saw were endless rows of consignment pods."

"And tell me again, where was it you came out?"

"I'd punched the pre-designated stop request into the consul and memorized the station's code number over and over again in my head, but when I got there I had this horrifying feeling that I'd messed up badly and had entered the wrong digits. Luckily, it was okay, so I got off the train and followed the signs along the platform to what were the places of exit. I thought it might be too risky taking the elevator, so I climbed up this endless concrete staircase and simply walked out through a door at the top. I couldn't believe it was so easy."

"No guards?" Charlie asked flatly.

"*Nobody!* The whole place was completely empty and silent. Even the door at the top of the stairs was unlocked."

"What did this place look like? From the outside."

"It was just an ordinary looking brown metal shack with a three-meter-high wire fence around it sitting fifty meters back from the roadside."

"I know the one he means," Joe said, turning to Charlie. "Looks like some kind of public works shed or something. Always wondered what it was doing just sitting out there in the middle of nowhere."

"What happened then Axel?"

"I buried the shirt and the sailor's hat and then walked off down the road." Joe just stood there looking amazed.

"How'd you know where Faye was anyway? … Svarte Kaniner?"

"No! Her best friend Elsbeth told me." Joe raised his brow with surprise as he shoved more cake into his mouth.

◆

Up on the roof, Joe, Axel, Charlie and I were looking out at the black plumes of smoke, which had become a permanent fixture on the skyline since that latest earthquake. Joe reckoned they were coming from a whole string of rupture points that had opened up along the Sea of Cortez between the Pacific and North American plates. Axel agreed but thought the increase in seismic activity around the East Pacific Rise was probably pushing the Baja California peninsula west, and away from mainland Mexico. They were talking in techno babble, but that was near enough the way I heard it.

We were waiting for Faye. She had a pre-planned afternoon training session with Hamada-san. This time though, sensei was giving instruction about naginata fighting on horseback. Obviously instead of riding on a four-footed nag, Faye would be doing her thing from the Martellare. I can tell ya, we were all pretty keen to get an eyeful of that.

The four of us sat there patiently, laughing at Joe as he told Axel bullshit stories about all the weird and horrifying things that live out in the desert that would kill you on the spot as quick as look at you. Axel was digging it though. Only a couple of hours ago he'd been freezing his nuts off (his words, not mine) in the cold, dark gloom of the Arctic. He thought the Mexican sun was fantastic, and all of this glorious heat had done wonders at thawing him out.

We all turned to look as a lone figure drifted out from behind the north end of the building and steered an almost funereal like path across to the grassy patch of the outdoor dojo. The figure, clad in a white hooded gown, looked ghostly and almost other worldly. We watched, intrigued, as the 'apparition' knelt serenely down on the edge of the grass and bowed its head forward in a sign of obvious grief or submission.

"Oh god, *that's Kiko*," gasped Joe as she pulled the hood back away from her head to let her hair fall down around her face and shoulders.

"She's puttin' on the dog, big time! Hamada-san must have gone straight back over and had words with her. She's all dressed up like a frick'n Noh performer or something. *Check out all that goddamn face paint will ya?*" Joe's voice pitch was going rapidly skyward. *"It's whiter than her kimono!"*

"Shini-shozoku," added Axel. "Clothing of death, or for those committed to suicide."

"*O-ooh*, she's not gonna like this. Faye's gonna freak." Charlie's words rolled from his mouth as I thought them.

"This is bullshit," Joe said, sounding really concerned. "She's a strange one Axel I tell ya. She's really changed her tack with this little drama though. Usually she'll just explode into tears, turn bright red, or slam her head face first into the concrete table. If she's going all over the top like this, next thing you know she might pull out a frick'n blade and actually do it."

It was right then, as Joe was cranking up the worry stick, Faye came cruising in towards her on her shiny, red motorcycle. You could tell by the way she cut the bike dead some distance back and walked in without the geirahöð that she was already aware of what was happening.

"That kid's a total flipper, I reckon," came Charlie's no-frills opinion.

Faye walked calmly over towards Kiko and sat down on the ground an arm or twos length in front of her. The four of us just stood there intrigued, watching, and waiting to see what would happen.

Even from this distance we could see that Faye was talking reassuringly to Kiko. The poor kid just knelt there, as still as a statue, with no sudden meltdown or dramatic explosion. Even so, it was clear her lips were going ten to the dozen, and I guessed, apologizing most profusely. From her body language you could see Faye was trying to impress upon Kiko that no real harm had been done and she wasn't cross or upset with her.

Unexpectedly Shintarō appeared out of nowhere, and stood behind Kiko, looking all very flustered and panicked. Faye gently raised her hand towards him, as if to say, *Please* Shintarō, just hang on a moment, please don't … Kiko's okay.

Shintarō wasn't playing ball, and launched himself forward, swallowing the young girl whole between his broad, protective arms. As he shuffled her away, Faye stood up, turned around to face us and shrugged.

"Come on guys, let's go, this is ridiculous. There ain't gonna be any kind o' horse fighting action going on now," growled Joe, disappointed.

◆

As the sun sank low in the west, Charlie and Joe were firing up the grill for a welcoming banquet for Axel. Joe had his hat on again, and hard as it was not to smile, Axel's furtive half glances, couldn't hide the fact that he obviously found the thing incredibly bizarre and as amusing as I did.

The big fella was in his element, bossing everyone around, and sending whoever was closest to go and fetch whatever it was that he needed. Even the guest of honor wasn't exempt, as Joe had ordered him to go look for any old sheets of newspaper, so he'd have something to wipe the grease off the hotplates.

I liked Axel a lot. He'd only been here a couple of hours, but right from the start you just knew everything about him was right up front, and completely on the level. He had that quality some folks have, where everybody who met him seemed to like him immediately. The fact that he was as good looking as a Madison Avenue underpants model didn't seem to hurt none either, I guess. But all that aside, he was the kind of guy you felt comfortable with and felt like you'd known for ages. Even Charlie had taken a shine to him, and that was as easy as cracking a Brazil nut with your teeth. Of course, all the women that had stumbled across him so far, seemed most impressed. From the middle-aged Mrs. Eduardo in the kitchen, to the normally extremely levelheaded Oppuam, who, when she first saw him, just stood there dazzled like a wide-eyed doe in the headlights.

To me Axel was the embodiment of some ancient Viking nobleman. It was easy to imagine him standing tall on the prow of a long ship, plowing its way through the salt air spray of the rough north seas. It's all in the genes, I guess.

Like moths to a flame, the drifting smell of chargrilled meat had lured some extra mouths for some supper. Oochie for one had hobbled in from the campsite pushing a decrepit looking wheelchair in which sat (and I really don't mean to sound callous), the even more decrepit figure of old Harry Pickles. I'd never seen him in person before, and I couldn't believe how old and physically frail he looked in comparison to Joe, who, give or take a year or two, was about the same age.

Joe poked around with his tongs immediately when he saw him and served up a plate of his finest cooked cuts. "Hey, hi there Harry, good to see you, old buddy. It's nice of you to come on over and join us. I know you like your meat medium rare, so get this lot down ya soldier. Can I get you a cold one to help wash it down?"

Harry lifted his hand feebly and attempted to talk. "Save you breath H. I know, half a glass of beer, *your usual*." Private Pickles grinned and nodded to the affirmative. I'm sure, if only for a second, a spark of fifty-year-old memory had just arced its way affectionately between them.

"What about you Ooch? I reckon you'd eat shit on a stick if it was free." Oochie roared with laughter at that one, as Joe piled his plate with enough meat cuts for two. "Go get some salad and a beer yourself Lieutenant Crawford, I've got better things to do right now than run around after the likes of you."

The other old soldier that had invited himself along was Wesley. I hadn't seen him around lately. His trance-like state seemed to have gotten even worse, but you could see he hadn't lost that sharp-eyed sparkle, and there was most definitely somebody still at home inside. Joe loaded Wesley's plate up too, and then dutifully helped him across to the concrete table bay where he sat him down on an end seat next to Harry Pickles.

"Hey Joe, where's little blondie?" boomed Oochie. "She's my favorite. Can't have all this meat and vittles without a good old helping of eye candy too."

"Watch it Ooch, this right here is Faye's big brother Axel, he's twice your size and might not take too kindly to a randy old—" Joe was halfway through his quip, when Oochie feigned an uppercut, right under Axel's chin.

"*Agh*, anyone as dog gone ugly as this bastard, *should* be worried about a good-looking old timer like me." This time Oochie-Cuchi nearly exploded under the power of his own bad joke, and dribbled half of his beer down the front of his beard as he did so. Then, as if mysteriously summoned by the wishes of the one-legged jokester, the thunderous sound of Faye's Martellare Angelus turned all heads towards it and its rider, as they came in fast against the last failing light of the sky.

"*It's blondie!*" cried Oochie getting all excited. "Who's that on the back behind her though?"

As Faye pulled up, I was surprised to see the passenger sitting behind her was Hamada-san, who, instead of her more usual solemn expression, had an ear to ear grin of excitement plastered right across her face.

Hamada-san not so elegantly clambered off the high, rear seat cowl of the motorcycle, and dusted herself down with her hands. She was wearing blue jeans, a checkered shirt, and a kid's cord-strung cowboy hat. If it wasn't for the fact she had the geirahöð strapped across her back, her get-up definitely made her look more like an over sixties, boot scootin' adept, instead of a high-dan, Naginatajutsu sensei.

"Where the hell did you guys come from?" asked Joe.

"Out there," Faye replied cagily.

"Grab yourself a plate darlin'. Get one for Hamada-san too, and then you can tell me *alllll* about it," Joe grinned, eager to know what they'd been up to.

"I took sensei for a ride on Hildisvíni."

"What did she think of it?"

"*Loved it!*"

"How fast did ya go?"

"I got her up to one hundred and fifty k's, she wanted to go even faster, but well, you know, it's not very safe to do that when she wasn't wearing a helmet and this motorcycle is really only designed for one."

"You can take me for a ride, *any time* you like li'l missy," blustered Oochie.

"You've been *out there* playing mounted cavalry, have you?" Joe said probing.

"Ja!"

"*Ooooh*, I love it when she goes all French," said Oochie.

Faye tapped him on the head with her paper plate. "Be quiet Oochicoochi, I speak Norwegian, I don't know any French."

"Well I'd sure be happy to—"

"That's it, Crawford, put a sock in it. Go and sit over there with Harry and Wesley will you," came Joe's stern rebuff. "Moses wept that guy can be a pain in the ass sometimes."

"There are one or two very sorry looking cactuses out there in the desert Joe," Faye said sheepishly.

"How many?"

Faye exhaled a puff of contemplation. "Maybe ten … *or twenty.*"

"That's an act of sheer, unmitigated, eco-vandalism Faye," Joe smirked teasingly.

"I know, I'm sorry, but they will grow all their arms and bits back again sometime … won't they?"

"That's cacti Faye, *cac-ti,*" interjected MacElroy, who had also been lured up out of his hole for a feed.

"Thank you Dr. MacExpert your input is most unequivocally appreciated," said Joe rolling his eyes.

"It *was* all for a good cause though Joe. Hamada-san showed me a lot about fighting on horseback, I mean on a motorcycle. If only in that one session. I can't believe she will be leaving here to catch her flight home to Japan in only three more days."

The pitch of Faye's voice sounded decidedly anxious.

"Hey, relax sweetheart, don't get upset, I couldn't give an S. H. I. T. about a bunch of frick'n cactuses. And as for Hamada-san, don't you worry yourself about *that*. I'll make sure she gets up to Puerto Penasco well on time and A.O.K."

◆

For even longer than I'd been standing near him, Dr. MacElroy had been badgering Faye's brother with an endless barrage of questions about devils and whatever else he knew regarding the ancient tunnel ways that ran underground across Europe.

Axel had been a paragon of virtue and engaged poor Eugene in conversation for a good deal longer than he needed to. I'd overheard him say that at one point when he was making his way up the long concrete staircase this morning, he'd passed by an almost circular, near collapsed cave that he thought might possibly be a chopped through section of one the ancient Sonoran passageways that he'd read about in a Svarte Kaniner transcript.

MacElroy went weak at the knees with excitement about that. Axel said under no circumstance would he go back underground at the mag-lev stop, but he had seen deep crevices in the above ground geology that most definitely would intersect at someplace with this archaic passage.

Suddenly a cheer went up, as somebody inside turned the little white lights on that edged out the shape of the building.

"Wow, I forgot about those little dinkies. Good call," said Joe in high spirits.

A pair of headlights almost went unnoticed until they grew larger down towards the roadway.

"Hey that's my truck! And within its bowels, art the prodigal son. I'd forgotten all about him too."

Vince came steaming in and pulled a half-baked attempt at a skid stop beside the driveway. He jumped out of the cab and reached over into the bed to lift something out.

"*More beer!*" yelled Oochie. "Bring me your finest ale barkeep, *immediately!*"

Vince plonked the six-pack down hard on the concrete table, knocking what was left of the beer inside Harry Pickles plastic cup all down the poor guy's pants.

"How'd you get on with little Prisciliana?" asked Joe.

"*Little* Prisciliana. That kids a full-on hellcat. From the moment I got there, she starts reading me the riot act and carrying on about 'La pena por la falta de respeto'. Whatever that means. She even threw a plastic chair at me at one point. I was ready to toss out the kegs and make a bolt for it while I was still in one piece."

"How'd ya get the six-pack?"

"Well she must've had a sudden change of heart I guess. Next thing I know she hands me the beers as 'a most cordial gift' for her new 'bestest, mejor amigo'. Vince shook his head dumbfounded. "Don't ever send me down there again, cos I ain't frick'n goin'." With that he ripped off the cap from one of the bottles and downed its contents in one.

"The road's back open then?"

"Yeah, they've laid some dumbass, pontoon bridge right across the crack. All these dickhead rubberneckers are stopping in the middle and leaning out of their windows taking selfies and shootin' videos down a black frick'n hole.

"I did see Juan-Carlos down there though, you know, Lil' Pepe's brother who's in the highway patrol. He told me about these two, fat little gringo kids they found wandering around, both balling their eyes out. It seems their olds had been eaten last night when they parked their van in the desert. When their campsite got hammered, these two kids were both fast asleep in those pull-down bed things. As the van started shaking, the beds slammed shut and hid them safely inside the wall space. Juan-Carlos reckoned that the two little turds didn't seem all that upset about what had happened to their folks. What had really set the waterworks flowing was finding that their gaming tablets, left on charge downbelow, had been totaled when the monsters got inside and smashed the place up."

"And what kind of state were the Jupiters in?" asked Joe.

"Who?"

"The parents."

"Well, going by what Juan-Carlos said. All of the woman's flesh had been stripped to the bone, and the skeleton left lying right across the campfire. At first they couldn't find any trace of her husband, until they followed these drag marks out into the desert. The only thing that they found left of the dude was a fingerless, half-eaten hand, bouncing up and down on a rock singing show tunes. Far out huh!"

A grimace fell on Joe's face. "I did try to warn him … I did."

◆

Joe was sitting on the couch drinking his morning brew and looking at a pamphlet. "Hey Wolfman, what do ya reckon to this?"

"What is it?" I said taking the little glossy brochure from his hand.

"The Western and Northern Carriage Company." He stretched out the words in a clear and silver-tongued manner.

I looked immediately at the pictures, which were impressive color photographs of those big old, 1960's diesel locomotives. The ones with the creepy, window slit eyes that stare blankly out into the distance. On reading some of the text, I learned it was only the outer steel shells of these brutish contraptions that had been left untouched. The engines, undercarriages, and interiors had all been stripped out, allowing each gigantic machine to be re-engineered, re-fitted, and transformed completely into an ultra-luxurious, fast-speed, highway mode of transport.

"Are these…?"

"Oh, come on Wolf, don't tell me you ain't ever heard of the *Moonlight Express*."

Now that name *did* ring a bell. I'd met this guy once in Vegas, who told me how he lived somewhere near Two Guns, Arizona, beside a long, straight stretch on interstate 40. He said it wasn't uncommon at night to see a Moonlight Express, all lit up like a Christmas tree, clocking one hundred and ninety miles per hour, as it sped eastward, out across the desert, on route to either Albuquerque or Santa Fe.

"Do you remember that old rhyme?" Joe asked curiously, before reciting it:

When the money was gone,
as the booze took its toll,
and she knew that he couldn't care less.
She packed up her things,
said her goodbyes,
and then left on the Moonlight Express.

"No."

Joe shook his head in disgust. "These little beauties have been around for near on twenty years now. They're the latest mode in *contemporary carriage evolution*, as they call it here, from the Western and Northern stables. Their lineage stretches all the way back to the wild west days. Back in the 1860s they started out as a single stagecoach operation that ran out of St. Paul, Minnesota," Joe said knowledgeably, filling me in on their history.

"They're all the rage with the trendoids now though. Movie stars, rappers, ball players, big moolah earners like that. The perfect, non-stop way to travel interstate, from a game, or a party or a gig. I've heard these babies are so luxurious inside, they make the old stretch limos look full-on, bargain-basement. Which one do you think I should book then, Wolf?" He sounded completely serious, so I took another look at the brochure. In total, there were four of these carriages in the Western and Northern fleet. They all looked pretty impressive, and had bold names like *Arrow, Goliath, Street Gang* and *Lion*.

"I dunno, what about Goliath?" It was all much of a muchness to me. That one had a slightly more bulbous front than the others, and I liked how its chrome-paneled sides sat boldly against the dark, red, roof paint.

"*Can't have it*. Completely booked up for the next three months. I looked them up on the web last night."

"Street Gang then?"

"Nope, that one's unavailable *'till next frick'n June*. I'm guessing all the well-heeled, wannabees like being seen struttin' in and out of that one, because of its *bad-ass* name." Joe made a feeble, impromptu attempt at some, hip-hopper hand signs. "Luckily, there's been a last-minute cancellation, so I'm getting Arrow."

"Where are you going?"

"Not for me Wolfman, it's for Hamada-san. She'll be flying back to Japan out of Puerto Penasco in a few days time, so I thought considering all she's done for our girl, the least I could do was show some appreciation and help send her off with a little bit of style. Trouble is, even a three hundred-mile, one-way trip on one of these beauties is gonna cost me a shit load of money, and what with Faye's twenty-fifth birthday party coming up in a couple o' weeks, I dunno how the hell I'm going to pay for it all."

"Faye's having a party?"

"Yeah, I asked her if she wanted one at the barbeque last night. Poor kid looked horrified when I suggested it. Kept trying really hard not to offend me or seem ungrateful. You know what she's like. Eventually after a bit of persuasion, she did kind of warm to the idea. *'As long as it was small, and absolutely nothing at all like Vince's.'* Oh yeah, and the other proviso is that it 'has to be classy'."

Joe chuckled affectionately, thinking just how top-shelf *everything* to do with Faye was compared to the likes of us.

◆

As it roared unexpectedly in from the road, the sound of the Martellare turned both our heads. I assumed it was Faye but was surprised to see that it was being ridden by Axel instead.

"Yeah I saw him take off north, about twenty minutes ago," Joe mentioned soberly.

Axel pulled right in beside us and turned off the engine. "Oooh, this is such a *nice* machine."

It didn't take long before they both started talking all technical about gear shift times, torque to weight ratios, and stuff like that. My ears heard nothing but babble.

"How was your sleep in that old bullet trailer Axel?"

Axel looked rueful. "Thank you, but it needs a lot of fresh air. It stinks."

"You're not wrong there boy," chuckled Joe. "I don't think anyone's even set foot inside that thing for two or three years."

"I bunked in with Freya, we had a lot to talk about anyway," said Axel.

Joe changed the subject. "I think we'd better rustle up some more clothes for this man too. I forgot he's only got the clothes he's wearing. We've got those Italian shirts, but I'll see if the boys can give him some of their stuff. Well at least Charlie anyway."

Axel nodded appreciatively. "But no old underpants please. I think I'd rather go commando."

Joe agreed wholeheartedly. "Are you still sweet with taking MacElroy off on his little adventure?" Joe filled me in. "After you left last night, Eugene was like a dog with a bone, hassling poor Axel with every frick'n conceivable question he could conjure up about that underground passage he said he might have seen. MacElroy kept going on and on about it. In the end, just to shut him up, I told Axel he was more than welcome to take the truck and lose the annoying little bastard somewhere out in the desert if he felt so inclined."

Joe turned back to Axel. "You can wear those grey coveralls hanging up in the garage for now if you like. They've just been washed, and there's a pair of work boots—" Joe stopped mid-sentence, as the doctor himself came bursting around the corner.

"*Hi, hi, hi,* how are you this morning Axel? … Hello Joe, hello Wolf," MacElroy added quickly after not even noticing us in his excitement.

"Loose the pith helmet Eugene, this isn't darkest Africa you know," Joe said critically. "I've got a boonie in the garage. You can take that."

"Thanks Joe, but I like the pith helmet, and I'm all packed up and ready to go." MacElroy was wearing a pair of great grandpa's leather ammunition bags on his chest, stuffed with far more crap than he needed. The ridiculous, khaki shorts hanging loose from his waist, made him look like an absolute bozo.

"Oh boy, an actual archaic, pre-Colombian, underground tunnel system. I've been waiting decades for the chance to go down and snoop around inside one of those," said Eugene excitedly.

"Maybe, maybe," Axel said tentatively. "I never said that there was a definite way to get down there from the surface. So please Eugene, don't set your hopes too high. There might be absolutely nothing to see back there at all."

"Oh, you're en Svart Kanin, a *black rabbit*. If anyone can find a way down there it's you Axel."

I got the impression Axel might be having second thoughts, but he was obviously a man of his word, and seemed resigned to go.

◆

Charlie got out of the pickup, which he had fetched from around the corner. As Faye climbed down from the passenger side, her hair was blowing all over the place with the strength of the cool morning breeze.

"Sexy overalls," she winked, teasing her brother.

"Yeah, if you roll 'em half down, and stick out your pecks—" Charlie said jestfully. He noticed we were all waiting for the rest of the joke, but there wasn't one, so he made some kind of incoherent mumble, and then got all shitty.

Faye pushed the Martellare into the garage and left it under the watchful eyes of Gutteka and Jenteka.

"Give Eugene his sandwich at lunchtime Axel, and then make sure he takes his nap," said Joe, picking on the hapless doctor. "Here's a machete, it might come in handy," Joe continued, casually lobbing it onto the seat. "Take my cell phone too, doesn't always work out there in the sticks, but it's better than nothing."

The expression on Axel's face was the same as when he saw Joe's computer mouse, but he took it with grace and leapt up into the cab.

"There's a six shooter, taped beneath the dashboard as well," Joe whispered through the open window. "But I didn't tell you that. Keep your speed down to what the signs say. If you stay below the limit, highway patrol cars don't even notice an old shit box like this."

Eugene was sitting there like a kid heading off on a school excursion. On the other hand, Axel didn't look all that keen. He gave a thumbs up, rolled his eyes resignedly, and then they drove off.

◆

I'd spent all morning in the garage, either helping Joe, or just watching Charlie, as he worked on the modifications, he was doing to Faye's Martellare.

The makeshift cruise control mechanism had now been replaced with a real one. Simply click the throttle forward, and the motorcycle would keep going, hands free, at whatever speed it was locked on.

Another radical thing that Charlie had done was install a holster type device for the little G-G, which allowed the weapon to tuck neatly into an air scoop channel on the right-side fairing. The perfect quick grab weapon tucked neatly down beside the rider's knee. Charlie had modified the one thousand round, ammo belt too. It now ran, virtually unnoticeable, from a more efficient bullet box that he'd attached up under the seat.

Faye was thankful, but said she wasn't all that convinced about the use of ballistic weapons anyway. Although they were obviously effective against the devils, she emphasized that she was reluctant to use them herself.

"When the dritt *really* hits the fan, I know intuitively, that the use of such weapons will have only a limited effect, and it would be very unwise for me to depend on them," Faye said, trying to sound diplomatic.

Charlie didn't seem the slightest bit peeved. It was hard to pick his mood at the best of times.

"Yeah, maybe," said Joe playing devil's advocate. "But the little G-G packs away so neat and clean don't you think? Trust me, 'the pointy-stick' has most definitely got its uses, but this little fire dragon will come in handy sometime, I can assure you."

Something else that Joe and Charlie had been working on together was a full-face motorcycle helmet with an added two-way radio system and a high definition, micro camera that sat almost unnoticed on top.

Shintarō and Kiko had jazzed it up even more, with some really wild artwork. They'd divided it into two separate halves with a yin and yang line down the center. Shintarō had taken the black side, and painted a large, white, skull face in the middle. On the white side, Kiko had balanced it perfectly, with a full bloom chrysanthemum flower in black.

Faye said it looked *wonderful*, and thought it represented at least one or two of the different dualities that were going on around here.

The hours raced by, and we had a fun time testing out the camera and the radio. Amazingly the sound and video worked perfectly, and it was Joe himself who made the point that it was an "absolute frick'n miracle," considering it was all connected up to his old, antique computer.

"Don't know about you guys, but I'm starving," said Charlie, patting down a rumbling stomach. The rest of us agreed, so post wash up, we were all in the kitchen diving into the fridge and the cupboards for last night's leftover cold cuts, bolillo rolls and whatever else we could lay our hungry little hands on. Joe was sinking his teeth into his very first bite, when the phone in his next-door office rang.

"Aww Faawwk!" Came an indignant, full-mouthed response. He plonked the roll down on the bench top and walked abruptly through to go answer it. Faye, Charlie, and I paid no attention as we were much more concerned with our lunch.

Not twenty seconds later Joe came running back. *"Forget that, quick, everyone back in the garage – NOW!"*

This didn't sound good.

"That was Axel. Him and Eugene are under attack. The phone connection was useless, but I got the gist of it."

Faye gasped horrified and demanded more information.

"Girl, get suited up. Charlie, you get the bike ready. All I could make out from what your brother said was that they were about one hundred yards north of where they'd left the truck beside the road. Something about rocks and a cave, and a swarm of frick'n reptile-like creatures. So you know what *that* means. *Okay let's move it, let's go, go, go!"*

Joe had transformed instantly back into staff sergeant mode, and Charlie and Faye moved as fast and efficiently as a well drilled, motor sport pit crew.

In no time at all, Faye had zipped herself into the white racing leathers and buckled up the motorcycle boots. Once done, she scrunched her hair back tight, and then pulled the helmet down securely over her head. She quickly slipped on her gloves as Charlie slung the quick-release strap that held the geirahöð, over her helmet and across her back. Only then did she climb onto Hildisvíni, who sat impatiently growling and straining to go.

"Give it some stick, like you did against Lucien, and you'll be there in fifteen, tops. *And be careful,"* Joe added in a tone of fatherly concern.

Faye nodded once in reply, and then screamed out at the top of her lungs, *"THORRRRRRRRRR! … RIDE WITH ME NOW!"* She let go the clutch and tore off like one of his thunderbolts.

Man, she was pumped.

Turning around, I saw Joe dashing back out of his office carrying a shotgun and a rifle and a couple o' boxes of shells.

Both doors of the Ouroboros were open, and Charlie was sitting in the driver's seat, running through what looked like some kind of pre-launch checklist. Joe placed the guns butts down into the passenger side footwell and wedged the barrels firmly up against the back of the seat.

As soon as Charlie had finished, he bailed out quickly so his old man could jump in his place. Joe fired up the ignition, and the full boom roar of the V8 engine hurled out a blast wave that reverberated around every wall in the place.

"Do you want me to come with you?" I said without even thinking.

"No Wolf, you stay here with Charlie boy ... but thanks all the same."

Joe closed the door, gave a snap thumbs up, and with a tire screeching wheel spin, launched the Ouroboros 359 away, leaving nothing but a belching cloud of acrid exhaust smoke behind him.

◆

Charlie and I ran back into Joe's office and manned the desk-top control center immediately.

"*Come in Ice Maiden, come in Ice Maiden, this is Mad Hatter, do you copy?*"

"*Reading you 5 by 5 Mad Hatter, I copy.*"

"*I don't have eyeball Ice Maiden, but go drop the hammer girl, I'm coming in fast on your 6.*"

"*10-4 Mad Hatter, over and out.*"

"Don't ya love all that voice procedure chatter," I said excitedly to Charlie.

"Ah, that's all *Bravo-Sierra* Wolfman, they're just making it up."

The feed from the helmet started streaming back in showing us exactly what Ice Maiden could see.

She was shifting alright. As Faye started laying the bike over left and right, going through the bends, I couldn't believe it. Her riding was ten times more exciting than some make believe, CGI video game.

Charlie clicked on his mic. "*Drop it down Ice Maiden, drop it down, your kph is hittin' 300. If you maintain that speed too long, you'll end up cooking the engine. Keep a little bit back in reserve.*"

"*Wilco! ... Any word from Axel?*"

"*That's a negative Ice Maiden.*"

"*10-4 Big Dain.*"

With that directive Faye eased off the speed for about ten seconds, but that must have seemed like an eternity right now, and soon the gauge started cranking back up.

"*Holy shit!* That blur that just shot by on the left was the truck checking station," Charlie looked at me in astonishment. "At this speed she'll be there in less than four."

All of a sudden, the pictures started bouncing up and down as if someone was shaking the daylights out of the screen. Charlie and I immediately felt the tremor ourselves, although luckily for us it was only a murmur, as the real epicenter had obviously come from somewhere further up north.

"That's all we need right now," came an enlivened Mad Hatter's voice, completely devoid of radio procedure.

"Come in Ice Maiden, do you copy, this is Mad Hatter, over."

"5-5 Mad Hatter, it's only by the grace of Óðinn, I'm still hanging on, that last quake almost sent me flying. … over."

"Yeah well don't get too comfortable sweetheart, off to your left, there's an opening fissure running your way and it's heading towards you pretty damn quick. It's on a direct course with that sharp right-hand turn in the road up ahead of you. If it gets there first it'll cut you off from the northern part of the road. I can see it moving about half a mile ahead of me … Smoke it Ice Maiden, that things coming in FAST!"

"10-4 Mad Hatter," Faye acknowledged as she zipped her head around swiftly to see what was coming.

Faye straightened back up and floored the machine to within an inch of its life.

"This is insane, *she's red-lining it, she's doing* three hundred and twenty ks!" Charlie gasped, with his eyes glued hard to the screen. Even through the radio linkup, we could hear the screaming wail from the overtaxed engine.

Ice Maiden took another quick look. The oncoming chasm was now only a bike or two lengths from her wheels.

"Oh my god," I cried out in panic. "That thing is right on her. It's gonna take her and swallow her whole!"

Suddenly the image dropped hard to the right, as Faye dropped the bike impossibly fast into the turn.

"She's made it. *SHE'S frick'n MADE IT!"* cheered Charlie, going berserk.

After straightening back up, Faye looked around to see exactly where the crack was. *"Oh no!"* came her horrified call. *"Its direction must have been heading straight down the middle of the road, and now it's charging right on my tail!"*

A brilliant white flash sent the screen pixels flaring. For a millisecond we saw the image of a car parked right across the road up ahead.

"Big Dain, Mad Hatter, I've got incoming. Somebody's taking shots at

me, I'm being ambushed!" A second even brighter flash exploded and completely snowed out the screen. *"Look*, it's that Baybecker. It's those two asshole agents," growled Charlie as soon as the feed came back online.

Faye kept right on her course.

"Start weaving Ice Maiden, start weaving, I estimate those hostiles at five hundred yards and closing." As Charlie spoke, the image on the screen began wobbling drunkenly, from left to right as she rode in the manner he said.

"That's good, now reach down for the little G-G's hand grip and arm it by flicking the green switch on."

"NO!" Ice Maiden screamed back defiantly. *"I won't kill them, I won't!"*

"Tell me she's joking," Charlie mumbled under his breath.

As Ice Maiden drew closer to her adversaries, she took another urgent glimpse at the crack. No words were needed, it was still there, right behind her, surging on relentlessly like doom's lapping tongue at her heels.

Faye was taking heavy flack. Thankfully, the incompetence of the shooters had saved her from being injured.

Crossing the two-hundred-yard line, she abandoned her evasive maneuvers and charged boldly straight at them. As the camera view sharpened, we could see the two demented morons, bouncing around on top of their vehicle like a couple of over-excited baboons. Travers was standing on the trunk, blasting away wildly with a pump action shotgun. His head was aqua-blue. *Literally.* He had one of those full face, compression bandage things on (post falcon mauling) which made him look even more psychotic than he already was. Likewise, Martindale was doing his bouncy, stooping thing, shooting wildly with a 12-gauge from his central perch on the roof.

"Use the gun Ice Maiden, use the gun Ice Maiden," Charlie repeated in a calm and monotone voice. *"Use the gun Ice Maiden, the closer you get, the easier a target you'll be."*

I flinched involuntarily as an on-target flash from a gunshot blast seemed to shoot its way straight through the screen.

Faye cried out in pain. She'd been hit.

"Use the gun Ice Maiden, use the gun."

"AAAAAAGGHH!" A defiant scream shrieked back through the radio. But there was something in the tone of the voice that signified that Faye was no longer out there alone.

We could see in the Martellare's mirrors that the fast, running crack was only inches away from her wheels.

"This is madness," cried Charlie, *"What the hell is she waiting for?"*

Then, with only moments left until she reached their position, Faye pulled out the little G-G, flicked it to green, and unleashed it's six bar-reled, one hundred rounds per second barrage directly towards them.

Well, not *exactly*. The shooting swathe had been well aimed and quite surgical. The intentional target seemed to be the entire strip between the doors and the roof line. Anything made of metal was vir-tually gone, and the pulverized windows had now turned to twinkle. Amazingly I think Faye still had some sway over the War Goddess, as miraculously the goons were both still alive and staggering around on the roof. Even so, they both looked pretty hammered, Travers made a giddy, disorientated shuffle sideways, and then tripped head over heels off the back. Martindale, still in the hunt, stepped toward the edge to take another shot. As he did so, the sinewy thread of the last remaining support column collapsed, and the entire roof section buckled like a ramp sending the unfooted idiot on a downward slide directly into the path of the oncoming motorcycle. Ice Maiden rode straight up his front like a launch pad, as he slipped out of sight down the crack. It was just as Hildisvíni took to the air, that I noticed a gun flash shoot out from where Travers was standing off screen.

"Look out Fa—" I yelled.

She was beyond quick, before I'd even managed to get all the words out, I saw the swirl of the geirahöð cut him down, accompanied by a loud and unnerving scream. Faye landed back on the ground and charged on ahead as if nothing had even happened. I could see in her side mirrors that the pulverized Baybecker had vanished.

"Come in Big Dain, do you copy, this is Ice Maiden."

"Reading you 5-5 Ice Maiden, I copy."

"I'm clear. The fissure has gone straight by. That thing was REALLY starting to piss me off!"

Charlie laughed with relief.

"Any updates from Axel?"

"That's a negative, but your ETA is now less than one minute. What's your status Ice Maiden, have you taken a hit?"

"Affirmative, a pellet or two winged my thigh, but I don't think it's too serious."

"Hey, Mad Hatter here. Do you copy? What's going on? Stupid radio

cut out on me a while back, I hope I ain't missing out on any action. I'm creeping along in the dirt trying to get around that crack so I can get my wheels back onto the ro—"

"Oops! The old man's radio's gone kaput again."

"*Come in Big Dain. I've arrived at Joe's truck, but there's no sign of Axel or Eugene,*" yelled Faye urgently.

"*Ride one hundred yards north, Ice Maiden, and look for rocks with some kind o' cave.*"

Faye picked her way impatiently through the rough terrain until it became impossible to ride any further. Eventually she parked the bike in frustration, and hurriedly took off on foot.

"*Ice Maiden, over on your right, what's all that stuff on the ground?*" Once again, I should have kept quiet, as it was clear she'd already seen it.

"Devils … devil bodies," Faye said soberly.

"*God there are dozens of them, that disgusting oily, black blood is everywhere.*" Faye followed the body trail over towards a mass of rocks.

"*AXEL! EUGENE! HVOR ER DU? WHERE ARE YOU? AXEL! … AXEL!*"

"*Eesh*, that girl's she's got a pair o' lungs on her," Charlie winced at the feedback squealing out of the speakers.

"*We're over here.*" An almost inaudible cry could be heard coming from outside the helmet.

Faye turned her head in the direction of Axel's voice.

"*AXEL!*" screamed Faye, as she pulled off the helmet and dropped it hurriedly on the ground and ran to his aid.

Luckily, although it was now on its side, the camera had landed still pointing more or less in the right direction. They were down in a tiny open gap between a boulder and a rock face. We could see by the frantic way Faye was crouching down in front of them that things weren't looking too good. But the longer we watched, it became obvious that it wasn't her brother who was in trouble, but rather the unconscious body of Dr. MacElroy who was the object of their desperate attempt to render some kind of improvised first aid.

"What's happened Charlie?"

"Looks like something pretty serious to me."

Just then Axel picked Eugene up as best as he could and tried to move him clear of all the devil bodies lying scattered around the rock face.

"Oh no, no," gasped Charlie turning deadly serious. "Those fucking monsters have torn off half of his leg."

Faye raced back to the helmet, picked it up, and then started speaking.

"Big Dain, we are taking Eugene down to Joe's truck. We've applied a tourniquet to his leg, but he's still bleeding very badly and needs to get to a hospital immediately. If Joe turns up—"

"No problem there darlin'," cut in the big fella, materializing right out of nowhere, as he scrambled onto the scene across some rocks. "Forget that old truck, I've got a two hundred miles per hour ambulance parked down there. Let's go pack old Eugene carefully inside it, and I promise I'll get him into the hospital at Nogales before he even wakes up."

27

Black Tie and Tinfoil

As we gobbled down our breakfast, Charlie and I filled Axel in on everything that had happened since he'd driven off yesterday with MacElroy. We watched the entire recording from Faye's helmet cam twice, and then replayed all of the best bits, at least a dozen times over.

Axel was horrified, not only finding out that his sister had been shot at by a couple of gun-toting psychopaths, but more so that she'd been hit, and hadn't even told him. He just assumed that all of the blood on her leathers was from Eugene's terrible leg wound.

"*Now* I know why she went straight over to the Indian camp when we got back. I slept in the other trailer last night, and I haven't seen her since."

As disturbing as all that was, another aspect of Faye's ride that completely bewildered Axel, was how on earth had she managed to get the Martellare around that sharp right-hand turn, without dropping through the gears and slashing down her speed. He was adamant that it was utterly impossible and defied every known law of mechanical physics. Axel put it down simply to the benevolent hand of the thunder god Thor, which really didn't seem too farfetched, considering that Faye was the vassal for a kindred Nordic goddess.

It was right on noon when Joe arrived back from Nogales. Even though he'd phoned in late last night to say that Dr. MacElroy had been operated on and that his condition was stable, it was only now that we got to learn all the details.

The most upsetting part was hearing that Eugene had lost his foot and most of his right leg up to the knee. Joe said he'd seen him briefly again this morning, and even though he was still doped up and very well aware of what had happened, he sounded surprisingly chipper and was being incredibly philosophic about the whole thing.

"Wow, he *sure* was singing your praises Axel," Joe declared with delight. "He reckoned you took on all those devils single handed with that machete. And I quote: *"He stood and fought as boldly as Heracles against the multi-headed Hydra,"* Joe chuckled teasingly, making Axel cringe with embarrassment.

"I'm so thankful you put it in the pickup Joe, if you hadn't there's no way on earth I'd be standing here now."

Suddenly the office door creaked open and Faye stepped in from the outside wearing her country farm girl meets Viking goddess dress and boots.

"How's your leg Faye?" I asked, pleased that I'd gotten in first.

"It's fine, thank you. I was lucky, it was only a glancing graze rather than a penetration wound … it certainly bled a lot though."

I was listening, but I couldn't take my eyes off her hair. She must have washed it again with that super strong Indian stuff. It hung straight and thick, like bleached out straw, from beneath Joe's hat which sat low on her head just above her eyes. She looked brilliant.

"Okay," Joe said keenly. "First up, what happened when you got out of the truck Axel? I get the feeling that I'm the only stooge around here who still doesn't know the whole story?"

"Hah, wait 'till you see the home movies pops," chuckled Charlie.

"You taped it? Good man Chucky boy … get that up on screen *now*, I wanna see it."

Axel looked momentarily over at Faye, who had sat herself down in Joe's swivel chair and rolled herself away from his desk. He turned back to me and made a wincing face that suggested she was definitely in some kind of a mood.

"Well, I pulled over at a spot where the striation patterns in the rock face looked like it might be a good place to start hunting around for a way to get ourselves down further into the geology. We'd only walked some sixty or so meters up a gradual slope when that earthquake struck. It didn't last long but it must have stirred up a nest of those creatures."

"We call 'em devils," Joe said matter of factly.

"Well these devils came charging towards us from everywhere."

"Out of the ground?"

"Possibly, I don't know, they just seemed to appear."

"Scaly frick'n bastards," snarled Joe angrily. "So, what happened to MacElroy?"

"It was obvious we had no chance of getting back to the pickup, or any real hope at all of fighting them off. All we could do was find a hole or somewhere extremely narrow to crawl into and try and keep them out with the machete. It was really as desperate as that."

"How was Eugene handling it?"

"When we reached that tight little crevice between the rock face and the bolder, I tried to get him to slip inside first while I held them off with the blade. But he wouldn't go. Instead he pulled out all of these golf ball sized packets of powder from his old ammunition pouches and started hurling them at the devils like a man possessed. I thought he'd gone completely insane and was trying to fend them off with flour balls or sugary snacks. Although I must admit, whatever that powder was, it *did* seem to react adversely on the skin of those creatures, very much like sea salt does to slugs and snails."

"Sodium fluoride … it's Eugene's secret ingredient. The hand grenade, splatter balls are a new one on me though, he kept them pretty quiet. I guess 'Big Bertha', that hand cannon contraption he made, just wouldn't fit in the truck," chuckled Joe. "Then what happened?"

"When he tried to squeeze himself in, after the powder bombs had run out, he got stuck. Those old, leather pouches got jammed between his chest and the rocks. I had to think fast, believe me those things were right there on top of us."

"What did ya do?"

Axel's face turned suddenly white, and his expression forlorn. "I dove through his legs and tried pulling him down from below. Please, believe me, there was *nothing else* I could have possibly done."

"*Woh, woh*, relax, take it easy there, tiger. We *KNOW*, you did your ABSOLUTE best. He's a bit of a green horn our Eugene. He'd be a saucer o' cat food by now if it weren't for you. Please, go on."

"Well he finally gave way and came crashing down on top of me, but those devils had locked their fangs deeply into one of his legs, it was truly, truly horrible, his screaming was—"

"How'd you get 'em off him?"

"Sheer luck I suppose. Somehow, I managed to pull him further inside with one hand, while I used the machete to hack away at the creatures with the other. It was so cramped, and there was so much noise, the devils were screeching, Eugene was screaming, and everything was echoing around like crazy. But then this other almost inaudible sound started building up outside as well, it sounded like—" Axel sat motionless as he searched his mind for the word. "I don't know, maybe a phasing drone or an electrical type noise, it was so hard to tell. It only lasted for a minute or two, and then it was over. When I chanced a quick look, only the dead were still lying outside on the ground, unbelievably the rest of those things had all gone."

"*Hmm*, well whatever it was, you're a frick'n champion in my book Axel, you did good," Joe said reassuringly.

"Well I'm sure we all wish MacElroy a speedy recovery," Charlie said seeing his chance. "I've got stuff to do, so grab yourself some popcorn old man, and settle back comfortably and watch the movie." He turned and moseyed off back to the garage.

Faye, who'd been sitting quietly, swiveling from side to side in the chair, got up soon after, took the ten-gallon hat from her head and placed it gently back onto Joe's as if she were crowning a king.

◆

The day of Hamada-san's departure arrived. For the past two days, from sunup 'til dusk, Faye had been honing her naginata skills with her tireless sensei, who's priceless tuition had now, sadly for all of us, come to an end. This evening was the time for her departure, and there was a hive of frantic, last minute activity around the place, mostly from Kiko and Shintarō who would be accompanying her as far as Puerto Penasco to see her fly off.

"I can't wait to see the look on everyone's face when they get a load of the Moonlight Express," Joe said with a chuckle. "We're the only ones, Wolfman, who know that the Arrow is coming."

Without saying anything, I handed Joe two gold coins. I'd decided earlier that it was the right thing to do. It was only money, and the poor guy really needed some help with this surprise goodwill gesture for Hamada-san, let alone footing the bill for Faye's birthday party as well.

"That's cool, just use it. It's all for a good cause."

"Thanks Wolf… thank you very much," Joe seemed really touched.

Eugene had come back that morning too. He'd gotten a lift down with a friend of Charlie's who was heading our way. He'd brought him down in his old J-Rider station wagon which fortunately for MacElroy, had buckets and buckets of room.

Years ago, he would have stayed in hospital for a week at least, but nowadays times had changed and very few places could offer that luxury. He said he'd almost decided to go back to the states, but with Faye's birthday looming he was quite adamant that he wanted to stay. Joe reckoned that the premium gold medical insurance cover MacElroy had, was "the envy of all mere mortals in the western world", so the hor-rifying problem of paying the medical expenses seemed, astonishingly, to be of little concern.

◆

Faye was bouncing back and forth, fussing over Eugene, who had been loaded into the spare wheelchair that belonged to the affectionately named "campsite cripples", and trying to sort out Kiko who was totally unorganized and acting like such a little drama queen you'd think it was her that was permanently leaving.

As evening drew near, Hamada-san quietly, and almost unnoticed, dragged her single, little wheeled travel bag out from the motel room across to the concrete picnic table and sat there just waiting in silence. One by one everybody started to appear and soon, a little throng of well-wishers had come to say their goodbyes.

When we were all there, Hamada-san asked Axel in Japanese if we wouldn't mind standing together for one group photo. She seemed very shy about it, but Axel was such an old smoothie and gladly organized everybody to stand up against The Alamo wall for the picture. He even grabbed a passing Tisac to take the shot so Hamada-san herself would be included.

We were *all* in it – Joe, me, Charlie, Faye, Axel, Eugene (sitting up front in his wheelchair) Hamada-san, Kiko and Shintarō, Mr. and Mrs. Eduardo, Sacramento and Oppuam. Even Vince and Oochie, who'd both turned up at the last-minute thinking there was a feed happening, were there as well. Hamada-san did that very grateful Japanese bowing thing and told Axel she'd send us all a copy soon, when she'd returned to Japan.

It was soon after nightfall when Joe pointed down towards the roadside. In the darkness, I saw a dim, slow pulsing amber light that somehow seemed to hypnotically beckon you over towards it. "That'll be the Moonlight Express," said Joe. "Better start saying our goodbyes."

One by one, Hamada-san clasped everybody's hands, shook them briefly and gave a little bow. Saying her farewells to Joe, she bowed a little longer and thanked him in Japanese for all his kindness. Kiko was interpreting but it really wasn't necessary.

Last in the line was Faye. The rest of us had mostly moved slightly away now, as it was obvious by the way they had bowed their heads down together and embraced each other so gently around the neck, that this was a personal and heartfelt moment for the both of them. As much as she tried to retain a modicum of formality, Hamada-san capitulated and threw her arms around Faye in a deeply affectionate manner. When she pulled back, she took something made of fabric from her pocket and presented it to Faye with a deep and most courteous bow of her head.

"What is it?" I asked Joe curiously.

"It's a tenugui, a kind o' cotton head scarf worn by martial artists."

This one was deep green with white Japanese brushed characters written down its length.

Kiko began speaking in English and relayed the words of her grandmother to Faye. "She wishes that you take special note of the inscription, on this, her own personal tenugui. Please remember these words blonde haired Tomoe Gozen, and no one will ever subdue or defeat you. *'Strike swiftly. Strike hard. Strike clever'*. Hamada-san has also asked me to tell you that even though you are not Japanese, she says that you are by far the most extraordinarily gifted practitioner of Naginatajutsu that it has ever been her privileged to teach. Even though being so tall and unorthodox it has very often made her head spin."

Kiko's face shone brightly with a rapturous smile.

Faye then responded in kind, by handing Hamada-san what looked like a plain white handkerchief, which, when unfolded, held inside a pencil thin, eighteen-inch braid of her long golden hair, held secure at each end by silver threads. Hamada-san nodded her head in deep gratitude, smiled thankfully, and then began to cry with unabashed emotion.

Both Faye and Hamada-san bowed long and respectfully towards each other for one last time, and then walked arm in arm affectionately down towards the roadway.

◆

"Holy hell, that thing's big," gasped Vince, gazing awestruck at the size of the Arrow. "How many wheels has it got?"

"Thirty-two," answered Joe confidently. "And each and every one is a road hugging fat-boy. Once she heads off it'll cut back inland and then crank up the speed heading north along highway 15 to Santa Ana, where she'll hang a left towards Caborca on highway 2, and then plow straight on north west all the way into Peurto Penasco. This baby won't stop for *NOTHING* the whole frick'n way."

"What about cops and red lights?" I said being a smartass.

"Don't matter, red lights are all programmed and synced at highway central, as to when these ironclad juggernauts are coming. And as for the cops, well, they're all sweet if you know what I mean. Yeah, some idiot took a pot shot at Goliath with a rocket propelled grenade once, can you believe that?"

"What happened?"

"Nothin', just bounced right off, didn't even scratch the paintwork."

"Far out."

Our whole little group had walked down to the roadway to see Hamada-san off, and to take a closer look at the Arrow, her most luxurious carriage. It was truly gigantic and appeared in the dark to be a deep ultramarine blue with a broad red line running down the side.

One loud blast from the air horn signaled it was now time to board. A single crew member, impeccably dressed in a crisp blue uniform and shiny peaked cap, unexpectedly appeared out of the small side door that had that opened up like a secret little drawbridge to collect the luggage, and politely asked, in fluent Japanese, for Hamada-san, Kiko and Shintarō to please follow him inside. We tried to sneak a look at the interior, but apart from some swish looking wall paneling and a lot of subdued, moody lighting, it was impossible to see much at all.

There was a last frenzied round of hugs and goodbyes as the three passengers walked up the ramp, which then began to rise and silently closed behind them. We all stepped back, as the low, ambient hum emanating from the stationary machine, changed dramatically when the large diesel engines fired themselves up into departure ready ignition.

"Check that out!" shouted Vince excitedly, as the whole of the massive contraption's undercarriage, began to glow eerily with a blue neon haze. Then, in fast running sequence, down the length of its tall, metal side panels, white and amber night lights came on, as well as the one enormous headlight that lit up the road ahead like daylight, for as far as the eye could see.

There was a single blast from the air horns, and amidst a departing cloud of diesel fumes and a gaggle of waving well-wishers, the Arrow sped off and was gone.

> *... She fine-tuned a goddess,*
> *and said her goodbyes,*
> *then left on the Moonlight Express.*

◆

It was early next morning when Banksie and the full contingent of dwarves pulled up noisily in their truck. The day for Faye's party was getting close and Joe had wrangled a deal with them to take care of the sound and lighting.

"Hey Banksie, will you and the four stooges shut the you-know-what up, and save all that racket for the party," berated Joe, striding out of his office wearing nothing but a pair of hiked up tighty-whities and his hat. "And don't even *think* of banging or crashing around 'till at least eight o' clock either, I've got a real frick'n headache."

I cracked up laughing as he slammed the screen door shut behind him and went back inside scratching his butt.

"Howdy Wolfman," said Banksie, seeing me sitting alone drinking a glass of juice at the concrete table. "What you doin' up at this hour anyway?"

"I do actually work, you know, and I'm always up early, when The Flying Moustache comes a-knocking."

"How 'bout some coffee?"

I just ignored him and took another sip of my juice.

"Hey Wolfman, come over here and meet the crew." I'd already met Señor Cheerful – he completely ignored me as usual, and was far too busy fiddling around in the bed of their truck with all kinds of boxes and tools.

The other three were introduced to me as Señor Funky, Señor Crazy and Señor Jazzy. Why they had adopted or been given these pseudonyms was unclear. Señor Funky did have an earring, although I was somewhat dubious as to whether or not that would have warranted him having such an illustrious title, but who knows. None of them were the slightest bit interested in knowing who I was anyway and went immediately back to sorting out all of their gear after Banksie's unwanted introductions.

Now a few minutes later, when Faye came past on her way to the kitchen, *that* was a different story entirely. All four of them, even Cheerful who had already met her, came bouncing and circling around her, grinning and ogling like the proverbial moths to a flame. So was Banksie for that matter, but he was acting like some kind of cool-headed hip cat dude.

Faye wasn't interested. Normally, despite all their inane comments and leering, she would have stopped and been all smiles and chatty. There had been a definite change in her mood and manner ever since she'd returned from yesterday's hell-ride. Whether it was anything specific, like striking down Travers with the geirahöð, or seeing his buddy slide off into the crack, I didn't know. I put it down to Freya. I think she was starting to take over more of Faye's mind and personality. I guessed only time would tell.

"*Dvergr,*" Faye whispered to me, looking unusually nervous and concerned.

"What's that?"

"Dwarves Fenrir. Four of them. They are not normal human dwarves either. Of that I am certain. I'm sure they are all above board," Faye shot a crafty squinting gaze out towards them as they went about their business. "*Hmm,* on second thoughts," Faye said suspiciously, "I bet they have come from the mines and mountains of Svartálfaheimr in the old Norse worlds. Crazy, Funky, Jazzy and Cheerful are probably only pseudonyms. I bet you their *real* names are Alfrigg, Berling, Dvalinn and Grerr. The one thing, or should I say the four things, that comes to my mind, is how Freya obtained the golden Brísingamen from the dvergr in the Eddas. There will be no repeat of those shenanigans on my watch I assure you."

She swished her hair back over her shoulder like some haughty little schoolgirl and stormed off inside towards the kitchen. I just laughed, Faye could be so unintentionally funny sometimes.

◆

Joe told me, quite off the cuff, that the party was scheduled for the coming weekend. Being a twenty-fifth birthday, traditionally everything was supposed to be silver. Faye had decided that was completely unrealistic, whereas *Tinfoil*, considering its obvious associations with our most secretive sombrero circle, would be far more appropriate, look almost as tasteful, and definitely be far easier to find and use.

Faye had given Shintarō and Kiko, the go ahead to take care of all the styling and decorations, as long as they made the whole thing look "classy and … *chic*". (In my whole life I've never understood what that word meant.)

Joe had agreed in principle to let Shintarō and Kiko decorate a few of the walls with some kind of *"Manga-skeletons meets Nordic-Vikings"* theme. (Well that was how Joe described it anyway.)

"I told them, only if you paint it *all* in acrylics. It never frick'n rains here, so if whatever they do looks like a whole bunch o' crap, at least I'll have some chance of hosing it off later." As he'd walked off to go around to the pumps, Joe turned his head back towards me. "Black Tie and Tinfoil. That's what she wants … Black Tie and Tinfoil."

Right at eight o'clock, Banksie and the dvergr moved the truck and their gear up to the rooftop and went to work immediately. It was the first I'd heard of it, but that was where the party was going to happen. The central, semicircular showroom was the obvious place for an inside dance floor, while directly outside the concertina doors, and down towards the further end of the roof, was designated the outdoor, open area for eating and drinking and partying.

Incredibly, by midday, the Four Señors had already run out all of the necessary electrical cables and wiring and were now darting around on a crisscrossing matrix of ladders and gantries they had set up, screwing in brackets and mounts in readiness for the connection of all the expensive sound and lighting equipment that they'd install on the day of the party.

Banksie pretended to be acting as foreman. He seemed perplexed as to why Faye hadn't hung around for as long as he'd hoped so he could strut his stuff and put on a show for her like the full-on poser he was.

◆

It was around four o'clock when Joe and Charlie invited me to "Get my ass around the front" and partake in a couple of late afternoon beers.

I hadn't seen Faye for hours. Charlie said that a small squad of Los Espectros Brillantes had arrived some time earlier while I'd been over at the campsite doing some chores. He reckoned they'd whisked her away in one hell of a hurry. I read the look on his face, and the shrug of his shoulders to say, "I'm not her boss or her keeper, so what the hell could I do?"

Joe, veering off on a tangent, revved himself up into one of his laughing sessions as he told us when *the seven dwarves*, as he called them, had finished their work and were ready to leave, they'd all hung around a tad too long hoping for one last gawk at our girl, while unbeknown to them, Faye and her entourage had already left the building at least an hour earlier. Joe almost cried with laughter at their hapless stupidity.

"Bunch o' deviants," came Charlie's no-frills summation.

◆

The sun was sinking low, and the blinding rays made it pointless to try and look anywhere westward. "Hear that?" asked Charlie.

"Chopper," Joe replied authoritatively.

"*Ah no shit!* I know it's a frick'n helicopter, I mean how many times do you ever hear one flying around that close to here?"

Joe listened attentively. "Probably military." We could hear it well enough alright but knowing exactly where it was amidst all the glare was impossible to tell.

Before their little tête-à-tête went any further, the point was suddenly crossed where we all just *knew* that it was unquestionably heading directly for us.

Amidst an ear splitting, cyclonic swirl of churned up sand and dirt, the sun reflecting form of a small insect like helicopter landed swiftly, not twenty yards out beyond the front of the pumps.

Against the blinding brightness, two sinister looking figures, one on either side, leapt menacingly out of the helicopter, holding what I can only describe, as some kind of hi-tech, space-age, blaster canons which were both aimed straight and threateningly towards us. "What the …?" were the only words Joe managed to say.

The two-armed men stopped ten yards apart, right behind the line of the gas pumps, their weapons trained keenly, with all of us in their sights. Nobody dared move a muscle.

Seconds later a third, unarmed figure emerged from beneath the slowly spinning rotors of the still idling chopper and headed in our direction. The two soldiers were all fitted out intimidatingly in black battle fatigues and dark, visored helmets, but this third person looked *entirely* different. He wore an impeccable white tailored suit, with an elaborate lace ruffled shirt underneath.

The man was in his thirties, tall, of medium build, and with dark straight hair that fell to his shoulders. He walked with an arrogant swagger, which, coupled with an unmistakably malevolent aura, *really* gave me the creeps.

He proceeded past his two guards and stood in the middle of the driveway for what seemed like an eternity, as if savoring our fear and giving us all adequate time to contemplate the fact that he was most probably our malign executioner. *"Look at the chopper,"* Joe said, daring to utter a whisper.

Inside the cockpit, behind the controls, was a third soldier-pilot, only vaguely visible behind the whipped-up ground surface. I also noticed twin rocket casings mounted ominously on either side of the helicopter's fuselage, with all four warheads pointing directly at us.

As the man in the white suit moved closer, the two guards crept onto the driveway, never taking their gaze from their scopes or their fingers from their triggers. The man in the white suit panned his eyes slowly across the three of us, as if to make us feel uneasy and completely demeaned. When he finally spoke, he drew his words out, long and pronounced with an old-fashioned lilt to his diction.

"I am here for the Vanadís. Bring her to me *immediately!*"

The manner of his speech was how I'd imagine a well-educated person from olden-days Europe would have sounded, maybe four or five hundred years ago.

This was most definitely Mimas.

"Ah go fuck yourself shithead," Charlie answered him back most succinctly.

The guards shuffled forward, awaiting his imminent order to kill us.

"Bring her to me *NOW!* or I will dispense with you pathetic—"

Suddenly, like a bull through a paneled-up dining room door frame, Axel burst out wielding a pair of wild west, six shooter revolvers at the ends of his outstretched arms. *KABOOM! KABOOM!* with two successive shots from each of the handguns, he blasted both of the guardsmen right in the face. They dropped like fresh felled logs to the concrete. Immediately Axel brought his hands back together and quickly fired two more shots directly at the pilot sitting behind the controls in the chopper *KABOOM! KABOOM!*

The moment Axel turned his guns towards Mimas, reality momentarily flipped into witchcraft and magic. Faye's unwanted suitor suddenly dematerialized into a spiraling zephyr and then disappeared. *Completely.* Even Joe stood agog, with his mouth hanging open and speechless.

"It's okay, it's OKAY," Axel said, trying hard to sound calm and reassuring to the rest of us. "Those three are *automata*. Robots if you like. They are not, I repeat, they are NOT real people." He placed the revolvers down on the ground and dragged the nearest "body" halfway back toward us. Tearing away the shattered visor he stuck his hand inside and yanked out a tightly coiled helix of microcircuitry.

"I've had a few run-ins with this type before. Fortunately, we now know their weak point, two or three shots, smack in the middle of their cranial CPUs. Unfortunately, that thing *there* is a much more immediate worry."

He was right. The blast from the gun shots had completely pushed the body of the helicopter's pilot away from the pedals, and now with nothing overseeing the cyclic and collective controls, it was really starting to pitch and list all over the place, about three or four feet off the ground.

Axel and Charlie ran fearlessly out towards it, armed only with the vague notion of somehow shutting the thing down permanently before it took off into the air and crashed, or fired off its rockets accidentally.

Too late. They'd only managed to get a part of the way there when the uncontrolled helicopter started listing further and further to starboard and then began walking itself drunkenly over on the tips of the still rotating but ever buckling blades towards the tall cactus wind break.

"Black Eagle down!" yelled Vince, getting his movie titles all wrong as he came charging out of nowhere to see what all the noise and the shooting was about.

The rotors had made complete chop suey out of four or five of the cactus plants, but thankfully the chopper had anticlimactically stalled on its side in the dirt and hadn't broken up or exploded. Joe immediately pulled his sergeant major's hat on again.

"Right, Axel, Charlie you two get those rockets out o' that bird now! I'm in two minds whether or not to keep 'em, but they might come in handy. Vince, you go get the tractor and chains, Wolfman, you can get the chainsaw and a broom and a shovel, that kind o' stuff, and make those cactuses, sorry, *cac-ti*, look like they've just had a bit of a haircut. That copter and our three robot friends here are all going straight down the hole boys. There's no telling who the hell knew that that thing was heading down here. I want this place looking as near as possible to normal in less than twenty. *Let's go, let's do it.*"

Even Vince jumped to it and didn't lag around asking a checklist of inane and pointless questions. "Who the hell were those guys, a will-o'-the-wisp, and three circuit-headed androids?" asked Joe, not expecting any kind of definitive answer. Well, not immediately anyway.

Once the four rockets had been carefully detached, Charlie and Axel lashed up the chains to the helicopter's skids, while Joe efficiently unfastened a good stretch of the fence wire, to allow them an easier access.

Then, after the tractor had pulled it out of the way, I got on with "Operation Cover Up". I know it wasn't as macho as the other guy's tasks, but I took it pretty seriously and I made a pretty good job of it.

"Excellent work team," came Joe's endorsement. With two minutes to spare we'd dispatched down the hole: one small attack helicopter; two Starling rockets (Joe said keeping all four was unnecessary, but we could hang onto a couple just in case); three synthetic humanoids (Vince thought it would be a hoot to keep them as driveway attendants, but that idea got knocked down immediately); two space age blaster type weapons (Joe was tempted to have a crack at bypassing their digital user recognition systems, but thought it far too risky and could only guess what kind of horrendous blow-back might befall us if they were ever discovered here); and last but not least, four and a half pieces of tree trunk sized, freshly chopped, cactus.

"Now don't go mentioning any of this to the girl okay," were Joe's last definitive words on the subject. "I think we should *all* leave that one for Axel. Anyway boy, how'd you get those two revolvers out o'... Ah don't tell me, I left the key in the frick'n lock again, yeah?"

◆

Since the incident with Mimas, Charlie was the only one amongst us who'd seen Faye at all. She'd taken to spending whole days and nights at a time out on the range with her army. Charlie said that he'd only spoken to her briefly a day or two back, when she'd come on in to pick up a few of her things, and to apologize profusely for not being around to help out with any of the preparations for her party.

He reckoned she seemed *mighty strange*, and in Charlie's own vernacular "She still looked frick'n hot, even if that goddess buddy of hers is burrowing deeper and deeper into her psyche."

◆

It was way after dark when Axel, Charlie and I drove south along some unused, desert back roads in the pickup, to try and track down Faye and see exactly what it was she was up to. We'd gotten a tip earlier from someone who'd pulled in to fill up with gas, that a massive host of eerie looking biker types had been seen heading out to a flat desert plain, somewhere north east of Bahía Kino. It took us ages to find them, but man when we did, what we saw was unbelievable.

"There she is," whispered Charlie excitedly when we spotted Faye sitting tall on Hildisvíni, up on a ridge against a clear desert sky. Alongside were gathered a host of her Lieutenant commanders, who as far as we could make out seemed to be watching some kind of mass maneuvers being conducted by an uncountable sea of Los Espectros Brillantes forces down on the flat lands below.

Even from here, some two hundred yards away, she made a most impressive and statuesque figure. I noticed she was wearing the black, haute couture coat that she'd bought in Hermosillo, its collar turned high, in stylish defiance against the winter's night air.

"Let's see if we can get a little bit closer along—" I cut my words dead, as a detachment of patrolling riders appeared unexpectedly out of nowhere. In no uncertain terms their feisty, but thankfully still self-restrained riding manner made it perfectly clear that our presence had been tolerated up until now, but that we'd outstayed our welcome, so we'd better turn right around and get out of here pronto.

"I still don't understand why you didn't hike your sorry ass out of the cab and tell those boneheads exactly what your relationship with 'super chick' is Axel?" teased Charlie. "They probably would have invited us all back over to their campsite for donuts and coffee."

We all got a laugh out of that.

◆

It was the night of Faye's party, which had been planned to coincide with the actual day of her twenty-fifth birthday.

Considering everything else that was going on, I was amazed how it had all come together so smoothly. Shintarō and Kiko had done a first-rate job fixing up the roof area and making it all fit in well with her theme. Well, that's what Joe had told me earlier. I hadn't been up there myself yet, I was saving it for a surprise.

Luis Escoto had driven down the day before yesterday, in that goofy looking pickup truck that I'd seen up on blocks in his garage. The bed was loaded high with a whole bunch of stuff, held tight beneath a khaki tarpaulin. The one thing I did see was an extra-long roll of industrial foil that was sticking out and leaning against the roof of the cab. I had visions of the whole place being covered from floor to ceiling in tinfoil, but I figured Shintarō and Kiko would come up with something a little more artistic than that and I was really looking forward to seeing it.

◆

We'd had an enthusiastic roll up that morning when the hire suit guy from Hermosillo arrived with his van full of fancy clothing.

Me, Vince, Charlie, Axel, Joe and Eugene, (plonked temporarily on the seat of his borrowed wheelchair) were all lined up keen and ready to pick out something that most suited our personal tastes. Bearing in mind of course that it had to be formal, and it also had to be classy. At one point I thought the poor clothes hire guy was going to burst into tears, when Vince started grabbing and pulling everything off of the clothes racks at once like some hyperactive nutcase. It was only the unexpected sight of Faye riding back in on her own, after one of her all-night forays with The Shining Specters, that had made him ease up and stop.

Faye looked completely exhausted. She pulled up alongside us, but stayed mounted on the idling motorcycle, mainly just to say a polite good morning and to have a brief chat with Joe and Charlie about some quirky little idea that she'd dreamt up herself for the party. Even so she had still received an ad hoc round of happy birthday wishes, and two or three congratulatory pecks on the cheek.

With a cute little bye-bye wave of her fingers, she leaned wearily forward, once again taking hold of the handlebars of the Martellare Angelus and chugged off slowly toward her trailer for a couple of hours of desperately needed sleep.

◆

My own ensemble was now complete with the addition of a pair of black drainpipe pants, a formal looking three quarter length tuxedo jacket and a matching string tie. They looked a treat and matched up fine with my embroidered red shirt and shiny polished boots. I'd spent well over an hour gawking in the mirror, honing up the high forward thruster of my near perfect, Rockabilly hairstyle.

I slid the door of the camper van closed, and headed over to the party wondering whether or not there was such a thing as arriving fashionably early?

Having almost reached the end of the wire fence, my attention focused on all of those pretty white lights that marked out the building's edges. Then unexpectedly down from the darkness, a low flying quad of squawking, black feathered birds, made a half-assed attempt to dive bomb my impeccable quiff. Horrified, I immediately did the old fingertip touch tests, but luckily, all of my painstaking hairstyle work seemed to have come through unscathed with no obvious signs of damage.

Out front of the garage I turned towards the bottom of the ramp, determined, (even though I knew it was early) to head right up and see what was happening. Up top I could hear the distant murmurs of a few people laughing and talking and what I thought were the ominous warming up cords of yet another dreaded mariachi band.

Over to my left at the concrete table, the tell-tale orange dot of someone smoking a cigarette, betrayed their unseen presence.

Three steps closer and I saw it was Vince, the glow at his lips was coming from a neatly rolled joint.

"What the hell is that thing on your head?" Vince asked.

"It's my gravity defying, deluxe, side roll special."

Vince took another drag on his joint. "Looks pretty cool dude…wanna bang on this?"

"*Uuuh*, not just now thanks, I think I'm tripping out already from this homemade Mexican hair cream. I kid you not, I just got strafed by four big black incoming birds, and *I swear to God* one of them said something to me in some odd foreign language."

Vince coughed out a lung full of inhaled smoke, and then had himself a bit of a chuckle. "Bullshit, what did it say Wolfman?"

"Like I said, it was in some weird foreign language."

"What sort of birds?"

"I dunno? What's the next one up from crows?"

"Buzzards."

"No, these were pretty much like crows, only a little bigger, and they make a loud kind o' quarking noise, you know 'QUARK! QUARK! QUARK!'"

"Man, you're fucked." Vince surmised my persona most astutely.

"*Ravens!* that's the ones I'm thinking of, yeah four talking, dive bombing ravens."

◆

At the bottom of the ramp I was surprised to see Bird's, or rather Shintarō's cousin, Galo. We shook hands warmly as he told me that he was working as the valet for any of the guests who'd be turning up in cars. And young Diego from over in the campsite, had been handpicked by Joe as his trusty, highly trained sidekick. They both looked smart wearing white cotton shirts and matching black ties.

I was halfway up the incline, cajoled to the top by the rhythmic pulse of ground-level, tube-lighting, when this skateboard type rumble came thundering up alongside of me. It was Vince, sprawled out lazily in a small, dimpled leather armchair on wheels, enjoying a push up the concrete ramp by an unfazed Galo Escoto and his highly paid assistant Diego. Vince just flipped me the bird and waved me goodbye as they passed.

"What was all that about?" I asked curious, upon reaching the roof.

"Chairlift. I thought that one up myself," Vince stated proudly. "For all of the cripples and lard asses who can't hike their fat guts up to the top. But it's mostly for any tight-dressed, nymphets who couldn't make it up there in those stupid, ten-inch-high heels. It's only right *I* should get to try it out first don't you think?"

It was only when he got out of the chair, that I got to see what Vince was actually wearing. He'd gone for a skintight pair of polka dotted pants, a square cut, silk lapeled jacket, with an electric blue shirt, and a skull toggled string tie underneath. The thing that impressed me the most though was his brand-new pair of two tone winklepicker shoes.

"Ah Vince, you're a frick'n classic … let's go get a drink."

Walking down toward the far end of the roof, where the first of the guests were already mingling, I noticed some of the party decorations that Shintarō and Kiko had come up with. In the corner, at the top of the ramp where the Fire Diamond had teetered on the wall after that very first earthquake, a large brazier made from a regular oil drum had been wrapped with the heavy, industrial tinfoil. A two-foot-long Fé rune had been cut out strategically through the metal and shone sharp and emblazoned with a bright golden flame. Hanging down from near unseen wires that zig-zagged along the length of the roof, shone a galaxy of colored paper lanterns, all glowing brightly in a multitude of different shapes and sizes. Down the far end was a fifteen-foot table, which seemed to groan beneath the weight of the most delicious looking spread of gourmet Mexican food that I'd ever seen. I knew Mr. and Mrs. Eduardo had overseen all of its preparation, but Joe had given the order that the pair of them were to behave strictly as guests for the evening. Quote: "You've done an absolute knockout job already. Please, leave all the fussing and fiddling to the serving staff, that's what I'm paying them for. You two just relax and have a great time tonight, it's Faye's party. And that's an order!"

The concertina doors of the dance floor were still pulled shut. Only the flicker of light through the gap underneath, and an occasional squeal from the PA system gave any hint there was somebody in there. Music for now was courtesy of the big Hombre with the guitarrón that I'd already met when the Fire Diamond broke down back at Bird-town. Although on this occasion, instead of a fiddle wielding skelly, he had prudently chosen a fellow human with a trumpet for an accomplice. The big fellow gave me a broad, sunny smile as we passed him. But it was only when he did the 'Call me!' hand gesture, that I was certain that he actually remembered me.

Hanging from a ten-foot-high rail, that ran the length of the far end wall and continued on around the corner behind the food table, was a

luxurious set of rich, burgundy colored curtains. They looked spectacular, and their placement gave the far end of the rooftop a more cozy and
intimate feeling. I think, judging by their height and length, they must
have come from an old theatre or someplace where the windows had
been quite substantial. Obviously, they must have accounted for most
of what had been covered up by the tarp' in the back of Lois Escoto's
pickup. As impressive as they looked on their own, Shintarō and Kiko
had gone that extra mile and attached dozens and dozens of tiny glit-
tering tinfoil Fé runes and stars, all meticulously cut out by hand from
the big roll of foil.

"Man, the fat guy *really* got stooged on that one," came Vince's only
comment.

The bar was nestled against the far wall next to the food table. The
look was plain and functional, on the left was a wide, flat dish full of
sliced up lemons and limes, on the right was a chintzy ceramic ornament
of an hombre in a sombrero riding a donkey pulling a little cart filled
with cocktail-swizzle-sticks and little paper umbrellas. Standing upright
behind that was a beautifuly handwritten menu board, showing a list
of all the re-named cocktails that were on offer for the occasion. You
could choose from a Chupacabra, a Ten Gallon Hat, a Fire Diamond, a
Honey Roller, a Hammering Angel or what Vince and I both settled on, a
Tequila Sunrise over Svaneke. Vince didn't get it, and thought the whole
idea was just a load of yuppie twaddle.

There was a lot of that *ONE-TWO! ... ONE-TWO!* stuff coming out
from behind the closed, dance room doors, as Banksie and whoever of
the Four Señors were fiddling about with his sound system. I hoped like
crazy we weren't in for another one of the Dog Man and Señor Cheerful's
excruciating duets.

Judging by the look on Vince's face, he'd seen enough. It was that
dormant, pre-anything time of a party, the fossil hour, where folks like
Eugene, Mr. and Mrs. Eduardo, and the obligatory handful of poor old
buggers from the campsite were up here sipping on a glass and having
a nibble or two, before heading back home to bed. Anyone hip, hot, or
remotely cool wouldn't be turning up for ages.

Joe was there too. He looked dapper in a sharp pair of black dress
pants, a white tuxedo jacket, and an old-fashioned western bow tie. Of
course, it goes without saying the ten-gallon hat took pride of place on
his head, which balanced out perfectly with the gleaming pair of white
cowboy boots stylishly peeking out from his pressed pant cuffs. Despite

his inclusion on Vince's list of boring old farts, Joe still seemed privy enough to be shown something that had just come in on Vince's cell phone.

"Juan-Carlos in the highway patrol sent me these," sniggered Vince as he flicked back and forth through the pictures. "They found this guy up north, about half a mile away from some giant crack in the highway."

"Hey Wolf, come take a look at this," Joe waved me over, as he snatched the phone from Vince's hand. "Look Wolfman, it's that Travers guy."

It was him alright. His head was still inside the aqua-blue compression mask we'd seen him wearing on screen at the ambush. The pictures were all pretty shocking.

"Look at the top of his head, look at the top of his head!" Joe pointed out to me excitedly. "Faye only half scalped the bastard; she didn't kill him at all."

"*Aaaah*, you're not telling me sweet little birthday cakes had something to do with this are ya?" Vince shook his head with disbelief.

"Oh yeah, they found this other dude too," laughed Vince commandeering the phone back from Joe and flicking quickly through the pictures. This guy was eaten clean to the bone as well, apart from a greasy, unruffled mound of hair on his head. Even on a skeleton I recognized those grinning super-white teeth immediately.

"That's Martindale," I said surprised, leaning in for a closer look. "That means he must have somehow managed to crawl his sorry ass back out of the crack. *So Faye didn't kill him either!*"

"Hey, Diego, come here," Joe called to the boy as he tried to slip unnoticed towards the ramp. Joe scribbled something quickly onto a paper napkin and carefully folded it twice. "Diego, take this over to Faye's trailer and slip it under her door. It's very important that she gets this immediately. Do that for me now and I'll pretend I never saw that bottle of beer you've got stashed down your pants leg okay? *Now git!*"

"That'll cheer her up no end," said Joe. "I reckon it's the reason she's been so moody lately. She deserves to have *that* weight lifted off of her shoulders on her one special birthday."

◆

The roof had now become a sea of chatter as more and more guests began to arrive. "Banksie's Disco" was now fully open, the deep pulsing beat of the sound system, combined with a kaleidoscope of brightly swirling lights, produced an irresistible, hypnotic magnetism that had already drawn a whole bunch of party folk inside.

"How the hell does she know all these people?" Joe asked bemused. "For someone that's supposedly lying low and incognito, she sure seems to have a lot o' friends. I reckon Vince must have rat lined a few of his evil little cronies in myself, but this lot all seem far too, I dunno … *normal*, to be any kind of associates of his."

It was then, just as I lowered a Hammering Angel from my lips, I saw the Birdman, Shintarō, strolling proudly, arm in arm down the center of the roofway with not just one, but two absolutely identical Kikos, one on either side.

"Holy hallucinations, fat man," I said seeing double. "I'd better ease off on these cocktails, or can you see that too?"

Joe laughed his head off and clapped his hands hard with joy. *"Well I'll be,* I remember that kid when he had nothing but a plump pair o' man boobs and a stupid purple hat. Look at him now. *Yeah!"* Joe uppercut the air, as he was prone to do.

Shintarō was coming straight towards us with a confident swagger. He was wearing the impeccable, top-notch, expensive clothing of some robust 1930's don, or an opera singer or someone of equal girth and style. He even had the waistcoat, the long white scarf around his shoulders and the two-tone spats and shoes.

"Check out his hair," said Vince with a grin. "Far out."

Shintarō was living up to his name. His black hair had been oiled to a shine and styled immaculately into what looked like some Japanese nobleman's hairstyle, complete with those tightly pulled side sections and a high bound tail at the back.

"You look *sick!"* Shintarō took Vince's appraisal as a compliment and responded with a dignified nod of his head. We all stood staring perplexed at the identical Kikos. Shintarō was loving this, he was having trouble holding back the massive grin that was blooming on his face.

The two Kikos looked amazing. Both girls wore the same body-hugging style cocktail dresses, the only difference being one was colored white and the other was black. On their feet they wore those super high heeled shoes that Vince had commented on earlier, although the black dress was paired with white shoes, and the white dress paired with black. The girls were both powdered up with identical makeup and their long, free hanging hair styles were both trimmed to look just the same, with their fringes cut low and running straight through the center of their eyeballs. The only difference I could pick was the black dressed Kiko had an intricately made, tinfoil brooch near the neckline, and the one in the white dress seemed to teeter a little more precariously so high on those shoes.

"Okay wise guy, we give up," said Joe. "Which one of you two is Kiko? And pardon me darlin', if you're *not* Kiko, who in tarnation *are* you?"

Suddenly the two girls burst out giggling, satisfied their ruse had been a success. "It's *you*, *you're* Kiko," I said when the girl in black put her hand up to her mouth out of habit when she laughed. Kiko nodded in agreement, and Shintarō grabbed her around the waist and pulled her affectionately towards him.

"... So?"

"It's ME, dummies, it's Oppuam."

"*WOW, Pocahontas*, you look...*HOT!*" Oppuam rolled her eyes despairingly, while Joe elbowed Vince extra hard in the ribs.

"Kiko came up with this great idea," spoke Oppuam in her usual eloquent manner. "It took me *ages* to convince the matriarchs that I really would like to try dressing up in clothes like this, if only just once for Miss Faye's special birthday. I've been practicing for days trying to walk in these crazy shoes."

"Oppuam, you look sensational!" Joe said tipping his hat forward complimentary. "Same goes for you Kiko. And as for what you and young Bird, sorry I mean Shintarō here, have done with the decorations, you should both be very proud of yourselves." Shintarō nodded in agreement, and Kiko just giggled.

◆

Turning around from the bar, with a lime colored, Chupacabra cocktail balancing perilously between my fingers, I was pleasantly surprised when two glamorous Mexican ladies who were both up close behind me, unexpectedly engaged me in polite conversation. Both women had an easy-going character about them that oozed charm and grace.

"I'm Wolf," I said trying to sound kind o' cool.

They both smiled warmly. "*THE Wolf?*" gasped the taller lady. "Señorita Faye has told us much about you."

I was going to say, "*All good I hope*", but caught myself in time. After the women introduced themselves as Consuela and Adana, they filled me in on all of the juicy things that Señorita Faye had told them about me. I kid you not, this was definitely the first time in my humble existence that *anyone*, let alone a goddess, had sung my completely over exaggerated praises. Even so, I shamefully lapped it all up while it lasted.

"We definitely must have a dance later on, Señor Lobo," smiled a cheerful Consuela as they moved on somewhere else to party and mingle. Feeling elated, I headed back over to where Joe was squatting down talking to Dr. MacElroy in his wheelchair.

"Wolfman, I see you've acquainted yourself with Adana and Consuela."

"Just saying hello."

"*Ooooh*, plays his cards close don't he," Joe said laughing and having a bit of a swipe.

"No, those two ladies are *way, way* too classy for you, Mr. Wolfman (swipe number two). They're right up there in the brains department as well. One of 'em's a neurosurgeon and the other one's an anesthesiologist."

"Seriously! How do they know Faye?"

Joe wound his finger around a couple of times.

"Tinfoil Sombreros?"

"You got it," said Dr. MacElroy sipping on a glass of fizzy soda.

"How's it going anyway Eugene?" I asked, purposefully not mentioning the word leg.

"It's coming on fine thank you Wolf. Lieutenant Crawford has kindly taken a keen interest in my onerous predicament and has been coaching me through a 'No bullshit' as he terms it, regime of exercise and rehabilitation."

"Yeah, frick'n Oochie fancies himself as some kind of latter-day Florence Nightingale," mumbled Joe under his breath. I didn't get it but laughed anyway.

"I was just telling Eugene exactly what happened when 'the boyfriend' dropped in unexpectedly the other day," Joe said flippantly, rising back to his feet. He looked me straight in the face and his demeanor turned unexpectedly sullen.

"Wolf, that chopper had absolutely no identifiable markings on it at all. It was *at least* half a dozen levels over black, … and I don't mean the color of its paint job either. That vampirical demon and those three automata, … *man*, now that I've had more time to think about it, I'm really worried this whole damn thing is starting to get way, way out of our league."

"Cheer up seňors," interrupted that Enrique guy who I'd met at Vince's party. I was even more impressed when I learned later on that he was the guy that ran the little orphanage, out there in the no dot, desert hamlet of Casa de Huérfa.

"*ENRIQUE*, how ya doing? Good to see ya buddy," Joe said, almost bursting his sides with sincerity.

"Not so bad thank you, Joe. Hello Wolf. It's nice to see you both again so soon."

"What about that battle out there on the plain hey?" Joe was forgetting it was only me and him who'd watched it from up on the ridge.

"You have no idea how thankful I was to Señorita Faye and Los Espectros Brillantes when I later heard that—" Enrique's words were cut short, as excited hoots and cheers of admiration went up from a predominantly female contingent of guests. A double lined squad of eight young men in evening attire were now marching in step, up around the corner of the ramp. Once at the top they turned, still in formation, and headed straight down the length of the rooftop towards us. They soon broke rank amidst good natured laughter and melted enthusiastically into the party. The Honey Rollers were here.

Two and a half cocktails worth of courage had been totally flattened. Consuela, Adana…Faye. Who was I kidding, I might as well chug this down like a pig, and head straight on home to the camper. Fortunately, my slump only lasted a few seconds, and I was back at the bar for another. Besides, this was Faye's twenty-fifth birthday party, and I should count myself "cock-a-hoop lucky" to be here. All qualms aside, it was good that the Rollers had arrived, their sparky gung-ho, exuberance had cranked up the already electric atmosphere of the party to a whole other level.

Lucien was unavoidable, everywhere he went, half a dozen guests seemed to tag along with him. Needless to say, they were mostly all women. I must admit, the black-sequined toreador jacket, paired with the leg hugging trousers he was wearing, did look pretty damn cool. On his head, Lucien's hair hung long and loose from beneath a wide brimmed, flat Spanish hat. I couldn't decide if he looked like a flamenco dancer, a well-dressed bandit, or some legendary Mexican hero.

A roguish, wispy haired dandy, who looked like he'd just stepped straight out of a Dickens novel, could only be Commodore Jack. His narrow wasted, high collared morning coat sat somberly in contrast against the knee-high leggings, a starched, old fashioned shirt, and his signature snow white cravat.

Young B with Dees, (or whatever his name was) looked equally impressive, all spruced up with his sand colored, freshly washed dreadlocks, and decked out exemplary in a kid-leather, blue-black tuxedo.

Although I didn't recognize four of the Honey Rollers, there was one other at the party who I did. Faye had never mentioned him, but I'd dubbed him Crazy Hawk, and I knew he was a HEXO mechanic. I remember watching him back at the canyon as he cut through a tangle of chains with his bolt cutters, only moments before an overarching, torrent of tires came slamming down hard, right in the exact same spot he'd been working. The baggy 1940's suit he was striding around in so confidently looked perfectly incongruous with his high combed, black Mohawk hairstyle.

All of the Honey Rollers wore a golden, nickel sized lapel pin on the left-hand side of their jackets. Either a hexagon or the double headed axe motif, to designate which particular clan of the Honey Rollers they were affiliated with. They looked understated, but extremely cool.

"Where's my little blondie then, Wolfman?" came the jocular tones of Oochie's voice, from right behind me. I turned around to greet him and was completely bowled over by what I was seeing. The old rascal looked immaculate.

"Woo-hoo!" howled Joe, coming back over with a piled-up plate from the food table. "Goodness gracious, you do spruce up nicely for an old-timer, don't ya."

And he did. Oochie was wearing a tailored three-piece suit with patch leather elbows, a string bow tie, and a squat bowler hat, tilted just at a favorable angle. While his long grey beard had been plaited to its tip, like some voguish, folkloric dwarf lord.

"Gotta look good for my girl on her birthday, right Joe?" insisted Oochie, feigning a doe eyed, "butter wouldn't melt" expression.

"Looking like that, she'll be putty in your palms Lieutenant. Where the hell did you get those fancy threads from anyway? I must say Ooch, I'm impressed."

"Mrs. Lieu in Saigon made 'em, back in the sixties. Don't think I've taken 'em out of their box ever since."

"What about me! What about me!" Once again, Sacramento seemed to appear out of nowhere. Joe just stood there dumbfounded.

"What?" said Sacramento, feigning indignation.

"You look fantastic," Joe said, shaking his head. "You never cease to amaze me mister."

Sacramento had arrived wearing the deep blue, double-breasted frock coat and pants of a wild west cavalry officer. It looked pristine, with two shiny rows of buttons running down the front, and shoulder boards that I guessed must have belonged to either a captain or a major. But that wasn't all. Gone were the matching, polished leather boots – instead, Sacramento had opted for a pair of soft-soled moccasins, while on his head sat a spectacular full-feathered, Indian war bonnet.

"I'm over getting typecast as an Indian. I thought I'd hedge my bets and turn up as a fifty-fifty."

"Is that your own personal war bonnet, or a sacred, ceremonial head-dress from your tribe?" I asked with virtue signaling sincerity.

"Where?" said Sacramento, sounding surprised, as he jerked his head around comically, trying in vain to get a look at whatever it was I was referring to.

"As if!" he said comically, "I picked *this* up at a flea market about two, *oooh* maybe three years ago. It is genuine though, no flies on Sacramento. Came with its own certificate of authenticity too. It says, Number 43 of 280, hand stitched, Indian, feathered bonnet. Made in Foiquan China … how cool is *that?*"

"You mean it's a frick'n knock-off," growled Oochie, sounding totally ripped off.

"No, it's a genuine Chinese prop from that famous 1950's western, 'Teepees Along the Potomac'. Download it sometime, it's excellent. There ain't a struck match between it and my other two favorites, 'Die Savage Die' and 'Injun's Scalped My Sideburns'. All good stuff, and *completely* accurate, right down to the very last detail."

"Come on dip-shit, let's go get ourselves a drink," scoffed Oochie, shaking his head with disdain.

"NO WAY! None of that pale face, fire water for me bro', that stuff's bad medicine."

They'd both started carrying on again like a couple of idiots, when the music coming out from inside Banksie's Disco, changed noticeably to a definite, slow pulsing beat.

"That's it, that's the signal. The birthday girls on her way," Joe nodded as he steered me over to the far end wall, where we stood with our backs up against the curtains. "Trust me Wolf, from here you'll get a really tip-top view."

The pulse of the beat began to intensify and the word quickly spread that Faye would soon be arriving. "Well about frick'n time, it's gone eight o'clock," hollered Oochie. "I can't wait around all night to give blondie a big smoochy kiss."

"Dream on Ooch," taunted Joe. "You'd never stretch that far up, you're too goddamn short."

"That's B.S. Joe, and you know it...more like blondie's just too goddamn tall."

Anticipation grew, as the Fire Diamond, with all headlights blazing, edged up the ramp, turned the corner and inched its way slowly toward us. (I was impressed how Kiko and Shintarō had artistically covered up all the scratch marks with a roll-on, glitter stick too. They looked like speed lines, shooting back down the sides.)

For some reason, young Galo, who I'd agreed could be the driver, brought her to a complete stop, just a car's length around from the turn. An enthusiastic hand clap, and high-spirited chants of *Faye! Faye! Faye!* started up as everybody urged the Fire Diamond to get moving, and bring her on in.

Suddenly the unexpected boom of a firework rocket exploded in the sky to our rear. As everyone swung around quickly to look, Joe threw open the curtains behind us to reveal the dazzling figure of Faye, standing high like a floodlit angel, on the edge of Charlie's tinfoil covered tractor bucket, that had lifted her up to the top of the wall.

The collective gasp of surprise from the party, changed spontaneously into an enthusiastic racket of whistles and cheers. Faye stood completely unmoving with only the gentle hint of a breeze at play through her hair.

She was wearing a knee length, black fitted dress, with a one-inch, circular collar that hugged firmly around the base of her neck. The right-hand sleeve ran all the way down to her wrist, while the one on the left was missing completely, highlighting the intricate Neolithic tattoos that wound down the length of her arm.

Swept entirely over to her right-hand side, Faye's long, magnificent hair was counterbalanced perfectly by a small silver bird's wing, that sat splendidly just above her uncovered ear. An obvious echo of an ancient, Viking helmet.

But the absolute clincher was the Brísingamen, that nestled perfectly around the collar of her dress. You could see the bright, white sparkle of the blue stones, and the captured rays of sunlight, that shone from deep within the amber.

"Ladies and Gentlemen," Joe spoke loud and proud without the use of any microphone. "Please put your hands together one more time for the birthday girl herself, the wonderful, the incomparable, the one and only ... *FREYA!*"

The applause that followed, went ballistic and was definitely the most joyous and sincere thing I'd ever heard. Man, I had no idea who half of these folks were, but one thing was certain they had the most fantastic party spirit, and they *really* loved Faye.

> *... She stood in the light,*
> *with hands on her hips,*
> *and her legs placed slightly astride.*
> *While down by her feet,*
> *sat her two little cats,*
> *looking sharp in their tinfoil bow ties.*

"Oh spare us, *please* ... the poet laureate strikes again," scoffed Joe, as we both reached an arm out to Freya, and helped her step effortlessly back to the ground.

She lip-synced a silent thank you, and then launched herself straight down the center of the rooftop-runway, for a shameless, one-off flaunt of her own stunning self. The entire crowd parted, as Freya, (which she'd reminded us a day or two back, was her real name, and that from the day of her twenty-fifth birthday, was what she then wished to be known as) presented herself to her friends.

Gutteka and Jenteka ran dutifully alongside, although less than a few yards in, Gutteka looked like he'd had enough and took a sharp angled leap off to the right onto an outside speaker. But then, as he made his second quick leap with intentions of making higher ground, Seiðr must have kicked in, as for only the briefest of seconds, he suddenly changed to a full-sized lion. Apart from me, only one other person seemed to notice. The confused girl looked up at the roof, back at her drink, and then reached down to the floor to pick up the discarded little tinfoil bow tie.

Jenteka's fast moving legs managed a get a little bit further, before she then ducked quickly away at the far end of the food table.

Freya was having a ball, she was struttin' her stuff and doing that long-legged, stridey type walk like a high fashion model. The whole place was hootin' and hollering, and when someone threw her a couple of long-stemmed lilies, she swirled them theatrically above her head for a moment or two, and then tossed them away to the stars.

Even Vince had come full circle, he was down on his knees with his mouth wide open, bowing in that imbecilic, double armed fashion you see all those tennis fans doing. I know he was hammered, but he was never, *ever* going to admit to this later.

"Banksie's sure picked the perfect song for this show," Joe yelled into my ear.

I was impressed, but I had absolutely no idea what the song was.

Apart from the music, the best touch of all, as Freya pranced down the rooftop, was the magic fluorescent path of an intricate Viking design that grew longer and longer beneath each and every one of her high stilettoed footsteps. It was only the unseen row of teeny-weeny black lights that ran along the length of a lantern cable, that gave any clue as to how it was happening. Kiko, Shintarō and Señor Funky, the electronics expert, had really outdone themselves with that one.

Reaching the end of her celebratory stride, Freya spun around and sat posed on the hood of the Fire Diamond. On cue, two male guests ran in from the sides and started blasting away with those old-style flash-bulb cameras, as Freya hammed it up perfectly, throwing her head back provocatively and striking a plethora of sexy, glamorous poses. Freya threw her hands in the air as if to say, *"That's it!"* and soaked up a final, gigantic round of applause.

"She's crazy, she's almost as crazy as you guys!" came a flat toned, Norwegian accented comment, as Axel appeared sipping on a martini, and looking ten times sharper in his cool, 1960's tuxedo than that suave, British, secret agent ever could.

It was just as the whistles died down, and Freya jumped off the hood ready to make her return, that both of the Fire Diamond's doors unexpectedly opened. Surprised as the rest of us, Freya swung around quickly to look, as two, statuesque young blonde women alighted from the car and stood with their hands on their hips beside the doors. Suddenly the seats flipped forward, and another pair of equally good-looking blondes stepped out, and assumed their stance right behind the two infront. You could have heard a pin drop.

Freya turned her head hard to the front and stepped away from the car. The four blonde women immediately strode forward and positioned themselves in a spaced-out square right behind her. If you were a fan of tall, long legged blondes, you could be forgiven for thinking you'd died and gone up to heaven (and that wasn't so far from the truth.)

Banksie, who had only turned the volume down momentarily, cranked it back up, and to the accompaniment of the perfect, still playing music, and yet another cocktail fueled crescendo of cheering and hooting, the five of them, bold as can be, came strutting back in, doing the most raunchy formation routine you're definitely ever likely to see on the roof of an old Sonoran gas station.

Halfway along, the five of them stopped on a dime, did a sexy little shimmy, spun around three-sixty, and then strode right into the party. (I think the little ditty was for the sole benefit of any superstitious guests to dispel their doubts that these four strangers might have been diablos or witches, or something even worse.)

Once back in the throng, Freya was mobbed by a tide of well-wishers, all eager to wish her a happy birthday and to give her a hug and a kiss. She obliged wholeheartedly but judging by the stony glances she cast now and then to the four blonde women, it was obvious that their presence wasn't at all planned or welcome.

When all of the congratulations had ended, Freya immediately turned to the four gatecrashers and confronted them. "What are you doing here? If you have come here just to ruin my day, please leave *now!*"

"*No,* please little Freya," spoke one of them, sounding almost condescending. "Why would we wish to do that?" She then changed from English and started speaking in a different tongue.

"*Stop!*" said Freya crossly. "Use a language that all of my friends can understand, I want them to hear everything that you have to say." A second young woman spoke up. "We've come all this way down here to help you, and all you can do is get angry with us dear Freya. You make us feel so unwelcome."

"I don't need *your* help. Thank you."

"Oh, we think you do … and besides, it really wasn't *our* choice to come all the way down to this ghastly, godforsaken place anyway."

"Well how did you get here?"

"We flew on feathered wings, isn't that right Fenrir?" giggled one of the women, feigning a wiggle fingered lunge for my still up thrusting quiff. An arctic chill surged through me, as the keen, darting eyes of a raven flashed for an instant, instead of her own.

"Who are they Freya?" I whispered quickly, trying not to be heard.

She just looked at me with surprise. "*VALKYRJUR!*"

Like moths to the flame, a whole bunch of curious men folk gathered around, checking out these four, completely stunning young women.

Freya soon relented and begrudgingly introduced them to anyone listening. "Please, may I introduce some *acquaintances* of mine. This here is Róta."

To me, Róta looked the most menacing of the group with blonde, rope-like braids that hung all the way down to her waist. She was clothed in a red leather tunic, matching kid gloves, and tapering, needle like heels.

"And may I introduce Sigrún." This Valkyrja *seemed* the most congenial. Although I was sure her charming smile could be deceiving. She wore her long fair hair pulled up high into an arcing ponytail that hung majestically right down the middle of her back. Sigrún looked striking in a black, long tailed jacket with a short, chain-mail dress underneath.

"This young lady is Göll." Göll was the shortest, and by that, I mean she was still *easily* five foot ten. She was the only one who could *maybe* fit that old American cliché of "the girl next door". Now don't get me wrong, Göll was as drop dead gorgeous as the others, but I did get the disturbing feeling that she, or for that matter any one of them, would rip your nuts off without a second thought if you dared take a look at 'em sideways. Göll looked splendid with her long, woven braids, and her body-hugging attire, fashioned out of white-leather strapping.

"And last, but *certainly* not least … this is Skuld."

Now if Freya was The Ice Maiden, then Skuld was The Thousand Degrees Below Zero, Glacial Queen. Such a cold, stoic beauty. So aloof, so completely unapproachable, and at the same time so incredibly beguiling. I knew right then and there she would *never-ever* condescend to even speak to me. Skuld stood right at the back and seemed completely uninterested in anyone or anything at all. I had to admit though, she looked truly stupendous with her dead straight blonde hair, her swan feather jacket, and those candy red PVC legs that just kept on going and going and going.

I'll never forget the look of utter disdain on her face when Oochie-Cuchi steamed straight on in and tried unabashedly to chat her up. She looked down at him once, as though he was some kind of bearded, talking elbow rest.

Axel was way out on point, as he soon returned from the bar with a tray stacked with glasses of sparkling champagne. "One for you little søster," he said kissing Freya affectionately on the cheek, and one for each of our most illustrious Valkyrjur."

"Well, well, well," said Sigrún flashing her wide, bright smile. "If it isn't little Heracles himself. Oh, he's even more handsome up close isn't he girls?" Róta and Skuld made no comment, but Göll ran her slender fingers softly around Axel's face, and without making a sound, stretched out the word *"Gorgeous!"* with her luscious red lips. Axel took no notice.

"Yes we all saw your most valiant stand, up there in the rocks the other day," said Róta "We came *this* close to taking you," she made a little pinchy, crab claw with her thumb and finger, "but Skuld decided that for now we would let you—"

"Enough!" scolded Freya "Cease this *NOW!* or Óðinn will most certainly hear of your willfully, ill-mannered attitude." The Valkyrjur swung their heads in unison and stared at Freya in absolute shock.

"Oh Great Dis, we know you so well, we have since... ooh, time immemorial," scoffed Sigrún. *"This* most recent vassal of yours is most certainly a beauty, but *HELLO!* Let's see it lose the attitude *huh!* (she did the "hoochie mama" head wiggle thing to perfection.)

Róta and Göll laughed most disrespectfully, but Skuld ignored their bitching completely and stared spellbound at the jewels around Freya's neck. Freya noticed her captivated eyes and rebuked her swiftly. "Don't even think about it, *chooser of the slain.* The Brísingamen came to *me* by rank and by birthright."

Another full-on exchange looked imminent, when Vince, horsing around with Commodore Jack, who was obviously his friend, pointed back down to the top of the driveway at a fancy looking couple striding grandly in towards us. "Get a load o' those two... *EXCELLENT!"*

The man was wearing a mauve-grey, gentleman's morning suit in the old wild-west style, that looked as if it had been tailored out of pliable steel. Sitting on top of his head was a tall top hat, made from the same fabric as the rest of his clothes. Add to the mix his scruffy black beard and he looked not that dissimilar to a charged-up version of Abraham Lincoln. I say that quite literally, as with every step he took the soles of his boots would light up and spit out a six-inch crackle of sparks, from right where the spurs should have been.

"Holy shit," gasped Vince, "it's Chucky boy!"

"My, my, my," Joe said smiling. "I had no idea the boy could doll himself up that well. I always thought a matching pair o' sox was Charlie's idea of style."

Charlie's companion was mysterious and silent, and dressed in no other color than black. At the center of her long, ruffled dress was a tight strung corset, from which opulent folds of black, shiny taffeta tumbled all the way down to the ground, but unlike the old cowboy day versions, this little ditty, was split up the center into two angled curves that allowed a glimpse of her long, slender legs underneath. Even so, we could still only guess what she looked like, as a towering mantilla of intricate lace work, hung like a shroud over her shoulders and face.

"Aren't you going to introduce us to your friend Charlie?" Freya inquired. Charlie didn't even have time to react.

Unexpectedly the woman flicked the trailing mantilla to the side with her lace covered fingers. "Hello little blondies, it's so *wonderful* to see you all again so soon."

"MORRÍGAN!" came a chorus of shocked surprise from the Valkyrjur.

"And before you ask, I've been sent here to keep a watchful eye on *ALL* of you."

I stared, disbelieving. My vision of how this wild and formidable, raven haired Celt would look, had now been utterly trashed. Her skin was a deathly pallor of white, (aided no doubt, by some kind of cream or powder) but the moody black makeup of her eyes and lips had been crafted with the most intricate and incredible detail. It was clear before my eyes that the war goddess Morrígan was (well at least when she got dressed up to go out) a full-on proponent of the late twentieth century's High Gothic art form.

"I know my entrance wasn't anywhere *near* as bootylicious or dramatic as yours, pretty blondies. Neither in a squash of silly giggling girlies, or on the top of a shiny mechanical bucket. I came instead on the arm of a *warrior!*"

Charlie's expression looked somewhat puzzled, but I'm sure his tall top hat grew a few inches taller.

"Have you all brought along your little flying horseys to help steal away the fallen? I know that's your usual forte, pretty, pretty shield maidens, or have you come here on this particular occasion to *FIGHT!* I remember when a Valkyrja wouldn't dream of riding into battle mounted on anything other than the largest and fiercest of wolves that hail from the depths of the dark, primordial forests. These romantic era, later day constructs, *uuugh!* If your great-great-grandmothers could see what has become of their lineage, they would most definitely rise forth from their graves."

"You have to move with the times ... dearest Morrígan," spoke Skuld for the very first time. "Róta is the only one amongst us here who has any fondness for those snarly, stinky creatures. They're so, uh, ... *beastly!*"

"Yes, that's right pretty Skuld, being a Norn you're far more suited to playing the part of a nice little pony girl, aren't you," taunted the Morrígan wryly.

That was it, quick as a flash Skuld lunged ferociously out towards her with the obvious intent of inflicting some grievous bodily harm. But Róta and Sigrún stopped her mid-attack and calmed her back down into line. Morrígan feigned complete indignation, but there was no doubt in my mind whatsoever, that if it really came down to conflict, she could easily dish out more than she'd get.

The whole dynamics of the music suddenly changed as Banksie shifted its direction into that mysterious, unknown world for me, the world of the techno, dance-beat sounds. Commodore Jack, who'd been waiting in the wings, suddenly stepped in sharply beside Freya.

"Hello Freya, would you care to dance?" he said in a cultured New England accent.

"Oh please, thank you," said a relieved looking Freya, grabbing him tightly around the neck, and quickly dragging him inside.

"Stupid dumbass. Why didn't you think of that?" was my thought, as I slapped myself on the face. Straight away one of the other rollers, who I didn't have a name for, moved in quick and asked the same of Sigrún. She whisked him inside even quicker than Freya did.

"This one's *MINE!*" screamed an excited Göll, grabbing Vince like a ruffian by the scruff of his collar and pushing him backwards forcibly over towards the pumping sounds of the disco.

Then Róta made a reach out for *me*, but only lifted up my sunglasses instead. She let them down quickly, took a step back, grabbed Skuld by the arm and led her off speedily in pursuit of the others. My heart dropped down like a stone. Maybe I was reading too much into it, but that little peep of curiosity, and rejection had ripped my already tenuous sense of self-worth up into a million and one tiny pieces.

"Pretty, pretty blondies," said the Morrígan pragmatically. "Trust me Fenrir, you're *far* better off without them."

◆

I stood back at the bar, but this time I was having a Ten-Gallon Hat.

My shoulder was bumping up against Lucien's, but he hadn't a clue in the world who I was. As usual he had a whole throng of sycophantic groupies hanging off of each and every one of his words. It made no sense, apart from his suave, debonair manner, his treacle thick charm, and his exotic Meso American good looks, I couldn't for the life of me see what all the fuss was about. ... Yeah right!

"Hey Wolfman," yelled Joe, tapping me on the back over the loudness of the music. "Me and Sparky Boots here are gonna mosey on in and show them our moves." He did a flawless, backwards moonwalk for a second or two, and then carried on talking as though nothing had happened. "Most of them young 'uns can't dance for shit."

I looked at Charlie, now on his own, and he answered my question before I'd even said anything. "The Morrígan apologized profusely, but apparently she's been called away on a most urgent matter from the *other* realm," grumbled Charlie. "How's that for an excuse for doing a runner. Although she did say she'll try her best to return ASAP if she can." Charlie shrugged his shoulders philosophically. "Frick'n goddesses, *far* too complicated for this little duck. Just love 'em and leave 'em, that's what I always say."

◆

The doors into Banksie's disco (as of right now) were closed – some bullshit about *"containing the atmosphere"* according to Señor Funky and Señor Crazy who were pushing their way outside as we were going in.

"Holy hell!" gasped Joe. This was the first time any of us three had even ventured inside yet, and for the unprepared it was like entering a full on, vertigo city.

The only thing *remotely* resembling this that I'd ever seen was the dance floor back at Snake Eyed Jacks. But compared to this whirling, kaleidoscopic cacophony of a million different lights and sounds, it wasn't even in the race. This humongous, psychedelic cement mixer, had you feeling like you were bouncing up and down like a super ball one minute, and then spinning around sideways the next.

"Ah well, when in Rome." Joe peeled off his crisp, white jacket and handed it over to young Diego who was moonlighting now as a part time cloak room attendant on top of his highly lucrative, chair pusher's job.

"Anything else I can get you Señor Joe?" asked Diego, batting his eyebrows suggestively.

"What's he—"

"Don't ask Wolf, I *really* don't wanna know," Joe said, shaking his head.

"Oh for God's sake. Get a load o' Banksie will ya," he said pointing over to the Grand Poohbah of all DJs up behind his opulent, shrine-like sound console.

Technically Banksie was shirtless, but the remaining dicky bib and matching cuffs, glowed whiter than white with an electro-fluorescent intensity. Perched precariously on his head, was a Turkish fez made of red cut glass, with a dangly tassel thing that pulsed green along its length like some bioluminescent sea creature. If that weren't enough, he had on a pair of those goggle-eyed, groover glasses, where little electric diodes the size of orange pips spun around the edges of the circular frames like balls on teeny weeny roulette wheels. Every now and then they would suddenly stop and start spinning back around in the other direction. Even looking at 'em from over here was making me giddy.

◆

Within minutes I'd been coerced out onto the dance floor, where my skills were on par with a hapless, ungainly twerp. But Joe was the absolute opposite. From that effortless bounce of his hips, to the salutary 'hands in the air' thing, he made it all look so simple and natural. I couldn't believe it. Every now and then he would spin around two or three times like a top, and do this forward, leg slits movement where he'd drop almost to the ground, bounce back up, and just carry back on with his dancing. All of his moves were as smooth as silk, he was a frick'n fabulous dancer for someone his age.

I was thinking that *now* was a good time to leave, when quite unexpectedly a cruisy, rush of what felt like a billion fluffy bubbles, surged through my body in a most agreeable manner. Not that I was complaining none, but at some stage one of my so-called compadres must have gone and slipped a mickey or whatever the kids are calling 'em these days into my drink. At first I thought I was on some kind o' trip, as I'd seen the Four Señors running all around the tops of the walls and up on the ceiling in these little matching wrestling outfits with their multi colored, pork pie hats on. Turns out they were using those little access gantries they'd set up so they could get at all of their electronic equipment and lights much more easily.

Once I realized that nobody in the sea of people around me could give two hoots as to whether or not I could dance, I must admit I was really starting to enjoy it. I dunno what it was, but I was suddenly feeling like the frick'n king of the world. All I had to do was stay in the exact same spot where I was, and sooner or later everyone seemed to eventually appear carousel-like, right there in front of me. Great.

At one stage Kiko suddenly appeared, and I compliment her as best as I could through the music, on all of the great work she'd done for the party. She looked at me, giggled, and then instead of speaking Japanese, started babbling away at a million miles an hour in what I presumed was an Indian dialogue. Shintarō, slammed me playfully on the back, and told me that I'd been "stooged." It seemed the two pranksters had swapped their dresses earlier, solely with the intent of confusing everyone even more. They fooled me for sure.

Dancing out in the middle, directly beneath the huge, rotating mirror ball were the Valkyrjur. They were more or less still in a group but with an endless supply of men folk dancing in and out all around them. Of course that included Oochie. Even allowing for the fact he had a wooden leg; he was an even worse dancer than me. But being the old chalker he was, you couldn't help but admire the diplomatic way in which he divied his attention up so evenly between the four of them.

Even Skuld had somewhat thawed and seemed to be getting right into it. More than once I caught a glimpse of her dancing provocatively where she would lean right back, exposing her taut, flat, stomach, and then pull herself back up again with long reaching air claws.

"Take my word for it," yelled Axel loudly with his mouth up against my ear. "That little foursome would be the biggest prick teasers in all the nine Nordic worlds. They'll *never* allow a mortal man to have his way with them, no matter how great his charms. They enjoy the good life in the mead halls of Valhalla too much. They know only too well that Óðinn would throw them out on their ear if they did so."

Freya came over and danced with me for five minutes, like I was the only other person in the room. She told me I was a really good dancer. *Hah!* I liked that, even when she lied through her teeth, she would always have something nice to say. But being the belle of the ball, she didn't last long and was soon whisked off and away. I tried to keep an eye on her whereabouts for a while but lost her when the one and only Sacramento himself came dancing by, half stripped off to the waist, and with his headdress that looked as if all of the feathers were ten feet long and trailing off like luminous swirls into space. He was having a great old time, acting like an idiot dancing with Oochie, the world's worst dancer, and Eugene, who for a dude who'd just had his leg bitten off, was putting in a real good effort out there leaning on a crutch and doing what looked like the twist.

Gaping back over to where I'd last seen Freya, I got the worst, most unwelcome surprise when I saw that she was standing off to the side talking and getting all kind o' touchy-feely with *him!* Yes, it was *Taurokathapsia* or my best buddy Lucien for short.

Pretending to dance eagerly with anyone and everyone, I tried as hard as was humanly possible to take no notice of them and keep that ugly green monster at bay. But on the *fourth* time I took another gut-wrenching glance over to see what they were doing … they were gone.

Instantly my intoxicated thoughts collapsed into a vomitous mush of self-pity. The music, all the people around me dancing, Banksie, the lights, Señor Cheerful's stupid, custard yellow hat, even the checker patterned tiles on the floor, all clumped together into one unbelievably giant irritant, and really succeeded in pissing me off.

Storming out from the dance room I jostled my way through all of the folks still happily partying outside, completely ignoring Mr. Eduardo who bade me a joyful good evening. I knew I was behaving like a petulant two-year-old, but I felt completely justified as that was *exactly* what I wanted to do.

I staggered down the concrete car ramp like a drunken idiot, past the long-abandoned chair lift at the bottom and set course more or less on autopilot in the direction of the campsite. As I drew level with Freya's trailer, the soft sound of music and the telltale flicker of candlelight through the down-turned venetians told me without a doubt she was home. The worst thing of all though, was I knew that he was in there too. I wanted to rip out my own teeth! It was only the last modicum of self-restraint that stopped me from screaming at the top of my lungs.

"She's a goddess, you asshole. A goddess of love and beauty. Do you *really* think in a million years she'd seriously want anything to do with a vole eyed, creature like you?" As I slid open the door to the camper van, and crashed out immediately on top of the mattress, the prophetic words of the Morrígan echoed around and around in my head.

"Pretty, pretty blondies Fenrir … trust me, you're *far* better off without them."

28

Just Call it Vigriðr

It had been almost three days since the night of Freya's party and none of us had seen hide nor hair of her since. We knew she was out there somewhere amidst the ranks of The Shining Specters, as she had taken the geirahöð, the Martellare, and Gutteka and Jenteka as well. But our concerns were higher than usual. Horrific reports of death and destruction due to an escalating amount of devil attacks had been coming in from all over central Sonora.

One guy who pulled in for gas told us that while he'd been out working in the fields yesterday, five of his amigos had been set upon and devoured by flying diablos that swooped down from the sky. He had escaped by diving unnoticed beneath a piece of farming equipment attached to the back of his tractor. There was no way of verifying if what he said about these flying devils was true but judging by the way this poor soul was still shaking like a leaf a whole day later, there didn't seem any reason to doubt him.

◆

Clutching the last six-pack of beers from the party, I walked back onto the roof where we were all sitting around watching the sunset. Well technically that wasn't true, it had already vanished behind a thick layer of clouds, some three hours ago.

"Thanks Wolfman," Joe said reclining in a deck chair, as I handed him a bottle. Charlie grabbed another for himself, and then threw one each across to Vince and Banksie, who was still hanging around at The Alamo with the rest of us as he'd been left behind to pack up the last of the equipment on his own. It seemed the Four Señors had been called away on "Urgent dwarf business," as he called it, to somewhere south of Tecoripa. They were due back sometime this evening. Even so, Banksie had still only made a half-assed attempt at sorting out the gear.

"I think Frigg must be in a somber mood this evening my friends," noted Axel, gazing long at the sky.

"Frigg is leader of the goddesses, isn't she?" I asked, not entirely sure.

"That's right Wolf, the Queen of Asgard. She who sits beside her husband Óðinn on the high seat of Hliðskjálf, where together they can keep watch on all of the kingdoms and doings of men as she spins her veil of clouds out wide across the universe."

"Are you serious?" scoffed Vince, taking a swig from his beer. "You really believe in all that bullshit about gods living up there in the sky don't ya?"

"Of course," replied Axel.

"How did things turn out with Göll the other night then?" asked Axel, immediately swinging a question back onto Vince. "From what I've been hearing, there isn't a single woman in the whole of Mexico or Valhöll who is immune to your roguish charm." Axel's low-powered sarcasm went straight over Vince's head.

"Aaaw, that chick was so frick'n hot, I—"

"No you didn't!" Axel cut in abruptly. Vince looked aghast. "Whatever you say I *know* it never happened … She's a Valkyrja."

"A wha'…?"

Right then, we all felt the faint, almost imperceptible rumble, of yet another earthquake starting to happen. "Man, that's three today," growled Charlie, climbing up out of his deck chair, annoyed at the inconvenience.

"No, *listen,*" Joe said attentively. "That's not a quake, that's definitely something different. Sounds like it's—"

"I know that sound," I proclaimed dramatically. I listened a moment longer but was certain that I knew what it was. "Joe, get those binoculars ready. Banksie, turn on that camcorder or whatever it is you record things on. Seriously, you ain't gonna believe what's coming."

Joe was leaning way out from the wall and peering into the darkness towards the south. *"Holy Saints,"* he chuckled, lowering his glasses, and turning back toward us. "The Wolfman's right, wait 'till you see this."

The rumbling sound grew louder and louder, until suddenly thirty or forty point riders came thundering past on the roadway out front. Behind this loose formation vanguard was an empty gap of a hundred yards or more, until the full, main body of Los Espectros Brillantes came magnificently into view as two endless columns of motorcycles and their torch-bearing riders stretched as far to the south on the roadway as our limited night-eyes could see. The noise was unbelievable, such a massive, massive body of riders and heavy motorcycles was clearly a force to encounter.

We just stood there taking it all in. Strangely everyone had placed their beers out of sight like some unspoken mark of respect. I recognized that eerie, yellow glow that hung low around their ranks, and the random pinpoints of light that flashed from their leathers, like it did that first night I'd seen them, hiding behind the rocks with Bird.

"This is excellent," crowed Vince excitedly. "I've never seen so many bad ass bikes. And I'm sure you've noticed, *Chucky boy*, every last one of 'em's a full-on American classic."

"What about the Brigantes and the Smithcrafts?" jibed Charlie.

"Yeah, well, I suppose there's a few good British bikes in there as well, but I sure ain't seen any ricers or fag-ass, I-tie ones."

A whole bunch of folks from the campsite had been drawn outside by the racket. They were milling around, a good distance back from the road, but all seemed intent on staying to watch this momentous event as the full Shining Specter army passed by.

"Unbelievable. This is unbelievable. There must be five, six, God knows how many thousands of them," uttered Joe, shaking his head in amazement.

Banksie, who'd been frigging around on his laptop, suddenly uncoiled a lead and mainlined it directly into the PA. The resulting feedback was easily tempered by the overbearing sound of the motorcycles.

I'd heard the track he was lining up on his digital thingamajig at least a hundred times before, but I didn't have a clue what it was. "That's the music from the pimple cream ad, right?"

"Yeah, the pimple cream ad, the kitty crapper ad. They've been puttin' the squeeze on this beautiful music forever. Same with all those CGI action movies. Well, this time it's different … It's MY TIME to frick'n well exploit it," tittered Banksie while he cranked up the volume and perfected whatever it was he had in mind.

"Oh hear me Wolfman, I know what's a comin' … I FEEL THE POWER!" he ranted comically like some overzealous hell-fire preacher.

"So what's it called?"

"What?"

"That track you're playing, *eesh!*"

"O Fortuna, the first movement of Carmina Burana. It's perfect for what this way a cometh."

"Not long now," said Banksie as the choral voices and the music kept on building and building.

It seemed as if this endless army would continue on forever, when suddenly the two columns began to spread apart, allowing clear passage for a third line of riders to advance through their ranks at high speed.

"Get a load o' these dudes," shouted Charlie.

With bright, yellow fire reflecting from domed iron helmets and blades, this unit looked truly formidable. I figured they were either commanders, or some elite detachment of the goddess's guards.

As Banksie's personal mix of 'O Fortuna' was building in volume and intensity through the PA, I just stood transfixed by the spectacle of mass raw power passing before us.

"Holy Lord of the Ages," mumbled Joe right beside me. "You'd better grab hold of those other field glasses Wolfman, I just *know* you're gonna want to see this." I did as he said and brought the binoculars up exactly where I ought to.

"Looks like something pretty heavy's coming up in that bright patch there, fellas," shouted Vince.

The first thing I saw was a rider holding a long, trailing banner that flapped wild in the cool, nighttime breeze. Upon its silver field flew the image of a golden falcon. I recognized it immediately as *Freya's* falcon, the one that Shintarō had sketched, that she had kept in the pocket of her brown leather jacket. How splendid it looked sewn anew in fine golden thread.

Then, directly behind the curl of her standard, came the goddess incarnate herself. I could not believe what I saw. At first, I thought she was draped in a loose piece of sack cloth. Although when I focused the binoculars a little sharper, it was clear that the garment was some kind of long flowing cape fashioned entirely out of that enigmatic hoard of falcon feathers. Even more impressive, around the base of its high feathered collar lay the splendid stones of the Brísingamen that gleamed ever bright amongst the firebrands with the mysterious enchantment of Seiðr.

The long golden locks were all gone. Everything below her scalp line had been shaven back raw to the skin. Her remaining hair now pulled high through the taut bind of Hamada-san's tenugui, held firm and hung down like a long matted horse tail, as red as blood. Yet it was her beautiful face, all painted white as a fleshless skull that shocked me the most. Not a playful mask, applied with a delicate artistry but one smeared on heavy by an urgent hand that looked crude and ancient, and frightening.

Just one look at the stoic figure crouched low upon her iron war-boar left me in no doubt at all that this truly was the manifestation of a war goddess from the age when the sun crossed the sky in Taurus.

We were all lined up watching. From down at the road the six of us must have looked like those old soviet fraudsters propped up along the edge of the Kremlin wall.

"Oh yeah! Here comes the goddess, boys. Here comes our girl," Joe yelled excitedly, his voice half washed away beneath the deafening noise of the bikes and the still rising music. Surrounded by her entourage of bodyguards, Freya was now coming in fast and almost level with The Alamo.

With my eyes still glued to the field glasses, I felt an overwhelming compulsion to try and attract her attention. I knew with all this noise it was pointless but feeling so charged with emotion I screamed at the top of my lungs 'F R E Y A !' Just for the goddamn hell of it.

Whether by coincidence, or through those inexplicable powers of Seiðr, she snapped her head around towards us, and immediately reared Hildisvíni up onto his rear wheel treads. Freya stood tall, and thrust the geirahöð skyward, holding it aloft in a magnificent sign of salute. The gesture coincided perfectly with the explosive highpoint of 'O Fortuna', and the chance rush of wind that unfurled the falcon feather cape to reveal a leather strapped, bare-breasted goddess beneath.

Freya held that stance for only a few seconds, then dropped Hildisvíni back down and continued on in formation amidst her flame wielding warriors. Such beauty, such terrible, terrible beauty. I knew in my heart, that as long as I lived, I would never forget that most splendid and glorious moment.

"Oh she's such a show-off," said Axel flatly. Completely ruining my reverie.

"*Nice pair o' tits though!*" added Vince, pounding it deep into the ground with a shovel.

"*I told ya Wolfman, I KNEW she was a gonna do it. I just KNEW she was gonna do it,*" chuckled Banksie, who was now, in my opinion, definitely the greatest living DJ the planet had ever produced.

"That was *supremo*. Absolutely perfect dude." I looked across at Joe, who was still returning her salute. He was saluting for himself, for his boys, and with the single twinkle in his eye from a tear that I knew was especially for Chester.

It wasn't until the very last riders had trailed off that Joe said anything. "Well that should put us in good stead with the boneheads. *Man*, that was something else. It don't need much figuring that this is The Big One. So are we just gonna let that little gal head on out there and take on all those devils by herself? ...Well, not counting them six thousand boneheads. Or are we gonna go and give her a hand?"

"ALRIGHT!" said Charlie, punching the air. "About frick'n time."

◆

As we hurriedly threw a whole bunch o' gear from machete blades and swords to a couple of armed rockets into the back of the pickup, Vince was telling Axel how he had been the one that had so kindly provided Freya with the raunchy body harness thing she'd been wearing when she made her salute. Axel simply laughed it off, as it was obvious he was talking a whole load of crap.

Charlie set him straight about the Martellare in the packing crate though, and how he'd found all those little extras stashed underneath. Then he took a rascally swipe at Vince and told a short version recap of how Faye had deprived him of the motorcycle boots when she'd flogged him out on the track at the time trial. That pissed Vince off big time.

"Well at least those black jeans were hers," grinned Axel. "She was wearing them the last time I saw her in Tromsø."

We all tried not to look as Banksie was taking a tongue lashing from the Four Señors, over near the driveway. They'd turned up in their truck in the wake of The Shining Specters and had gone completely ballistic when they'd realized that apart from coiling up a few leads, the "Planet's Greatest DJ" hadn't done anything. Poor old Banksie, who literally towered over his bosses, was twisting back and forth like a washing machine, taking flak from all sides, and the occasional boot in the ass for good measure.

"I had a feeling something might happen tonight," said Axel, wiping sweat from his eyes with his T-shirt.

"Why so?" I asked, intrigued by his resignation.

"We are at the crucial point in the Winter Solstice."

"Yeah I've heard of that. But so?"

"Well, it's winter's darkest day when the sun reaches the southern-most point in its cycle. Ancient peoples regarded it as a day of extreme importance. Solstice just means 'the sun stands still' which it appears to do for three days before it starts to move northward again, and the days grow longer and longer."

"Do you think all those centuries ago that *hidden-sun* might have been referring to the solstice? Is that the same thing?" I said trying to sound mildly intelligent.

"Most definitely. I remember when we were children, our bestemor would sometimes repeat this little rhyme to Freya that mentioned something about a hidden sun, but I just can't recall how it went."

"Right, DONE!" yelled Vince from inside the back of the pickup as he'd finished bolting down the detachable gun column that was to be the mount for the RODS-7d.

"Check out little brother will ya," sniggered Charlie. "He's really gett'n off on all o' this. There's a picture he drew of himself when he was a kid in the old man's office somewhere. He's got himself standing in the bed of a truck with a fifty cal', blasting away, shooting the shit out of everything. Stupid idiot loves all those ridiculous war movies."

Joe came charging back out of the garage. He looked impressive in his ten-gallon hat, camo' pants and a black T-shirt, with a copy of Chester's army dress photograph printed on the front. Below it read THIS ONE'S FOR CHESTER.

"Yeah, I know it looks a little goofy, but I've been saving this up for a special occasion. And I reckon this is as good as any. Come on ladies, *let's roll. Let's roll. Let's roll.*"

Joe was at the wheel of the Fire Diamond, and I was riding shotgun. I'd already agreed with a palm-spit handshake to swap the '58 Special for his unseen shack on the beach, so now she was technically his. Behind us in the pickup were Axel, Charlie, and Señor Vince. I could hear him yelling something insulting out of the window at poor old Eugene. The hapless guy who'd just lost half his leg and made the effort to hobble on down to see us all off.

"Do you think they'll be okay if there's another big earthquake or attack Joe?"

I've left Rosalina and Mr Eduardo in charge, with the two love birds as deputy sheriffs. Kiko's *way* too flakey, but I'm certain Shintarō and Rosalina will keep a trusty eye on the place. No problem. They both know where all the emergency food and essentials are, and if need be MacElroy's lab can double as an impenetrable safe room."

We hadn't even reached the road, when a solitary figure stepped out from the darkness and into the beam of the head lights. Joe pulled up alongside. It was Oppuam, unusually wearing her finest traditional clothing. At first, I thought she was holding a stick, but I soon realized that it was the old shovel that I'd used when I fought off the devils.

"Hello Joe, hello Wolf. Sacramento said that he is most certain you will be needing this and asked me to come and hand it over to you personally."

I got out of the car, thanked her, and took it from her hand. I noticed immediately the vertical row of dime sized glyphs that had been etched along the handle, below the newly sharpened blade. But when I looked across to ask what they meant she was gone. A feeling of dread washed over me, as I realized I hadn't a clue what I was in for.

◆

Instead of heading north like I'd expected, we'd hurtled off a by-road that took us south on a long sweeping stretch out into the scrub. I hadn't said anything, but after ten minutes driving in the middle of nowhere, it seemed like a good time to ask. "So where exactly are we going Joe?"

"*Hmm*, been wondering when you'd say that."

Unexpectedly, Freya's yin and yang motorcycle helmet, which was sitting on the seat between us, started talking with a life of its own. Actually it was Vince's voice, coming out muffled through the radio. I turned it upside down like a bowl, so we could both hear what it was he was saying.

"*Hey, you two, where the hell are we going?*" Vince had no use for any kind of voice protocol and just babbled away as per usual. I sat it up on my lap, as Joe shook his head, indicating to me not to reply.

"*Hello, H E L L O … anybody there? Ah for fuck's sake, answer the call will ya? Stupid assholes,*" Vince yelled, getting more and more irate.

Joe roared with laughter. "Got no patience at all that boy," Joe's mood quickly changed back to business. "Those abandoned buildings we passed back there. That's El Calienta, or at least it was in its day."

"*Yes?*" I stared unblinking, feigning unwavering interest in his very next words.

"*Oh goddamn it, I was WRONG.* I just had a feeling they'd be somewhere out around these parts. *OKAY.* A customer came in late before we left saying he'd seen a whole bunch of motorcycles heading out in this direction, I thought it'd be The Shining Specters for sure. Probably some club of weekend joyriders cutting across to Punta Chueca on the coast somewhere. *Yeah, yeah*, I know, it'll be twenty minutes wasted by the time we get back to the road but, *aah*, don't frick'n hassle me Wolfman, we'll find 'em eventually."

"I know where they'll be," I said matter-of-factly.

Joe looked at me sideways. "You do huh?"

"Yep!"

"Well would you care to partake or is it some kind o' secret?" inquired the helmet. I could hear from the tone of his voice coming through on the radio that even Charlie was getting ticked off now.

"Roger that," answered Joe accordingly. "Please go on," Joe continued calmly, ready to hear what I had to say.

"When Faye took me out into the desert that day to watch The Honey Rollers, we stopped on the edge of this enormous crater thing, so she could check out these prehistoric rock carvings. Well scratchings, really. When she came back to the bike, she looked at me strangely and said, 'This will be the place Wolf.' Gave me the willies at the time, but I *know* that'll be the place where they're heading."

"A crater! I've never seen one around here. Was it a maar crater?" asked Joe.

"A what?"

"Volcanic crater. The only cones I know of in Sonora are at Sierra Pinacate and that's right up near the Arizona border."

"Well Faye reckoned it was a crater," I said knowing that would more likely convince him.

"What did it look like?"

"It was, *ooh*, about three quarters of a mile in diameter, it had higher ridges further up towards the northern end, but right where we were, it was a lot more shallow. If you weren't paying attention you could have easily driven right by and not even noticed."

"What else?"

"There were long sweeping curved sections around most of the rim. They reminded me of the banked-up parts in a velodrome or something."

"Go on."

"It was a bit too glary to see very much. There were a few rocky out crops around where we'd stopped, a couple of cacti maybe, that was about it."

"It must be fifty million years old at least to have weathered down to that kind of level." Joe was dumbfounded that in all the years he'd lived in Sonora he'd never seen or even heard of it. He still wasn't entirely convinced it was where we should head for either.

◆

Our misguided detour behind us, we now headed north with the pickup following at a safe and sensible distance. Joe figured the chance of getting pulled over by the highway patrol was negligible. Even so, loaded up with such a healthy-sized arsenal of weapons, we kept our speeds down to the limit, which at this hour seemed barely more than a crawl.

I hated trying to pick out any kind of distinguishing feature in the darkness but eventually I thought I recognized a familiar bunch of pot-holes looming up ahead beside the road. "Hey, better slow down a tad. The place Faye and I turned off is right around here."

Joe sighed resignedly. "Okay Mr. Wolf, you'd better be right, radio the others and tell them we're turning off into the scrub."

We left the road too early, but soon picked up the Martellare's tracks from when Faye and I were out here before. But beyond the spot where the Saguaros cacti were growing, we lost the rest of the trail. I was sure I could wing it. "This here is the spot Joe. If we head straight for that ridge up ahead, we'll be there. Trust me."

"Another half mile Wolfman," growled Joe, getting impatient. "If Faye and the Specters aren't there, we'll ask Charlie and Axel where they think we should frick'n well go."

I got that half mile, then we stopped and got out of the car. Vince and Charlie parked right alongside us. "Zip it will ya," asserted Joe, shutting down Vince's tirade of smart-ass comments.

"Do you remember how we went over the edge of that lip back there?" I said, pretending to sound like it was obvious.

"No. What lip?" asked Charlie.

"*Exactly!* We're not heading toward that crater, we're already in it. We've driven right in through a section where the rim must have completely eroded."

"Crater! What are you talking about? This ain't a *crater,*" came the knowledgeable outburst from Vince.

"Oh yes it is, boy," answered Joe. "I'm amazed, completely amazed, I never knew this place even existed." Then, with impeccable timing, the moon momentarily poked its head out through a parting of the clouds and lit everything up bright as daylight.

"He's right little brother," said Charlie. "Check out those curves over there, they look like the high banks at Indy."

"Faye reckons this place is an important node point, where a whole bunch of ley lines intersect," I mentioned unashamedly to try and gain myself some more cred.

"Well if it's *SO* goddamn important, why isn't she and her ten-million-man army here, dickbrain?" Touché! Vince had me there.

"Come on pops, let's get out of here, this is pointless," barked Charlie, agreeing with his brother.

I looked across at Joe who'd walked on a few paces further and was puzzled at what I could see. Either the clouds were playing tricks in the moonlight, or the ground up ahead was surging toward us, and bobbing up and down as it did so.

"GET BACK! Get back into the vehicles FAST!" yelled Joe turning on his heels and running for his life. "There's frick'n thousands of 'em." As we pulled the doors shut, a frenzied barrage of devils smacked hard into the front of the car.

"Grab the little G-G, *QUICKLY!*" yelled Joe, urgently starting up the engine and slamming the car into gear. "It's loaded, don't waste time—" We immediately heard the electric whir of the little G-G's bigger brother, the RODS-7d. Vince had obviously dived straight into the bed of the pickup and come up shooting.

"That boys gotta frick'n deathwish." Joe hit the gas and tried to smash his way through the pack.

Joe yelled into the helmet's radio ordering Charlie and the others to get themselves out anyway they could. The moment he said that, my passenger side windows were pulverized by a barrage of fast lashing talons, with yours truly half sprawled over the top of the seat fiddling around trying to get a proper hold of the G-G, pinned beneath the shovel pole lying right across it. Luckily, the gun was pointing in the right direction so all I had to do was flip the green button and let rip with a deluge of gunfire.

"HIT 'EM. HIT 'EM HARD!" screamed Joe. "Let the bastards have it!" At close quarter, the little G-G mashed the onslaught and splattered everywhere inside the car with their disgusting black sludge. The shell cartridges were flying around hot and distracting, but at that moment when the belt ran out of ammo, I knew we were all out of time.

Right then, the most mournful wailing noise you could have imagined, moaned loudly from somewhere outside.

"That's an air-raid siren!" yelled Joe, completely baffled. But more than that, as if in some far-fetched scene from a sci-fi movie, the woeful sound had somehow cast a debilitating stupor over every last devil and frozen them still in their tracks. We both sat looking around in disbelief unsure of what had just happened.

"Yeah, we're all fine over here pops, no sweat. Thanks for asking," came Vince's smart-ass voice from inside the helmet.

"Perhaps these things aren't as bright as we thought they were," whispered Joe. "Just one trick ponies that have been lying under the ground for so long they don't have the capacity or term of reference to process loud noises."

"You mean it kind of overloads or shorts out their circuits?"

"Shhh!" winced Joe with a finger to his lips. "Maybe they've just got piss-weak ears. I dunno."

"What are you whispering for, that siren's making a hundred times more noise than you ever could."

"Yeah, good point Wolfman."

As we looked around trying to see where the air-raid siren was coming from, Joe caught sight of something that was making its way down towards us from the lip of the rim to our right. *"What the hell is that?"* he said wide-eyed and losing the whisper. It looked like a circus trailer, but one wrapped in a cobweb of pulsing blue neon, with a light splaying mirror ball out front for effect. As it moved closer towards us, the air-raid siren eased off and the whole shining contraption exploded loudly into the up-tempo piano music of an old fifties jump-blues song.

"WOO-HOO! Alright," came enlivened voices from beside us in the pickup.

Immediately after the intro' bars, none other than the irrepressible Banksie himself, came bursting down the length of the extended metal roof rack, miming to the lyrics of the Little Richard classic 'Good Golly Miss Molly' with the Four Señors right behind laying down some unbelievable b-boy dance moves that would have blown any contenders out of the park.

He looked even more ridiculous than usual, wearing that floppy eared dog mask with the front ripped off so you could now see his face. And apart from the bright fluro underpants, the only other thing he was wearing was a pair of super-shaggy, knee-high fluffies that made Kiko's dinosaur stumps look almost tame. We looked on amazed as the van kept on coming, cutting an extremely noisy but steady path through the mesmerized devils like Moses parting the sea.

"I don't like this Wolfman, it's *waaaay* too weird. Get that little G-G reloaded as quick as you can boy. These critters could snap back out of it (Joe clicked his fingers) just like that!"

As the mobile music-machine drew right alongside us. Banksie, who'd been gyrating about and lip-syncing like crazy to the song, dropped himself precariously over the side for a couple of seconds to speak to us over the racket.

"Hey, how's it hangin' dudes? Slip your sorry asses in behind Banksie and the Señors. We'll guide y'all out." He burst out laughing and then jumped back up on top to continue his most unusual performance with the dwarves.

We did as he said and followed up close on their tail.

"Jeezus get a load o' the little guys," nudged Joe, getting me to look up from reloading the G-G. The Four Señors were going off big time. All bouncing around and spinning on their heads like a bunch o' frick'n propellers. It really wasn't the place to sit back and watch, but they sure had some pretty hot dance moves.

"How long does this song go for Wolf?"

"Two, three minutes tops."

"Well, I reckon we've got about two seconds left, so these jokers better have another record in the stacker or we'll—" Joe stopped mid-sentence. "*Hey!* I just realized, if Banksie and the Seven Dwarves are all up there working the room, then who the hell's driving their van?"

With our vehicles in convoy, the still pumping disco wagon took the most direct route up the incline. We'd just passed beyond where the closest devils still stood immobilized, when for some unknown reason the disco wagon slipped backwards and crashed hard into the front of the Fire Diamond, which in turn smashed back into the pickup.

"Hell, I was intending to restore this car, not *completely* rebuild it." Joe was annoyed, but to make matters worse, the impact had knocked both of the driver's side wheels tightly into a narrow crevice, and due to the cars low ground clearance he couldn't manage to drive her back out.

"*What's your call old timer?*" yelled Charlie on the radio. "*Those critters back there'll be waking up REAL soon.*"

"Okay, *one*: we can high-tail it out in the truck. Or *two*: the whole frick'n lot of us jump onto the funkster mobile with the dwarves. Which, my dear compadres, seems to have driven off out of sight without us."

Joe sent Vince up to the top of the slope to see where they were waiting. "Hey you guys, you're not gonna believe this," Vince said returning in a matter of seconds. Despite all the previous good intentions, it seems Banksie and the Four Señors had scarpered like thieves in the night.

"Well something must have come up. They've probably got another gig to go to I guess," Joe said astonished. "Seriously Wolf. Did the last five minutes *really* happen, or did I just imagine the whole fuckin' thing? *Jeeeeeeeesh!*"

Immediately the five of us began clamoring for weapons as we knew exactly what was about to go down. Vince had finally gotten the RODS-7d up on its gun column and was itching to cut loose with some well balanced, wide angle blasting.

"Hey!" said Axel, darting his head around looking for imminent signs of attack. "I can't see any sign of them. Where in Ragnarök are they?"

We strained our eyes in the darkness back to where the devils were massed, but in those few frenzied moments we'd been grabbing our weapons it seemed that they'd vanished completely, back to wherever it was they had come from.

"Melted away like a late summer snow," commented Axel poetically.

"GOOD! Wherever they've gone is fine by me," grumbled Joe. "Maybe Vince's hairy legs scared 'em off."

"It wasn't him that scared them off Joe, take a look up there behind you," came the familiar cackle of Oochie as he hobbled out of the darkness at the top of the bank. We all turned to look at where he was pointing.

"Holy cow!" cried Charlie excitedly, seeing that the top of the northern ridge straight ahead was now rimmed with an uncountable line of Los Espectros Brillantes. They looked formidable sitting silent and still against the moon's somber sky.

"Look, over there towards the west, there's a whole bunch more of them," pointed Charlie enthusiastically.

"Yeah they're here alright. Apologies Mr. Wolf looks like you were right all along. *But where's the girl?* That's who we're here to keep an eye on," asked Joe, as he turned his attention to Oochie. "So it was YOU that pranged that heap o' shit into my '58 Special. Why the hell were you driving it anyway? I know for a fact you're *way* too cunning to get conned by that pack o' dipshits. What gives Crawford?"

"Ah come on Joe, I couldn't miss out on *this*. I just told the little dwarf guys you'd all gone out in the desert to help rescue the blondies as they were being held hostage by a whole pack o' those nasty devil critters. You know how much they—"

"Yeah they're as deluded and lecherous as you are. How'd you manage to smash up the Fire Diamond then?"

"Well I'm pretty short, granted. But the custom shift stick and pedals on that thing were kind of weird and way too high up and close even for me to operate properly. So when my old prosthesis slipped right off the pedals, and—"

"*Oh please*, don't try and play the sympathy card Ooch. How come they just pissed off and left us here?"

"Well apart from realizing they'd been had, they went completely ape-shit when I supposedly dinged up their truck. Especially that Mr. Cheerful, he's a piece o' work ain't he? Banksie tried to talk 'em 'round, but they were adamant. All four of 'em told me to f-off out of the cab and find my own way home."

"And how did they know loud noises and lights would send the devils bye-byes?"

"They are Dvergr," interjected Axel, sounding all very mysterious. "They know about such things. Since ancient times, their kin have delved deep into Svartálfaheimr's interior. The stories they tell of who and what live down there will either enthrall or scare the living daylights out of you. Svarte Kaniner take their advice on such things very seriously."

"*Hmmm*," mumbled Joe. Satisfied for the moment with both Oochie and Axel's explanations. "Okay let's get the Fire Diamond out o' this crack and down on the level. Wooden leg or not Crawford, you're doing most of the pushing."

◆

We'd scooped up a whole bunch of slime from the car's interior, and were now just sitting, waiting for something to happen.

Axel stuck his arm out of the pickup's window, pointing out where to look as more and more riders began to appear. Joe darted his head around fervently looking at their latest deployments.

"Impressive, yeah, but I'd guess that makes only five or six hundred at most, so where the hell are the rest of 'em?"

"*Look!* Look up there," I said excitedly. "There she is." The goddess had arrived amidst a heavy contingent of guards and a dozen of her senior lieutenants. There was no doubt as to who the commander in chief was. Once they'd taken their positions Freya sat magnificently upon the war boar Hildisvíni, unmistakable beneath the light of the cloud covered moon.

"What's with all the white shit on blondie's face, Joe?" questioned Oochie straining his eyes through the binoculars.

"It's Neolithic, the face of the War Goddess," I answered authoritatively.

"Umm, can't say I like it," grimaced Oochie. "No goddess I've ever known would have been seen dead wearin' *that* frick'n hair-do neither."

Joe turned his head and noticed Oochie had a .44 sitting on his lap. "Hey! How'd you get a hold of that gun again you little—"

Oochie's chastisement stopped dead, when once again the ground began to shake from another tremor. But then, as quickly as it started it stopped. Even so, it was enough to breach the ground surface, and through momentary glimpses of moon light we could make out what looked like an up-rush of fast gushing oil. Unfortunately, experience left us in no doubt as to what we were actually seeing.

"Devils!" barked Oochie unperturbed. "If this ain't the mother lode of the sons o' bitches I don't know what is. We sat watching in silence as their masses began to spread like a flood across the entire surface of the crater.

"They're heading this way fast fellas," observed Joe. "I do realize they're still some three hundred yards away, but due to their *ridiculously* overwhelming numbers, I think it's high time we get the you-know-what out of here." He ground the column change into reverse, right as a dozen pinpoints of light shot up from Freya's command position, and arced slowly across the dark, winter's sky.

"Flaming arrows!" scowled Oochie. "That's different." But his misgivings soon vanished, when the down coming fire brands landed silently amongst the swarms, igniting random swathes of their forces with the fury of the most intense and incinerating fire storm imaginable.

"Holy ...!" gawped Joe, bewildered by the unexpected scene of ignition up ahead. "Good tactics there, girl. Pre-dousing the ground with incendiary, that one's straight out of the ancient's play book. That wasn't any type of old-fashioned lamp oil Wolfman. That was some kind of super grade, military napalm on steroids. Where the hell d' they get *that* from?"

It wasn't long before the force of the firestorm had burnt itself out, leaving a patchwork of still burning flames. "Here come the stragglers from the barbeque," said Oochie peering over the seat through the binoculars.

"Yeah, but get a load of what's charging up behind 'em," added Joe uneasy.

Charlie bipped on the horn of the pickup, as Axel indicated with his finger towards what was heading our way. This new emergence was nothing like the free swarming, all teeth and claw devils which we'd encountered up until now. These monsters were as big as super-sized linebackers and marched in battle formation like the mass phalanx legions of old.

"The bastards are *RED!* They're bright, crimson red," yelled Joe almost bursting a blood vessel. "Well ain't that just perfect, they've probably got horns and long pointy tails as well."

"Take a look for yourself," said Oochie handing Joe the binoculars.

"Yep, they've got the horns and the tails, but I guess they must have forgotten their pitchforks, 'cos these red rascals are all armed with *SWORDS!* There's gotta be five or six hundred of 'em, at least."

I could see the flaming eyes of Señora de las Sombras burning redder and brighter than they had ever done before. Despite what the others would think, I was holding on in terror to the door handle, ready to do the world's fastest bolt. Luckily, Joe pointed up to the ridge and said those six most unforgettable words, "Here we go boys ... *she's engaging!*"

From the command position, I saw Freya raise the geirahöð high above her head, and then point the blade towards her most northerly positioned forces. The signal to attack. She then did the same to her riders in the west, and then directly past our location towards an unseen force in the south.

Oochie and Joe turned their heads instinctively to look, and in a matter of seconds, we were passed by a fast-moving wave of Shining Specters charging forward from out of the darkness behind us. Even so, my attention stayed unwaveringly fixed on the goddess, captivated by her dignified poise and how aloof and strikingly regal she looked.

From these three cardinal directions, long waves of armed riders were now pouring down from their positions, heading directly in towards the middle of the crater. Only a reserve flank, stretched out along either side of Freya's central position, had been held back in readiness for the command to attack.

"There ain't enough of 'em Joe," said Oochie sounding worried and fidgeting around in the back. "Even with blondie's division still sitting up there, I still don't reckon ... *HOLY frick'n CRAP!*"

As if to quell his concerns, an unexpected deluge of the held-back force of Los Espectros Brillantes came pouring in over the ridge tops and cascaded like an unstoppable torrent into the crater. I can only liken it to pushing an empty bowl into a tub of water and watching it flood in over the sides. The escalation in the noise level from the mass arrival of four or five thousand extra motorcycles was incredible.

"Good girl, she'd just been toyin' with 'em Ooch. Conceal your disposition, *never* reveal your true strength, then catch the dumb-ass bastards off guard."

"Yeah, frick'n oath Joe." Judging by the grin on his face, I think old Oochie was ribbing him.

Freya held the geirahöð aloft once more and signaled a command to her own division as she led them down to do battle in a well-practiced peeling maneuver that looked like the fast-breaking curl on a wave.

"Oh yes. Very nice! VERY nice! Take a look at *that* will ya?" Joe was loving all this. *"A swooping falcon breaks the back of its prey. Such is the precision of its timing."*

"Sun-Tzu?" asked Oochie.

"Sun-Tzu," affirmed Joe.

"Hey look, check out Gutteka and Jenteka," I said pointing across at Freya's cats, which had now been transformed by the magic of Seiðr back into an even more fearsome and ferocious pair of lions, almost three times bigger than when we saw them out on the plane at Casa de Huérfa.

"Woe betide any red devil that tries getting in between Freya and that pair o' kitty cats," remarked Joe wittily. "And I think it might be prudent to start calling 'em by their full names too, huh?"

"Guttekatt and Jentekatt it is then," I said sounding smug, being the only one who could remember exactly what their names were.

We sat there, staring straight ahead, knowing that at any moment these two most bizarre armies were about to mortally collide. "What's that up there?" asked Joe, distracted by a bird-like shadow that glided menacingly in front of the moon. "Its wingspan must be what, twenty feet? Looks like a giant crow," Joe said ducking around in his seat, trying to follow its path.

"Looks like a thunderbird to me," answered Oochie.

"Aaah! They were all killed off a hundred years ago," growled Joe.

"Nah, they're still out there. That son of a bitch Sacramento reckons he used to keep one as a pet," chuckled Oochie, with an affectionate shake of his head. We watched it circle the sky for a few moments longer, but soon turned our focus back onto what was happening on the ground.

The giant bird quickly regained our attention when unexpectedly it dropped from the sky like a rock and landed with a god-almighty thud on the hood right in front of us. Even though I was certain I'd seen the tell-tale flutter of feathers, I was completely unnerved when confronted by the sudden apparition of a most fierce looking woman, crouching, and peering menacingly at us from the other side of the windshield.

"That's the witch!" yelled Oochie, pointing his finger straight at her. "Me and the little fellas caught a glimpse of her in the headlights by the road, with her hands drenched in blood."

We sat there like bunnies as this truly intimidating woman shifted her gaze slowly back and forth between the three of us. Her appearance and demeanor were startling. Coal black hair hung wild and untethered, her well-toned body encased in a primitive armor, fashioned from dark leather bands that clung like a taut second skin. Her flesh and face were painted in the rich, woad blue war paint of the old Celtic tribes.

I knew straight away it was the Morrígan.

Suddenly she pushed her fingers in through the damaged, top corner of the windshield and with one super strength heave, ripped it out from the frame as easily as the skin from a freshly killed stag. Joe sat there dumbfounded, with his back pushed as far as it would go into the seat. Lunging forward the Morrígan twisted and turned her head staring long and intently at us through the wide-open gap. I was struck by how her eyes looked so distant and terrifyingly devoid of any connection. I didn't know what the Celtic equivalent of Seiðr was, but either way, I figured this war goddess was most definitely under one of its spells.

She glared at us for what seemed an eternity, and then in a deep, raspy voice began to recite some kind of verse:

A warrior's blood still runs through your veins.
Have the years turned you feeble … and weak?
Or are you still fearless and strong,
like Cassivellaunus or the Great Cú Chulainn.
Come, come with me now … come join the fray.

◆

Man, things really started getting scary, when Joe, completely bewitched by her spell, immediately got out of the car, plonked his hat on his head, and drew a gigantic civil war cutlass out from under the seat. Oochie clambered out behind him, lured also by her enchanting words, as she beckoned them to follow her and *"Come join the fray."*

By the time I'd gotten out of the car and over to the pickup, Charlie had lifted the largest machete I'd ever seen out of the back and was following right on the tail of Oochie and Joe. "It was the Morrígan, she's cast some kind of spell over them," I blurted out quickly to Axel.

"Yes, it was the Morrígan Wolf, she was also here working her spell on poor old Charlie too."

"What? ... so who then?"

"She can appear as just *one*, or as one of the *three*. She can appear as just one, or as one of the three." Axel said it twice to try and hammer it home. But by now all this ancient mythological gobbledygook was really starting to do my head in.

"I think it was Macha who paid you guys a visit."

"Who the f—"

"Macha is one of the Three Morrígana ... they are all sisters. Although on the other hand it could have been Badb. But the one who visited us was most definitely Nemain."

I was amazed at Axel's knowledge. "Well whoever it was, our three old soldiers are heading out there, zonked off their gourds with only a cavalry sword, a .44 revolver and the world's biggest machete between them. How come you weren't hypnotized Axel, you've been a soldier?"

"Yes I was, but it doesn't matter. You'd *never* believe me anyway."

"*COME ON, LET'S GET A MOVE ON*. I wanna blast the shit out o' some of those big ugly red ones," screamed Vince, already locked and loaded, bouncing up and down in the back behind the RODS-7d.

Axel and Vince took the lead in the pickup, and apart from the defiant little figurine of Señora de las Sombras, still hanging from the rear-view mirror, I was alone in the Fire Diamond, heading forward on my own. We'd only moved a short distance before we caught up with the others, who had now thrown themselves headlong into the skirmish with the first pack of devils they'd run into.

As Vince blasted a devastating swath of cover fire through the monsters with his RODS-7d, Axel and I were now boots on the ground. Armed with only a shovel and Joe's replica Viking broadsword, we threw ourselves in alongside Joe and the others like a pair of crazed berserkers. No doubt spurred on in some ancillary way by the Morrígan's mysterious powers.

Thankfully our foes were the familiar fang, claw and scales type devils we'd already fought. The bigger, sword-wielding red bastards were still some distance behind them, engaged in a wide fronted battle with a mounted brigade of The Shining Specters.

Amidst all this fury, it was the first time that I'd ever seen any of the riders go down. I couldn't wrap my logic around how a bike riding compressed-smoke-skeleton could be brought to an end. And what did "undead" *actually* mean? I filed the whole thing away as a paradox of the metaphysical and turned my attention and shovel, back to the fray.

Fighting beside Joe he glanced at me almost furtively as if to say "The Morrígan huh. I know you know, but *please* never mention it again." Even so, he was a pretty dab hand with that old cavalry cutlass, slashing away like a wild-man at all attackers, and hamming it up theatrically with his classic fencer's stance and parries, as he neatly ran through any devil that foolishly got in his way. Charlie was no slouch when it came to a blade fight either. At one point I saw him swirl that giant machete around with such a ferocity he chopped two of the devils in half with one single blow. Needless to say, young Heracles showed effortless skill and finesse with a broadsword, (even a mail-order replica) he truly was blessed by the gods.

I was going ape, I felt like I'd been time warped back to the battle at Faye's trailer when these ugly sons o' bitches first appeared. I think I must have unconsciously taken in a few tips watching Faye and Hamada-san practice, as I was definitely aware of an improvement in my shovel skills.

Oochie on the other hand had blasted off all his ammo *way* before we'd even arrived, but for a pint-sized guy with a prosthetic leg, he was really getting stuck in with the long-handled axe Charlie had given him as a backup.

All in all, despite the fact we were fighting under moonlight, and that evil black blood-slime was flying around everywhere, the six of us were doing a damn good job of holding our ground. Engrossed in our own little battle, our delusions of being some kind of latter-day Spartans soon came to naught when the ammunition belt of Vince's Rapid-Ordnance-Deployment-System, eventually ran out of bullets.

We felt the surge of the devils immediately and, to make matters worse, The Shining Specters who'd been holding back the gigantic red buggers had begun to sweep further forward towards the north western section, leaving us all on our jolly lonesome.

Unexpectedly, like an energized young-blood, Vince came charging out from around the back of the pick-up and threw himself hard into action swirling a homemade chain-mace in one hand, and a trash-can-lid shield in the other. Add to that Freya's motorcycle helmet, combat boots, a pair of psychedelic board shorts, and a "Mr. Ed" T-shirt, this modern-day Sir Galahad was a sight to behold.

"You GO boy! You GO!" laughed Joe, encouraging his youngest, as he went completely ballistic, smashing the living daylights out of anything

that moved. The guy wouldn't stop, he just kept on bashing and belting. "Take out the batteries. *Quick!*" heckled Charlie, "before little brother here gives himself a frick'n cardi'."

Knowing this amusing respite wouldn't last long I took the moment to look across to where the major engagement was happening. The entire area was bathed in an eerie red light, some from the fire of battle, but also from something unseen. From something not of this world.

Right in the very thick of it, beneath the shining swirl of the gei-rahöð, I saw Freya upon Hildisvíni locked hard in the midst of battle. I saw Guttekatt and Jentekatt, her devoted feline companions who fought savage and true by her side. I even caught a momentary glimpse of the Morrígan armed with her spear, as she effortlessly sprang fleet-footed from backend to backend of The Shining Specter's motorcycles, rallying and drawing the riders ever further onward into the turbulent heart of the fight.

I saw other things too. Evil looking things that crept out of the ground, amidst all the smoke and fire. But I couldn't make out what they were. The whole scene reminded me of those ginormous, biblical war paintings where everyone portrayed within their borders seemed condemned to writhe in perpetual turmoil, from now 'til the end of all days.

Inevitably a three deep ranked force of the red demons made a surge straight toward us. We fought hard against them like six men possessed, as these evil brutes were in a whole different league. The swing of their weapons was vicious and forceful, and they were by no means lacking in skill. This was nothing less than a full fury state of kill or be killed warfare, and it was obvious that right up until this savage onslaught we'd only been battling their B teams.

I couldn't determine whether we'd been fighting for hours, or relatively no time at all. I only knew I was fast running out of steam, and that my chances of coming out of this mess in one piece or even alive were beginning to look pretty shaky.

Out of the corner of my eye I saw Oochie drop like a stone, from a most vicious blow to the head. I swung my shovel around to retaliate, but before it had even made contact, the boy-wonder came storming in hard from behind me and smashed the culprit to pieces with blows from his spiked iron ball.

"Wolf! Get Ooch out o' there *NOW!*" commanded Joe. I lifted his head off the ground and dragged him quickly out of the fight and back to the vehicles. From the neck up the poor guy was completely covered in blood, I had no way of knowing for certain, but I was pretty sure he was dead.

Enraged by what they'd done to poor Oochie, we hit back with even more zeal. Miraculously, we must have turned the tide somewhat as their attack lost its momentum and was finally starting to falter. But as if jinxed by my own wishful thinking, over to my right I saw Charlie curl forward and fall in a heap to the ground. Thankfully, it didn't seem to be from any blow or sword strike. Judging by the familiar shaking of his body, he'd been struck by a most untimely coughing convulsion brought on by his dreadful sickness.

This time Joe moved straight in himself and pulled his boy back by the scruff of the neck, all the while covered by Axel's slashing broadsword, and the over tenacious swirl of Vince's chain-mace. It was then that the devils seemed to completely lose all interest, and amazingly retreated off somewhere else. As Vince saw 'em off on his own, Axel and I followed behind Joe to help with our wounded companions.

Joe gently propped Charlie's back up against the side of the Fire Diamond and gave him some water, which he coughed back up straight away. "Easy son, you'll be okay, you'll be okay," he reassured Charlie calmly as he dabbed his eldest boy's face and forehead gently with a scrap of wet cloth. I was touched by his true devotion.

"How's Ooch?" asked Joe, flipping his attention across to his old buddy.

"Oocher-Coocher is unconscious but he's still alive," answered Axel, attending carefully to the old soldier's wound. Joe moved away from Charlie and looked around in disbelief at the jumble of devil bodies that we'd somehow managed to kill. "Hmm, impressive, but disgusting all the same."

We were about to try and get Oochie and Charlie inside the car, when out of nowhere, came a swoop from what I thought was a lightning fast jet fighter, *literally* four feet over our heads.

"*FAST MOVER!*" cried Joe looking up excitedly as the following wind rush ripped the hat right off his head and straight into a puddle of bile. As the aircraft zoomed northward toward the center of the battle, we saw that it wasn't a jet fighter at all, but an air-borne, flying Valkyrja.

"*O lordie, lordie!*" exclaimed Axel, attempting some unidentifiable American accent. "*THE AIR-CAV'S ARRIVED! I really didn't think they'd show. The girls don't get stuck in all that much now-a-days. But when they do PHEW-EE! Roll 'em all in with the war goddess Freya and that there*

Morrígan, and those devil varmits out yonder sure ain't gonna know WHAT IN TARNATIONS is about to hit 'em."

Joe laughed heartily at Axel's most unusual outburst. "What are they packin'?"

"Spears."

"Spears!" gulped Joe unbelieving.

"Yah, but it's not the *size* of the weapon, it's what they can do with them that counts," grinned Axel, reverting unperturbed back to his normal Norwegian-English. "Besides, it's the flying stallions they ride that are their most formidable weapons."

"How so?" Joe asked intrigued.

Axel thrust his chin forward. "See for yourself."

"HOLY frick'n!" Joe's arms sprung up in shock.

We looked on in disbelief, as right in front of us, like an enormous, unstoppable scythe, a three strong formation of flying Valkyrjur sliced a merciless wing to wing swathe right through the middle of the devils. Even from here the image of hundreds of headless devils convulsing around in their death pangs was a profoundly disturbing sight.

"So, what are—"

"They are a symbiotic-hybrid of the biological life form *Equus Ferus Caballus*, and the purest Ulfberht crucible steel. The same unassailable material that Thor's mighty hammer Mjölnir was forged from. Add to that a high-powered booster of Seiðr magic and *that's* what the Valkyrjur are riding."

"So where's the one that dissed me at Freya's party?" I said, momentarily forgetting her name.

"Róta?" said Axel. "Look over there." If death wielding blondes, riding steel-flying-horses didn't do it for you, then Róta the exemplary force on the ground most probably would.

"The beast that she rides is called Mánagarmr," explained Axel. "He is the reincarnate of the largest and most fearsome of the ancient Moon Hounds. It is only Róta who maintains such an unwavering link with the oldest of the old ways. She alone has the pluck and determination to go anywhere near, *let alone* manage to ride him."

As for the Moon Hound, that description doesn't even come close. This creature was basically a ferocious and severely pissed off wolf, that stood as large as an oversized buffalo-bull. We looked on in awe as this most frightening of creatures ripped every devil it snatched in its jaws to a dismembered tatter of shreds.

Mounted high on the back of Mánagarmr, Róta's pale skin literally glowed in the moonlight. She controlled the beast as best as she could with one hand, as she fought hard with a double-bladed axe in the other. From where we were standing, it appeared that her limbs were bound in a crisscross of taut, leather armor much like that of the Morrígan. Around her shoulders hung the matted grey fur of a wolf's pelt that trailed long down the length of her back.

Joe shook his head despondently. "God almighty, what the hell have I gotten us into. Just cast your little peepers on *THAT!*" Then Joe reverted to command mode. "Come on you two, push all that broken glass and crap onto the floor will ya. I'm letting Charlie stretch out along the back seat until he feels better, and we're gonna stash old Oochie Iron-Head here safely away in the trunk."

It really was the best place to put him. Axel had cleaned and bound up his head wound and, still completely unconscious, we laid him out flat and made it as comfortable as possible. Although after the fender-bender with the Four Señors work truck, the lid wouldn't stay shut, so we weighed it down from the top with the two large unopened sacks of sodium fluoride which we quickly transferred from the pickup.

"I doubt very much if those bastards would tear their way through all of that stuff to get at him," declared Joe with a rascally snarl. We held a hurried confab around the door of the improvised field ambulance as to whether, all things considered, now would be the most sensible time to make a retreat.

Axel wasn't going anywhere because of his sister, and when he cajoled us saying things like, "It is entirely your choice, but believe me, you have not seen *anything yet*. If you leave now, you will most surely regret it one day." The rest of us, right or wrong, all made the unanimous decision to stay.

I couldn't put my finger on it, but there was something about the heartiness of Axel's voice with his lilting Norwegian accent that could convince you of just about anything. Even so, when I pressed him to elaborate a little more on what he'd been inferring, he stood looking pensive for a moment, then tapped me on the shoulder and said simply, "Just call it Vígríðr." I had no idea what that meant, but as if to give his words credence, a deep hollow boom from the bowels of the earth blasted forth from the middle of the crater.

"That can't be good," winced Joe, as what at first looked like an upchuck of dirt, soon took the shape of a swarm of nasty looking bat-winged creatures, no bigger than the size of your thumb. Like some pestilent surge from the end times, they shot high up above the battle and then swooped down en masse to attack The Shining Specters as well as anything else that dared move. When we encountered these things up close, they were repulsive. Their scrawny body carried an oversized head that looked as ugly as a newly breached hatchling, but with the added blight of bulging red eyes and fast snapping razor sharp teeth. When one of these horrid little creatures managed to get in close and take a bite out of you, it felt like when that sadistic asshole in your past jabbed you with a lit cigarette. They were pretty gutless though. A few angry swipes with your hand and they'd back off quick and try and attack someone else. Irritating as they were, these little turds were the least of our worries.

We could see much larger things flying amongst the swarm as well, we just *knew* they were gonna be a whole different ball game. Suspended beneath pterodactyl-like wings, the wretched brutes looked like vicious emaciated hellhounds, only stretched out in length, with a long tendril tail, and *easily* four times as big as a dog. Their skeletal heads had red bulging eyes like the hatchlings, but even more revolting than their appearance was the spasmodic convulsions that they'd induce in their stomachs, before vomiting up countless numbers of those vile hatchling-things from their guts. The only thing these monsters had going for them was that they weren't armed with pitchforks and swords. Even so, their ugly sharp teeth and articulated claws looked about as welcoming as falling into a drawer full o' steak knives.

Joe looked on in disgust. "If that ain't the most repugnant thing that I've ever seen, I truly don't know what is. *GET – ME – MY – SHOTGUN!*" ordered the big fella. "I'm gonna blast that monstrosity a new one."

"Look, there's a whole bunch more," I yelled pointing towards the north. "They've gotta be the same things that attacked those farmers out in the fields? How many do you reckon there are Joe?"

"How the hell should I know. Two hundred, a thousand. As many as you want, I guess." Fair call. It was a ridiculous question. Not unexpect-edly two of the creatures dropped out of the sky and took a halfhearted lunge at our heads. Vince made an overstretched swing with his chain-mace, but missed them completely, and slipped shin-deep in guts for his troubles. As he hauled himself up, he pointed high at something coming in fast from right behind us. Turning to look, I was expecting more claws and teeth. Instead, in a full throttled dive came two Valkyrjur.

By the time we managed to duck, they'd already shot past like a couple of incoming comets. Whipping our heads around we looked on amazed as one of the flyers banked hard to her left in pursuit of the "flying monstrosities" as Joe had so eloquently named them. The moment the Valkyrja caught up with them, one of the creatures threw up its guts, while its sidekick pulled back and circled, waiting for an opportune moment to strike.

There was no way of telling which Valkyrja was which, but the one who was engaging slammed her spear hard into the center of the disgorger's chest as it reared to attack with its claws. It let out a bloodcurdling shriek as it flapped around erratically ready to drop to the deck. By now the other Valkyrja had performed a most magnificent loop-de-loop and returned unexpectedly at the rear of her still unchallenged prey.

"Inside loop!" said Joe excitedly. "I saw a crazy Huey helicopter pilot do that one time back in 'Nam."

We looked on intently as three more creatures dropped menacingly down from the sky. Outnumbered two to one, Óðinn's handmaidens didn't seem fazed, especially when the *third* Valkyrja, flew in as swift as a hawk from the darkness and struck hard with her Ulfberht blade. Another creature fell dead into the battle, with its head severed clean from its neck. With the opposing numbers now even, the demons feigned a half-assed attack, before they turned around quickly and fled. The Valkyrjur followed on in pursuit, but soon broke from their chase and returned to our position where they landed gently like soft, settling feathers on the ground.

Now flying metal horses ain't the kind of thing that you see every day, but they barely raised a glance when Sigrún and Göll sprung down from their backs to the ground. Only Skuld remained mounted, aloof, and decidedly distant as she kept a watchful eye open for any sudden attack from above.

As they strode up beside us, I couldn't believe how shit hot this Valhalla strike squadron actually looked. Naturally, Vince made the stock standard wolf whistle, to which Skuld glared back with a look of steel-cold contempt.

They looked even more magnificent than any CGI envisioned warrior women I'd ever seen. Apart from enough blonde hair to go around twice, the Valkyrjur were all dressed the same in winged Viking helmets, that sat low on the brow and gleamed in the moonlight like chrome. Their shoulder and breast armor had all been well fashioned and forged from the pure Ulfberht steel. But most noticeable of all were the chain-mail breechcloths that hung in two separate parts front and back, that weren't even the size of a hand towel.

"Check out their feet," muttered Joe under his breath.

I knew they were fly-babes, but I couldn't believe it, the pointy toed boots they were wearing, came stacked up with six-inch high heels.

"We've come for those missiles," said Sigrún in a tone that was all strictly business.

"Missiles?" replied Joe playing dumb.

"Yes, the two little Starlings you have in the back of your pick-up."

"Oh, *the rockets!* They work on a completely different system you know; you can't just drop 'em like bombs over—"

"Excuse me," interrupted Sigrún most authoritatively. "The proximity fuse on a Starling JX-93b can be adjusted to enable detonation of the warhead either before, on, or after contact. *You* know that as well as I do. The delivery method is irrelevant."

Joe looked impressed, the expression on his face was a classic. "Tell you what… seeing as we're *alll* on the same side here, and *alll* wanna help out young Freya, I'm gonna give you just one of them rockets for now. If you can make it go boom, you're welcome to come back any time soon for the other. … Deal?"

"Deal!" said Sigrún sealing the agreement with a splendid, hair flicking nod of her head.

"Okay. You boys get one of the projectiles out of the truck, and I'll go get my pack of teeny-weeny screwdrivers out of the car, so I can adjust the goddamn prox'-fuse."

"Hey Axel, how come they wanna use rockets? It's a bit of a shift from the ways of old Norse isn't it?" I said, somewhat curious.

"Well at one extreme there is Róta, who, as you have seen, is a Valkyrja wolf-riding purist. The rest all fall more or less somewhere in the middle, but there's a faction of about five or six, who for reasons known only to themselves, are obsessed with dabbling in 21st century high-tech. Apparently Óðinn isn't all that impressed, but they've cajoled him, at least for the moment anyway, with reassurances that it's only a fashionable, digital-age plaything and no disrespect to the unchallengeable power of Seiðr. Have you noticed these three all stay in communication by radio? Check out those discreet little stem microphones on the left-hand side of their krigs hjelmer."

"Their what?"

"Their war helmets," laughed Axel, tapping his knuckles on the motorcycle version that Vince had just pulled from his head.

"Vincent!" came an elated greeting from Göll, making like she had no idea he was here. "How nice to see you again, my little hunky chunky."

You could have driven a bus through the shameless insincerity, but *uugh!* the way she was struttin' her stuff and running her fingers all soft and sexily down the side of his face like she'd done to Axel at the party, would have dumb struck a three-legged sailor. She was buttering him up big time for something, although I was damned if I knew what it was.

"Vincent darling, I'm just a girl and obviously far too weak to take the reins and hold onto a silly old rocket as well. Being the big … strong … man that you are, how would you like to come for a ride with me on my little flying horsey? There's plenty of room for you, right up behind me."

"Go for a spin up there?"

"Yes, little Vincent."

Of course, having no faculties of discernment whatsoever when it came to the flattery of a good-looking woman, the twerp fell hook line and sinker for everything Göll had just said. *"FUCK'N A … let's GO!"*

Vince lifted one of the Starling rockets out by himself, but as soon as he turned to approach Göll's flying horse, a sword wielding demon, lying half dead amongst a bunch of bodies right out front, suddenly jumped to its feet and made a full frenzied lunge for whoever it thought it could stab. Like a bolt of white lightning, something shot past, half an arm's length away from my face. As my eyes turned quickly to follow, I saw the creature fall dead in its tracks, skewered straight through the neck by a spear. Stepping formidably out of the darkness, Skuld placed her pointed heel firmly onto the face of her kill, and with a no-nonsense yank, pulled out the imbedded blade. She never said a word, but the dispassionate smile on her face, chilled me right to the core.

"Frick'n screwdrivers," grumbled Joe, emerging victorious from below the dashboard. "They were in … What's going on? Where's Vince? Where's the Air-Cav'?" Axel pointed a finger skyward.

"Oh, tell me you're joking, he hasn't. That damn fool. Axel, you're the expert, has any other still breathing person, actually, *willingly* flown away with a Valkyrja?" Joe shook his head in amazement.

We stood beside the vehicles, looking up at the plague swarm of circling demons, trying to pinpoint the three flying Valkyrjur and where above the crater they were heading. Joe almost had a seizure when he heard that Vince had also taken one of the rockets up there with him.

But despite all the bluster, you could see he was genuinely wracked with concern for his son.

"What are they expecting to do with it anyway?" Joe asked rhetorically. "It *might* explode if they drop it, but either way, it ain't got enough oomph to … *ah!* never gonna happen anyway." Joe turned his attention quickly back to what was at hand. "Okay groovers, I think it's time to get our asses back in the vehicles."

An excruciating stabbing sensation suddenly pierced me hard along both shoulders. In panic I looked around quickly and realized I'd been plucked from the ground by some maverick, low swooping demon. Thankfully, I'd been holding on tight to my shovel, which, even when I'd pulled Oochie away from the battle, had never left my hand. I made a token swing at the creature but realized that if for some reason it decided to let go of me, considering the speed I was being lifted skyward, I would surely fall straight to my death on the ground. Eighty feet, a hundred feet, two hundred feet. *Ah god*, this was easily the most horrifying thing of my life. I was even more petrified that at any moment my head might be ripped from my neck for a snack. Yes, I can endure the stabbing pain, but please, please, whatever demonic brand of evil creature you are, *"DON'T FUCK'N DROP ME!"*

From up here I could see the entire expanse of the battle, which in the sulfur, stinking darkness appeared as a gigantic cauldron of fire within the ring of the crater below. Unexpectedly the creature plunged downwards as it banked off with speed to the right. I caught a quick glint of something metallic and heard Vince's dulcet voice yelling excitedly from directly above.

"Eat that asshole!" In horror, I witnessed the head of my captor pummeled with only a couple of blows from his mace. I immediately dropped like a stone. Going into a tumble I crashed terrified into something hard that was obviously not solid ground. My momentum flipped me onto my side and I kind of rolled along something flat for a second or two, and then dropped back again into free fall. Everything happened so fast. The only thing I could see was the quickly receding underside of a Valkyrja's horse and the reflections of fire dancing on its spread metal wings. I was ecstatic that either Sigrún or Skuld had been there to catch me, or if unintentional, at least break my fall.

Dead on the hard ground of Hell, or alive amongst a pack of devils. I was glad I'd been granted the latter and jumped up swinging the moment I was dumped back on *terra firma*. Completely alone and disorientated, sheer desperation had cranked up my shovel skills to the point where surprisingly I was fighting with some cracking-hot moves that I never even realised I'd mastered. Only trouble being, my impromptu skydive and the blood-gushing wounds in my shoulders had left me in a whole lot of torment. I was getting hammered and smashed from all sides, but I battled on regardless. I fought like a madman. The putrid taste of sulfur seared poisonously down the back of my throat, and mixed in with sweat, it clogged up my shades, and stung unbearably in my weak vole like eyes. My whole existence had now been reduced to an inescapable crush of blood-lusting devils, unadulterated terror and ab-solute, mind-numbing pain. But then, right on the verge of collapse, I was certain I'd caught a glimpse of someone or something fighting their way through this endless sea of demonic malevolence towards me. I was overjoyed when I clearly saw the sleek, rearing bodies of Guttekatt and Jentekatt destroying all around them with their ferocious attacks. The steady growing rumble of approaching motorcycle engines was the most beautiful sound I could imagine. I dared another glance from my own private mêlée, and saw the most magnificent, incoming formation of Los Espectros Brillantes, with the Great Dís herself riding majestically out on point.

"It's Freya! It's Freya! She's gonna save me!" I mumbled to myself overjoyed. Now you hang on Wolfman, you hang on, just endure for a little while longer.

For every yard gained, my incoming rescuers fought hard against the relentless onslaught of devils. Standing upright astride the girth of Hildisvíni, the goddess continued to battle her way forward, wielding the geirahöð with such perfection and speed that the dual blades of the naginata appeared as no more than a whirling blur. Freya pulled up close, dismounted quickly and strode the last few yards towards me with her guards, scything down almost casually any fanatical demons that persisted with the attack. Drained of all energy, and certain that the tide had now turned, I let down the shovel, and looked up to the sky with relief. I'd been saved, saved by my good buddy Freya, everything would now be okay.

"WHAT ARE YOU DOING HERE, *FOOL?*" came her most unexpected rebuke. "Why do you meddle in affairs that are *NOT* your concern? It was only the incessant urging of the vassal, that has diverted our attention away from matters far more important than coming to *your* individual aid." The unnerving voice that was getting stuck into me from behind the white skull mask was that of Freya the goddess, most definitely not my dear friend at all.

By now dozens of Shining Specters had completely encircled our position and I felt terrible that my rescue was regarded as no more than an unnecessary distraction. Even Guttekatt and Jentekatt looked annoyed, and circled closely around us, making low rumble growls from deep in the back of their throats.

As she stood there in front of me, with her near naked torso running with sweat, the goddess unexpectedly began to knead and claw back and forth along my blood sodden shoulders with her fingers. It felt like absolute torture, but for some reason I kept quiet, and never once cried out with the pain. Then, with an outstretched finger, running red with my own blood, she drew two long diagonal lines across my forehead, and one down the length of my face.

"I will send a squad of my riders to escort you back to your companions. Tell them to depart from this place of power *IMMEDIATELY!*"

Riding pillion, I pulled up alongside the truck. I noticed that since I'd been gone, they'd moved themselves further over towards the western side of the crater but were still very close to the action. Nobody seemed too elated that I'd miraculously come back alive. The only comment from Joe being, "How was the joy-flight chief? I love the war paint." And Axel's response was hardly much better, although he did say "You look like shit, but it seems that the goddess has paid you an honor."

"Why's that?" I said unsure of his meaning.

"That blood-rune she has marked on your face." I glanced in the pickup's side mirror to see it for myself. It looked like an up-pointing arrow. A broad upside-down V on my forehead, atop of a vertical line that ran straight down my nose and lips to the end of my chin.

"It's the Týr rune," explained Axel. "Among other things it signifies courage, victory in battle, and an unassailable determination to succeed."

WOOOW! I felt like a star-struck teenybopper who'd been touched by a rock god, I was adamant I was never-ever gonna wash my face again. "Take off your jacket and T-shirt Wolf, I'll see if I can do something to patch up your wounds."

Axel bound up my shoulders with some clean bits of bandage and tape. It was only when he'd finished I realized that the excruciating level of pain I'd been feeling, had miraculously just about gone. Axel reckoned it was the nurturing powers of Freya that had healed it. I was pretty well sure he was right.

Joe came blustering over with Charlie, who thankfully was back on his feet. *"How!"* he said mockingly, thinking I was some kind of wannabe brave.

"I saw your shenanigans up there earlier," commented Joe with a grin. "You're *so* lucky one of those fly-babes managed to get her bird between you and the tarmac. I'm in two minds about that doofus son of mine though, clubbing your ride's head into a raspberry smoothie. Even though he's an idiot, he's still my boy, and I sure hope he's all in one piece." Joe raised the brim of his hat and made a wide arcing scan of the sky. "With all that smoke and those hatchling things flying around up there, I ain't seen nothin' of Vince nor any of the Valkyrjur since that one broke your fall," Joe said feeling more and more anxious.

While I was struggling to pull on my jacket, a flash lit up the crater like daylight. It lasted only a moment, but the shock wave that followed hit like a twenty-ton truck. "That weren't no Starling rocket," barked Charlie, spinning around to see a glowing green column of pixel-like smoke, that billowed up into the darkness.

Straight away the bizzare looking smolder began to transform into the shape of a colossal sized man, complete with the head of a crocodile. "Oh, tell me I'm seeing things will ya?" Joe said, while shaking his head at this new, unknown protagonist. "That's it, this is the game changer boys," he declared, sounding worryingly like he'd thrown in the towel. "I can't see any way our girl and the boneheads can turn this around now."

"That's *Sobek!*" cried Axel as he noticed the form become more solid.

"Who?" I said, beginning to shake like a leaf.

"The Egyptian crocodile god. He was ferocious and vicious. They say he created the world."

"As if!" scoffed the ever-pragmatic Charlie. "I reckon that's more likely our black-magic, underworld bullshit artist just trying it on for size."

"*Hmm*, that would make sense," nodded Axel in agreement. "Even so, I'm pretty sure the Old Kingdom Sobek carried an ankh and a scepter, certainly not a long-handled scythe."

"I've seen some pretty weird shit over the last couple o' days," came a musing, even-keeled comment from Joe. "Devil-demons, skeleton-bikers, bug-eyed, dive-bombing hatchlings. Not to mention half-naked blondes flying around on shiny metal horses. But a luminous, sixty-foot asshole sporting a bad-boy alligator head? Man, that really does take the cake."

We looked on uneasily, waiting to see what this latter day Sobek was intending to do. It stood there, still as a statue, only the enormous head panned back and forth as if it were searching for something specific amidst all the smoke and the mayhem.

All of a sudden, it lunged swiftly forward and with a wide arcing swathe of its scythe indiscriminately cut down a whole division of The Shining Specters, and any of the devil hordes that happened to be in its way. The horrible action was repeated a second and third time with even more merciless zeal than before. An unassailable rampage seemed imminent, but the towering figure refrained from any further attacks, as coming right out of left field, its gigantic crocodile head morphed unexpectedly into that of a man.

"Holy shit, that's *MIMAS!*" I yelled, shocked by what I was seeing.

"I told ya!" said Charlie.

The head spoke loud and menacing in a language that I was pretty certain was Old Norse.

"What's he saying, what's he saying?" we all pestered Axel annoyingly. Axel raised his hand slightly, as if to say, *"If you'd just shut up for a minute, I might be able to hear."*

"I can only understand bits and pieces, he's using an archaic dialect of old, West Norse."

"Yeah well, but *what's he saying, what's he saying?*" hassled Charlie, doing a pretty funny mimic of yours truly.

"He's laying down the old, jilted lover ultimatum. You know, *'This is your last chance Freya, leave all of this foolishness behind you and come with me now. Or I will destroy YOU, and everyone you know, and send the whole lot back to the Ginnungagap.'* ... That kind of stuff."

"That's the great nothingness isn't it?" I commented fittingly.

"Well yes, the void of all voids, the primordial emptiness, that which was there before even the cosmos came into being. How on earth do you know that?"

As I began to relay my extensive knowledge of coffee-table-book Nordic mythology a long mournful wail from a battle horn blew distinct and loud above the noise of the fighting. It's sounding seemed to signify some point of crucial importance in the goddess's battle strategy, as from all-over the expanse of the crater The Shining Specters immediately began to mobilize their widely dispersed motorcycle divisions in accord with some kind of tactical, pre-planned maneuver.

Joe climbed up onto the pickup's roof to get a better look. *"No darlin' NO!"* Joe said distraughtly. "She's pulling all of her forces back together into a single, central position. That's madness, she'll get herself completely surrounded and that's the last thing she should let happen." Joe watched unmoving, as he took a moment longer to ascertain exactly what was happening.

"Oh well," he mumbled, shaking his head despondently, "if it worked for General 'Chesty' Puller back in Korea... What was it he said at the battle of Chosin? 'We're surrounded. That simplifies things.'"

Standing on the edge of the pickup's door frame, I stretched up to take a look for myself. At first it seemed disorganized, like a ginormous massing of motorcycles, but as the riders maneuvered themselves into formation, it began to make the unmistakable pattern of three, long arcing spirals. "I know what she's doing," I said fairly confidently. "She's playing the tafl!"

"She's *WHAT?*" barked Joe.

"I know what I'm talking about Joe. Freya's gettin' ready for the world's most humongous game of Hnefatafl. And she's *really, really* good at it too."

"She was the Norwegian high school champion," threw in Axel as the cherry on top.

"High school champion," muttered Joe flatly, as he scrambled down from the roof. "Well will one of you two jokers explain to me in the next twenty seconds exactly what *the f—*"

Joe was about to let rip, when an all-pervasive racket pulled our attention instantly back to the sixty-foot Mimas, who, apoplectic with rage at Freya's obvious and most humiliating rebuff, had begun to strike out violently again. Now, mid outburst he unexpectedly morphed into a creature even more bizarre than the last one.

"Oh for the love o'... What the hell is *that?*" shouted Joe, now really starting to lose it. All eyes turned to Axel, as this new bag of laughs was so unbelievably ridiculous, we figured he'd be the only one that would have even the slightest idea what it was.

"It looks like a ... Typhon." We never asked any more questions, as there really didn't seem any point.

The top half was still basically human, with a six-packed torso physique that looked so fake it was laughable. Instead of one single neck there were twelve. *TWELVE!* Long wriggly things that stuck out wide from the center of its shoulders. Half of the heads on the ends looked like Mimas, although distorted, as if they were puffed up on 'roids, and the other six had curly-whirly, oriental type dragon faces that snorted flame-thrower volleys of fire. The lower half of this creature's body was no more than a writing tangle of uncountable snake coils that made you feel sick when it moved.

Charlie started laughing "Oh come on, this is such a load o' bullcrap, there's no-frick'n-way-Jose *that* thing is real." There wasn't even time to debate it, as within seconds of its appearance, two fast flying Valkyrjur and the Morrígan, soaring swiftly beneath her enormous spread of crow wings came in hard for a three-pronged attack. We looked on in awe, as a fearless Morrígan dropped herself right in amongst the necks, where with a ruthless ferocity, she plunged and gouged her battle spear deep into the mishmash of heads.

The Valkyrjur were just as aggressive and gave no quarter at all. To witness the unleashing of such devastating fury, really was something to see. At one point I saw Skuld dive headlong from her mount, and with her long legs wrapped tightly around one of the Typhon's necks, actually hack off not one, but three of the oversized Mimas heads with her spear and a regular shortsword. Even Róta, mounted shakily on the back of the fierce Mánagarmr, was down there at ground level, battling hard and untiring with her war axe amongst the slithering snake legs and the never-ending onslaught of demons.

I don't know if there was something inherent in the pattern of the geometry, but as the spiraling formations of Shining Specter motorcycles began to tighten up and grow ever larger, the devils were becoming increasingly disorientated and rattled by their movements. As the out-coming riders passed slashing and stabbing through the demons on one side, their fellow riders who had already reached the furthest end of the spiral would then double-back tightly, adjacent to their brethren maintaining the perpetual fighting cycle on their return. The three conjoined spirals were definitely having a most adverse effect on their foe.

Joe thought the mathematics of this never-ending structure was intrinsically linked somehow with the mesmerizing racket Banksie and the Four Señors had been making earlier. "Too much unfamiliar information for the limited mindsets of the devils to process I guess."

"You don't think the ancient European tribes held the Triskele in such high esteem merely because of it's pretty pattern, do you?" remarked Axel knowingly. "If you understand it's secrets, it is a most powerful transducer for—"

"There's the boy!" cried Joe, sounding both relieved and excited, as Göll out of nowhere came careering overhead into view. "He's still up there, and the son-of-a-gun's still got a hold of that Starling rocket."

Göll and Vince banked hard to their right and did one circumnavigation flight around the Typhon. As they came back around straight and level, we looked on in disbelief. Like a seasoned circus performer, Vince stood himself upright on the back of Göll's flying horse and was holding the rocket high up over his head like a javelin.

Their incoming sortie seemed no more formidable than any other of this whole airborne attack, but for some reason the gigantic monster lashed out noticeably quicker and more aggressively with one of its tendrils, catching Göll completely off guard, sending her, the flying horse, Vince, and the rocket all tumbling off fast into the high reaching blackness. We stood there in silence, despairing, and fearing the probable worst, all the while listening to the remaining, unsevered heads of Mimas ranting and raving through the din of the battle, as one loud, unintelligible voice.

After what seemed an eternity, it was Joe who finally spoke, fighting hard to hold back the tears. "Okay! That's it, I've had enough of this crap. You're going down now ya sack o' shit! I don't understand what he's saying but listen to the way that oversized piss-ant talks will ya. He ain't no *GOD*, he's just some jumped up turd that's trying his darndest to piss off poor Faye by playing his own little sob-story, wild-card on top of all this other bullshit going on already. He had me going for a while back at The Alamo with that will-o'-the-wisp disappearing act. But I know for a fact that this dematerialization hocus-pocus is as old as my hat. Black ops have had it at least since the seventies."

"Joe's right," nodded Axel, "its security rating is only level two restricted. Even so, it's common knowledge in my circles that Mimas, whatever he is, has been around in some self-serving guise, pissing people off for more than three hundred years now."

"Okay, maybe the son-of-a-bitch does have some kind of weird, demonic pedigree," added Joe getting more and more angry. "How the hell would I know. Like they say. You can fool most of the sheeple all of the time, but I'm sorry sunshine, Uncle Joe's about to pull the plug on this little dog and pony show. All that prick out there is trying to do is scare the living bejesus out of us with a whole frick'n smorgasbord of high-end holographic CRAP! Charlie, you get the cloth tape and I'll get the other rocket. Then I'm gonna go shove it right up that smug bastard's ass!" The look on Joe's face as he taped the rocket onto the Fire Diamond's hood was grimmer than I'd ever seen it before.

"Those motorcycle spirals seem to be heading this way pretty quickly now boys. If you want my advice, I think you should get yourselves into that central, eye of the storm point right there with young Freya. She seems determined to go all the way with these Hefa'...whatever you call them tactics. As for me, I'm going straight for that son of a bitch over there, and quite frankly I couldn't give a shit anymore whether I come out the other side or not. Like it says on the shirt, THIS ONE'S FOR CHESTER, and now I guess it's for young Vincent as well."

"I'm coming with you pops," roared Charlie, throwing his arm awkwardly around Joe's shoulder. "In for a penny, in for a pound. I'll probably cough my lungs up and be dead in a year or two anyway." Joe looked his son long in the eye. "You really don't have to do this Charlie."

"*Bullshit*, we'll be sweet old-timer, we'll be sweet."

"Well grab that other shotgun out of the pickup then boy, and let's get rolling."

"What about Oochie?" I blurted, suddenly remembering that he was still lying unconscious and flat out in the trunk."

"Don't you worry about me none, Mr. Arrow face," came a chuckling voice through the shattered side window. I figured he must have woken up, sometime earlier, and crawled his way into the back through the pull-down part of the seat.

"I've got my ol' .44 and a handful of ammo. So I'm coming along for the ride," grinned Oochie tapping the door with the end of the barrel.

"*My .44!*" scolded Joe.

"*Yeah, yeah*, and besides, I sure won't get to see all those blondies in action up close if I stay here with these two numbskulls now will I?"

"Cut open those two sacks of fluoride will you Wolfman," ordered Joe. "Hopefully, we can choke up some of these mongrels if we don't get to run 'em down first." Joe nodded a silent goodbye and slipped behind the wheel of the car. Axel and I stood there in silence, as the Fire Diamond took off to the hard metal sound of Mötorhead, with the powder from two bags of sodium fluoride swirling out from the trunk like a tail.

◆

It was only when you drove up closer, that you could fully appreciate just how massive this triad of Triskele spirals actually was. They reminded me a little of the buffalo herds that used to roam wild on the plains.

Although it seemed somewhat limited, our plan was to skirt around the edge of the nearest spiral, and then follow its course right into the small patch of land in the center. Freya had moved there already with her Los Espectros Brillantes bodyguard. There could be no doubt that the Great Dis was positioning herself tactically to 'act as the king' so to speak, in the middle of the Hnefatafl table.

As Axel and I tried to make our way in around the edge towards the center, it became obvious that the three gigantic spirals were all interlinked and rotating in a counterclockwise direction. Axel said the ancient Celts would advance that way in their war dances to show their intentions were hostile. The going was harder than we'd expected. Like moths to a flame, the devil swarms would continually climb onto the hood or into the bed of the pickup. They were slamming themselves against all of the windows, which by now had been totally shattered, although miraculously they hadn't caved in, so the devils couldn't get at us. Even the flying hatchlings were getting more brazen. A handful had managed to crawl their way up through the air vents. The little shits were way more aggressive than any we'd come across earlier. They took a whole bunch o' chunks out of both of us before we finally managed to smash 'em.

Axel was hanging out of the open door, slashing away tirelessly with his broadsword, trying anything to hold the devils at bay. All I could do was try and keep the wheels moving and not let them get bogged down in a whole bunch of bodies. Unable to do much more, Axel swung quickly back inside and glared at me prophetically.

"This is unbelievable Wolf. There's no turning back, if we don't get through to where Freya is soon, well I don't think—" Right then, I heard something that, at first, I thought was my imagination playing tricks on me, but even through all the racket I was convinced that I heard it again.

"That's Cavalry Charge!" shouted Axel, as his face lit up with excitement. "Someone out there's got a bugle. Maybe the cavalry really is coming." I almost wrung my own neck, as I twisted my head around trying to see where the distant calls were coming from.

Turning back to my driving, I looked on in horror as right down the center of the hood, a massive, horned devil, was heading straight for a full impact collision with the windshield. I instinctively flinched and braced myself for the crash, but when it didn't come I opened my eyes and saw its dead ugly face pressed right up against the glass with two feathered arrows lodged in its head. *Arrows?* I thought, hearing once again the unmistakable, bugle sound of "Charge". Looking out of my driver's side window, I thought I was seeing things when no more than ten feet away I saw the magnificent image of an Indian chieftain, resplendent in a full-feathered warbonnet, complete with red and black war paint, mounted atop of a feisty Appaloosa stallion.

Axel seemed even more impressed at the sight of this war chief than I was. "Open the window Wolf, open the window, isn't that—"

"*SACRAMENTO!*" we both said together, and then burst into laughter. I guess as a sign of relief.

Two long streams of mounted Indians were now passing quickly, one on either side of the truck. Any devils that stood in their path had been cut down mercilessly with either a lance or a tomahawk, or a hard-hitting salvo of arrows. The thirty or so in the vanguard looked exactly how I imagined warrior-braves of old must have been. But as the columns began to taper, the still blowing bugler appeared, wearing traditional Indian clothes for the most part, except for a ridiculous, high riding ball cap that seemed to just perch on the top of his head. After him, the only other standout of note that galloped past was dressed in a raw buckskin breechcloth and a matching rig of iridescent, thermoplastic ice-hockey armor. The rest of the tail enders had all but ditched anything Indian, in favor of fur collared lumber jackets, and stock-standard blue jeans and trainers.

Sacramento sidled his horse close to the window and lowered himself down for a look. "Evenin' Wolf. Evenin' Axel," he said feigning a tip of his war bonnet as though greeting a guest on a still summer's evening. "What brings you folks here?"

Axel just cracked up laughing. *"I love this crazy guy!"*

"We would've been here hours ago, but most of these clowns wanted to get takeout and watch the late-night re-run of *Dancing with America's Greatest Home Renovators,* or whatever that stupid show is called."

"Well now that you're here, perhaps you could give us a lift," I said pointing over to the eye of the storm. "'Cos I don't think we can get there alone."

"You're going in *THERE?*" queried Sacramento, with an expression of mock surprise. "Zeeesh, you two really are loco. Okay, I can get you in most of the way, but all these skeleton dudes are freaking the life out my guys. Wolf, you come with me, Axel you can ride pillion with 'Son of Satchmo' here. That tin bugle of his is a champion, it's so bloody noisy it spins the diablos right out."

◆

Watching from the back of the horse, it was obvious that the gigantic

Triskele was exacting a punishing toll on the devils. With every action they seemed more and more confused by the unwavering regularity of the lines of oncoming riders. Within minutes our Indian escort had taken us most of the way down the gap between two of the spirals. I was expecting that they would take us further in, but unexpectedly only a short distance from where we could clearly see Freya and her bodyguard, Sacramento and the other braves pulled their horses to an immediate stop.

"That's it, folks, this is as far as we can go," declared Sacramento, sounding grim and unusually serious. "One of the boys just received a text message saying that his village is under attack. We have to leave and go there right now so you'd ...' Suddenly a flash and the thunderous boom of an explosion, turned our heads to the north. With gut wrenching sickness, my intuition told me that the detonation had surely been triggered by Joe and Oochie and Charlie. Sacramento knew nothing about the missiles, I tried hurriedly to explain what Joe and the others were intending but the urgency of our own situations, pared my words down to only the most basic of facts.

Unimpeded by the violent explosion, Mimas just stood there, silhouetted unmoving, against the high curling column of flame. Then, with a blood curdling shriek he unfurled an enormous spread of black wings and rose like a curse to the sky.

Whipped up by his fervor, what seemed like a million flying demons swooped down in wave after wave, unleashing an even more vicious bombardment at anything that moved on the ground. For once, even Sacramento looked shocked, but when he raised himself high on his war stallion to fight them, his prowess as an exemplary warrior was obvious for all there to see. As he wielded his war lance, in the style of a bo staff, not one of the vile, swooping creatures could lay a claw slash or get anywhere near him.

"*Go! Go now!*" said Sacramento straight faced and forceful, as he and his warriors repelled the attack. "Oh yeah, say a big *howdy-hi* to Super Chick for me will ya."

◆

As Axel and I made our dash on foot for the center, we were exposed to constant attack. Not only from devils, but from every type of dive-bombing demon as well. Even so, we still kept a watchful eye fixed on the now high soaring Typhon, as there was no way of telling what this lunatic Mimas might do. At the spot where the spirals linked up, we passed through the riders and into the small piece of land in the middle. It was roughly the size of a ballpark diamond and most definitely the eye of the storm.

"Welcome to the inner circle," shouted Axel sarcastically. I knew this spot held some kind of strategic importance, although I was still in the dark as to why. Any hopes of respite were dashed, as even here in the eye of the Triskele it was still swarming with devils and we'd have to fight every step of the way before we could link up with Freya. What made it worse was the Great Dis and her entourage weren't holding any kind of secured position in the center. Instead, they were moving across to a low, nondescript hillock further toward the edge.

"What the hell are they going there for Axel?" I yelled with frustration.

"Look at the ground Wolf," he answered hurriedly, more preoccupied with the onrush of a half-headed sword-wielding devil.

Apart from the red, glowing cracks still spewing up demons, a pattern of luminous bands had begun to appear over what I could see of the ground. They all seemed to converge more or less in our direction. "Those things are *LEY-LINES*, right?" I yelled, trying to be heard over the overwhelming noise of screaming devils and motorcycles.

"That's right," answered Axel. "You see how they intersect at the spot where Freya is now?" he said quickly wiping a whole gulp of devil gore from the battle-stained blade of his sword, "That little rise is a NODE POINT. It's imperative, that's where The Dis has to be."

We were only a stone's throw away from reaching Freya's position when Mimas, who'd been circling menacingly high above the battlefield, suddenly dropped down to attack. *"FRRREEEEEEYYYYYYYYYAAA!"* came the pathetic, almost synthesized wail from what was left of his unsevered heads. As he dived, Mimas screamed out a tirade of words in old Norse.

Axel poked a finger down his throat and pretended to gag. "Same old, same old. He just *LOVES* little sister. He's so unoriginal. He keeps on ranting about, 'If I can't have you, then nobody else will!' … et cetera, et cetera."

"Seriously?"

We both looked on helpless, knowing that armed with only a replica broadsword and a shovel there was absolutely nothing at all we could do. "Why don't the skellies blow the shit out of the bastard with a collective volley from their shotguns?"

"They won't function anymore Wolf. Nothing with moving mechanical parts will work this close to the node point. Why do you think all the riders in here and on the hillock have dismounted on mass from their motorcycles? This is why Freya had no intention of relying on guns, she knew it was all going to be only swords and Seiðr from here on in."

As we clambered our way over the circular wall of closely abandoned motorcycles, I stopped momentarily to look up in fascination as this monstrous, fire breathing Typhon hurtled straight down towards us. Axel goaded me on towards the middle, where, without even saying, I knew unquestioningly we were about to join Freya and The Shining Specters in some redemptive moment of willful self-sacrifice.

"*Hey!* Hey Wolf! snap out of it," nudged Axel. "Your drifting off, it's affecting you."

"Wha ...?"

"The Triskele. The energy fields they generate can play unusual tricks on the mind, especially our perception of time. Just stay focused and be aware it can easily creep up on you." He was right, for a moment I was back home in Vegas, watching my neighbor's son and his friends moving their painted figurine armies around on a table-top war game. Although it had taken some hits, the thousand-point Typhon was only a single dice throw away now from a game changing strike on the opposing high scoring goddess. But on the very next dice roll a squadron of nubile, warrior women, resplendent on magnificent, winged flying horses came—"

"*WAKE UP MAN. Watch the Triskele,*" screamed Axel. "It obviously affects you so easily." Affected or not, I looked up ecstatic as the real time Valkyrjur came screaming in fast from the south. I strained my eyes hard to pick out which one was Göll. It didn't seem to matter much really, as all three were now flying solo. It was the final, unwanted confirmation that Vince was now most definitely lost.

"Those three better re-route that idiot pretty quickly or—"

Mimas was dropping fast. The audacity of being attacked for a second time, set him shrieking with rage and firing off all of his remaining flame jets at once.

Skuld flew in first, skillfully corkscrewing her horse around one of the long, deadly columns of fire. For a moment she was hidden from view by the smoke. She emerged suddenly alongside the head that was flaming. It was gone in an instant, hacked clean from its neck by her sword.

Wing tip to wing tip, Sigrún and Göll climbed rapidly skyward, positioning their steeds right in the path of Mimas's unstoppable dive. As a collision seemed imminent, both Valkyrjur unexpectedly spun their mounts upside down and sliced their wings like four giant razors through the necks of their plummeting target. We could hear them laughing and screaming as they hung on tight to the reins of their horses with their legs dangling free in midair.

He was still aiming straight towards Freya, but Mimas was not looking good. More than half of his heads were now missing, and the ones that were left started sparking up bright from within.

"Look, here comes the Celt," shouted Axel excitedly.

No glint from the flames marked the Morrígan's presence. Invisible amongst the absolute black of her wings, she swooped in low but changed her trajectory to avoid the gaggle of fire breathing necks and went straight for the underside belly. As Mimas became more translucent, we could see clearly as the Morrígan plunged her battle spear forcefully right up inside the Typhon's guts, letting her blade and the pitch of his dive do the rest.

"I can't *believe it*," said Axel in his finest Norwegian accent. "That woman is just so unbelievably *TOUGH!*" The Typhon was still dropping hard and on course. The Morrígan's spear had undoubtedly spliced right through the mainframe or something, as the whole holographic shemozzle was sparking and firing up big time, and rapidly coming apart at the seams.

"SEE! … I told you it's not frick'n real," said Axel, doing a well-meaning impression of Charlie.

Reaching the top of the hillock, I looked across at the relentless ocean of devils that swarmed up towards us like a disgusting, unstoppable tide. Thankfully, Guttekatt and Jentekatt showed an unfaltering dedication to their mistress. Any demon that came even close was set upon immediately and literally torn to shreds. Disorder was rife as Freya's Shining Specters guard were failing in their efforts to escort, or more aptly drag, her away from the spot where in about ten seconds time this most deadly of fools was about to crash and explode like a comet.

The goddess commanded them back and stood poised with the geirahöð angled low and still by her side. With her gaze fixed firmly on Mimas, Freya took a few paces backwards, raised the weapon high, and then at the end of an urgent dash forward, leapt straight into the air beneath a magnificent spread of unfurled falcon wings that I wasn't completely sure I was seeing. The cloak that hung down from her shoulders had sprung back into life. Not by a chance draft of wind, but by the fully energized powers of Seiðr. At first, I thought it was the Triskele, messing around with my head, but Axel was seeing it too.

As Freya soared straight towards Mimas, she morphed spectacularly back and forth in appearance between herself and an enormous Peregrine falcon, both sharing that same spread of wings. When the two foes collided, it was obvious this battle would be over in seconds. Failing to completely engulf her amidst his flame bursts and tendrils, his one option now was to smash Freya hard into the ground with sheer force and size. Despite his momentum, the goddess countered with a ferocious and deadly attack. The lightning fast speed of the geirahöð and the falcon's raptorial talons completely ripped the ill-fated Typhon to pieces in an absolute one-sided maul.

The whole thing crashed to the ground. Immediately the enormous pile of spluttering wreckage began to dematerialize into a fast-fading shadow.

Such a weird and anticlimactic ending for such a self-aggrandizing demonic... mage?

"Well at least *that* thing's kaput," said Axel, snatching unsuccessfully at a holographic shard that digitally fluttered past. "I'm so glad it ended so easily, albeit with the magnificent efforts of Freya, the Valkyrjur and the Morrígan. Unfortunately, I have no doubt Mimas would have bailed himself out in time with his archaic magick and skulked off back to—"

Axel's words were cut short, as Freya dropped from the sky and landed firmly beside us. She was still holding onto the geirahöð, but the falcon feathered cloak had now gone.

"Hei little søster!" Axel wiggled his fingers and greeted her amusingly. But the goddess was in no mood for mirth. She just glared at us with obvious displeasure, saying only "I thought that I'd told you to *LEAVE!*" The encounter with Mimas had been no more than a pathetic, but most dangerous, sideshow. But now with that distraction over, I could see Freya's resolve as her focus shifted immediately back to the main task at hand.

Freya seemed anxious, as she studied the eastern sky. It was only then that I noticed the dim red glow of pre-morning light, banding wide across the horizon. Freya turned quickly and signaled to someone that I sensed had moved up behind us. Two mighty blasts from a war horn soon followed. As I looked back to see who it was, I froze on the spot, as only inches away from my face snorted the wet, drooling snout of Mánagarmr the ancient Moon Hound.

"Róta. Hurry!" ordered Freya to the Valkyrja sitting attentive on the enormous beast's back. "Ride out and escort them through *NOW!*" At first, I thought she was sending me and Axel packing, but as I strained my eyes across to where Freya had been pointing, I could see a long string of tiny black dots skirting in our direction around one of the curved inner walls of the crater, but it was still too dark to see what they were.

"*C I R C L E !*" screamed the commander in chief, as yet another even more aggressive onslaught of devils surged up from the ground straight towards us. Freya's order was followed immediately. In moments, her skeleton bodyguard formed a steel wielding ring of defense around the very most top of the hillock. The area inside the skeleton circle was no more than forty feet wide, and along with Freya and Guttekatt and Jentekatt, Axel and I were the only ones in there.

"Welcome to the *inner*, inner circle!" laughed Axel hysterically, obviously succumbing at last to the powers of the Triskele. "This is the end of the line Mr. Rune-face, there's nowhere to run to, NOWHERE TO HIDE." His laughter turned to maniacal cackles, filling me completely with dread.

Despite the courageous stand of the skeletons, devils were pouring through everywhere. So vast were their numbers, they were climbing up over each other in a fervor to get into the circle and kill us. Axel and I fought hard beside Freya, her skill with the geirahöð was sublime as she mowed down the demons like corn. I took a quick glance at the wall face, hoping desperately that it was Sacramento and his warriors riding back now to save us. But this single line phalanx moved swiftly without any horses and were already arcing their way across the floor of the crater with both an air and ground Valkyrjur escort around them.

"*Who the hell are those guys?*" quizzed Axel, as he skewered his sword through a devil. Now they'd come closer, their distinctive silhouettes revealed who they were straight away. "*It's THE TIRE BOYS!*" I yelled excitedly.

"*Who?*"

"The frick'n Honey Rollers."

"How are they going to help us?" he scoffed, bursting my bubble immediately. "Maybe those things they've got there are *bombs*."

"Do ya think so?" I said, looking back like a moron to check.

The Rollers were moving through on their big wheeler blade skates, but this time they were teamed up in pairs. Between them they carried two long poles on their shoulders from which hung an oval shaped object as big as a medium sized barrel.

Freya smiled, as more and more Rollers appeared. They were some fifty yards off to the north, but instead of heading straight in toward us, they turned east and sliced their way unimpeded between what was left of The Shining Specters still fighting on outside of Freya's inner circle. I recognized Lucien the moment I saw him. His towering, Mezzo-American hairstyle was unmistakable, but he was also the only Roller not in a pair and seemed to be acting as leader. The HEXO and DOAX contingents were all out there somewhere, but in this pre-morning half-light it was impossible to tell who was who.

"What's happening Axel? I thought they were coming to help us." Axel said nothing, he was back in the fight with the devils.

As the Honey Rollers moved eastward, a strange, animated mist began to disperse from all of their oval shaped cargos and merged into one single cloud.

"What in God's name is it?"

"Bees!" replied Axel, somewhat blasé. "Those oval things they were carrying must have been hives. I can only suppose they are going to dive-bomb together and sting all the devils to death." Axel roared loudly at his own stupid joke.

"Bees!" I said, feeling cheated as they converged into an enormous black swarm above us. I looked once again for the Honey Rollers, but by now their one-way foray had continued right through unabated, as they were now on the far eastern side of the crater. Freya's eyes were glued to the east, when unexpectedly she made a hurried retreat a half dozen paces, to a spot where the glowing white bands all converged.

"That must be the middle of the node point," I said, amazed that I hadn't seen it before. Axel ignored my astuteness and half pulled me back, near to where Freya stood poised in the center.

Gradually the top of a bright, golden disc appeared upon the horizon. The wait seemed interminable, but then, when the two blades caught the first dawning rays of the light, the Great Dis lifted the geirahöð skyward. It was clear something of great significance would follow. I noticed the gleaming stones of the Brísingamen that hung magnificently around her neck and remembered the prophetic message that Freya had nurtured in her memory since she was a child, which now, at this moment had finally come to fruition – *"At the rising of the hidden sun, be ready Freya, your time has now come."*

Standing astride the node point, Freya began to rotate the geirahöð above her head. At first the gyrations were slow, but the speed soon got faster and faster. Axel and I moved in as close as we could without getting sliced, while Guttekatt and Jentekatt defended the area between us and the skeleton's now rapidly weakening defenses.

I had no idea what the goddess was doing, but to witness such resolve in the way she handled the geirahöð, reassured me that hopefully all was not lost. Hearing the angered buzz of a squadron of bees doing battle with a bunch of those horrid, little hatchling creatures, I looked up at the sky to see what the rest of their buddies were doing.

"Axel check that out!" From the shapeless black shadow, the massive swarm of bees had formed themselves into an ever-accelerating circle that shone brilliantly in the first morning rays overhead. But as they built up more and more velocity their individualities blurred completely as they then transformed into a golden, spiraling cone that drew its midpoint closer and closer down towards the geirahöð. I knew there was obviously some kind of link between their synchronizing rotations, but as the goddess's blades reached an impossible speed, a wispy stream of dazzling blue light began to build and corkscrew upwards from the spinning geirahöð towards the counter rotating spiral that was descending from the bees up above. When the two spirals came in contact, they immediately locked in together and formed a towering shape of bright light that looked like an old-fashioned hourglass.

"PLASMA!" said Axel, as he sliced the head off a devil.

"What's that?" I asked, aggressively gutting an onrushing foe with my spade.

"Well it's the fourth state of matter, ionized particles interacting with the Earth's geomagnetism. I think the goddess is trying to create some kind of hyper dimensional torsion field vortex."

"Keep talking." I ducked beneath a free-wheeling sword swipe.

"Well, supposedly if two counter-rotating plasma spirals come into contact, the stress on the neutrino particles can create anomalies in the space-time continuum. I'm no expert, but that's how I heard it."

I was distracted momentarily as I struggled with a duo of high vaulting demons. "Are you serious? I thought bees only made honey." Axel didn't comment, waylaid incommunicado by more of the same.

Despite all the dangers, I felt an overwhelming compulsion to just turn and stare at the goddess. I understood now why Freya had been sent back in time to the Neolithic. The rigorous training with that huge wooden stave had made it mere child's play for her to now spin the much lighter and well balanced geirahöð, and fine-tuned the abilities needed to create this torsion field vortex. I stood there enthralled by that impeccable motion and besotted by her incomparable beauty.

"Wolf. *WAKE UP!* Stop ogling my sister, we're still in a fight here you know." I knew I'd fallen back under the influence, but as Axel's voice brought me around, I became unnerved by the tug of the vortex, and was convinced it would suck us both in. "Exactly how dangerous is that thing Axel?" I yelled above its shrill, howling noise.

"Normally we'd be dead in two minutes from the emerging gamma rays, but this honeybee assisted momma is most certainly a creation of Seiðr."

Unexpectedly the vortex shot out some kind of colossal, high pressure blast-wave, which smashed us hard to the ground with its force. Prone to attack I lifted my head up immediately and was shocked to see that the fast rolling, out-surge of plasma had nearly blown every last devil from the top of the hillock, and those a short distance beyond. Unbelievably, the goddess's Los Espectros Brillantes bodyguard weren't spared from its impact either. The force of the plasma had torn it's way outward and through them, scattering the Triskele formations, their bones, and their bikes to the wind.

Clambering back on my feet, I turned to Freya. How could she possibly do this? They were her most loyal of forces. Noticing that Guttekatt and Jentekatt were both gone as well, my reason slipped into panic.

It was then that Axel suddenly let out a most awful, blood-curdling scream. I turned towards him and saw to my horror, a long, jagged blade skewered deep into the small of his back. He'd been stabbed by some malevolent devil that had been lying in wait playing dead. Enraged I jammed my spade straight through its face, but with its assassin's job done it made a last dying gasp and fell in a heap to the ground. I dropped my weapon without thinking and lowered Axel gently along one of the glowing, ley-lines. I figured all this earth energy stuff might help him *somehow*, although in my heart I was sure he'd been killed.

As all this unfolded, Freya stood firm and maintained the geirahöð's rotation. But an obvious struggle was going on between the will of the goddess and the need of the vassal to break free from her commitment and rush to the aid of her brother. The need was too strong, and as Freya took only two or three steps from the node point, the vortex immediately slipped away from its pivotal rotation and pitched unbalanced on its side out of kilter. The moment this happened, everything around me seemed to dissolve to a thin, smoky veil. Except for a bizarre onrush of recognizable cameos that threw themselves straight out of the plasma towards me. Amongst them I saw a fish-eyed distortion of Sacramento as he crouched down on his horse and looked in through the pickup's window, I saw Francisca, an ex-workmate of mine from Vegas, as she tripped and dropped a full tray of glasses. I saw Johnny Hollywood talking in tongues to Navette, and the image of a hearty young boy with a crewcut, sitting in the back of his dad's brand-new Fire Diamond, who I knew was most definitely Joe. The whole thing was over in seconds but seemed to play on for much longer.

Unwillingly Freya moved back to the node point, her desperate wish to help Axel had been overruled by the goddess, as the need to restore equilibrium to the vortex was deemed as much more important. The devils were heading back in force, but now with Axel gone and the skeleton circle obliterated, there was only the goddess and myself left to face them.

As the sun climbed higher, I quickly scanned around the battlefield, desperately searching for a contingent of The Shining Specters that were charging back in on their motorcycles to help us. But my hopes came to nothing, as in every direction this endless outpouring of devils had now forced all of the still remaining riders to abandon any kind of formation and to continue to fight toe to toe on the ground. I glanced across at Axel, hoping that by some miracle he'd made a sudden recovery, but was chilled by the unexpected presence of Skuld, who must have settled her flying stallion down beside him, unseen amidst the overwhelming distractions. Indifferent to Freya's presence, Skuld sat firmly mounted, while in a calm and well-practiced motion, drew Axel's lifeless body up onto the back of her horse. I remembered from reading Joe's book that this was what Valkyrja did. Their role since forever had been to choose the bravest from amongst the fallen warriors, and carry them back as the Einherjar, to practice their war crafts, and drink mead in the great halls with Óðinn.

Understandably this was all way-way too much for the vassel. Even through the heavy white smear of her skull mask, I could see the terror on her face as her brother's lifeless body was taken away right before her eyes. Freya dropped the geirahöð and dashed across towards Skuld. She tore the dazzling Brísingamen free from her neck and held it out in a desperate offering of exchange for her brother. But Skuld just gazed back at her with a cold expression that erred on the edge of contempt. The vortex was now going haywire and threw me back down on the deck. With my face full of dirt, all I could see at ground level was the urgent scurry of Freya's boots as the goddess pulled her back once again to the node point.

Holy crap! When I lifted up my head, I felt as sick as a ten-gallon drunk. Nothing else even registered except for this blue spinning nightmare around me. Man, I thought that first little twister was trippy, but this untethered beauty was in an absolute class of its own. Luckily, it stayed spinning around madly at ground level, like some unpassable, high voltage blockade. But knowing that every last devil from the bowels of the earth was out there on the other side just busting to get through and gut me, was pushing my nerves to the limit.

As my eyes adjusted to the blinding glare, I became aware of an increasing number of indeterminable figures emerging out of the plasma's electric-blue wall. Transfixed by the ease of their motion, I watched them circle and tried to make out what they were. At first I panicked, but I just knew without question that they were in some way supernaturally connected with Freya's Specter bodyguard and were hopefully not on a course to attack me.

A white glowing skull appeared right before me. Startled I slammed my head on the ground, as only inches in front of me the specter began to develop sinews and muscles and flesh, and within moments a fully formed face of a man with a Hispanic appearance was smiling and peering straight at me. Suddenly his head exploded with what I suppose was a blast from a gunshot. Immediately another skull took its place, but when the facial features grew back again, it was that of a middle-aged black man. He managed a sad smile before a sturdy, rope-noose strangled his neck and yanked him away out of sight. I started to freak out severely, as yet *another* skull appeared in its place. This one grew the features of a pretty young Asian woman. I cried out in panic as the face was then smashed to a pulp by a fist. Then came a fair-headed white man, I saw him quake and his eyes roll back in his head as a blood splattered blade was drawn hatefully from one side of his throat to the other. This most horrific cycle just kept on repeating and repeating and seemed destined to go on forever, when in an inverse appearance to all of the others, a fully fleshed man, wearing army fatigues dived towards me from out of the distance. But right at the moment I saw who it was, this incoming soldier exploded in flame and his face peeled away from his skull … it was Chester.

Looking directly into the eyes of these tortured souls, I understood perfectly that I was being shown a lesson by the space time continuum about unbelievable hatred and cruelty. Eventually it got so damn horrifying that I shouted and pleaded for the visions to stop, which thankfully they did, but only when the vortex had regained its equilibrium.

I jumped to my feet straight away. It didn't take a genius to figure that the moment the plasma spirals reconnected, I'd be completely overwhelmed when the devil hordes came charging back in.

My only options were to stand here and hope that whatever it was the goddess was trying to do would succeed, or high tail it over to her and fight side by side 'till we fell. I felt humbled by Freya's commitment. Only moments after the horror of losing her brother, she was back standing strong on the node point, with the geirahöð rotating above her at an even more unimaginable speed than before.

Within moments the plasma flipped skyward, and an all sides attack, came charging in hard for the kill. Bellowing a wild-hearted roar, I began swinging like mad with my shovel, and for the first time in my life I felt unhindered by any notion of fear, which was ironic as this most certainly would be the very last thing that I'd ever do.

For some unknown reason I was moving more quickly than they were. The difference was minimal, but that small, priceless edge helped me to hold them at bay on my own. Even so, the assault kept on coming, but when I noticed that their physical bodies were becoming drawn out and stretched, I realized it wasn't me moving faster, but rather the devils were going slower, due to the increasing pull of the vortex. Within moments entire ranks of demons were getting wrenched from the ground and sucked up into the shrieking plasma spiral.

I could feel it's unnerving tug now myself, so unable to stand on my feet any longer, I let go of the shovel and saw it hurtle away out of sight. I dived headlong towards a half-buried rock which was the only fixed thing I could hang onto. *Man-o-man*, the draw was so unbelievably strong, that as well as a hell storm of devils, it was now sucking in whole lines of Shining Specters and their fast flying motorcycles from every part of the crater. As my body began to lift skyward, I felt the firm touch from unseen hands that had come to my aid and were holding me back from a one-way ride into the vortex. I had no way of knowing but I was certain they belonged to a Valkyrja.

The roar was so loud I could taste it, but as the pitch seemed to flat line, I could somehow make out the twinkling sounds of the most beautiful music that I knew I'd heard once before. I managed to turn my head and look back towards the center where it was coming from. I was astonished to see not only the goddess as she maintained the fast spinning geirahöð, but also the luminous image of a most beautiful creature that shared both the same space and time.

I recognized her immediately as the manifest spirit of the little music box dancer turning slowly to the lovely Moonlight Sonata. This phasing duality was unquestionably the workings of Seiðr, but to explain it was *truly* beyond me. Nevertheless, I looked on completely enchanted as in a state of loving symbiosis they turned around and around and around.

Suddenly the vortex exploded. The *WOOOOOOOOOOOOOOOOOMPH* of the electric blue shock wave hit like a low flying wall and blew me away with its force. With a much-lessened thump I crashed to the ground, right at the base of the hillock. Awkwardly, still half in shock I clambered back onto my feet and looked up. I wasn't thrown far, but unbelievably my course across the sky had collided with an aerial buffer of thousands of tightly packed, still glowing and unharmed honeybees. Everything in this surreal, cacophony of otherworldly madness that had held my very being in a state of absolute terror had, in an instant, suddenly ceased.

Apart from the smoldering remnants of the fires of battle and some scattered wreckage of motorcycles here and there, there was no sign of anything. *NOTHING!* No Shining Specters, no cohorts of devils, absolutely no-one. Nothing at all. I realized only then, that was obviously what the vortex was intended to do, blow the absolute shit out of everything, and send it all back to the unfathomable, primordial void.

FREYA! My gaze shot straight up towards her. At first, I could only see smoke, but as the plumes broke apart I saw her standing there as still as a stone against the bright golden dawn. I took a few paces forward but stopped when unexpectedly she began to make her way down towards me. She pulled up short and dropped the geirahöð uncaringly on the ground beside her. She was *completely* exhausted. The black on her eyes and the red through her hair had mixed in with sweat and streaked down through what remained of her white painted skull mask. I stood there just staring, transfixed by such raw ancient beauty.

"I've killed them all Wolf. I've killed my brother, I've killed Joe, I've killed Vince, I've killed Charlie and Oochie." Her eyes were now welling with tears and her body was starting to tremble.

"No, *not* you. I mean, YOU didn't—" I was hopeless. I took off my jacket and wrapped it awkwardly around her shoulders. Not just to keep her warm and cover her half-naked body, but to divert from my own pathetic inability to express any real comfort or solace.

Freya looked inconsolable, I thought I had to say something. "You only did what you had to. You tried to warn us all away, we were all here of our own free will, the goddess was calling the shots, and you defeated them. No, I didn't mean—" In desperation to say something comforting, I dug myself in even further. "Well maybe they're all safe now together in Valhalla," I said crying out loud like a baby.

Unexpectedly Freya's eyes opened wide. *"FENRIR! that's it, you're a genius!"* She then kissed me, sweet on the lips with elation.

Freya pulled her arms out from under the jacket and examined them hurriedly. "They're gone, all of the tattoos have gone. What about The Sun Wheel on my back, is it still there?" she said turning around quickly and flipping off my jacket. *"Is it still there? Can you see it?"*

"It's nowhere as strong as it was, but yep it's still visible."

"Good, then She's still with me." Freya strode a few steps away to the north, and then raised her head to the sky.

"Óðinn … Óðinn!" For a moment there was only silence, but then a long, low rumble echoed down from the heavens above.

With the authority of a victorious goddess, Freya stood grandly and bowed down to no one, not even the ruler of Asgard, Óðinn the King of the Gods. Whether from a last fleeting remnant of Seiðr I do not know, but curiously I was able to make out most of what she called out to Óðinn, even though she spoke in the old Nordic tongue.

"Allfather … I have fulfilled my commitment and cast the pestilent horde to the Ginnungagap. Although not by myself, but with the aid of the powers of Seiðr, as sanctioned by the High Goddess Council. There were others who stood with me too. Los Espectros Brillantes, the host of unrested spirits, who in a pact of exchange for their loyalty, I made a promise to help send them back to their own gods and kin. Brave, indigenous tribesmen and other courageous humans helped me too. I am most thankful for the aid of the Celtic war goddess Morrígan and the Valkyrjur strike squadron, who, without their allegiance I am uncertain as to how things may have fared. But *as-well-you-know,* 'all seeing' Óðinn, they have acted as 'the choosers of the slain' which of course is their role."

Freya's deliberation was poised and oozing with dignity. Surely it must have done something to hold The Lord of Asgard's attention. "Óðinn, as a high-ranking goddess and Queen of the Valkyrjur I am going to remind you of our age-old agreement. That it is *my* first right of choice, to one half of the fallen Einherjar, who I welcome warmly to my green and sunlit fields of Fólkvangr. But this time, I request most respectfully Allfather, that they *all* go with you to Valhöll."

She then thrust a spread fingered hand in the air. "Except FIVE! The men folk who fought by my side. Please return them straight back to me now Óðinn. There were many of our own fólk amongst the unrested spirits, please, receive them all with my blessing, just send me those five fallen men back... *alive*." Freya then turned and walked back towards me. Her striking figure looked regal against the heavy black clouds that were rolling in fast from the north.

"That plea you just made was amazing," I blurted out stupidly in an attempt to lift her out of her woes. She glared like she was ready to go at me, when suddenly amidst a side show of lightning, Thor struck his hammer, and down came a deluge of rain. With a toady effort at chivalry I moved sideways to pick up my jacket for Freya, but as I looked into the hard-falling downpour I noticed a blurry, grey form, unmoving at the top of the hill. "Look, up there," I pointed naively, as if a war goddess might not have noticed.

"I see her," Freya said calmly. "It's Skuld. She appeared when the rain started falling and now she is making me wait." For the first time in ages, I ripped off my shades, to try and see more through the rain. It wasn't much better, but I could now make out the winged metal stallion with a Valkyrja perched on its back. After a moment, one of the great wings unfurled, and the body of a man slid sideways down its length to the ground.

"*AXELLLLL!*" screamed Freya with mad elation, as she charged through the rain up towards him. A thought crossed my mind, that Skuld's intentions might not be friendly, but when I looked back I saw she was gone. I ducked as another Valkyrja zoomed low overhead. I knew it was Göll by the way that she giggled, as she rolled her mount sideways and let something drop to the deck. It landed smack bang in a puddle, and I could see it was most definitely human.

A half-gargled groan wailed up through the water. "Wha?... where the fuck am I?"

"VINCE, *you're okay!*" I burst into laughter and with gladness lobbed myself over to help him. "You're alright, you're back on the ground with me and Freya, and Axel's here too," I added as they both appeared right there beside us.

"*Vincent!*" cried Freya excitedly as she struggled to support the weight of her brother. "You're safe and in one piece, this is *wonderful*, I'm so glad to see you!"

"How come it's raining?" quizzed Vince still only half compos mentis.

"It's a most welcome gift from the gods, Einherjar," beamed Freya. "Óðinn most surely took heed of my words."

"Ein *what?*" mumbled Vince lifting himself up on his elbows.

"I too am Einherjar now Vince," smirked Axel rubbing his back. "We were both on our way to the mead halls of Asgard, but unexpectedly the Valkyrjur have thankfully brought us back here."

"You mean we were *DEAD!*" scowled Vince, pointing a forefinger skyward. "*Cooooooool!*" Vince looked bewildered. I could see him trying to rewind his memory through all that had recently happened.

"*Hey!*" came a faraway call, as two blurry figures strode towards us through the pouring rain. The shorter man carried a bundle, and the other one walked with a stick. "Who said you can throw away my shovel? We found it lying around back there in the dirt … it's a good shovel."

Freya and I jumped up and down, laughing and waving with joy. It was Joe and Charlie. They were alive, and as they came closer, we could see it was Oochie, slung like a sack over Joe's shoulder. Vince climbed up from the puddle, loosened his strides and promptly proceeded to moon them.

"*Is that the boy?*" shouted Joe gruffly, as best as he could through the rain.

"Why you little toe rag, and there's me and your brother here both thinking you were dead." He handed Oochie over to Charlie and jogged the rest of the way in on his own.

◆

It felt good to be a part of their reunion. Besides all the backslapping and bravado, it was the first time that I'd ever seen them show any real affection for one another. There were even more joyful greetings when Charlie walked up, with Oochie hobbling along on one leg, using the shovel as a make-do crutch.

"Stupid asshole's gone and lost his leg," teased Joe.

"What happened Oochicoochi?" asked Freya with genuine concern.

Joe jumped in first. "Get this, the Fire Diamond's locked on auto pilot and just about to smash straight into that frick'n sixty-foot Mimas character. Charlie and I rolled out through the doors like a couple o' well-seasoned jump-chumps."

"I really thought you were going on a one-way mission that time Joe," I butted in excitedly.

Joe shook his head, with feigned belligerence. "Why-o-why Mr. Wolfman do you always think I have this penchant for doing myself in? *'AAAGH! Joe's gonna set himself alight with gasoline, AAAGH! Joe's gonna blow himself up like a missile!'* Geesh! I do have some sense of self-preservation you know." The accompanying routine he'd performed was hilarious, and everyone burst into laughter.

"Where was I? Oh yeah. Me and Charlie bail out fine, but when it's *this* guy's turn, the doofus gets his frick'n foot caught up under the seat. He's half hanging out of the door frame gettin dragged through the dirt like a rag doll when the leg straps give way and he slides smack bang straight into an onrushing detachment o' devils. After the Fire Diamond explodes, Charlie and I move up to help him, but right out o' nowhere leaps Freya's buddy Róta on that frick'n Mánagarmr thing, who proceeds to take them all on by herself."

"That's bullshit Joe and you know it. I blew the frick'n brains out o'… *ooops*, language, I'm sorry Miss Faye. I took out seven of those mothers by—"

"*Yeah, yeah,*" interjected Joe with a grin. "You got two with one shot, I saw it. You should have seen the old timer, wiggling about like a worm blasting away with *my* .44, right underneath the legs of that god-awful Moon Hound."

"Yeah," added Charlie. "But when the rest of the blondies flew by, the old bugger just gave up his shootin' and layed there copping an eyeful."

"I was playin' possum. I'd run out o' bullets, ya numbskull," Oochie laughed hardest of all at that one.

"So what happened then?" I asked, intrigued.

"Ah, we can swap stories later, let's just say we fought on five legs for as long as we could, but when we were literally swamped by the demons, the only choice we had left was to get ourselves down into one of those cracks and do what we could to survive. Kind of ironic ain't it, old lieutenant Crawford here thought he'd tumbled all those years back in a time warp. There he was crawling around on his belly with all his old tunnel-rat training kicking back in. Amazing. We were only a few feet deep below ground, but he sure saved my ass once or twice down there."

Joe changed the subject and gently outstretched his arms around Freya. "Hello darlin'… you did it kid, you did it. But *boy* you look dreadful."

Joe handed Freya a soaking wet handkerchief and she wiped away most of what was left of the mask on her face. "Better?"

"Beyond gorgeous," chuckled Joe teasingly.

"Even when we were ferreting around like a bunch o' prairie dogs, we still managed to catch an eyeball of you conjuring up that vortex thing. *Man*, you sure kept that one a secret. From where we were it looked like this brilliant blue whirlwind swirling around in the middle of a whole sea o' uglies. But then when that blast wave blew the daylights out of everything, *holy bejesus*, it was only by dropping back down a hole that we're standing here now."

"It was as much a surprise to me Joe, truly. I knew I had to be right on the node point, and I knew that I'd been trained to maintain the geirahöð's rotation. But when Axel fell right there before me, I was mortified. It was too much to bear, knowing it was imperative that I had to keep on going and going."

"Well you sure tore those devils a new one, sweetheart."

"Bigtime!" added Oochie.

"Come on everybody," ordered Joe, making himself the boss as usual. "We'll probably all drown if we stay out here much longer. The Fire Diamond's had it, and I ain't seen hide nor hair of the truck so we're gonna have to walk home on our tootsies." As we tramped our way to the edge of the crater, Axel stopped quickly, responding to a noise he'd heard coming from a low heap of earth to our left. "Did you hear that? I think we've got company."

Suddenly Gutteka and Jenteka popped out from behind a small, level boulder and began doing that weird circling thing that cats always do. *"My babies!"* cried Freya as she ran out towards them. It was joyful to see them back together, but Freya called us over as there was something half buried in the quickly forming mud near the rock. "Look, this is what they were guarding for me. *Aaagh, thank you, thank you my little darlings."* Freya went all goo-gah and kissy-kissy with her two cats.

"ALL RIGHT!" yelled Charlie as he burrowed with his hands, while I stood doing zip with the shovel.

"Hildisvíni," laughed Joe. "How the hell did them crazy critters manage to find you out here."

"They are very smart," replied Freya most indignant. "Besides they're not just any old cats you know."

After we'd dug the motorcycle out and got it running, a ridiculous argument ensued over who should be the one that was going to ride it. Freya decided that obviously Oochie should at least be allowed to sit up on the seat, and we'd take it in turns to keep the bike upright.

"Check that out," shouted Joe looking up at a flock of four ravens that were circling directly above us. "Is that who I think it is?"

"Ya never know," answered Charlie. "Ya never know. Those blondies were sump'n else, but the Morrígan, man, now *she* was my kind o' woman." Charlie was about to elaborate, when the little peregrine falcon that looked out for Freya made a lightning fast dive through the ravens, and then spiraled out of sight up ahead.

"*Oh yeah!* Victory roll," said Joe flipping his hat forward comically, as if it had been pulled from his head by her wake.

"You guys are so crazy, I love you all to bits," laughed Freya hysterically.

I raised the question that nagged in the back of my mind: "So, was that *finally* the end of the devils, Freya?"

"Oh no!" She answered quite confidently. "It's only a respite, they always come back. All we can do is stand on the side of goodness and do our best to hold them at bay. But they *will* re-emerge around an earth chakra or a ley line somewhere, sometime. It's part of the nature of things. Even though I had the insight of the Great Dis, I'm still not entirely sure how this will all play out in the end. But I do know the High Goddess Council and their allegiance serves only the good. Maybe on some other level the whole episode was no more than a manifestation of the dualism that plays out within all of us. Love and hate, good and evil. I really don't know Wolf. Already there is a little girl in Mexico or Britain or Japan, or in some other place on the planet that will grow up and soon take my place. But that's it for me. I've done my bit."

As she sighed with content, I could see a momentous weight had been lifted from Freya's shoulders. "*Ooh,* I can't wait to get home now Fenrir," she said with an impish grin. "I'm going to have the world's longest hot shower, put on some warm comfy clothes, then have breakfast and toast, and tea with a big blob of honey."

29

Callings

Six months later

Things hadn't changed much at Joe's place. Whenever it was mentioned, the battle we fought with the devils was nearly always referred to as "that night in the crater" or "back there at Freya's thing."

On the surface, nobody who'd been there appeared any different. I guess the upshot of being part of such a weird and otherworldly event like it was, is that it had affected some of us quite deeply, whereas with others it seemed to have just rolled off the bat.

◆

We never saw Banksie again. We heard he'd had the most humongous falling out with the Four Señors and told them all to go and you know what themselves, and then he took himself, his charm, his music and presumably what still remained of his Dog Man outfit down to an upmarket nightclub in Monterrey. Apparently he'd been pulling capacity crowds every weekend with his own incomparable brand of Banksie DJ spectacular.

Oochie went straight back over to "Beverly Hills" and carried on as if nothing had happened. After he'd acquired a new wooden leg, he took up running a mad looking flock of these polka dotted Spitzhauben chickens. Joe reckoned "He was a few sandwiches short of a picnic." Even so, he relished the seemingly never-ending tribute of eggs, and thought it was wonderful to see the old timer happy.

Not long after "that night in the crater" Kiko flew back to Japan to enroll in her freshman year at graphic design school. Luckily Shintarō's passport had come through, so Kiko was able to take the big fella with her. Last time Vince got a postcard, it was an invitation to his first solo exhibition of his Día de los Muertos style artworks. Apparently, the Japanese can't get enough of his art and pay handsomely for every last thing that he paints.

Dr. MacElroy went back to the States and took up a position as a biology lecturer at a private college on the outskirts of San Diego. He described the facility as being, *quote*: "Passionately unestablishment and completely open-minded in its educational criteria." I'm sure he's dined out more than once on his epic saga of how he'd lost half his leg in the desert, battling against underworld demons.

Oppuam really surprised everyone a few months back when she told us that Eugene had asked her to attend his college for a semester as a guest lecturer in Southwestern American Anthropological Studies. She's still there. Even more amazing was the announcement that soon after she comes back to Sonora, she will be getting married to a man she'd been in love with for years. His name is Kotori and he is the second son of a chief from a neighboring village. She sure was a dark horse, that one.

Sacramento insisted he knew nothing about it, but even when you *knew* he was making up stories, he had that incorrigible, straight-faced ability to make you want to believe him. He told me last week, that he was still only acting chief, while "the boss" as he called him, was still away in Switzerland of all places, renovating an old mountain chalet. And then there was the ongoing lark with Oochie and his Spitzhauben chickens. Sacramento told him that they were the only breed of poultry on the planet, that if you repeat something over and over to them, they will eventually start saying it back like a parrot. Ooch reckoned he was "Way too long in the tooth to fall for that load o' bull twang." But Joe caught him out one time sitting on a fruit box, surrounded by chickens, squawking *"Polly wants a cracker! Polly wants a cracker!* Oh for God's sake TALK, you dumbass chickens, TALK! … *Polly wants a cracker!"*

All of his shenanigans aside, I knew firsthand that Sacramento was one proud and formidable warrior, and as an inspirational friend I rated him right at the top with the best of them.

Charlie hadn't changed much at all. Back in February he'd "gone and seen the quacks" as he contemptuously called them and was informed that every last trace of DU infection had completely disappeared from his lungs. Charlie didn't believe them and was convinced he was being used as a guinea-pig in some kind of morbid, psychological experiment.

But as the months went by and the terrible coughing fits never returned, and he realized he was breathing like normal again, he conceded there was no other possible explanation to his recovery, other than it was all down to the powers of Seiðr.

Joe was over the moon, thrilled about the new lease on life for his son. On the day we came back from the crater, Joe said he'd "Hence forth retired and was never-ever, going to pump gas again." But before it was even midday, he'd hitched up a flatbed trailer, and headed back out for what remained of the '58 Special. Joe said he was going to completely rebuild the whole car from scratch and was planning to sell off the Ouroboros to pay for it.

In the process of retrieving the Fire Diamond, Vince, who had gone back there with him, had found a whole bunch of The Shining Specters motorcycles which, like Hildisvíni, had somehow escaped from being wiped from the face of the earth. I remember Joe's comical description of how he'd seen one of those giant cartoon light globes switch on over Vince's head. "Oh, he helped me load up the Fire Diamond okay, but the little bastard was *far* more interested in those bikes and lashed as many of 'em onto the trailer as possible."

With a spit handshake Charlie was roped in as the mechanic, and when the dozen or so motorcycles were all cleaned up and serviced, the brothers went into business selling second hand American classics from an open-air show line they'd arranged along the length of The Alamo's rooftop. Ironically, the only point of disagreement was which one of them should keep the highly coveted British Brigantes for himself.

Yeah, Vince had changed the most out of everyone. The positive change in the way he saw and conducted himself was undeniable. Almost overnight he stopped with the derogatory comments he so enjoyed dishing out to everyone. Especially the racial ones.

Obviously being killed in battle and carried away by Göll to Valhöll as an Einherjar wasn't something that happens to everyone, everyday either. But when Joe reminded Vince that his mother's parents were both Scandinavian, Vince threw himself wholeheartedly into everything "Olden day Nordic" as he called it, and the Nine Noble Virtues of Ásatrú, which he adhered to as best as he could.

Axel, with whom Vince shared a unique and most special bond, was more than happy to help out with an almost incessant barrage of questions that pertained to Vince's newfound infatuation for his own people's past.

◆

Two weeks after "that night in the crater," I was drawn to a pretty young woman standing alone with a rucksack beside the concrete table, who asked me if I knew where she could find Freya. She said her name was Elsbeth and that she'd travelled all the way from Denmark to see her.

Holy Jesus! I've never in my life experienced such an over excited, girly-whirly carry on as when those two came into contact.

Only a couple of days later, when the elation had settled, Freya, Elsbeth, Axel and I headed off on a south-easterly tour across Mexico, in the old blue camper van that up until then was my home. The trip was a hoot, and undeniably the best time that I'd ever had. I really didn't want it to end. We travelled all-over the place without any kind of hassle or bad will at all. The only disturbing thing was, when we visited the pyramid sites at Teotihuacán and those in the Yucatan. Freya stayed with the van and wouldn't set a foot anywhere near them. She said she could sense "a most terrible unease" and felt "surveilled by the powers of darkness."

We said our good-byes to Elsbeth in Veracruz, where she was taking a leisurely catamaran trip over to Cuba. The parting was all cheers and smiles, as they'd all meet up again soon back in Norway. It wasn't long after we'd returned to Sonora that Freya and Axel had to leave too.

Up in the showroom the guys had parked Hildisvíni on active display, with the geirahöð and Freya's fire-singed falcon standard arranged artistically on the wall space behind it. The kicker was a make-do frame holding an eight by ten photograph of the goddess making her wheel stand salute on that evening she rode off to battle. Apparently Oppuam had been down by the roadside and taken the snap with her cellphone. Freya was overjoyed by the gesture, but even so, made Charlie promise that he'd take the Martellare Angelus out now and then for a long and vigorous workout.

On the evening that they left, Freya knelt down and gave Gutteka and Jenteka one last affectionate stroke and a hug. When I asked her how badly she'd miss them, I found her reply most curious. "Oh of course I'll miss my darlings, but they'll both be waiting for me at Fólkvangr, by the time I get back to Norway."

Joe had planned on hiring another Moonlight Express, but they were all booked up for months, so he gave them the keys to the Ouroboros and said he'd arrange to have someone collect it from the airport. Using his Svarte Kaniner connections, Axel had wrangled a couple of seats on some obscure Scandinavian cargo airline, which flew straight over the pole back home, bypassing Freya's big phobia of biometric harassment completely.

At the moment we all said our goodbyes, the two of them looked like the coolest pair o' dudes on the planet. Freya had on the curl straw hat that I'd given her, along with the magical stones of the Brisingamen that hung perfectly around her neck. As they drove away north, I can still see Sacramento as he came charging out of nowhere on his war stallion. Silhouetted sharply against the red-orange sunset, he looked magnificent in his full feathered bonnet as he galloped like the wind alongside them. It was only when the Ouroboros started to pull too far ahead that he reared up his mount, thrust high his lance, and bade them a heartfelt farewell.

As for me ... *man*, I sure was going to miss her. "You really smashed the ball out of the park that time Fenrir." I'd say to myself in an unfitting analogy of my own unrequited love. Soon after Freya and Axel went home, I'd moved south to the shack on the coast that Joe had traded me for the '58 Fire Diamond Special. At first, I went into a panic as to how I'd survive, but I did manage to pick up the occasional bit of work here and there.

One day I got a visit from Crazy Hawk and Prins Eugen of the Honey Rollers. They'd come down to tell me that if I so wished, I'd been approved by their guild masters to act as a bona fide merchant and authorized to sell on their honey. And if things all went well, it would be highly likely that I'd be permitted to keep my own apiary of hives next year too.

Even though I knew "Jack's shit" about bees, I was thrilled at their generous offer. Obviously, Freya had pulled some strings somewhere, but hey, I'm not complaining. Another thing that came as a shock was when Joe told me that the newly elected governor of Nevada had thrown out most of the unconstitutional laws that had crept their way into the system and called an amnesty on arrest warrants for ridiculous charges like mine. To cut a long story short, I went straight back to Vegas and applied for a passport. With the aid of my last few gold coins, I'll be heading off to Norway in a few months time. At Freya's invitation I'll be staying for a while at her grandmother's home outside of Tromsø, where she promised to show me the *Shining Armor of the Valkyrjur*, the Northern Lights for those who aren't in the know.

◆

On reflection I really don't know if my efforts back there in the crater added up to a low hill o' beans. But one thing's for sure. One day when I'm eighty or ninety in some old folks home, sitting locked in a wheelchair, or hanging over the john in a sling watching my dentures slip out of sight around the S bend, I'll always remember that for one night, for one single night in my life when I was a much younger man, I stood tall with the greatest bunch of guys you could ever have the privilege of knowing. Along with my dear friend called Freya, the goddess incarnate, and helped plug a hole full of demons.

For the moment though, I can stand by my fireplace and look at all the things that are dear to me. Along with the shovel that Joe had given me for a keepsake, he handed me the little figurine of Señora de las Sombras which was the only thing he'd saved before he bailed out through the door of the '58 Special. I took it willingly, but the more I think about it, I'm convinced she belongs more with the car than with me. So when the rebuild of the Fire Diamond is finished, I'll hand her back over to Joe along with the winged V badge that I never did put back on the hood.

The thing I look at most fondly though, is my copy of the photograph Hamada-san had sent back from Japan of us all standing in line by the wall of the garage. But one tiny object that sits back at the rear of the mantelpiece means more to me than anything else that I own. It is my precious symbol of acceptance and the everlasting bond that I've come to cherish with every last one of them, that most useless of objects Freya bestowed upon me that time we "took tea" in her trailer.

My very own tinfoil sombrero.

ACKNOWLEDGEMENTS

A most grateful thank you to my persistent editor Marcia Ruf, designer and old mate Graham Rendoth, and especially Toni Hope-Caten for her decades of friendship, and encouragement of my writing. Without their help and expertise this book would not have been possible.